PAST JUSTICE

Part 1

The Asylum Fight Club
Book 20

TIBBY ARMSTRONG

BIANCA SOMMERLAND

Copyright © November 2022

Tibby Armstrong & Bianca Sommerland

All Rights Reserved

Cover by I'm No Angel Designs

License Notes:

This is a work of fiction. All characters, places, actions and events are from the author's imagination and should not be confused with fact or recommendation of the activities herein. Any resemblance to persons, living or dead, events or places is purely coincidental.

All rights reserved. No part of this publication may be reproduced in any form, in any manner by any method, existing or not yet envisioned, without the written permission of the author.

WARNING:

This book contains adult language and themes. This book is for sale to adults only, as defined by the laws in the country of purchase. Store books and secure devices where they cannot be accessed by under-age readers.

Prologue

PAST

Book filled boxes warped with dampness covered every inch of the basement like small bloated bodies. Noah Crawford stepped around the puddles soaking the cardboard from the flood, the damage twisting in his chest as though a serrated blade had taken root there, slicing the organs in the way. Each of those paperbacks with the pretty covers had been lovingly chosen by his mother on trips to second-hand bookstores, the only thing that brought light to her dark gray eyes for…as long as he could remember. And the only thing she ever fought with his father about.

Raised voices from behind a closed bedroom door and his mother crying gave Noah some pretty twisted fantasies. If his father ever hit her…

The bastard will find me a lot more interesting.

For about five seconds. Until a kitchen knife carved a permanent smile.

Across his throat.

'*You're sick, Dude.*'

One of the kids at school said so when Noah'd joked about doing the same thing to a bully—first clue he should keep those kinds of fantasies to himself. He didn't really get what the big deal was. His father and his buddies talked about killing people whenever his mother wasn't around. But maybe only *'manly'* men could do that.

Dad never failed to remind Noah he wasn't one. At twelve he was supposed to be into something other than books and learning 'fancy fighting'. Noah knew 'fancy' was his father's way of saying gay, but the man never came right out and accused him of being queer. He just didn't want Mom's books giving him 'ideas', so they were kept down here, out of sight.

The compromise had been to make the space all nice for her. Noah'd lost count of how many times bookshelves were supposed to be built for them, but the promises were lies.

Like everything Dad says.

Today was no different. Dad had *promised* Mom he'd take Noah to the park. He always complained about the 'martial arts shit' Noah was into—never showing up for competitions or wanting to hear what level he'd reached—and was gonna teach him how to play a 'real' sport.

The idea of them throwing a football around together made Mom so happy, Noah didn't have the heart to say he wasn't really into that kinda thing. Or that he was scared his Dad would use it as an excuse to rough him up, like he did with his cop buddies the couple times he got wasted and told Noah to show them some moves.

Only thing Dad cared about was making sure Noah never forgot his place. No matter how skilled Noah got, he was too small to take the man down. Or impress him.

Hefting up one of the less messed up boxes, Noah grinned when he spotted his favorite book, *The Count of Monte Cristo.* Mom loved reading, but Dad thought it was for nerds and losers. Doing it in front of him was a good way to get one of those *looks.* Like his son was pathetic and he couldn't believe he'd gotten stuck with him.

But Dad was hanging out with his cop buddies now, so Noah could hide out in Mom's sitting room, where she did all her knitting when she wasn't feeling so good. Dad never really went in there, which meant no looks or cutting remarks he acted like Noah couldn't hear. There wasn't much space in there, but maybe Mom would be happy if Noah brought up a box of all the books that weren't ruined?

The rest would have to be replaced, but Noah would ask his sensei about working for him. Maybe cleaning the dojo or teaching the little kids. His dad wouldn't be able to control that money, and Noah could buy his mom tons of books. Build the shelves for her himself.

Then she'll smile more often. I miss seeing her smile.

Dry books in the only sturdy box he could find, Noah crept up the stairs and slipped into the hallway. Avoided the creaky floorboard, the same way he did whenever he snuck out at night with a flashlight to read in the big tree in the backyard. Out there, he didn't have to hear the men downstairs laughing, the thin walls never enough to keep out what they found so funny. Some homeless guy they roughed up. A kid they made piss himself after hauling him in for shoplifting. A body jerking after being filled with bullets.

But I'm the sick one.

Door closed quietly behind him, Noah placed the box with all his mother's Romance and Fantasy novels on the pink armchair by the window, and sat on the floor beside it with his own book, the way he did whenever he spent time with her in here. He hated the days she wasn't home. His father was unpredictable and so were all the assholes he came home with for a few beers after work. Noah refused to admit he was scared of them. If they really messed with him, he'd show them he wasn't small and weak.

Some of these books tell me all the best ways to make someone bleed.

But so far, all he'd done whenever they got loud or rough? Was cower. Because they were big and mean. And had guns. And if Noah pissed off his dad, where would he and his mom go? Maybe one day he'd be strong enough, and smart enough, to create a better life for her, but not yet. He was still just a kid and, if nothing else, he understood who had all the power.

The men behind those shiny badges.

Power was everything. Until Noah figured out how to get some, he'd have to be patient. Find little ways to make his mother happy. He couldn't impress his father, but at least he could avoid pissing him off.

If I could make him happy, too, things would be better around here.

Except that was impossible. The only time Dad even *pretended* to like him was on the days when things were good between him and Mom. That's when stuff like going to play football came up. All kinds of pretty lies Noah could tell his mother was desperate to believe.

Shoving away the hopeless thoughts, Noah focused on his book. Having read it dozens of times, slipping into another world was like coming home. Even the musty scent of the pages faded away, replaced by what he imagined the ocean would smell like. Fresh and salty, the waves rocking him, the sounds from the harbor, handsome men all around in old fashioned clothes, filled his senses.

Warmth at his side jolted him to reality and he stared up at the very real man who'd sat on the floor beside him. A big hand covered his mouth.

"Shh. I won't hurt you." The man, Officer Darrel Emmit, spoke in a whisper, his lips curving into a smile that was probably meant to be friendly, but with him so close all Noah saw was the threat behind it. "What are you reading? You mind if I keep you company?"

How could Noah say anything except what the man wanted to hear? If he told him to go away, Darrel would tell his dad he was in here. And Dad's attention would be on him for all the wrong reasons. Shaking his head slowly, Noah glanced down at the pages.

Before he could answer, the book was taken from his hands and placed on the chair. Somehow, the man was closer.

Panic wrapped around Noah and darkness warped within his skull like a black sea. At first, everything played out in fast clips, as though he'd stepped away from his body, observing the shores of reality from a distance. Waves of action crashed into reactions. Devoid of fear. Of hesitation. In a detached way, his mind answered one subconscious question, always lingering along boundaries he set without even knowing.

What happened if someone went beyond those limits?

Now you know.

As his vision cleared, he became aware of the weight. The taste of copper on his tongue, in the air, hot and wet pools pulsing all around him. His hand was fisted around lengths of metal. Mom's knitting needles.

Rough hands on his arms dragged him to his feet. Then there was a familiar smile. His father, clapping him on the back as he looked at the other men crowding the hall. "Well fuck. Maybe my boy's not a complete waste of oxygen after all."

"I told you, you stupid bastard. No kid who gets that look in his eyes is normal." Stepping into the room, the bald cop his dad always called Bubba spread out a few towels. The pretty ones Mom embroidered flowers on. Thick white fabric soaked up the blood and the man laughed when Noah glared at him. "Just look at that. If you let him loose, you'd have two bodies to clean up, Crawford."

Chuckling, his father guided him down the hall. In the living, he gave Noah's cheek a sharp smack and took hold of his chin. "He's right. I thought your mother had turned you into a little pussy, but I've got a killer on my hands. I'm impressed, son."

"You are?" Noah blinked, staring up into eyes that weren't like his. They *weren't*. He'd decided a long time ago his eyes must be like his mother's, because he didn't want her seeing this man when she looked at him. But right now, they weren't...cruel. Weren't hiding anything.

The pride in them made all the confusion, all the doubt, disappear.

Nodding, his father, Joseph Crawford, squeezed his shoulder and smiled. "I am. And we're going to be spending a lot more time together, Noah. I'm your father and it's past time I teach you how to be a real man. But we'll keep this between us. Your mother never needs to know what you did. Or how we're going to give her a good life." He held Noah's gaze. "That's what you want, isn't it?"

That was *all* Noah had ever wanted. He smiled back at his father, lifting one blood slicked hand. "Does that mean I get to do this again?"

For some reason, his father seemed to find that hilarious. He shoved Noah toward the bathroom. "Go get cleaned up, you little fucking psycho. If you're good, I'll let you have all kinds of fun. But if you don't want to upset your mother and get caught? You'll do exactly what I say."

After that, life changed. Became much better. Over the next three years, he understood what his father had always wanted from him. It was so very simple. He earned the man's attention, his respect, and most importantly?

The very power he needed to protect his mother from him. And other men like him who came into their lives. He never trusted his father—over time he realized he'd be a fool to give that kind of trust to anyone. Other than his mother, everyone around him told nothing but lies. Lies that brought pain, that tried to steal what he'd gained. Lies to take advantage of him, except...no one could use them for that ever again. He was too strong. Too deadly.

His smile became a warning, and he loved the reaction whenever he aimed it at someone bigger and stronger than him. How quickly they understood the mistake of underestimating him.

Until the day someone came into his life to save his mother in ways he never could.

And took all that power away.

Most would have seen two options. Welcome his savior and reclaim what was left of his childhood, or fight to the death to hold on to whatever control he'd gained. But the choice was never his to make. Inside, the little boy who'd picked flowers for his mother, who sat at her feet and listened to stories of the kind of life no one could possibly find in reality, waited for a chance to break free. While something much stronger shielded him, knowing what would happen if he ever let down his guard.

Things hidden in the darkness, locked behind a vault, could destroy them both.

Noah hated his uncle for coming into his life. For his efforts to make Noah into something vulnerable. For the risk he posed to all those carefully crafted walls. Until he let someone break them all down and build new ones. Ones where the horror was erased, the void became a different kind of strength, and he began to see himself as…more.

Not a thing with no purpose except to destroy.

Someone who could create. Noah Leonov discovered the truth within those pages, even though the darkness was never too far. In some ways, the men who came into his new world proved the darkness wasn't something to surrender to. It didn't have to swallow him whole. And he could…love it a little bit, without overindulging. Sip it like aged whiskey.

But first, he had to be rebuilt with a solid foundation. Imagine a future to hold the only thing he'd ever really wanted. A dream beyond a few bookshelves in a flooded basement.

A sanctuary. One his mother didn't need anymore, she'd discovered her own.

For men like him, there needed to be a haven. A place beyond the reach of those who'd use the twisted parts within against them. Where love didn't come with a price.

The Asylum.

Chapter One

PRESENT

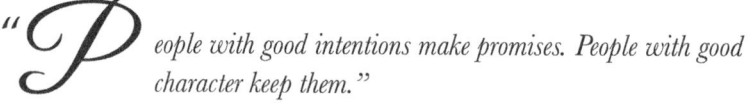

"*People with good intentions make promises. People with good character keep them.*"

For as long as Sinaan 'Sin' Persaud could remember, his father always repeated that same phrase. Nothing had been more important to him. Sometimes it didn't seem like the smartest thing, and friends and relatives were constantly saying he should let up. Not take on so much.

Especially after he and Sin's mother became foster parents. Between the house and tons of experience, both of them being the oldest siblings in big families, they were ideal for the job. But things had been tight. Having the space and time for a bunch of kids didn't always mean having the money or the skills. Sin couldn't remember how many times he'd been on leave from the Air Force and walked in the door, only to walk back out to go to the grocery store.

Since most of the foster kids had been teens, they went through *a lot* more food than his aging parents could keep up with. The house was kept pretty clean—underneath the random games and clothes the newer additions tended to toss around—but there was always the feeling of being right on the edge of chaos.

From having only one kid, to turning their house into a home with a revolving door for children in the system who were harder to place, there was no denying his parents had been in over their heads.

And as much as Sin had wished they'd made things a little easier for themselves?

He loved them for all they'd been willing to give.

I'll never live up to that. But I'll damn well try.

Only five of the dozens of foster kids who'd come in and out of that home ended up a permanent part of the family. They weren't blood, but he'd always be their big brother.

And right now, it was one of his sisters he was trying to pull rank on. But she wasn't having it.

Voice low so he wouldn't disturb their mother—who looked a lot more relaxed in her new room, sitting in a floral armchair staring out the picture window—Sin shook his head as Bethany fussed with the new cushions she'd made for the bed. "It's too soon for me to leave. She's still getting settled in and—"

"And *I'm* here." Bethany shot him a sideways look, straightening and smoothing her hands over the long tie-dye skirt she'd paired with a peasant blouse, her hair a shiny blonde cloud around her head. "I suggested you move her to Santa Fe because this new facility is exceptional and I'm close enough to keep an eye on things."

Sin rubbed his hand over his face. "True, and I feel a lot better with you around, but there are some amazing places up north and—"

"Let's not go there again. We swore to her we'd find her somewhere warm." Bethany's eyes narrowed when Sin opened his mouth to come up with another suggestion. "You're not moving here. You have your whole life set up in New York. You're going to do like the rest of our siblings and visit once every other month. Every month if you can. That's the deal we made with Mom. We keep living."

Of all his siblings, Bethany was both the bossiest and the most down-to-earth. She'd been brought to the Persaud household when she was almost fourteen, rejected by her own family when the research she'd been doing for her transition was discovered on her laptop by her 'egg donor'. Within hours of her walking in the door, Sin's father, Rayyan Persaud, was showing her the research *he'd* started when he'd learned that she'd be joining them.

His father had always been big on unwavering support. If he didn't understand something, he'd learn about it. If he didn't have the answer, he'd find it. There'd been a lot of crowdfunding, part-time jobs, and saving up, but he'd fought nonstop to give Bethany what the family who'd never really loved her wouldn't. Exactly what she needed.

A chance to live as who she was.

The woman who now held the Persaud family together.

But Sin couldn't help feeling like that should be *his* job. "What if I *did* move here, though? I can set up another shop. I don't want you taking on too much."

"Sinaan Persaud, you are not uprooting your whole life. The deal we made with Mom when she got her diagnosis was that we find her somewhere nice and warm to live, and we keep doing what makes us happy." Not giving him a chance to argue, Bethany continued fussing with the cushions. "Besides, you promised her you'd take care of Tay. It would break her heart if she knew she'd pushed him away because of that asshole he got stuck with as a twin. I'll make sure to call when she's present enough to talk to him, but it wouldn't be good for either of them to drag him here. And you're not leaving him alone in Anniston Falls."

Shaking his head, Sin sighed. "I hadn't planned to, but... you're right." There was no use arguing anymore, so he held out his arms, pulling his sister in for a hug. "I'll be here once a month. And I'll call every day. And—"

"I'll let you know if I need anything." Bethany kissed his

cheek, then shooed him out the door, acting so much like his mother had before every deployment he couldn't hold back his grin even as she scolded him. "Drive carefully when you're back in that snowy wasteland. And give Tay a kiss for me. Tell him the doctors here have been working with Mom and he'll be able to visit. She'll be happy to see him. And so will I."

Those last words were the only ones that could get Sin out the door and booking the next flight. As much as he wanted to be here for his mother, he'd already been away from Anniston Falls for two months. His mother had his sister here, and his other siblings took turns visiting, enough that his mother was never without company, but not so much to exhaust her.

Tay had…no one.

His lips thinned as he considered his last call with his little brother. No, apparently he had *someone* now. Not that Sin didn't like River, but the guy didn't seem to settle down for long. And with how fucking head-over-heels Tay sounded already? He was going to get hurt.

I promised I'd look out for him.

But the worst thing was, Sin had no room to judge. He was as commitment-phobe as a person could be. In his twenties, keeping things low key with various lovers had seemed ideal. After leaving the Air Force, and starting his own tattoo parlor, his life was pretty damn perfect. He set his own schedule and did what he loved.

The men he was with were left satisfied and with zero expectations, just how he liked it.

Or…how he'd liked it for a really long time. Not so much anymore. Getting tangled up in the very complicated relationship between Garet and Ezran hadn't been too bright. Looking back, he knew he should've paid more attention. He shouldn't even have *considered* messing around with Garet, no matter how tempting that sexy fucking body was. Or the way the sub melted against him when they danced. Or how good it felt to wake up with the young man in his arms.

The way both Ezran and his brother, Reed—one of Sin's fun flings in the past, until Reed hooked up with Curtis and Lawson and going there was another dick move—had reacted told Sin he should keep his distance. And he'd done just that.

Usually, it wasn't this fucking hard. He couldn't stop thinking about that morning when he'd pulled Garet back into bed. Not for another round, but just to hold him. Kiss him.

Wonder what it would be like to have a boy like him for his own.

No, you wondered what it would be like to have him.

For the first time, he'd actually stopped by Blain's shop to do more than catch up. He'd been looking at collars.

Laughing at himself, Sin pulled out his phone and checked his texts, most of them from his siblings. A few buddies from the Force. None from Garet.

Yes, because he knew how things were going to be. You made that perfectly clear.

What if he'd changed his mind? Would the young man want to give them a real chance?

In the airport lounge, Sin considered his phone before tapping on Garet's number. Instead of his usual one-ring, Garet answered on the third, the sound across the line from somewhere noisy, like the college cafeteria.

"Hey! How's your mom? How're you?" Garet's voice held its usual exuberance. Someone shouted about not touching their 'fucking stuff' in the background. "Sorry. One sec." There were footsteps, then a few doors opening and closing. The other end of the line grew quieter. "Okay. Let's try again now I can hear."

Sin chuckled, gaze going to the planes lining the runway. From the bright sun glaring down, he'd thankfully avoided another insanely hot day by booking his flight today. "I'm doing all right. And my mother loves the new place. The staff here are much better equipped to manage her condition and since my sister works freelance as well, she has plenty of time to stick around and keep an eye on things. Or so she's been insisting for the past month. How about you? Doing anything interesting besides welding?"

"Nope. Same old, same old, you know?" Garet cleared his throat. "I, um, I'll be around. When're you coming back? Or are you turning into a sunshine Sally?"

The question had Sin snorting loud enough to get him a few sideways looks from impatient travelers. He lowered his voice. "No. I considered it, but this place isn't for me. I miss New York and my shop." He paused and decided to just go for it. "And I miss you. What would you think of meeting up for coffee or something when I get back? I know there were some…issues about the two of us… Well, you know what I mean. But I'd like to see you. Away from the club."

"Away from the club…is good. Yeah." Nervous laughter bubbled across the speaker, Garet's voice a bit breathy. "I, um, I miss you, too. You know I'm always up for whatever."

Shaking his head, Sin sat forward. "I'm not talking about 'whatever', Garet. I want to spend some time together. Actually get to know one another. Is that something you'd be interested in? I understand if it's not, you have enough to focus on with school. But if you are…I'd like to see where things could go. Besides the bedroom."

The silence stretched, only the rhythmic exhales rushing over the line to indicate Garet was still there until he spoke again. "It's everything I ever wanted, but you don't have to feel sorry for me. I don't know who said anything, but I really am okay with whatever. I don't want to lose that when—" He could almost picture Garet's shrug. "Well, just when."

Sin frowned, his brow furrowing. "Why would I feel sorry for you? Yes, I regret how awkward things were with some of the Core members, but this isn't about them. It's about you and me. There's nothing to lose, but I'm hoping there might be something to gain." He took a deep breath. "Look, you don't have to decide anything now. I'm asking you out on a date. One that can be kept short so you don't have to text someone to rescue you if it doesn't go well."

Laughing, Garet drew out his, "As if." Sobering, he made a thoughtful sound. "Yeah. A date sounds nice. Ain't never been on one of those. Where do you want to meet?"

"As much as I enjoy your brother's coffee, having it there would be...a bit uncomfortable. There's a nice place on the other side of town. I'll send you the address." Sin relaxed back into the stiff plastic seat, resting a foot on his small suitcase. "Now that that's settled, tell me what's been going on while I've been gone. Any interesting club drama I missed?"

"Nope. Everything's the same." A few creaks sounded, like Garet sat on a wooden piece of furniture or maybe paced badly nailed down floorboards. "I haven't really been going. It's no fun without you, and I've been heads down working on stuff. Sorry to be boring as fuck. I'll try to find out some interesting gossip before you get back so you won't make me go halfsies on the coffee."

That drew a soft laugh from Sin as he shook his head. "I don't see how it's boring to hear my absence makes the place less appealing. I wouldn't mind getting caught up a bit, but you don't need to go digging just to have conversation fodder. I'd be happy just to hear about *you*. And I'm waiting for my flight now, so feel free to tell me all about Seattle and what it was like being in a whole new state. You haven't gotten to travel much, have you?"

"Matt would love it. Coffee everywhere, you know? And the landscape is so different in some ways. I was really homesick, and it felt like everyone knew what they were doing but me. I thought it was going to be about the art but there's so much math." Clearing his throat, Garet blew out a long breath that rushed like wind across a flat terrain. "I didn't see much, to be honest. For real. I was locked up most of the time."

Sin's brows lifted. He liked to think he was pretty up to

date with the 'lingo' of younger generations because of Tay, but that was an odd term to use for courses revolving around working on cars. "'Locked up', huh? I guess I imagined the classes being a lot more fun than they actually were. Maybe not when you start out, but you should be getting past the theory and into the good stuff soon, shouldn't you?"

Another stretch of silence, this one seeming more uncomfortable than the last. Getting Garet to talk about himself had always been difficult, but it hadn't really mattered because they were together to have fun. Not go deep. This, though, was a whole new level.

"I'm taking a break."

Sin blinked and sat up a bit. "That's...that's a shame. I know how excited you were about this whole thing. But spending some time at home figuring things out can be good, too." He paused, trying to come up with a topic to bring back the easy conversation. "Have you been spending much time with your brother?"

Garet's voice brightened. "I think he had the right idea, opening his own business, you know? Matt's always been so responsible, and I think coffee and desserts are his thing. The ice cream? People talk about it all over Anniston Falls. He's all over TikTok, too, because of Jamie. Oh! I heard Tay's joining Jamie's gig."

That had Sin's brow lifting even more. "Really? That little fucker—I'm going to have a few words with him when I get home. All I heard about was that he's staying at the club and he's got a new Dom. And why I shouldn't worry. I'd be a lot less worried if I'd known he had other things going for him. Damn."

Sin's phone vibrated against his palm, Garet's voice coming across at the same time. "I just sent you one of the videos with him and Danny. I never knew Tay could sing. Or dance. It's sexy A.F."

"Thank you, I'll have to check it out." Sin's lips curved in a soft smile. "I knew, but he never seemed interested in doing anything with it. This will be really good for him." He breathed out a laugh and shook his head. "Little brothers will drive you up the wall. You just spared me a whole lot of stress, though. I appreciate that."

"Then I'm glad I knew a little something." Garet's smile was evident in his voice, which had gone soft. "I can't wait to hug you. And if Tay bails on ink, I could always apprentice with you. I can do all the flames." There was some teasing to his tone, but also an edge of a more serious question. Like he fished for whether Sin might actually be interested in that kind of arrangement. "Hey, did you know there's a whole redevelopment campaign going on in the old part of town?"

"No, I'm completely out of the loop with everything." The edge of Sin's lips curved. "Working on skin is a lot different than working on metal, but if it's something you're into, I could teach you." His chest tightened at the thought of Tay leaving the shop completely. His little brother was talented and he'd spent so much time perfecting his skills. Sure, the band gig was a great opportunity, but he'd miss having the kid around. Garet would have been a good addition to the team. He could learn a lot from Tay as well. "So should I brace myself for a whole new Anniston Falls or did they manage to hang on to the best parts?"

"Well, your shop is still there, natch, but the strip mall is gone. Some new investor said it was a 'cultural eyesore' and bought it out. Tore it down." There was some wistfulness in Garet's words. "Tracey used to take me and Ez there to the thrift store and there's talk about tearing down the brick building with the hardware store and the candy store."

Sin let out a heavy sigh. "Jesus, they're really gutting the place. I'll have to get together with some of the shops around mine and make sure we don't end up on the cutting block. I get making some improvements, but Phil's been there for… hell, like twenty years? Reed's gonna be crushed."

"Yeah. If I had the money, I'd do something. But—" A door slammed, cutting Garet off, then another couple people entered whatever room he was in.

"If you can't follow the rules, we'll talk to your parole officer and see if there are other options, but you can't stay here." The man's voice was firm but kind.

"Fuck off, Jordan."

"Shit." Garet swore softly, and the voices receded as he left the room. "Sorry. Yeah, Reed will think of something, though." He walked outside, the sound of traffic rushing by steadily. "Maybe Matt can work with him? That'd be a great dessert thing, right?"

Standing, Sin rolled his suitcase with him to the window, speaking quietly. "Are you in some kind of trouble, Garet? Who were those people? They're not part of the club, I know most of the members. And Lawson wouldn't allow anyone in who's still under parole."

"I'm not at the club." It was an answer, but not. "They're my roommates."

Roommates?

Sharing a place with Ezran when they'd been away for college was one thing, but why the hell would Garet need random roommates now? "There's something going on that you're not telling me. I won't push, you don't owe me any explanations, but I hope you know you can come to me if there's…anything. Even if it's just to talk."

Garet's hard swallow was audible. "Thanks, Sin. I really want to meet up for coffee, and I want, well, a lot. But this stuff is something I have to do on my own, you know?"

"I get that." Sin braced his hand against the window, burying the urge to go into fix-it mode. At Garet's age, he'd still been in the Air Force, with little room for error, his every day planned out for him. But he'd made his fair share of mistakes. If that's where Garet was, the best thing to do was let him work it out. And be there for him in whatever way he needed, without taking over. "We've got us a date, then. It sounds fucked up, and I'll probably be complaining the first time I've gotta dig my car out and clean the snow from the front of the shop, but I'm looking forward to the cold weather. It'll feel fucking good after barely avoiding sunburns for two months."

"You're in luck, because it's cold enough to freeze balls." Sounds of traffic receded, Garet's footsteps clipping against pavement. "Not a lot of snow so far this year. But we got some last week. If you want, I'll dig out your car though." There wasn't any sex in that offer, but it sounded like there was more than a little 'sub'. "Will you be home tonight? I'd pick you up from the airport, but I have...things I promised."

Nodding slowly, Sin did his best not to look too deep into what might be behind Garet's words and simply took them at face value. Whatever else the young man wanted to tell him would come when he was ready. "If you get a chance, I'd really appreciate that. The car thing. It's parked behind my shop and it gets buried pretty easily. It'll be a pain in the ass to deal with after spending the day in three different airports. Remind me *not* to grab the cheapest deal on flights next time? I'll be back by tonight, but holy shit, I think I got every single connecting flight possible."

Warm laughter gusted from Garet. "Well, if you're not flying home by way of Australia and South Africa, probably not. But I would never contradict my— I mean, *a* Dom." A crosswalk signal chirped, and Garet's footsteps quickened. "I'll get you something to heat up for dinner, too. Sounds like you'll be in late. It's cold enough out. I can put it in the newspaper box on your back porch and it'll be alright."

"*Or* you could get the key from Tay and bring it inside so I don't lose it to a stray. Not that there's many, but enough that I've lost a few deliveries when I wasn't fast enough." Sin didn't want to ruin the whole date plan by having Garet at his place mean more than...well, him stopping by to drop off something tasty—which would be more than welcome after enough takeout for him to dread the sight of any paper bag with a logo—but having him around would be nice. "Let's make a deal. We took shit really fast before. I want to switch things up and take them slow now, okay? So if you do swing by my place, it's to do me a favor. Maybe hang out a bit. Let me ease into the fact that the place will feel empty as fuck without Tay there."

Garet's footfalls slowed. The shout of kids and the sound of the town clock's chimes said he walked close to Old Main Street, where the Center and Sin's shop were located. "Sure. I can see if Tay's at the shop and grab the key if he is. I'll make sure it's all cozy and doesn't feel empty when you get home." There was a pause. Then a gusty sigh. "I have to be back before dark."

"Back?" Sin repeated the word, not sure he'd heard right. But no, he definitely had. "You got some uptight roommates or something? Which you don't have to answer, but fuck. I had more freedom in the military when I had days off. I won't keep you too late, though, either way. I probably won't be the most entertaining host. I'm dying to crack open a beer and reacquaint myself with my couch."

"Promise you'll let me handle stuff, not freak out, and still be my friend even if you don't want to date me?" Garet's words came out in a rush.

Without a second of hesitation, Sin answered, his voice low and soothing, the one he used when a sub safeworded out of a mild scene and got embarrassed. It felt like Garet needed the same kind of reassurance. "I promise, Garet. However this goes, for either of us, we'll always be friends. I'm told I'm a pretty damn good one. So let me prove I can be that for you, too." His lips quirked and he continued before the guy ended up thinking he was being stuffed in that zone already. "I think we can be more, but one step at a time."

"Good. That's...really good. Thank you." Wind buffeted

the speaker during Garet's long pause. "I'm...living in a halfway house."

Sin pressed his eyes shut, making sure his breathing didn't change. He didn't let the silence lengthen, but it was a struggle not to demand what the fuck had happened. How the hell Garet's family had allowed...whatever had happened to him. That wasn't reasonable. Or helpful. "I'm sorry. Like I said, you don't need to give me any details, but... Are you all right? Are they treating you well?"

The wind died down as Garet clomped up onto wooden floorboards like Sin's shop porch had. "Yeah. They're decent. It's sponsored by the rehab place. And I just have to follow the rules. Therapy, AA, look for a job every day, be home by dark, do my chores. No car and no drugs or alcohol. No violence or weapons."

"That makes sense. A few of the kids my parents took care of had arrangements a bit like that. It can be tough, but it'll get you where you need to be." Sin cursed himself for the mention of the beer. Also unreasonable, but he wouldn't go there again. But he had another idea that might give the young man a good distraction, considering his submissive nature. "I doubt Tay's at the shop, I didn't want him there alone, for several reasons. And he's not staying at my place anymore. Give him a call—I'll text you his number—and have him meet up with you. My place has been gathering dust for a while, so if you've got some time on your hands, freshen it up a bit. And I'd love a cup of hot chocolate when I come in. Maybe some freshly made cookies. I remember you telling me Tracey taught you and Ez how to make your favorites."

"Yeah? That sounds like a cool way to spend the day. I'd like to do it for you..." There was a brief pause. "And I think I'm allowed to talk to him. Rhodey never put him on the list, not explicitly anyway."

Sin's brow creased. "'The list'? What list? And of course you can talk to Tay. I don't give a fuck what Rhodey, or Tay's new Dom, have to say about it. If they have a problem with that, I'll deal with them."

"I sort of lied. About talking to Matt." Voice tight, Garet sniffed. "I don't know what's been going on at The Asylum because I'm not allowed there anymore. It's okay. I get it. So don't be mad, okay? But if Tay's living there now, then I don't know if I'm allowed to talk to him. Rhodey got me help, and made everything pretty clear, but not that."

Sin rested his forehead against the glass, taking a few deep breaths. There was a lot about this situation he didn't know, so he shouldn't jump to conclusions. But he'd damn well hold on to the control he could, no matter how the Core might feel about it. "Then I'll make it clear. I don't know Tay's whole situation. Or yours. But I've been looking out for my brother for longer than any of them have known him. And you're my friend. If they start trying to choose his for him? I'll be dealing with that *very* fucking fast. So don't give it a second thought."

"Thanks, Sin. I'm sorry. And I'll make sure you have something nice to come home to. Food and cocoa and a clean place." Sincere remorse and a willingness—no, a *need*—to please were in Garet's offer. "Don't worry about a thing."

"I won't, but, Garet?" Sin let his small smile come across in his voice. "I'm glad you felt comfortable telling me all that. I know it can't be easy. But you've got this." He let out a soft laugh, lightening the mood. "I like cinnamon on my hot chocolate. Just to make sure you get it right. And marshmallows, but don't use Tay's colorful ones. They're probably stale."

"Got it. Cinnamon and marshmallows that don't look like a unicorn ate something that disagreed with it." Garet snickered. "Reed likes those, too. I bet they're getting into all sorts of shit with food and glitter."

Picturing just that drew a grin to Sin's lips. "Fuck, I hope so. I hope things are good for him there. And they'll be that way for you again. Soon. I promise."

"Sin, they already are. I have a friend. In you. So, there's all the good. Right there." Clearing his throat roughly, Garet stomped his feet a few times, his shoes echoing against what sounded like porch floorboards. "I'll text Tay once you send his number, so I don't get him into shit if he's gotta let me in on the sly."

Humming the song Garet's words immediately reminded him of—with how often Tay'd watched *Toy Story*, it used to be permanently stuck in the back of his mind—Sin inclined his head. "I'll get that right to you. But as good as it feels to have you say all that, I meant what I said. You're going to be back in that club before long. Enjoying all the silliness subs there like getting into. Flirting with all the Doms." He breathed out a laugh. "So long as you save the last dance for me."

"Dude, you *are* the dance." Garet let out a gusty laugh. "What time do you get in?"

"Around eight." Sin frowned, shaking his head. "Which means you'd better not be there when I get back. I don't want you in that kind of trouble. We'll put a raincheck on the hot chocolate."

"If I put out all the ingredients, and pour some milk in a measuring cup in the fridge, will you make it so I can think of you enjoying the marshmallows?" Garet's suggestive tone drew a mental image of the sub licking the sticky whiteness off Sin's upper lip with the point of his tongue.

Sin chuckled, shaking his head. "Behave yourself. You remember the 'slow' part of our conversation, yes?"

"Yeah. Sorry. It's a gear shift. I'll be good." There was still a warm smile in Garet's voice, but he clearly meant what he said.

"Good boy." Not exactly the words to use for someone Sin wanted to take his time building things up with from scratch, but he'd said 'slow' not 'glacial'. "I'll send you Tay's number now and let you get to it. Thanks for taking care of my place for me. And I'm looking forward to our date."

"Me too. Have a good flight. Text me when you want to get together." A shop bell jangled, Blain's deep tones registering in the background. "I'm free most of the time, until I find work."

Nodding, Sin glanced over to the gathering line in front of his terminal. He'd missed the boarding call at some point during the conversation. "Will do. I've got to get going, but I'll text when I land. And send the address to the café. And generally spam you with messages whenever it pleases me."

"Coffee and spam. The perfect combo. I'm gonna go before you miss your flight and I say something that Blain will object to." Snickering, Garet spoke quietly. "See you later, Sin."

Suitcase rolling beside him, Sin made his way to the back of the line. "See you, Garet. And take care of you." He rolled his eyes at himself. "Sorry, I'm not trying to *'Pretty Woman'* you. My little brother is a bad influence. It's hard not to let movie quotes slip out with how often he latches on to them. But it's not quite so cute when I do it."

"Am I allowed to contradict that statement?" A sub barked in the background, making it clear Garet was close to the pup play aisle.

Sin used a mock stern tone which had the lady in front of him casting him an amused look. "No, my word is law. And if you dare call me 'cute' you'll regret it."

"'You're killin' me smalls.'" Groaning, Garet likely shook his head, judging by the rustling sound. "Now you've got me doing it."

As the line crept forward behind a large family who seemed to have misplaced all their passes—*been there*—Sin moved with it and muffled a snort. "Careful doing that around Tay, you'll end up down a rabbit hole. And he'll have you watching movies that were complete busts, explaining exactly *why* they were so terrible. Not to say it can't be fun, but I figured I'd be nice and give you a head's up."

23

"Noted. But I wouldn't mind." Something jangled, chain-like. "What movies do you like?"

Sin fished out his boarding pass as he got closer to the attendant, letting out a quiet sigh. "Ask me again on our date. I've gotta let you go now. But it's been really nice catching up with you. I'm looking forward to doing it again. In person."

"Will do. Bye, Sin. Safe travels."

"Bye, Garet. See you on the other side." Sin ended the call and slipped his phone into his pocket. By the time he was seated on the plane, exactly what he was heading back to hit him for the first time.

Not like he'd expected to leave for over two months and have everything remain the same, but part of him had… hoped not too much would change. Instead, not only did it sound like there was stuff going on at the club he had no clue about, but Anniston Falls itself was different.

He'd been through much bigger changes in his life, though. And he'd always adapted. Whether it came to his family, to the club, or to a sweet young sub who was facing some really difficult challenges, he'd do the same now. Because as much as he enjoyed his life being nice and uncomplicated?

I still have a few promises to keep.

Chapter Two

PRESENT

Give me something to kill. Anything. A fucking rodent, I don't give a fuck.

Long strides took Rhodey Leonov through the gym, with freshly polished floors and the harsh stench of paint lingering almost a mockery of what the place had looked like barely six weeks ago. Just closing his eyes for a second brought it all back, so fucking clearly. The smoke and dust hanging in the air. Fallen beams, twisted metal, the ring now in perfect condition again ready to take a dive into the pool on the bottom level.

Going down there might make shit feel a little less surreal. The pool had been drained, but no one had the time to clean or refill it. The cells—the once-local shrink's room and office—still looked like part of a warzone. As close to being whole again as The Asylum was, under the surface, there was still damage to repair.

Flaws. Weaknesses. Not just in the fucking building.

And one wrong move, pressure in the wrong spot, would expose it all.

Maddox being in Anniston Falls was more than a bit of pressure. The man was the equivalent to strapping explosives along the entire foundation, on a timer just out of sight. With no wires to cut and no fucking warning when the whole thing would come crashing down around him.

But like fuck would he give the bastard the opportunity to catch the one other person he could throw completely off balance at a glance unaware. Shoving into the clinic, Rhodey picked his way around stacks of boxes that had come in that morning to restock the place. He glanced around, the edge of his lips quirking a bit as he took in the clinic that had been expanded for a third time.

His nephew knew *exactly* where he could exert control without resistance. A 'proposal' to make sure the main doctor of The Asylum had as much space as he needed to comfortably treat members? That had gotten a unanimous vote from the Board.

Shit was all shiny and neat. Everything in its place. An area for people to sit and wait, several closed off rooms. Jared was probably in one of them.

"You can quit jerking off over the inventory now and get your ass out here." Rhodey spoke loud enough for Jared to hear him, no matter where he'd burrowed himself into his new medical kingdom. "We need to talk."

The one spot he hadn't expected the man's voice to come from was completely out of sight, under a cabinet on the room's far side. Hidden by a low table, Jared's stillness made his legs almost blend into the furniture. "Hand me that pipe wrench, Rhodey. There's a leak... Dammit, Curtis. You're going too fast, not paying enough attention."

Rhodey grunted and cut across the room, reaching into a nearby toolbox for the wrench. But he didn't hand it over. "Get out of there. You're a doctor, my man. You've got to baby your hands when you're not punching people. I'll deal with it."

Scooting out from under the cabinet, Jared rose up on his elbows. The beard he'd grown before everything had gone to absolute shit was absent, cheeks smooth except for the scars and natural age lines, the whole Daddy-Santa-Clause look erased.

Thank fuck.

The subs had enjoyed the novelty, but to Rhodey? As good as the beard had looked, it didn't fit his once best friend. It softened his edges too much.

Edges that were familiar. Needed. If the man ever wanted to be let out of what the Core subs liked calling a protective 'bubble', anyway. Not that Rhodey minded blowing enough for the lot of them...

Analogies are bullshit. Stop while you're ahead.

Yeah. Good idea. Rhodey gave the man a slow once over, latching on to the familiarity and the signs that time had passed. Both which he fucking needed to avoid getting dragged back into that place where Maddox had way too much power over them both.

Jared's salt-and-pepper hair was a little longer now, sticking up in soft tufts. Those ice blue eyes, however, hadn't changed a bit since they'd lost the last bit of childhood naiveté, lasering into Rhodey now with the man's level look.

"Isn't that supposed to be my line?" Lips slanting, Jared affected an imitation he'd been perfecting for as long as Rhodey had known him. "'Dammit, Jim. I'm a doctor, not a plumber.'"

Despite the FUBAR that was about to go down *again* if he couldn't figure out how to stop it, Rhodey grinned. "Does my nephew know what a nerd you are? I didn't think he was into that, but the less I know, the better." He nudged Jared with his foot. "Move. And you should help River's boy work on that impression, he's terrible at it."

Jared pushed to his feet, his wry laugh a bit breathy with the movement. A cough followed, and he cleared his throat, waving Rhodey off. "It'd take a few more years of hard whiskey to really get it right. I've been drinking toward that goal my entire life." He stepped out of the way and moved to one side, sweeping his hand toward the sink. "Be my guest, but be careful of the p-trap. It drips in your eye."

Couldn't be worse than fixing up a Hummer in the middle of a snowstorm. Rhodey lowered to the floor, the now familiar sharp ache in his healing leg making it less *graceful* than it would've been otherwise.

No more dance parties for me.

Shoulders too fucking big for him to get a good position, he twisted into much the same angle Jared had managed to reach in. Ignoring the cold drip against his cheek, he began inspecting the pipe. "You're gonna want to sit down for this. And no fucking freaking out or I'll have Seth come in here and drug you."

Because the medication in the clinic got a brand new home in a safe Seth could restrict access to. Another new addition, but Rhodey wouldn't remind his best friend about the need for it. Casual threats were just their thing.

There was a pause, then the sound of a short, sturdy table scraping back as Jared lowered himself to its surface, the only place that hadn't been piled with boxes and pouches of medical supplies. "I already know the portable MRI machine was fried. Vani said something about donating another one if we could train her new Resident."

"No. We're not letting her send in any more people. Not now." Rhodey shifted over a bit, undoing the pipe completely and dragging the small bucket under it to let the rest of the water leak out. "And no fucking favors from her or anyone else. I'll get you a new machine. And whatever else you need. Write me a list."

"Fine." Jared's sigh was gusty, but resigned. "You're doing too much. But nothing I say is going to slow you down. At least let me get you a vitamin regimen." Caretaker mode in high gear, the man started to rise. "If you don't want to take them, we can do IVs but you need to sit still for those."

Sliding out from under the sink, Rhodey tossed the ruined piece of pipe in the direction of the closest trash can and grabbed another from the pile of supplies. He measured it, then lifted the hacksaw to cut it down to size. "I don't know why the fuck I need more vitamins, but sure. Give me whatever you want. I'm fine. You're the one coughing. Why don't you do those oxygen treatments all the fancy L.A. people are into? Pretty sure your boy could tell you all they're good for or whatever."

At the mention of his second sub—ex-boy-band member turned indie artist—Jared's gaze softened. "I'm sure he would, but he's not part of that world any longer. Let's not make him feel like he needs to go back there just so we can experiment with vodka colonics." He went to a cabinet, pulling out a couple of unopened cardboard boxes. "The cough is nothing. What were you going to freak me out over?"

"Bullshit, but whatever. You're the doc. I only play one when I run out of real ones." Rhodey sighed and rolled his neck to get rid of the tension gathering there. It would be better if Jared wasn't being all mushy, but there was no helping that. Might as well just spit it out. "Maddox is in town. He paid us a visit. I got rid of him, but...yeah. He won't have gone far."

The box cutter Jared held stilled, its point between the cardboard flaps. Back to Rhodey, he said nothing for several long moments. His next movements were smooth. Efficient. And brutal. Slicing the box into three pieces that fell away as if he'd peeled the supplies from its carcass to remove them.

"What do you want me to do?" Calm coating his words in a way that would make ice itself shiver, Jared began plucking boxes of sterile gauze from the counter to shelve.

Lifting his shoulders, Rhodey watched Jared for a bit. At least his head was in the right place. He'd need it that way for a while, which fucking sucked, but there was no helping it. Now was not the time to let soft underbellies show. "There's not much you can do. Be prepared. Keep an eye on your men. I don't know what the move will be, but... Damn it, I wish I could give you something. He's...he hasn't changed."

Shelving the supplies with jerky movements, Jared all but punched them into place. There were times the man became unhinged, but this subject...

One of the many good reasons I ordered him not to lose his shit.

"What does he—" Cutting himself short, Jared shook his head. "You. Does he want you?" He turned, arms crossed, a dark scowl twisting his lips. "No, Rhodey. Absolutely not. You swear to me right now you will not give yourself to him again to save our asses. It might placate him for a while, but he'll only find a way to engineer it into a mindfuck of monumental proportions. Then ask for something more."

Cut pipe placed on the floor by the tools, Rhodey shoved to his feet. "It's tempting, but no. I can swear to you I won't go there. He already has River and that's going to be enough of a fucking mess. I don't know how far he'll push the man—at least him being Vani's puts some limits on it. But I trust Seth to manage that side of things. There's someone else he has that's going to make things a lot more complicated."

"Christ." Proving himself very much mentally present, Jared thinned his lips. "River? He knows too much, Rhodey. About...everyone."

"I'm aware. His mother also sent him here to fall stupid in love and he did. Maddox will use that if he can, so let's not let him. I'll give Seth a heads up, but I have a feeling he'll get an earful from his boys. Both Pike and Tay were there when he showed up. So was Curtis." Rhodey didn't want to have to lay the rest of this shit out, but he had no choice. And he fucking hated it when that happened. "I think it hit Curtis hard, seeing Ez with him? River might know a lot, but Ez? He knows everything. If that boat's gonna sail? It's already out to fucking sea."

"Ezran..." Reaching behind himself, Jared curved his hand

over the counter, using his other arm to shove the unshelved supplies from its surface. Memory leeched color from his skin, anger and the edge of fear warring in his expression. "No."

Yeah, pretty much the reaction I expected.

Fucking kids, growing up and not doing what they were supposed to. There should be a law against it. He was gonna work on one before his own kid even considered doing the same. "The boy's obviously in deep. In other news, the old shithole club you rescued Reed from? Maddox bought it. We've been invited to the grand opening. Ain't that sweet?"

Jared's hand spasmed around the counter, expression turning murderous, his eyes going nearly black with rage. "I'm going to kill him, Rhodey. He's a dead man."

"No, you're not. It's a pretty thought, but impossible. I'm well-set-up. Vani is even better. Maddox is fucking untouchable." Rhodey lifted his shoulders, his own mental minefield leveling out as he focused on the facts. "All the security we have here depends on the balance we've found with her and... well, more people connected to Maddox than I care to think about. We can't fuck with that. We have to play by his rules, like it or not. And I sure as shit don't like it, but I'll do what I have to so you don't lose..." He gestured vaguely around them. "All of this."

Raking both hands through his hair, Jared lowered them to cover his face and breathed deep. "What does he want?" He dropped his hands. "Exactly?"

That part was a whole lot tricker to nail down. Rhodey understood how Maddox operated, to a point, but his exact goals right now? "I wish I knew. This could all be part of Ez's training. It could be...because of me. If he thinks I've gone soft and will make him look bad, he'll fix the problem. He implied having his hands in a few other things that would've been long term moves, but..." Inhaling roughly, he shook his head. "I don't know what to believe. It's like...my whole reality is being fucked with. I need to get a grip on that before I deal with him again."

Of course, that last bit would make Jared sit up and take notice. "How so?"

Whatever else he'd been about to say was stowed away, his demeanor turning clinical on a dime. Though he hadn't pulled out the blood pressure cuff and stethoscope yet, he was a hair's breadth from getting out a notepad and anal probe to plumb the depths of Rhodey's *'feelings'*.

Rolling his eyes, Rhodey crossed the room, going into Jared's expanded personal office, another new addition to the clinic. To keep the peace, he'd made sure Seth had one too, giving the men space from one another when working close together might end up with one extra body. Quint had quietly laughed at the suggestion of him getting his own, suggesting an extra room for the patients' comfort instead.

Soft motherfucker.

Going through the drawers, Rhodey found a flask of whiskey and uncapped it. He plunked down in Jared's nice big leather office chair as he took a swig. "Maddox knows everything about Tay. He was also talking shit like Pike ending up here was planned, which…fucking *how*? I just…" He took another swig, cursing when he hit the last drop way too soon. "And Seth and Quint, all of it. As if he was behind the curtain, pulling strings. I would have noticed. I had to have… But what if I was just too fucking cocky?"

Jared joined him, opening a side panel on the desk with a soft press of his fingers. A door sprang back to reveal a minibar complete with several Glencairns, a small humidor, and all the whiskey Rhodey could want. Pouring them each a glass, Jared harrumphed.

"Of course he knows. Every day of my life that I've awakened, being able to believe he might not have a list somewhere of what I ate for breakfast, and how many times I took a piss, was a day I thanked you for." Plunking Rhodey's glass in front of him, Jared gave him a long look. "As for the string pulling, it doesn't matter. Either he did it, or he's trying to reactivate the paranoia he instilled in us both. Thinking about it will only make both of us crazier than we already are."

Bringing the glass to his lips, Rhodey let out a frustrated sound he would've held back if he was sitting with anyone besides Jared. Here, now, he didn't have to pretend he was some kind of damn all-powerful fucker. He was good at what he was good at. Losing control of his own home and family wasn't one of those things. "Whether he planned it or not, he has information he can use to break down our people. He'll use it right when we least expect it. Noah... Fuck, he's been doing so much better. I won't have him tested by that fucker."

Having taken several large swallows, Jared began to lower his glass, seemed to think better of it, and took a few more. When he set the half-full glass on the desk, positioning himself on a curved antique side chair carved with angel faces at the end of each arm, at least the color had returned to his cheeks, even if the murderous gleam hadn't left his eyes.

"Why now? He's known where you were for years. He can't still hold a grudge over you bartering for my freedom." Toying with the edge of the leather blotter, Jared stared at it with a faraway look. "And Noah... He always wanted him, but he never had him. Going to these lengths for that...it doesn't make sense."

Rhodey lifted his brow. Finally, something he could answer. "I was his greatest accomplishment. The shining example of what he can create. The place everyone knows I protect was blasted open by someone else he trained. That was more than enough to draw his attention. And losing her? I should have made the connection when Vani had such a hard-on over stopping Karliene. She never makes shit personal. So Maddox's reputation as a recruiter—as *the* recruiter—is in jeopardy. He won't take that lightly."

"He's here to...babysit you? Us?" Jared's left eye twitched, the fingers curved around his Glencairn spasming. "Or does he want you to work for him again to prove yourself?"

Grinding his teeth, Rhodey turned the glass in his hand against the desk. "Of course he wants me to work for him. But not unless he has full control over me, like he has with River. And he'll have his eye on a few others. Noah is obvious. Seth. Anyone who can fill up his ranks. Anyone he can own. He'll find where each of us is most vulnerable and offer solutions that seem simple. Break 'em down and build 'em up. It's how he's always done things."

Gaze raised to meet Rhodey's, Jared shook his head in small movements. "We have to keep Noah away from him. He *is* better, but he's also too easy. There's too much history. Too much...*he* knows. Tracey's...would he be safer there?"

"No. So long as I keep Tracey out of this, there won't be any issues. Vani will help keep her safe. But if I try to hide Noah there it will make him look weak and— No. We can't mess around with that." Rhodey brought one hand up to rub over his eyes. "It would help if we just had to worry about keeping your boys out of reach. We've been doing it for years. But we're dealing with some new weak spots and we've got to make sure they can't be exploited."

"Boy, Rhodey. You know how to ruin a day." Jared took another drink. "What's the most pressing problem, to your mind? Let's start there." At least the man wasn't crumbling under pressure. Maybe they should blow up The Asylum more often. Hard shit seemed to pull the bastards together. "It'd be good if it was both pressing and easy, but I won't ask for miracles."

Snorting, Rhodey shook his head. "None of this will be easy. Not with who we're dealing with. We need to make sure he can't get to anyone, can't draw them out or make them owe him shit. I don't know what his play is with this new club. I'd say it was to give Ez another reason to be in debt to him, but the boy never had that kind of ambition, as far as I knew. We need to either get Ez out from under his thumb, or make sure our men cut ties. There's no middle ground."

Already shaking his head before Rhodey finished his last bit, Jared sat up. "Reed will *never* abandon Ezran, so you can cut out that option. Neither would Noah. The second he finds out where the boy is, he'll try to drag his backside home. I'm surprised Curtis hasn't tried already."

"He'd better not. I need to have a chat with him about how precarious his own position is, since he has certain agreements with Vani for training him. Maddox won't bother with him for that reason alone, unless he starts stirring shit up." Rhodey brushed a few droplets of whiskey off the arm of the office chair. "I'm debating whether or not to bring Seth in on this. He could help, but again, he's Vani's man. Both a good thing and a potential pain in the ass."

"What you need is for Vani to owe you a favor, for a change." Toying with the cap to the whiskey, Jared pressed the edge into his own thumb, staring at it with open curiosity as crimson welled—something he hadn't done since the last time he and Rhodey had this type of conversation. "Where can I help besides keeping Noah stable and unaware?"

Swiping the bottle cap from Jared—because watching him bleed wasn't as fun as it'd been when they were stupid kids— Rhodey dropped it on the floor to join the whiskey puddle. "Not giving me another person to worry about would be a good fucking start. Can you keep *you* stable?"

"Shut up. I'm fine." Jared swiped up some whiskey with his thumb. "It grounds me. Helps me think better. I need to think right now. Not feel." At least he was aware of why he did it, but they still needed to get the fucking shrink his own *real* office nearby. "I'll put together a spreadsheet of the issues, without being direct in case someone sees them. And our options. I say we go on the offensive now. If there were any gang members left, I'd pay them off to torch his club. Let's hit him when he's not expecting it, and from directions he won't be able to trace."

Rhodey pushed to his feet, shoving back the chair and standing over Jared to hold his gaze. "You're not hearing me. This isn't war, my man. This isn't an enemy we can shoot at, or strategize against. We can't attack him unless you want to lose every bit of protection we have here. Wren, Quint, Curtis, Lawson…should I keep going? If we do anything against Maddox, they'll be picked off, one at a time. And he never really gave a fuck about collateral damage."

Jared tipped his chin up, his strong jaw dark with stubble. "Then you only have one other option, because we're not the types to sit here in our hair curlers on Friday nights waiting for the gentlemen to call."

"Why did you have to go and put it that way? Jesus, Jared." Rhodey stepped back a few paces, bracing his hip against the edge of the desk. "I'm not saying we do nothing. Mounting a good defense isn't *nothing*. Making sure our house is in order needs to happen one way or another."

"I have no idea what you mean when you say that. House in order?" Jared pointed in the direction of the side parking lot, where the newly installed fence would require a lot more than a semi to knock it down. "We let people in here five days a week. And that's not going to keep *him* out. He's got Seth, who has a membership, is on the Board, and can bring any damned fool in here he pleases. Or Vani requires." His hand lowered to his thigh. "We're the same crazy sons of bitches who enjoy bleeding for a living in one way or another. I'm not sure what else to do other than offer that man up a vein to drink from."

Rhodey shook his head, drawing in a measured breath. "He can't have you. That never was an option and it never will be. I'm giving you a head's up. That's what it comes down to. I'm letting you know where he might come at us. Let me deal with the rest."

Searching Rhodey's gaze, Jared sat back slowly, clutching the chair arms. His voice was quiet. "You won't see him coming, husky."

"Probably not. I never do." Rhodey let out a bitter laugh. "But he's never had so much he could take from me before. I was always in the strongest possible position. I need to find a way to get back there without..." Damn it, that would be so much easier. If Rhodey didn't give a fuck, if he could walk away without looking back, this would be over. Maddox wouldn't be in control of him, but he'd still be his crowning achievement. Except...Rhodey couldn't give it all up. Not yet. "I have several options. Some I hope I won't have to use. For now, just...be here. That helps."

Smile full of regret, Jared nodded. "Not going anywhere. This time." He wet his lips with a pass of his tongue. "But if you do...take your boys with you. You don't need to be alone, Rhodey. Not anymore."

That was the problem, though. By having 'his boys', by having anything that tied him down at all, Rhodey had become just as weak as Maddox likely suspected. He couldn't remain completely detached. Fine, he was still damn good at his job, but that wouldn't be enough for the fucker. He'd still see him as lacking.

"Leave this fucking mess for the subs to take care of later." Rhodey held out his hand to Jared. "Come with me. Let's...I need to see what I'm fighting for. That he hasn't somehow managed to ruin it by...walking through those doors."

Taking Rhodey's hand in a solid grip, Jared let Rhodey pull him to his feet. "He's going to die trying, but he won't succeed. Not this time."

Sounded good, but Rhodey wouldn't count on it. The worst thing was, he could never quite tell the impact Maddox actually had on shit, or what he just saw, lurking in the shadows, every inch of his life within the man's reach. Already, it felt like his power was leaving its mark. The stench of whiskey too heavy in the air from being spilled, Jared's blood, the pristine atmosphere of the clinic marred by the topic and the tension hanging in the air.

He rubbed the back of his neck, glancing toward the door to the gym. "I'm going to have some vodka. Want some?"

"Vodka." Jared looked at him with worry for the first time, banking the expression after only a blink. "Thought you'd never ask."

A tight smile curved Rhodey's lips as he motioned for Jared to lead the way out of the clinic. "'Course. I haven't taken you out for drinks in way too long. My treat. Only I ain't paying, because we own the fucking place. I'm a cheap bastard."

"Do I get lucky, too?" Reaching back as he stepped into the gym, Jared flicked off the lights to the clinic.

"Yes, very lucky. I like you alive. Gonna make sure you stay that way so you can keep fucking my nephew and the stable of subs you're collecting." Rhodey made his way across the gym at Jared's side, smirking a bit as a thought hit him. "Came close to keeping it in the family. Good thing Seth works faster than you do."

"Excuse me?" Brows raised, Jared stopped with his hand on the gym door, half turned toward Rhodey. It only took a split-second before the expression fell away into something resembling wide eyed surprise. He barked a laugh. "Shit, Rhodey."

"Shh, the walls have ears." They didn't, except for the ones Rhodey'd had Avery plant there and he had full control over, but no need to risk it. "Couldn't help it. I know how much you're into the cute little ones. And I see how much you enjoy getting under Seth's skin. It's kinda hot."

Humor sparking in the light blue, eyes crinkling at the corners, Jared shook his head. "You should see when we fuck."

"Is that on the schedule? Because I wouldn't mind." One hand on the door above Jared's head, using the few inches of height he had on the man, Rhodey blocked him from going further. There was one more thing they needed to hash out, that'd been eating at him. Not life or death, but still a fucking problem. "You two need to get back in the ring. Show you can level up your game against him. Like hell am I letting him keep your spot."

"Lot of good it'll do if you don't get between the ropes with me like you promised."

"Kinda had the floor caving in fucking up all my good intentions." *The floors are solid now.* Rhodey'd keep reminding himself—without double-checking if his eyes were playing tricks on him. No one would twist his reality within these walls. Not with the most real man he'd ever known right in front of him. The edge of his lips kicked up. "But we'll get right on that. Soon as neither of us has any booboos."

For most of Rhodey's life, he'd gone with the flow, bracing for whatever shit might come at him, damn sure nothing could ever knock him down for long. Unless it killed him. And he'd gotten damn good at doing it alone.

He might be an arrogant fuck. Emotionally bankrupt. A killer. A ruthless merc.

But he wasn't too proud to admit this place made him stronger than Maddox ever had. Whatever blood he spilled from here on would be like another layer of mortar between the goddamn bricks.

One of those bricks being the man he'd never let out of the steel trap of his heart, no matter how cold and hard it had become.

And whatever kind of wrecking ball Maddox wanted to swing in their direction?

I never fucking will.

Chapter Three

PAST

A cupcake and a card on a birthday wasn't customary in the Jacobson's home, but there was one tradition Jared's foster parents never failed to observe. The eighteenth birthday gift of an Army surplus duffel filled with second-hand clothes, a new toothbrush, and twenty dollars for bus fare.

Albany, New York, in the late springtime could be filled with drizzle, snow, or weather on the temperate side. At least tonight was the last. Sitting on the bus bench outside the ramshackle triple-decker that had been his home for seven years in the rain would've sucked.

He should've expected it. Should have been prepared. Truth be told? Birthdays were such a non-event, he'd forgotten he had one at all. So when he came home from the library, the duffel and his walking papers that had met him at the door, along with Vic Jacobson's gruff, "Take care, son," hadn't just been unexpected. They'd been a shock.

But no way was he leaving without saying goodbye to the one person who would notice he was gone. He'd wait until Rhodey got off his shift at the local supermarket—where he'd been promoted from bag boy to butcher as soon as the manager figured out how much he enjoyed slicing things up. Thinking of his best friend brought a tug to the hollow place behind his chest wall, which he knew from studying anatomy books housed his heart. Rhodey was the only person who had a place there. The only one who ever would.

Having to go back to their foster home alone tonight would suck for him, and though Jared never would've said it out loud, *not* going back sucked for him just as much. A world without Rhodey seemed inconceivable. There were things to look forward to, though, and he consoled himself that someday, not too long from now, his friend would have a share of every single one.

Hazy twilight heralded the glitter of streetlamps down Main Street, and the arrival of the dinner crowd at the pizza joint across the way. The scent of pasta sauce and oregano made his stomach twist, and he imagined the meal he'd have tomorrow night.

Steak. Filet mignon. And a massive baked potato.

No. After tomorrow night, he'd have a personal chef. Who'd make fancy dishes, like duck with the French orange sauce. Not the kind from the Chinese restaurant he and Rhodey always joked was made from squeezing ducks, but the kind reduced down, using real fruit and cloves. Or some other spice he had no idea what it tasted like.

He just knew he wanted it.

Taking out the map he'd hand drawn, he used the light of the street lamp to study the bank layout one more time. The guards changed shifts just before noon for lunch. First Albany National didn't get busy until ten after. Which gave him fifteen minutes with minimal civilians, and the ability to impersonate the security guy who'd come to pick up the cash.

He'd spent years imagining this, planning for it. Tomorrow, he'd put it all into play.

Quiet whistling in the distance alerted Jared to Rhodey's approach. Like he often did when he didn't feel like waiting for the bus, he'd taken the miles on foot, his heavy boots clunking along the sidewalk. Even from here, the bloody apron he enjoyed wearing home just to freak people out gleamed eerily under the street lights.

His hair was starting to curl again, since he hadn't taken the clippers to it in a few months, and sweat had several strands sticking to his temples, giving him a more boyish look. He was already well over six-feet, and still growing, if the size of his hands and feet were any indication. Kinda gangly, but with thickening muscles from lifting heavy carcasses out of trucks at the supermarket.

In one hand was something thick, wrapped in brown paper. And something smaller folded up in the comics section of the newspaper. His dark gray eyes brightened when he spotted Jared and jogged the rest of the way to shove both at him. "Hey! Gotcha a couple things. Happy birthday, old man."

As Jared reached for the packages, the wind plucked his map out of his fingers. Sent it sailing into the air, across the street where a succession of passing cars kicked it further down the block.

No matter. He'd memorized it a long time ago.

"Hello, husky. You didn't have to do this." A grin split his face anyway, because damn it felt good to be remembered, even if he'd just spent the last couple hours telling himself it was just another day. "Do I get three guesses?"

Cocking his head, Rhodey scratched at his jaw. He always kept it shaved, but by the end of the day it darkened a bit with scruff. Which looked really good, but drove him nuts. He eyed the escaping map. "Yeah, but shout 'em while I go grab that for you." He darted into the street, flashing the middle finger at a driver who swerved and honked at him. "Don't pretend you didn't fucking see me, asshole. I'm *huge!*"

Jared pressed his fingers into the first gift. "Your deli manager's right quadriceps?" He called out his first guess, holding up the brown paper wrapped package. "Or Vic's missing balls?"

Snatching up the map and barely avoiding another two cars, Rhodey snorted, taking his sweet time crossing the street. "They ain't that big, but probably that flat from being kept in a purse for so long. That was two and you wasted them both on what's obviously meat. And not people meat, but maybe for your next birthday if that's your thing. You don't gotta share, I'm good."

"Ha!" Shaking his head, Jared placed the steak he'd been wishing for on top of his duffel on the bench by his right hip. "I know, but I really enjoyed those guesses, so they're worth it as long as it doesn't mean I don't get to eat the prime rib inside."

Rhodey shot finger guns at him as he looped back onto the sidewalk. "And the first win goes to the birthday boy. I'll give you a hint for the other one. It's not a really small dildo."

Snorting, Jared felt around the contours of the dry inked package wrapping. "I might be a tightass, but I can take a dick bigger than that, I bet."

"I hope so." Rhodey's lips slanted as he plunked down on the bench. He put his hand on Jared's shoulder and gave him a little shake. "Hurry up, I've been dying to see what you think. The only way I could get it was unloading all the boxes for Jimmy, since he's still messed up from getting his arm caught in the forklift. I saved his job so he owed me, but… yeah, figured I'd do him a solid."

"Gruesome." Gaze going wide with fascination, Jared refrained from asking for the detailed description he might have once tried to pry out of Rhodey—who would have given it willingly. Instead, he focused on the package again, shaking it a little. "Um. Lock picks?"

Tipping his head back, Rhodey groaned. "That's so far off it's not even funny. Open it. I…like, if it's not the right kind, just tell me. But it's supposed to be real good. And it ain't legal or something. I stopped listening when Jimmy started giving me a whole history lesson about trades and Cuba and all that shit. Quality is goals."

Excitement—true excitement—trilled down Jared's arms, his fingers shaking a little as he tried to gently pry the package open and finally gave up to tear into the paper.

"You're joking. Rhodey. Really?" Before he even got the paper off all the way he could smell the sweetness of the tobacco. Holding up the box to the light, he couldn't help his gasp. "Christ. You have to share it with me. Holy... Where did you get this, husky?"

"I just told you. Jimmy. He's making a sweet amount of cash on the side selling 'em. Maybe I can do that, too, one day. Get us enough money for our own place." Rhodey made a face. "I'm almost old enough to get the fuck outta dodge. And you..." He frowned, seeming to notice Jared's bag for the first time. His gray eyes darkened as he glanced back at the house. "They didn't... I'm gonna fucking snap his neck."

Licking dry lips, Jared split his attention between wanting to try the cigar so bad he could already taste it, and needing to walk Rhodey back from the edge. He held out his hand for the paper, feigning an indifference he'd perfected over the past several years studying for his undergrad among students who'd often been more than four years older.

"I'll take that, thank you. And it's perfect timing. I needed someone to frame for the bank job." His grin slid into something colder. "It would've been a terrible time, having a conscience and trying to stay cool when I'm questioned by the police."

Rhodey sat back, studying Jared's face before rubbing his hand over his mouth. "You're serious about all that? I mean, it was fun to talk about, and it would solve a lot of problems, but... Man, you're one of the smartest guys on the fucking planet. You can do a lot of shit. You sure you wanna chance getting caught?"

Not saying a word, Jared gave Rhodey his best level look. And waited.

"Okay." Rhodey inhaled roughly, then inclined his head. "Let's do this. But…" He leaned in, brushing a soft kiss over Jared's lips. Not the kind he did sometimes, when he wanted more. The kind that felt…different. "Cigar first. And we can go to the park and cook the steak. It's still your birthday and we gotta celebrate it right."

"You'll get busted for curfew." Jared hooked his thumb toward the house behind him, where the living room lights had come on and the television flickered blue and white through the curtains, over the crooked porch onto the lawn. A laugh track played to whatever 'shit-com' Vic watched, while drinking his watered down loser beer. "It's something I can do, but I don't want you to lose the roof over your head. Just in case."

That earned him a hard look. "You don't seriously think I'm letting you do this without me? Come on." Rhodey stood and flung Jared's bag over his shoulder. "We do this thing and we never have to come back. We won't have to wait to get a place together." He started walking down the sidewalk toward the park, effectively holding Jared's stuff hostage and forcing him to follow. "You be the brains and I'll be the muscle. It's the perfect plan."

Momentarily stunned, Jared sat on the bench for a full three seconds before shooting to his feet to catch up with Rhodey's long strides. "Hold up. Hold up." He tapped Rhodey's arm, walking ahead of him and turning to force him to stop. "I don't have a uniform for you, and I only ever planned this out as one person. I'll take you wherever you want to go—and I hope it's with me—but other than carrying the cash, there's no guns or muscle."

"Oh…" Rhodey pressed his lips together, holding Jared's gaze. "If I coulda gotten that gun from the Army surplus store, would that've made a difference? I could try again. But if all I can do is carry stuff, I'm okay with that. Just...tell me what you need me to do and I'm on it."

"See..." Looking around, Jared lowered his voice, making sure no one could hear. "I have it figured out that unarmed robbery as a first offender would carry simple jail time. Especially for someone with my academic history. But armed robbery is guaranteed prison time. So, it's got to be no guns or knives or violence, right?"

Rhodey nodded, his expression serious. "Sure. I can do that."

Giving him an approving look, Jared continued. "So, I got a hold of a Destine Security Company uniform. The ones they use for the money trucks. And I'm going to come in at shift change, and just tell them I'm there for the money." Now that he thought about it, there was a useful thing Rhodey could do. "They're going to think they're about to be hit with the lunch rush, and the bank manager is a real uptight S.O.B. So he'll get on the head teller who'll be all worried about losing his job, right?"

"That makes sense." Rhodey stood a little taller, bringing himself just above eye level with Jared. "And you throw me the bags? We gonna have a car waiting? I could probably figure out how to snag us one, but..." His lips twitched. "That'll add auto theft to the charges. Against me, not you. You gonna visit if I get locked up? We'll get married so we can enjoy ourselves. Gonna have to go up to Canada for that, but it'll be worth it."

A soft smile curved Jared's lips, just thinking about all the ways he could tease Rhodey about wearing a white dress. "It's a date. Does that mean we're engaged? I like the sound of Mr. and Mr. McCleod."

Rhodey huffed, nudging Jared with his shoulder and continuing toward the park. "We'll get engaged before I go to jail. Only way I'm doing shit like that. I don't want you stuck with me like she's stuck with that asshole who made her ditch me. Not that I'm ever gonna be that kind of dude, but... Wait. Is that something you want? I don't wanna reject you on your birthday, that would suck."

Going from planning a bank robbery to marriage proposal to jail time to birthday had Jared's head spinning a little. Enough so he stammered when he answered. "I m-mean... It's you. I'd go anywhere and do anything with you, husky."

"Good, because that's where I want you." Rhodey brought his hand to the back of Jared's neck, massaging lightly. "I gotta stop by the store near the park and see if they've got charcoal. Do you know how to cook steak?"

"I think you put it on the grill and keep flipping it until it stops bleeding?" Even if Jared had known, with Rhodey touching his neck like that it wasn't likely he'd remember anyway so he went with what the beer commercials all looked like. "Hell, if Vic can do it, it can't be that difficult."

Stopped in front of the small corner store, Rhodey eased Jared's bag off his shoulder and set it on the sidewalk at his feet. "I'll figure it out. Stay here, I'll be right back. I'll get chips to go on the side. See if there's some paper plates and stuff. Since I ain't going back, I can keep my paycheck, so I'm gonna spoil you."

"I love you." The words came out so naturally, with zero effort, it was a second before Jared realized he'd said them.

In that slow motion moment, raw panic and horror overtook the naked devotion Rhodey's going all-in on something so inconsequential and everyday—on a planet of *billions*—as a birthday set up within him. But there was no way to take it back. For once, there was zero traffic. No screaming teens with boom boxes shoved their way down the street. Absolutely nothing between himself, his best friend, and those three words.

Eyes widening slightly, Rhodey opened his mouth, then closed it. He ducked his head, a blush spreading across his cheeks. "Yeah? I mean, I guess I kinda hoped you did. Not that you had to for us to mess around, but I'm happy 'cause... I love you, too."

"You do?" Stunned that Rhodey hadn't taken the opportunity to leg it back to the house—in fact that *anyone* in the world had said those three words to him for the first time in memory—Jared blinked fast. "Shit. I mean... Wow. Yeah. Okay."

Rhodey lifted his shoulders, shifting awkwardly. "So...do we gotta act different now that...that's out there? Because I kinda like how things were before." He swept a hand absently over his bloodstained apron. "I don't really wanna start holding hands and being all gooey. Unless you do?"

Frowning, Jared shook his head fast. Trying to picture them both in a Rom Com, skipping through some French lavender fields, was nauseating. "Can we just eat steak?"

"Fuck yeah." Rhodey leaned forward, pressing a kiss to Jared's forehead. "Stay with the stuff, 'kay? Spoiling you time. That's as gushy as I get."

"Hurry up, then. I don't want to get mugged and end up doing time for murder if someone steals this cigar off me." Jared grinned and ran his hand down Rhodey's arm, his eyes on the motion, unable to hold Rhodey's gaze. "I'd rather plan out a kill and enjoy it. Prison free."

Which had Rhodey tugging his hair to make him meet his eyes. "Don't let things get weird. We're us, got it? And you only go to jail if you get caught." This time, Rhodey's kiss landed on his lips, with a bit too much teeth, like it had been their first time. He let Jared go and jogged into the store, his voice carrying back as a woman let out a soft scream. "I'm a butcher, chill."

Chuckling to himself, still a little high on Rhodey, Jared imagined the wonder there was in the world for him and his best friend—his *man*—to explore. All they *would* explore after tomorrow, when they had the money and the freedom. He leaned against the brick wall to the right of the door, taking out his map to stare at it again. They wouldn't need a car right off. Escape on foot was unexpected, and the cops couldn't run as fast as they could if they showed.

Several alleys near the bank led to fire escape ladders Jared had scoped out. Those could be climbed. He'd opened an account under Vic's name so it'd make sense for him to be in and out, squirreling away the small amounts he'd managed to save. All of which could stay there for as long as he needed it to. Someday, he might come take it out, just to see the place again.

A small storage shed on one of the industrial warehouses near the train depot could house them for the night. Then they could jump a train and be on their way to Boston.

And Harvard. Where medical school awaited. Where the future awaited them both.

Plastic crinkled as Rhodey came out of the store, both hands full of bags and a heavy thing of charcoal balanced on one shoulder. Somehow, he managed to grab Jared's bag again and add it to his load, a huge grin on his lips. "I never knew how much stuff you could get when you've got money. Usually I just get to keep a twenty I gotta spread out for lunches. Thank fuck my boss gives us a discount on some stuff so I can have a decent meal, but it's never nothing like this."

"We're never going to go hungry again after tomorrow. They have a cafeteria at Harvard that's all you can eat. I'll forge a pass for you and you'll eat there with me." Medical school might take up a lot of the money, but there'd be enough left over for a nice place on Massachusetts Avenue, along with some trips so Rhodey could see his sister. "I bet, when we find Tracey with that money, too, she loves Boston."

Worrying his bottom lip with his teeth, Rhodey nodded slowly as he led the way to the park. "I just gotta figure out how to get her away from her bastard of a husband. It'll be hard with the kid and all, but since I ain't gonna be trapped here anymore, I can come up with a plan."

The park off Main Street was closed this time of night, but there weren't any gates and the cops pretty much stayed out of there. Why bother to protect a bunch of people who didn't have money and couldn't raise a stink if their precious property was defiled by vandalism? Thankfully, a few of the grills hadn't been kicked over, and still functioned. The picnic tables were carved with initials and more instances of 'fuck' and 'dick' in square letters than Jared could count, but in the summer it was a really nice place to get away from the house and the screaming of the younger kids.

"I can help. If you want." Grabbing his duffel, Jared placed it on a bench seat. "You're the Russia expert, but I'm pretty good at poking holes in things to make sure we don't get into a jam."

Setting all the bags on the closest table, Rhodey glanced over at him as he opened the bag of charcoal. "I don't think she went back to Russia—I wish she did, I think we've still got family out there. Last I remember, her husband was trying for a job down south. Nice place for a dirty cop to raise a kid and all."

Jared knew nothing about the South, but if movies were anything to go by, there wasn't a single good thing about law enforcement there. Probably they couldn't *all* be bad though.

"I guess there are good and bad people everywhere, but it'd be less cold at least." He blew on his hands, warming them as the temperature fell. "I sure would like to meet her though."

"You'll love her." Rhodey's expression warmed, the way it always did when he talked about his sister, even though he hadn't seen her since he was six. "She's tough, but really nice. She likes hugging a lot..." His lips twisted in thought. "I didn't mind it so much back then. I guess I'll have to practice before I see her. You can help." He gave Jared a hooded look. "When we're not doing *other* stuff."

"Mhm. Okay, *jailbait*." Snickering to himself, Jared untied the twine from around the steak's brown paper wrapping. "I should start calling you lambchop—young, tender, and underage."

Dumping a bunch of charcoal in the grill, Rhodey shot him a dirty look. "Don't mess with the cook, man. And it's a few months, so fuck off with the 'underage'. You're joking, right? I had more gifts. But I couldn't wrap *me*."

Jared skirted around the table, standing on a tree root to bring himself and Rhodey eye-to-eye. He leaned in with a soft kiss, ending with a saucy sweep of his tongue across the pronounced peak of Rhodey's upper lip. "You're all wrapped up in that apron. But I already know what's inside the package."

"Exactly. So nothin' changes with that either. Shit, you scared me for a sec." Rhodey huffed out a laugh, drawing a lighter from his pocket. He squirted some lighter fluid on the charcoal, a spark sending the flames up high, but he didn't jump back. Just stared at it until it burned down to a manageable level, one arm slipping around Jared's waist. "I hope you're hungry, because it's a really big steak. The best cut. Obviously, 'cause it's for you."

Sneaking his arm around Rhodey's hip, one thumb hooked in his belt loop, Jared watched the glow. The acrid scent of the fluid combined with the smoke, and he knew he'd always remember this moment when he'd had nothing and everything at the exact same time.

"Nope. Nothing will ever change us. I never lie, and I never break a promise. I'm yours 'til I die." Jared nodded once, to himself. "And I'm starving. Patty didn't have enough breakfast bars for everyone today. I think she took a couple extra for her sister."

Rhodey's eyes narrowed. He trailed his fingers up and down Jared's side. "Why don't you start on some chips, or the other snacks I got? This won't take long." He stepped forward, laying the massive steak on the grill. "There weren't any veggies, but I kept some money so we can have breakfast at the diner. The one that always smells so good when we walk by? Maybe we could manage lunch, too, but I want a *huge* breakfast. And you're having one, too."

Mouth watering just thinking about that breakfast, and the steak, and *hell yes* his favorite chips with the cracked pepper—that he always wanted ever since they'd had them at the Fourth of July picnic given by the City Founders—Jared squeezed Rhodey's hip. "You thought of everything. I can't wait to share that cigar, too. Only thing we need is three years on us so we can have some brandy with it. Promise me for your twenty-first we do brandy and cigars? Just like this? With a steak every year until we're a hundred and two?"

Jared spun dreams like cotton candy, life heady with possibility for the first time. Indulgence was something he'd never given himself, and tonight he wanted to revel in it. With Rhodey.

"You've got yourself a deal." Rhodey grinned at him, using his fingers to flip the steak. He hissed in a breath, then laughed. "Remind me we're gonna need kitchen stuff at our new place. A bunch of silverware, too, all fancy and real silver because I know you're into that shit. I'll eat all proper at the table with you. But we'll have good beer, not wine. That stuff's disgusting."

Pulling open the bag of chips, Jared stuck his nose in to inhale deep. "Mmm...hell, yes." He plucked a chip out and held it up to examine the thick wave of the perfectly deep-fried potato, glistening with oil, and flecks of black pepper. "Real Glencairn glasses and crystal brandy snifters. And—" Popping the chip in his mouth, he grinned at Rhodey, then went a little weak in the knees as the taste burst over his tongue. "God. Fuck, that's good. Better than I remembered."

"Yeah, well there hasn't been twenty other kids with their grubby hands in them." Rhodey fished a plastic fork and knife out of one of the bags, then used them to poke at the steak. "I think it's done." He awkwardly used the plastic utensils to lift the steak to a paper plate and brought it over to Jared. Then he held up a finger and dug into the last bag, which was full of marshmallows and different kinds of cookies. Opening a small box, he took out a single candle and stabbed it into the steak before lighting it. "There. Now it's official. Happy Birthday. Make a wish. And then tell me what it is so I can make it happen, because fuck fate."

Candlelight danced over Rhodey's sharp features, making a primitive spell of the moment when Jared believed somehow he absolutely could and would do everything he said. "My wish is for a family. Not kids or screaming or people tearing each other down, who can't wait to get away from each other, but people who chose each other. Who can't get enough of loving and supporting each other every damned day, and doing exactly this. Seeing dreams and making them come true." He blew out the candle. "With you."

"That's a big wish." Rhodey sat beside him at the table, resting his arm around Jared's shoulders. "But you've got it, my man. All of it. Nothing but the best people for you. We're gonna find them and if they don't treat you good... Well, we can always keep a great big freezer in case you still wanna grow up to be a cannibal."

A bark of laughter escaped. "I'd forgotten about that. I think I figured if I ate Steve and Dan we'd have enough to live off of for a while."

Rhodey scraped his teeth over his tongue. "It's all those weird books you read giving you fucked up ideas. Besides, they'd've tasted like shit. Because they were full of it."

Full-on laughter shaking him now, Jared nudged Rhodey. "Stop. I don't want to, but I can actually picture it. Taste it. I need that steak now just to get them off my tongue." He mock shuddered. "I was never so glad as when they aged out of the house."

"Me neither. I thought for sure I was gonna get shipped

off to a group home that time I broke Steve's nose. But I guess I'm still worth something." Rhodey wrinkled his nose. "I bet the parentals knew I'd be good at manual labor and bring in some cash. Gonna suck to be them without it."

"I hope they don't call the cops when you don't come home. They might... Because of that." Trying to plan for disaster came naturally, which was why he knew already he had to specialize as a trauma surgeon. Seeing forty possible things wrong at once was a skill. It had to be. Otherwise, it was the wrong kind of nightmare, and that wasn't an option. Besides, even if he was fixing people, the more blood and gore the better. "Maybe you should go home tonight and get shit for being late, then meet me at the bank? Otherwise, there'll be every cop in the city looking for you."

Rhodey gave him an arch look. "You ain't getting rid of me, so cut it out. Eat your steak before it gets cold. I'm seventeen. The cops won't do shit unless I'm gone for a while, and even then. I'm not going back. *Ever.*"

As much as Jared hated to admit it, that was the exact answer he'd hoped to hear. He might be an asshole for taking Rhodey down with him, but he'd only been alone a few nights in his life. Where he came from was bad. That had been worse.

Even with the plastic knife and fork, cutting into the meat was like slicing through air. The steak was that expensive of a cut. "My man, you've outdone yourself. This is going to be amazing." Knowing Rhodey would want him to have the first bite, he popped it into his mouth. "Oh, God." If mouths could orgasm, his had just died and gone to heaven. Though it was crass, he spoke around the mouthful. "Thank you, thank you, thank you."

"You're welcome." Rhodey's gray eyes shone with pleasure as he watched Jared eat. Elbow braced on the table, he plucked a few chips from a pile on another plate and crunched on them. "I woulda gotten you a cake, but I thought I had to hand over my paycheck, so...yeah. But I got some little snack cakes. The brownie ones and a couple other kinds. I think that counts."

"That more than counts." Distracting himself from tearing up—because the size of Rhodey's heart made him the best and biggest gift Jared could've wished for in a lifetime of birthdays—he held a bite of steak to Rhodey's lips. "Here."

Rhodey carefully took the meat from his fingers with his teeth, letting out a quiet moan as he chewed. He didn't say anything for a while, like his focus was all on the taste. Then he made a thoughtful sound. "It's really good, but can you imagine how much better it would be with spices? And all kinds of sides, like...those funky looking noodles. Obviously potatoes. Maybe I'll learn to make all of it. Or...maybe just bring you to fancy restaurants a lot."

Chin propped on the heel of his hand, Jared chewed his next bite, studying Rhodey's face. "So many options. What'm I going to do for *you*? Hmm?"

"Reattach my fingers when I cut them off?" Rhodey shrugged, digging into the chips again. "You're gonna be a doctor so I gotta make sure to get a job that'll give you plenty of practice. For now? I'll just get another job as a butcher wherever we go. And train somewhere other than back alleys."

The idea of Rhodey getting hurt twisted Jared's guts, up high under his solar plexus, making it harder to breathe. He sawed into the steak, cutting a bigger piece for Rhodey. "Free medical care for life. You have my word as a gentleman and a future doctor." He held out the bite, then retracted it when Rhodey tried to take it, meeting his gaze. "But you have to promise to *try* not to get hurt, husky, because it hurts me, too."

Catching his wrist, Rhodey brought the steak closer, hardly blinking as he closed his lips around it. "When I've gotten all the training I need to save Tracey? You've got it. I'll be too fast and strong to ever get hurt...which I guess means the practice thing will be temporary."

"Good." Wrist still tingling where Rhodey's fingers had touched, Jared didn't sit back. Straddling the bench, he leaned a little closer, waiting for Rhodey to swallow. "Do I get any other presents?"

Rhodey blinked fast this time, looking at him, then the table. "Umm... I mean, I could probably think of something? I didn't have the money for anything expensive."

Utensils placed on the plate, Jared framed either side of Rhodey's jaw and claimed his mouth. Salt and sweet, the buttery oil of chips and steak lingering on his lips, his best friend tasted of a promise of power and the warmth of a home neither of them had ever really known, but had found in each other. Needing to gather up every drop of that feeling, Jared cupped the back of Rhodey's head, digging his fingers into the thick, short strands to control the kiss until both of them were breathless.

Chest heaving, lungs burning, he sat back with a short laugh. "I think this'll be the only gift I ever want."

"Oh, good." Rhodey grinned, adjusting himself a bit in his jeans, then reaching out to stroke his hand up Jared's thigh. "'Cause I can give you plenty of that, even when you're a fancy rich doctor and I'm... Hmm, not sure what I'll do with all my training once I've got Tracey and the kid somewhere secure. Maybe I can be a bodyguard or something. Or a bouncer at a really swazy club. Do you think they get paid well? So you don't gotta pay for everything for my ass?"

Take care of Rhodey the way he took care of me tonight?

That sounded like the best reason to become a doctor in the long, *long* list of reasons Jared already had. Rhodey needed a purpose, though. There wasn't a chance in hell he'd go along with any of the million justifications on the tip of Jared's tongue.

"If I'm a doctor to only the rich and famous, maybe you can be the bodyguard or chief of security?" It seemed like a halfway decent plan, so he shrugged. "We have a year or two to work it out before I graduate Harvard Med. There are a lot of brilliant people there. I'll ask them what kind of personal protection businesses pay the best, so you and I can fight over who gets to buy the diamond studs."

Rhodey snorted, picking up another fork and trying to hold it all proper, which looked strange in his big hands. "I'm gonna have to learn manners like you or they won't want me around. But I can do that, I'm smarter than I look." He pointed at Jared with the fork. "But you'll be getting the diamond studs. And the nice clothes. And no one will ever look down on you."

When Rhodey said it, that wasn't difficult to imagine. Even if the students in the local branch of the state university he'd just graduated from had called him strange, his best friend never had—at least not in a way that hurt.

"I don't mind being different, as long as I can take people apart and sew them up." Opening his mouth, Jared let Rhodey feed him a couple chips, crunching around them while he talked. "I bet they don't make fun of rich people who are weird though. It's going to be nice after tomorrow."

"Damn right it is." Rhodey looked around the park, his lips twisted to one side. "Tonight's a different story. We can't sleep here. Maybe I can call Jimmy and see if he'll let us crash in his garage? He doesn't have a lot of space with a wife and three kids, but a garage would be plenty comfy. And his kids aren't like the kids back at our place. I mean, some of them weren't too bad. Just noisy, always pushing and shoving the littler ones." His expression darkened. "Now that you're an adult, maybe you can report the shit that happened there. Get the little ones out before they starve."

Staring at his plate, Jared picked up his fork to toy with it, wondering from his own experience in the system whether or not the kids were better off where they were. "Or maybe we can find a place for them. After tomorrow." Another bite of meat, this one for Rhodey, saw him switching gears. They still had planning to do to make all this happen. "Tonight, we do reconnaissance of the bank to make sure nothing changed like street construction. I can get us up onto the roof where I have a sleeping bag and the uniform hidden. What you'll need to do tomorrow is be my partner and come in to bark at me that someone wants the truck moved. We don't have a truck, but they won't know it because you'll come from the side of the bank without windows."

"And then kiss you because it'll freak them out and they'll cover their eyes and we'll make off with everything?" Rhodey spoke around the mouthful of steak, like he'd forgotten the whole 'manners' thing in his excitement—and amusement. "It's a good idea, don't get me wrong, but I just hope you're right about not needing guns or a car. They're gonna assume we've got all that."

"But that's the thing." Jared snatched a handful of chips, the bag rustling with the rapid motion as he surfed Rhodey's energy. "They think we're there to pick up the money. Nobody's gonna know until the real guys come an hour later at the normal time."

Rhodey nodded, using the back of his hand to wipe his mouth. "Okay, cool. This is your plan and you've been working on this for a while, going by the map and everything. I'll follow your lead."

"Next one, I'll involve you. I just laid awake so many nights figuring this out and I didn't want you to be implicated. Just in case they came to question you." Though Jared didn't know much about law enforcement, it wasn't hard to intuit they'd possibly figure out who he was and start questioning his foster parents. "After, we have to use some of the money to get new identities."

That had Rhodey showing the first bit of doubt he had so far. He turned his attention to the bags, pulling out the boxes of snack cake and two glass bottles of Coke. He snapped the tops off with the edge of the table and handed Jared one. "If I get a new identity... I mean, what if Tracey gets away before I find her and comes looking for me? She'd never find me."

Indulging in the chips, Jared chewed slowly, savoring the layers of flavor as he considered the problem. "I hadn't considered that. You're right." Bottle on the table edge after a sip, he twisted his lips. "Nope. There's nothing for it. You'll have to stay out of sight and I can execute the original plan alone."

"Or I just get a hat so no one sees my face." Rhodey's lips thinned slightly and he folded his arms over his chest, turning so his back was to the picnic table. "We're not getting caught so we don't need to go into hiding after. We can keep our names. You're gonna be Doctor McCleod and that's final."

When Rhodey talked like that, things just *felt* true. Even things that weren't logical and meticulous. Jared plucked up one of the chocolate snack cakes, tearing into the thin plastic wrapper. He broke the square in half, handing one portion to Rhodey. "Okay. We'll get you a hat when we get your uniform tomorrow morning." Traffic on the road had died down, the park dark and quiet except for their voices and the red coals burning in the hibachi-style grill on its crooked metal stand. Jared held up the cake in cheers. "To success."

Holding up his own cake, Rhodey bumped it against Jared's. "To success. This is gonna be awesome, my man. I can't even imagine half the things you've got planned, but I'm looking forward to all of them."

"Did I tell you I memorized all the illustrations in *Gray's Anatomy*?" Jared licked chocolate off his lips, preferring to talk about this topic, if only to remind himself why he was going to jump feet first into a life of crime when he'd never so much as told a lie in his entire life. "Even the footnotes."

Hands braced on his knees, Rhodey sat forward a bit, his expression intent. "Yeah? That's really cool. You're gonna ace all the tests."

That was a given, but it was nice to hear Rhodey say so

anyway. Jared beamed. "Thank you." A few more chips and he patted his stomach. "Too full. It's the best birthday of my life. We should clean up and get to the bank before it gets too late and we look weird for being out walking around."

"Good idea." Rhodey stood and began shoving stuff back into bags. His lips slanted a little as he stood back. "At least we're tall enough most people think we're a lot older. Jimmy bet Stan once that I could buy smokes without getting carded. He won. I got myself an extra ten bucks—remember the day I brought home donuts?"

"How could I forget? They were fresh, not stale, and not covered in plastic. I almost didn't get one though, when everyone else smelled them." Still able to taste the Boston cream donut—which would remain one of the best memories of his life until he died—Jared licked his lips again and stood to help Rhodey. "Donuts. Tomorrow night. Linguini with clam sauce—which I never had but it sounds so good. Just the word. *Linguini.* I could say it all day and night and never get tired of hearing it."

Rhodey grunted his agreement, grabbing Jared's bag and heading out of the park. "I want to try all kinds of stuff. I'd be happy with just a burger with ground beef that's not flat and frozen first. And every single topping you can think of. And real potato fries."

Groaning his appreciation for Rhodey's imagination, Jared matched Rhodey's pace as they headed in the opposite direction of the house. Knowing he'd never see it again, he still didn't glance back. The sooner he could forget the mildewed, noisy, overcrowded space, and the two miserable excuses for substitute parents who owned it, the better. Starting now.

"Rhodey?" A slow smile spread over Jared's face, uncontainable, and his steps developed a lightness to them he'd never remembered feeling before.

Giving him a sideways look, Rhodey shortened his strides

as they passed under one of the few working streetlights on the block. "Yeah?"

"We never have to take a shower in that scummy mint green and chalk pink bathroom again."

Or mention it.

That got him a snort and a nudge to his side from Rhodey. "Nope. We can find somewhere with nice white tiles. And a big bath and a separate shower, like in the movies."

Playing 'we never have to' the rest of the walk downtown, they traded old horrors for new dreams until the bank building came into view. Its windowless granite flanks were unbreachable, that much Jared knew from years of research. Which was how he'd come up with the idea of walking right in. Of course, around its perimeter not a single light was out, and the sidewalk was a little wider and more even. The place looked and smelled like…well, *money.*

Jared stood at a distance, staring down his dreams. "Tomorrow, I'm going to tell a lie. So I never have to again."

"I think…" Rhodey set Jared's bag down between his feet, along with the plastic ones. "Being honest is good. I love that you don't lie, because…fuck, it's hard to trust people, ya know? But sometimes you *have* to. Like, to save someone. Or… maybe to your patients. Telling them they're shit outta luck probably wouldn't be the best idea."

A quick bark of laughter echoed off the surrounding office buildings, warning Jared to lower his voice, or risk being overheard in his giddy excitement. "I think they teach you about bedside manners. Which is how to tell the truth without kicking someone's legs out from under them. I tried to do it with one of the kids I tutored in the college math program for extra money, but I ended up having to tell him that he either needed to cheat or drop out, because there was no way he was passing."

"Harsh truths are just as important as nice lies." Rhodey shoved his hands in the pockets of his jeans. "I bet it saved the guy wasting a ton of time there. He'll get to figure out what he's good at and do that instead."

"He had enough money to pay someone to take the test for him." Kicking a loose stone into the street, Jared scowled and jammed his hands into his jeans pockets. "Someday he'll be running the accounting department for some big firm and bring the entire banking system to its knees with his stupidity."

Rhodey made a face. "One of those, huh? Okay, well, that's different. You shoulda told him he'd pass with flying colors. See? Nice lie. For humanity."

"Dammit. I never thought of that." Not a little in awe of Rhodey's wisdom, Jared widened his gaze. "You need to go into diplomacy. I bet you'd stop a lot of wars with the cold, hard facts. People wouldn't be able to deny them, and you'd know how to be gentle when it was required. Like..." He glanced around. "You'd tell me if you thought robbing this place was a stupid idea, right? I could just go into the Army and get them to pay for my training. It's just...I always... It's *Harvard Med*, you know?"

Rubbing his hand over his mouth, Rhodey eyed the bank, then motioned for Jared to keep walking. "Where's this stash of yours? We can't get caught hanging around out here. And yeah, I'd tell you. But I'm smart enough to know when someone's smarter than me, and you've got this figured out. So I don't think it's stupid."

"Thanks. That helps. It's down this alley and up that fire escape." Jared motioned toward a darker patch of pavement that led around the building, and they stepped past a glass office tower's revolving door. Bright yellow light spilled onto the street, painting the night with artificial daylight. "You can climb up the first ladder and I'll hand stuff up to you. Tomorrow, we'll have to take a different route around there." He pointed. "Because this is too visible."

"That'll work. And we can head straight out of town and get lost in a bigger city—Boston, right? I think if we're careful for a while, the trail will go cold and we'll be free and clear." Rhodey climbed the ladder, reaching down to grab the bags as Jared handed them up. "We can enjoy some of the money, but we should probably not do anything crazy right away. It'll make people suspicious. We don't exactly look like we come from money."

"But we will. Someday. If we want. I already have etiquette lessons planned with a blue blood from Beacon Hill. She teaches them in her home." Swinging up, Jared gripped cold iron. "I'm going to sound like and look like that rich asshole who bought his way through school, but I'll be smarter and more powerful than all of them."

Rhodey wiggled his brows at Jared before continuing up the fire escape. "That's hot." He stepped onto the roof, walking up to the very ledge and looking over, closing his eyes and breathing in a deep breath. "Feel that? It's freedom, man. And it's fucking amazing."

Joining Rhodey, Jared tucked his fingers inside his best friend's back pocket. The skyline stretched in broken spikes that got shorter and shorter off toward their foster home. He looked in the opposite direction. East, toward Boston. "I can't wait to see it for real. I get butterflies in my stomach when I think about walking through the quad the first time."

"Those will die rather quickly once you lose that precious freedom." A deep, calm voice spoke from behind them, on the roof even though there hadn't been a sound. But now there was—light, even footsteps as a man who was taller than even Rhodey strolled halfway across the black surface. His hair was pure white, but his face seemed like that of a middle aged man. Maybe forty. His all black clothes were the kind of quality that belonged on screen, even nicer than what the rich students Jared had met wore.

There was something in those deep brown eyes that held the kind of intelligence Jared couldn't help respond to. Like his favorite teachers, who recognized something in him and would give him extra coursework so he could complete his studies earlier.

Smile warm and disarming, he stopped a respectful distance away.

Held up his hands when Rhodey growled and tugged Jared behind him. "I won't come any closer, young man. I'm simply here to give you some advice."

Chapter Four

PAST

"What did you hear?" Panic turned butterflies into a herd of wild horses as Jared saw the all-too-rapid death of his dreams with the man's arrival. He fisted his hands, surprised at the number of violent images crossing his mind in defense of his plans.

Harvard...
One little push.
No, they'll find the body.
Actual murder? What the hell are you thinking?
Christ.

"Everything." The man tilted his head to one side as he caught Jared's gaze, the edge of his lips twitching. "It's a clever plan, from your limited experience, but it won't work. And if you still want to try it, I'll leave and not alert anyone. Not that I'll have to. You were both caught on camera, looking at the bank. There was an inquiry yesterday into the bank manager, who was helping himself to the funds of some of his less wealthy investors, hoping no one would care enough to look into it. Banks tend to care very much when you disturb their bottom line. Security has been tightened and they're using a different service for transfers. Perhaps this information will be useful to you?"

Feeling a bit like he'd run into Batman on a rooftop in Gotham, Jared stepped fully out from behind Rhodey. Chin lifted, he narrowed his gaze, trying to puzzle the man out. He had too many skills and knew too many things.

Except he didn't look like he worked for the FBI...or the bank.

"How do you know all this?" In order to have overheard all their plans—which it was clear the man had—he would've needed to watch them in the park. Yet, neither Jared nor Rhodey had noticed a thing. "Why were you following us? And how do you know so much about the bank?"

The man gave him a level look. "When I'm investigating a potential employee, I'm always thorough. Nevermind two. When I heard your ideas I was curious how it would pan out and I made a call. I didn't need that much intel to tell you the simple facts, though. You'd already risked being identified the second you walked down the street."

After all this planning, all these years, to be felled by one careless mistake. Jared had been so damned sure of himself, and he'd wanted to show off to Rhodey, if he were honest. One good steak, a beautiful kiss, and he was thinking with his heart instead of his head. Or his ego, at the very least.

Jared turned to Rhodey, one hand smoothing down his chest. "I have the tutoring money. Take it back to Vic and he'll never know. You'll get kicked around for being late, maybe get the belt, but it's better than being homeless."

"Like fuck. I'm not leaving you." Rhodey spoke under his breath, for Jared's ears alone, then raised his voice as he addressed the man. "Who are you? And what did you mean by 'employee'? This isn't how any job offer I've ever heard of works. I have a job and Jared—"

Shaking his head, the man took a step closer. "*Had*. You

had a job that was wasting your skills. You have no intention of going back to it. And Jared wants to go to Harvard. He's ranked the top of every advanced class he's taken, and his IQ is the highest on the East Coast. For people like you? Yes. This is how jobs are offered."

Rhodey laughed, staring at the man like he'd lost his mind. "Sure. Being a butcher put me right on some list of people with special skills."

"No. The street fighting in back alleys did." The man chuckled when Rhodey blinked at him. "I've sent three of my men to challenge you. You beat all of them. With their training, that should have been impossible." He let out an irritated sound. "You should have had the money to get yourself and your friend into a much better position, but you bet on other fighters. And you are *not* as skilled at picking winners as I am. But we can work on that."

Taking a step back, then another, Jared looked for a place to sit.

Rhodey grabbed him by the back of the shirt, hauling him away from the ledge.

"Christ." Limbs shaking, Jared threw Rhodey a grateful look. "I don't think this is real. And street fighting isn't a career... Is it?"

Red spread over the tops of Rhodey's cheeks. "I mean, some people make pretty good money off of it. I figured if I invested in the right fighters, I might be able to, but it never worked and I had my job so..." He lifted his shoulders. "It's fighting. I didn't think it was that special. I'm kinda big so why wouldn't I beat a lot of people?"

Letting out a heavy sigh, the man walked in a semi-circle so he could stand by the ledge, looking out over the horizon. "Your size has nothing to do with it. A smaller man with the right skills and training can take down a much bigger one. Your advantage is your instincts. Your ability to read people in a split second. It's raw talent and, properly honed, it is very 'special'."

Pride in Rhodey swelled Jared's chest. "I *told* you that you had your own kind of intelligence. See? I'm not the only one who sees it."

"Okay, fine. But why do *you* want to 'hone' it?" Rhodey jutted his chin at the man. "What's the job? And you still haven't told us your name."

The man inclined his head, smiling with warm approval as he looked from Rhodey to Jared. "You're very observant, Jared. I'm pleased that he had someone who could see it. You've both given one another the support you needed to get through some difficult challenges. Which will end now if you accept my offer." He went quiet as he studied both their faces, like he was making up his mind over whether or not he still wanted to give it. "My name is Robert Maddox. And the job is not important right now. The training is. It will include housing, funds, and whatever support you could possibly need to reach your full potential. But I will only offer it once." His gaze settled on Jared. "You have value, but Harvard is expensive. I don't make bad investments."

Trying to suss out whether the man—Robert Maddox—had just offered to pay for Harvard, or had called him a bad investment, Jared blinked a few times. Reading so much for school had been hell on his vision, and he hadn't been able to afford new glasses. He wished he could see the man's expression better.

"I apologize, Mr. Maddox. I don't usually have trouble understanding what people say to me." Jared cleared his throat, glancing at Rhodey, whose expression seemed like it might be as confused or wary as his own. The scientific principle mandated he have more facts, but he had a feeling the man wouldn't like it if he looked his gift horse in the mouth. "Are you saying Harvard is a good or a bad investment? And how long are the terms of this arrangement for?"

Maddox let out a soft laugh. "I suppose having all your plans falling down so abruptly might make it difficult to wrap your mind around anything else. I'm saying *you* are a good investment. Sending you to Harvard would be worth the cost —if you're willing to put in the work. And we will discuss the terms of this arrangement once I see how your training goes. For now, that's the only answer I need. If you're willing to come with me, be put in suitable accommodations, and show up to your studies with the same dedication you've shown in everything you've done so far."

This is definitely an international spy ring.

Punting away the absurd thought, Jared held up a finger to Mr. Maddox and turned to Rhodey, speaking out of the side of his mouth. "What do you think?"

Rhodey scowled, taking Jared's hand and lacing their fingers together. "I think if it's real? That would be fucking awesome. And I get why he'd want someone who's gonna be an amazing doctor one day. I'd do this just for you, to get you to Havard. I'm just having a hard time believing this guy's got the kind of power to do all that."

"Yes, I can see why that would be hard to take at face value. And I have offered you nothing at all. Yet." Maddox slid his hand into his pocket, pulling out a cell phone. One of those fancy phones with the screens not many people had. He turned it on and an image appeared, a technology the newspapers said was available in Japan, but seemed like science fiction. "I know where your sister is. With my help, you'll be able to free her from her marriage to a man who is much worse than… What did you call him? A 'dirty cop'? In any case, the situation is sensitive and will take some careful maneuvering to get her and her son away to safety. But if you come with me now, if you do the training, you will be able to accomplish it."

The color left Rhodey's face as he stared down at the photo. The woman, with soft, flowing, curly dark blonde hair was familiar from the one photo Rhodey kept of her in his wallet. She was smiling, her arms around the boy with short, wilder curls, but the smile didn't reach her dark gray eyes. Looking a bit like he'd been grabbed and forced to hold still for the picture, the boy, about eleven or twelve, glared at whoever was taking the picture, his light gray eyes flashing with anger.

"Let's do it, Rhodey." Staring down at the screen, Jared decided even if Mr. Maddox was full of shit about Harvard, he definitely knew where Rhodey's sister was. Somehow, they could get that information and get Tracey even if everything else didn't go to plan. "If he doesn't do what he said, we're free to go. No harm, no foul." He met the man's eyes. "Right?"

Maddox inclined his head again. "Absolutely. But I keep my word, Jared. It's a quality you have as well, which I admire. I expect that to remain true between us." He put the phone away and gave Rhodey a sympathetic look. "I'll have a copy printed up for you. If it's any consolation, your sister is doing well. Her marriage is not a pleasant one, but he does not physically harm her. The boy...well, from my intel, no more than what it takes to keep him in line, which appears to be quite challenging. Once we get you and your sister away from the toxic influence, I'll offer her my assistance with him."

"He's a kid." Rhodey inhaled roughly, closing his eyes. "I don't...I can't think about stuff like that yet. Just tell me what I've got to do to get her out of there. I'm in. Whatever you want, I'm fucking in."

Lips thinned with displeasure, Maddox motioned for them to follow him back to the fire escape. "You can start with improving your language. It won't be acceptable in your training." He cast Jared a warm smile of approval. "I've noticed that is not something you struggle with."

"I—" Pausing to grab his duffel off the rooftop, Jared checked in with Rhodey to make sure the whole not swearing thing wasn't too weird for him. "I swear. It's just that I think of other words first a lot, so those are the ones that come out of my mouth, most of the time."

Rhodey rubbed his hand over his mouth and met Maddox's eyes as they reached the metal steps. "If that's one of the conditions of training, I won't swear. It's not a big deal."

"Having that kind of control over yourself is a very big deal." Maddox gestured for them to go down ahead of him. "My driver is parked in front of the bank. He's been working with me for a long time and he's loyal and dedicated, but he doesn't have patience for children. Don't chatter at him, and be very polite. Show him you're young men with standards, yes?"

Being a guest or an employee definitely had rules that Jared hadn't quite understood until he'd picked up a few etiquette books from the local library in his mid-teens. He enjoyed reading Rhodey the more absurd tidbits, but secretly reveled in all of the arcane seeming rules that danced off the page to show him other possibilities for another life. Being able to demonstrate some of the things he'd learned, making Maddox happy so he'd teach Rhodey how to rescue Tracey more quickly?

Will be a sincere pleasure.

Nodding politely, he met Maddox's steady stare with one of his own. "Yes, sir. We can do that."

"Good." Maddox gave Rhodey a pointed look when he stopped at the bottom of the stairs and still hadn't answered. "Will this be difficult for you, Rhodey? You are only seventeen, so I suppose expecting you to behave as an adult might be asking a bit much."

Rhodey pressed his eyes shut, looking a bit like he was counting to ten. When he opened them, his gray eyes had darkened, like they did sometimes when he was really pissed, but his voice was level. "I can behave. And I'm an adult. I don't think you'd be offering me all this if I wasn't."

For some reason, that had Maddox's lips twitching with amusement. "I've trained younger men and women. When someone stands out and has particular skills, they draw attention from different agencies. Waiting too long can end up with them being assets for rivals. But obviously a younger asset needs to be handled quite differently. I would have someone much more…patient with me if you were a child. And we'd be discussing this over ice cream. I hope that won't be necessary. My last 'Mary Poppins' was swept up by the CIA."

"I knew it!" Jared snapped his fingers—the sound echoing off the buildings around them—then winced. He lowered his voice. "Sorry. I knew you were a recruiter for some sort of international agency or spy ring." Re-adjusting his bag, he glanced at the driver, who'd emerged from a dark sedan. "I guess even spooks need schools."

There was some indulgence in Maddox's gaze as he turned his attention to Jared. "Yes, I suppose they do. You're close, Jared. But not quite. The training does open up several opportunities, but we'll discuss this further when the time is right."

On their side of the car now, the driver opened the front passenger door for Maddox. "Any difficulties, sir?" He eyed Rhodey, standing head and shoulders above both him and Jared.

"Not at all." Maddox slid into the smooth leather seat, glancing up at the driver. "I shared your concerns that they would be more of a product of their upbringing than of their talents, but I'm pleased to see it was unwarranted. They're actually quite pleasant to converse with."

Completely bald, with no facial hair, including a complete lack of eyebrows, the driver seemed more an endless expanse of pasty white skin and thick neck than a man as he nodded.

"Good to hear." Leaving the door open, he faced Jared. "Hands against the side of the car. Feet shoulder width apart."

Rhodey stepped forward, losing the calm expression he'd been holding on to. "Why? We haven't done anything wrong. Is this a trick? You have to tell us if you're cops and we're under arrest. We want a lawyer."

"I must say. That *is* a new one." The driver glanced over his shoulder at Maddox. "One hears so little that is truly novel these days."

Chuckling, Maddox regarded Rhodey with seemingly endless patience. "This isn't a trick. It's a precaution. I'd be a fool to have either of you sitting behind me with a weapon. You will learn, quite quickly, I am many things, but never that. You're right, you've done nothing you could be charged with. But you were planning to rob a bank. You're going to have to earn my trust."

Feeling dirty and low was something Jared had gotten used to in his life, but it wasn't a feeling he'd planned to need to confront again once he and Rhodey had the money from the robbery. Shame heating his cheeks, he turned with a reassuring glance, then placed his hands on the side of the car a bit more awkwardly than he would've liked.

"At least you're not wearing too many layers." Sighing as if the entire thing put him out, the driver began his patdown, leaving no part of Jared untouched.

Tone conversational, Maddox took something out of the dashboard. A cigar. He clipped it deftly, then brought it to his lips. "I have a feeling you got their sizes right, as usual. I think once they're set up and changed into something more comfortable, this will all be much easier for them to absorb." He glanced at Rhodey. "Jared can enjoy the cigar you gave him while you're being checked. After this, the rest of the night will be much more pleasant, I promise."

The only person who'd ever made him promises in his life had been Rhodey, so in Jared's experience when someone gave him their word it stuck. He wasn't sure what passed for 'pleasant' in Maddox's world.

Only one thing was certain. It had to be better than where he and Rhodey had just come from.

No way could it be worse.

Chapter Five

PAST

*O*ne day, this fancy car with smooth leather seats would be a birthday gift. Or...one just like it. Rhodey cracked open his window, not sure why the things were so dark, gripping Jared's hand as they were driven...who the fuck knew where. With two strangers, offering the equivalent of candy.

A good life, one that didn't include robbing banks and risking Jared landing his ass in jail the day he fucking turned eighteen. Rhodey didn't really care if he ended up there himself, except it might've delayed him finding Tracey for a little bit. Until he found a way to escape.

Like fuck was anything keeping him from looking for his older sister. Or taking him away from Jared. He wasn't sure how he'd accomplish a lot of the shit he planned to do, but he would.

This dude was offering a way to reach both his and Jared's goals. Believing him might be a dumbass move, but fuck, they didn't have a whole lot of options. Mastering jailbreaking seemed a whole lot more complicated than doing...whatever it was the rich guy expected from them.

He squeezed Jared's hand a bit tighter, glad the two

strange men were in the front seat, leaving them in the back behind a roll-up thingy like they were the fancy people, getting chauffeured around. "If this is all some kind of twisted sex-murder-plot, you stay behind me while I gut them. We don't want to mess up your hands."

Jared's eyes momentarily widened, the owlish expression raising the heavy rimmed eyeglasses he'd worn for as long as Rhodey could remember up on the bridge of his nose. "And miss the show?" He leaned closer to Rhodey, whispering darkly in his ear. "If you twist the knife in the heart, it's a hundred-percent kill shot."

Grinning, Rhodey let his eyes drift shut and made a thoughtful sound. "That's the organ that pumps blood when you get hard, right?"

Jared didn't snicker often, but the sound escaping him now definitely couldn't be mistaken for anything else. "It's always doing that, but yes." He slid his free hand up Rhodey's thigh. "Yours is still working okay?"

"Hell yeah." Rhodey patted the middle of his chest. "Hasn't failed me yet. Especially when you're around, using that voice. Do it again. Teach me other stuff."

"Severing the Achilles tendon is the quickest way to make certain your victim can't run." Leaning forward, his face nearly in Rhodey's lap, Jared inched his fingers up Rhodey's pant leg, then down inside his tubesock to trace the back of his heel. "Right here."

Lips curving, Rhodey hummed his understanding and pleasure. There was no better feeling in the world than his best friend's hands on him, even if it was just somewhere like his ankle. Best fucking way to learn anything. "Like that old guy you told me about? He was the…king of something?"

"Achilles was a warrior. Like you." Jared's voice was husky, his lids heavy like he'd just gotten off, as he massaged the spot he'd traced. "A demigod. His mother dipped him in a magical river to make him invulnerable, but someone shot him in the spot she'd held him that the water didn't touch. He died. That's where we get the term 'Achilles heel'."

Rhodey huffed, shaking his head, his gaze locked on the side of Jared's face. "She must've felt shitty about that. Did she toss the rest of her babies in the water? Make sure to do a better job? Pretty sure they float."

Three small lines creased the spot at the bridge of Jared's nose and he sat up. "I don't know much about babies. I don't care for them. No obstetrics for me, though you do need to do a stint interning at each specialty. I'm still trying to figure out how to get out of using speculums on women."

"Well, if you've gotta do it, at least they'll know you're not some creeper trying to get off when they're all, you know, uncomfortable." Shifting a bit, Rhodey got *more* than a little uncomfortable with the topic. If his sister had to deal with that shit, maybe he'd rid the world of a few of the less ethical doctors. Jared alone would be better than a dozen of those fuckers. He gave his head a little shake. "As for the babies, find out if you can do some…what's that damn word? Buoyancy tests on them?"

Hands on his knees, Jared rubbed his palms back and forth like maybe it helped him think. Or would conjure answers, like a genie lived in his kneecaps. "Hm. Babies are born underwater sometimes. They know how to swim and hold their breath and things, I've read. They forget how after some weeks or months."

Rhodey nodded, liking this conversation a whole lot more than anything involving speculums being used on anyone. He twisted a bit to lean against the door. "Make sure you get 'em when they're fresh, then. You could—"

The partition slid down, Maddox shooting them an amused look over his shoulder. "Remind me to keep both of you far away from children. And avoid conversations like this in the future." He chuckled, shaking his head. "You might give people the wrong impression."

"What impression would that be? Intelligence?" Jared sat up straighter, his huffiness around all things intellectual showing. When he got a smack in the mouth at home it was usually when their foster parents said something against smarts, so it wasn't surprising now. "The empirical method is the strongest educational and scientific discovery tool we have, and much of what separates men from the neanderthals."

Rather than take objection to Jared's tone, Maddox looked...kinda impressed. "Absolutely. But none of the knowledge you will need to succeed in this life will require any kind of experience with infants. Or children. You would do well to consider all the weaknesses you're aware of about the human body. That information is useful to everyone."

'Huh?' wasn't a look Jared wore often, but he sure as hell wore it now as he blinked back at Maddox. "In a good way or a bad way?" His snooty tone slipped a bit, Exposing his born and bred Upstate cityboy heritage. "Because I don't think physicians usually think of it in those terms."

"No, I suppose they don't." Maddox inclined his head, then faced forward again. "Ah, here we are. Let's leave this discussion for another time. We have arrived at the place you will call home for the near future."

The dark windows made it really hard to get a good look at the place, but the second Rhodey opened the door, he almost closed it again at the sight. A long, round driveway surrounding an actual fountain, the big kinds he'd only ever seen in the park—where assholes pissed at night, only a lot cleaner and well kept. The place was a fucking mansion, with pillars and huge stone steps, so big Rhodey got a bit dizzy looking up at it.

"Holy shit." Closing his eyes and rubbing his fingers against them, Rhodey shook his head before opening them again. Nope. He wasn't dreaming. "Kinda not caring if you brought us here to murder us. Could we check out the place first, though?"

Maddox let out a deep, rumbling laugh, stepping up behind him and Jared and putting a hand on each of their shoulders. "I'll do you one better. I'll even let you see your rooms." He motioned to his driver. "Crispin, get them both settled in and have the cook prepare something filling. I have some matters to attend to, but I will join you for breakfast in the morning."

"We'll make them quite comfortable. Rest assured." The driver—Crispin—looked him and Jared over, then sighed as if he were picturing all of the dirt they might get on whatever fancy carpets were inside. "Fetch your things. We won't want to keep Lewis waiting."

Grabbing Jared's hand again as soon as Maddox moved away, Rhodey tugged him close, speaking under his breath. "Great, we're meeting more rich people. Is it bad that I don't give a fuck if I ain't got all the pretty manners they do? I'm gonna become a super spy without all that shit."

Ahead of them, Crispin paused on the steps and snapped his fingers. "You will refrain from swearing. This is the last time you will be warned." He kept walking without turning around to see if they followed. "Now. Tonight, you will dine in your rooms. Tomorrow, you will be expected to dress for dinner and be at table at eight sharp. Meals are at eight, one, and eight. Miss them and you will miss the opportunity to eat. Understood?"

"Yeah... So is swearing part of the eating rules, too?" Rhodey twisted his lips, not loving the idea. "If I slip up, you gonna feed me to your dogs? Rich people got those wicked dogs, right? Hate to tell you, but I'm real good with animals. You'll have a fu—" Okay, maybe he'd save testing the dude's rules until *after* he and Jared got some good food in them. But the orders itched. "You'll have an animal uprising."

"What a singular idea." The dude spoke like Rhodey had only ever had one idea in his life and he'd managed to share it right then and there on the mansion steps, inspired by their grandeur. "No. You will not be starved for your slips." He opened the front door with one hand, motioning them through ahead of him. He waited until Rhodey passed inside before rumbling in his ear, "Mister McCleod will."

Breath catching, Rhodey almost tripped onto the marble tiles, a low growl rising in his chest as he spun to face the man. "Try it. Your boss man didn't snatch me and my guy up for nothing. How much blood is in a human body, Jared? I'm too dumb to know that stuff, but I bet I could learn through practice."

"One point two to one point five gallons. Exsanguination is a messy business, however. If that's what you're referring to. It takes spilling far less to induce death, however." Jared stared up at a giant chandelier, hanging from a thick silverish chain in the middle of a giant foyer, complete with sweeping double staircases. "I believe the training will be difficult and our hosts are attempting to leverage what we care about most to make us give our full attention to it. Spies are..." His lips twisted like he tasted something bad. "Hardcore?"

Crispin didn't comment this time, preceding them up the stairs to the right and down a long gallery type hall. There were bedrooms on either side, some visible through open doors with men and young men inside. Some studied at desks while others did calisthenics or recited things they'd memorized. They went up another set of stairs, then another to a third floor where the rooms were cramped and the temperature chilled.

"You'll earn your way down." Opening a door, he motioned Rhodey inside. "Your meal will be brought to you. Make yourself comfortable. Good night." The door shut and a lock turned, separating him from Jared. "Sleep tight."

A wave of panic smashed into Rhodey's chest. Not even bothering to look around the room, he slammed his shoulder into the door. Twisted the knob and yanked before slamming into it again. "You motherfu—" No. No, he couldn't risk swearing and having those bastards take it out on Jared. Not until he was sure he could get to him. "Open the door! You mess with him and I swear I'll rip off your arms and stuff them down your throat. I'll cut you into little pieces and fry them to feed to all your minions downstairs! Let me out!"

The only sound to greet him was the drip-drip of the faucet in the porcelain wall sink. A twin bed with a lumpy looking mattress, wool blankets with one pillow on top, the only furniture in the room. A window without a latch. A bulb in the ceiling socket had a pull chain. That was it.

Pacing the room, Rhodey raked his fingers through his hair. Went back to the door to shout until his voice went hoarse, then strode up to the bed and tore the mattress off it, tossing it across the room. He lifted the bedframe, shoving it into the window, but the fucking thing wouldn't break.

One prison sentence traded for another. Rhodey kept his cursing in his head, but used every single swear word he knew, along with more he invented, the sensation of being trapped getting him about ready to lose his shit. If Jared were here, he'd say something smart. Come up with a plan.

But he wasn't. Rhodey was alone and...

Fucking helpless.

A feeling he didn't like very much.

The sound of metal squeaking against metal preceded a brush of cool air against his ankles. A portal at the bottom of his door opened, a tray sliding in with a mug of stew and some plastic utensils.

Someone whispered to him. "Psst."

Dropping down on the floor on his stomach, Rhodey shoved the tray aside and looked through the small space. "Who are you? You gonna open the door or you gonna piss me off and keep giving me time to come up with nasty ways to pay you back for it?"

A young woman with a long, dark braid seemed to mull that over before a broad grin showed even, white teeth. "I was going to say, get some rest. They let you out in the morning. Welcome to basic. You're gonna love it."

"So far, I'm not a fan." Rhodey huffed, dipping his fingers into the stew and snatching up a chunk of meat, ignoring the stinging heat as he shoved it in his mouth. "You training to be a super spy, too?"

That earned him a chuckle, and her black eyes sparkled with humor. "Mercs. Not spies. And yes. Why? You think a girl can't kick your ass?"

Rhodey shrugged and grabbed another piece of meat. "With the right training? Sure. If the wrong body parts get in the way, I guess you just get rid of them. Or...like, maybe girls have some kind of extra advantage, because they already know how to work around the extras. And most of you are small, so you gotta learn how to work with that. I don't hit girls, which would mean I'd get dead."

"I have no idea what you're talking about, except for the hitting girls part. I hit boys, and I hit hard, so when we fight you'd better be prepared." She turned her head, looking toward a sound down the hall like a clanging door, then back. "Look. I'll do you a solid. They brought you in with your friend, which means if you want him to have that fancy room downstairs and good food and not to get the crap beat out of him...or worse, by Crispin, you gotta eat with a fork and be a good boy. Your little tantrum already got his ass beat. So man up, Leonov. They're watching you."

Gritting his teeth, Rhodey thunked his head against his arm. "This is messed up, you know that, right? No one explained anything to us. Except about the swearing, and I didn't do that." He pressed his eyes shut. "And I meant tits, but I was trying to be polite. Why's everyone around here gotta treat me like I'm dumb?"

Fine boned fingers with scars across dusky knuckles slid through the door to squeeze his arm. "You're not dumb. And there is no merc 101. You'll catch on fast." A door slammed and she scrambled back before kicking some gray sweats through the door to him. "Gotta go. Name's Vani. See you tomorrow, Leonov."

"Sure. See you." Rhodey picked up the clothes, tossing them toward the mattress as he sat up. Back against the wall, he picked up the tray, scowling at the utensils. Rolling his eyes, he grabbed the fork and dug into the stew. Wasn't the worst thing he'd ever eaten, but he wanted better for his best friend. More steak. Pastries that melted in his mouth. A meal under that chandelier...okay, maybe not the one in the hallway, but this fucking place probably had a bunch.

If eating properly got Jared any of that stuff, he'd do it. Then, they could lock him in this stupid room for as long as they wanted. Maybe the girl would come back with Jared next time and show him he'd earned his reward of freeing his best friend.

The idea of being let out in the morning seemed like nothing but another trick. He was stuck. Things were exactly like they'd been when he was smaller. Bigger, stronger people had all the power and could take away whatever they wanted to, and there was nothing he could do about it. Except...get bigger and stronger.

And take it all back.

Next step to hopefully earning Jared some perks was fixing the room. Rhodey put everything back in place, washing the stew cup in the sink, along with the tray, and drying them with the hem of his shirt. He changed into the new clothes and laid down on the bed, staring up at the ceiling.

Sleeping wasn't on the agenda, but pure irritation, exhaustion, and boredom finally dragged him under. He had a dream of racing a sweet, slick black car down a country road, Jared in the passenger seat and a heaping bag of money clutched to his chest. Cigars between their lips, sweet smelling smoke creating a haze around them as they gazed out at the long road ahead, imagining the kind of freedom they would have for the rest of their lives.

Reluctant to wake up when morning light shone through the window, Rhodey groaned and dragged his pillow over his head. "We shoulda just robbed that bank. Was a good freaking plan."

A buzzer sounded, loud and near his head—a hidden speaker in the wall he hadn't noticed the night before. The racket stopped, then started again three times before his door popped open, and the thundering of dozens of running feet echoed from beyond.

Not wanting to risk getting locked in again if his door opening had been a fluke, Rhodey bolted from the bed, tripping over the blanket and stumbling out into the hall. He reached back to snatch up his boots, shoving his bare feet in them as he trailed after the last person racing down the hall.

"Jared?" Rhodey glanced in the direction Crispin must've taken his best friend after locking him in. Fucker probably had to drag Jared. Hopefully, his man had gotten in a few hits. Right to Crispin's hoity-toity ballsack. "Jared!"

The chick from the night before popped out of a room, still doing her braid. "Shh! Do you want to get us all hosed down?" She motioned Rhodey with her, breaking into a jog. "He'll be in the dining hall with everyone else. We're late. Come on."

"Guess you didn't want an answer to that question." Rhodey jogged with her, mood lightening a bit with the knowledge he'd get to see Jared. And neither of them were prisoners anymore. "Wouldn't mind a hose. They don't believe in showers in this place or what?"

"You have to earn those. I got a demerit two days in a row and lost my first floor privileges." Tossing her braid over one slender shoulder, Vani shrugged one lightly muscled arm. "Ugh." She stopped at the doorway to give the monitor there a pleading look. "Come on, Sanders. I'll give you my bag of licorice if you let us in. We're only thirty seconds late."

The door opened, a tall, sandy haired man blocking the way with his arm and giving Vani a long look. "You can't bribe your way out of everything, kiddo. And you're setting a bad example." He glanced at Rhodey, then back at Vani, lowering his voice. "I'll let it slide this time, but if you get me fired, I'm going to wait a couple years, hunt you down, and cut off your pinkies."

Wiggling said pinkies, Vani sashayed past Sanders. "And if you play nice, I'll hire you and make you a very rich man, so you can retire in style with seven doting grandbabies and a pet llama."

"I know." Sanders chuckled, shoving Vani's shoulder. "Why do you think I put up with your nonsense? It's called an investment."

"Smart man." She bowed and motioned Rhodey with her. "C'mon. We're at the bad kids' table. Porridge and bacon bits for you today. The top table gets all you can eat steak and eggs. Lucky bastards. Gotta earn my way back there. It's hard to bulk up on gruel."

A shadow fell over them, Maddox's voice strangely soothing as he snapped his fingers and brought Vani's attention to him. "It is, and I'd hate to see you fall behind. How about we make a deal? You perform well in all your training today, and I'll have a talk with your instructors. But *only* if I am very impressed." He motioned to Rhodey. "I did mention you were having breakfast with me? Whatever are you doing in here? Come, Jared's waiting for you."

Seeming to understand her response wasn't necessary or desired, Vani gave Rhodey an impressed look behind Maddox's back, before making her way past several long tables to one in the far corner, where a few uninspired looking recruits spooned up said gruel. She slid into her seat and took up the spoon to eat with a gusto they all lacked.

"You have some skill at making connections. Very good." Maddox led the way out of the big dining hall, down a massive corridor lined with expensive looking statues and vases, everything gleaming and holding a faint, clean, pine scent. Two huge double doors opened for him before he could even step up to them. He brought Rhodey into another dining room, this one a bit smaller, but even grander than the other. "I understand last night must have been very confusing. Some lines were crossed, but I hope I can make up for it. As you can see, your friend is no worse for wear. Ground rules do need to be established, but there will be certain…concessions for you both."

Appearing no worse for anything, much less wear, Jared stood from his seat with his, "Husky!"

Dressed in a charcoal gray suit complete with pocket square, he looked like he'd been born to live in the mansion. His white shirt was crisp enough to give some fucker a lethal papercut, and someone had replaced his klunky glasses with a sleeker pair.

Closing the distance between them with a few long strides, Rhodey tugged Jared into his arms to hug him. Put his hands on his shoulders to inspect him for a damn *hair* out of place, then yanked him to his chest again. "You good? Did anyone hurt you? Point 'em out and I'll wreck 'em."

"I'm okay. Nothing too bad." Jared smoothed his hands down Rhodey's arms. "Where's your suit? Or clothes? This looks like prison garb." He made a face like he tasted something bad, then shook his head. "Are you okay?"

Before Rhodey could say a word, Maddox cleared his throat. "You may continue this conversation while we eat, but please do sit down. The cook made you both a very nice variety so we can explore what you like. We wouldn't want to upset them by letting their hard work go to waste, now would we?"

Rhodey scowled, grabbing the chair next to the one Jared

had left, not sitting until he was sure his best friend wouldn't be dragged away again. "Look, man. I appreciate the nice food, but I don't get how things are around here and...I don't like it. Are we training or prisoners or...? Hell, I don't know what. I need to know what I'm...what *we're*...dealing with."

Inclining his head, Maddox took his own place at the head of the table, unfolding a napkin and placing it over his lap. "All very reasonable questions. Just as my request was quite reasonable. You will do what I asked you to and then you will have your answers."

Mimicking Maddox with precise motions like he'd been taking notes, Jared unfolded his napkin and smoothed it over his lap. He stared at the plate in front of him before carefully choosing the outermost fork and a steak knife to cut into a very tender looking sirloin. The meat sliced like butter, and juice ran out into some tiny potatoes with little green ferns on them.

"Thank you, sir. This is a very nice steak. I will enjoy it very much." Under the table, Jared toed Rhodey's boot with his foot, prodding him to pick up his own fork. "Did you have a nice evening?"

Maddox gave Jared a warm smile and nodded, taking a sip of what looked like orange juice in a tall wine glass. "I did, thank you, Jared. All things considered, it ended with several successful endeavors." He forked a small bite of the thick omelet on his plate, the rich scent of cheese and roasted vegetables combining with the aroma from the steak to make Rhodey's mouth water. Which the man seemed fully aware of when he lifted a brow at him, nodding his approval when Rhodey started to eat. "Are you pleased with your accommodations?"

Glancing sideways at Rhodey, Jared seemed to be looking to him for an answer, but ended up taking a deep breath and answering himself. "We never slept in different rooms since we met, sir. Would it be okay if we shared?"

"I will consider your request." Maddox took another bite of his omelet. "But you didn't answer my question."

"It was warm and comfortable, sir. Thank you." Jared spoke around a bite of the steak, washing it down with a deep drink of milk. "The blankets were a little itchy, but I think I'll get used to them. Maybe I'll pull the sheets up a little higher tonight."

Maddox clucked his tongue and shook his head. "Nonsense. I'll have a selection brought to your room so you can choose something more to your taste. Unless Rhodey would like to insist along with you that you share a room? I don't believe his will need to be adjusted."

The piece of meat Rhodey was swallowing almost stuck in his throat. Without hesitation, he shook his head, grabbing his own napkin to wipe his mouth. Manners. They wanted him to have good manners. "No. Maybe...maybe separate rooms would be good. We're gonna have different kinds of training, right? And Jared's gotta study and all that. But...we can still hang out sometimes?"

From the way Maddox's lips curved, he'd just passed some kind of test. He made an affirmative sound. "Yes, of course. I hope you understand, I am committing considerable resources to make sure you both reach your full potential. Some of our methods may seem strange, but they are very effective. I do not recruit anyone who does not excel in some manner. The path they take, how difficult it is, is entirely on each individual. But if you trust the process, we will get you both exactly where you need to be."

Jared toyed with his potatoes now, seeming lost in thought. "I guess until last night I always thought I'd be alone, so Rhodey making his own way in this makes sense." He glanced up, his dark hair falling across his brow to partially hide one blue eye. "Sure. We can...hang out sometimes."

Appetite gone, Rhodey stared down at his plate, wishing he could tell Jared why he wasn't challenging Maddox on...

anything. The idea of being separated from Jared at all made his chest hurt, and air didn't want to fill his lungs right, but the alternative meant Jared being in one of those rooms. Eating slop. Maybe getting beaten for real.

Their new... Boss? Teacher? Head honcho? Whatever. He was giving Rhodey a choice. And no way would Rhodey pick the one that made Jared's life harder. He was gonna do important things with it.

"Come now, you needn't see this like you're being sent off to live on opposite sides of the ocean. If Rhodey does well with his training, and you do well with yours, you may have all your meals together in here." Maddox lowered his voice, like he was sharing a secret. "Which is highly irregular, we usually maintain the same system for all the recruits, but as I told you, you're both special. I also have need of a skilled doctor to join the ranks, so Jared is in a unique position. Not that I won't challenge you, but not the same way I would a recruit who's in a position that could be filled by anyone."

"What position will Rhodey be filling, sir?" Steak half gone, Jared paused to refold his napkin on his lap, obviously being very careful not to mess up his new clothes. The way his dark hair curled against the collar was out of place with how neat the rest of his appearance was. "Is he going to be someone important? He should be. He knows a lot of ways to punch things, and he can be very intimidating. Also, he's a very good listener and sees things about people I sometimes don't."

Motioning to someone out of sight, Maddox didn't respond as several men and women in waiter uniforms came in, clearing the table and putting fresh plates in front of them. He motioned to the covered trays in the center of the table. "Please, help yourselves to anything that appeals to you." He turned his attention to Jared. "Those are some very keen observations, young man. You have your own skills at reading people, in a different way, and we will be honing that. As for

Rhodey, the goal is for him to eventually take up a leadership role. I am very selective with those I choose for specialized training in a broad number of fields, but like you, I believe he's well suited for it."

Rhodey ran his tongue over his teeth, ignoring the food as he studied the older man. He liked the sound of everything he said, but what was the catch? Other than the crappy room and seeing Jared less. They'd still be having meals together, and maybe it wouldn't always be like last night. If Rhodey wasn't locked in, he could find out where Jared was staying. Learn how to be sneaky and spend the night with him anyway.

But he had a feeling he wouldn't get the chance if he didn't follow whatever rules this place had. Which he still couldn't figure out. It was like...like part of the training was picking them up along the way. Not being sure of anything until you fucked up. Then, at least that could be scratched off the 'what *not* to do' list.

He didn't like it, but for the chance of Jared becoming a doctor? Yeah, he'd deal. And he'd earn the privilege of being near him any way he could.

"So you want me to learn to be in charge of the other kids in there?" Rhodey lifted the lid off a tray, frowning as he took in the little pastries that smelled spicy and a bit cheesy instead of sweet. "What are these?"

Taking one, Jared broke it open with his fork and took a bite, making a thoughtful face. "I'm not sure, husky, but they're really good." He pushed a little toward Rhodey with his fork. "Here. Have some."

While Rhodey took a bite, Maddox watched him, a hint of amusement in his smile. "They're cheesy jalapeño bites. Careful, the heat creeps up on you."

Tongue on fire, Rhodey nodded, huffing and grabbing his milk. He gulped it down, laughing and shaking his head. "You did that on purpose."

"Yes. I had a feeling Jared would find the sensation more

tolerable, but you'll adapt. Part of your training will be identifying various flavors. It's important you know when something doesn't taste right." Maddox sat back in his chair. "You will not be 'taking charge' of any of the recruits, you still have a long way to go before you're ready for that. But you may work with some of them in the future."

"Are we your youngest recruits right now, sir?" Jared lifted another lid, taking out a gelatinous mound that appeared to have a small brain in it. "Oh. Sweetmeats. I've heard about these but I've never had them."

Maddox's smile widened. "You will have to tell me what else you've heard of, that you'd like to try. We can make it a special treat whenever I dine with you. Unfortunately, it will not be a frequent occurrence. Aside from the 'school', I have several projects in the works, but I will be keeping up with your progress, along with seeing to some of your training myself once you're further along."

A glint appeared in Jared's eyes at the mention of Maddox's special treats. "Thank you, sir. Do they need to be all food related?"

Sitting forward, Maddox held Jared's gaze. "No, my boy. But some things will take a considerable amount of effort to earn. To answer your previous question, yes, you are the youngest. But I do not personally trouble myself with children. The rare times someone has shown potential at a tender age, I arrange for them to begin a less intense form of training with those qualified to handle…well, let's just say children can be sensitive and I have no tolerance for pointless tears or wayward emotions. Keep that in mind when you are trying to earn my favors."

Chewing thoughtfully, Jared nodded, swallowing the bite of brains and clear gelatin like he'd been doing the zombie schtick his entire life. "Yes, sir. I don't cry too much. Our foster parents didn't like it either, and it just made them madder."

"Ah, but you see, they were terribly unqualified to help

either of you develop in *any* way. Emotions, when properly controlled, can be useful. But that is a conversation for another day." Maddox lifted his napkin and laid it beside his plate. "Finish eating, as much as you want, and then go find Crispin. He will let you know your schedule. I'd also like to make it clear, when I am not present, Crispin has the authority here. You will treat him with all the respect you would me. And that is as a man who will provide absolutely everything you need to not only reach your potential, but thrive."

At the mention of Crispin, Jared chewed more slowly, his skin losing a bit of color. "You're very different in your approaches, sir. Is that deliberate?"

"For now? Yes. You're not ready for me to train you on my level, yet. Crispin will help you get there." Maddox stood, walking around the table behind them and squeezing each of their shoulders. "I have very high expectations for you, which means the trials you go through may sometimes seem almost unbearable. But you will get through them, and find yourself stronger, sharper, and more resilient when you get to the other side. So long as you never forget that, I believe you will find there is nothing you cannot face."

Finished chewing another pastry, this one sweet and sticky and tempting him to go back for more, Rhodey cleared his throat. Tried to wrap his mind around what Maddox was saying. "So…Crispin is giving us the beginner's level? *He's* the easy one?"

Maddox chuckled and shook his head. "He is not 'easy', so do yourself a favor and do not test him. But in some ways, he will be putting you through your paces at a lower level, increasing the intensity as he sees fit. He is very good at his job, so even when you are uncertain about one of his commands, or his methods, know he is doing it for your benefit."

"But he likes it, too." Jared made the observation without emotion. "He gets off on it."

"Very observant." Maddox patted Jared's shoulder and stepped back. "I see no reason for one not to enjoy their job, within reason. Learning those lines is the important thing. And that is something I would like you to focus on, my boy. You need to pay very close attention, because it would be very easy for you to find yourself beyond that edge. Crispin will make certain you see where it is. And when I work with you, I will make certain you find the balance you need. That you crave. Further than most would even consider, but not so far you can't come back from it. Enough to sate you." His lips curved as he gave Jared a knowing look. "If you're uncertain what I mean, I will clarify the next time we speak. For now, that should be plenty to pique your interest."

The door to the private dining room opened, Vani slipping in to deliver a note to Maddox on a silver platter. Crispin entered behind her, walking up to jingle a bell on her heel. "Very good. Not a sound. We'll start with a quick jog next."

"Here." Maddox picked up one of the honey pastries, handing it to Vani after taking the note. "You'll need your energy. If you can run quietly enough that Crispin can't find you, the rest will be waiting for you in the kitchen."

"Thank you, sir." Pastry in one hand, Vani adjusted her tank top with the other. She'd ditched the sweatshirt matching Rhodey's, and looked like she'd done some kinda physical training while he and Jared were eating. "I won't disappoint you."

Maddox inclined his head. "No, you won't. Go on now, you have a room to earn back. And no more making Crispin waste his time correcting your language. He is a very busy man."

Something flashed in Crispin's eyes that said he didn't mind that part of his job at all, but his expression remained pasty and bland. Vani bowed, eating the pastry as she ran out of the room on soundless bare feet, and disappeared from view.

"I'll give her a head start. She always gets cocky when I do." Crispin gave a set upon sigh. "We'll cure her of it someday."

Rhodey cleaned his fingers with the napkin, avoiding looking at either man, afraid his thoughts would show all over his face. He hoped they failed at getting rid of Vani's cockiness. If they did, maybe he stood a chance of holding on to some of his own identity.

Looking at Jared, in the suit, eating all proper, he couldn't help being a bit scared he wouldn't recognize his best friend when they were done with him. Maybe, once he was able to spend time with him alone, they could come up with a plan together to stop that from happening.

But months passed without any kind of opportunity. Rhodey wasn't sure how it had happened. They ate together, as promised, but a lot of the time their schedules forced them to eat fast and hardly say a word. Until his birthday, days rolled into one another, a nonstop cycle of things he couldn't explain becoming perfectly normal. The blast of the hose when one recruit stepped out of line. Nights without sleep, learning hand to hand combat in the worst possible weather, the first time he felt the whip on his skin and…so many times after.

This was his life now and he could hardly remember it being any other way.

Somehow, even though a lot of the other recruits did end up earning other rooms, Rhodey never managed to impress Crispin enough to do the same. The space had become familiar, though. And it wasn't like he ever spent enough time in it to appreciate it if it had been a nicer one. He did get better clothes, though, thank fuck. Recruits stuck in gray had a real hard time doing recon and stealth exercises.

If Rhodey got a say, he'd never wear anything except

black, ever again. The color made it easier to hide a lot of sins. And more importantly, weaknesses.

Blood never bothered him, but one of the first lessons to stick?

No matter how much was spilled, either his own or others, he could never let pain, regret, or sympathy slow him down. Because as 'special' as he was? In this place?

The only thing easier to do than lose himself...

Would be to disappear.

Chapter Six

PAST

$\mathcal{I}$nside the private dining hall, Rhodey took his place at the table, brow furrowing as his gaze slipped to Jared's empty seat. Was this a new kind of training? Showing him his birthday didn't matter? Like...whatever, but...he really needed to see his best friend. It was the only gift he could ever want.

Instead, what he got was that fucker, Crispin. Coming in with a velvet box. On a tray. The man set the thing in front of him, then motioned for someone else to join them. A guy about Rhodey's age, but a lot smaller—especially now that Rhodey had begun to bulk up with all the exercise.

"Where's Jared?" Rhodey didn't usually bother questioning the man. If he got any reaction at all, it was never a good one. Today? He didn't give a damn. *My own present to myself.* "He's never late for breakfast."

"He's with your lord and master." Crispin nodded at the box as the brown haired, green eyed guy he didn't recognize took up a stiff stance to Rhodey's right. "Be a good boy and you can see him when he's done with his test."

Blowing out a breath, Rhodey picked up the box. "Okay, but does this dude need to stand so close? If I'd already had my breakfast, I'd smash his face on one of these pretty plates. How does anyone here not know better?"

That got a rare laugh from the man. "Tell him where you want him to stand. Be specific. And do not send him from this room."

All right, it wasn't often the games Crispin played—and Rhodey *knew* some of them were really fucked up games— were any fun, but this one sounded like it could be. He glanced up at the small guy. "Stand on the table. Like a flamingo. I don't like the table setting, it's boring."

Without so much as a blink, the guy climbed a silk covered dining chair, straight onto the mahogany wood table. His feet were bare, the regular bells on one ankle not making a sound, the black leather covering his thighs clinging like a second skin. There was something different about him...his whole demeanor nothing like the trainees Rhodey spent most of his days with. His pretty face remained stoic, lithe muscles flowing in a graceful display as he bent one knee and lifted his arms into crane-like wings. And...just stood that way.

"Weird party favor, but thank you, Crispin." Rhodey was supposed to call him 'sir', and he might end up getting clocked for not doing it—*again*—but as far as he was concerned? Totally worth it. He grinned at the older man for good measure. "This present from you? You shouldn't have."

"Oh, no. I really should." Crispin's grin was wolfish. "The boy is Aldin. He is yours. From the Master. His job is to attend you. In whatever way you choose. But his presence is not a choice. You have responsibility for him now. The thing in the box? Well, that's just so you can have a little more fun with him." On his way to the door, Crispin glanced over his shoulder. "If you don't like using him, I'll take care of it myself and you can watch."

Wetting his lips with his tongue, Rhodey shook his head, his stomach dropping as he looked up at the smaller man. This game definitely wasn't fun anymore. Maddox's recruits might never fail, but those who didn't do so well tended to drop off the face of the planet. And no one who'd been here longer than a day believed they'd been sent back home to mommy and daddy.

He inhaled slowly, keeping his tone level. Not giving Crispin the damn reaction he was always trying to get. "Aldin, get down now. Come sit on the chair beside me. Move it over a bit, though. I don't like anyone sitting too close."

Anyone except Jared.

Aldin obediently lowered his arms and leg into a more natural position, stepping off the table onto the chair before he set his feet on the floor and adjusted the furniture to suit Rhodey's specifications. He sat, hands folded in his lap. "Thank you, sir."

"Ugh, don't call me that..." Rhodey opened the box. "My name is Rhodey. Use it."

"Yes, Rhodey."

In the box was an ebony handled switchblade with his initials carved in it and mother of pearl inlay. The card inside simply said, *Happy birthday. Don't fail. Xoxo C.*

Swallowing hard, Rhodey looked over at Aldin. "Do you know what this is about?"

Glancing at the box, Aldin licked his lips nervously. "No, s — No, Rhodey."

"Great. Guessing games. My favorite." Rhodey palmed the knife, enjoying the weight of it in his palm despite the sinking dread from the note, and the uncertainty of yet another test he had no choice to be prepared for. Those were a lot more common than...hell, hot water? More than four hours sleep? Going outside on an actual sunny day? He made a face. "All right, it's too quiet in here. Tell me about you. Why are you here? Got dreams of being a superhero or something, because if you do, you came to the *wrong* place."

"I like to serve." Aldin ran his palms over the arms of the chair, leaving a glossy sheen of sweat behind. "I was a rent boy before I came here." He looked around the room. "It's nice here. Better." A shrug seemed to sum everything else up for him. "Crispin said they were training me for someone. I think that must've been...must be you?"

Rhodey rolled his eyes and nodded. "Probably. And unless you've got some deep, dark, secret I've gotta torture out of you, I doubt they'd've done all that if they wanted you dead. He's probably just messing with me." He tucked the knife in the pocket of his black jogging pants. "Grab a plate and serve yourself. You're not a puppy, so I ain't feeding you. And if you've got any ideas about anything else? I got a boyfriend. Kinda. So...you know, you gotta handle your own thing."

Shadows moved behind Rhodey, Crispin stepping up, having reentered the room unseen from another direction. "You're sure about that?"

"What?" Rhodey scowled at him. "You gave him to me. I'm his boss or whatever, so I get to tell him to eat. What's your deal?"

"About having a boyfriend." Threading his fingers in Aldin's hair, Crispin tugged the guy's head back, exposing his throat. Leaning down, he held Rhodey's gaze as he ran his tongue up the length of Aldin's jugular. "About us not wanting this one dead?"

Rhodey stood, jaw hardening as he stared at the instructor who made the mean nun he'd had as a teacher in grade school —who believed rulers were for little hands and not measuring shit—look like an actual saint. "Unless you tell me he did something to deserve it? Yeah, I'm sure. You pounded it into the heads of the recruits who are fucking psychos that we don't hurt civilians. Seems like he counts as one."

"You're certain he was telling the truth?" Grazing with his teeth, Crispin left little wounds behind as he bit and suckled up Aldin's neck.

This cute little twink?

Rhodey spat out a laugh. "Look at him. Yeah, I'm sure.

Now cut it out. He's mine, so you don't get to hurt him."

"All right." Releasing Aldin so quickly that the guy nearly fell headfirst into the syrup pitcher, Crispin stepped away. "Remember. He goes everywhere with you. Sleeps in your bed. Washes your laundry. Serves you in any way you please. You may do with him and to him anything and no one will stop you. You will not be punished unless you lose him."

Rhodey grunted, sitting back down and grabbing the lid off a plate, glaring at the pancakes that smelled fucking amazing. They'd probably taste like sawdust with how pissed he was. "He's not a damn sock, I'm not going to lose him. And unless you're here to tell me when Jared's coming? You can go away."

"It will be rather amusing to watch you run your obstacle trials without leaving him behind. So many definitions of 'lost' and I am rather looking forward to playing target practice with him." Crispin slipped from the room without answering about Jared. "Such a shame."

Slapping two pancakes on his plate, Rhodey glanced over at Aldin again. "I hope you're fast. Eat up, I can't have you passing out on me. I'm not the doctor one. You'd've been better off if they'd given you to him."

Nothing else had seemed to really affect the guy, but mention of Jared had him leaning away from Rhodey. "Thank you. I prefer to take my chances with you. Even if they did say I'm supposed to try to poison you. I won't. Please don't tell them I told you that."

Rhodey stopped with his syrup dripping piece of pancake halfway to his mouth. Set it back down. "I won't, but because I'm not as dumb as some seem to think, how about we share?"

"Share?" Aldin turned in his seat. "I am happy to listen. Thank you for letting me share my story with you."

Blinking at him, Rhodey tried to decide if Crispin had clocked small guy in the head a few times before delivering him. "Huh? Food." He pointed at the fork. "Eat that."

Lifting the fork, Aldin popped the bite of pancake in his mouth and chewed it. Swallowed. Then drank all of Rhodey's orange juice. He was so skinny the meal would probably have his hollow stomach bulging out. Dude seriously needed to pack on the carbs.

"Try a bit of everything else. Like I said, you need your energy. And I need not to be poisoned today." Rhodey chuckled to himself, just because he was tired of things being so serious. At least when Jared was here, they could sometimes make this whole fucked up situation seem a bit brighter. And he never got tired of watching Jared enjoy every bite with quiet dignity, finding the status he deserved in so many little ways. "Try poisoning me tomorrow. Might be entertaining."

Aldin took up the lids on a bunch of the platters, some with their own serving utensils. The ham platter released hot steam when he got to it, the curls of white creating a fog that would've coated Jared's glasses. Carving off a piece of the ham, he took a bite. Moved on to the stack of waffles to the right.

Metal flashed. Fire slid across Rhodey's throat. The carving knife created a shallow wound. Deep enough to bleed, but not to kill. Moving too damn slow, Rhodey shoved his chair back. Knocked over his plate as he hit the ground. Scrambled to switch gears. Figure out how to keep himself alive.

"I graduate." Aldin grinned in his face. "You lose. Next level? You snooze and you die."

Slow clapping, Crispin stepped into view. "Go shower, Aldin, while I deal with our birthday boy."

Hand to his neck, Rhodey stared at the smaller man he couldn't have read worse if he'd tried. All his training, all the things he thought he understood, and in a split second he was back to square one. Completely clueless.

"I thought..." Rhodey shook his head, getting dizzy. "I

thought I was supposed to take care of him. Protect him. Why—?"

"Trojan horse." Sitting in Maddox's seat, Crispin took the bloody knife from Aldin's hand and used it to spear a piece of ham for his plate. "You never accept gifts from anyone. Never let an unknown—or even someone you think you know, for that matter—handle a weapon that close to you without being on alert. Your biggest mistake though? Caring about him enough to think he needed you. A sob story is a sob story, and the only person who needs you is you. You are the only person you can trust."

Clearly, Rhodey needed to work on his people skills, and he'd definitely fucked up by believing Aldin was harmless. Still, he didn't agree with Crispin. Jared needed him. His sister needed him. His nephew…

But they weren't here now and he'd be useless to them if he didn't get through this thing.

Nodding slowly, he pushed to his feet. Hand moving in a swift motion Vani'd taught him, during all their quiet moments of running silently out of reach, he palmed the knife. Flicked it open and flung it at Aldin.

His instincts might need work, but his aim?

Always spot-fucking-on.

The blade sank into the center of Aldin's throat. "Graduate that, asshole."

Surprise widened the guy's gaze. A gurgle accompanied blood gushing from his mouth as he fell backward onto the expensive foreign rug. The mess would leave a stain that wouldn't come out anytime soon—such a damn shame.

Crispin continued eating his ham as two of the ever-present lackeys came in to drag the still twitching body out to wherever they disposed of the corpses around here.

"I do hope they return the knife. That was expensive." Crispin dabbed his mouth. "Sit. Eat. Jared's waiting for you."

Rhodey plunked down in his seat, shoving a piece of

pancake in his mouth and speaking around it. Screw manners, it was his birthday. And there had to be some leeway for first kills or some shit. "Why didn't you stop me? Did you want him dead? If he was graduating, wasn't he important or something?"

Slowly putting down his mimosa, Crispin gave Rhodey a long look. "He should have caught the knife. His mistake was not killing you when he had the chance."

"Ah...yeah. Didn't know he was allowed to." Rhodey picked up a napkin, pressing it to his throat as the cut began to sting. Adrenaline really needed a longer shelf life. "You really don't like cocky recruits. Except for Vani. And me."

Crispin shrugged. "You're both special."

"Aww. See, I knew I'd grow on you." Rhodey grinned as he took another bite of pancake. "Not that you'll cry at my funeral or anything. But we can be pals when I'm too big and strong for you to rip up my back anymore. Mind telling me where they keep the bodies? I really did like that knife. Thank you."

Though he didn't crack a smile, the light in Crispin's eyes shifted to something less...dead. "The basement. Furnace room. Funny you should mention. Jared's there now having a little fun of his own."

Scrambling from his seat, Rhodey paused on instinct, having learned after his first few weeks not to leave the table when either Maddox or Crispin were in here without asking. Not that he didn't still do it sometimes just to be a shit, but with all these 'tests' he didn't need to add healing whip lashes to make it more challenging. "May I be excused?"

"You may." Crispin waved him on, calling out to him when he reached the door. "Rhodey."

Stopped short with his hand on the doorknob, the other on the expensive napkin turned bandage against his neck, Rhodey looked back at the man. "Yeah?"

"Remember one thing." The carving knife landed in the

wood of the door to the right of his head. "I didn't have to miss."

"No." Rhodey's lips curved as he opened the door. "But I couldn't enjoy the show if I was dead. See? We're becoming better friends already."

Crispin gave a very uncouth grunt, neither agreeing or denying.

And because there were other potential weapons on the table for him to 'show off' with—maybe to a completely different audience—Rhodey slipped past the door and closed it behind him. Hopefully, he hadn't used up all his birthday luck already. He still had to live through lunch and dinner.

With Jared, or I'm gonna be throwing a few more knives.

In the direction of their 'host' if he kept breaking his word. Everyone else might call Maddox 'Master', but so far, Rhodey got away without doing it. Which he would continue to, so long as it didn't fuck with Jared's future. Or finding Tracey.

Down in the basement, Rhodey made sure to breathe through his mouth, suddenly understanding the weird stench he hadn't been able to place the times he'd come down here to 'take out the trash'. Lumpy bags filled with ash.

Guess I know where the guys who flunked out go.

Voices in a room past a brick arched doorway with a glass door reached him. Faint. Muffled. Jared's laughter was as light and happy as Rhodey had ever heard him. Actually, at first, he almost didn't recognize it.

Thick glass gave a narrow, warped view into the wine cellar with its oak casks and gleaming bottles. Hundreds, maybe thousands, of them. Sitting at a round table with Maddox, and another man whose back was to the door, Jared glanced up, a goofy grin on his face. A bunch of little glasses of wine were lined up in front of him and Maddox.

Standing, Jared crossed the room. The unknown man listed to the side a bit. On the middle of the table was a birthday cake with 'Happy Birthday, Husky' written in an elegant scrawl.

After opening the door, Jared motioned him in. "Happy birthday, husky. Come in, please. Join us."

"Uh...sure." Rhodey glanced around the room, an uncertain smile tugging at his lips. "Were you going for some kind of theme? Industrial...corpse?"

The wine cellar was nice and all, but the rest of the basement, what happened down here...? Then again, Jared liked things that were a bit creepy. And Rhodey enjoyed how into it he got. The death row vibe, along with the fancy cellar, would definitely hit all his buttons.

Maddox chuckled and motioned him over. "Not at all. Come, sit down. The air is filtered in here and it's much more pleasant, but you'll eventually get used to the other smell. We'll have more privacy down here. Some of the students are going through their trials and it would be a shame to be interrupted."

Giving him a dry look, Rhodey held up the bloody napkin he'd still been holding to his neck. "You don't say."

Making a concerned sound, Jared seemed to notice his neck for the first time. "What happened? Let me see. Sit down." He glanced over at Maddox. "May I have a med kit, please, Master? Some infections are interesting, but not on my best friend."

"Of course, my boy." Maddox's fond look toward his best friend was the only thing that kept the whole 'Master' thing from rankling. If the guy treated Jared good, Rhodey...was cool with how their relationship had developed. Not that he was really sure what'd changed. Whenever he let off that he wondered about it, Maddox would give him an amused look, like he was doing now. "You don't intend to use your birthday as an excuse to be difficult, now do you, Rhodey? Don't force me to repeat myself, you're not a child anymore."

Rhodey pressed his lips together, grinding his teeth before

pulling Jared in for a hug. He wasn't so good at following orders, but Maddox never seemed to mind as much as he let off, so long as whatever task was set in front of him got done. "I got you something interesting to work on for my birthday. Aren't I sweet? Much better than skinned knees and splinters."

Humming his approval, Jared nodded. "Yes. This isn't deep enough for real sutures, but we'll need some surgical glue in a few places. That was close." He ran the pad of one finger over a sensitive spot, his eyes glinting when Rhodey gave a barely noticeable flinch. "Oh, yes. This is lovely. Thank you."

"Damn it, I love you, man." Rhodey laughed, shaking his head as he settled into his seat. He didn't want to get all emotional, 'specially in front of Maddox. In the moment, the man might brush it off. On occasion, even seem indulgent or kind. But Rhodey had realized months ago the direction his training took always lined up with removing those particular 'frailties'.

Still, having Jared taking care of him, while also treating him like a fascinating science project, was just like old times. "You should see the other guy. Or maybe you already did? I got lucky, he was cockier than I am. Not going there until I can back that shi—crap up."

Pouring Rhodey a glass of wine, Jared nodded. "Yes. I believe Stewart here would agree with you. He learned a similar lesson a little too late." Jared threw an award winning smile toward the guy at the table no one had bothered introducing. "Didn't you, Stewie?"

The first sign something was seriously off was Jared using any kind of nickname with anyone other than him. In their foster home, he'd pissed off a few of the other kids using their full names, but Rhodey made sure they never got in his face about it.

'Stewie' wasn't gonna be complaining about anything, though. After taking a longer look at the dude, Rhodey caught on that he wasn't moving. Or breathing. Or…well, *alive*.

Lifting his brow, he tipped his head a bit to give Jared better access to his neck, ignoring the hot, throbbing ache. "And I thought my breakfast was weird. You doing some medical thing with the guy?" He glanced over at Maddox. "Or you too stingy to get him a proper doll to play with?"

Maddox breathed out a laugh, shaking his head. "With Jared's considerable skill, there is very little I would deny him. But no. He is not prone to playing with dolls. He is, however, impressing me with how comfortable he is around death. It's a natural part of life, and I would be very displeased if he'd been squeamish."

Hands gloves in latex, Jared worked some glue into one of the cuts and pinched the skin together. This close Rhodey could feel the wine-sweetened puffs of air on his jaw. Crouching, Jared glanced up at him. "He's my first, Rhodey. I didn't want to let him go so soon, but I need to learn a little more finesse. Though I got the required information from him, his weak heart proved a liability I hadn't predicted. I suspect I will be corrected later, but that is only to be expected. I won't make the same mistake again."

Glancing at Maddox, Rhodey found the man studying him, as though waiting for a reaction. In the beginning, Rhodey might've given him one. Gotten angry over Jared suffering in any way. Wondered if things like this would mess with his best friend's head. But Jared was tough and he always seemed fine when Rhodey saw him. Also, no one innocent died here. Other mercs-in-training didn't count—they knew what they were signing up for, and letting trained killers loose who were undisciplined or unstable?

Would be a really bad idea.

This guy wasn't familiar, and if he'd had intel? Probably a bad dude. Which meant Jared had leveled up to *real* jobs.

Rhodey was proud of him, but...he couldn't help worrying a little bit. Not that he'd let it show in front of

Maddox. His friend enjoying his work a little *too* much was something they could talk about in private.

"Hey, we all gotta start somewhere, right?" Rhodey wrinkled his nose and huffed. "I'm not counting the guy I threw my new knife at as my first. He wasn't dead when they took him away. And if Crispin hadn't been there, I'd probably be the dead one. I got kinda…careless." He wrapped his arms over his chest, still not sure what to do with the feeling of having someone he'd been trying to take care of turn on him. So he tried to laugh it off. "Gotta watch out for those cute twinks. They're quick."

Nudging Rhodey's chin to the other side, Jared frowned up at him. "Does he require medical attention? I would be happy to keep him alive for you to practice on."

"Unfortunately, Rhodey's friend is no longer with us. He was disposed of." Maddox looked toward the door, motioning over a server. He lifted something from one of the fancy silver trays that were used for pretty much everything. Leaned forward to place it on the table in front of Rhodey. "Don't lose this again. As your training intensifies, you'll find yourself in need of it, and you won't be given another."

"Yeah, thanks." Rhodey palmed the knife, bringing his attention to Jared again. "I wasn't into him or anything, I told him I was with you. But…Crispin said he was mine to take care of. I thought…he needed me."

Stripping off the gloves, Jared neatly folded them up, then placed them in a plastic biohazard bag with a red medical seal. Took the seat to Rhodey's right. Across from Maddox and close to his newer friend. "Perhaps he meant the other interpretation of 'take care of'? As in to dispatch?" Leaning over, he plucked something from the corpse's lap to place in front of Rhodey. "Happy birthday. It's cigars. I'm glad I'm with you, too. In both senses." He glanced at Maddox. "Sir? May Rhodey and I share a room this evening? I would like to give him another birthday present."

"Oh? Do you find yourself in need of privacy?" Maddox lifted his brow at Jared. "From your Master?"

Tension radiated through Rhodey as he stared at the man who already had complete control over every aspect of their lives. No matter how much he appreciated what being here did for their futures, right now? Being so powerless was smothering. And it took everything in Rhodey not to tell the dude to go fuck himself.

The only thing stopping him *was* the fact that if they had to escape—and they would, there would be no coming back from that kind of disrespect—everything they'd gone through so far would be for nothing. And Rhodey refused to do that to Jared.

A shying of Jared's gaze and his momentary hesitation weren't something Maddox would appreciate, but his friend's head shake might save the day. "I don't, sir, but...we haven't had much time together lately. I thought it might be nice to be able to take care of him in all the right ways when we had that." Jared glanced back at Maddox as if to see how his words had gone over. "There are some things we haven't done. Together."

"I am aware." Maddox stood, stepping around the table and leaning over Jared. He lifted his face with two fingers under his chin. "But I feel like you don't appreciate the time I am allowing you. Is that true? Maybe some distance would be good for you, so you can learn gratitude."

Rhodey growled, fisting his hand around the handle of his knife. "You promised we could see each other for meals. You already made him miss breakfast."

"Did I?" Maddox waved his hand over the table. "There is cake. For breakfast. The time being adjusted changes nothing. I haven't broken my promise, but I will remove the privilege if I find it detrimental to either of your progress. Now, I suggest you apologize for your tone. Watching Jared suffer for it would not be a very pleasant start to your birthday, now would it?"

Shaking his head, Rhodey stuffed the knife back in his pocket. He might be getting more skilled, faster, deadlier, but he was nowhere near Maddox's level. And the man was way too close to his best friend to take any chances. "No. I'm sorry, I shouldn't…shouldn't be talking to you like that."

Lips slanting, Maddox brought his hand to Jared's throat. "'I'm sorry…' who? You know how you're to address me, Rhodey. I've tolerated your disobedience long enough."

Jared swallowed against Maddox's palm, his adoring gaze never leaving Maddox's face. Almost like he'd been completely taken over by the man, without the ability to reason for himself. Which had always been one of his strongest qualities. Thinking. Reasoning. Seeing through things Rhodey struggled with sometimes. "It's okay, husky. I don't mind paying for your sins. I learn something each time I do."

"Oh, my sweet boy." Maddox tightened his grip, to the point Jared clearly couldn't get any air in at all. "You have to be alive to learn. Maybe this is the day I will have to decide who's worth more. Sometimes, choices can be difficult. Your mind, or breaking him of this idea that he can stand against me. A very kind gesture for his birthday. Leaving the decision up to him."

Maddox's methods were never straightforward. His casual observations could mean anything. He'd never made it a secret how valuable Jared was to him, but right then? Rhodey wasn't sure he wouldn't kill him on a whim, just to prove a point.

Shaking his head, his voice broke as he stood. And did the one thing he always told himself he wouldn't. Not with his foster parents. Not with the cruelest trainers here, including Crispin. But with Maddox's hand around Jared's neck, squeezing the life from him?

He did it.

He begged.

Chapter Seven

PAST

"*I*'m sorry, Master. Please..." Rhodey dropped to his knees, fully aware nothing less would satisfy the man. "Please, Master. I'll obey. I'll do whatever you want. Let him go."

Maddox gave a satisfied nod and released Jared's neck. "I don't think I will. But let him live? Yes. Because he is precious to me. And he has also proven quite useful for keeping you in your place."

Rattling breaths came on paper thin gasps from Jared's lips. Slumped in the chair, he visibly fought to get oxygen through his bruised windpipe. But his fingers found their way to Rhodey's shoulder, squeezing lightly before they fell away.

"Now then, who would like some cake?" Maddox returned to his seat as though nothing out of the ordinary had happened. "Get off the floor, Rhodey, and cut everyone a piece. Jared, fetch us some wine."

Jared struggled to his feet, swaying toward the bottles laid out in a semicircle on an oak cask. His fingers shook as he worked the corkscrew to decant a very old bottle, clearly having been tutored on proper protocol. In that moment, figuring out whether Maddox intended to keep him as a personal body servant, or let him become a doctor, was almost fucking impossible.

A bit steadier than his best friend—because Crispin had cured him of exposing physical cues anything in this fucked up place shook him up—Rhodey stood and stepped up to the side of the table. Holding the knife and cutting the cake instead of sliding the blade right through Maddox's amused eyes was almost harder than the kneeling and begging had been. Somehow, he managed.

He served a piece at each of their place settings. Including the corpse's. Because why the hell not? Right now, he was the luckiest fucker in the room.

"Why don't you tell Rhodey what you learned from our guest, my boy?" Maddox gestured at the body with his fork before taking a bite of the rich, Black Forest cake. "I did enjoy seeing you make him sing. It was truly lovely. He had such a pretty voice once he got past his shyness."

A white towel over one arm, Jared poured a bit of the wine for Maddox to taste. "Yes, Master." His gravelly tone sounded like he had a two pack a day habit. "He was a lower level flunky of a cartel in San Diego that has decided to branch out into child pornography. His associates kidnap youngsters to use in their online videos."

Making a face, Rhodey put his own fork down, his appetite immediately gone. "Holy shit—" He jumped when Maddox clinked his wine glass hard on the table, giving him a sharp look. "Sorry…Master. I just…I'm glad Jared dealt with him. I hope he suffered. Did you…get enough information to take them all down?"

"He did." Maddox reached out, the affectionate way he stroked Jared's arm sending a chill right down Rhodey's spine. His soft smile made him ever hurting Jared seem impossible, which was all kinds of fucked up. "I wouldn't say this in front of any of your peers, but I know it won't bother you. Jared is my rising star. I've never had anyone quite like him. I will allow you to spend more time with him, whenever possible, simply because the others may become jealous of his special treatment. And we wouldn't want anything to take him from us, now would we?"

Rhodey shook his head. At least that was one thing they could agree on. "Anyone hurts him and I'll take them down, Master."

Except you...for now.

Pouring the rest of Maddox's wine when he approved the vintage—by doing the whole mouthwash swish thing fancy people did—Jared turned his adoring smile to Rhodey. "Same, husky. We will make a formidable team. Those lowlifes won't stand a chance."

"Damn right we will." Rhodey managed a real smile for the first time since...hell, he wasn't sure when. Sure, he still found things to joke about, but a lot of the time he had to shut down and go with the flow. Pretend things were fine, even when the voice in the back of his mind told him nothing was. And might never be again. But no matter how messed up things were, Jared was here. And getting to spend more time with him would be amazing. "I can't wait to see the expressions on their faces when they figure it out. You're untouchable and there's nothing they can do about it."

Maddox chuckled, sliding his hand down Jared's side to rest on his hip. "Indeed. But that will only remain true if you *both* perform to the highest standards. The privileges can be taken away as easily as they were given. Your status must be earned or it is meaningless."

Usually, Jared wasn't exactly touchy feely, but he didn't seem to find Maddox's affectionate gestures at all strange. Actually, from how little Maddox's touch bothered Jared, maybe the two were a lot closer than Rhodey'd thought.

"We're here to work, Master, and we'll remember that." Jared gave Maddox an owlishly serious look through his glasses. "Thank you for the privilege."

Patting Jared's thigh, Maddox inclined his head. "It is my pleasure, my boy." His lips curved as he sat back in his chair, resting his hands on the arms of it and giving Rhodey a thoughtful look. "Now that you are officially an adult, I suppose it's time we treat you as one. As Jared mentioned, there are things the two of you have not had the chance to indulge in. Things Jared has been *pleading* to do for me, but I find my tastes lean more toward less carnal things when it comes to him. Perhaps now he can show you what he's desired for so long."

How did the bastard always manage to twist things up and make a 'gift' into a double-edged sword? Like, he'd let Rhodey and Jared be together, but not until Rhodey understood he could keep it all for himself if he wanted to. And whatever they *did* share would be on his terms.

Wetting his bottom lip with his tongue, Rhodey caught Jared's eye and kept his voice low. "It's cool if you don't want to...like this. I don't mind waiting."

"I...it's your birthday, and we don't want to disrespect the gift our Master is giving us." Jared clearly had the Maddox 'line' down cold. But he still didn't seem all that hot about the idea of getting it on in front of the man. "I just wanted him to teach me so I could... I didn't..." Stammering, Jared verbally backed himself into a corner. "I can do whatever you like, husky."

"No, you will do whatever *I* like, my boy." Maddox lifted his brow at Jared. "What was it you told me, once? Ah, yes. The merits of the 'empirical method'. I believe that will serve you well now. Nothing like experience to learn how to perform well. Show Rhodey how nicely you kneel. At his feet. The birthday boy should be given whatever pleasure you can think of on this special day, don't you think?"

"Yes, Master." Light pink tipped Jared's ears as he tore his gaze away from Maddox to meet Rhodey's. "What gives you pleasure, husky?"

With Jared kneeling in front of him, Rhodey was torn between needing this moment, this closeness, and wishing he could take him away somewhere. Beyond Maddox's control, his gaze, his touch. But they both knew what was out there. The life they'd lived in foster care hadn't been ideal, but it could get so much worse.

Not that he really believed Maddox would ever let them go.

Which meant playing along with his sick games. Surviving by learning all the rules. And one day, hopefully, discovering how to break every single one without being crushed by his limitless control.

At eighteen, Rhodey wasn't anywhere near that point yet.

One day, I will be.

So would Jared, except he was too lost under the man's spell to even consider it yet.

Cupping Jared's cheek, Rhodey met ice blue eyes, praying he could see something of the young man he'd grown up with in them. Something more than Maddox's perfect little puppet. The edge of his lips twitched. "Gee, I don't know. That mouth's gotta be good for something besides kissing ass."

Jared blinked, then glanced at the man he'd iced. "That wasn't a very nice thing to say, was it, Stewie?" He returned his focus to Rhodey. "Please accept Stewie's apology. He's not feeling very well."

Damn it, Maddox really had Jared all fucked up in the head. Rhodey raked his fingers through Jared's hair, jerking his head back and bending down to speak against his lips. "Stewie can't answer the phone right now. He's fucking dead. I'm the one who's here." He pressed his lips to Jared's, slanting his mouth and adding enough pressure to bruise. Enough teeth to draw blood. Anything to bring Jared back to him. "Me, Jared. Pretend it's just you and me."

"You and me." The hoarse whisper, muffled against Rhodey's mouth, came with a groan of longing so deep he could almost feel Jared's toes curl. "We did it. Harvard is lovely in the fall. Can you smell the leaves? So crisp."

Rhodey closed his eyes, wishing Jared was already there. Anywhere *but* here. Only...he couldn't give that to him alone. "Soon, my man. You'll have it all. Soon. Right now, I need you to stay with me. You're scaring me, Jared."

"No." Maddox slapped his hand on the table, shoving his chair back as he rose to his feet. "None of that. I won't tolerate any pathetic displays. Pull yourself together. Both of you. Jared, you were told to use your mouth. Do it. *Now.*"

The spark in Jared's eyes guttered and went out as he reached for Rhodey's belt. The practiced motions said he'd done this with someone else, even if it wasn't Maddox. Crispin, maybe. He freed Rhodey's dick, reaching in to stroke him with deft, sure movements of his chilled hand, bending at the same time to tongue the slit. Sucking the head into his mouth, his tongue continued to toy with him.

Jerking at the surge of arousal way beyond anything they'd shared in their more curious explorations for so long, Rhodey curved his hand behind Jared's head. A groan escaped him and he hated himself for the sound, even more when he saw the smirk on Maddox's lips. This was nothing like what he'd expected their first time, being together as adults, to be. He didn't mind things getting a bit rough, or trying out whatever, but this felt like...like he was just using Jared. Like the Jared he knew and loved wasn't with him at all.

And the only way to change that was to somehow bring him back. Ignore Maddox and find a way to escape into their own little world.

"God...you feel good." Rhodey stroked Jared's hair, speaking to him softly. "I always knew you would. You don't do anything halfway. Even down there like that, you completely own me, you know that?"

A trill went down Jared's spine that registered as a pulse of connection where his mouth joined with Rhodey's body.

The pleasure he gave became less mechanical and more teasing, as if he'd found a power source in Rhodey's words and plugged himself into it. He hummed, the back of his throat slipping around Rhodey's shaft as he swallowed and swallowed again. The fist of sensation a kind of control all its own.

"Yeah, just like that." Rhodey kept his gaze locked on Jared, blocking out everything else in the room as much as he could. If Maddox wouldn't let them be alone, he'd find another way for them to slip away to that space, where the man wasn't in charge of anything. He slid his hand down to the back of Jared's neck, digging his fingers in and holding him down as he thrust in deep. "Fuck...I could come just watching you, but I won't. You can't make me until I've got you bent over that table."

Curious, hungry eyes full of life and recognition rolled up to meet Rhodey's gaze. Jared's mouth was a sculptural masterpiece, stretched wide around his dick, slick saliva pooling around reddened lips. He sucked Rhodey down, hollowing his cheeks to increase the pressure, his tongue flicking and teasing, all without lowering that ice blue stare.

Until those eyes caught his, the lust was kept at bay. Almost too vulnerable to indulge in, but Rhodey couldn't hold anything back when he saw the man he cared for more than his own life in those depths. Like plunging into a frozen lake, every inch of him coming alive, his blood rushing as something invigorating took over. An urge to keep moving, to surge through the depths, except he didn't want to get to the other side. He wanted to stay right here with Jared and let the darkness swallow him whole.

"Take him, my boy." Maddox's voice slipped into the haze, becoming part of it, not commanding this time. Not triggering Rhodey's impulse to reject his unbreakable hold, but a subtle temptation he didn't want to resist. "I am giving him to you. This time. Right here, in his element, where not even his most depraved desires will be judged. You want that for him, don't you?"

Pulse quickening, Rhodey nodded, dragging Jared to his feet. "Yes. I want that for you. All of it."

Chin wet, eyes bright, lips swollen, Jared gave him such a look of adoration and love it was impossible not to feel it like a physical force. As if he'd taken his fist and somehow slammed it right through Rhodey's chest to release the energy inside. "Give it to me, husky."

A wicked smile curved Rhodey's lips. He fisted his hand in Jared's shirt, ripping the expensive fabric as he tugged him close. Biting Jared's bottom lip, he smiled at the taste of blood. "Give you what? You want me to fuck you? While the man you killed and your *Master* watch?"

"I want you to fuck me so hard, while I stare at them both, that you make our Master want nothing more than to come, too. He's going to want you as much as I do. Because you're beautiful, and no one can resist you." Jared glanced at the corpse. "And I can think about the power I felt when Stewart's heart stopped beating and I knew he'd never hurt anyone again."

Rhodey inhaled roughly, his fingers working open Jared's belt almost like they didn't want to wait for his brain to catch up. He nodded, his pulse thundering in his ears. "Yes, that's what I like to hear. That power is yours. Promise me. Promise me you'll hold onto it, no matter who tries to steal it away. Because it'll always be inside you. That's the man I know and love."

Clutching the table's oak edge with both palms, Jared nodded, the wings of his shoulder blades flexing with each rough inhale and exhale. "I promise. I'll remember."

"Good." Rhodey lowered his jogging pants, his own clothes a lot easier to get out of the way than Jared's. But his hard dick made it difficult to consider anything except the heat as he pressed against his man. He hissed in a breath, the resistance frustrating, part of his mind reminding him not to hurt Jared, while another whispered he'd enjoy it.

Or maybe that was Maddox, who observed them with no little amusement in his dark eyes. "Blood can suffice, if you are really that desperate, but there is some risk to it." He jutted his chin at a silver canister on the table. "Oil might be more comfortable, but you are the one in charge."

Rhodey glared at him, snatching the oil and tipping it, not being careful about the suit, or the silk linens on the table. He let it spill over Jared's ass, slicking his hand over the round, pale flesh and stroking his dick so everything was covered. Then he guided himself back into position. "Tell me you want this, Jared. I need to hear it."

Fingers flexing, Jared nodded, sweat dampening his hair and trickling down the back of his neck. "Please, Rhodey. I've been waiting so long. Wanting this forever. You are my forever. Fuck me. Fuck me, dammit. Please."

At each word his man gasped out, Rhodey pressed in harder, stretching him open. He gripped Jared's shoulder, easing in and out, giving him an inch more every time, mostly so he could watch the way his dick disappeared into his body and hear the sounds he made every time he took it away. The sensation was fucking incredible, a tight grip, a pulse driving his own deep within, but even more drugging was the feeling of owning the sensations Jared craved. Being able to give him it all. Or deny it until he begged.

"This is what you want, isn't it?" Rhodey slammed in, bringing his body fully against Jared's and whispering in his ear. "All of me, taking you. Do you like it?"

Wine glasses crashed, rocking off the table, Jared fully bent over it now, one hand on Stewie's chest over his heart. Fingers digging, he growled out Rhodey's name. "I'm going to show you a beating heart someday, husky. I'm going to crush them all in my hands until yours is safe. Take this. Take me... Fuck!" Jared shuddered, his body clenching around Rhodey's dick as he found his release. "Motherfucker!"

"I can't fucking wait, my man." Rhodey growled as his own arousal reached a breaking point, faster than he'd wanted, but he hadn't learned how to draw things out and Jared's body was dragging him down with him. His words shattered any of the resistance he might've found. White flashed into the red darkness behind Rhodey's closed lids as he slammed in, his grip on Jared's shoulder the only thing keeping him on his feet when he came. All his strength spilled out with the intensity of his climax. "Fuck, Jared... God..." He struggled to suck in air, laughing as he kissed the side of Jared's neck. "Who's your master now?"

Mumbling, his cheek mashed into the white linen stained red, Jared answered. "Always you."

"That's enough now." Maddox rang a little bell, and the room filled with the serving staff that was never too far. "Pull yourselves together and finish your cake. Jared, Stewart will need to go now. But I will have others for you to practice with. Would you like to watch him burn?"

"Yes, please, Master." Jared practically knocked Rhodey off him in his rush to stand. That eager, pleasing tone had returned. He made a face, looking down at the mess of his wrinkled suit and ripped shirt, with its cake and wine stains. "Oh, dear. This will never do." He sighed, giving Stewart a regretful look. "I'm afraid I will be less than presentable for your big moment."

Rhodey straightened himself up, meeting Maddox's eyes. His jaw ticked as he read the message conveyed very clearly in that slightly amused look. He might have given them this time together, but he'd taken something, too. A moment that should have been special, that could have brought their relationship to another level, had been warped in subtle ways Rhodey didn't fully understand yet. All he knew was Maddox had granted him the illusion of control. Only to prove how easily he could snatch it back.

"It's still my birthday, and I like you a bit messy." Rhodey cursed internally, pretty sure he sounded like a sulky kid, rather than a man with any kind of power, but it was damn frustrating to have to accept how weak he was, compared to Maddox. His training had given him some confidence, and even the way the other trainees responded to him made him believe maybe he approached the man's status. But he wasn't even close. "We used to talk about this kind of cake all the time. Do you remember?"

Please tell me you remember. When it was just us and all kinds of simple dreams.

Jared sat, adjusting his jacket and tie. "It's a Black Forest cake with brandy soaked cherries." The first part of his best friend's answer was spot on, but that wasn't difficult considering the cake was right in front of him. "Our Master got it for us." Throwing Maddox a grateful smile, Jared corrected himself. "He got it for you."

"Yes, but you were very helpful in letting me know what he would like, my boy." Maddox sipped his wine, giving Jared an indulgent look. "And as I mentioned earlier, there's nothing I won't do for my star. Rhodey is very lucky you consider such things for him. He is not nearly well behaved enough for me to grant him any favors on his merits alone."

Grunting, Rhodey stabbed his piece of cake with his fork. "I'll take that as a fucking compliment."

"Really, my difficult, hard headed boy. Must you make things harder for yourself?" Sitting back with a resigned sigh, Maddox made a vague gesture with his hand. "You may return him to his room, Crispin. And let him know how we feel about spoiled, ungrateful children, since that is how he chooses to act."

Disappointment in Rhodey flickered across Crispin's gaze —he'd probably made some kind of bet with Maddox about

Rhodey getting through the celebration without royally fucking up. Behind Rhodey, he slid his hands under his arms, lifting him from his seat to zip tie his wrists at the base of his spine in a quick, efficient maneuver. "This will be a novelty at least. It's been a while since I've diapered and bottle fed a recruit."

Rolling his eyes, Rhodey didn't resist as he was led out of the basement, and kept his mouth shut until they reached his room. Actually, he was kinda glad he'd been sent off with this man. Because he couldn't look at Jared right now. Or whoever that shadow of him was.

He gave Crispin a cold look as he plunked down on the edge of his bed. "Do whatever you need to. You can't humiliate me worse than he did. The only thing I care about is already gone."

"Not yet. But our Master is good at taking what he wants, piece by piece, and rearranging it to make his own art from our skins." Taking out a box from a cabinet someone must've rolled in, Crispin spoke as he set up for whatever fucked up shit their 'session' would entail. "He will do what he needs to in order to make you comply. It really would be easier on you both if you gave in and played the good boy for once."

Rhodey lifted his shoulders. "Maybe it would be easier, but then wouldn't I be like the rest of your little lemmings? If you wanted me to be nothing but more cannon fodder, I don't think you'd waste so much time on me." His brow furrowed slightly. "It's the same thing with Vani. You don't treat her like the others either. And she doesn't play the 'good' anything. We can both pass you little tests. Except for being brainless idiots."

Pushing Rhodey back on the bed, Crispin snapped the zip ties, then dragged out chains to secure him to his headboard and footboard. He took his time adjusting the metal links as he appeared to consider his response. "Have you ever seen Vani disrespect the Master? How do you think leadership happens? By undermining those above you, or by winning their trust and respect in return, so they know they are able to give you the freedom to act in their stead. To make decisions when they aren't around to do so?" Sitting back between Rhodey's thighs, he took out the birthday switchblade from Rhodey's pocket to slice his clothes off in long strips. "You are no leader. And you never will be."

Eyes narrowing, Rhodey lifted his head. "I will. You might think I need to crawl in front of *him* to prove it, but I don't. And I *won't*. I'll take whatever you throw at me and I'll earn that respect and trust my own way."

"Fuck you." Crispin's swear was startling, issued so close to Rhodey's face his breath was a hot puff in his eyes. "You think you're better than him? Than everyone who has given their lives to save the people he's been saving? They crawled. They licked his boots to prove they had his back, and the backs of the kids we protected. You want to skip that step? You'll skip, but it won't be to anywhere but an early grave. And I will have the supreme pleasure of being the one who puts the bullet in the back of your skull." He mimed a finger gun to Rhodey's forehead, pulling the trigger. "Because I was the one who advocated for bringing you both along and not just your friend. And I can't wait to see what he thinks when it's your body he's dumping into the incinerator."

Lips parting, Rhodey stared up at the man above him. He'd never been afraid of him, not really, and he wasn't now, but…his words hurt. Something inside Rhodey liked knowing he'd earned his special attention. That he wasn't seen as beneath his notice, like so many of the others.

The earlier disappointment hadn't reached him, because he'd been too wrapped up in his feelings about the changes in Jared. But now there was nothing between him and the knowledge that he'd failed the one person who still believed he was worth anything.

Losing Jared made it hit even harder.

"What do you want from me?" Rhodey inhaled roughly,

shaking his head. "I can't...I don't think I'm better than him, but the groveling, the...hell, the giving up control like everyone else does? I can't do it. If that's what you expect from me, you're right. I won't ever be anything. You might as well just use that knife now. Save yourself the bullet."

Twirling the knife in his fingers, Crispin considered him. "Are you listening? Because I'll only tell you this once. Next time we have this conversation, it will be much less pleasant. And you won't learn anything other than where your spleen is."

"I'm listening." Rhodey couldn't help himself. He really did try though, biting back a smile. "Could you teach me where it is anyway, though? Seems like something I should know."

The knife sank into his flesh about an inch deep. "Right beneath this layer of muscle."

"Okay, got it." Rhodey sucked in a breath, careful not to move, because with the wounds he already had? PT later today was gonna suck. "One of these days, I'll come see you and give you the same scars you've given me. Just to let you know how much I care."

That got him one of Crispin's rare lip twitches. "You need to live through basic first."

"Yeah, I figured as much." Rhodey dropped his head back against the bed. "Can you...teach me how? Please...sir?"

Plucking out the blade, Crispin cleaned it on Rhodey's sheets before folding the knife to set it aside. "Bravado is a piss poor substitute for competence. You've got bravado in spades. Lose the ego. Lose the bravado. Focus on the job. You don't need to grovel to the Master if you're doing the work. He won't ask it, and he won't care if you don't give it, because you'll be showing your loyalties in other ways." He sat back against the footboard, drawing up his knees into a mountain Rhodey only saw past because he slanted them to either side. "The rest of us like it. You don't. Got it. But you don't have to be a prick about it. If you don't respect him, then you don't respect the work. And we have zero use for you."

"I like things straightforward. You...I get you. Even though you're tough, it's simple." Rhodey turned as much as the chains would allow, dragging himself up the mattress a bit to put some slack in them so he could face the older man. "Maybe that's why Jared likes Maddox so much. They're both smart. I can't get what he's trying to do sometimes and I can't... I'm strong, not intelligent like them. So I use what I've got."

"You're intelligent or you wouldn't be here." This was the nicest Crispin had ever been with him, and he almost looked human if you didn't count the way his eyes never moved when he spoke. He stared and he didn't blink. "Maddox is teaching you to read people. By being the hardest person of all you'll ever read. After him, we'll all seem easy. Who cares why he's doing what he's doing? Stop thinking about it so hard and stop trying to win against him. He's not your opponent. You are. You're the one keeping yourself from getting out of here and getting to work. You should've been on to stage three by now and you're at the beginning of stage two. Get your head in the game. You don't have much rope left."

Rhodey huffed and closed his eyes. "I never wanted to play any damn games. I wanted Jared to have the opportunities I couldn't give him. I wanted to be able to find my sister and get her away from her bastard of a husband. Instead, I'm stuck here and screwing up. I thought I wasn't doing all that bad, but...obviously I was wrong. That's what he wanted to show me, wasn't it? That I'm not all that?" He opened his eyes and nodded. "Message received."

"You're not 'all that' *yet*. You haven't put in the work. As it stands you're a bundle of raw potential with an ego the size of Russia." Crispin unfolded his legs, swinging them off the bed to stand. "Your sister. Thank you for the reminder." He drew out his phone, pressing some buttons, then held it up to Rhodey's ear. "Say 'hello'."

Blinking, Rhodey hauled in a breath, positive this was another trick, but...

What if it isn't?

He swallowed hard. "Hello?"

"I can't talk long, but they said you'd call...is it really you?" Tracey's voice hitched. "Rhodey? You sound... God, you sound so grown up."

Closing his eyes against the sting, refusing to cry in front of the man—one of the men—he needed to impress if he was ever going to get to his sister, Rhodey forced a smile and nodded. "Yeah, it's me. You sound...just like I remember. Are you okay?"

A light laugh carried across the line, not at all like the soft one from his faded memories. More hollow. Strained. "Of course I am. But I really need to go. Can you...can you have the people taking care of you arrange for us to speak again soon? If I have more time to plan, I...we'll be able to talk for longer. I want to hear all about your life. How you've been. I miss you, little brother. So much."

"I miss you, too." Rhodey glanced at Crispin, keeping his tone steady. "And I'm sure something can be arranged. I need to get back to...class. But, yeah. We'll talk again soon. I love you."

"I love you, too. And I have to tell you...I'm sorry. I'm so sorry, Rhodey." Tracey went quiet, then whispered. "I have to go."

The line went dead.

Crispin pocketed the phone. "So what'll it be? Bravado, or the work?"

"I'm doing the damn work, but..." Rhodey's voice was rough, almost like he'd been strangled, just like Jared. Except Crispin had found something other than his hand to do it with. "I'll do it without the attitude. Without…the ego. I'll do whatever you need me to, just…I have to get to her. Please."

"Confidence looks good on you. Learn the difference." Crispin tossed the key to the chains onto his chest. "Let's go. You're with me. We're going to San Diego."

Bucking his body to toss the key close enough to grab, Rhodey maneuvered until he could get it in the lock and free himself. He pushed off the bed and went to grab some clothes that weren't all cut up.

Fucking Crispin. That was my only spare set.

Except…instead of his regular matching black sweats, he found some black jeans and a black T-shirt. Boots instead of canvas sneakers.

He grinned at Crispin as he tugged them on. "Another birthday present?"

"A graduation present." Leaned against the door frame, he watched Rhodey change. "Open the compartment in the bottom of the wardrobe. Your Glock's in there." He tossed the phone he'd used to call Tracey to Rhodey. "That's yours. Don't abuse it."

Clutching the phone to his chest, Rhodey shook his head. "I won't, sir." The honorific didn't jam in his throat like it had the first few times he'd tried using it. Not after talking to Tracey and being reminded he actually had his own reason for being here. For going through all this. "Thank you."

Crispin inclined his head. "Thank the Master. I am his instrument." He pivoted, nearly running down Vani, who stepped lightly out of his way.

She wore an outfit similar to Rhodey's, her gun tucked at her side. When Crispin wasn't looking, she rolled her eyes and mimed playing a violin.

Coughing into his hand to muffle his laugh, Rhodey crossed the room to Crispin's side in the hall. He stared Vani down to let her know he wasn't gonna mess around. And slid his finger across his throat for good measure. Which fucking hurt.

She considered him for a moment, then fell into step with him and Crispin with an approving nod. "Let's do this, then."

One successful mission checked off, taking down the marks Jared's good friend 'Stewie' had given up. More training, then another, each one cutting into the brutal, soul crushing routine, enough to remind Rhodey the purpose of the intense conditioning, whenever his conviction began to falter. A new aspect was added to the regime, clearing up the power dynamics until it all made sense in some fucked up way. Those who were deemed leaders, learned to submit to give them a strong foundation and respect for the position, then instructed in the responsibility of dominance.

Submission never fit comfortably, but Rhodey understood the reasons behind showing the strength to be able to wear another man's collar and practice obedience. He made a shitty sub, only Crispin and Maddox ever gaining anything resembling submission from him.

Thankfully, it didn't last long. And it didn't change the core of who he was.

A core melded into solid steel, with a sharp, deadly edge.

There were still kinks to work out—not the fun kind—but age and experience would refine those. Crispin warned him personal bonds, weak emotions, would be his undoing, but Rhodey refused to surrender the two most important ones.

His sister. And Jared.

Keeping in contact with Tracey, taking steps to separate her from her husband, was a long process, but the money Rhodey earned—more than he could've possibly imagined growing up—paved the way. The accounts he set up for her, which Joseph Crawford didn't know about, gave her the opportunity to develop a skill for investments, which in turn gave her a sense of security and independence she'd been denied. Crawford's position made him dangerous, and she couldn't escape just yet, but as Rhodey gained his own strong connections and resources, he got closer to destroying every obstacle to his sister's freedom.

There was someone else's freedom he needed to work on, though, which became clear the less and less he recognized the man Jared had become. He was trained as a Dom as well, and the power he wielded gave Rhodey some hope, but he couldn't ignore the way Maddox kept him under his thumb, more than anyone else he trained. The man continued to indulge Jared's darkest impulses, until torture and death became an obsession, eroding every bit of Jared's personality. Rhodey wouldn't pretend the potential hadn't always been there for Jared to become a ruthless, indiscriminate killer, but his mind had a firm grasp of right and wrong. Enough to keep him in check.

Maddox claimed every bit of control, leaving him without the ability to make those decisions for himself. And when he wasn't there, Jared sometimes found his own ways to satisfy those needs. At least he had his pick of prisoners to toy with—though some of them were supposed to be kept alive, and for a doctor-in-training, Jared had a hard time keeping them that way once he got in the zone. Part of Rhodey admired his methods—his own hands weren't exactly clean, so he had no room to judge—but every time Jared went too far, Maddox chipped away at him a little more.

All of the man's recruits were weapons, but Jared was becoming his own personal one. Harvard was still the goal for him, except...Rhodey knew it would only make him completely indebted to Maddox.

And the man already owned what was left of his soul.

So Rhodey came up with a plan, one that would put him in debt with several power players, including Vani, but would give Jared back control over his own life. There weren't many things Rhodey was afraid of, not anymore.

The man he loved, his best friend, being completely erased?

Terrified him.

The only problem now?

Whether or not what he had to offer would be enough for Maddox to let Jared go.

In the Master's office, Rhodey strode up to his desk. Slapped down the paperwork with Jared's acceptance for a military commission. He'd had to pull a few strings to get it, but with Jared's grades and track record, none of the brass had been too put out over him walking all over procedure.

Not looking all that surprised, Maddox sat back, an indulgent smile on his lips. "I appreciate the incentive, but what makes you think I will allow this? Jared is very special to me. I don't believe I'm willing to lose him so soon. This would require him committing his future to a cause other than my own."

"Yes, sir." Rhodey had to tread carefully. One wrong word, a hint of anything other than complete subjugation, and the Master would hold steady to the methods that had worked for him from the beginning. When all else failed, he could always use Jared against him, or him against Jared. He'd be able to tell if Rhodey was bullshitting him. But he wasn't. "It'll be years before you can use him as a doctor, and Vani has her eye on two other ones who will be available to be recruited by then. That sub Jared's been working with is damn skilled at extracting information. You don't need to keep him."

Maddox let out a soft laugh as he slid the paperwork closer and began to flip through it. "Oh, but I want to, my boy. He gives me a great deal of pleasure. What in the world do you have to offer for me to give that up?"

"Me." Rhodey squared his shoulders, stripping all emotion from his tone. Every bit of fear and doubt. "You've been training me to become independent. To lead my own team. Take on any contract I choose. You know all I care about is freeing Tracey. Once that's done, I'll give you the next two years. For any mission, no questions asked. I will belong to you."

"You already do."

Holding his gaze, Rhodey risked playing his last card. He had nothing left to lose. "If you've trained me as well as we both know you have? I won't. Not anymore. You intended for me to build something of my own and I did. You don't want another lapdog, you have plenty." He braced his hands on Maddox's desk, leaning forward. "I will be your weapon. The most lethal one in your arsenal. No one will ever be able to question your power again."

Making a thoughtful sound, Maddox stood, walking around the desk at a languorous pace. He curved his hand under Rhodey's jaw, bringing them to eye level, forcing Rhodey to remain slightly bent over, since he was a few inches taller than the man now. "Such arrogance. But I'm pleased you haven't lost it. And I believe Crispin is right. That confidence is justified. More now than it was when you came here, with nothing but desperation to be needed. By your sister. By Jared. What will you become once I take all that away?"

Rhodey's lips curved. "Fucking unstoppable."

"Yes." Maddox patted his cheek. "Very well. Go tell Jared to pack his things. You are aware you are leaving his future in his own hands? If he's anywhere near as messy in the military as he was here, that freedom you're sacrificing so much for won't be worth a damn thing."

There was a real chance Jared might not be able to regain his humanity. The part that kept him from becoming a straight up fucking serial killer. But Rhodey had to believe his best friend, the one who knew how to walk that careful line, was still in there somewhere.

And he'd give him every opportunity to find himself again.

"Jared wanted to learn how to save lives, not take them."

Rhodey put every ounce of conviction into his tone, his chest aching with how hard it was to hold on to. "That hasn't changed."

"You'd better hope you're right, my boy." Maddox gave him a pleasant smile. "Because if he becomes a liability, you will be the one to eliminate him."

Rhodey kept perfectly still. Didn't let a single one of his thoughts show. He'd cover up a hundred kills for Jared. A thousand. Under only one condition.

That none of them were innocent.

To Maddox, any unsanctioned kill would be enough cause, but Rhodey wouldn't worry about that now. He had faith once Jared got a taste of holding a life in his hands and dragging it back from the brink of death, those more twisted urges would be held at bay. And the discipline the military provided would appeal to the side of him that thrived under the structures of command.

Besides, the Jared who Rhodey remembered, who he still loved?

Would ask Rhodey to finish him off himself if he went too far in the other direction.

So he made the only promise Maddox needed from him. No matter how much it hurt to know there was a chance he might have to follow through with it one day.

Please, Jared. Don't ever force me to take you down. It's supposed to be you and me. Forever.

Only, it couldn't be. Not anymore. The distance between them had already grown, their lives on two very different paths. And the choice Rhodey made for Jared now would only push him further away.

But he had another promise to keep. One that gave Jared a family. A future.

Which he'd never have if he continued on the path Maddox had laid out for them.

"I swear to you, if he becomes anything other than an

amazing doctor, saving more lives than he's ever taken?" Rhodey put the final lock in his own chains with his last words, placing the key to his future in his Master's hand. "I won't hesitate to pull the trigger."

Maddox inclined his head and squeezed his shoulder. "Then there is only one thing left for you to do."

Frowning, Rhodey fought not to jerk away. "And what's that?"

"Say goodbye."

Chapter Eight

PRESENT

No matter what changed, a sharpened edge defined Rhodey's life, like a blade whet against stone, which otherwise became a useless chunk of metal. The difference now? The weapon he'd become protected something precious. And, unlike in the past, Rhodey wasn't forced to appreciate all he shielded, all he cared for, from a distance.

But sticking close exposed his vulnerabilities to the one man who could use them against him.

Or worse, take it all away.

Not today. That fucker's not taking anything from me today.

With Jared by his side, Rhodey crossed the bar, lips slanting as he observed a man who likely wouldn't see himself as one of Rhodey's weaknesses. Mostly because, after all Noah's work toughening the bastard up, there was no way Rhodey would treat Lawson as anything other than strong and capable. Because that was exactly what he was.

None of that equaled superhuman, though. Rhodey pulled out Lawson's chair, nudging him to sit a lot gentler than he would've even a year ago. Somehow, after a month in a cast, the man hadn't figured out he couldn't carry a bunch of ledgers and manage it himself, but Rhodey'd had plenty of experience with overachievers.

Still, he kept his tone a little gruff so the man wouldn't wonder about him being too fucking nice. "You're lucky I don't plan to shoot you today, you'd be shit out of luck."

Blinking at him like he was speaking Russian instead of English, Lawson sat and plunked down the heavy books, along with the laptop he tended to treat like an alien invader in his more traditionally cultivated space. His starched, dark blue button-down contrasted with his slightly rumpled black hair and bleary expression, but at least the jeans kept him from looking like an overworked business stiff. "No, thank you, I don't want a shot. Coffee would be fine."

Would laughing at him be mean?

Rhodey wasn't sure, but he held back anyway. This side of Lawson, one he only relaxed into when The Asylum felt safe, was more than fucking welcome this morning.

Who knows how long it'll last?

For now, the biggest obstacle the man faced was keeping The Asylum from accumulating more debt, getting around the red tape preventing the Club from officially opening, and avoiding using any of the untraceable money Rhodey offered. The man liked going the more difficult 'legit' route, for some fucked up reason. Something-something about how investigators constantly paying this place visits made it a little harder to get kinky.

The stubborn bastard would have a lot less stress if he'd just let me handle shit my way.

But Rhodey admired his tenacity. Between Lawson and Dallas, things would work themselves out. Until then, maybe Rhodey could lend a hand by digging a little into who was throwing those particular road blocks in their path.

You already know, Leonov.

Probably. But getting to the bottom of it?

Requires hard liquor.

And a trip down memory lane he wasn't ready for, just yet.

Smooth and quiet, more casually dressed than his Dom, in a blue T-shirt that matched his eyes, Matt slid a steaming mug on a coaster in front of Lawson, reaching out to adjust the ledgers so they wouldn't get in the way of the necessary morning ritual. "Good morning, sir. What can I get you?"

"Vodka." Rhodey left the seat next to Lawson for Jared and pulled out the next one over. "We're spoiling ourselves for breakfast."

Still snuggled together on the stool beside him, Pike and Tay were much stickier than they'd been when he'd left the bar earlier. In colorful, animal themed onesies, both seemed to have abandoned utensils at some point. The mess they'd made was...pretty impressive.

River would have his hands full with both deep in little headspaces, but after his time with Maddox?

Bring on the sweet distractions. Every fucking one of them.

The man must've been ready to fucking lose it, keeping his wild, devil-may-care nature under lock and key during those missions. He'd welcome all the mess and mischief his boys threw at him.

I know I will.

From the sounds of sizzling frying pans and laughter drifting past the partially open door, the man was in the galley with Curtis. Whenever things got a bit quiet, Tay stilled, looking over as though his Dom might've disappeared.

By the time he got comfortable enough with River being around to stop checking, Maddox would probably steal the man away again. His timing was usually just that perfectly fucked up to do the most damage.

"I coulda gone and gotten the chocolate milk myself." Pike followed Tay's gaze, lowering the forkful of pancake he'd been holding up for his co-sub. "So Papi could stay with you."

Tay blinked, then shook his head before resting it on Pike's shoulder. "Papi's gonna stay with us both. He missed us, but he missed Curtis, too, so we're gonna have to share him a little bit."

"Okay, but only a little." Pike spoke in a mock whisper. "We gotta be careful for my cuz. He gets around and he might seduce Papi before Daddy even gets to see him."

Glass to his lips, Rhodey almost choked on his vodka. He'd like to see Curtis try, if only for the entertainment value. But how Seth would actually react once he saw his man was anyone's guess. The bastard could be unpredictable.

Which might be exactly what we need.

Coming out of the galley, River glanced between his subs and groaned. "*How?* I was in there for five minutes. Did you two take a bath in the syrup?"

Licking Tay's cheek, Pike nodded. "Isn't that what it was there for, Papi?"

Wetting a bar towel, Matt nodded toward River to catch his attention. "Here you go, sir." He wrung out the towel, and handed it over. "It's warm but not too hot."

"Thank you, my boy." River gave Matt a warm smile, brushing a hand over his overgrown blond hair, which got a warning grunt from Lawson. He smirked, coming around the bar with the towel. "I get it, hands off before you have your coffee and can speak in full syllables. I'll wait until you're coherent before I try to steal a kiss."

Lawson grumbled into his coffee, not fully coherent now, but saying something along the lines of, "No kissing my subs. All mine."

Hand to River's cheek, Tay brought his Dom's face close to his, smiling as he met his eyes. "We don't tease Lawson before his first cup of coffee, sir. You'll get in trouble."

"We wouldn't want that." River touched his forehead to Tay's, whispering against his lips as he kissed him. "Fuck, I missed you, my tiny teddy. Should I save all my kisses for you?"

"And Pike." Tay spoke between kisses, his eyes sparkling

with laughter as River's claimed a sticky kiss from his co-sub. "And Daddy. Maybe Quint, if he's not upset that we made a big mess. He'll want to kiss you bunches if you help us clean up, though."

River gave his boy a very serious nod. "That's some good motivation. After you're done eating we'll get right on it."

The door to the upstairs opened, Avery coming through with his outerwear on, Curtis emerging from the galley at the same time. His eyes landed on the ice breaker Avery held, and he lifted up a finger. "Gimme a minute. I'll come help you spread the salt and get those ice jams from the downspouts."

"Leave it." Rhodey noted the way a few of the subs stiffened and softened his tone. He didn't want the Core on edge, but he was claiming as much of everyone's time as he could. With them all, right fucking here. He held out his hand, beckoning Avery to him. "Come sit with me, my boy. I'm feeding you breakfast. Maybe that way you won't get as messy as the rest of 'em."

Rising up on his knees, Pike stretched out to grab the ice breaker. "Here, I'll do it for you." The motion tipped the stool, almost knocking him and Tay to the floor before River grabbed them both around the waist, dropping the towel he'd made a valiant attempt to clean Tay with. When the stool clattered at his feet, Pike ducked his sticky head against River's chest. "Sorry, I was gonna help."

"You're very helpful, my boy. But you're not dressed for that kinda work" River adjusted the subs in his arms, syrup shining on his scruffy jaw and his light brown skin, ruining the hard edges of his black on black, standard merc getup. He looked nothing like the too smooth, cocky bastard he'd been when he'd first gotten here and everything like an overwhelmed Daddy Dom, with no clue what he'd gotten himself into. But the tenderness in his eyes and the patience in his tone showed he intended to make every effort.

Hard not to respect that.

Shucking the coat, Avery hung it on a peg before joining Rhodey. He cuddled back into Rhodey's lap, his small frame relaxing instantly. "Good morning, sir."

Curtis popped out of the galley again, this time with a giant platter of pancakes and bacon, Drew bringing up the rear with a plate of Keiran's pastries and a pot of what appeared to be raspberry jam. "I put chocolate chips in these. Smiley faces." He set the platter down on a placemat on the bar, within Pike's reach. "Marshmallow noses."

"You're the best, cuz." Pike leaned toward the bar, almost unbalancing River. "Those look yummy. Clean us after, Papi. I'll sit nice."

Bouncing a bit to get a better grip on Pike, River slid Curtis a dirty look. "You're timing is fucking *perfect*, my man. Thanks *so* much." He moved closer to the stool. "Can you climb down, Tay?"

An impish grin on his lips, Tay exchanged a look with Pike, then shook his head, wrapping his arms around River's neck. "No. It's cuddle time. We've gotta make Papi as sticky as we are."

"Mission accomplished." Lawson spoke over his mug, humor in his eyes as he finished off the last gulp. He slid his mug across the bar. "Pour me another cup, my love, then come sit with me. You can enjoy some of those pancakes before Pike changes his mind about tarring and feathering his Dom and goes for second breakfast."

One hand already on the coffee carafe, the other holding Lawson's mug, Matt beamed at his Dom. "Yes, sir. May I have a cup of coffee with you, please?"

"Of course." Lawson smiled at him as he tugged one of the ledgers in front of him, opening it a bit awkwardly. He frowned, looking around the bar. "Where in the world did I put my pen?"

Reaching over, Avery plucked the pen that hadn't been

there before from behind Lawson's ear. He held it out to Lawson. "Here you go, sir."

While Lawson took the pen with a sheepish 'thank you', Rhodey began taking off the rest of Avery's layers so he wouldn't get overheated, tossing them in the direction of the abandoned, sticky stool for good measure. A shame, it would have to be cleaned before his boy could go outside again. He snugged his boy against his chest, nuzzling his neck with a light kiss. "I'm feeling greedy. Don't expect to be very far from where you are right this moment anytime soon."

Curving into him, every bit the little snake, Avery nestled into Rhodey's arms. Eyes closed, dark lashes rested against his pale cheeks, he sighed happily. One hand crept up under the hem of Rhodey's shirt, Avery settling the flat of his palm over Rhodey's heart. "Thank you, sir."

The door to the gym opened as Rhodey was swiping some pancakes to feed his boy, Quint's smile bright as he came in, not fading as he glanced at River, who still had his subs clinging to him like spider monkeys. Actually, if anything, the sub seemed a little satisfied at the sight as he approached, drawing Pike's attention to him.

But unlike the animosity he'd shown to River before, the look he gave the Dom held understanding as he eased Pike into his arms, clearly unbothered by the mess. "Welcome back, sir. Next time, text me. They can be a handful and you're not used to the way they tag team when you're not prepared."

"I can see that." Red stained River's cheeks as he adjusted Tay again, but he laughed quietly as he rubbed at the syrup sticking his black T-shirt to his boy's fluffy blue onesie. "You'll have to teach me all your tricks, my boy."

Fork positioned to Avery's lips, Rhodey fed him a bite of the cutesy food with too many empty calories. Not something any of them could do on missions, but...this wasn't a mission. Home was a place to indulge in these little pleasures. And it had fuck-all to do with Maddox that every single one was even more precious today.

Opening his mouth in a way that made his tongue ring flash, Avery managed to grin at the same time. "Mmhm..." He chewed with relish, eyes fluttering closed again. "Very yummy, sir. I got a piece of the nose."

The ridiculous comment brought a soft smile to Rhodey's lips. The man in his arms at the moment was pure sub, not a trace in sight of the razor sharp merc he'd been conditioned to be. With some tender guidance from Dallas and Keiran, his little snake had come a long way from being constantly locked and loaded. Become more than another weapon.

Bringing his coffee with him, Matt rounded the bar to join Lawson, and Curtis took his place to serve up their breakfast. He leaned across the bar to steal a kiss from his man, placing a plate and a little carafe of syrup with their bundle of silverware. "Morning, Papa Bear."

"Good morning, Mama Bear." Lawson breathed out a laugh, shaking his head. "I'm pulling rank. Let's never do that again. The 'mama and papa' part, not kissing, before you try to be a smartass."

River snorted as he slid onto a non-sticky stool with Tay, Quint sitting on the one beside him, holding Pike. "He's got your number, my man. You'll be old and boring before your time if you're not careful."

"Does that mean our baby bear has to play Goldilocks instead?" Curtis tipped his head to one side, managing to find a crack to squeeze that sarcasm out anyway. "I know everything about him is *just right*."

Lawson arched a brow at Curtis, then glanced over at River. "You give me too much credit. But I'll keep working on it. Without a tighter leash and a gag in his mouth, he always seems to find a way. I should keep them handy."

Adjusting his jeans, Curtis grinned at River. "Those just make me hot." He winked, heading back toward the galley, where Drew had quietly disappeared seconds after slipping into the bar. "Anybody need anything besides this sexy bod?" He turned, flexing his pecs at Rhodey. "Clean enough to eat off."

The man really did entertain himself, which might have annoyed Rhodey once, but now it was part of the 'normal' he needed to soak in. His lips slanted as he glanced over to where Pike had settled down a bit with Quint's calming influence. "Hey, trouble. Your cousin missed out on all the sticky fun."

"No he didn't, we're not done yet." Pike squirmed out of Quint's hold, reaching out to grab a half eaten pancake off his and Tay's original plate. He flung it at Curtis. "Food fight!"

Leaning back with a fighter's quick reflexes, Curtis caught the edge of the pancake in his mouth where it flopped down like the tongue of one of the Saint Bernards Tracey'd adopted last summer. Tearing it with his fingers, he slurped the remaining piece up and chewed with an open-mouthed grin. "Thanks. I was hungry."

Arms looped around Pike's waist, Quint clucked his tongue. "No food fights. Do you want Daddy to be upset with you? It's time to sit nice and eat now. I know you're excited that Papi's back, but he's tired. Let's show him what a good boy you can be."

Pike huffed and plunked down on Quint's lap. "Daddy won't be upset. And Papi was having fun. You're being a meanie."

A tap on Rhodey's arm brought his attention to his little snake. "Sir?" Avery cocked his head as if listening to something. "Dallas wants to know if he should send Keiran down for his breakfast, or if I can bring something up for him?"

"No, tell them to both come down." It was rare Rhodey didn't keep a round-the-clock watch on the place, but the new security system and reinforced gates even a tanker would have trouble getting through made it unnecessary. If he was going to be greedy, might as well go all in. "Don't ask why, but I need this. Us. Our people. Without any bullshit."

Unquestioning as always, Avery nodded, smiling as his gaze went soft when someone replied. He met Rhodey's eyes again. "Dallas says, 'One bullshit free badass coming right up'."

With a one-armed hug and a kiss to the cheek, Rhodey let his boy feel his appreciation without words. Around here, it was tricky to demand anything so simple as a quiet—or quiet*ish*—morning, but he'd damn well paid in blood more than once for the right.

His lips quirked as the galley door opened, Reed's voice trailing out with his bright laughter. "You need to let me do the other side, fireball. I promise, the sparkles won't get in the food, you just gotta let the sticky stuff dry a bit."

"They're edible." Curtis added on the mollifying comment.

Drew made a doubtful sound, halfway between a whine and an, "Umm..."

Gym door opening, Dallas sauntered through, stomping his feet and blowing on his hands. The layer of snow on his closely trimmed black hair and the shoulders of his jacket brought out the rich brown of his skin. "It's cold out today. I warmed up the car for Connor, and good thing. Jamie'd be asking to move back to L.A."

Phone in hand, Jared glanced up, mid-text. From the long replies he was getting that took up most of the phone screen, he chatted with Wren as he nursed his breakfast vodka. "Let's install an autostart on all the vehicles. It's easier to warm them up, and safer to start them when we're not in them."

"Most of them are set up that way already. If Connor kept his car here often enough, I would have done it by now." Rhodey fed Avery another bite of pancake, licking a bit of syrup that trailed from the corner of his lips just to make him giggle. Not a sound he made often, but it was a pleasure to hear. He kept his eyes on the door to the stairwell as soft voices sounded, but no footsteps.

Like most mornings, all doors seemed to become revolving, the next one the front, Keiran slipping through with Wren bundled in his arms, the other sub still texting. Short, light brown hair sparkling with melting snow, Wren's cheeks were rosy red, his glasses completely fogged up. At least there were shoes on his feet, but Keiran's puffy black jacket was the one wrapped around him, meaning he'd forgotten his own—likely rushing out the second he got the alert for snow.

Coming to Rhodey's side, Keiran pressed a cold, wet kiss to his cheek, then Avery's. "Good morning. Have we decided to live dangerously today?"

"There's nothing fucking dangerous. Sometimes I like being overly cautious." Rhodey tossed back his vodka, shrugging. "Now I don't."

Settling an arm around Keiran's shoulders, Dallas pressed a kiss to the top of his boy's silky, dark hair. "Morning, sweets. I can't wait to warm you up." Smile wide, brown eyes glistening with the good humor that seemed to follow him everywhere, Rhodey's man met his gaze. "We doing shots of Jägermeister after this?"

"No, I just wanted a taste of the old country." Which was kind of fucked up. Rhodey had done some pretty intense training in Russia. Both alone and with Noah. But Maddox hadn't been there. Stephan would have a fucking field day with that shit. He shoved the thoughts aside, arching a brow at Wren as he handed Keiran his jacket. "Did we forget to dress ourselves before we went to watch the snow fall again?"

Not taking his eyes off his phone—which he could only text with and very little else—Wren nodded. "I was only stepping out for a moment, sir. And it's not terribly cold, just…beautiful."

Jared stood, meeting Wren halfway to guide him to the

seat to his left. "Let's get you something warm to drink. Black coffee spiked with something, perhaps?"

"That would be very nice, sir. Thank you." Wren lowered his voice, leaning a bit closer to Jared. "The baby is very cute, but I don't think I could spend as much time speaking to her on vid cam as Noah does. I'm very happy he and Jamie decided not to have their own, it would be much more difficult to excuse myself. And L.D would not like having a baby in the loft at all. He clearly has no paternal instincts. I can't fault him with that, though, neither do I. Are you drinking vodka?"

"At last, something you and L.D. have in common." Jared raised a glass to Wren, Curtis handing the sub his spiked coffee.

Rhodey took a long swig of vodka, enjoying the burn as he met Keiran's inquisitive gaze and shook his head, letting his boy know there was nothing to worry about. There was a conversation to be had with all three of his men, but for now, he didn't want them on high alert. It would wear them down before Maddox even made his first move.

This morning didn't count. If anything, that was nothing more than a courtesy, in the most fucked up way possible. Rhodey hated not knowing, which...also might be part of Maddox's plans.

He held Avery a little tighter, nursing his drink and letting the conversations flow around him.

"I'm telling you, Law, it's not as cut and dry as it looks." Leaning on his forearms, Curtis had the fight book open. He tapped it with his finger. "It's going to be Tappan. Not Ward. I think he's going to make it this time."

Lawson chuckled, picking up his pen, then putting it back down to grab another ledger and flop it open. "You're going to regret betting against me on this, my man. But sure, let's put it on the books. Tappan is a strong fighter, but he's about to get a promotion. His head's not in it."

"*Or* it'll give him the confidence boost he's needed to go

the distance." Smirk fully in place, Curtis watched Lawson enter the bet. "If I win, you don't come for a month and you watch me fuck our boy every night."

Choking on the mouthful of whipped cream he'd slurped from the massive mug of hot cocoa in his hands, Reed stared at his Doms. "Damn, that's hardcore. What's wrong with just betting cash? Then no one gets hurt."

The sex talk seemed to make the boy uncomfortable, like it'd been doing for a while, but as usual, he tried to brush it off. Something his Doms didn't always catch, but Maddox wouldn't miss. And could definitely use.

Stop fucking letting that fucker in your head.

"This makes things more interesting, my boy." Lawson spoke to Reed, but his gaze never left Curtis'. "Very well. If you lose, you don't get to fuck him. Or anyone else. If you beg, very nicely, I might take mercy on you. At my pleasure. I don't enjoy seeing you suffer…*too* much."

"I thought I was the sadist around here." Giving Curtis a thoughtful look, Jared sipped his vodka. "We should talk."

Curtis shrugged a little, slapping the bar with both palms as he straightened. "I'm always game to learn something new. And I owe Lawson. He just doesn't remember."

That got him a brow lift from Lawson, who finished his second cup of coffee, setting the mug down beside the ledgers. "If I was racking up how much you owe me, we'd never get anywhere. I'm enjoying your eagerness to 'learn something', my man. I'll enjoy teaching it to you even more."

Leaning in, Curtis nipped Lawson's bottom lip then turned the gesture into a deep kiss. "Mhm…" He leaned back a little. "What a damned shame you keep breaking your ass."

Reed winced, glancing at Matt, his gaze skimming over the scar on his co-sub's brow. The redness had gone down, and the young man wasn't getting as many headaches as he had over the first few weeks, but between his recovery and

Lawson's cast, how close they'd all come to losing both men was still pretty raw.

The remark from Curtis gave Rhodey a pretty good idea where his headspace was at, likely a bit on edge between seeing Ezran and how damn obvious it was Maddox wasn't a welcome presence. This was the kind of shit Rhodey didn't know how to deal with. Beating some sense into the man was an option, but probably not the best one.

Maybe.

Having more people on the mend would be bad for morale. Or some shit.

Hands over River's ears, Tay spoke up. "We need to keep you out of the betting pool, Papi. None of us will ever get laid again. Pike, make sure Seth hears nothing."

"Hears what?" Coming in from the stairwell, Seth headed for Pike, then came to a stumbling halt. Surprise widened dark blue eyes fringed with thick lashes, the alluring charm within having fooled more than one of Vani's mercs into believing they could lay the man out. "River. You sonofabitch. You promised you'd text—" Cutting himself off, he crossed the bar. Grabbed both Tay and River at once, sending the stool teetering dangerously. "You're really fucking here."

Raw emotion in his eyes, River wrapped an arm around Seth, steadying them all and holding him and their boy tight. Like he could absorb all the love, all the affection he'd missed in his absence, and return it in a breath. The parts he shielded from Maddox were damn clear. Given the chance, their trainer weeded out vulnerabilities like this, leaving only enough to maintain some humanity. Enough to be useful.

But never enough to get in the way.

River's connection to Vani was probably the only thing sparing him from his whole personality being gutted and reformed, and only so long as he could do the jobs laid out for him. Now that Maddox owned him, any perceived weakness could change that.

Either River didn't know, or—more likely—didn't give a fuck at the moment. His lips slid over Seth's, his tone a soft caress. "I wanted to, so fucking much. But I'm here, my man. I'm home."

What River didn't say was how long he could stay, or if he would, which wasn't surprising. Maddox had likely left things uncertain, and the bastard loved tearing any plans his people were foolish enough to make for themselves to shreds. The Doms of The Asylum might get off on control, but the power exchange with their boys never went beyond what a sub was willing to give.

Limits like that never applied to Maddox.

If not for the fact the man's operations managed to take down some truly dangerous fuckers, and save countless innocent lives, Rhodey might've set his targets on him as his one final goal. With no question as to whether he'd survive, because he knew he wouldn't. The loyalty Maddox's people had for him would leave Rhodey a hunted man for the rest of his very short days.

It'd be worth it to gain men like River, and...Ezran...their freedom.

But the cost to those still within Maddox's twisted net of protection, even though half the ropes were formed of barbed wire?

Was too fucking high.

Whatever else the two men who hadn't seen one another in months had to say was lost in the relaxed din of the bar, too quiet for even Rhodey to catch. With one last meaningful glance exchanged, River began to catch Seth up on the conversation he'd walked in on, while Tay playfully tried to cover his mouth with small, sticky hands.

Damn, it's fucking nice to see the men around here just...having fun.

Mercs didn't tend to take any opportunity for granted, whether their pleasure was sex, alcohol, or...cute, sticky little subs. Hard to take life too fucking seriously in the moments between bombs and bullets.

Finished greeting River, Seth swooped in on Pike with a kiss. He licked his lips, forking up a dripping piece of pancake. "Open wide."

Without hesitating, Pike devoured the forkful, his eyes glinting with laughter at Tay's groan.

Pushing Tay's hands down, River met Seth's eyes, his lips twitching. "Lawson and Curtis are betting each other into a dry spell. Our boys are afraid we'll want in on that. I don't. Whoever you think will wind up on top? You win."

Seth chuckled. "The only dry spell I want is for all this early snow to stop." He glanced Wren's way. "Sorry, my boy. I just came six inches from getting an icicle in the eye. We need to do something about those downspouts catching the water."

"On it." Subdued, Curtis walked around the bar toward the gym, gripping Lawson's good arm on his way by with a quiet, "Sorry."

Catching him by the waist, Lawson pulled him in, so he was snug against Matt's side and close to his own. "Don't be. You'll lose, but it will be fun. Trust me to take care of you, my man. In any way I can. I want more of this for us."

"Me too." Curtis pressed a kiss to the top of Matt's head, then Lawson's cheek. "Let me take care of some things. I need...to burn off some energy."

For a few seconds, Lawson studied Curtis' face, then finally nodded and let him go. "All right, but come see me after." His lips curved. "And don't forget your jacket. Or your gloves. Reed, make sure your Dom is dressed nice and warm before he heads out."

"On it, sir." Reed took another quick gulp of cocoa, sliding his mug onto the bar before half skidding around it. He hopped up to kiss Curtis' cheek on his way to the stairwell. "I'll get your knit hat while I'm at it. And your scarf. You'll be all cozy."

Curtis looped his arm loosely around Reed's shoulders, reeling him close. He lifted Reed's chin with two fingers. "I love you, sparkles."

"I love you, too, sir." Reed grinned at him, leaning in for a kiss and speaking against his lips. "Don't take your hat off this time or I'm telling Tracey. Like she always says 'you'll catch brain freeze and we all get our heads knocked around enough around here'. Do you want me to get suited up and come help?"

"She says that when you eat ice cream too fast, too." Smile back in place, Curtis shared another kiss with Reed. "I could use your help with the salt spreader. And it'll give me an excuse to peg you with a few snowballs." He held up one palm in Pike's direction. "Don't even say it. You know what I mean."

Mouth empty, Pike licked his lips and gave his cousin his most innocent look—which he didn't pull off very well. "Hey, it's none of my business what you two wanna get up to in the snow. Ice dildos sound kinda painful, but I ain't judging. I'm open minded, so long as no one's coming near me with them."

Tay shook his head, picking up a big piece of pancake with his fingers. "You've gotta stop giving the Doms ideas, man."

Finished with his vodka, Jared sat with Wren in his lap now, running his fingers through his boy's hair in a meditative motion. He'd been doing that a lot since getting him back from prison, seeming to need to touch him as much as possible, to assure himself he was really there.

"I have an ice mold for that very thing, Tay..." Closing his eyes briefly, Jared seemed to remember himself—and who he spoke to. "Rhodey can borrow it to use on you if he feels like collecting more subs." The last was an obvious dig, because there wasn't a chance in hell Rhodey would be touching the boy. "Unless he's gone soft."

Rhodey snorted, arching a brow at Jared. If the man was

in the right mindframe to start taunting him, he wasn't vulnerable. Thank fuck.

Glancing at Tay, he made a thoughtful sound. "My schedule's a little full right now, but he'd be a treat for someone with more time on their hands. If he's bored with his Doms already, I'm sure we could find someone for him."

Pike sat up a bit, his eyes narrowing. "He never said he was bored. Stop messing with him. If *you're* bored, maybe you should, you know, do some shit with your own subs."

Turned part way on his stool, Jared gave Pike a long look while Seth covered his eyes with his hand and groaned. It was Curtis who spoke up from where he still hugged Reed close by the stairs. "Rhodey and Jared only mess with people they like, Pike. Don't fash yourself over something that's nothing, as gran would say."

"Yeah, well…" Pike chewed on his bottom lip as River exchanged a look with Quint. He ducked his head when River stood with Tay in his arms. "Corner time?"

River shook his head, bringing Tay to Seth and lifting Pike off Quint's lap. "Nope. We're in the bar. I might be new around here, but I know the rules and so do you. Come on, let's get this over with. Give Seth a break from having to remind you how to behave."

"It was *one* swear word." Tay grabbed River's sleeve and tugged. "Can't you pretend you didn't hear it?"

Wiping a smear of syrup off Tay's chin, Seth brought his head around. "He swore *at* a Dom. If Rhodey chose an apology, he'd be within his rights." Seth met Rhodey's gaze, something shrewd flickering in his blue eyes. "Which I would support."

Rhodey demanding that kind of apology would serve the brat right, but when Tay's eyes met his, something disturbingly familiar in them had him treading very carefully. The sub was pretty well behaved, but he tended to follow Pike's lead—a tempting little bundle of trouble holding out a juicy red apple, making the milder sins sound harmless. Which they usually were. Except, nothing here was ever fucking uncomplicated enough for a bit of naughtiness to slide.

Strange thing was, any of the other Core subs pulling this shit would get a very different reaction. His own subs could maneuver their ways out of most situations, and he and Dallas had no problem handing out all the 'Free Passes' they might need. For others, discipline would be swift and delivered without much drama. On a good day, anyway.

These two were a whole different story. Not only because they were littles. There were times Rhodey struggled not to lay Curtis' past mistakes on Pike's shoulders. To avoid judging both of their actions by the O'Rourke legacy. Rhodey had kept clear of Curtis when he was this age, and it was a damn good thing. He wasn't sure he could've stood back the way Jared had and let Noah and Curtis work through all those damn issues together, learning and growing in their own fucked up way. No point denying it, he probably would've tucked Curtis in for a dirt nap to avoid him dragging Noah down with him.

But he would've been wrong about him, like he'd been wrong about his nephew.

For these two young men, there was no avoiding how the past impacted the way everyone handled them. Some was warranted, because the whole nurture versus nature thing couldn't be ignored. Rhodey could see the potential for both the best and the worst parts of Noah in Tay. The fucking twin? That one had been waking, talking proof of how personal choices, accountability, and character played into what a man could become with the questionable 'gift' of Joseph Crawford's genetics.

Tay had lived most of his life trying to make up for how cruel and selfish his twin had been. He was only now getting a chance to define himself as his own person, but there was no escaping the lengthening shadow he'd stepped into once the

Core discovered the truth of his origins. Not all of it was bad, and maybe, one day, when Noah was ready to be told who Tay was, those similarities would give him some comfort. Allow him to see the good in himself when reflected in someone without his scars.

Until then, integrating the young man into the Core came with several challenges. He couldn't seem to help doing the exact fucking things that would expose his secret. The defiant edge was...

Hell, just like his big brother.

If Tay believed he was taking a stand for someone he needed to protect, there'd be no getting him to back down. Short of beating it out of him, which Seth would likely object to. And probably wouldn't be very effective.

Stubborn little thing.

Rhodey couldn't handle Tay the way he had Noah—not that he wanted to. But the boy *was* a sub in The Asylum. When it came down to it?

Maybe treating him as one, and nothing else, would be the best place to start.

Couldn't hurt to try, anyway.

Much.

Chapter Nine

PRESENT

The strangest thing about the whole fucking living arrangements in The Asylum? How different the close quarters impacted everyone within these walls, compared to how it'd been in Maddox's mansion. Or even in Vani's compound. Maddox discouraged connections with no long term value—or any loyalties superseding the ultimate ones to him. Vani liked her teams to be tight, and preferred to avoid emotional pitfalls, so her people tended to be good friends who could share a beer, but intimacy was rare.

Here? Those tight bonds were an essential part of how the Core functioned. No one had to be trained to belong within its ranks, they only had to share one common goal. Love this place, what it meant to everyone who stayed here, who came here, enough to contribute whatever they had to offer.

Something Rhodey reminded himself whenever he was tempted to treat any of the subs like he might've the ones he'd dealt with in the mansion. No matter how pure Maddox's cause—saving the innocent and burying the bad guys—in the end, the man dealt in death. Those under him had to be able to deliver the final blow without hesitation.

The place Noah had created was about life. Freedom.

Family. And none of those things required mindless obedience.

Just the regular kind.

But Rhodey wasn't a regular kind of Dom. And it took everything in his power not to fall back on harsher forms of discipline while holding the gaze of the small sub, with the eyes of the same young man who'd once craved nothing more than to spill *his* blood. His jaw hardened.

. "Careful, Booboo. We're having a pleasant morning. Let Pike take his punishment. I'm being nice, letting River give it to him."

"What really fucks with them, little cuz? When you make it a game and start blowing bubbles out your nose." Winking, Curtis ushered Reed through the door.

Over by the sink, River poured some soap into his palm, casting Tay a concerned look. "He'll be all right, my tiny teddy. If he found it completely unbearable, he wouldn't do it so often."

Cheeks going red, Tay glanced over at River, then blew out a breath. "He *doesn't* do it that often anymore. He's been good. He was sticking up for me because of…of whatever these two are playing at. Which isn't fair."

"Who are you referring to, exactly, boy?" Coming out of the stairwell, Noah gave Tay a hard look, ignoring the soft groan Quint let out as he tried to get Tay's attention, shaking his head. "You've been welcomed into this club and I don't have an issue with you being here. Don't change that."

Tay lifted his chin. "Sir, no disrespect, but this doesn't concern you."

Out of his seat with a lethal swiftness retained from his past training—a default flow of movement he likely wasn't aware of—Jared leaned over Tay, practically nose-to-nose with Seth. "Since you are concerned with the way I was playing with you, would you like to take it up with me?" Voice silky smooth, deceptively calm, Jared lengthened his spine. His serpent tattoo came into view above his collar, a visual of his willingness to strike, concealed by layers as easily shed as the fabric. "Please do. I assure you, I shall refrain from being anything but *very* serious with you in the future."

"Dammit, Jared." Seth scooted back a bit. "We're fine. Everything's fine. Tay, you're on speech restrictions. Pike, take your punishment and let's resume our morning. Unless you'd rather I left? Things seemed to go sideways when I arrived, so perhaps it would be best."

Shaking his head, Pike caught Tay's eye and made a zipping motion across his lips. He took a deep breath and gave Seth a pleading look. "Don't go, we were just… Things got weird, but it wasn't you. We're excited River's back. And I… I'm sorry. I'll be good so Tay doesn't hafta try to distract everyone from me being a brat." He squared his shoulders, lifting his gaze to River. "Please punish me, sir? I'm a bad boy."

"You're not a bad boy, pixie." Pressing his eyes closed, Seth shook his head. "Jared. Back off, please. Noah, good morning."

Glancing at River, seeming satisfied when he began washing out Pike's mouth, Noah inclined his head and turned his focus to Seth. "Good morning, my man. But do refrain from telling Jared how he can deal with your subs. It looks like they both needed a reminder this morning that it's not a fucking free-for-all." He pulled out the stool next to the one Jared had left Wren in, sliding into it and giving Tay an assessing look. "I expect an apology from him, to all the Doms in the room, for the attitude. Since I'm in a good mood I won't make him give it on his knees."

Thank God for small fucking favors.

Seth breathed deep, then exhaled slowly. "When I take him off speech restrictions, you can have your apologies, Noah. Let's give him time to settle. We don't need any more drama. We were having a nice morning, enjoying River's homecoming."

If Tay's temper was anything like his brother's, it would take a while, but at least Seth had bought his boy some time. Smart man. Rhodey stroked his fingers up and down Avery's thigh, tamping down his own urge to hold the stormy gaze of the young man who was sitting stiffly on Seth's knee, watching River doing a much too thorough job of cleaning Pike's mouth—like it was a dish covered in grease instead of inner cheek, teeth, and tongue. Newbie Doms were amusing when they tried too hard.

Noah huffed out a laugh, shaking his head as he rose from his stool. He brushed a kiss over Jared's lips in greeting. "Drama? No, this was simply a couple of subs being too bold. They're being handled." He gave Seth a pleasant smile. "You might want to try doing it yourself before someone else has to step in for you."

The way Tay was grinding his teeth would cost his Dom some serious money in dental work. But other than glaring at Noah, he didn't do anything that could be considered disobeying his Dom.

Nodding slowly, Seth licked his teeth. "You have a point. But we're not doing anything but enjoying each other today. River just got home and we'll be spending the day as a family. You do know what that word means, right my man?"

"I have a feeling I need to get into the flow of everyone constantly sniping at each other. Can't we just go back to poison cookies?" River's lips twitched upwards as he focused on the mouth soaping. "If you don't need Tay working around the club, we'll steal him for some family time, but I haven't forgotten how important it is for him to feel like he's doing his share."

Lawson's brow lifted slightly. His expression softened when he glanced at Tay, who'd lowered his gaze. "Tay has been very helpful around here and there's plenty for him to do. Chin up, my boy. Matt, after he's gotten himself cleaned up, why don't you bring him to reorganize the storage room with you? We just got a new shipment in and the inventory needs updating."

"Yes, sir." As calm as if nothing at all unusual had gone down in the last ten minutes, Matt glanced up from his phone where he'd been texting someone. "Would you like us to take care of liquor or dry goods inventory? There's too much for one day. We have to unbox a bunch that lost their labels in transit."

Slipping around the bar, Quint spoke quietly to River, who nodded and began helping Pike rinse out his mouth. Then Quint looked over at Lawson. "If I may, sir, I'd planned to help Keiran with the dry goods inventory. Matt and Tay can take care of the liquor."

Quietly standing with Dallas, Keiran made an affirmative sound. "It saves time when he can inspect everything before I put it away. With labels missing, it'll take a bit longer, but we can handle it."

Yes, that would be the better option. Keiran knew what to look for, but Quint had more experience. Between the two of them, they'd find anything that might have been tampered with.

Catching Rhodey's nod, Lawson inclined his head and jotted a few notes in one of the ledgers open in front of him. "That works out perfectly. I don't have you scheduled for anything until tonight, Noah, so you can enjoy the day with your boys."

Noah gave him a dry look as he pulled on his jacket. "Thank you so much, my man. Appreciate you allowing me the leeway."

"I didn't know you needed it, but you're very welcome." Lawson winked at Tay before going back to his ledger. "Curtis, when you and Reed are done outside, I have a few repairs I need you for. If you're up for it?"

On his way to the front door with Reed, Curtis threw

Lawson a double thumbs-up. "I'm yours, whenever you want, however you want, my man." He paused, doing a double take. "Oh. Good morning, Noah. I was just going to ask you for your help ripping down a gutter I need to replace. Probably not a good idea to do it in your leather jacket though. I'll be too turned on to pay attention, and I don't want you to get hurt."

"Dallas can give you a hand." Rhodey patted Dallas' thigh. "Make sure the fool doesn't break himself. Reed won't be able to catch him if he falls."

"I was going to say, didn't he rip open his leg the last time he played with sheet metal?" Standing, Dallas gave Keiran one last kiss. "Sure. I'm already dressed for it."

Reed rolled his eyes, sticking his hand in the back pocket of Curtis' jeans and pressing close to his Dom's side. "That was an accident and he's more careful now. Let's not make this a 'pick on the O'Rourkes day', 'kay? I swear, there's something in the freakin' water this morning."

Ignoring him, Noah turned his attention to Rhodey. Thankfully, he couldn't see himself, or there was no way he'd have missed he was giving him the exact same damn look Tay had earlier. "I don't need you to plan my day out for me either, uncle. I'll help Curtis. You can keep your man for… whatever you think needs watching."

"We'll get it done faster if all three of us do it." Dallas clapped Noah on the back, squeezing his shoulder in a friendly gesture. "Besides, I have a few things to run by you for some upcoming club entertainment."

This was the part of the being more in touch with his humanity or whatever—which Dallas did well, and Rhodey fucking sucked at—that came in handy in situations like this. Rhodey didn't react when Noah relaxed and nodded, going to the coat rack to trade his leather jacket for the sturdy one he'd left there. But internally, he allowed himself a silent sigh of relief. Club matters would keep Noah distracted. And hopefully, seeing Curtis *carefully* managing the outdoor upkeep would get him out of his hypervigilant mindset. That was not a headspace any of them wanted him to stay in for long.

By the sink, River dabbed at Pike's mouth with a bar towel. "I might have overdone it a bit. I'm sorry, my boy."

"Shh, Doms don't apologize for punishments." Pike pressed his fingers to River's lips, making a face. "That'll keep me from being naughty for at least an hour. Maybe even *two*."

Bringing Tay with him behind the bar, Seth sat him on the ledge just beneath the lip. "Well done, pixie." He reached in his front pocket, pulling out a tube of lip balm and uncapping it. "Pucker for me."

Lips pursed, Pike held still for his Dom, closing his eyes when River petted his hair. No worse for wear from the punishment, the sub had calmed down and was soaking in the attention. Which had Tay looking more relaxed as well, leaning against Quint's side when he moved closer and laid a hand on his shoulder.

Almost out the door, Noah paused to observe them. Sometimes, he liked to push the other Doms, or the subs, expecting certain standards. He wasn't as uptight about it as he'd once been, but Tay's getting on the wrong side of Jared pushed all the wrong buttons. Rhodey would have to talk to the boy about that. He didn't have the liberty to test his boundaries like some of the other subs. Not with those two, in any case.

With one last satisfied nod, Noah continued out the door.

Laughing at something Reed said, Curtis scooped up a snowball and pegged Noah squarely in the back, white bursting across the threshold with the impact. Dallas shouted, "It's on, my man!" his own laughter echoing off the security fence before the door closed.

Coming out of the galley with a giant copper stock pot in his hands, Drew whispered into it. "Don't worry, Marco and Petris. I've got a nice tub of water for you to escape into upstairs. Where no one will boil you alive." He navigated surprisingly well around the tables until his pajama bottoms slipped below his hips, forcing him to tug them back up. The pot tipped sideways as he reached Rhodey's side. "Eep!"

Chuckling, Rhodey swooped the pot out of the sub's hands. He lifted it over his head to hand to Keiran so his boy wouldn't be tempted to find the closest object to throw at Drew for stealing his lobsters. "No great rescue today, sparky. Go upstairs and get dressed before your Dom shows up and has to save *you*."

"My pots do not leave the galley." Keiran cursed under his breath in Spanish, shaking his head as Rhodey nudged him forward. "I need you, Wren. The passcode is getting changed. I'm reclaiming my domain."

Wren lifted his head, immediately slipping off his stool. "That's a good idea. I should change all the access points in the building again, it's been at least a week. Maybe longer. I think I wrote it down somewhere." He put his phone on the bar by Jared for his Dom to tuck away and smiled at Matt. "I'd like to hear more about the icicle impaling incident. Maybe with enough details I can picture the exact scenario and how a wound like that would need to be cared for. And what the survival rate would be."

"There's someone being impaled by icicles?" Stairwell door open, Danny gaped at Wren, almost managing to trip both his Doms as they came down behind him—an almost daily occurrence, the two needed a fucking refresher in their training. Danny put his hand over his eyes as Shea lifted him off his feet so he and Jacks could pass. "I can't see this. Ugh, I don't *need* to see it, I can already picture it. It wasn't Jamie, was it? Is he okay? No, of course he's not… Can I go visit him?"

"No one is being impaled by anything, little Despereaux." Meeting Shea at the edge of the bar, Jared held out his arms to take Danny with a fond look. "May I, my man?"

Shea nodded, passing Danny to Jared, clearly biting back a laugh. Intelligent of him. If Jared didn't punch him for making light of his boy's fear, Rhodey definitely would. The man glanced around the bar, his tone light. "No disasters yet, little mouse. No one's even bleeding. It's safe to look."

"It was at my junior high school a long time ago. At least ten years. Ancient history, Danny." Matt winked at Wren. "Otherwise I'd totally tell you that they had security cameras and footage of it you could review."

Before Wren could even ask, Rhodey shook his head. "No. Fucking do a search on YouTube if you need graphics. You're not hacking security cameras for entertainment."

Wren gave him a level look, as though he was being ridiculous. "I hadn't intended to, sir. My freedom is conditional on my adherence to the very specific rules I agreed to. I wouldn't risk..." His gaze snapped to Jared. "I wouldn't risk that, sir. I swear, not for...for something like this."

Leaning forward, one arm around Danny on his lap, Jared brushed his fingers through Wren's hair, ending with a tiny tug. "I know, love. I know."

"Come, mi alma. Let's get those codes changed." Pot against his hip, Keiran took Wren's hand and smiled at Jared. "If you don't mind me stealing your sub, sir?"

"Eyes on him every second." Jared held Keiran's gaze.

Keiran gave him a very serious nod, drawing Wren close to his side. "Always, sir. I won't let him out of my sight."

Easing back against Jared's chest, Danny finally lowered his hands, looking around the bar. He wet his bottom lip with his tongue. "Did Jamie leave already? I was going to head to the Center with him, but my tarot readings took a bit longer. Shea said I had to start over because they were all coming out bad. I told him that's not how it works, but...well, they *did* seem a bit better after the third time."

"He did, I'm afraid." Straightening Danny's sunglasses, Jared fussed over him.

Jacks spoke up from the booth where he'd already laid out a project he pieced together, his fingers moving over the fabric, inserting pins so quickly it was difficult to tell where they hadn't been before they suddenly appeared. "Let's have a quiet day at home. I'm sure Jamie and Connor can do something to prep for their wedding instead of working on the new release. I kept you up late last night and you need some sleep."

"Mhm, but it was worth it." Shea went around the bar, grabbing a glass, then fetching the container of orange juice from the fridge out of sight. He straightened and filled it to the rim. "There's a new client Connor wants me to take on, so I might get a few hours in, then check that out. Thanks."

Sharing a look with Rhodey, Jared changed the topic. "Are we opening tonight? Am I in the ring, dungeon, club, or clinic? The schedule has been so sporadic while we fixed things up that I can't remember the staffing rhythm. It's making my teeth itch."

A sigh came from Lawson as he shook his head. "Not yet, I still need to schedule a final inspection before we're allowed to open back up in an official capacity. It's been delayed again, but I'm working on pushing it through sooner. There's still a few things to do before we're ready, but…it shouldn't be much longer."

Avery's weight became heavier in Rhodey's lap, his cheek pressed more firmly into Rhodey's chest as soft wuffles came from his lips. He turned his face, making a contented sound, the hand he still pressed to Rhodey's chest under his shirt slipping down a bit.

"Looks like Shea and Noah aren't the only ones missing out on sleep." Matt met Rhodey's gaze. "Would you like me to get a blanket, sir?"

Lips curving as he adjusted Avery into a more comfortable position, Rhodey nodded. "Yes, please, pup. Thank you." He waved a hand to catch Pike's attention. "Go tell Keiran to put on some steak for me. And whatever Jared wants for breakfast. Probably porridge or something fucking boring."

Returning from the stairwell, Matt quickly stepped aside to let Drew pass. "Watch out, Clifford Junior."

Wearing a blue knit cap with a pompom on top, the sub carried a small canvas duffle while texting one-handed on his phone. Frowning, Drew lowered his phone as the door closed, staring after Matt. "I'm seriously shaving my head, and earning my first punishment from Stephan. Who wants to help?"

Even as Pike shifted his to Drew, Quint clucked his tongue and shook his head. "You are *not* shaving his head for him."

"No, he isn't." River put his hands on Pike's shoulders, guiding him toward the galley. The edge of his lips twitched as he considered Drew. "But I will, if you're serious about it. Nice little buzz cut. I'm sure Stephan will *love* it. Not like he's not going on all the time about how soft your hair is or how he enjoys the way it brings out your eyes."

Making an uncharacteristic frustrated sound, Drew all but stomped his foot, causing his jeans to slide down a few inches past his boxer briefs. "Everyone makes fun of it. Maybe I can get a wig and only have my natural hair when we're alone?"

"You don't gotta do that, I think your hair is wicked." Tay grinned at Drew, his smile fading as he gave Seth an apologetic look. "Sorry, sir. I'll start over."

Seth cupped Tay's cheeks with his palms, tipping their foreheads together. "You'll be good now. That's not a question. Apologize nicely, and all will be forgiven."

"Yes, sir. And I will." Tay held Seth's gaze. "I'll be your angel, Daddy. I...shouldn't have said all that stuff, no matter how pissed I was. I'll apologize to everyone and do better next time."

"That's my sweet boy." Kissing his nose, Seth patted Tay's cheek, and lifted him off the bar. "When you open your mouth, what you say tells people what kind of respect you hold for me and for Papi. I didn't hear a lot of respect today.

If we need to work on that, you let me know and I will help you."

Worrying his bottom lip between his teeth, Tay nodded. "I wouldn't mind...working on it, Daddy. I want to have the kind of manners that make you and Papi happy." He scuffed his sneakers on the floor. "Can I tell everyone how sorry I am now?"

"You may, my good boy." Hands on Tay's shoulders, Seth turned him, not letting go. "Chin up, make sure everyone hears you."

Taking a deep breath, Tay lifted his chin, his gaze flicking from Lawson, to Rhodey, then settling on Jared. The regret in his tone had his voice hitching, but that wasn't what made listening to him difficult. It was looking into those damn eyes and seeing how much he needed them to believe him. Fuck, it had taken so long to get anything like that from Noah.

Except...Rhodey hadn't been able to see it, even when it was there. Not at first.

Jared always had.

"My behavior was out of line and there's no excuse for it, sir...sirs." Tay inhaled roughly. "My Doms expect better from me and so do you. I won't speak to any of you that way again. I'm sorry and I'll do whatever it takes to make it up to you."

Jared's blink, subtle as it was, might've been amusing—if not for how quickly anyone who knew him as well as Noah did would catch on if he didn't get a better at masking his reactions. "I accept your apology, my boy." He cleared his throat. "It is never wrong to speak up as long as you do so respectfully. The humor wasn't meant to upset you, but it did, and for that I am sorry."

"It didn't really bug me, sir, I'm just...not used to you joking with me like that. And Pike probably thought it was a thing." Tay lifted his shoulders, the edge of his lips curving up a little. "If I can get him not to freak out about it, can you...?

I don't want you to be different with me. You've always been really cool. Please don't stop?"

"We will never lose that, Tay. You're part of this place, part of us now. You can relax. We all will look out for you." Leaning on one forearm, Danny on his knee, Jared brought his gaze level with Tay's. "Sometimes it will feel better than others, but we take the bitter with the better, yes?"

Tay nodded, then glanced over his shoulder at Seth. "Is it all right if I give everyone hugs now? I think it'll seal the deal. 'I like warm hugs.'"

"As long as you ask people before you hug them. If they're part of the Core, that is fine with me." Squeezing Tay's shoulders once, Seth let him go. "And you did a good job. I'm proud of you, my boy."

A bright smile lit Tay's face, washing away the resemblance to Noah so fast, it was like it hadn't been there at all. Rhodey's nephew had always sought some approval, but never the way a sub did. And he definitely never jumped up for kisses before dashing around. By the time Tay reached Jared, the ghost of the past hovering around him—probably all in Rhodey's messed up head—was gone.

And those familiar eyes were shining with mischief as he stopped just short of climbing into Jared's lap with Danny. "Can I hug you, sir?"

Shifting Danny to his other knee, Jared widened his free arm. "I believe there is room for two here."

Seth snorted. "Greedy Doms are as unattractive as greedy subs."

"Says you." Jared's tone was a little too light, the strain showing around the edges of his expression as the sub gave Jared a quick hug, then a sweet kiss on the cheek before slipping down and going to Lawson. Those actions weren't like Noah either, which would help. As would having Danny to hold on to.

When Tay stopped in front of him, Rhodey cut him off

before he could ask. "Yes, you can hug me, silly little cub. Then go snuggle your Doms or something. I've never seen anyone so needy."

The dismissive tone didn't seem to bother the boy at all. Moving carefully to one side to avoid disturbing Avery, he wrapped his arms around Rhodey's shoulders. Then brought his lips close to Rhodey's ear. "You're not as mean as you pretend to be, sir. But it's okay. I won't tell."

Another thing Noah never would have said, but the boy didn't know him very well. Holding him was…strange. Rhodey couldn't help feel the warm, trusting weight of him and realize…he'd never had this with Noah. And never would.

If Rhodey was any other man, it'd have…

Fucking hurt.

"All right, enough." Rhodey patted Tay's back, blowing out a breath when he climbed down. "I'll pretend you apologized to everyone else and not me. I don't accept apologies. I expect actions to prove you'll do better. You won't get any more warnings."

Tay gave him a sharp nod. "I gotcha, man. And that totally works for me."

"Don't call me 'man', sub."

Yep, Noah *definitely* never went red like that. All right, this was much better.

Still, as the sub returned to his men, a strangely well-matched group that had become part of the Core, but remained at the fringes of the tighter bonds within, Rhodey couldn't stop another stab of regret from piercing in deep. Tay's life might not have been exactly easy, but there had always been someone doing their best to shield him from the worst of it. Those strippers, Sin's parents, all teaching him about love and trust.

By the time Rhodey had gotten to Noah, the chance of

him learning either of those things had seemed fucking hopeless.

Eventually, he'd seen his nephew as more than a lost cause. Spared his life, making choices that would impact him for the rest of it. How far Noah had come over the years since could have Rhodey believing he'd done the right thing. He'd convinced Jared as much—only, the man didn't know all the facts. The price not only Rhodey, but *Noah*, had paid to get him where he was today.

With Maddox's return, one thing was certain.

There was no way to ignore the final cost. Only pray to higher powers Rhodey didn't believe in…

Another payment wasn't due.

Chapter Ten

PRESENT

*B*eing back in Anniston Falls wasn't so weird anymore, but walking past The Asylum's gates on his way to Matt's coffee shop was its own kind of awkward. Every moment, Garet half expected Rhodey or Noah to come out and moonshot him all the way to Manhattan where he'd end up on the streets like a junkie.

Which I am...

It hadn't started that way. Some kids at a college frat party had spiked his drink with narcotics, and he'd awakened in a bed with a stranger. Aching all over and covered in the mofo's crusty spunk. Something about that morning—the way the light had seemed more gray than yellow, how the scent of the guy never seemed to leave him—had him searching for something. Anything. Just to get away from the memories.

He knew all that now, even though it hadn't registered then. All this therapy shit was actually worth something. Even if it had caused him to remember things he didn't want to. Like his mother's death, Matt's leaving, and how their dad had taken out his anger on Garet once his brother had ditched them. Of course, Matt hadn't actually done that, but to Garet's mind as a kid the cause and the effect were separate.

"Some things really should be left alone." Hands jammed in his jeans pockets, he hunched in on himself against the cold. Some fucker had stolen his jacket back at the halfway house, along with the money he'd earned washing dishes. "Stop whining. Be happy. People like you when you're happy."

Pasting a smile on his face, Garet jumped up and down a few times to warm his blood and his mood before he shoved through the door into the Roughhouse Café. Inside, steam and heat, along with the rich aroma of fresh brewed coffee, hit his nose. He breathed deep, noting how the scent of new paint underlaid it all. Behind the counter, Matt had his back to the door, working on one of his concoctions for the line of customers Garet found himself swept into.

There was plenty of time to look around at the hand carved oak stools Curtis had made, and the beautiful lettering and drawings Pike had created on the chalkboards above. Black and glass, dark oiled wood and gleaming chrome equipment, shone with all the pride Matt had poured into the place along with the rest of The Asylum. Garet ignored the hole in the pit of his stomach, a chasm where his relationship with his brother had once been. They hadn't really seen each other since the day Matt had come to bring him some clothes and Garet had preferred it that way at first.

But it's time...

The line moved quickly now, with the next few customers ordering easy beverages. A few black coffees, then a mocha. Garet knew when Matt spotted him, tossing his bangs out of his eyes. His brother's gaze landed on him, widening for a moment, his grip tightening on the curved metal handle of the milk pitcher.

Gaze flicking to the door, like he wondered if he was going to need backup, Matt broke Garet's stare and rang up the customer. Then, they were face to face, only the rubbed oak counter separating them. "What can I get you?"

Blinking, Garet rolled his lips between his teeth.

This is how we're gonna play it?

He lifted his attention to the board, noting the prices of the drinks. Which were fancy. Definitely no nickel cup of joe here. Bouncing on the balls of his feet, he remembered to bring the effervescent expression everyone expected from him to his eyes as he met Matt's. "Just a small black. Thanks."

Punching away from the counter, Matt whirled with one of his dark scowls. He would've shit himself to know the expression looked so much like their father's. He returned with the paper cup stamped with the café's logo, lid already affixed.

Voice lowered, Matt slid the coffee in front of Garet. "You know you're not supposed to be here."

Shelling out the money, Garet left it on the counter. "No. I'm not supposed to be across the street." He took a sip, enjoying the burn to his tongue as a distraction. "I wanted to say hi. I'm around, if you want to talk."

"About what?"

Thankfully there weren't any customers to back into when Garet took his step away. He shrugged. "Anything. Nothing. We could just hang out."

Matt tossed his bangs out of his eyes again, revealing their deep blue. "Sure. I'll think about it. Where can I reach you?"

Prepared for this question, at least, Garet slid the card he'd jotted the halfway house number on out of his back pocket, snapping it onto the counter next to the money Matt hadn't touched. "Either here or at Sin's maybe? He's coming home and I was going to hang out with him a bit."

Taking the card, Matt didn't look down at it. "You hurt a lot of people, Garet. You fucking wrecked me. I wasn't sure I ever wanted to see you again. Was getting used to not having you around. Now you walk in here like you don't have a fucking care in the world, expecting me to take your number like you're my fucking dealer and you think I'm gonna want a goddamn hit?" Matt's voice rose the way it did when he got upset, his face getting red and his eyes glistening. "Get the fuck out of my shop."

They'd said this might happen. In group. It did a lot. Apparently. When you really hurt people, they didn't seem to want to come back for more if they were healthy. Which, it was really good Matt was, because he'd need all of that strength in a place like The Asylum.

Trying not to make it about himself, Garet nodded. "I get it. Sorry. You know where to find me."

Outside, the cold made itself known, quickly cooling the heat of the paper coffee cup. The trudge back across the railroad tracks toward the center of town was going to be a bitch with his sneakers already soaked. He stood staring at The Asylum's gates longer than he should have, until the coffee grew colder and he tossed it into the bin by the sidewalk.

Walking up and asking to be let in was tempting. Ringing the buzzer, or testing his code. Except he didn't have a death wish. Rhodey'd been clear he wasn't to cross that line. Taking out his phone, he noticed the draining battery and groaned. He was supposed to text Tay about Sin.

Hi. It's Garet. Sorry to bug you. Sin wants you to know he's gonna be home tonight. I'm shoveling his place and need a key to deliver his dinner.

Apologizing for breathing had started to feel natural, and he held said breath waiting to need to do it again for delivering Sin's message. No way in blue fucking balls would he have believed him if he were Tay. Who'd want to give a junkie the key to their house?

There was a long pause, the little dots bouncing, then stopping, either like Tay was typing a lot or changing his mind about his reply. Finally, a single word popped up.

Sec.

A brain blowing up emoji followed. Another pause, then a full response came.

Sorry, needed to find a way to get somewhere private.

Pike saved my ass and fell off the bar...not sure if it was on purpose or not. He told me what happened and...anyway, I get it. I gotta figure out how to come meet you, but the Doms are always talking like being sneaky is good so...practice?

Shifting from one wet, frozen foot to the other, Garet nodded like Tay could see him. It wouldn't go well for either of them if the guy was caught sneaking out to meet him. Maybe...maybe this was one of those cases where one-hundred-percent honesty would be best?

Might be better to just tell them where you're going and why. It'd piss a lot of people off, you going to meet me on the sly.

This time, the reply was almost instant.

Dude, a lot of things piss people off. Sin wants me to get you the key, I'm getting you the key. Better to beg forgiveness and all that. You there now?

Garet shook his head.

Believe me, it's not.

No. I'm outside the gates, across the street. Just said hi to my brother. Fun times.

A few gifs with different celebrities rolling their eyes popped up, but it was a bit unclear whether they were in response to the whole forgiveness thing, or stuff with his brother being 'fun'. At the side of the club a door opening and closing with a bang joined the noise of shovels and ice being broken.

Reed's laughter rang out, followed by a groan. "Not you, too, Simba. What's it with all the subs trying to slip out without winter gear? Wren I get, but you... Are those Seth's boots?"

Ugh. I knew he should've just said where he was going.

Stepping across the street, Garet dodged a few ice puddles, saving himself from another dunking. He approached the gate, standing at an angle to see through the crack between the fence and the hinges. Keeping his voice as quiet as possible he called out to the pair. "It's me."

Eyes going wide, Reed snapped his gaze toward him, huffing against Tay's palm when the other guy slapped a hand over his mouth. He took off his jacket, laying it over Tay's shoulders, covering up his onesie as he directed him close to the gate.

He glanced over his shoulder, then back at Garet. "Please tell me you didn't convince him to get you back in here. You'll get both your asses banned for life. Which will start Asylum Wars…hell, I've lost count."

"No." Hands balled in his pockets, Garet tried to muster some energy to be bouncy and utterly failed. "I need a key to Sin's place."

Tay shot Reed a stubborn look before pulling out a key he must've taken off the ring before coming out. "If he needed to get back in here, I'd help him. Sin told him to text me, like fuck am I not helping him out however I can. My brother knows which people are good. He obviously thinks Garet's good and that's enough for me."

You're too effing trusting, pipsqueak. It's gonna get you hurt someday.

But Garet swore it wouldn't be by him. He ducked out of sight as Curtis came around the corner with Dallas carrying some bent metal and some hand tools. The former was whistling a tuneless tune while Dallas tried to drown him out with some much more on-key singing of his own.

"Hey! Stop trying to upstage me, my man. It's rude." Curtis grinned, then spotted Reed. "Hey, sparkles. Did Teddy Ruxpin decide he likes the snow? Get him his own coat."

Reed's lips parted, then shut, like he couldn't bring himself to lie.

But Tay didn't seem to have that issue. "I was just coming to see if the mailman was here yet, sir." He yanked off the jacket, back to the gate, and poked the key through the bars with one hand while holding the jacket out to Reed with the other. "He...he's a nice guy and I try to say hi to him whenever I can so he doesn't feel bad about that whole thing with Pike. I think he was totally traumatized. I'm gonna save up and get him something nice. Like...umm...a new...socks?"

The confusion racing across Curtis' face would've been funny if the situation weren't so dire. Dallas glanced up at the rooftop, Avery leaning over with some sort of hand signal that had the man's eyes going wide as he looked over his shoulder toward the gate. Knowing the jig was up, Garet snatched the key from Tay's fingers without a sound and ran across the street without looking.

A car horn blared, and water splashed, but the only thing damaged was the driest portion of his jeans. His ass. Wincing at the cold, he kept going, feet flying to take him away from The Asylum as fast as his legs could move.

The train tracks were a bit clearer, so he took them a ways back toward town, until downtown's sidewalks appeared and he could claim them again. He stopped first at the Chinese place to grab Sin's food, then the free box at the church to rummage around for a sweater. The pink one he found was dotted with posies, but at least it was warm.

On the way past the Center, he slowed to check out the program on the old services board out front. The acapella group was having a concert next Tuesday. Looked like things there were in full swing again, which was nice to see. At least the developers couldn't get their hands on the place and tear it up.

Sin's porch didn't take long to shovel, but his car took a bit longer. The driveway had a few layers of ice between several layers of snow and the stuff was heavy. By the time he'd finished, Garet was toasty warm from the exercise, but his feet were numb. Inside, he stripped off his shoes and socks, then rolled up his pants. No sense tracking dirt everywhere only to have to clean it up again.

The apartment above the tattoo parlor wasn't big. Only

one bedroom, one bathroom, and an open living room and kitchen kinda set up. Not a horrible bachelor pad, but the worn out, dark blue sofa bed, with the cushions slightly askew like someone had put them on in a rush showed the sleeping arrangements hadn't been great. On the walls there were movie posters in plastic frames, along with tattoo sketches in glass ones, more of the latter in the small bedroom which contained a full-sized bed and a tall dresser, half the drawers partially open and emptied.

Walls all painted in darker shades of blue and green gave a strange 'manly' atmosphere to the place, but somehow made it more welcoming and warm. Other than the quick job of Tay's stuff being moved out, things weren't messy, just lived in. And a bit dusty.

Brown paper sack of Chinese food stowed in the fridge, Garet made a mental note of the items Sin would need. Milk, bread, looked like butter and mayo were low too. He didn't have the cash after buying the dinner for Sin, but he made a list and left it under one of the magnets on the fridge before rolling up his sleeves to get to the cleaning. He powered through the bathroom and kitchen, dusted the few horizontal surfaces and the poster frames. All that was left was vacuuming.

Garet found the vacuum in a kitchen broom cupboard—an older model that seemed to leave a few crumbs of everything no matter how many times you went over the floor. He used the broom to get the rest, and by the time he'd finished it was nearly dark. Shoes on, he left the key on the little table by the door and locked up before shutting everything behind him. The porch light came on automatically as he walked through the shadowed recesses and jumped off the steps to land in a new, soft pile of snow that had fallen while he'd been inside.

There was no time to shovel that up. Sprinting he made it to the halfway house just as the clock in the entryway geared up to strike four-thirty p.m. Inside, the space was nothing like Sin's. It smelled of chemical cleaners and plastic. In a cleaning mode, Garet took off his shoes and decided maybe there was a way to make the place a little less like a prison and more like a home.

Shifting his peg from OUT to IN on the whiteboard by the kitchen, he listened for sounds of life about the place. A television played in the living room, and someone talked on their phone in one of the bedrooms. The house monitor wasn't around this side of the place yet, so must've been locking the doors and alarming the windows on the other side of the house. Group therapy was in thirty minutes. Dinner at six. Looked like pizza again, judging by the menus out on the counter.

Cool air creeped in from the back door, which looked closed at first glance, but quiet muttering coming in along with the rising howl of the wind proved otherwise. The muttering stopped and the door opened, eyes so dark they seemed almost black meeting his through a damp spill of golden blond hair that had come loose from a usually snug, low ponytail.

Finn's wary gaze slid past him, then back as he spoke in a whisper. "Are we in the clear? I'm not getting back in that cell until I got no choice. Not really getting the point of staying out of prison if I can't leave this fucking place. At least there, things were entertaining."

Garet supposed he was lucky Rhodey had arranged for him to only spend thirty days in the county lockup before having him transferred to a rehab facility. Going through withdrawals in a cell without medication to lessen the fall had been the kind of hell he never wanted to live through again. So, not a bad decision on Rhodey's part.

Glancing over Finn's shoulder, Garet tried to decide whether the guy had been outside using and whether it was really any of his business. Deciding it wasn't, he ducked for the under sink cabinets instead, taking out the pine scented cleaner and a scrub brush. "Maybe we can ask for some groceries and learn to cook a few things from some online videos?"

"Your idea of entertainment is fucking weird, man." Finn sighed as he came fully into the kitchen, closing the door behind him and stepping over Garet to poke his head in the fridge. "Maybe I can boost Mal's car and cruise town for a few hours to remind myself what freedom's like. You wanna come with? You're dressed all cute and shit, shame not to show off."

Trying to read Finn was a full-time job. It was hard to tell when he was joking or serious. He always sounded the same. "Thanks. I flew down to Manhattan fashion week special to pick this up." Garet gave a lopsided grin, standing to set the bucket in the sink. "How about you wait five weeks until you get your walking papers and I help you build your own car. I'm good at it. Better than rotting in prison for the next five years for five hours of fun."

Finn came out of the fridge with a juice box, letting out another sigh as he stabbed the straw into the top, looking at the thing like it offended him by existing. "I kinda get why Mal says I should hang out with you, you're good people. And you might convince me to keep my next... 'adventure' off my permanent record. Building a car, huh? That's some mad skills. Wouldn't mind trying that on for size, even though nothing beats that look on a guy's face when he's watching you peel out with his fancy ride."

Pulling the faucet forward, Garet turned off the rushing tap and unscrewed the top off the cleaner. Pine wafted on the air, and he breathed deep as he poured a capful into the steaming water. "You know...my buddy Jamie took me street racing once. Said he wanted us to go to a track. I sometimes dream about what it'd be like to put that look on someone's face by winning a race. Like...when I blow past them? And then get a fat trophy and a wad of cash."

"Yeah?" Finn sucked on the straw, giving him an interested look. "So this dude loaded? We can make both our dreams come true. Steal his car, get you on a track, and let you fly. Unless, like, he's a real pal or something. I'm not a complete asshole, no stealing from friends. But if you're here?" He lifted his shoulders. "Not thinking you have any good ones. And *same*."

Swirling the scrub brush in the water, Garet watched the oily residue spin on the surface along with a bit of foam. "Nah. I wasn't a good friend to them. My fault. But I hope I can do better, and then maybe someday he and I can race in Lawson's McLaren. You know?" Hefting the bucket, Garet headed toward the hall where all the muddy boot prints were. "Until then, I can save up to build my own ride, and give it a sick custom paint job. Maybe race on the local circuit."

Only a half-formed idea, and one he hadn't let himself hardly think about, much less mention out loud. Having someone to talk to like Finn—who he might help by showing there were other options to consider besides grand theft auto and a life behind bars—made the fantasy come to life. If he could do something besides be a fuck-up maybe Matt would want to see him. Talk to him. Be his brother again.

That was an even better fantasy.

Picturing it, he got down on his knees and began to scrub, dunking the brush in the water and listening to the sound of the bristles against the scarred linoleum. It felt like praying. Those few times he'd been to church with his mother were hazy, but if he'd done something other than play with his toy cars in the pew he bet it would've felt like this.

Quiet footsteps moved away from the fridge, Finn's threadbare black socks coming into view before shuffling toward the table, where he began picking up the chairs and turning them upside down on the surface to get them out of the way. "Promise I can see your car when you're working on it, even if you gotta mail me pics when I'm back in?" His tone sharpened as his attention shifted to someone else. "Can't you see he's cleaning the fucking floors, asshole? Take your shoes off or I'll make you eat them."

Unable to help the thought, Garet wondered whether Rhodey needed another kid. Finn would be right at home with the Dom. Possibly kneecap-less, but definitely at home. "It's okay, Finn. I'm working off a lot of energy. I appreciate the chairs and stuff." He threw a grin over his shoulder at a young man he'd never thought to consider a friend but had rapidly come to want to see do well. "If you want to build the car with me, racers always work in teams. You wanna be my team?"

Surprise, then excitement, filled Finn's eyes as he nodded. "For real? Yeah, that'd be cool. I'll even show you I'm serious about it and not skip group again. Might shock the fuck out of Mal. He'll keel the fuck over and today will be the best day ever!"

"He'll think it was his idea, but we'll know something he doesn't." Sitting back on his heels, Garet plopped the scrub brush into the bucket of filthy water, noting they were alone again. "Which is always the best. Having a secret someone else doesn't know. And you can kinda smirk when they're all pleased with themselves thinking they made it happen when really it was you."

Lips around the straw of his juice box, Finn braced his hip against the counter and nodded as he sucked the thing dry. "If I ever get out of here? I'm making sure the credit goes where it belongs. You kinda make me want to be all…legit and stuff. If it wouldn't get you in all the wrong kinds of trouble, I'd find a fun way to thank you, but…well, you're a good guy. And breaking the wrong rules means something for some dumbass reason."

Smelling like pine cleaner and Sin's summer cotton dryer sheets from the load he'd done to freshen the bed while he was there, Garet decided to do something he hadn't done in months. He stepped up to Finn, wrapped his arms around his waist, and gave him a tight squeeze. "Thanks. It's all you, man, but I'm glad to be along for the ride."

Throat clearing came from the hall even as Mal's sharp steps approached, his hard-soled shoes snapping against the worn wood floors. "We respect each other's personal space, boys. I'll give you a warning. This time." His dull green eyes swept the space before he gave a satisfied nod. "Didn't I tell you focusing on something productive would be good for you? It'll be nice to have something good to tell your parole officer, Finn." Gray hair slicked back from his face, wrinkles deepened when the old man's gaze went over Garet. "What are you wearing? There's no need to make life more difficult for yourself, son."

Still smirking at Finn with their shared secret, Garet clicked the heels of his socked feet together three times. "Just looking for my ruby slippers. I thought maybe the tornado might come to Kansas and sweep away the wicked witch."

Finn snickered, holding Mal's gaze as he slid his hand into the back pocket of Garet's jeans. "You're just jealous. He looks hot, but you're too old to get it up anymore so you won't let the rest of us enjoy shit either."

Mal let out a heavy sigh. "No, I am trying to keep all of you *out* of prison. Give Garet some space, Finn, you know the rules. You are not being a very good friend to him by behaving inappropriately in a way that *he* will suffer for, simply because he's slightly older than you are. Finish up your time, keep out of jail past the date when you'll be tried as an adult, and you can 'enjoy' all the 'shit' you'd like."

Eyes widening briefly, Garet realized that Mal had basically said he was somehow coming on to a minor. To Finn. Age in friends wasn't an issue. He and Finn had each other's backs. The whole lover thing though... Why did people assume just because you were gay you were out to screw everyone you met?

Rage licked at Garet's nape, making it heat, and understood what Matt must feel every time someone pissed him off. It didn't happen to him often, but when it did he could give his older brother a run for his money. "Come on, Finn. I'll finish the floors in a bit. It's time for group." Giving Mal a dirty look, Garet stepped around him. "We want the bean bags. I call purple."

Jerking his hand away like he'd been burned, Finn hooked his thumbs to the pockets of his own jeans, shoulders hunched as he kept close to Garet's side. "I'll take the blue one. And... sorry about that. I was just playing, but...yeah. I don't want to get you in that kind of trouble. Didn't think he was gonna make a thing out of a few damn months. Not like he caught me sneaking into your room...not that I'd do that, but..." His cheeks went red. "Yeah. Anyway."

"It's okay. My conscience is clear. Whatever anyone else makes of it, that's their issue." Garet flopped down on the oversized purple bean bag closest to the large cast iron radiator. Heat contrasted with the cold and damp of his jeans, making him aware exactly how uncomfortable he was. "I didn't know you were gay." He held out a fist. "It's nice not to be alone."

Bumping his fist to Garet's, Finn nodded, looking more than a little relieved. "It really is. I couldn't be out with my old crew, or in juvie—obviously—but here? You make it feel safe. I also saw...some of the movies you did. Mad respect, man. It was super...anyway, I'm gonna keep my not-quite-legal trap shut."

It was Garet's turn to blush. He squirmed a little in his bean bag, changing the subject. "I have a whole new crew for you to hang out with when you're out. There's a garage where we work on cars, and it's safe to just be you. Ez does a mean custom paint job, and Curtis..." He trailed off as he realized he wasn't welcome in that space or any others with his 'crew' any longer. "Anyway...they're going to love you."

"We'll see. Hard to picture *being* out, you know? Or...well, *you* probably can. You weren't in that long." Finn made a face. "I wasn't all that worried when I kept getting caught as a kid, fucking regular hot meals and a bed to sleep in? Not too shabby. But third strike and you're doing hard time's got me... a bit freaked the fuck out. Thanks for...making me feel like I might have other options."

As the other guys began to fill the room, Garet leaned over, voice lowered. "You have all the options. No matter what, when you get out of here you find me at the tattoo parlor downtown. You're never gonna be hungry or cold again."

"I will." Finn lowered his own voice, sinking down a bit into his bean bag chair and tucking his socked feet under the edge of the carpet as one of the guys passed, lifting it enough to trip him. He tipped his head back, whistling as he stared at the ceiling. Then he winked at Garet. "He won't forget to take his shoes off in the house again."

Garet couldn't repress a naughty snicker, though he knew it would only egg Finn on. Licking his lips, he felt the sparkle return to his gaze and the colors in the dingy room brightened. He might not be allowed back in The Asylum, but he realized one very important thing. It had taught him how to form bonds like these, and shown him who was worth protecting.

Which meant no matter where he went?

Home was right there with him.

Chapter Eleven

PRESENT

*C*ustomers... *Gotta stay cool for the customers...*
This adulting shit was next level. When he was younger, Matt figured the worst thing about being a grown-up would be having to pay bills, but the bonus of staying up as late as you wanted, and getting to eat the last piece of chocolate cake after the kids went to bed, would be worth it. He hadn't counted on things like a deadbeat and drug addicted gangbanger of a brother, or taking care of problems that definitely weren't his own.

Like where Mrs. Karver had left her baby's 'blinky'. Whatever the fuck that was.

Matt raked his hands through his hair, glancing around the overcrowded café. "Where did you say you'd last seen it?"

"He left it on the table, I'm sure of it." Mrs. Karver struggled to keep the squalling infant from pitching himself out of her arms, his hand pressed to her mouth in his attempt to take a nosedive into the hard floor. Red-faced, the harried mother adjusted her hold. "Unless I left it by the changing table..."

A better advertisement for birth control and being gay never existed.

Stepping through the front door of the café, Lawson took one look at the mother and child, and the growing line of customers, then shot Matt a bracing smile as he joined them. He held his arms out for the baby. "Here, let me take him while you settle whatever the issue is, Mary. Toby, what have I told you about giving your mother a hard time?" Holding the baby with one arm, Lawson waved his tie in front of the tiny, scrunched up face. "What's all that noise for? There you go. Chew on that for a bit."

Throwing Lawson a grateful smile, Matt returned his attention to Mrs. Karver. "I'll check the booth, and how about you check the restroom? If we can't find it, I can probably have someone grab one at the convenience store... Unless it's something handmade?"

Blinking at Lawson like he might've cast a spell over her now contented infant, Mrs. Karver nodded. "Please and...it is. I could make another one, but I don't have nearly as much time or *hands* as I thought I did before I had him." She laughed and shook her head. "Thank you, Mr. Gaumond. And...Mr. Gaumond." She looked between him and Lawson, ducked her head, and seemed to get even redder before she dashed toward the restrooms.

"I've never been Mr. Gaumonded before." Watching the woman go, Matt blinked a few times, then did his own pivot to duck and weave past tables people moved around to suit their little groups throughout the day.

At nearly five p.m. the place was a freaking wreck, and he hadn't even had time to top off the sugar decanters at the coffee station. A square of blue paisley catching his eye, he bent down to peer under the rear booth where a baby blanket or quilt...or something, was under the foot of a customer.

"Hi. Excuse me. Sorry." Matt pointed to the blanket. "Do you mind if I just grab that?"

Not even looking at him, the teen lifted the edge of the quilt with the pointed toe of her shoe and kicked it in his general direction, speaking around hard sucks of her 'specialty drink'—an iced monstrosity he'd had to remake three times.

"Can you *believe* the guy's a teacher? I've started walking my little brother to school just to see him and his boyfriend. Like...O.M.G. Red hair just does it for me. But *all* the hot ones are gay. I'm not even joking."

Blinky in his fingertips, Matt glanced over his shoulder toward the register where Drew talked with Zandi, and wondered if he was about to have a modern version of a 1960s style teen squee fest on his hands. Zandi rang up the guy, having finished making an iced mocha latte and a regular coffee for the sub and his Dom, Stephan, who spoke quietly with Lawson while doing some cutesy finger movements to keep the baby entertained.

Somehow refraining from rolling his eyes, Matt shook out the blanket, muttering to himself. "If this baby thing is catching, I'm finding a vaccine."

The edge of Lawson's lips quirked, as though he'd caught Matt's words, despite the noisy chatter in the café. His deep laugh carried as he bounced the baby in one muscular arm, his cast used to hold the little thing steady. "I know The Asylum isn't exactly childproof, but would it be terribly inappropriate to arrange some kind of babysitting service?"

Stephan snorted and shook his head. "I'm going to assume you're joking and not answer that. But if you want my opinion? Enjoy these little moments. I can guarantee you, Mrs. Karver would be all for it, and you'd regret offering within the first twenty minutes."

Submission wasn't something Matt made obvious in his workplace, but he had little ways of showing his respect to his Dom and to Stephan as he stepped carefully up to them, standing just a hair outside their circle when he handed the soft handmade blanket to the grasping infant.

Who promptly spit up on Lawson's tie.

"You found it!" Mrs. Karver rushed over to them, her brilliant smile fading as she took in the mess. Easing the baby into her arms, she stuttered an apology.

Which Lawson waved off. "That's quite all right. We were all small and…" He held his tie away from him with one hand, awkwardly trying to undo it with the fingers of his casted arm. "Messy at some point."

Standing on tiptoe, Matt made a soft sound to let Lawson know he had the situation under control. "Here. Let me, s— sweetheart." His face flamed, the endearment feeling somehow kinkier than the honorific.

"Thank you, love." Lawson glanced at him over his shoulder as Stephan distracted the mother and child, leading both to a recently cleared out booth near the door to help her bundle the baby back up. Giving Matt a soft smile, Lawson lowered his voice. "If you missed it, I need to make something clear. I enjoy visiting Tracey and playing with Azalea. I don't mind lending a hand to an overwhelmed young mother. But I have absolutely no interest in having children of our own."

Relief gusted from Matt with his accidental, "Thank fuck," as he handed Lawson his rolled up and ruined tie. "Doesn't count. I'm at work." He grinned, momentarily forgetting his own grumpiness and the reason for the disturbing amount of churn in his gut. "For another ten minutes."

"Mhm." Lawson made a face as he grabbed a few disposable napkins before wrapping the tie in them and going around behind the counter to tuck it away beneath. "Two things? That's Noah's policy, not mine, but I'll let you have *one* free pass." He went to the sink to wash his hands. "And two, we really should consider extending the opening hours here. I'd like to arrange it so the café is…more independent from The Asylum. Financially. I have some ideas that will make it a smooth transition, but we can discuss that later."

Behind the counter now with Zandi—who'd managed to make a pour over and a few lattes for a group of business types without breaking a sweat—Drew started restocking the straw container.

"Drew? Thanks, dude, but..." Matt threw Lawson an apologetic look, holding up a finger. "You don't work here."

"But I could?" Ducking down, Drew seemed not to hear the meaning behind Matt's words, which was basically *customers don't belong behind the counter*. He came up with the box of sugar packets and a few boxes of creamers. "Excuse me. I'll just refill these and be right back."

Matt opened and closed his mouth, watching the redheaded guy with the secret fanclub skirt around the tables to the coffee station. He pulled at the back of his neck, frowning. "Well, I mean, I guess we could extend the hours if we have enough help. It's really Saturdays and Sundays that are crazy like this."

"You have enough business to justify hiring at least another barista or two. As well as cleaning staff." Lawson pulled out the ledger he'd set up for Matt, laying it on the counter before turning to put two muffins in a bag and hand them to Zandi for a customer. "If it feels overwhelming to go through the applicants, I can handle that for you, my boy." He stepped aside to let Drew pass with the refilled sugar containers. "And if Drew would like to join the ranks on the weekend, that will save you having to deal with too many unfamiliar people."

Or the familiar ones...

Recalling Garet's unexpected presence at the counter, Matt paled. Seeing his brother, looking healthy and whole, had almost been enough for the briefest moment. More than enough. *Everything*. Until memories came crashing back of the nights Matt had spent nursing drunken stupors, spending bail money meant for the car he wanted to buy so he could get the better paying job, and wondering how many gang members would be inside his house the next time he came home from working a double.

Fingers shaking, Matt pulled the ledger closer. "I trust you, Law. If you think that's the right business decision, that's what we'll do." He lifted his gaze from the numbers he wasn't really seeing, the hum of conversation mingling with the buzzing in his ears that had never quite left since the accident. "Why now though? I thought you wanted The Asylum to diversify? The club has a lot of seed capital in the Roughhouse."

"It does, but we're facing several issues and I don't want your business caught in the crossfire. Keiran had to reapply for his liquor license the other day. The new mayor seems to see putting obstacles in our path as his way to secure his position, and the café and the restaurant being seen as their own entities will avoid those issues spreading any further." Lawson's brow furrowed as he studied Matt's face. He snapped his fingers, beckoning Zandi over and holding the pink-haired sub's gaze. "Matt and I need a moment. Drew will help you. Keep things running smoothly until we return. Stephan can assist if you have any trouble."

Zandi nodded with his usual earnestness. "I have this, sir. We can close up. I know how to cash out and clean up."

At one time the impulse to argue with Lawson would've surfaced, but Matt found himself merely grateful to have a husband and a Dom who could read him so well. He didn't need to put on a brave face or to pretend to have all his shit together. Lawson would make sure that things were handled, and he didn't need to do everything on his own. They were a team.

"Thanks, Zan." Grabbing the bottle of antacids from beneath the counter, Matt popped two, crunching their chalky disks into powder as he followed Lawson out from behind the counter.

Leading the way to the small office in the back, which Lawson had designed personally, making it almost like his own, except without the chairs in front of the desk for interviews, his Dom waited for him to step in, then closed the door behind him. Instead of going to the office chair, He braced his hip against the side of the desk and held out his arm. "Come here. Tell me what's going on. You've dealt with crowds like this before without looking this stressed."

Moving quickly into Lawson's hold, Matt took a moment to bury his nose in the warm, slightly prickly skin where his husband's jaw met his throat. Breathing deep, he inhaled the scent of cigars, whiskey, and...baby powder.

"That does not belong on you." He pulled back a bit, giving Lawson a shaky smile. "You smell like talc."

"Better than regurgitated breast milk. Or any kind of sour milk. I don't discriminate." Lawson chuckled and pulled Matt back in to give him a firm hug. "Something's bothering you. And it's not how I smell. You manage just fine with Curtis and he likes to show off when he's particularly ripe."

Unable to help himself, Matt snorted with laughter. "Please. Don't remind me." Being near Lawson was helping. A lot. Just having his Dom's steady presence and warmth refilled the well of composure his little brother always seemed to empty out just by being in a room. "I love you. Thank you. I needed this. And to answer your question..." Glancing away, he puffed his cheeks, letting out a noisy breath. "Garet was here. I threw him out."

"I see." Lawson's jaw hardened, and he put his arm over Matt's shoulders, drawing him around the desk with him. Lowering to the big leather chair, he pulled Matt down to sit on his thigh. "Between him and Ezran, I have a feeling things are about to get...very complicated. But I need to make something clear. And I may end up saying that a lot, because I won't let uncertainty come between us." His dark green eyes met Matt's. "You do not owe your brother, or *anyone*, anything. Not forgiveness, not your time, and not your energy. What you give is no more or less than is right for you. That can change from day to day. From moment to moment. It took me a long time to learn that. To understand...I have nothing to offer if I can't protect myself. Honor my own feelings, my own boundaries. Does that make sense?"

Settling on Lawson's thigh, Matt looped one arm around the back of his Dom's neck. Nodding, he leaned into Lawson's chest, barely able to speak above a whisper. "I'm so angry, Law. It scares me how angry I am. I see him...and it's like I was before I met you. I want to just... The stuff that happened a few weeks ago, I can't deal with all that and Garet." His brother's name tasted bitter on his tongue. "So much happened that you don't even know about. I didn't want to taint everyone's feelings about him, and I was so proud when he finally straightened out with everyone's help. I'm so mad at him for throwing it in our faces. I can't trust him again. I just... He hurt me so much. All of us."

"Yes, he did. And whenever you're ready to tell me those things, I hope you know I'm always here to listen. To sort through your feelings." Lawson brought his hand up to cup Matt's cheek, his thumb gently stroking back and forth. "I had a hard time being who Ezran needed me to be when he was still a child. But he's a man now. I'll still try to be there for him, but his choices are his own because he's not a child anymore. And neither is Garet. At some point, we have to let them own the decisions they've made and decide...if we're willing to keep them in our lives despite them." He took a deep breath. "I'm reserving judgment, for the moment, but it's hard. I know what it's doing to you. I know what it will do to Reed. Curtis. Noah..." He pressed his eyes shut. "If I had my way, I'd shield all of you, but that's beyond my control."

Turning his face, Matt kissed Lawson's hand, enjoying the way his broad palm seemed to form a well where he could hide. He leaned back, lifting his gaze to meet Lawson's dark green eyes. "I came home from work one night... We didn't have a lot from my mom. Just a hope chest with her wedding gown and a blanket she'd made. His friends had been cutting coke on it and doing lines. I never knew if Garet had been using with them."

Even saying the words was difficult. Memories he'd stuffed

down for so long just so he could be there for Garet and have a relationship with him welled to the surface, threatening to overwhelm his ability to breathe or speak. When he managed to get in an even breath, he continued.

"I feel it here." Matt pressed a fist to his own chest. "Like a rock of anger. I want to throw it at him and watch him bleed. That scares me, because I know I'm capable of horrible things where he's concerned. I gave him everything I had to give, and I'm so damned scared he's coming for the rest whether I want to give it to him or not."

Lawson shook his head and slid his hand to the back of Matt's neck, the grip not painful, but more secure. Solid. Reminding him where he was and who he was with. "Those thoughts, those emotions, come whether we want them to or not. It's what we do with them that matters. I need you to know, the things I share with you are *never* to make you feel like what you're going through is less. But I can relate because I felt very much like that with Curtis. For longer than I want to admit."

Bringing his other hand around, fingers only partially showing above the cast, Lawson laced them with Matt's. He let the silence stretch, the office soundproof enough to become their own little sanctuary despite the chaos steps away from the door. A comforting kind of peace.

"A lot of the time, knowing why he was with Noah, seeing Noah as my savior, while he had a man who'd done something so terrible there, was…to put it plainly? A mindfuck. Noah helped Curtis become someone other than who his family had raised him to be, but all I could see was my rescuer constantly fighting with a…thug." His throat worked. "The violence, the conflict between them, I didn't understand it. And in the end, I didn't have to. Curtis and I built our own friendship because…I was able to see past what he had done. And I understood why Noah was finally able to. But that's not the point I'm getting at. I…I often wondered if that understanding meant I should have…handled my ex showing up differently. But I did what I could, with the information I had at the time. And…I do not forgive him for what he did to me. I never will. For me, it is not part of my healing. If it's not part of yours? That's okay."

The whine in Matt's ears picked up, and he shook his head, using the tiny motion to knock it back to a manageable level. "Thank you for telling me that. About you and Curtis and Noah, and about not forgiving." He squeezed Lawson's fingers lightly, careful not to hurt him. "I feel like a bad person for the thoughts I have, and I kind of worry that my brain is all screwed up because of the accident. I wasn't this bad before…" A shaky breath stretched his chest, burning with his inhale. "Sorry. Stephan says it's normal to have emotional dysregulation with trauma. I just don't expect how strong it is. I feel like I don't own me. Does that make sense?"

"It does. And you also had a bit of a knock to the head." Lawson leaned in to kiss the scar on his temple. "So don't be so hard on yourself. Yes, he's your brother. That adds several layers to how you process things between you. But you gave him all you could. For a very long time. It's more than fair to say 'That's enough. I can't do this anymore'." He kissed Matt's cheek. "Maybe, one day, the effort he puts in will make a difference. Maybe it will feel safe to open up to have some kind of relationship with him. But only on your terms. When *you* are ready. Not before. If you don't feel strong enough to draw those lines? I will."

Matt found himself nodding before Lawson finished speaking, needing to lean into his submission. Maybe he was using it as a crutch, but one he very much needed with his metaphorical legs knocked out from under him.

Reaching up, he straightened the buttons at the points of Lawson's collar. "If it pleases you, sir, I could stand to feel like your boy right now and not a business owner. Or a brother. I know you've got the control so I don't have to, if I'm unable to…" He gave Lawson a rueful smile. "But I'll still take care of you, too."

"You are *always* my boy, my love." Lawson kissed his lips, smiling against them. "It's healthy for you to be in charge of your own thing, now and then, but I like knowing I can step in and claim it all for myself when it pleases me. This might come as a surprise, but I'm kind of good at it."

Laughter puffed across both his and Lawson's lips, breathy and light. "I have kinda noticed that, sir." Matt sobered for a moment, needing to claim one other thing for himself. "The Asylum… Our home. It's ours, right? He can't come back unless you and I say it's okay?"

Lawson's lips drew into a firm line. "On my part? No. He can't. But this isn't a decision I can make on my own. I can't see him getting around Rhodey—he has to know what it would do to Noah to have that young man around—but if he somehow manages that, there's still Jared. I'll speak to the other Core Doms as soon as I'm able and explain why it would be a very bad idea to let him come back."

"Thank you, sir." Relief gusting from him, Matt leaned into Lawson's chest, his head on his Dom's shoulder. "I know I sound selfish, and my mother would be pissed as hell at me…but my head is too full and I don't want to lose myself. I feel too close to that sometimes already without adding anything else."

Nodding slowly, Lawson stroked his hand up and down Matt's back. "That's understandable. The way I see it? Garet was…he was here, with us, given…so many chances. Before either of you came to The Asylum, yes, I can see how, with how hard and how much you worked for you both to survive, he might have been vulnerable. Not known any better. But after that…" His jaw worked as he stared straight ahead. "Curtis alone showed him, taught him, a better way. Noah… he made sure both he and Ezran understood where *that* path could lead. He ignored everything we did, everything we said, and went back to what was easy. And, believe me, I get where you're coming from. Part of me says I should be more compassionate. But another part of me is...frustrated. Fed up. I have seen those who've taken the opportunities they're given and make something of it. *You*, for example. So many others. I don't give a fuck about the money I poured in to his schooling. I care about it being thrown back in my face, your face, as though it meant nothing."

Palm flat against Lawson's chest over his heart, Matt did what he always did when he worried he stressed his man out too much. He felt the steady rhythm of his heart, drinking in the life beneath his fingers. Warm cotton and the thub-dub reassuring him, he made a thoughtful sound. "How'd you do it, sir? Forgive Curtis? I don't know a lot about what he did, but I know what he was like when I got here. You two weren't in a great spot, and he was...edgier?"

"He was. But I'd already forgiven him for a lot. We were..." Lawson's lips curved slightly, his gaze softening. "We were struggling to fill up the power vacuum left with Noah's absence and doing a terrible job of it. Things would've been a lot worse if we weren't coming from a better place. We both might have...regressed a bit, but what saved us was having a common ground. We both wanted to hold The Asylum together. That made everything else secondary. I don't think either of us realized it at the time, but if we didn't love one another, at least a little bit? We wouldn't have managed for as long as we did. You...when you showed up and he nudged you in my direction? It was the first step to both of us being able to move forward. Together. Not knowing what would happen when Noah came home. If we hadn't done that...I don't think The Asylum would still be there. We couldn't have kept it going for him. Or for ourselves."

Matt snorted quietly, remembering those early days. "If that was a nudge, I'd hate to see what his shoves look like." Tipping his head back, he settled into Lawson's arms and took

195

in the professional yet cozy office that he retreated to whenever he needed to feel his Dom's presence and to think through something difficult. "Thank you. For everything you've given to me, and to everyone. You never quit. On any of us... Not even Curtis when he was being...a mob rat. Maybe that's why giving up on Garet feels so awful. I have you as an example, and I'm just not good like you. I have so much anger and hatred." He met Lawson's eyes, his own shying away for a moment. "I'm not the boy you deserve, but I'm really glad you're my Dom anyway."

A soft clucking of Lawson's tongue was followed by a sharp slap to Matt's thigh. "Are you questioning your Dom's taste in subs? That's what it sounded like to me, but I might be mistaken."

Saying 'no' would be lying, but it hadn't been what Matt *intended* to imply. Passing his tongue over his lips, he shook his head in a Jamie-like circle, then almost rolled his eyes at himself. The dude was catching. "I don't mean to, but I guess that's what it amounts to. I'm sorry, sir."

"You're forgiven. I expect you to be honest with me, and with yourself, and that's exactly what you're doing. There's no wrong way to feel, especially when you were caught off guard like that. It's what we do with those emotions that matters. Sharing them with me was a good start." Lawson patted Matt's thigh, much lighter this time. "I'm going to go over the books for you and you're going to kneel at my feet and relax for a bit. Your only job is to keep me company. Is that understood?"

"Yes, sir. Am I allowed to talk to you?" Seeking clarification, Matt waited to be dismissed from Lawson's lap.

Lawson inclined his head, snapping his fingers and motioning to his feet. "You may."

Sliding off Lawson's lap, Matt went to his favorite place in the world, by his Dom's feet, next to strong thighs and high end wool slacks that smelled like the warmth of home. Taking position, he lowered his head, hands resting palm-upward on his thighs.

"I love you. So much." He had to say it, or the feeling was going to burst his chest open, spilling all his feels in a gooey puddle across the thick burgundy and azure carpet beneath his knees. His lips curved softly. "Husband."

Fingers brushing lightly through Matt's hair, Lawson spoke in a quiet, soothing tone. "I love you, too. Husband." He chuckled as he opened several ledgers on the desk, the light scratches of a pen on paper filling the brief silence. "At the moment, we are the only married members of the Core. We'll have to be sure to set a good example. Maybe I'll carry you over the threshold a few times to show them all how it's done."

Matt's answering snicker shook his shoulders. "You better not let Jared see you do that until your cast is off." He glanced up from beneath his bangs at the blue sling. "I'm looking forward to seeing you all patched up, sir. Do you think you'll need PT? I did after I broke my arm when I was—" He cut off, shaking his head when his ears began to ring, loudly. Several more shakes seemed to clear the sound, and he let out a shaky breath. "I broke my arm *after* a tournament once. Not during. I was running around with the trophy, looking for my mom and tripped on my gym bag."

"Doing that after the tournament sounds like it was both good luck and bad. Before would have made winning a bit more challenging." Lawson's lips curved as he slid his hand down to massage the back of Matt's neck, light teasing in his voice. "I'm sure you would have managed it anyway, though, my stubborn boy. We have that in common." He sighed and the writing stopped. "I will likely need it, but I'll be doing everything in my power to expedite the process. I'm tired of everyone thinking I need to be taken care of. It might not seem like it, but even with this damn thing, I'm still quite capable."

Hearing that he had *anything* in common with Lawson was pretty fucking awesome, but Lawson's last comment drew Matt's attention away from saying so. "Sir. Of course you're capable. Who's treating you like you're not? I'll have a word with them." *With my fists.* "Nobody puts The Law in the corner."

Lawson arched a brow at him, a small smile tugging at his lips. "I'm not sure how to feel about my name replacing 'Baby', but I appreciate the sentiment." He rolled his neck and shook his head. "No one is doing it intentionally, love. Everyone's on edge and it brings out those protective urges. I can't fault anyone for that, but I need to be back to my former strength so I can contribute more. Get back in the damn ring. Paddle my own subs. Knock Curtis on his ass now and then to remind him that I can."

"There's no rush on the paddling, sir. I'm enjoying Curtis' lightweight swing." Matt bit back a grin, wiggling his ass against his heels. "I haven't had bruises in forever. It's novel being able to sit down without wincing." He nudged Lawson's knee with his nose, rubbing his cheek against the soft gray wool of his trousers. "You contribute a ton, sir. I can't wait to see you in the ring again, but it'll happen."

Giving him a long look, Lawson slid his chair back a bit, curving his fingers in Matt's collar and tugging him between his thighs. "Curtis has been careful with you because you were injured. If Jared clears you for more intense scenes, I'll see to it that you get them. Let's not have Rhodey or Noah's subs influence how you view your own. You know very well Curtis can be as hardcore as you need him to be."

The urge to pull a bit on the collar was strong, but Matt refrained, taking only what he was given. "Yes, sir. But it's fun to tease. I know you're the best Dom in the Core and Curtis is a close second. I'm very grateful." Mention of the dungeon had need pooling in his groin, tightening the muscles there. "I miss apologizing to him in the bar. We stopped that when

Noah came back. Is it weird that I don't need as much privacy as I used to? I'm good with what you want, but I kept meaning to tell you."

"No, it's not weird at all, and I'll take that into account. As a matter of fact, I believe I'll have you apologize to him for the 'teasing'." Lawson tapped Matt's nose with the back of his pen. "From you, I know it's meant to be playful, but with some of the others, I'm tempted to put them in the damn stocks for the way they speak about their Doms. And the rest of us."

Paling, Matt tried to think of who'd be enough of an asshole to insult their Doms. The Core were the best of the best, and anyone who had one of their men was damned lucky. "I haven't noticed it, sir, but if I do in the future I'll make sure to say something to whoever it is. And I'm sorry. I'll gladly apologize to Curtis."

"That's my good boy." Lawson leaned down to kiss his forehead. "I'd very much like to see you on your knees for him, right in the middle of the bar, not giving a damn who's watching. Except for me. I very much want you aware that I'll never take my eyes off of you."

A needy sound escaping, Matt rose up a bit off his heels to nuzzle Lawson's lips. He took, only because he couldn't help it. The peaks and valleys of Lawson's mouth were too tempting, and right fucking *there*. It had been so long since the three —or four—of them had enjoyed each other. There were a few other things he knew he had to apologize for, but now didn't seem like the right time to bring them up. He and Lawson were having a good day, and his Dom seemed happy.

And keeping things this way?

Meant more than opening *any* cans of worms.

Chapter Twelve

PRESENT

"*D*o you really need to do the books now, sir?" Matt gazed up at Lawson, a hopeful lift to his brow. "We could go home?"

Letting out a soft, considering hum, Lawson claimed another, deeper kiss. "I do, but I suppose it's unfair of me to put all those thoughts in your head and make you wait. Well, wait for *everything*, in any case. It wouldn't be much of an apology if I didn't offer you to Curtis a little needy." He nipped Matt's bottom lip. "I could always let you practice while I work. We wouldn't want your performance to reflect badly on your husband, now would we?"

Matt's dick thumped against the seam of his jeans like the wagging tail of a needy puppy. He shook his head slowly, earnestly, trying not to show how excited the idea of pleasuring Lawson made him. Since it was supposed to be a practice apology, he *tried* to treat it with the weight it deserved. "No sir, I would never want to make you look bad."

"That's *very* good to hear." Lawson glanced at the desk. "I have a feeling Curtis made this big enough so our boys could fit comfortably underneath. He's a fan of multitasking. Why don't you make use of your other Dom's ingenuity and get under there. Then show me what you can do with that pretty mouth."

Mindfucks—even mild ones—were a rare but delicious twist when they came from Lawson. Having his Dom's thick thighs surrounding him, the musk and heat of him all around, was the kind of gift Matt craved. Lawson giving him this here, now, in a space they could call all their own, made it next level. The need to forget the events of the day even more so.

Sidling under the desk, where light became shadow, and Lawson's face disappeared entirely from view—only sculpted chest muscles under quality fabric, and the glint of his belt giving any clue to his identity—Matt settled in and reached for the fastening to his Dom's trousers. Leather gave way, the belt jangling, then the zipper creating sharp sounds that cut through the silence. Pages flipped—another mind fuck—as Lawson at least pretended to work.

Heat and musk invaded Matt's senses, the silken smoothness of Lawson's flesh in his palm its own reward. He freed the thick length of him, reveling in the proud flare of his dick, the way the base had its own darker contours with bulging blue veins that painted their way up to the place he longed to taste. Dipping in, he flicked his tongue against the slit to lick up the subtly sweet saltiness, a taste all Law's own, and hummed his approval.

"I really have to call the distributor for those sugar packets, you should be getting a much better price for the amount you're ordering..." Lawson's tone remained casual, but the fingers he slid under the desk to rake through Matt's hair, forcing his dick deeper down his throat, betrayed his arousal. "And why do you need two different kinds of sugar? What is cane sugar? Isn't all sugar from canes?"

Answering was impossible with the way Lawson fucked his mouth. An incoherent gurgling sound all he managed, Matt swallowed fast as he slid the head of his Dom's dick past his throat. They hadn't played this way in a little while, what with the tensions of the past weeks. Reflexes honed over years took over and only a momentary panic increased Matt's heart rate to panicky levels. When Law let him breathe, he took in great inhales through his nostrils, gathering up his man's musky scent. Underneath the desk, his world was small, controllable...controlled. By his Dom. He didn't need to think or feel. He just existed for the pleasure of a man who was his everything.

That solid grip guided him down again, Lawson's breaths a bit faster now, a low groan escaping his throat before he resumed his writing. He inhaled deep, pure willpower radiating from him with every inch of composure he latched onto, as security as he held on to Matt.

By the time he spoke again, he probably could've taken a business call without anyone suspecting a thing. "I believe in saving money wherever possible, but I'll have to concede with Noah on this expense. Those napkins you ordered aren't up to standard, I'm going to get you a refund, especially since you've had to use some from The Asylum ever since you ran out of the better ones. I'll get you an account with our printer—they haven't been taking on anyone new for a while, but I'm certain I can get them to reconsider."

Lawson being all...*Lawson* while doing dirty things to Matt's lips and mouth, smearing sticky precome so thoroughly over and around both he swore he was going to need one of those napkins before he could leave the office, had to be the hottest fucking thing ever. Mind spinning with visions of Lawson forcing him to leave the café just like that forced a warning shot up his own dick, making him gasp and choke around his Dom's length. The wide girth stretched his mouth, making what he knew from watching in a mirror was an obscene display. Fuck him sideways, but he so got off on it. On the secret things they did together, on imagining Lawson making him into his little come slut in the middle of the bar while talking to Noah, or some other Dom, just like this.

"Careful, pet." Lawson jerked Matt's head back with a sharp tug, so the head of his dick rested on his bottom lip, dangerously close to slipping away completely. "You do *not* have permission to come. If you do, I'll put a ball gag and a cock cage on you and neither me or Curtis will use you until you can be our good boy again."

"I'm sorry, sir..." Breaths labored, Matt laved Lawson's dick in apology between words. "You're so sexy. I can't help it. You make me so hard, thinking of all the ways you could use me." Reaching up, he grasped the base of his Dom's shaft, sucking on just the tip, then flicking his tongue rapid-fire over and around the most sensitive places as he met Lawson's gaze. "Please? I don't want to be able to see straight, sir. I just want to feel. To make *you* feel. So good."

Lawson inclined his head, cupping the back of Matt's and shoving him down until his dick sank deep into Matt's throat. "Then let me help you, my boy. You will not lift your head again until I'm done with you."

Hand slipping to Lawson's thigh, Matt reveled in the feel of rock hard muscles and the grip of Lawson's palm against the back of his skull. The grip was unyielding, and even though he couldn't see his Dom's expression, he knew it would be that steely one he wore when he faced down a fighter in the ring. So much control it almost shimmered off of him—a different kind of glitter. Dark. Dangerous. Every bit the Dom.

Fingers curling, he clutched Lawson's ankle with his opposite hand, the glide of expensive shoe leather its own kind of erotic torture. He imagined licking the black shiny surface until every speck of snow was gone. Tasting the mellow richness of the hide. Obscene, messy noises, keening sounds that would've registered as begging had he been able to get enough air, filled the office. There would be no doubt as to what went on inside if anyone approached the other side of that door.

Sucking in air through his teeth, Lawson increased the pressure on the back of Matt's head, his fingers digging into his scalp. He fucked into Matt's throat, unrelenting, growling as he came, leaving no choice but to swallow. "Fuck, my good boy. That's right. Take it all for me. Exactly what I'm giving you."

With how far Lawson was down Matt's throat, it was impossible to taste, only to feel how much he came. Swallowing for what seemed like forever, he kept going until the universe consisted of the scent of musk and all the blissful sparkles of light that could possibly exist. When the first sweet, cool burst of oxygen hit his nose and tongue, expanding his lungs, he expelled it with a shout of his own, the sound all that kept him from tipping over the precipice into oblivion.

"Very nicely done." Lawson did up his pants, leaving his belt open as he settled back into his chair with a satisfied sigh, stroking Matt's hair as he pressed it to his thigh. "If Curtis can't forgive your little slip after that, he's a fool."

"Mph..." Lids closed, Matt floated in a blissed-out haze. If he said anything at all right now, it'd come out sounding like he'd been turned into a frog.

He was an absolute puddle for who knew how long. By the time he blinked open his eyes, he had a crick in his neck and Lawson was absorbed in the books, the street noise dampened enough for his internal clock to mark the time as early evening.

"I'll be bringing these home with me to finish up." Lawson lifted his suit jacket from where he'd laid it over the back of the chair at some point, his brow creasing with irritation as he attempted to pull it on one arm without putting down the books. "Go make sure Drew and Zandi left the cafe up to your standards and we'll get back to the Club."

Pulling himself to his feet by the edge of the desk, Matt stepped up to Lawson, daring to smooth his hands away from the jacket. Unclipping the sling, he adjusted the strap so it wouldn't be in the way while making sure that he didn't jostle the position of Lawson's arm. He helped his Dom shoulder on the jacket, then repositioned the sling before rising up on tiptoe to brush a kiss over the dark shadow along Lawson's jaw.

"Thank you, love." Lawson gave the collar of his jacket a little tug, his lips curving into a rueful smile. "I fully intend to master this damn thing at some point. Possibly before I find a way to remove it myself."

"I know you're superhuman and all, Law, but even you need to obey the laws of physics...or whatever you call them?" Matt dared to give his husband a little cheek, his saucy grin feeling like Curtis, but probably looked nothing like him. "If you could grow a third arm, you might have a prayer. Until then, you'll have to let me do what you don't pay me for."

Lawson huffed, holding the ledgers against his chest as he nudged Matt toward the door. "The lip on you. I'd do something about it if I hadn't just enjoyed it so much. If your Dom wants to disobey any laws, he will. Including physics. And logic." He shook his head and laughed. "Realistically, I'll have to work on becoming completely infallible. Then little things like broken bones won't be an issue again."

In the cafe, adjusting the machines and instruments on the counter to just where he liked them, Matt made a mock thoughtful sound. "I like you being infallible. That means you'll get the books done quicker and can have more time to figure out ways to tame my mouth." Looking up from the register, where he locked the til and pocketed the key, he grinned. "Did I tell you I figured out what I want for my birthday? Even if it's a whole-two-and-a-half months away?"

"You did not." Lawson gathered both his and Matt's jackets, bringing them with him to wait by the end of the counter. "And as for taming your mouth, I have ball gags for that. If you need a little more to convince you to be my good boy, I'll have Noah use his clothespins on your tongue. His are even more effective than the ones I used to use on you and Reed."

Mock shuddering, Matt helped Lawson on with his parka

before putting on his own. Even though the walk across the street was short, the wind had been biting lately. Some of the Core prided themselves on being able to go in and out without one, but when Matt made the attempt one too many times, Curtis put his foot down, saying nobody needed to be 'fashing themselves' about him getting sick.

"Well...I'd say that's hot, but yeah no. Definitely not what I want for my birthday." Locking up, Matt frosted the glass with his breath, then drew a quick heart with his initials and Lawson's.

Lawson inclined his head as he stepped over a mound of snow on the sidewalk, from where the plows had pushed it off the street. Holding out his casted arm, he steadied Matt as he did the same. "What is it you'd like? If it's to make all the snow go away, it might take me a bit, but I'll work my magic."

"Funny how your 'magic' always seems to take until June." Matt snickered, leaping over a puddle and sliding to the gate where he waited for Lawson to join him before tapping in his code. "If it pisses you off, please say so? I don't mean anything by it. But it'd be super cool to spend time in the dungeon with you, Curtis, and Noah."

Brow furrowing slightly, Lawson slowed his pace as they approached the front door. "No, it doesn't piss me off. I'm not going to lie, I don't know how I feel about doing a scene with Noah. We're...better. But I'm not sure we're there yet." He smiled softly as he pressed his cold lips to Matt's temple. "You sharing the desire gives me very good motivation to work on it, though. I like the relationship the two of you have now. Things here feel much more secure for you, which has always been one of my priorities. And it's hard to stay angry with him when he treats my boy so well."

Over the past weeks, the man had become something of a confidante. A friend even. The sexy times he and Noah had weren't all that many, but the undercurrent had been there ever since the poker night. That feeling of protection wrapped around Matt when the trio were in the bar was second to none. If he were honest, he longed for a peek into the past. Into a time when he hadn't been a part of things, and their relationship had an energy he sometimes glimpsed humming below the surface. To be right in the middle? Yeah. That'd be a way to rock a birthday.

"I don't want you to force anything. Ever. But yeah. He's really different now that I know him." The door to the bar buzzed, the lock clicking, and Matt waited for Lawson, holding it open for him. "But if all I get is cake and you, that's more than enough."

Inside the bar, Lawson went to his stool, laying the ledgers down in front of it. He glanced back at Matt over his shoulder. "I love hearing that, my boy, but you will be getting more than cake. And you always have me. The dungeon will happen, in some form. And presents. Whether or not Noah overdoes it might be the deciding factor. He can't seem to help himself." He rolled his eyes and breathed out a laugh. "Not that I mind you being spoiled, but I insist on being the one who spoils you the most."

Matt shucked his own coat, hurriedly throwing it on the peg, then helped Lawson with his own. "You can't really blame him. I mean, until Wren found dolls, there wasn't much he wanted, and Jamie can't stand anything that reminds him of that day. Since it's on the biggest gift holiday of the year, the man is in a capitalist desert with a ton of cash and nowhere to spend it."

"If he didn't already invest a healthy amount, I'd suggest he spend less and save more, but he knows what he's doing. Even if what he's doing is often buying the most ridiculous things." Lawson settled on his stool, a fond look in his eyes. "If I didn't know how much he enjoys all those gadgets, and surprising everyone with randomness, I'd think he did it just to mess with me. I got in the habit of being very careful with money…except for with my cars, but those are a different kind of investment."

Never having had much himself until he'd come to The Asylum, Matt couldn't fathom being comfortable with throwing money around on anything. Cars or what-not. He skirted the bar, shaking his head as he put on a cup of coffee for his Dom. "Let's just say I like it that I leave all the finances to you. I was reading the other day online about some people who are in D/s relationships who don't get to touch money and their Doms control it all." He glanced up, the paper filter between his fingers. "I have to say it had its appeal."

Lawson's lips slanted. "I'd say it works out for us both, since I like being able to take care of you in every way. You spent enough time dealing with uncertainty and having all the responsibility on your shoulders. It's my pleasure to make sure you deal with as little as possible now."

Coffee's nutty aroma wafted on the air as the machine began to gurgle and drip. The bar's warm lighting and all the gleaming wood made the moment feel cushioned and safe, as only this place and time with Lawson could. Matt took his time adding a shot of Lawson's whiskey to a mug and poured the first cup for him before answering.

"I really appreciate that you do that for me." Matt slid the black mug with its white Asylum logo onto a coaster in front of Lawson. "I know you enjoy numbers, but it can be a lot sometimes. If it really bothers you that we order the sugar in the raw as well as the natural cane sugar, I'll just get the natural cane sugar. People don't realize sugar in the raw is actually white sugar that's had molasses added to it. There's nothing unprocessed about it."

Shaking a finger at him, Lawson gave him 'the look' before picking up his coffee and taking a sip. "It does not bother me at all, and whether or not it's a gimmick, customers enjoy the options. I was looking for topics that wouldn't require too much of my focus, while I was very much enjoying having the majority of it on you."

Matt leaned on the bar, forearms stacked on top of each other, and stared into Lawson's gorgeous-as fuck, deep green eyes with lashes that should've been illegal on a guy. "I was enjoying having it on me too, sir."

The door to the upstairs opened, Curtis' raised voice rumbling like a snowplow over the moment. "No, I am not dressing up as Cupid Curtis at your Valentine's Day wedding, Jamie. I don't care how many times you decide to hitch your horse and wagon to some guy, the answer is always going to be a great big emphatic fuck off."

"Incoming!" Noisily trampling down the steps, Pike stumbled past his cousin into the bar, grunting as he hit the ground. He shoved to his feet and rushed over to the galley door. Tapped the code, then groaned. "Ugh, I forgot he changed it." He ducked behind the bar. "I'm not here."

Lawson's eyes shone with amusement as he leaned close to Matt over the bar, coffee mug in one hand. "I was beginning to think we might need to check a few pulses, things were much too quiet."

Entering a step behind the cousins, Jamie carried his guitar in one hand, adjusting it as he passed Curtis. "If you want to dress up as Frank Sinatra, then you have to learn to play at least one song. It's either that or Cupid. Everyone else has already chosen their costumes."

"I'm going to murder you." Turning sideways to include Lawson in the conversation, Curtis spoke to his man. "You talk some sense into him. Or beat it into him. Who ever heard of a costume party wedding? Why can't we just wear penguin suits and eat canapés like normal people for once?"

Lips parted, Lawson started to answer, then sat back as the stairwell door opened again.

River grinned as he clapped Curtis on the back on his way by. "Who we killing?" He strode around the bar, hefting Pike up and throwing him over his shoulder. "No hiding, tiny devil. We're only discussing a dentist appointment, you're not there yet. And you can't use a Tic Tac to replace the tooth. You scared the hell out of Quint, trying to shove it in there." He gave Pike's ass a light smack. "I'm all for the look, but it won't be so cute if you get an infection."

At mention of Pike's tooth, heat crept up the back of Matt's neck. Recalling his promise to Noah that he'd tell Lawson and apologize to Pike's Doms, Matt opened his mouth.

A strange resonant *TWANG* vibrated through the bar, cutting him off. He cringed and whirled toward the sound. Standing over his guitar, Jamie's mouth hung open in a silent scream. Snow tracked in from Matt and Lawson's boots formed small puddles, causing a slip hazard. The other sub must've lost his balance on the slick floors. And landed with his foot in the middle of the instrument.

"I don't think that's how that's meant to be played." Plucking Jamie off his feet, Curtis separated him from the guitar. "But you have lots more where that one came from. Don't cry. Then I'll have to stop being mad at you, and I was having fun."

Sipping his coffee, Lawson caught Matt's eye. "When we renew our vows, we are doing it without telling anyone besides our men again. If it pleases everyone, we'll take more pictures, but a big, elaborate wedding couldn't be less appealing."

"No babies. No weddings. No instant coffee. Hard limits." Matt kept his distance from Pike, the moment broken when he might've said something. Tonight was a good night. There was no reason to ruin it. Everyone seemed to be getting along in their own way. Even Curtis cuddled Jamie on his lap now, examining his foot. "But you? Me? No limits at all."

Still holding Pike over his shoulder, River bent down to grab the ruined guitar. "Mind if I keep this? I bet we can cut it into small pieces and make funky cars to add to your and

Tay's train set. Gonna give me a hand with that, Curtis? It might distract your cousin from any thoughts of evil men poking inside his mouth."

Ugh... Just say something! Matt busied himself wiping down the already clean bar.

"I don't mind if you make something of it." Jamie stared forlornly at the guitar. "It's better than junking it. That's the first guitar I got. Me and my dad picked it out on the day that-won't-be-named. He had a friend who had a music store."

Curtis made a sympathetic sound, holding Jamie closer to kiss his temple. "I'm sorry, Jamie. I'll do something cool with it so you can still remember it."

Hands braced on River's back, Pike lifted his head. "We'll make a new line of tracks just for the guitar train and call it the Jamie Express. You can get little people in fancy old clothes to ride it all over. They'll be, like, uber fans."

"Thanks, Pike." Jamie smiled at the other sub, clearly making an effort. "I can't wait to see it."

"Who wants ice cream?" Matt spoke up, needing to do something other than feel guilty about Pike's tooth. "I made Brownie Brittle Battlefield and Core Caramel."

River sat Pike on the edge of the bar, giving him a considering look. "I guess you can have ice cream. I haven't been home long enough to be the mean Dom." Moving in close to his boy, he spoke in a mock whisper. "But don't tell Seth I'm giving you treats when you were being naughty."

"I won't tell him until I'm finished it all, Papi." Pike leaned forward and kissed River's cheek. "And he won't be upset. He's too happy you're home. And so am I."

The next time the stairwell door opened revealed Jacks, coming through with Danny in a cute panda hoodie riding on his back. A leather work bag bulging with material slung over one shoulder, Jacks somehow maneuvered the bar with a huge bolt of fuzzy fabric under one arm, the combined loads making him look like a thoroughbred packhorse.

"I'm going to need you to read the cards for me, little mouse. I don't know whether finishing the mockups for the department store Halloween costume line or doing Amanda Kirkwood's wedding dress for her Vogue cover shoot is the right thing to do." After putting down the mass of fabric while his sub slid to his feet by his sewing table, Jacks frowned in thought, his hair slightly mussed and sticking up in back from rubbing against Danny's hoodie. "Which project is most likely to make me stay up all night in frustration and die of exhaustion?"

Danny chewed on his bottom lip, pulling two stacks of tarot cards out of the pocket of his panda hoodie. "I could already tell you it will be the wedding dress, sir, but I'll read the cards just to be…" His eyes went wide as he spotted the guitar in River's hand. "Is that… Jamie, what happened? Are you okay? This is the worst thing ever, you loved that guitar." He rushed over, carefully taking the thing from River and holding the instrument close, like he could hug it back into one piece. "We can speak to a specialist. Or maybe bring it back to the store where it was made, only it's a terrible time to travel. We might drive off a cliff and get buried under an avalanche…"

Dishing out the ice cream, Matt set a giant bowl with two spoons in front of Pike, with all the toppings just the way he liked them. "There you go, sport."

"Thank you." Pike gave him an uncertain look, scooping up a huge spoonful and bringing it to his lips. He smiled as he flicked his tongue out to taste it. "Ice cream fixes everything. I'm glad you don't mind making it for us and all. And you're super good at it."

Leaning down so he was at Pike's eye level, Matt braced himself against the bar. The guilt in his middle threatened to consume him from the inside out. "You know, even though the money didn't pan out, you're still my business partner, right? You're the best taste tester, and you have loads more experience than I do knowing what's a good food investment."

"Yeah?" Pike licked the spoon after clearing it of every bit of ice cream, then dipped it back in the bowl again. "I'm good helping you whenever, man, just say the word. Not sure I'll be a good business partner, but I'm a decent sidekick. For the cafe, the band…it's my thing. Like a really naughty cheerleader. Tay would look better in the skirt with those legs, but I could probably pull it off if Jacks' got time between dressing all the stars to make something cute."

"I'll make you pom poms to match your hair!" Jacks called out from his corner booth where he'd started laying out Danny's tarot cards himself.

In the sub's corner, Jamie talked quietly with his bandmate, the two of them looking over his phone. "It's just a thing. Everyone important is here, and I can replace the guitar. It's okay, Danny. Let's just have fun."

"I know, but still." Danny petted the guitar like it was a bird with a broken wing, his fingers moving carefully around the splintered wood. "We could try to get it fixed. Then maybe we should keep it out of the bar. Or put it in a case in the studio…"

"Or make it into The Jamie Express." Pike huffed at Danny's horrified look. "What? It's a good idea. It's like reincarnation. Trains never die."

Coming through the door with Tay, Quint not far behind, Seth made a thoughtful sound as he swung the smaller sub up in his arms to bring him to the bar. "I don't know. I once derailed a train in Vermont and made it look like a landslide washed out the tracks. High body count, but they were all assholes. The train didn't fare much better."

"Fuck, that's hot." River bent over to brush a kiss to Seth's lips. "I love it when you say 'body count'. Of bad guys, of course. And the train probably made a pretty epic mess. Your favorite."

Focus on his ledgers, Lawson spoke into his coffee cup. "The mercs will avoid talking about dead bodies in front of the reformed mobsters, thank you very much. We don't need any more bad influences around here."

"Aww, he called us 'reformed'." Pike grinned at Curtis, who'd left Jamie cuddled up in an afghan on the sofa to join Lawson. "Your man is so sweet."

Taking his seat on the stool at the end of the bar, Curtis winked at Pike. "We should have a Sub 101 module called Reform School Reprobates." He looked across the bar toward Jamie. "Hey. Why don't you have a naughty nurse themed wedding? We can all dress in tear-away white pants with edible g-strings underneath."

Jamie scowled. "I kinda hate you a little right now."

Popping his brows, Curtis grinned. "Nah. To know me is to love me."

"Not sure what white edible g-strings would taste like, but I'm in." River snatched Pike's spoon, taking a bite of the ice cream and groaning. "Fuck, this is incredible. I haven't had anything this sweet in months. I swear, the only thing aside from the obvious that makes leaving suck so bad is missing out on the amazing food."

Tay worried his bottom lip between his teeth, looking his Dom over. "But you ate enough, didn't you, sir? You don't look like you lost any weight. Seth should probably check. And you can have all my meals until you're...you're back at a hundred-percent again."

"You stayed at the Chateau?" Surprise widened Seth's gaze as he looked River over himself. "Did you...hear anything interesting?" His voice lowered so that only Matt, who dished up ice cream for Lawson and Curtis, could hear him. "About this place?" He motioned to Matt, noticing his presence. "Get the man a slice of cake to go with his ice cream, my boy."

"Yes, sir." Matt didn't know what the Chateau was, but if it was so fancy then they should've had cake. Maybe the guy had been on a diet, staying in one of those luxury places while out on his mission.

No need to sleep in the mud just because you spent your days spilling blood.

Five seconds later, Drew emerged from the galley with a slice of Black Forest cake and a glass of milk. He somehow avoided tripping over lowriding trousers, displaying bright blue underwear with pink rabbits hopping all over his ass. It was kinda cute how he always removed his belt and shoes when he was at The Asylum.

"Hi, Matt." Drew grinned at him as though he hadn't just seen him at the cafe, and placed the cake in front of Pike.

"Hi, Drew. Are you and Stephan here tonight?" Glancing around, Matt didn't see the guy, but sometimes he did his sessions as house calls now. Koda and Bram were nowhere in sight. "Want some ice cream?" He placed the scoop in a half-empty container, bringing Curtis and Lawson their portions, which he'd doctored with some buttered-rum candy and brandy soaked cherries. "I made you some vanilla, since I know you don't like things with bits and pieces in them."

That got him an enthusiastic nod. "Yes, and please, and root beer. I'll have a float. Even though they make me sick to my stomach, every once in a while it's worth it."

Shaking his head, River slid onto the seat next to Curtis, lifting Tay onto his lap and letting his sub give him a thorough inspection. "We stopped there a couple of times to check on the new recruits, but we didn't stay, thank fuck." He shuddered. "Can't stand the place. I'll take The Compound over that any day of the week. We didn't go there at all." He nuzzled the side of Tay's neck, his lips slanting when Tay pulled his shirt up, exposing some nice hard abs, the toned six pack tensing and relaxing under the small sub's gentle touch. "There's always talk, but less around...certain people. I did hear you guys have drawn a lot of attention, but Vani's best team coming here to pick through the rubble, that was gonna happen."

"Whose attention?" Matt frowned between Lawson and River, the soda wand limp in his hand as he fixed Drew's root beer float. "That doesn't sound good. Who do we need to clobber?"

River stabbed his cake with a fork, bringing a big piece to Tay's lips, then shaking his head and eating it himself when Tay frowned at him. He tickled his sub as he glanced over at Matt. "It's nothing to worry about. With some of the Core members being…let's say, high profile, there will always be eyes on the place. But between Rhodey, Seth, and…well, now me, it's a less appealing target. Those who matter want to keep it in one piece." His gaze swept around the bar. "Which they should, it's a damn nice place."

"But you…weren't somewhere nice." Tay rested his head on his Dom's shoulder, his throat working. "And you can't… give me any details, can you."

Sliding the float in front of Drew, who'd taken a seat next to Pike and Seth—the former not even having touched River's cake when the guy had mistakenly put it in front of him— Matt gave Lawson a worried look of his own. Then Curtis. "Can *you* say anything, sir? You went to the Compound for stuff, right? Before everything?"

Curtis cleared his throat, glancing up toward the rafters like he was checking in with Rhodey, but without an earpiece, there was no way for him to actually communicate with the man—unless there was some kind of merc-mind-meld that happened when you got your first kill. "Yeah. What River said. I was there for a bit. Glad I survived. That's all."

"I was only ever there with you to heal, my love." Lawson put his hand over Matt's, his reassuring smile not quite erasing the haunted look in his eyes. "Sometimes, not having the details is best. Our priority, no matter where we…end up? Is always to come home to you."

Sometimes, being a sub sucked. When you couldn't protect the people you loved, and you were protected instead. Except being here with Lawson and feeling the security of his love never sucked, so Matt 'took the bitter with the better', as Curtis said.

Heaving a sigh, Matt nodded. "Yes, sir. I'm glad you weren't." His gaze skated to Curtis. "And I'm glad you survived...not having cake."

Someday, those words would become a euphemism for hardship. Because when shit got rough, subs like Pike and Reed could keep things light with sayings like that. Sadness tipped Matt's stomach into a roller coaster drop when he thought of his co-sub. They hadn't exactly been on the best of terms lately, and that sucked balls. Having him to chat with about this right now would've been really nice.

"Where's Reed?" Matt looked to Curtis. "Up in the loft?"

Digging into his sundae, Curtis shrugged. "Last I saw him, he was with Wren."

Tay tensed, giving Matt an unreadable look before reaching out to take Pike's hand. He ran his tongue over his teeth. "They were talking about having some work to do. That's not a bad thing."

Matt blinked, feeling for the first time in his time at The Asylum—at least since he'd become Lawson's boy—very much on the outside. Which was probably only fair. Even Jamie wasn't too happy with him, giving him a wide berth until he read Matt's mood.

"Sorry, guys." Timing his apology to when Curtis had Lawson's attention with some questions about supplies for the pool, Matt ducked his head. "I really am."

Shrugging, Pike scooped up some ice cream, slipping it past Tay's lips before he could speak. "It's all good. I'm sorry, too." He spoke quietly, even though there was no way Seth and River didn't catch every word. His lips tipped up at the edges as he leaned closer to Matt. "Kinda. Just because something's funny, doesn't mean I should do it. Or something like that."

"Want some cake?" The best peace offering Matt could come up with, at least in Pike currency. He gestured to the galley. "And the code?"

Pike nodded, feeding his co-sub another spoonful of ice cream, which had River's eyes shining with tenderness and humor. "Hells yes. And maybe we can try the whole watching a movie together again sometime when we're all not busy? I like it when we get to hang out."

Warmth like sunshine spilled into the empty spot in Matt's middle. Nodding with the kind of enthusiasm guys like Jamie and Pike usually displayed, he snatched up a pen to jot down the galley code on a napkin, then folded it in half to hand to the sub. "You got it. And I'll bring ice cream."

"You speak my language, man." Pike grabbed the napkin, jumping off his stool while trying to kiss Tay's cheek, which ended up with the two subs head butting. He rubbed his forehead as he scrambled toward the galley. "Keiran said he was making some fruit salad. I'll grab some for Tay, it'll make him less grumpy."

Fingers lifted to rub his own head, Tay didn't respond at first, but his eyes darkened so the blue in the gray depths almost disappeared completely. He slipped off of River's lap. "I'm gonna go get a puzzle, Papi. I need quiet play."

"Go ahead, my tiny teddy." River cast his boy a concerned look as he disappeared into the stairwell, then forked up a bit of cake, glancing over at Seth. "My being gone was hard on him. I wish I could've kept in touch, told you what I was doing, but…you know how it is. I'll make it up to you, and them, in any way I can."

Seth turned from his conversation with Lawson, brow lifted. "Hm? Oh, yeah…" He reached over to squeeze River's thigh. "It was, but he's got a lot on his mind. Still processing Sin being gone, and all… Though, I hear he's back? Something about Garet cleaning his place and them hanging out."

Stiffening, Matt ground his teeth. Was *that* why Tay wasn't happy with his apology? He thought Matt should be cozying up to his brother? "Fuck that noise." The words fell from his lips and he cringed immediately, gaze snapping to Lawson's. "I'm sorry, sir."

"Don't be, I think this is the perfect opportunity for what we discussed earlier." Lawson motioned to Curtis with his coffee mug. "Though it would have been much more pleasant if your other Dom didn't have to wash out your mouth with soap *before* he gets to enjoy it."

Still a little nauseous from having heard Garet's name on Seth's lips, Matt shook his head.

Curtis threw Lawson a sideways look as he stood from his seat. "And I'm the lucky winner of a blowjob because...?" He grinned. "Or is this one of those 'don't look a gift sub in the —' well I'd *have* to look in his mouth. Shit. I'm out of one liners." Reaching over, he lifted Seth's hand to slap it to his forehead. "Take my temperature. Am I warm?"

"No." Jerking his hand away, Seth snorted. "I'd say you're right on target."

"Fuck, I missed this place." River breathed out a laugh, folding his arms over his chest, lips slanted and he looked at Curtis. "You never told me about the joys of bubble baths in a sub's mouth for your dick. I'm looking forward to being educated."

"It's a nice, slick experience. Don't use the pink stuff though. We don't want to kill them." Behind the bar, Curtis motioned for Matt to kneel as he reached over to grab the milder soap kept under the counter for the littles. "What am I punishing this pretty mouth for? And why do I get to take an apology from you, mo ghrá?"

On his knees, though he didn't really know how he'd gotten there, Matt realized Curtis had positioned him so he

219

wouldn't be in full view of everyone. At that moment he didn't know whether to be sad or grateful. Rubbing damp palms against his thighs, he answered quietly. "I was joking about something with Lawson that concerned you, and it wasn't entirely respectful, sir."

Lawson's brow lifted slightly, though the tilt to his lips and the soft glow in his dark green eyes showed he wasn't upset. He lowered his coffee mug to the bar. "He implied you were going too soft on him. I won't have our subs speaking badly of how we handle them, unless it's an actual issue. He was joking, but it's a habit around here I'd like to nip in the bud. Not only does it have us questioning if we're being good enough Doms, but it is not something we want the members to overhear and start spreading. Status, like it or not, means a great deal within these walls."

By the time Lawson was finished, Matt's face felt like it was on fire and there wasn't an ounce of defiance left in his posture. Curtis ran his brown-eyed gaze over him, nodding slowly. The gentle seriousness in his expression said he was on board with Lawson, but wasn't pissed off with Matt, even a little. He motioned with his hand, palm flat, to signal Matt should stand.

"Let's get everyone else down here. I think this calls for a demo. Out of class. Think of it as a pre-101 reboot for everyone." Curtis gripped Matt's wrist, tugging him around the bar to a spot more toward the center of the room.

River exchanged a look with Seth. "Did I miss something or did the dick bubble bath just get a bit more intense? Our boys are littles, they shouldn't have to—"

"Sir, if I may?" Enjoying a bit of quiet time to himself, Quint looked up from where he'd settled at a booth with what looked like several patient files. "Even as littles, Pike and Tay are part of the Core. They also do much better when they can understand which rules are not to be toyed with."

Phone out, Curtis nodded. He must've sent a group

message, because everyone's phones in the bar buzzed. He slid it back into his pocket, settling one shoulder against a nearby hand-hewn support beam that no longer held the aged sugar-laden patina of the old building. "This isn't harsh, is it my boy?"

Kneeling again, Matt shook his head. "No, sir. It's pretty standard. Though we haven't done it in a while, so River probably doesn't know about the traditions."

"He's aware of them, but not necessarily why his subs need to be careful of the power balance here." Stephan came in through the gym, motioning Drew to his side, and giving River an encouraging look before turning his attention to Curtis. "I spoke to Rhodey and I agree his men shouldn't participate. They understand the way things are around here and the distraction wouldn't be good for any of them when they need to focus on security. The rest should be fine, but I'll keep an eye out."

Jacks stood, lifting Danny from his seat at their booth and tugging his hood to almost cover his eyes. He whispered something reassuring to the sub, moving to a place where he was part of the group rather than separate.

Coming out of the galley with a bowl of fruit salad, a box of Lucky Charms, and what looked like a big chicken leg between his teeth, Pike tripped to Seth's side, almost dumping the fruit on his Dom's lap. He spoke around the chicken leg, but it was so incoherent, he might've been either talking about the apology or discussing trains again.

Taking the bowl and the box, Seth set both on the bar before he plucked the chicken leg from Pike's mouth. "Up here, pixie pie. We're going to be very good right now so we don't end up with you kneeling for your cousin next." He winked to show he was joking, then nodded toward the subs' corner. "Come on, Jamie. Stand up here by the bar."

Clearly trying to disappear in his own gray hoodie, Jamie set aside his broken guitar and dragged his feet to join everyone. He stood closest to the galley, giving Matt a bracing look and a covert thumbs-up.

A bit breathless, Connor came jogging in through the gym, a sheepish smile on his lips as he lifted Jamie into his arms. He kissed his cheek, speaking softly to him. "I had to wait for Avery to replace me in the security room, but I came as fast as I could. And I'm glad I double checked the message. For a second I thought you were in trouble and I fully intended on staging a rescue unlike anything this place has ever seen."

Jamie snickered, his face pressed into Connor's neck. "No, sir. Not yet, but you can never be too prepared where I'm concerned. We could practice."

"Are Wren and Reed in the security room?" Curtis brushed the back of his hand along Matt's cheek, eyes on him as he spoke.

Trying to get comfortable, Matt shifted from knee to knee. Kneeling on the floor wasn't so difficult, but someone had spilled something granular, which brought the sensation of pins and needles after several minutes.

"No, they were doing some research on local deaths." There hadn't been a sound from either of the doors when Noah entered the bar with Wren and Reed, but the scuff of Reed's sneakers from the direction of the stairwell made it obvious they'd come down that way. From the dampness to Noah's curls and the redness of his cheeks, he'd been on watch on the roof. "Shea's taking his shift with Dallas. Rhodey and Avery are resting." He lifted Wren to sit on an empty stool, his gaze following Reed as he hopped up on the far end of the bar. "This should be everyone who needs to be here."

"Thank you, my man." Curtis returned his attention to Matt. Tapped under his chin with two fingers. "Open that naughty mouth so I can get deep inside and make sure it's nice and clean before you apologize to me."

A fucked-up mixture of arousal and fear trilled down

Matt's spine, pooling at his tailbone. Heat flooded his groin, his dick fattening in a way that would never be appropriate for a real punishment. Which this wasn't. Suspending his disbelief, however, came easily as the intensity of Curtis' stare deepened. A look that said this would be as real as Matt wanted it to be. None of his men would ever leave him wanting. Which made him feel absolutely one-hundred-percent seen, and loved, and safe.

With the Core—his real family—all around him. Giving him exactly what he wanted and needed. So he could be whole again. Complete.

And forget the pieces of himself he'd left behind.

Chapter Thirteen

PRESENT

From the floor, the congregation of boots, sneakers and jean-clad legs was like being in a sea of leather and denim. Matt's dick sat up and took notice because it was a sick little fuck, even though he knew he was about to be gagging on soap and cock. Everyone watching was what it got off on.

Opening his mouth, working his jaw side to side, he squeezed his eyes shut.

Curtis tsked. "Nope. Eyes open. I want to see those gorgeous baby blues so I can tell when you're sorry. I'll come when I know I won't be getting any lip from you after I take my dick from your mouth."

Oh shit, that's hot.

Eyes flying open, Matt felt his nostrils flare on his deep inhale. His gaze landed on everyone's faces before hitting Curtis'.

His Dom traced a thumb over his bottom lip. "Oh my. Someone's very interested in this. We'll have to do this again sometime for more pleasant reasons."

"We will be. Very soon." Stool turned to face the center of the bar, Lawson gave both Curtis and Matt an approving smile, his eyes resting on Matt for a few seconds longer, as though to double-check his headspace. "I'd like our boys to set the standard for the rest, so we'll be keeping them on their toes. Which won't be easy, but there will be plenty of advantages to meeting our expectations."

"I'll take that challenge." Seth slanted a smile at Tay before his dark blue eyes landed on Lawson. "We'll institute a demerit book. Sub with the least demerits in a month wins, and his Dom gets to lead us while his sub gets to wear the Head Boy crown for the next month."

Lawson's lips curved, interest sparking in his eyes, as though he very much liked the suggestion. "That's an excellent idea, my man. And good incentive for us all."

Brow furrowed, Reed traced his fingers over the Head Boy pin attached to his T-shirt, a self-conscious gesture he probably wasn't even aware of. Legs twisted in his favorite pretzel position, he remained silent, looking everywhere except at Matt.

C'mon dude. Forgive me?

Matt willed Reed to look his way even as Curtis took out the length of his dick to drizzle dish soap on the tip. The blue liquid smelled like someone's fucked up idea of flowers, and looked like troll snot. A strange contrast on Curtis' pale skin, his member less wide, but just as long as Lawson's. Where Law was darker and had a sexy landscape of thick veins, Curtis was more...well, cocky. His dick jutted and swayed as he held Matt's chin between his thumb and forefinger, before gliding past Matt's lips and over his tongue to work up a froth.

Unable to help himself, Matt made a disgusted sound, gagging a bit as the taste of springtime dish soap spread over his tongue. He closed his eyes and a sharp tap to his cheek made them fly open again.

Careful, dude. I might be submitting, but it doesn't mean I can't accidentally bite you.

Curtis' brows rose. "You'd better fucking not."

"The soap is all natural, though consuming it in excessive quantities would have unpleasant results." Wren sounded a bit like he was observing some kind of fascinating experiment, though by River's thoughtful sound, he was likely responding to either the Dom's expression, or something he'd said. "It's one of the reasons it's used for the littles…or more specifically, Pike. Repeated exposure to the one you used for him this morning could be problematic."

River blew out a breath. "That's good to know. Though, I guess we'd better work on *not* fucking swearing if he's gonna be avoiding those demirit points. Sucks, because that looks fun."

Hips barely moving, Curtis eased in and out of Matt's mouth, for maximum suds action until Matt figured he looked like a rabid dog. Lips curving, Curtis got a heavy lidded look as he played with the bubbles with one fingertip. "That's a good look on you. I might do this every day just as a maintenance thing. We'll keep you nice and clean, my boy. I've got you. We'll get your Dom that crown, won't we?"

"Considering how messy Seth likes his subs, you might want to find other ways to amuse yourself, my man." Noah put his hand on River's shoulder, his light tone saying he was enjoying the show. "Besides, Lawson's more suited to royalty."

Jamie began to hum Billie Eilish's *You Should See Me in a Crown*.

Trying to stay in the zone with a peanut gallery wasn't easy. Dick flagging, Matt only tasted, smelled, and felt *soap*. And Curtis' hard length feeding it to him. On the next glide, his Dom pulled a fast-one, slipping down his throat before he was fully aware. A fan of the whole 'gag and choke on cock' scene, the man was a fucking sadist when it came to blowjobs.

Hands coming up automatically from behind his back, Matt reflexively gripped Curtis' legs. Easing back, he let Matt get a stinging lung full of air that ended with him coughing and spluttering out soap bubbles, before his mouth bulged with dick again.

"Oh, yeah. Let's do that again." Curtis filled his throat again, but this time Matt was ready, and his Dom made a disappointed sound.

But the one from Lawson held approval. And no little amount of pride. "Very nicely done, my love. Keep your focus on serving your Dom, on showing him how deep your submission is. Don't let anything distract you from it."

Removing his hands from Curtis' muscled thighs, Matt took a deep breath through his nose, and placed them behind his back again. One hand latched around his opposite wrist, he arched his chest and lengthened his throat like Lawson had taught him, giving the prettiest display he could. Curtis fucked his mouth and throat in rhythmic bursts, at first seeming haphazard, but had a pattern to them. He was allowed to breathe every fourth stroke, though his mouth was never empty, and Curtis barely left the back of his throat.

One hand curved over Matt's shoulder, the other gripping firmly around Matt's jaw, Curtis held his gaze. Heat warmed the caramel kissed brown of his eyes, saying he was as pleased as Lawson with Matt's performance. His submission.

"This mindset. Right here. It's what you give to every Dom around here. I want to see this look in your eyes every time you say, 'Yes, sir'." Not flagging at all, Curtis increased the pace, giving him a breath every three strokes in a show of approval with Matt's affirmative groan. "That's my good boy. We're getting that dirty mouth clean and that submission in lockstep with what Law expects now, aren't we?"

For some fucked up reason, his eyes decided to start leaking, along with his hard as nails dick. The whole thing was so twisted, it made him want to get down on his belly and crawl for the man, and he knew without a doubt that the second his dick got in touch with the floor—with any pressure at all— he'd fire his load like a rocket launcher.

"Nothing feels better than when you can reach that level of submission from your subs." Noah spoke softly, admiration in his tone. "Very impressive, Curtis. He responds well to you."

"He's always been sweet underneath it all." Not even out of breath, Curtis carried on the conversation like it was over a pint at the bar instead of with his dick crammed in Matt's mouth. "You'll need to play with him sometime. I bet he responds like he was kitted out in a show ring as your prize pony."

Cheeks flaming, Matt made a needy sound, and adjusted his grip on his wrist. Curtis poked at the insides of his cheeks, getting him messy and gurgling with the motion. Withdrawing, he slapped Matt's face with his dick, then shoved back between his lips hard enough to go right down his throat.

A few puzzle pieces plinked against the floor as Tay gathered the rest from the table, speaking in a harsh whisper. "I'm going to the nursery, Papi. This isn't an apology and I…can't do this right now."

"Let him go, River." Stephan's voice was just as quiet, but held a calming quality. "Reed, go with him. We can sort through the underlying issues later. Curtis, try to keep your boy in this headspace."

Shoulders already bowing, Matt battled the boulder of shame crashing into his chest. He wasn't doing it right. Wasn't good enough. This was why he hadn't been able to keep Garet in line, or safe. There was no way to even keep himself in line. His entire fucking family was a laughingstock. An Asylum joke. Everyone knew it.

Tears came faster now, wetting his face in a steady stream. Dick no longer hard, he submitted and tried to find within himself something—*anything*—that would be worth his Doms' notice. His family's respect.

Making a sympathetic sound, Curtis eased his strokes,

whispering for his ears alone. "Let's get through this my boy. We'll talk later. You've got this."

The sound of a stool dragging was cut off by Noah's words as he stepped up behind Matt. "I have him, Law. You've helped me often enough. It would be my pleasure to return the favor."

Warmth spread over Matt's back from Noah's chest as the Dom knelt behind him, securing Matt's arms in a firm hold. On the outside, the whole scenario was much more like the standard Club Apology, one Dom offering their sub to the one who'd been wronged.

But the grip was somehow comforting, along with Noah's deep voice, his lips brushing Matt's ear. "You are Lawson's boy. And Curtis'. You are in this club, so you are mine as well. You will not let *anything* pull you away from being everything we know you can be. Please your Dom, pup. That's all that's required of you, and it's all I'll allow you to do."

Feeling Noah there behind him, absorbing his authority, his sheer *presence* that was so much like Lawson's, but with an edge all his own, Matt relaxed. His brain slipped into a state of acceptance much more in line with the kind of mindset required in a punishment. The feelings Curtis instilled with his movements—deep thrusts, meant to force him out of his head and into a space of sheer submission. Almost sharp slaps of his dick meant to test Matt's willingness to submit despite embarrassment and discomfort—became ones of gratitude, respect, and a bone deep need to please this man. To do better by him and by Lawson in being respectful in all things, mindful of his place and how he supported them as well as The Asylum.

"Beautiful. That's my boy." Curtis breathed the praise, his gaze never breaking from Matt's, his fingers never leaving his skin.

Air ceased to be a necessity as his Dom fucked his throat, finding a rhythm to let in sips of oxygen without Matt consciously recognizing he'd taken a breath. As if they became one, he was in tune with Curtis. With his needs. The moment the man decided to let go and chase his own release, Matt sensed the shift. The way his pupils blew, his grip tightening just that fraction along Matt's jaw. Thrusts became less even, shorter and quicker, dragging at the back of Matt's throat until swallowing them down turned into a kind of sport. If he hadn't been so in sync with Curtis in that moment, he wouldn't have been able to keep up.

Curtis' "Right there...right...yes...fuck..." preceded a deep inhale. Denim pressed against Matt's face, the softness of his Dom's pubes right there as long ropes of come shot over the back of Matt's tongue and down his throat. He swallowed every single drop until Curtis collapsed a bit, stumbling against him, then withdrawing to a safer distance. "Good boy," his Dom rasped, breathing out his praise as he patted Matt's shoulder. Then again, "Good boy."

A few minutes passed while both of them caught their breaths. Matt sagged back into Noah's warmth, wondering how in the world Jamie could've ever traded this in for Connor. It felt so safe right here. Like between Lawson, Curtis, and Noah, nothing could or would ever rock Matt's world off its foundation again. Almost making him believe the rabid dog side of himself, which snapped and growled at everyone who rattled his internal cage, could be tamed. The boundaries keeping him separate and safe wouldn't need such sharp fangs.

When Curtis approached him again, his jeans were zipped and his belt done up. He cupped Matt's jaw more gently this time, cleaning up the edges of his mouth with his thumb. Pressing it against Matt's lips, he issued a command. "Suck."

Drawing him in, Matt tasted salt and musk, Curtis' essence. Everything in him yearned to be forgiven, to be allowed to say the words he'd been physically unable to while Curtis fucked his mouth, occupying his body with his control.

Nothing was uncertain when those options were taken away, his Doms using his body in whatever way they wanted. Giving to him exactly what he needed and—even though some might think otherwise—taking nothing but his submission in return.

Thumb clean, Curtis popped it free with Matt's wet slurp echoing in the completely quiet bar. "I'll take the words now."

Matt's first attempt to speak came out as a tight squeak. He cleared his throat, wincing at the rawness there. The taste of Curtis had replaced the soap, to the point he didn't even need to rinse. "I should have done better, sir. I disrespected you, even though I didn't mean to. Your way of disciplining me, of keeping control over our family and The Asylum, is perfect. I don't ever need anything other than what you give to me. You know best and I won't ever question that, even joking, again. I love you and I'm sorry."

Leaning down to bring his lips close to Matt's, Curtis breathed against his skin. He searched Matt's eyes, his own brown ones so near that the flecks of gold and the tiniest hints of green were visible around their rims.

His, "Forgiven," was issued with a brush of his lips against Matt's, before he met Noah's eyes. "Thank you."

"You're welcome." Noah rose to his feet, petting Matt's hair before he stepped back. "You and Lawson are damn good Doms. Any sub of yours knows that, sometimes they simply need a little help showing it. I didn't mind holding the leash for a little while so he could feel it there."

The washed out feeling of being a bit apart from everything and more than a little unmoored cushioned Matt's awareness of everyone in the room as he climbed to his feet. Punished subs weren't coddled and given so much aftercare as expected to get on with things. What had started as a something that had felt like a *funishment* had somehow taken on the aspect of a full blown actual thing, which was a mind fuck all on its own. Probably leveled up because of the swearing.

As Matt passed Jamie to go behind the bar, the other sub's

gaze followed him, his bright green eyes unreadable. If he knew his frenemy-turned-lover, the guy was probably wondering if Matt had replaced him in Noah's eyes. The two hadn't been spending much time together, while Jamie and Connor settled into their fiancé thing. Matt knew if he were in Jamie's shoes, he would've had feels about what had just happened. And about the whole distance that had seemed to grow between him and his Dom. Even if it was a settling in, readjustment period. This coming on the heels of having accidentally punched the guy in the mouth meant now Matt had rockiness to deal with in most of his Core sub relationships.

Great.

"You want a cherry soda, kitten?" Matt asked the question with a voice that sounded like it had been run over a nutmeg grater.

"Sure." On his Dom's lap, Jamie rose up a bit, reaching across the bar to squeeze Matt's arm. "You did good. That was intense...but I hope you don't mind if I say it was super hot, too." A fragile wistfulness skated across his expression, quickly replaced with a soft smile. "Keep making them happy, okay? They need some of that. The three of them. So do you. It's a good look on you."

Snorting quietly, Matt nodded, pouring Jamie his soda. He stuck a straw with the wrapper still on the top into the drink before handing it over. "You got it. And you look pretty good where you're sitting, yourself." Not even lying, because Connor and Jamie just melded together like they'd been weirdly separated at birth with their Hollywood sculpted looks —all golden and gorgeous even when they'd just woken up in the morning, and stumbled into the bar on the rare days they slept over. Matt plucked a twin cherry from the garnish well and added it to the drink. "Happy?"

Glancing at Connor, Jamie smiled even more broadly. "Yeah. Happy."

"Good. You deserve to be." Needing a few moments to

himself, Matt waited a decent amount of time before he slipped into the galley to 'check on dinner' for Lawson and Curtis. Wishing Reed were there to talk to. To share his thoughts with, or just to hug, he pulled out his phone, then remembered his co-sub had lost his. Again.

Inside the galley, everything was cozy, warm, and gleaming. The pot roast Keiran had left in the warming drawer smelled mouth-wateringly good. All sweet carrots, earthy potatoes, and glazed meat that fell apart under the fork. Setting out a couple plates, he dished out hearty portions and separated some fluffy biscuits from a pile. A butter plate and napkin wrapped silver on a tray, along with the dinners, he emerged from the galley, gaze lowered, to serve his Doms.

"That looks incredible, my love. Thank you." Lawson's tone was a bit strained as he straightened his stool and patted the one beside it. "Come sit between me and Curtis and join us for dinner."

Matt glanced toward the galley, intent on getting himself a plate, but Curtis was already up off his stool. "I got it. You sit." He patted Matt's shoulder on his way past, and motioned toward the seat for emphasis. "*Sit.*"

Taking his place on his Dom's right, Matt found his gaze going everywhere but to either man as Curtis disappeared into the galley. "It smells good, sir. I think there's lemon meringue pie in the fridge."

"I believe you're right." Lawson glanced down at his plate, his throat working. Then he turned to Matt. "I'm sorry, my love. I know it's difficult while I'm still like this. I intended to step in, but…Noah was right. He was able to give you the strength I couldn't. But it won't be for much longer."

"Sir…" Shaking his head, Matt tried to get his Dom to see it wasn't him or his injury that were the problem. "If it's okay, I can't talk about it right now because that was a lot and my head is in the wrong place, but what happened there with Curtis and Noah was amazing and everything. I just…I need to make some things right, and there are other things bothering me. Things that make me feel like I'm like Garet. I can't get it out of my head, and when Reed and Tay left...that was the real punishment. I'm so sorry." He knew Lawson wouldn't have the foggiest what he apologized for, but he said the words anyway. "It threw me, and I made a mockery of how you'd want me to behave on so many levels. Today. B-before. I just need you to know I'm going to try to do better, and I will. I'll do better."

Lawson reached out and put his hand over Matt's. "I could tell it got to you. My focus was on you, so I'm not sure why Stephan told the other subs to leave. And I won't tell you not to let it bother you. We can discuss everything else when you're ready, but for now?" He squeezed Matt's fingers. "You made me very proud with the way you took your punishment. And you were stunning, on your knees. For me and Curtis. Regardless of anything else, I need you to know you're everything a Dom could want. Even when you make mistakes. Because you learn from them, you accept them, and that's all I will ever ask of you."

Flipping his palm up, Matt clasped Lawson's broad palm. One side of his mouth tipped up in wry amusement. "Why'd he have to make it so hot?"

"Because it's Curtis." Lawson chuckled, shaking his head. "And he likes bubbles. There was no way that wasn't going to be a pleasure, no matter *why* you were in that position. If I was a different kind of Dom, I'd find ways for you to get in trouble, just so I could enjoy a repeat. As it is, I'll just count on that mouth of yours to continue to provide plenty of opportunities. There are only so many free passes to go around."

"Who's giving out free passes?" Seth spoke up from where he teased Pike with a piece of Reed's red licorice, dangled to make him snap for it, and jerked up right before he got it between his lips. "What?" He mock frowned at Lawson. "We're playing go-fish."

Shaking his head, Lawson gave Matt's fingers one last squeeze, then picked up his fork and knife. He cut a nice-sized bite and brought it to Matt's lips. "My boy gets a certain number of passes for his language, which you well know. I've considered giving him an extra one a day, because the response to some of *your* boy's antics can only be 'what the fuck?'."

About to take the tender bit of meat between his teeth, Matt spat out a laugh, smearing the gravy against his lips.

Seth growled, letting Pike capture the candy. "You know, two can play at that game. I could give him *unlimited* free passes, and no one could say a word about it."

Returning from the galley with Matt's plate, Curtis hooted. "Oh, you do not want to know what Reed would do with that kind of license. Careful, my man."

"I don't need free passes, Daddy." Pike chewed on the licorice with a thoughtful look, his lips quirking as he leaned in to badly whisper in his Dom's ear. "Not for swearing, I like trying to use the good words for you and saving fuck for when you're giving it to me hard. Or shit for when I fall down. And if I got free passes for when I was naughty, you'd get bored. And a bored Dom is a very bad thing."

Chewing the tender morsel Lawson had fed him, Matt grinned around the mouthful, keeping his voice to a proper whisper. "Popcorn."

At the other end of the bar, Jamie mouthed, "Yup."

"Free passes, my boy. All the free passes." Seth's words were kids on the playground claiming they'd touched 'home' and were 'safe' when they were clearly out.

"Aren't we supposed to wear free passes?" Setting Matt's plate down in front of him with a bundle of silver, Curtis sat and smoothed his own cloth napkin into his lap. "On our collars?"

Glancing over from where he'd been admiring Connor and Jamie's wedding rings, Noah straightened, his expression making it clear he wasn't at all pleased with the conversation. "If Pike can't control his mouth, and you're unwilling to correct him, he can go eat in the damn nursery. Matt just showed how a submissive should behave in the bar. Your boy either learns from his example or he gets the fuck out."

Sliding his seat back, Seth stood, setting Pike down in his place. "You win in the ring, I'll do what you want and send him up. You lose, and he gets to do what he wants for the next twenty-four hours."

"For Christ's sake, can we enjoy *one* meal?" Lawson shoved his chair back, moving to stand between Seth and Noah. "If the two of you want to fight, save it for when the Club is officially open. We had Sub 101 because we were setting a standard for our boys." He visibly tensed when Noah's brow lifted, his lips curving slightly. "This isn't a challenge, Noah. You're spending time with your boy. Have something to eat. Let me handle this." He faced Seth. "Let. It. Go."

"What the fuck, Lawson?" Grumbling, Seth paced away from the bar and back, gesturing to Noah, arm outstretched. "He's a fighter." He jabbed his thumb at himself. "I'm a fighter. We have a ring. We enjoy the ring. It was an excuse to get him in there. Just wait another week and you'll be training to be back in there yourself. Why are you so worried? I won't break him. He'll probably break me. And I'll enjoy every minute of seeing what he's got."

Moving in closer, Lawson spoke in a harsh whisper. "You're right, he'll probably break you. And your boys need you. Tay can't seem to help testing him and it's the last thing we need right now. You want to fight him? I'll let you know when you'll have a fight and not a fucking blood bath. I know him, Seth. Please trust me on this."

Jaw working side to side, Seth finally nodded. His response was jerky, but Matt let out a breath when the Dom relented and lifted Pike from his seat. Bundling him to his chest, he stalked out of the room, jerked the bar door open, and came a hair's breadth from slamming it shut behind him.

Matt clutched his fork, his gaze swinging to Noah, then Jamie—who clenched the velvet covered ring box in one hand, the joy over the moment he'd been sharing with his Doms completely erased.

"I think we need to acknowledge that Seth can be a supreme asshole." Curtis stabbed his fork into his pot roast and lifted the whole slab to tear off a piece with his teeth. "It's a good thing he knows how to shovel a mean driveway. Next time, I'm holding him by his feet and making him do it with his face."

Stephan massaged the back of Drew's neck, his observant gaze sweeping the nearly cleared out bar. "That would be less than productive. And from a professional standpoint? I'd say that label could easily be passed around, but that wouldn't do anyone much good, either. Emotions are running high. Let's try to take it down a notch." He kissed Drew's cheek. "Go get us some of that roast, Dujour will have already eaten with Tracey. Jamie, is there any chance you and Danny could play us some music when you're finished with your own meal?"

Nodding, Drew separated from Stephan, moving with his own kind of respectful grace toward the galley—the door temporarily propped open with a stool, since he'd been forbidden the code—as he got dinner for his Dom and himself.

Jamie ducked down to peer into Danny's panda hoodie. "Want me to go get the instruments? You sing, I'll play harmonica. I've been practicing blues stuff and Connor says I'm getting kinda good."

"I said you gave me a whole new appreciation for the instrument." Connor patted Jamie's thigh before settling back into their booth. "My only exposure's been when one of my sisters wanted to torture another by getting one for my nieces and nephews. I thought you wanted to punish me for something when you first brought it home, but I was pleasantly surprised…after the first few times."

At the booth, Stephan pulled out his phone and sat next to Noah. "Some blues music would be very nice. But first? I thought you two and Jamie would like to see some pictures of Dujour with Azalea. She's hoping they can be your flower girls together. Ana came up with her own title for the role she'll fill. Petal Stomper. It was a very…lively discussion."

"As long as it wasn't Pallbearer. Around here you can never tell." Curtis winked, clearly teasing as he scraped the rest of the potatoes and gravy from his plate, practically inhaling the last of his food. "Speaking of starving, I completely forgot to eat today other than that ice cream sundae." Reaching over, he ruffled Matt's hair in the way Matt hated and loved in equal measure. "Good stuff. How about that pie? You want some?"

Matt nodded, using both hands to straighten the mess of his bangs. "Yes, sir—"

"Drew! Pie, please!" Curtis shouted before Matt could get off his stool.

"Don't holler at my sub, Curtis." Stephan shook his head, leaving his phone with Noah, the other Dom's expression softening as he flicked his finger across the screen, taking in what must be dozens of pictures of his baby sister with Stephan and Drew's adopted daughter. Crossing the bar, Stephan poked his head into the galley. After the lobster incident, Keiran wouldn't be thrilled by the man's sub being alone in there for any length of time. "Drew, love, hand me that tray and get the pie for Curtis. He's forgotten a growing boy needs three meals a day."

"Sir, he's old enough that soon he'll only be growing wider." Though Drew whispered, his voice echoed from the galley. "A little fasting wouldn't be a bad thing. Our digestive systems need to rest sometimes, and between him and his cousin there aren't many desserts left in the fridge. Keiran is going to have a fit. And didn't he already have ice cream? Sugar rots your teeth."

Connor cleared his throat, picking Jamie up and sitting him on his lap, raising his voice like it would somehow wipe the anxiety from Danny's face. "So, how about that? We'll have two flower girls at our wedding. And crushed pedals. It'll be...original at least. And the scent will be incredible. The only issue will be coming up with outfits that will be...somewhat coordinated."

"I didn't know fasting was good..." Danny chewed on his bottom lip. "I should have fasting days if I'm going to have cheat days. And what if my teeth are already rotting? I need to go check, please excuse me."

"Ep. Hey, Kung Foo." Curtis stood, leaving his napkin and letting out a quiet burp with the side of his fist against his chest. "Stop right there." He lifted Danny off his feet before Jacks could utter a word. Holding him in his arms, he seemed to weigh him, head tipped to the side as he settled him up and down before putting him on the floor again. "Nope. You're not nearly the weight you should be. You gotta eat. Drew's not in a place to say, because he's delirious from staying up all night with crying babies. You and me are on the pie train. Not the protein shake train. Toothbrushes though?" He held his nose, waving his other hand in front of his face. "We should probably carry those around with us and practice better hygiene."

Finishing his last bite of pot roast, Matt slid a sideways glance at Lawson, mouthing, "Wow. Seriously?" That was the best the Dom had? He was off his game. No way would Danny buy it.

Lawson inclined his head in agreement, likely guessing Matt's line of thought.

In front of Curtis, Danny was already shaking his head. "Stiletto. I can't have pie, sir. But you should, you're very healthy and you have nice teeth. I need to..." He pulled his hood up over his head and darted over to Jacks' table, slipping underneath to tuck himself against his Dom's feet.

Reaching down, Jacks threw Stephan a pleading look as he petted Danny's...black and white panda ears. "Little mouse, you know I would never lie to you, right? I look at your backside more than anyone else on the planet, and I promise...I *promise* I'd tell you if you started to look like Jamie and needed to lay off the Whoppers."

"I am going to need to bring my appointment book the next time I visit." Stephan let out a heavy sigh, then gave Jamie a pointed look. "You do *not* need to lay off anything. One of your Doms is a doctor, so please ignore any unhelpful comments about your ass." He rubbed his hand over his mouth. "And Drew, fasting is best under the recommendations and supervision of a professional. Let's be more careful when speaking of things like that. Not only here, but you wouldn't want Dujour or your students to get the wrong idea."

"No, sir. I mean, yes, sir." Drew's voice was small as he came out of the galley, carrying a tray much too large for the few very small pieces of pie on it. He threw Jamie an apologetic look. "You have a very nice ass, sir." Then moved to Curtis' side where he deposited the two pieces of pie in front of him. "And you too, Curtis."

Lawson's jaw worked, and he glanced over at Noah—who was thankfully still distracted with the photos—then brought his attention to Drew. But his words were for Stephan. "I would appreciate if you'd practice the proper address for the Core members with your boy. I'd hate to have to keep him out of the bar as well once the Club opens."

Disappointment shadowed Stephan's eyes as he inclined his head. "Yes, we'll be working on that." He motioned for Drew to join him and eat. "You'll be on speech restrictions until we head home, my love. We'll enjoy some quiet time with our meal—unless Jamie still wants to play us some music?"

Jamie perked up, nodding, clearly not worried about any

comments about his ass. Guy's physical self esteem was hardcore. Not that there was anything wrong with him. Matt grinned to himself at the thought, digging into the pie, muttering to himself, "Deeper the cushion the better the pushin'."

"Danny, you want me to get your guitar?" Standing, Jamie peered under the table. "Or just my 'monica?"

Voice quiet, Danny shifted away from Jacks' legs, just enough to view his face in the shadows. He smiled at Jamie. "I'd love to hear just you play, you're getting really good."

"Okay, but you know you're awesome, right? And my bestie? And I don't know about a single thing about you that there isn't to love? And I've known you for freakin' ever?" Hand outstretched, Jamie hooked Danny's pinkie with his own.

Danny took a deep breath, letting it out slowly. "You're my bestie, too. And I…guess I know some of that stuff, it's just… Things people say gets messy in my head. But you get that."

"I do." Crouched down now, Jamie wrapped one arm around Danny's shoulders. Matt watched them, admiring their bond. They'd been friends for so long, it was like they were brothers. Which had him remembering Garet and swallowing hard. "And you help me when things get messy in my head. I trust you completely."

After a brief hesitation, Danny slid a bit closer to Jamie. "Same. And…if you really want me to play with you, I will. It'd be a good distraction. I also want to get another look at your ring. And show you all the fabric Jacks picked out for your wedding… If that's okay with him. You're gonna love it."

"I'd really like that. When you do, I feel the music more. You're part of the beat in my head, even when we're not together. I play and you're there with me." Reaching up to the table, Jamie brought down the ring box and handed it to Danny. "So when you *do* play with me? It's an entire freakin' orchestra. Like BOOM."

Kissing Matt's cheek, Lawson spoke for his ears alone. "This is much better. These moments of peace, of feeling like a family, makes all the rest bearable. It's all I thought of when I..." He shook his head and laughed. "Being here with you, like this, with the people we chose to have in our lives is priceless. I enjoy when we can all remember how important it really is."

Knowing that, seeing that, made it even more important no one *ever* disturb that happiness again. Maybe a few weeks ago, before the explosion and wreckage had happened—before all that peace had nearly been destroyed for good—he might've found his way to peeking around the corner of his anger toward his brother in the direction of forgiveness.

Looking around the bar, The Asylum, *home*? And seeing how much the place meant to Lawson? To them all? There was no way he could invite trouble back to their doorstep.

My brother made his choices.

Now?

Matt made his own.

Garet is never, ever coming back.

Chapter Fourteen

PAST

Years on the job, a few dozen missions under his belt, and more than enough blood on his hands to fill a fucking swimming pool. Still younger than most've the mercs he'd worked with, Rhodey's reputation as a ruthless operative was spreading. A reputation he'd fought damn hard for.

His soul paid the price of Jared's freedom. Rhodey's own freedom meant perfect performance.

Not good. Not even just successful.

There was absolutely no room for errors.

Pulling that shit off was the only reason Rhodey could be here, right now, without anyone breathing down his neck. He'd used a lot of resources to find his nephew. Called in every possible favor. Then a few more to keep the little fuck from ending up as an easy payday for some lowlife headhunter without Rhodey's moral standards.

He might not have many, but there were some things he wouldn't do. Certain kinds of torture. Careless collateral damage—no blowing up a fucking hospital to take out one mark.

And no killing kids.

That his own nephew might be the only exception to the last one pissed him off. He didn't really care about Noah trying to shoot him. Hell, under any other circumstances, he'd admire the effort. What made him sick? Knowing the kid's father, Joseph Crawford, had been conditioning his own son—*Tracey's* son—to become a gun runner for years. But grit and determination could be advantages on either side of the law.

Rhodey could've worked with that.

To hear Tracey talk of her son, he'd been sweet and affectionate as a little boy. Smart, energetic, a fighter with considerable skill from the start of his training in martial arts, always looking for a new challenge. She'd even mentioned how sensitive he'd been, always wanting to take care of others, compassionate in a way that disgusted Crawford.

Something in her voice told Rhodey she suspected a dramatic change, but not *what* exactly. Crawford had rejected his son for the longest time, only maintaining enough control over him to make sure Tracey would never leave. But, at some point, Noah'd become desperate for his father's approval. And Crawford had seized the opportunity to mold his young mind. Destroyed the loving, sweet child Tracey remembered and turned him into something else. The closest comparison Rhodey could make was some of the child soldiers he'd pulled out of warzones—who could be pretty dangerous, but still had some sense of humanity left. Might take a shitload of therapy, but they turned out all right.

Bringing Noah to a therapist wasn't an option. Well, unless it was a therapist Rhodey wanted dead, but there were ways to get the job done without sending the boy even deeper into whatever dark pit he existed in now. Having him locked away was another option, but he couldn't bear the thought of Tracey's son spending his life drugged up and restrained in a padded room to keep him from going on a fucking killing spree.

He'd be better off dead.

Grim, but Rhodey didn't see any point in sugarcoating shit. The reality was, the kid was running out of options. Rhodey wasn't ready to give up on him just yet, but...fuck, he was getting there.

I don't know if I can work with...whatever the fuck he is now.

Rubbing his hand over his face, careful not to disturb the IV line feeding blood back into his body, Rhodey kept his expression blank as a needle was poked through the skin at the back of his arm and given a sharp tug. The pain didn't bother him, but the little smirk on the lips of his makeshift 'doctor' reminded him why he avoided working with other mercs at all cost.

Even though this one was technically a friend, Rhodey liked it a lot more when her visits were kept short. Especially when he was dealing with personal shit.

Vani was the only other merc even close to his level. And the only one he trusted near him when the blood spilled was his own. She could've killed him a few times and hadn't used the opportunity—with the price on his head, she'd've been set for fucking life.

But they had an understanding. Keep things professional. Always.

Not that he wanted to talk about how frustrated he was. Or how shitty it felt to break his promise to his sister. A promise to get her son away from his father and the influence he'd had on the kid.

"Right to the bone." Vani brushed her sleek, dyed blood red hair away from her face with the back of one gloved hand, her black eyes fixed on the wound running up the length of Rhodey's tricep. "He's fast. It's been a while since anyone could even knick you from this close."

Yeah...so apparently we're discussing this.

Positioning himself so he could twist his arm and give the woman easier access, Rhodey grunted. "He's fifteen. I didn't

245

realize he'd come at me like that. I got sloppy. It won't happen again."

"Mhm." Vani smirked, lifting an elegant dark brow at him. "You don't have it in you to handle him. Not the way he needs it. Why don't you ask—?"

"No." Jaw clenched, Rhodey glared at her. "Fuck no."

Ignoring the look, and his tone, Vani shrugged. "Suit yourself. Kill him and get it over with. You'll never be able to look your sister in the eye again, but you know I'll watch out for her."

"Leave it alone, Vani."

"Stop being so sensitive. I'm just making conversation."

"Why, exactly?"

"You're entertaining. I don't often get a chance to poke at your sore spots."

Fuck, why did I call her again?

Because he'd been fucking bleeding out and there was no one else. He couldn't leave Noah alone. Couldn't go to a hospital and risk being taken out while he was weak from blood loss—or have the kid finish him off and go out into the world. A ticking time bomb with bronze curls and a disarming smile—until you looked into those light gray eyes and saw the void beyond the storm.

Rhodey needed time to recover, in the safehouse he'd spent years making secure enough to disappear to in times like this. Only Vani knew about it. There was one other person he'd have trusted enough, but Jared was probably overseas somewhere. The safest place he could be. In the middle of a war, but still…himself. He'd never have to surrender parts of who he was again to become a weapon. Sure, a soldier could be considered the same, but…they weren't. They could still have lives. Fall in love. Fucking retire one day and do normal shit.

A merc didn't retire. Any who tried were erased. Often along with anyone close to them.

Which was fine. Rhodey's one attempt at a relationship after Jared left—a year with only his own hand to get off made him stupid, had nothing to do with his heart being fucked up—ended with him laid out for a month. Recovering from a lethal cocktail of poisons. Without Vani, he'd be a rotting corpse in an unmarked grave somewhere.

Love meant either putting someone vulnerable in danger, or finding someone strong enough to survive by your side. The latter meant they just might be strong enough to kill you.

Or somehow be a mix of both, like Jared had been.

Fuck, I miss him.

There were less than a handful of people in Rhodey's life he could say he'd really loved, who'd loved him back. Jared had been one of them. Keeping him would've been so much easier than letting him go. Wouldn't have come with a shitload of pain and a debt he was still repaying. But as little as Rhodey knew about love, he did know one thing.

If the fucking word meant anything? The easy way was never an option. Selfishness and love didn't belong in the same goddamn sentence. Letting Jared stay would've been selfish. The man deserved better, whether or not he'd agree if he knew the whole truth.

Vani let out a heavy sigh as she finished the stitches. She stood, tugging off her blood slicked gloves with her teeth. Probably to see if it would freak him out. And also because she was more than a little twisted. Her black eyes leveled on him, her ever-present smirk fading as she looked him over. "From what you've told me, you can't handle that boy right now. Call Maddox."

"Damn it, Vani, you know I can't do that." Rhodey rose to his feet, grabbing a wipe from the questionable looking, blood-stained white leather medkit the woman had dumped on his kitchen table. He was pretty sure it was the same kit he'd seen her bring to interrogations. "I'll owe him. Even more than I already do."

That got him an irritated look. "So what? You do the jobs he wants you to do for a few more years. It'll save you time on gathering intel and getting the necessary clearance." She huffed when he just stared at her. "Do you want me to try?"

"No." Rhodey's blood ran cold at the thought. If he had to put Noah down like a rabid dog, he'd do it quick. And part of him, the small part that flashed to Jared now and then, made him think twice before pulling the trigger, wishing he was half the hero the man once thought he could be... It wasn't ready to give up.

Noah would test Vani's nonexistent patience. She'd kill him within minutes of meeting him.

At least Maddox would consider his value. He had plenty of patience. His methods might work. But Rhodey wasn't ready to go there yet either.

Vani dumped all her supplies into her med kit, hefting it up and passing him with a backwards glance. "The number you have still works. He kept it connected in case you ever needed him. And I think you do."

For the next twenty-four hours, Rhodey fought not to let his mind wander to how simple making that call would be. To let Noah be someone else's problem. If not for Tracey, he would've done...*something* other than lock the little bastard in a cell in the basement—one he'd had to adjust twice just to hold the fucker. His nephew had a sharp mind and he was sneaky. Resourceful. Observant. All things Rhodey would consider strengths if they weren't making this whole situation that much harder.

He'd sliced Rhodey's arm open with a piece of wood he'd broken off his bed frame. This after weeks of trying to use isolation, building Noah's reliance on him, creating a routine he could set an internal clock to that might build trust.

It kinda had, only...in a backwards way. *Rhodey* had trusted Noah's calm. The attentive way he listened when Rhodey explained how fucked up what Crawford had him doing was. His quiet thanks when Rhodey brought him three square meals and snacks. Clean clothes. Sat with him to watch movies. Gave him wax crayons to do crossword puzzles and draw—wax because Rhodey wasn't stupid enough to give him anything sharp yet. Or he'd tried not to be.

The second he'd started to relax a bit with the kid, he'd regretted it. Only his own training got him out of that room alive. And when he'd shut and locked the door after slamming Noah into the cement wall hard enough to stun him...

The little fucker laughed.

A weaker man would have nightmares about that laugh for the rest of his pitiful days.

Recalling it only made Rhodey sad. Not something he'd ever admit to anyone, but his determination was shifting into hopelessness. Which he fucking hated. He'd started all this with some fantasy of walking through Tracey's front door with her son, who looked so much like her it hurt. Seeing Noah hug her. Seeing Tracey smile to finally have the piece Crawford had stolen back.

Rhodey poured himself a few fingers of vodka, taking a couple gulps as he made his way to the basement. He stood in front of the door with the bolted slot he'd installed to slide in food. On paper plates. Nothing needing utensils. Water in a paper cup.

Excessive? Maybe. But he was done taking chances with the kid.

Polishing off the vodka, Rhodey set the glass on the small, round wooden table in the dimly lit hall. He glanced toward the empty space where there was a pool table, still in its box, leaning against the wall. A ridiculous indulgence, from when he'd seen Noah's rehabilitation going much differently. He'd almost bought a few arcade games, too. Imagined installing them down here as he gave Noah a bit more freedom. The kid getting all excited, checking them out and having fun just being, well, a *kid*, while they finished the work to get him ready to go back out into the world.

It was looking less and less likely that would ever fucking happen.

Crossing the space to the door, Rhodey opened it. Did his best to move naturally. To not show a single sign he'd ever been torn open in this room, despite the dried blood on the floor.

Laid out on the bed, Noah didn't bother looking up from the papers he had spread out in front of him. Each one was covered in words, written out neatly in dark blue wax crayon—thank the higher powers for small miracles. Tongue between his teeth, the teen looked lost in thought as he read over one page. Then flipped it and held it against the headboard. His writing was precise, making use of every millimeter of space.

Rhodey couldn't help himself. He asked the first thing that popped in his head. "What are you writing?"

Gaze locked on the page, Noah lifted his shoulders. "Seeing how much of *Silence of the Lambs* I can remember. It was the first book Dad gave me. He said if Mom was going to have me reading stupid books like she does, he was going to choose them. It's a fascinating story."

'Fascinating' was a good word for it. Rhodey hadn't read the book, but he'd seen the movie. Noah was fifteen, so…well, fuck, he wasn't a parent. He didn't know how appropriate it was for a kid his age. But to have remembered it by heart?

"You have a good memory for stuff you read?"

Neutral topic, right? Good place to start.

Another shrug. "I guess. I've been reading it since I was twelve. Over and over. I wanted to find out why he *wanted* me to read it." A smile curved the edge of Noah's lips. "I think I know."

"Yeah?"

"Don't pretend to be stupid. It's annoying." Noah

dropped the page on his bed and flung his legs over the edge, sitting up. His smile spread when Rhodey held his gaze. "I like that. No reaction. This wouldn't be fun if you were afraid of me."

Rhodey snorted and shook his head. "I'm not, but I don't see how any of this is fun either way. You just made your stay here longer."

"Hmm. We'll see." Noah cocked his head to one side. "I'm happy you didn't die."

"Are you?" The hairs on the back of Rhodey's neck rose. He knew he could take the little fuck, but his instincts were less than impressed with him being even this close. There was something very wrong with the kid. Something his mind had been trained to eliminate. And rejecting the impulse felt wrong, too. "Is this a new game you're playing?"

That got him a chilling laugh. "I think so. I want to see if I can do it again." Noah nodded, almost to himself. "I'll let you put in all the work. Try to make me good. Pat yourself on the back over your success. Then, when I'm free, I'll find every way possible to make you regret it."

Folding his arms over his chest—which fucking hurt, but he didn't let it show—Rhodey eyed the teen. "You think telling me all this will get you anywhere?"

"Why not? You have a job to do. You're arrogant, you don't believe you'll fail. You'll see something that isn't there." Noah stretched his arms over his head, rising in a fluid motion. "And I'll let you believe it, for a little while. But you'll never have a moment of peace because deep down, you know exactly what I am. Exactly what you see in the mirror every day. A soulless killer. One you stopped from doing what I was made for. We're the same and that's why you hate me so much."

Rhodey sighed, shaking his head again. The kid was trying to fuck with him. They'd get nowhere if he played along. "I don't hate you. And you're not 'soulless'."

Rage flashed in Noah's eyes as he stepped forward. "Don't lie."

"I'm not."

"You are. You hate me because she chose me and left you behind." Noah walked in a slow semi-circle, not coming close enough to present an actual threat, but still setting Rhodey's nerves on edge with the languid prowl. "You hate me because I'm proof my father won. He decided you were worthless and you're reminded of that every time you look at me."

Taking a deep breath, Rhodey followed Noah's pacing with his gaze, not moving a muscle. Crawford couldn't have been the one to convince Noah of the shit he was spouting, he didn't know what Rhodey had become. But Noah did know Rhodey was responsible for his father being behind bars. For his parents getting a divorce with unprecedented ease. For his mother changing back to her maiden name.

Noah had refused to do the same. Which should've been the first sign of something being off. The kid hadn't seen how miserable his mother was with his father. How he'd abused her. Not physically, as far as she'd told Rhodey, but mentally. Emotionally. The child wasn't aware he'd been a pawn in his father's manipulations. A weapon used against her.

Or maybe he didn't care.

The latter would be a lot more difficult to fix.

"Your mother was sixteen when she had you. I was only six. She was too young to take care of either of us. I don't blame her for choosing you. I don't blame you for it either." All true. For as long as Rhodey could remember, all he'd wanted was for his big sister to be okay. For her to find someone who would love her and take care of her. He'd been too young to do it. He'd wanted to grow up so he could at least help, and now...that's exactly what he was doing. Only with her son. "She deserves better than what your father made you. Can we agree on that at least?"

The way Noah studied him made it clear the kid wasn't

talking out of his ass. He'd seen something, a twitch, a blink, a reaction Rhodey wasn't even aware of that he'd equated with a lie before. Now he was looking for more of the same.

Finally, he inclined his head. "Yes. She deserves a good life. And she won't have one if you bring me there. To that house I'm sure she has now. I know the kind of place she's always dreamed of—my father laughed when she told him. She was very sad. I think part of her imagined their relationship to be very different than what it was."

The cold, clinical way Noah laid out the reality of his parent's relationship stunned Rhodey. And not much fucking surprised him anymore. He'd seen too much in this fucked up world. But he didn't expect *this* out of…a child. "You know this and…it doesn't bother you?"

"Why should it?" Noah's brow creased slightly. Then he spat out a laugh and shook his head. "Ah, I get it. I'm supposed to react some kind of way. He had a job to do. She didn't understand it. She didn't have to. We were a family and we all played our part. I learned to play mine. She didn't." He tilted his head to one side. "I wish she had. It would have been…more pleasant."

"'*Pleasant*?'"

"Yes. She would have been safe. Provided for. I would have been part of that." Noah gave him an irritated look. "You changed everything. It was simple. She would have accepted it eventually."

Rhodey's eyes narrowed. "If you loved her, you wouldn't have expected her to."

Another one of those looks, like he was being stupid again. "I learned to be practical. I couldn't do the things I did if I let 'love' get in the way. The best way to protect her was to become someone who could. I did that." He arched a brow at Rhodey. "So did you."

"I don't think you know what love is."

"No. Maybe not. But it's useless anyway." Noah returned

to the bed, sitting on the edge. "But you know that. Remember when you told me about that tattoo?" He nudged his chin toward Rhodey's forearm, covered by the long sleeve of his black shirt. "Poison. What a lazy way to try to kill someone. You have horrible taste in men."

The kid was trying to get under Rhodey's skin. And, damn it, he was doing a decent job. Rhodey had told him what happened on one of their better days, encouraged by the seemingly genuine curiosity. They'd watched *An American Tail*, for fuck's sakes. One of Rhodey's favorite movies.

But Rhodey should have been paying more attention. He should have noticed Noah didn't react to anything that happened on screen. He analyzed it. Asked the right questions. But he didn't seem to…*feel* anything.

There was only one thing he needed to know, since the kid was being so *honest* with him. Which, come to think of it, he always had been. Sometimes, he'd be quiet. Refuse to answer questions. Change the subject. He'd pretend to be relaxed, and that smile was hard to read, but…fuck, Noah was right. Rhodey had wanted to believe they were getting somewhere.

Nothing Noah had said or done should've actually made him believe that.

So he asked the one question he needed an answer to. "Noah…what will you do when you're free? What do you want? Your mother is waiting for you. She's building a life she wants you to be part of."

"I want to do my job." Noah braced his hands behind him on the bed. "The one my father put so much time and effort into training me for. Don't send me back to her. I'm sure we can agree she's not fit for this life. I can't promise I won't hurt her in some way. *She's* not stupid, though. I'm sure she'll get out of my way and let me do what's necessary."

Every muscle in Rhodey's body tensed. For an instant, all he wanted to do was cross the room and snap Noah's neck. End this shit. Tracey could have another kid. One not completely fucked up by whatever Crawford had done to him. This was more than Noah *wanting* to be the perfect son for Crawford. He'd become it.

Emotionless. He didn't care if he hurt his mother. The worst thing was, it seemed like, intellectually, he knew he *should*. But it just wasn't there. Whatever feelings Noah ever had for her, or anyone else, had been buried. If not completely wiped out.

And that smile just kept getting bigger. "You see it now, don't you? But let's keep playing. There's not much else to do. I'll say the things you want me to. I won't make who I am so obvious. You can feel better about the work you've put in."

"Is that what you want, Noah? To fool me? To get back to her and…what?" Rhodey crossed the room and put his hand on Noah's shoulder. Gave him a hard shake, like that might do…*something*. "I'll kill you before I let you hurt her."

Noah held his gaze. His tone was lifeless. "Do it. Either let me go or do it. You want the truth? You can't make me into anything but what I am. And if you keep trying? Someone will get hurt." He flashed a smile abruptly, sitting up. "Since I know you're too weak to decide either way, can we watch another movie? I promise I won't cut you open again. I want to watch the one with the horses. I really like the music in that one."

Swallowing hard, Rhodey pulled out his phone and removed the chip. He'd copied the movie on the device, so he could leave the thing with the kid and not worry about him contacting anyone who might try to get him out of here.

That Noah didn't react, or seem bothered that he didn't plan to stay and watch with him, was good. Rhodey glanced toward the end table—which he needed to get out of here, along with the bedframe, to avoid any more improvised weapons—where there was a half cup of water and a few bites leftover from the roast beef sandwich he'd served the kid for lunch.

"Are you hungry? Thirsty? I could get you some orange juice."

Glancing up from the phone, Noah shook his head. "No. I would enjoy it, but you're playing your hand too early. Let me work for it."

Somehow, the suggestion only made Rhodey feel empty and cold as he left the room and locked the door behind him. He wasn't getting anywhere with his nephew. And, if he really thought about it, the kid was right.

I do hate him.

Not for the reasons Noah believed, but because he'd seen this as another mission. A simpler one than he usually took on. With a grocery list of goals to accomplish.

One. Get child away from bad guy.

Check.

Two. Show child life can be good and happy.

Not even close.

Three. Send child back to mommy.

Like fuck.

Four. Happily ever after.

What a goddamn joke.

But when he really looked back on everything he'd done so far, he could see in fucking neon highlights where he'd fucked up. Crawford had finally gotten Noah on his side. Not just that. He'd killed any part of the kid that gave a fuck. About *anyone*.

Including his own mother.

Tracey can never know.

Vani had offered two solutions. Kill Noah. Or let Maddox work on him.

But what will he be when Maddox is done?

More than what he was now. Sure, Maddox's training fucked with a person's morals, but they still had them. He didn't want mindless machines. He wanted operatives who could take down targets and preserve assets. Or shield victims.

Rhodey and Vani were his pride and joy and both of them could comfort a child saved from a sex trafficking ring. They weren't great at it, and those trained for the job always took over, but the point was, they cared enough not to do more damage.

Fifteen. Noah was only *fifteen*. His job had been to transport guns across the border. Nothing too nefarious—even though it was illegal and put weapons in the hands of a lot of assholes Rhodey would've had to deal with later. But his conditioning went beyond that. Crawford hadn't turned his son into *this* just to make deliveries. He'd created his own personal enforcer. Noah had several black belts. He was more than willing and ready to kill on command. His father's command.

Crawford's ambitions might have been cut short, but he'd been setting himself up for something bigger. Likely had all kinds of ideas about having a strong son, who'd stand by his side and wipe out his enemies.

He'd almost succeeded.

In Noah's mind, he had.

And so long as that was Noah's focus, nothing else could reach him. He—whoever *he* might have been—was shut down behind his father's expectations. This was 'making Daddy proud' on a whole new level.

However Crawford had figured out how to create his perfect little soldier, whatever Rhodey felt about it, the priority needed to be making sure he couldn't do it again.

Rhodey was good at his job. Exceptional even.

But Vani was right. He couldn't fix this. He couldn't stop it.

And protecting Noah—or himself—from Maddox was weak. If Maddox could reach whatever humanity was left inside his nephew? Rhodey couldn't be too proud, or too *afraid*, to ask.

Taking out his phone, he made the call. The conversation

was brief. He had a feeling Maddox had gotten some intel from Vani. Likely without her having thought twice about it. Not like what Rhodey was trying to do was a secret. He'd had to do some serious digging to find Noah when his nephew had been on the road, ready to deliver military grade weapons into the hands of the highest bidders.

When Maddox showed up at the door with Crispin and a few suitcases, Rhodey did his best to hide how much seeing them step into his sanctuary fucked with him. This was supposed to be a place where he had full control. Where he didn't have to be perfect.

But between Maddox and Noah?

That place doesn't exist anymore.

One of the suitcases in hand, Maddox gave him an expectant look. "Lead the way."

Rhodey eyed the suitcase. "You can't bring that in the cell. He'll—"

"Rhodey, I understand what I'm dealing with. I heard what you didn't say." Maddox patted his cheek. "I promise you, when I'm done with him, his mother will be able to hug him. And see her little boy." His lips twitched. "But we won't lose a priceless asset. You've always been exceptional. I have a feeling he'll be no less."

Exactly what Rhodey had been expecting. And his answer was prepared. "This will be *his* choice. And if you get an actual human out of whatever the fuck is in that cell? He'll be able to decide for himself. One way or another."

"Agreed." Maddox slid his hand down to squeeze Rhodey's arm. The one that was still a mess. And even though Rhodey didn't flinch, Maddox lifted a brow. "Ah, I see. You let him being your nephew soften you. I understand. You would do anything for your sister, and he's part of that. Your idea of 'family' is a weakness. One I'll allow. For now."

It was so fucking tempting to argue with him, but Rhodey didn't bother. He'd found himself backed into a corner too often. Then faced Maddox reminding him of all he'd done for Rhodey. His intense training, his introductions to all the right people, even his finding Rhodey a Dom in Russia and getting him enlisted in the military there. The dead bodies Rhodey had left behind weren't the point. Tracey would still be trapped with Crawford if not for all Maddox had done.

He'd never let Rhodey forget that.

And however he 'fixed' Noah?

That wouldn't be forgotten either.

Chapter Fifteen

PAST

For two months, Rhodey hardly saw Noah. Crispin brought Noah's food. Not always enough, but any objection from Rhodey was shut down. Maddox had it handled. The first few times he'd heard Noah scream, he'd tried to get down to the cell, but Crispin put him in his place, much like he had when they'd met, all those years ago.

One day, out of nowhere, Maddox came up from the basement. Into the backyard, where Rhodey was chopping wood for the fireplace.

"It's done." Maddox took his white kerchief from his suit jacket, wiping blood off his hands. "I had to make sure. His grip is fragile, but it's there."

Rhodey snapped his gaze from Maddox's hands to his face. "What do you mean? You said you'd 'fix' him."

"Oh, and what did you *think* I meant by that?" Maddox lifted a hand to Rhodey's cheek. The blood, which was obviously Noah's, still dampened his palm. "The damage a parent can do is always considerable. One with a goal and the methods to do what Crawford did? It's something else. He forced the child to shut off all his emotions to please him. I would love to learn exactly how he did it, but I can guess. At first, it would have been small rewards and punishments. 'Please me and you are my son. Don't and I'll abandon you.' More and more, likely using trusted 'associates' to enforce his power. The safety he could offer. Protection. Then tests. So many tests. Noah had to learn who was 'on their side' and who wasn't. If he got it wrong, he paid dearly."

Rhodey felt sick. But he had to ask. "How?"

"One of his father's men attempted to *'use'* him. Bigger. Stronger. But Noah saw what he planned to do. From what I've gathered, no one was around either your sister or Noah who wasn't completely loyal to Crawford. It was a setup." Maddox sounded a bit amazed, shaking his head with a soft laugh. "Noah stabbed the man with a knitting needle. Crawford made him disappear. Then, Noah understood the game."

That's... Rhodey pressed his eyes shut. Tried to remember everything Jared had taught him about playing chess. He'd always sucked at those games. Or maybe Jared was just that good. Either way, he couldn't wrap his mind around what Maddox was saying now. "What did it mean? What does it mean now? Can I...is he...?"

"A fifteen year old boy who needs a hug?" Maddox let out a soft laugh. "Maybe. But don't give it to him. You need to enforce the training I've done." His lips slid into a slow smile. "He'll respond to Russian commands. Automatically. If you want him fully under your control, use that."

Right then, Rhodey finally understood what Maddox had done. What he'd *let* him do. "You didn't fix him. Or *help* him. You...did what his father did. This is...you fucking brainwashed him? Was that..." He looked over at the boxes Maddox's driver had been bringing in and out every other week. "Damn it, Maddox. What did you do to my nephew?"

"I put him in a position to make a choice. Like you asked me to." Maddox drummed his fingers on a tall, wooden box. "It will stick this time. I won't ask for a 'thank you'. Right now. But I will at some point."

Rhodey met his mentor's eyes. Let out a bitter laugh. After being sent to Russia to continue his training, he'd ended up killing not only his 'new Dom' but his fellow sub. He'd learned it was all planned. A year of getting close to people. Finding out all their secrets. And killing them before they killed him. "If I have my way, he'll reject any offer you give him."

"We'll see." Maddox motioned his driver to his side. "Call Vani. The child needs her tender loving care. This last stage was difficult."

Long after the door was closed, Rhodey couldn't look away. But then there was another sound. From below. He went over to the door to the basement. Opened it to listen.

Crying. Noah was…crying. He never cried.

Descending the steps two at a time, Rhodey got to the door of the cell and threw it open.

Whenever he opened this door, no matter how much noise he made, Noah never reacted.

But he did now.

Tears glistened his cheeks as he hunched into the mattress, laid out on the floor in a room bare except for that and a bucket for him to pee in. Showers, shaving, and shits were done under Maddox's careful supervision. Rhodey had only seen Noah twice during these past months.

Both times to make sure he was still breathing. He'd been fast asleep.

"I'm sorry." Noah pressed his hands to his face, stifling his sobs. "I'm sorry, I…I rolled over in my sleep. I'll be quiet now."

That tone…wasn't one the kid had ever used before. Once Rhodey had learned the difference, he could never mistake it again. Noah was 'real' when he felt like he'd caught Rhodey in a lie. And…maybe he really had.

Before tonight, Rhodey hadn't decided whether or not the kid would be better off dead.

That smile, the one Noah always had on his lips right

before he tested Rhodey's resolve? Yeah, Rhodey wouldn't lie. He could've killed that guy.

But this one?

So often, while Rhodey had been training under Maddox, he'd said those words. 'I'm sorry I didn't move faster.' Or 'I'm sorry I didn't expect that.' Then 'I'm sorry, sir, but no. I won't hit him.'

Curled up under the blankets, Noah tensed at Rhodey's approach. Something he never did.

"Please just...I won't be a problem. I'll stay. I won't fight you." Noah turned a bit to look up at Rhodey. "I get it, okay?" His voice hitched. "People are dead. Because of me. I'm... sorry. I'm so fucking sorry."

"Don't say that word." Rhodey's voice broke as he took in Noah's back. He'd been trained on the whip and several other tools. Under Crispin, Maddox, and his Dom in Russia. Matvey. Only one name. He'd often wondered if the 'M' was intentional. Matvey had been a good Dom. He'd taught Rhodey all the rules, along with his co-sub, Yaroslav. To live? Rhodey had to kill them both.

He'd sworn the last time he'd apologize for anything was at their funerals.

"What word?" Noah spoke in a whisper, flinching when Rhodey lifted the blanket to bare his back. It was covered in whip lashes. Some still bleeding. Others scarred over. Worse than Rhodey's had ever been under any of his 'Doms'.

"Fuck, Noah. I'm—"

"Don't. Please don't." Noah pressed his eyes shut, tears trailing down his cheeks. "You're...I don't do well when I'm weak. Everything goes black. I don't remember what I do. I need...I'll be whoever you want, but please...not yet. I can't. It hurts so bad."

Lifting a hand to Noah's shoulder, Rhodey pressed his eyes shut at the heat under his palm. "This will never happen again."

Instead of relief, Noah jerked away and twisted to stare at him. "No, you don't understand. I need this. I won't...you don't know who I am without this. Don't make me beg. The blackness...it comes out. It doesn't like it when I'm weak. It takes over. Someone...did you find me?"

"Find you? No, you weren't..." Rhodey didn't know who he was talking to. This wasn't the Noah he knew. And he didn't trust the kid. No way would he go there again. But he could give him...some reassurance. "You're fine. You don't have to beg. Just don't tell me killing people is part of the job. You want that job? Learn who needs to die and who needs to live."

Noah stared at him. "You don't get it. *I* don't want to kill *anyone*. My dad wanted me to be able to. We talked about it all the time. Whether I could. I was...so tired. But I wanted to make him proud. I...don't anymore. I..." His voice broke. "I want my mom. But don't bring me to her. Not yet."

"I won't." Rhodey's throat tightened. Was it...was it possible Maddox had succeeded? Or was this another trick? "You stay here until I can trust you."

Trembling, Noah nodded. "Okay, I'm good with that."

"Do you...need a drink? Some painkillers?" Rhodey would've offered a shot of vodka if the kid was older, but he was barely sixteen. And they weren't in Russia. "Talk to me."

"I need...just let me sleep? Please?" Noah laid down and tugged the thin blanket over himself. "Can I...watch the horses again? My mom loves horses. She loves all animals. They're so much easier than humans. My dad didn't let her keep any. But she said one day she'd take care of a bunch." He closed his eyes. "Tell me she has that? She...maybe if she has a whole bunch, she can forget me."

Smoothing his hand over Noah's hair, Rhodey shook his head. "She won't forget you. You'll get there, plemyannichek."

Another shiver and Noah twisted away from him. "You want what he wants. Me to be a different kind of weapon. I don't... I'm begging you..." His whole body shook. "Stop. I need it to stop. I want to...just be me."

A simple request. And fuck it all, it felt real. This person Rhodey was talking to wasn't a cold, hard chunk of a person. Rhodey wasn't sure he was whole. He didn't know what Maddox had done.

But he did know one thing. Maddox had left his mark. Not an easy repair. One clinging to life. Either Rhodey would have to bring Vani in, hope Noah didn't slip, or...

You can't do this alone.

Vani could probably do a decent job.

You know better. If you're lucky, he needs to be rebuilt.

And I can't do that.

Let the boy suffer, as he likely deserved, or find him real help?

You know the answer.

Rhodey left the cell and sent a numeric message to a number Maddox had given him ages ago. Jared was brilliant. He'd get it. He wouldn't call back on the phone their once shared Dom could trace.

He would find a payphone. And call the number to Rhodey's *other* phone. One he'd set up after he'd finally clued in to the fact Maddox owned him. And made steps to make that a little *less* true while paying off his debts.

Something Jared would also get. Both of them understood the price. Only, Rhodey had made sure Jared never had to pay it.

I will never say that word. One we had to say, so many times.

'I'm sorry for questioning.'

'I'm sorry for having any doubt.'

'I'm sorry for loving anyone else more than you.'

If I get my way? That useless word will be erased. Forever.

But as Rhodey brushed his hand over Noah's hair, he knew, if he got through to Jared, he had to say something.

The phone clicked. Rhodey wasn't sure if it was voicemail

or Jared himself. "Hey... Umm...you busy? I don't want to bother you, but remember when we talked before you went out again? I found him. I...did something. To help. It didn't... well, it kinda did. But he's..." He laid his hand on Noah's forehead. He felt like he was on fire. "I need you, Jared. I hurt him. Really bad. I thought I had to. I was so fucking wrong."

Rather than an overseas number, the return call came from Bethesda, Maryland. A payphone, as Rhodey had predicted. The question as to whether Jared would answer if he ever needed him? With how damn fast the man had gotten back to him, there was zero doubt.

The second Rhodey picked up, Jared spoke in a rush. "Hurt him how, husky? I'm—" A crowd of voices echoed like he stood in a concrete hallway. "—Christ. I can't wait until I'm a C.O. and can make everyone shut the hell up. What are we dealing with? Broken bones? Infection? I don't know if I can get a weekend pass, but I just ruined the curve for everyone again, so I probably have a little leeway. The General would probably like to see me fail a few exams, but he won't. I already have all the course materials memorized. Why are people so stupidly slow? Don't they know they need to be intelligent to be in medicine?"

Rhodey's lips twitched as he listened to his best friend, just the sound of his voice soothing the tension in his muscles and twisting his guts. While Jared talked, Rhodey shot off another message on his spare burner. He used to get so irritated with Maddox and all his fucking phones, but he was starting to get why they were needed. "I'm sending a plane to pick you up. Can you be at the hangar in an hour? I'll have someone drive you to the closest gas station once you land and meet you there."

"A plane?" There was a moment of stunned silence, then Jared breathed deep. "How bad is this? Of course, I'll be there. Sorry for fucking talking so much. I am on so much caffeine right now, I feel like I could fly there myself." The swearing didn't sound like Jared, but neither did the verbal torrent. "I've been awake for thirty-six hours. This is not Harvard. At all. My three bunkmates enjoy trying to gas me out of the room. Speaking of, which gas station? I haven't left base much."

Pacing the length of the hallway, Rhodey took a deep breath, mentally calculating the time it would take Jared to get here. He should have considered a doctor wouldn't get much sleep. "Fuck, I hate that I'm dumping another patient on you. I wouldn't ask if it wasn't... It's a little gas station just outside of Colorado. You can take a nap on the plane I guess."

"Who needs sleep when there's caffeine? Amazing stuff. Comes in pill form, too. What will they think of next?" The man was obviously full of sarcasm, but in a good-humored way. "I'll bring my med kit, but do I need to get it through security?"

Rhodey shook his head before remembering to answer out loud. "No. Just have a cab drop you off." He gave Jared the address to the private air strip, which wouldn't take more than half an hour to drive to. "If you don't have any cash, my guy there will pay the fare. Thanks for this, my man. I fucking owe you."

Snort registering loud and clear, Jared clucked his tongue. "You owe me nothing. You're my best friend and always will be. Even if you don't answer my emails." There was a pause. "I'll take care of him, husky. We'll make sure he's okay."

"Yeah..." Rhodey stepped out his front door, looking over the wild landscape. The air was crisp, like winter wanted to remind him it hadn't been gone for long, but everything was nice and green. He preferred places like this. So many of his missions brought him to ugly, broken down spots, moving through darkness, smelling shit and blood. At least he wasn't dragging Jared anywhere like that. But he should still warn him about what he *was* dragging him into. "He's...I don't know what he'll be like after this, Jared. But he's not some sweet little kid. He's...pretty fucked up. Not just physically."

"I'm a doctor, not a therapist, but something tells me that anyone who went through what he did just needs a little trust." More people walked by, one of them singing a cadence that had Jared growling. "They let anyone enlist, I swear." Then, "I have to go grab my things. See you soon."

Rhodey nodded, sighing as he disconnected the call. He kept himself distracted making all the arrangements to get Jared here, then checked on Noah. His curls were dark with sweat, sticking to his face, and his sheets were damp, both with sweat and blood. Carefully moving the kid, Rhodey changed the bedding. Got a cool cloth to put on his head, and another for his back. Probably didn't help much, but it was the best he could do.

The call came when the plane landed and Rhodey secured the house, getting in his nicest car—a sleek, black Lincoln he'd always thought Jared would like. Driving out to the gas station, he had to rub his hands on his jeans a few times when they got slick on the steering wheel. Fuck, he could stakeout a target for a week, shoot them right between the eyes in the middle of a crowd, and be perfectly calm, but he was nervous about seeing his best friend?

He laughed at himself as he parked. Gave himself a minute to pull himself together. Then stepped out of the car, nodding to the driver who was standing a few feet away from Jared, looking bored. The man, a decent guy who'd done transport jobs for Rhodey in the past, nodded back and got into his own car without a word before driving off.

Hefting a military issue canvas duffel with enough gear inside to make his shoulder and arm muscles flex under his tight, black button-down, Jared approached Rhodey with a question in his ice blue eyes. Eyes that were much more prominent beneath the sweep of his dark brows with his military buzz cut.

A foot short of Rhodey's boots, he stopped, leaned in, and brushed a soft kiss over Rhodey's lips. "Hello, husky."

Rhodey wasn't sure what he'd expected. Either from Jared or himself. This was the first time in…fuck, way too long that anyone besides Vani had touched him. And with her it was all for patch jobs. The last person who'd kissed him had tried to kill him, so maybe he should be on guard. But he wasn't.

Being near Jared felt safe. Good. He grinned, yanking Jared in for a hug. "Hey, Doc. It's…really fucking good to see you."

Chuckling, Jared shifted the duffel, using both arms to lift Rhodey off his feet in a python-like squeeze. "I have a two-week leave. Bastard said he expects me to flunk out when I get back, but if I maintain my average he'll bump me up to the next cohort and I'll graduate early." Rhodey's boots touched the ground again as Jared pulled back to study him. "As if I wouldn't have anyway. Now I'm going to make him move me up two."

"I'm surprised you're not running the place already." Rhodey let out a soft laugh, reaching out to brush his hand over Jared's hair. This short, the black strands sharpened Jared's features, making him look older. But his eyes, his smile, hadn't changed. Not like they would've if Maddox had gotten his way. Curving his hand around the back of Jared's neck, Rhodey briefly touched their foreheads together. "For some reason, I thought you'd be…I don't know, out in the jungle. Treating soldiers for weird diseases. While getting shot at."

While Rhodey studied Jared, Jared's gaze ran over him in return, likely not missing a thing. "That comes after I finish my specialization and residency. I'll be there next year. Possibly December of this year."

Lowering his hand, Rhodey took a step back and nodded. The man had a life to get back to. They hardly knew each other anymore—getting too familiar would probably feel weird. How Jared'd sounded on the phone wasn't…the best friend Rhodey remembered. If Jared had acted like that back when they'd spent every possible second together, he'd guess he was...masking or whatever they called it. But Rhodey couldn't assume anything. Maybe this was just who Jared was now.

Either way, he didn't sound like the soulless Maddox flunky he'd once been. He'd taken time off to help Rhodey out and he'd probably need every bit of it to put Noah back together. Blowing out a breath, Rhodey motioned toward the passenger side of his car. "We should get going. He was still breathing when I left, so...I'm guessing that's a good sign. But he's burning up."

"Infection." Tone assessing, gaze curious, Jared settled into the seat, letting his bag rest end-up between thighs much more muscular than the last time Rhodey'd been with him. "I brought antibiotics. Do you know if he has any drug allergies?"

Climbing in behind the wheel, Rhodey shook his head. "Not that I know of. Other than being a little psychopath, he seems healthy. In good shape. He's stronger than he looks, so don't let your guard down. I'll stick close, but...just in case. Don't leave anything sharp within his reach."

"If I don't trust him, he won't trust me." Jared bumped his shoulders against the seat like he found being in a car confining. They hadn't had access to many as kids, but at least the Lincoln afforded his broad frame lots of space. "Have cars always moved this fast?" He squinted out the window as the trees blurred by, then turned his head to study Rhodey's profile. "How are you doing? This can't have been easy for you, either."

Rhodey shrugged, keeping his eyes on the road while turning off the main one, onto a narrow one that was almost impossible to find if you didn't know where it was. The trees on either side were close enough that the branches made soft scratching sounds in the silence. He cleared his throat. "No, it wasn't easy, but the alternative... I couldn't let Tracey see him. It would destroy her. He's... I don't think you understand. You *can't* trust him, Jared. You don't know what he's capable of."

"I understand. *You* can't trust him, Rhodey. He hasn't broken any trust with me. I'll be vigilant, but I'm not going into a room with him putting him on the defensive. If he's suffered as much as you say he has, he's going to need a safe space. I'll try to be that, if I can. If you need to be the bad cop, I won't object, but you have to give the boy a place to land." Jared's hand slipped over the one Rhodey had on his own thigh, thumb brushing his knuckles. "I missed you."

Swallowing hard, Rhodey slid Jared a sideways look. He couldn't help smiling a little, even though he had a feeling Jared would see him much differently after he saw the condition Noah was in. It couldn't be helped. And hell, maybe Jared's approach would actually work. Had to be better than Maddox's. "I missed you, too. More than I can say."

Parked in front of the house, Rhodey stepped out, waiting for Jared in front of the car. He shoved his hands in his pockets, for some reason suddenly really worried about what his best friend thought of the place. It was a decent sized house, bigger than the one they'd grown up in, but not as nice as a doctor would have. Comfortable, but more practical than anything.

Does that even fucking matter now? He's not gonna care about any of this if he ends up having to help you bury the kid in the backyard.

Right. Priorities.

Rhodey cleared his throat. Said the first thing that came to mind. "Just a head's up... He's in the basement. I made a... cell for him." He gave Jared a hard look. "Don't let him out."

The look was returned with one of Jared's best acerbic stares. "Your relationship with him is your relationship with him, Rhodey. You know what's best for that and I'll always trust your judgment. I hope you know that. Just...let my relationship with him be mine."

"Fine." Rhodey led the way inside, blowing out a breath as he reached the door to the basement. He wrapped his hand around the handle, but didn't turn it. There was one last thing his best friend needed to understand. "No pressure, but this is his last chance. If he…loses your trust, he's done for."

A few blinks showed Jared's surprise, but he eventually nodded. "Alright. But you let me determine that. Unless I explicitly tell you he's lost it, you don't act. Swear it."

Rhodey frowned, holding Jared's gaze. He wanted to refuse. But he respected Jared too much to dismiss him like some flunky he'd been forced to deal with on a mission. The man was intelligent. He'd listen to reason. "We'll discuss this again when he's healed. When I can tell whether or not there's anything in him worth saving. I'm not letting you put too much time or energy into a lost cause."

"He's a human being, not a junk car, Rhodey." Jared's gaze skipped around the room. "I can't believe you got a house before I did. Bastard." There was no heat in his words, only admiration as he slid his gaze to Rhodey's face. "Tell me you have a giant, comfortable bed and I'll get on my knees right now."

Despite how messed up this whole situation was, Rhodey chuckled. He nodded toward the other end of the hall. "My bedroom's over there. If you don't take that offer back once you see the kid, I'll show you it. I don't spoil myself often, but I damn well made sure I got a bed that fit me right. My feet don't hang over the edge. It's fucking awesome."

Jared literally groaned with pleasure, the sound almost like a purr. "God. I've been curled up on that sorry excuse for a twin bed for so long I'm surprised I'm not permanently folded in half." Before Rhodey could take them further into the basement, Jared put a hand on his shoulder to make him turn. "Hey. I know you did whatever you thought you had to, and it sounds like that was a lot. I don't judge you. I love you. We'll get through this. We've been in worse spots, right?"

"I guess." Rhodey met those pale blue eyes, the cold in the color, like a frozen over lake, not hiding the warmth he found within them. He was prepared for that to change, but until it did, he'd soak in all he could. "I'm not...sure how I'm supposed to feel about any of this. I should care because he's my nephew, but it didn't take me long to shut that shit down. I would've been useless to him if I didn't face the facts. He's more Crawford's son than Tracey's. I'm hoping that'll change, but if it doesn't..." He sighed, then lifted his shoulders. "We'll see."

"Then we weed out Crawford so the part of him that's Tracey's has room to grow." Jared made it sound simple, and maybe it would be. But first? Noah would have to live. "You be the bad cop. I'll be the good cop." Reiterating his earlier statement, he motioned toward the darkness where the security lights hadn't yet flickered on. "I could use a roast beef sandwich and a beer after this, if you don't mind?"

Rhodey nodded, bringing Jared to the door of the cell. He unlocked it. Kept his tone as light as possible. "I've got you covered, my man. Good food, a comfy bed, and a 'bad cop' coming up."

Opening the door, he glanced in before letting Jared pass. It took a few seconds, but...yeah, Noah's chest rose and fell. He'd rolled onto his back, which had to fucking hurt, but he was sleeping so maybe he didn't notice?

Either way, he's not dead.

He opened the door a bit wider when it was clear Noah wasn't going to jump up and make a run for it. Or even open his eyes. "You can go in."

"Tell him I'm here. He'll hear you, and it'll relax him to know who's taking care of him." Jared stood back a little from the bed, his gaze fixed on Noah. The expression on his face was different from any Rhodey'd ever seen. As though he'd seen a small kitten in distress and was determined to make certain it survived at all cost. Nothing like the young man he'd been in Maddox's basement. "Be gentle."

Lifting his brow a bit, Rhodey almost asked Jared if he'd been listening at all when he'd told him what he'd be dealing with, but he knew better. His best friend never missed anything. But he'd have to learn for himself. Only, not the way Rhodey had. Keeping himself between Jared and Noah, Rhodey crouched down and spoke softly. "Hey, kid. You awake? I brought a doctor. He's a friend of mine and he's gonna take care of you."

Still not opening his eyes, Noah tensed. He turned away from Rhodey, his whole body jerking, as though the motion renewed the pain. "I don't need anyone to take care of me. I'm just...a little sore. Did you really think it would be that easy? Just...go away."

Well, at least he's not crying anymore.

Behind Rhodey, Jared spoke up. "My name's Jared McCleod, Noah. Let's get that back looked at and then you and I can get to know each other over the next few weeks. I promise you'll feel better once we get some medication in you."

"Medication..." Noah moved slowly, like he was testing how much his body could manage. From how the color left his skin, he clearly wasn't faking. He positioned himself to look up at Jared, half sitting for less than a second before lowering back down. Tears wet his lashes, but he brought his hand to his mouth, biting into his palm and taking a few sharp breaths. When he spoke again, he obviously tried to hide how much pain he was in. "You give me nothing without telling me what it is first. I'll know if you're lying. Don't lie or this is over. I won't let you touch me."

Duffel hitting the ground with a soft *whump*, Jared lowered to his haunches to bring himself to Noah's eye level. "I promise I will never lie to you, and I will never touch you without your permission unless you touch me first. Whatever I do to treat you, you'll be fully cognizant of, and if there's a treatment you refuse, I will respect your decision."

Noah held Jared's gaze for a long time before he nodded. A small smile curved his lips. Not the fucking creepy one. Almost...shy. Like he was a normal kid, meeting someone for the first time he was...impressed with. "You have really cool eyes. I never thought I'd like the way glasses look on anyone, but they suit you." He rested his head on his folded arm. "You're not a doctor, though. You're too young. But you seem more intelligent than my uncle. I believe you know what you're doing."

"Mhmm..." Jared's lips twitched, his gaze warming with his repressed smile. "I'm a doctor, but you're right. I'm young. Thank you for the compliment. I almost didn't get into the military because of my vision, but someone convinced them refusing me would be a bad idea." He glanced up at Rhodey, including him in the joke. "I graduated university at eighteen." Jared held up one hand and pointed at his bag, attention returning to Noah. "Would you be okay with my getting out my kit and taking your temperature? I'd like to get you some IV antibiotics if you're not averse to needles."

That got a small laugh from Noah as he shifted again. "I'm not bothered by needles. I can take a lot of pain, so don't worry about that." He shivered, biting hard into his bottom lip. "Since you're a doctor, you're in charge, right? Can you tell my uncle to turn the fucking heat up?"

"I'm right here." Rhodey straightened, frowning at the kid. "And the temperature is fine."

The little bastard completely ignored him. "And will I be allowed a blanket? I'll let you take my temperature if you'll get me one."

"Rhodey, he has a fever." Jared opened his bag, the zipper making a toothy sound in the barren cell. "I'll need clean sheets, comfortable blankets, a pillow, and the heat set to seventy-four. I don't want it too hot in here so it won't spike his fever more. Also, water, ginger ale for sugar, and some broth."

Turning his focus to Jared, Rhodey inclined his head. "Fine. Do what you need to and I'll get all that. Once you're out of the room. I'm not leaving you alone with him."

"You're an idiot." Noah pressed his eyes shut, his voice almost too soft to hear. "Use your eyes, uncle. I can't even sit up. And Jared's more than twice my size. If I could take him down in this condition, he'd fucking deserve to die. But I don't want to. He seems...like a good person. Not like you."

Pain ghosted Jared's expression at Noah's assessment of Rhodey, but he nodded toward the door. "Let me have some time with him, husky. It will be fine. We'll get to know one another a little better."

The worst thing was, both of them were right. Even though Rhodey knew what Noah was capable of, he couldn't do anything now. He didn't have the strength to use more than words as a weapon. And Rhodey was too well trained to let that fuck with him.

Or he should be, anyway. But he was having trouble remembering anything he'd been taught. Between having Jared close, and the kid Rhodey was supposed to take care of lying there, shaking, torn up, spitting attitude while clinging to life...

Yeah, maybe letting Jared be in charge this once would be a good idea. Rhodey didn't trust his own judgment right now. He couldn't look at the teen without seeing a threat. Where there wasn't one.

Not right this second, anyway.

Giving Jared a quick nod, Rhodey spared Noah a last glance before stepping out of the cell. He closed the door, but didn't lock it, not wanting to trap Jared in there.

The prison for two they'd once shared, Rhodey'd gotten the key to set Jared free.

Like fuck would he lock him in another.

Chapter Sixteen

PAST

Taking his time, Rhodey collected all the supplies Jared'd asked for. Paused outside the door, his heart in his throat at Noah's soft words to Jared.

"I want to know what it looks like. Rhodey never seems bothered by anything, but I can tell…it's fucking with him." Noah paused, inhaling roughly. This was it. He was going to tell Jared about Maddox. Instead, his voice broke. "I want it to. I won't ever forgive him. Not unless he…he fixes me. He said he would, but I'm not fixed yet. Tell him…tell him I can do it? Please? I'll…try harder."

Jared made a soft sound that was one part sympathy and one part agreement. "Your relationship with your uncle is your responsibility, my boy. Just like my relationship with you is my own. When we mix ourselves in each other's relationships, they grow more fragile because the bond is stretched in too many directions. It has too many seams." There was a hiss like Jared might be prodding at Noah's wounds. "I believe you can do this. You can fix yourself with our support. It will be hard, but few things worth having are easy." A packet tore. "As for your stripes, when they heal they'll remind me of who you fought to become. A tiger, free to prowl the jungle on his own terms. To protect those he loves, and to experience what the world has to offer."

There was silence. Then barely a whisper from Noah as he sniffed. "I'll show him I'm worth something, but...you're right. That's my job. I don't know about loving anyone yet, though. I haven't decided if I ever want to feel that. It's... weak. I'm not weak." He made a muffled sound. "Don't tell him...Jared, it hurts. So fucking bad."

Rhodey pressed his eyes shut and rested his forehead against the closed door. He wanted to fucking kill Maddox. Except, the man had done what he couldn't. Maybe...maybe he should thank him. The kid still sounded a bit disturbed, but nowhere near what he'd been like before.

I can only imagine what Jared must think of me, talking to Noah now.

"Let's see if we can't get you more comfortable. I don't want you taking pills on an empty stomach, and you'll need to take care that the IV meds don't make you think you can move more than you should." Another packet tore, this time a bit sharply. "Once I suture these, you'll need to move carefully, as little as possible without help." The mattress creaked like Jared sat on the bed by Noah's side. "Love? That takes strength. Bravery. Not because it's weak, because it's the most vulnerable place we can be. We risk everything, pain worse than what you're feeling now, when we're brave enough to love."

Only a bit older than Noah was now, Jared wouldn't have been talking about vulnerability like this—except maybe to explain a few creative ways to make suffering last. How fragile the human body could be. He'd loved Rhodey, but...not as much as he'd worshiped Maddox.

There were hints of their 'Master's' training, but barely a shadow compared to the traces of the boy Rhodey'd known. The one who'd patched up his skinned knees. Who he could talk to about anything. His best friend.

Fully a man, about to become a doctor, and a...damn good human being.

A better one than Rhodey could ever be.

You were worth selling my soul for, Jared. If I could go back?

I'd make the same choice, all over again.

Hearing Jared open up to Noah, discussing love like it was something special, something he might've even experienced, brought a soft smile to Rhodey's lips—the kind of smile he was surprised his face remembered how to make. But, damn it, this was everything he'd wanted for Jared. The teenage fantasies of being the man in Jared's life were long gone—mercs were better off sticking with other mercs, and breakups got messy. Making a valuable asset disappear cost time and money and who needed the fucking hassle?

See, this is why me and my nephew can't have 'the talk'.

The love one, not sex. But the latter could wait until Noah was less likely to gut his first boyfriend. That'd be messy, too.

Jared being here meant the kid might actually live to do all that normal shit. He was getting through to him. Without threats, or restraints, or...whatever Maddox had done.

Fuck...I should have called Jared first.

More quiet. Another sniff. "You're right. My mother...she loves, so much. She still loved me, for some reason. And my father." Noah paused, then let out a bitter laugh. "She'll regret both. I could see it. I couldn't feel anything about it before... I don't like this. I...I watched her get completely drained by him. By me. I was able to be detached and now... Use one of your drugs. Make it stop."

"Oh, tiger..." Jared sighed softly. "No one could ever regret you, beautiful boy. I can't make it stop, because it's what makes you human. What you're feeling is the pain of consequences that will help you make better decisions in the future. Wanting to? It comes from love, and having a soul. Welcome to the human race."

Hope flared up and was snuffed out in the blink of an eye

as Rhodey sensed the energy in the room shift. He opened the door in time to catch Noah latch on to Jared's wrist. The kid was still weak, but that look in his eyes... Rhodey wouldn't force Jared to deal with that.

Or the fucking smile.

"You saw what you wanted to see, heard what you wanted to hear." Vani's black eyes held his—once enough poison cleared from his system for him to tell her what the fuck had happened. Her words, her tone, sounded enough like Maddox to shut down the pain of betrayal. Focus on the facts. *"We're too well trained to buy into the bullshit. Don't do it again. I'll only get flowers for your funeral if you die a good death."*

Which meant no flowers if he ended up done in by a feral teenager. And if Maddox found out the life Rhodey'd purchased for Jared with his own had been wasted over trying to save the little shit? He'd take Rhodey out himself.

And I'd fucking deserve it.

Crossing the room, he wrenched Noah's hand away from Jared.

"Slower than I thought you'd be, uncle." Noah tilted his head to one side. "I knew you'd be listening. And you don't trust your friend's strength at all. If I was at my best, you might have a reason to worry. He wants to believe it, so much." He rolled his neck, stretching as though the pain he'd been feeling before was gone. "A soul. That's funny."

Rhodey ground his teeth. "Grab him again and I'll snap your neck. Don't fuck with me, boy. We both know who out of the two of you I care about keeping alive."

"May I have the ginger ale for him, please, Rhodey?" Jared behaved as if nothing at all had changed. "And a hook for the IV bag. I neglected to bring one." The formality of his speech was the only thing that gave him away—maybe there was more than a bit of Maddox's training left. Except it was hard to tell if he was shaken, or if his feelings had been bruised. "Noah, I'll need you on your stomach so I can inject anesthetic before I begin the sutures. Are you comfortable with that?"

Eyes widening slightly, Noah brought his focus back to Jared. He looked like he wanted to say something at first, likely one of his cutting remarks—which would have Rhodey punching him in the face if they were aimed at his best friend. Instead, his smile faded. And he suddenly looked confused. "Why are you doing this? He cares about you, he wouldn't risk you. Not for me. I don't understand this game. Play it properly. Defend yourself."

"Thank you." Taking the ginger ale and straw from Rhodey, Jared popped the top. He stuck the straw inside the fizzing can before holding it to Noah's lips. "Sip. You need some blood sugar. Not too fast or it'll make you sick." He waited to see if Noah would comply before he answered the question. "Just because it is a game to you doesn't mean it's a game to us. And if you believe your uncle holds me in such high regard, then I think you must know he wouldn't, as you say, risk me, unless he cares about you as well. Enough to give you every opportunity to have a happy life."

Sucking on the straw, Noah kept his gaze on Jared's face. He swallowed, easing back, then hissing in a breath. Almost like he'd been snapped back into his body and felt it around him all over again. Tears trailed down his cheeks. "You don't get it. I told you to make it stop and you…you won't. So this will…just keep happening."

"What will?" Rhodey's brow furrowed when Noah turned his head to face the wall. "Damn it, kid, just fucking talk to me. You were getting better. Then… I don't understand."

"Yes, I know. I just fucking said that." Noah wiped his hands irritably over his face. "Why don't you tie me down so you don't have to worry about me hurting your friend? Or just knock me out. Make it easier on you both."

"Hush, now. Both of you." Jared held up his gloved hand. "We're all going to take a breath and focus on the next thing in front of us, which is getting you on the road to recovery, my boy. Can we focus there for a bit?" Peeling off one glove, Jared hovered his fingers over Noah's temple. "I'm going to touch your face, alright?"

Noah nodded slowly, flinching even though Jared hadn't moved a muscle. Fist clenched at his side, he lifted his gaze to meet Jared's. "I won't hurt you. Maybe one day I won't have to say that, but right now...I need to tell you. Because I don't lie."

"Thank you for trusting me." Rather than making it about whether Noah could be trusted, Jared peeled back a layer from the conversation, his fingers combing gently through the curls at the boy's temple. "It means a great deal to me that I can trust you as well. I won't do anything to make you feel like you need to take that trust away."

Whatever part of Noah had been so cold and mocking before was replaced by something... Well, like Jared had said. *Human.* As the tension left his body and more tears wet his cheeks, he looked so much smaller. Which was weird, but it was almost like his presence had taken up more room when he lashed out. And now he was...just a teenager.

"I...need your help." Noah shifted a bit closer to Jared, wincing at the slight movement. "I can't lie down on my own. It hurts too much. But that doesn't mean I can't defend myself if I have to, just so we're clear."

"I understand." Continuing the rhythmic stroking, Jared appeared to use featherlight touches, his voice quieter than Rhodey had ever heard it. Gentler. "No one will hurt you. They'll need to come through me. I take your care seriously, and that means making sure no one can abuse your vulnerability while I do." He adjusted, leaning over a bit so Noah would be able to see his face. "May I help you get onto your stomach?"

Noah nodded, going completely still. "Yes. And...I appreciate you asking. It's better when I know what you're going to do. It fits in my brain and things stay in the light. I wish I could make it that way all the time, but I have a feeling you won't do what I need for that. Because you want me to have all the emotions, don't you?"

"Of course. It's what I promised. We have that in common. We don't lie to each other. Ever." Shifting his hip, Jared traced a finger down Noah's ear, over the shell. "My hands are going to your hip and shoulder now. This will feel fiery, but not as bad as if you did it on your own." Handing Rhodey the ginger ale, Jared then placed his hands where he'd said. "Here we go."

Eyes closed tight, Noah reached out, bracing his hand on Jared's shoulder. He took a deep breath, then nodded again before relaxing as Jared moved him. The care the man took was clear when he lowered the teen onto his stomach. Still, Noah buried his face in his hands, his shoulders coming up as he stifled a sob.

This had to be good, right? It seemed like the more Noah felt, the more present he was. Rhodey wasn't sure how he could use that to keep Noah grounded, keep him from backsliding into becoming a cold, detached weapon, but he'd figure it out. At least there was *something* to work with, now.

With Noah on his stomach, the full expanse of his back was exposed. Jared's expression never wavered, his gaze taking in the criss-cross of scars and open wounds before he met Rhodey's gaze. They'd both learned how to submit to heavy beatings under their Dom, and Jared's thoughts didn't need to be spoken out loud for Rhodey to know he thought of the man now.

"Noah, I'm going to inject the pain meds into your IV port now. You won't go to sleep, but you'll be relaxed. Is that alright?" Jared didn't move toward his kit, his hand still on Noah's hip above the line of his soft gray joggers.

Blowing out a breath, Noah turned his head a little to gaze up at Jared. "I think so. I haven't tried to be this way without the pain yet. Just don't...don't test me. We can do the 'feelings' thing some other time. If I'm relaxed, I need to focus on staying where it's bright." He made a frustrated sound. "It would help if the room wasn't so dark. How can you even work like this?"

"If you would prefer it brighter, I'm sure it can be arranged. I can work with a headlamp otherwise. It focuses the light where I require it." Jared leaned over his kit, rummaging in the very neat trays to access one beneath. "Don't laugh. I have a woman's emery board with me. It can be useful for everything from a ragged nail before surgery to filing little bits off a needle to make it shaper." He held the oval shaped piece of cardboard with its sandpapery surface in front of Noah's face. "Hold this between your thumb and forefinger. Run the pad of your thumb lightly over it. It's a grounding technique they teach us for treating patients who dissociate due to PTSD. And I promise. No feelings."

Taking the emery board, Noah examined it, the edge of his lips curving slightly. "What makes it a woman's? The flowers? I like them. So do you, or you wouldn't have chosen it. I'm sure there were more 'masculine' options."

"I enjoy provoking my peers with stereotypes of my homosexuality. They can't ask, and I don't tell, but I make certain they know I won't compromise on who I am." Warm humor and determination formed a steel core in Jared's response. "You'll feel a warm sensation in your arm, and then about five seconds before things get nice and drifty. Those antibiotics I gave you earlier, along with the ibuprofen, should be bringing that fever down. Are you still cold?"

Noah blinked, putting down the emery board like he couldn't focus on both things at once. His brow furrowed. "Not as cold as I was. Actually...it's a lot better. I hardly noticed when I was...you know. But without the distractions it's almost comfortable. Or as much as it can be with my back all fucked up. But I'm not complaining. I really...even if I act different later, please know I really appreciate what you're doing for me."

Now that the situation was under control, and Noah seemed stable, Rhodey backed up a bit to give Jared the space he needed to work. Even slipped into the hall to turn up the lights. With all those meds, the chance of Noah being fast enough to grab Jared again was unlikely. He also appeared to be...*aware* in a new way.

There was no telling how long that would last, and Rhodey wouldn't get his hopes up again, but he couldn't help catching Jared's eye and smile a bit. Mouth his own thanks. He didn't want to remind Noah of his presence and ruin whatever progress had been made, but he needed his best friend to know how fucking grateful he was.

Jared's slow blink acknowledged Rhodey's thanks, a small smile of reassurance following. "Pressing the plunger on the drugs now, Noah. Let me know how you're feeling physically."

"No feelings. Sensations." Noah picked up the emery board again. "I'm all right. And you can call me 'tiger'. I like that. But only you're allowed."

"I like that. Thank you, tiger." Jared's smile broadened, his gaze for Noah and Noah alone. "Sensations. How are they?"

Wrinkling his nose, Noah rubbed the emery board against his lips. "Fuzzy. And floaty. I'm not sure I like that. Next time, let's try this without the pain meds. I can take it and you probably can't always numb patients. Not when you're in combat zones, right? But you haven't been, yet."

"True. Next time we'll do just a topical. I wanted to get you a little more comfortable, but I understand not enjoying the sensation." Producing his suture kit, Jared laid it on the mattress in front of Noah. "I'm going to apply that topical now, where the skin isn't open. Then, I'll be using the kit there to stitch you up."

Noah stared at the bag, then wet his bottom lip with his tongue. "Jared, please... Don't put that where I can reach it.

Just show me what you'll be using. I need to know you'll be careful with yourself, too. I won't hurt you...if I can help it. I mean that. But you need to understand what you're dealing with. You need to keep yourself safe."

Stepping forward, Rhodey did his best to judge whether that was some kind of threat or if the kid actually...*cared*. Nothing he'd seen out of Noah so far made the latter seem likely, but he'd started to get the sense, more and more, they were dealing with someone he didn't know at all anymore. And it was kinda messing with his head.

"Thank you for letting me know, tiger. You can be assured that I am aware of how quickly you can and cannot move right now relative to myself, but I am happy to make you comfortable by being extra cautious." After plucking up the kit, a plastic sanitary barrier fell away as Jared opened a box. "When we stitch children, they give us rainbow colored sutures. I have been known to practice on myself with them. I'm going to assume you'd prefer standard issue white?"

Brow furrowing, Noah stared at Jared. Like he was weighing every single word. Then a broad smile spread across his lips, lighting up his whole face and brightening his eyes in a way that made him look...kinda sweet. "You're fun. I mean that in a good way, not like fun to fuck with. I'm glad you don't think I'm a child. But I like colors. Use the rainbow. Maybe it'll make this more enjoyable for you, too?" He bit his lip suddenly, shifting a bit and lowering his gaze. "Is it weird if I ask you a question?"

Jared shook his head, gaze on the needle he threaded. "Not at all." He glanced at Noah. "Oh, and I should tell you, I enjoy my work. I don't like causing people pain that they don't like, but medicine has always fascinated me, and you're a fine canvas."

"Yeah?" Noah grinned, and he blew a few curls away from where they'd fallen over his face, fluffier now that they were dry. "Some girls in school told me I was handsome. I wasn't interested in them. I was interested in some of the boys for a while, but I didn't have time for that kind of thing. Dating." The edge of his lips twitched. "I think I'll have more time now. Are you dating anyone?"

"Stay still, tiger. I'm going to work on this longer gash along your shoulder first to stabilize the skin around it before I work on the smaller ones." Regloved, Jared gave Noah a warm look as he inserted the needle in precise movements into the area he'd numbed. "No. I am the one without time to date at the moment. I'm finishing up my specialization and interning nights in a hospital in Maryland. Have you ever been?"

Noah made a face, looking a little frustrated, and Rhodey fought not to laugh. Shoulder against the wall, he folded his arms over his chest, seeing the way Noah changed his approach play out clearly over his face.

The determination in his eyes was almost cute. "A man like you shouldn't be single. You're..." Noah's cheeks reddened. "Well, you know. You've looked in a mirror. I'm glad you're too busy to bother with all the pathetic guys who'd want a piece of you. Stay that way for...at least a couple more years."

Though he'd stitched Rhodey up countless times when they were teens, Jared's sutures had never been so precise as they were now, his fingers moving quickly to align and repair the skin of Noah's back. "As long as you don't force me to date the pathetic ones after? I would like that to be a hard limit for a lifetime, if you don't mind?" Jared winked at Noah. "And I thank you for your compliment."

"Maybe when I'm better I can visit you and discourage anyone from even thinking they have a chance." Noah nodded firmly to himself. "I can be very convincing."

Yeah, they were verging into dangerous territory if Noah was going to start thinking about that kind of 'convincing'.

From what Rhodey knew of both him and his father, they used methods only Vani would approve of.

If Noah was a normal teen, this would be harmless, but he wasn't.

Rhodey glanced at Jared, hoping he wouldn't have to remind him. So far, the exchange had been going well. And he didn't want to mess with the delicate balance his best friend had found with the kid.

"Hmm..." Jared made a thoughtful sound, as though considering how best to answer. "I think when you find the person or persons who are right for you, you don't need to own them. You just trust that they will meet your needs and you meet theirs. It's more of a dance that way, not being constricted. What do you think?"

Noah went quiet for a bit, resting his chin on his arm. He finally inclined his head. "I don't like the idea of owning anyone. Or anyone owning me. But that could be…interesting. Being who someone needs." The shy little smile was back. If the kid kept doing that, Rhodey was gonna have a hard time not liking him. "What do you need, Jared?"

Threading another needle, then applying a little more disinfectant, Jared glanced at Noah. "I guess trust is a big one. Someone intelligent, who likes to read and to play chess would be fulfilling. People who strive to grow, because it makes them not static. More interesting." A smile flitted across his lips as he focused on his work. "Good manners. No swearing. Care for others is another big one."

"Ah…that's…" Noah sighed, turning his head so his face was between his arms, his voice echoing in the space. "A lot, but reasonable. Ugh. Fifteen is a stupid age. We're gonna be playing a lot of chess for a really long time, aren't we?"

"Whenever I'm not deployed? Yes. Absolutely. And reading books, and getting to know each other…and ourselves." Cool blue eyes met Noah's light gray ones when he turned his head. "I promise I won't be nearly as boring as I sound. Do you enjoy any hobbies?"

The look Noah gave Jared as he lifted up on his elbows was incredulous. "Boring? You're not boring. You're... I'm going to learn to love chess and get really good at it. I loved reading...I wouldn't mind having some books in here. Tell me all your favorites so we'll have something to talk about when you visit. You'll visit a lot, right? I won't be fifteen forever."

"I get a weekend a month when I'm deployed." He met Rhodey's gaze. "If you're working hard to stay present and earn privileges, your uncle will send a plane to get me so we can spend that time together. And I'll bring you all the books you want."

Rhodey gave Jared a slight nod, the edge of his lips twitching. He liked the idea of Jared being around more often. And he definitely wanted to be here when his nephew proposed to the man before he hit sixteen. "I've got no problem with that. The visits or the books. So long as it's something other than books about serial killers."

"Books on the psychology aren't bad. I can do without the gruesome details, however. It's much more fascinating to save people than to kill them, I've found in medical school. Much more difficult and challenging." Jared shrugged a little, getting back to work, his posture perfect even when he worked on the edge of a tiny mattress. "Rhodey, I'm going to need something to eat soon. My blood sugar is dropping, and I don't want shaky hands to ruin my work. How about you, tiger? Are you hungry at all? Or have the meds dulled your appetite?"

Noah cocked his head. "I could eat. Maybe we can start with the soup my uncle brought in that thermos he forgot about. Then he can serve us something more substantial." His eyes widened with feigned innocence when Rhodey frowned at him. "What?"

"If you want to show Jared you've got manners, you've got a long way to go. I'm not your fucking servant, kid. 'Please' and 'thank you' are as fucking basic as it gets." Rhodey crossed the room to get the thermos, opening the top and pouring some of the broth into it. He went to Jared's side, holding it for him to take a sip. "I'll go fix up that sandwich for you, my man. But this should help for now."

The way Noah's eyes narrowed at Rhodey was the first indication that his mood was about to snap into the direction Jared had successfully steered him away from. His tone was sharp as he began to move like he planned to get off the bed. "Would you *please* fuck off, uncle? Jared can drink the soup on his own. I'd *thank you* to get up to the damn kitchen and make some real food. You dragged him all the way here just to stand around and let him suffer while dealing with *your* problem?"

"Careful there, tiger." Jared leaned back, the thread and needle still in his fingers, but attached to Noah's skin. "Let's get this line finished before we try to get up. I don't fancy either of us losing an eye to this." Tone even, calm, he waggled the bit of metal between his fingertips. "Rhodey, a sip of the soup would be great, thank you. And I'd hate to trouble you, but coffee with sugar would be heavenly. Noah, please tell me what you'd like to eat and drink?"

Noah's expression softened as his gaze returned to Jared. "I'll let him hold the soup for you if it'll help. I guess I can't do it from here." He carefully lowered back down. "I want what you're having. Thank you."

Rolling his eyes, Rhodey held the makeshift cup close to Jared's lips again. "I hope he keeps up the effort for you, because if he ever throws this kind of attitude your way, this is over. There's no way I'm forcing you to put up with this shit."

That had Noah tensing again. But instead of lashing out, he buried his face between his arms. "Don't. Please…don't make that a condition of him being here. I'll try harder, I promise, but I might…I'll screw up. Ugh…" He rubbed his eyes against his forearm. "It's happening again. Maybe you need to just fucking sedate me before my uncle comes up with a reason to take you away."

"Use the emery board, Noah. Breathe." There was a soothing, almost lyrical quality to Jared's voice. He kept working, as if the moment didn't worry him, but Rhodey saw his sutures multiplied more quickly now. "This is fatiguing for everyone, so we're all going to be as patient as we can for each other." He threw Rhodey a quick look, shaking his head slightly in warning. "Roast beef, rare, on rye bread with Swiss, if you have it, Rhodey. Which, knowing you, my man, you do. Then, when we're finished, I'm going to read to you from *The Hobbit*, one of my favorite books."

The emery board back between his fingers, Noah rubbed his thumb hard over the surface. His breaths were rapid at first, timed with the rubbing. Then slowed a bit as though he'd just absorbed part of what Jared had said and it shifted his train of thought. He peered up at Jared over his arm. "You'll read to me? I'd...like that." He rose up a bit, resting his chin on the palm of his hand. "I don't really like books from the point of view of the serial killer. I read those because of my Dad. And I know talking about him messes with my uncle. He's in control of everything, I need ways to take some of that back." He shifted his gaze to Jared. "Don't let him control you."

Rhodey moved away from the bed, putting away the rest of the soup and giving himself a minute to regain his balance. On some level, he'd known *why* Noah pulled the shit he did, but it was fucking frustrating. And hearing Noah was aware of it too was a total mindfuck. He needed to stop letting the kid get to him.

"Have you ever studied game theory, tiger?" Snipping the last suture, Jared glanced over his work, using light touches to press the skin in various places.

Frowning, Noah shook his head. "No. Is that another book you like? Will I be allowed to read it?"

"There are a great many books on it. It's often used in economics, when trying to outbid a competitor on a contract, for instance. There are other uses, of course, but when you hear about it it's in that context much of the time." Peeling off his gloves, Jared made a small bundle along with the leavings of his work, stashing everything in a small plastic biohazard container to tuck away. Then he sat on the floor to bring himself to Noah's eye level. "You figure out what you want, then pick your best strategy for getting it. Sometimes, corporations have a vested interest in things in addition to profit. Like saving the environment. So they make their plays for control or a contract based on both monetary and environmental considerations. Others only want profit, for their own gain. When you think about what you want from Rhodey, or any relationship, do you usually think of it in terms of yourself only, or a bigger picture? Do you have other considerations?"

The emery board against his lips again, Noah visibly considered the question, looking like he was trying to solve a complicated math equation. "People are threats, obstacles, or allies. I'm the same for them. Only more dangerous. That's why Rhodey needs to stop me. The big picture is...convincing him I'm not, I guess. Except that would be a lie, so...we're stuck." He blew out a breath. "Which sucks."

"I'm going to teach you one of the most valuable—no, *two* of the most valuable, lessons you can ever learn about yourself and people that will help you to set up any board in your favor." Bending one knee, Jared draped his wrist over it. "As long as you're feeling up to it? Would you like some more ginger ale?" He held up the can with the straw so it was level with Noah's lips.

Noah leaned in and took a long sip, making a soft sound of enjoyment. "Thank you for this, by the way. I almost forgot how much I liked it. Stuff like soda. Rhodey gives me juice sometimes as a treat. Mostly just water. Maybe you can convince him to get me root beer one day?" He took another sip from the straw and smiled at Jared, holding his gaze. "I want to learn whatever you want to teach me."

"One." Jared held up one finger. "The word 'yet' is very powerful. You can accomplish anything you set out to in life if you don't limit yourself with absolutes." He leaned in closer, voice going quieter like he shared a secret. "You have not convinced him, *yet*." The second finger went up. "Two, figure out what you have in common with your opponents, and rather than battling them—which is a waste of resources—make them your allies. Or at least less of a threat or obstacle. They might never be your best friend, but they won't use up your energy getting in your way."

The way Jared laid things out seemed to appeal to Noah's intellectual side. His expression was intent, but not calculating, which Rhodey liked seeing. If the kid only had three boxes for people, he'd already put Jared in the 'ally' box.

But be damn nice if he didn't have to put people in boxes at all.

They'd get there. Jared's approach worked better than anything Rhodey'd tried so far.

Reaching out, Noah stopped with his hand just over Jared's. "Can I...? I just want to touch your hand. It feels..." He made a face and drew his hand back. "That's pathetic. I'm sorry. That's good advice about how to deal with people. I'll keep it in mind and work on it."

Flipping his hand palm up, Jared opened his fingers so only the tips curled up. "You may hold my hand anytime you wish. I would enjoy it, tiger. It's not often I have the privilege."

"Really?" Noah stretched his arm out again, placing his hand in Jared's. "No one could say you're weak. Or pathetic. Why do you enjoy it, though? It doesn't serve any purpose."

"It's like the emery board. Only more pleasant." Tipping his head back against the wall, Jared exposed his throat, eyes fluttering closed as he swiped his thumb lightly over Noah's. Back and forth. "Thank you."

The soft smile on Noah's lips was another new one. There

was a tenderness to it. He watched Jared, his expression, his whole body relaxed. "You're welcome." He glanced over at Rhodey, speaking quietly. "Could you…? If you go get the food, I won't move. I want him to rest after what he did for me." His gaze flicked to the med kit. "Take that with you, though? Please?"

Rhodey nodded, stepping over to pick up the med kit and the neat bundle of trash Jared had set aside. "I have root beer if you want some. Your mom told me how much you used to like it." He cleared his throat, not sure what to do with the surprise morphing to sadness in Noah's eyes before he schooled his features. "I won't be long. I'll bring my copy of that book Jared's gonna read you while I'm at it."

That got him a brow raise. "You read?"

"Not in English. And not often. But yeah…" Rhodey let out a quiet laugh on his way out the door. "I can read."

As calm as things were in the room, Rhodey got the food together as fast as he could, putting everything into an empty box he'd used to get supplies the other day. He grabbed a bean bag chair at the last second, wanting to give Jared something more comfortable than the floor to sit on. Arms full, he made his way back to the cell door, using his foot to 'knock'.

There was no answer. And the door didn't open.

Rhodey ground his teeth. "Damn it, get the door for me, boy."

"No." Noah's voice sounded like it was still coming from the other side of the room. He hadn't moved. "That would not be a good idea."

"Oh, shit…your back. Yeah, okay."

"Not because of that."

Was the kid already trying to fuck with him again? Rhodey let out an irritated growl and dropped the bean bag chair. He opened the door, using his foot to drag the thing inside. "Then why the fuck—?"

Noah stared at him. "Close the door."

Chapter Seventeen

PAST

"Don't tell me what to do, nephew." Rhodey strode across the room, leaving the door wide open. "I'm still in charge, let's not forget that."

"He's asking you not to tempt him. Close the door, husky." Jared kept his gaze locked with Noah's, still holding his hand. "You're drawing an acceptable boundary. I'm impressed, tiger. Very well done."

Lips parted, Rhodey looked from Jared to Noah, putting the box down by the bed, then going to the door to close it. He rubbed the back of his neck. "I thought we were working on trust. It wasn't a test."

Lashes wet, Noah inhaled several long, deep breaths and shook his head. "*I* don't trust me. I need…more time." He wiped his eyes, blinking a few times before turning his focus to Jared. "You meant that. You…were impressed? It was a small thing. Why should it matter?"

"Trust happens in the small things. It's not built by grand gestures that are flashy and often cost us very little." Gravel in his voice, Jared cleared his throat like he was as moved by the moment as Noah, though for different reasons. "Those little things build a foundation over time, and they prove you are paying attention to details. Not only the large, easy to spot things. You knew yourself well enough to ask for help. That takes courage. Awareness. And trust in the person you're asking to help you."

Sitting on the floor, Rhodey dragged the box closer and started dishing out the food and drinks. "I'm gonna tell you something, Noah. It might come as a shock, but…" He took the top off the plastic bottle of root beer, then handed the soda to his nephew. "I make mistakes. I'm not perfect. You telling me stuff like that? It helps a lot. Then I know where your limits are and you can learn mine. I'd feel a lot better if I knew we were working on this together."

Noah wrinkled his nose, awkwardly trying to tip the bottle to his lips, like one of the limits he'd apparently reached was asking for help. "I was with you until you brought up feelings. You feeling anything besides irritated about this whole situation doesn't fit in my head."

"Here." Jared poked the straw from the ginger ale into the root beer, then sat back to take the sandwich Rhodey offered, never letting go of Noah's hand. "Your uncle's default is irritation. It's like the asphalt of his emotions. He paves over all of the hard stuff with it so he can drive right on past."

"Thank you." The edge of Noah's lips twitched as he pulled the straw between them. "That makes sense. And it's practical. I like practical."

Shaking his head, Rhodey took a big bite of his sandwich, chewing and swallowing before he spoke so he wouldn't touch on Jared's sore spot about lousy manners. "He's not wrong, but it's more complicated than that. People have layers, Noah. Yeah, sometimes this whole thing pisses me off. But do you think I'd've kept trying for this long if I didn't—"

"Stop." Noah almost dropped the bottle of soda. "I don't need your reasons. They won't make sense to me. I need to… just know you'll be able to do what you need to. And I'll do my part. I'll get better at it. But I'm still *this*. You're opening yourself up for damage if you forget what I am, uncle. So stop."

"May I ask a question?" Half his sandwich already uncharacteristically wolfed down, Jared made a happy noise as he leaned back against the wall.

Noah pulled the straw between his lips again, giving Jared an expectant look. "Aside from the one you just did?"

"Well played." Jared grinned at him for his cheek, taking another, more careful bite of his sandwich. "Yes."

Rolling his eyes at them both, Rhodey polished off his sandwich and got started on the bowl of kettle chips. He slid another bowl over to Jared, this one full of the pepper chips he used to love so much. "Just fucking ask, damn it. The both of you enjoy hearing yourselves talk way too much."

"Perhaps we just enjoy hearing you grumble." Popping his brows, Jared crunched on a chip and moaned. "As good as I remembered. Remember when the price of a bag seemed like an entire paycheck?" Swallowing, he shook his head and refocused on Noah. "So, the question for you, tiger, is why it feels good to connect with me but not with Rhodey? I have a theory, but I'd rather know for certain."

Bottle set on the floor, Noah turned his attention to picking the meat out of his sandwich. He chewed on a large piece, his expression back to the math quiz one. "If anything happens, if I stay...all wrong in my head, he will be the one who has to make the hard decision to end this. People who care can't make hard decisions without breaking part of who they are. This makes it easier. You wouldn't be happy about it, but...I hope you'd be able to forgive him one day." He shrugged. "It would be silly not to."

For the first time since he'd arrived, Jared's full spectrum of emotion played over his face as Noah spoke. By the time the kid finished, Jared's skin had mottled and his eyes sheened. "You're no fool, Noah, but I'll revise that assessment if you ever say again it wouldn't crush both of us irreparably were that to come to pass. There's a difference between not caring and doing what we have to. Your uncle and I—" He shared a watery glance with Rhodey, emotions he'd never been allowed to display with Maddox right there on the surface, like he reveled in them now with the freedom to experience them fully. "—we never had it easy, so we don't waste our time on things we don't care about. No matter what you think of our ways of expressing it. It might make you damned uncomfortable to know it, but what you do? It matters to people. It has an effect on people. Because you matter. To both of us."

This was one of those times Rhodey was damn grateful Jared had gotten the fuck away from Maddox. Somewhere, deep inside, Noah's view of what strength and weakness was, his view of himself, fucking hurt Rhodey worse than any bullet. But he'd been taught how to manage those emotions. The kid wasn't wrong, he *would* be capable of doing whatever he had to. And it wouldn't destroy him.

It would never be *easy*, though.

But explaining that would only confirm Noah's way of thinking. Which wasn't healthy. And wasn't what he needed from anyone.

Noah glanced at Rhodey, his gaze assessing. Then he looked at Jared. "You're right. It's very uncomfortable. Can I just put all feelings as another boundary? This was a lot more fun before we had to deal with them. I can't make you not care. I just…don't get it. And I'm not sure I want to. It's not useful."

"*Yet.*" Giving Noah a lopsided grin, Jared ate two more chips, washing them down with a sip of coffee. "But I agree. Feelings can take a backseat for the rest of the day. We have a book to read, as long as you don't mind my eating these chips and reading at the same time. They're my drug of choice."

Grinning back at Jared, Noah shook his head. "No, I don't mind at all. I like the sound of your voice. But before we start, I want to ask you…" He took a deep breath. "My answer wasn't what you expected. It upset you. Please don't let me do that? And...tell me what you think the issue is. With me and Rhodey. Maybe it's part of his layers. You both have them I guess. It's fascinating."

"The risk of caring about someone is that you'll get hurt, by accident or on purpose, by things they say or do. You thinking that you could disappear from my life and it wouldn't matter, especially when you have gifts you don't see in yourself yet, is painful." Chips forgotten, Jared launched into his explanation in a rush, not hesitating for a second to answer Noah. "And it makes me sad that you haven't had the opportunity to know the man your uncle is because of circumstance. I want that for you, someday. It would be wonderful to see where you go, what you become, and to watch you discover who he is."

The silence stretched as Noah stared at Jared, like he was trying to make sense of his words. And it was clear they'd hit their mark by the way Noah's throat worked. He bowed his head, tugging at the edge of the sheet, like he wanted to make wiping his eyes discrete and doing a terrible job of it. "Thank you. I...appreciate you explaining that to me. Maybe it'll... help me not hurt you again. I don't like hurting good people."

"Remember that, when you're struggling to think of good things about yourself." Giving him a small smile, Jared leaned in and brushed a soft kiss against Noah's cheek before he leaned back. "We've got you. It won't be easy, but we're in this together."

Noah lifted his hand to his cheek, right where Jared had kissed, his expression a bit bewildered. The kid didn't seem to know what to do with affection. Which Rhodey hadn't been much help with, but was fucked up because he couldn't see Tracey not having been affectionate with her son. Crawford had somehow managed to steal that away from both of them. More damage that would take a lot to repair.

He sensed Noah watching him and shook his head. "Don't ask."

"I don't have to." Noah reached out to steal one of Jared's chips, addressing him instead. "My uncle doesn't expect very much from me. What he did…he didn't know whether or not it would work. It must have, because I don't want to torture him anymore. And I don't want to torture you at all. You wouldn't think I was worth the effort if you'd met me a couple months ago."

Holding up another chip to Noah's lips, Jared shook his head. "I know all about torture, and I don't believe in easy. Except when it comes to exams. I'm far too smart to be learning from half the jokers teaching my classes, but they make me jump through hoops. I see the end goal, so I jump. You, however, are a prize worth the fight."

Noah carefully caught the chip between his teeth, pulling it into his mouth with his lips. He let out a happy little hum as he chewed. "These really are good. And I'm not surprised to hear you're smarter than them. Goals I understand. And I can respect. I respect you a lot. Maybe…I can have goals one day. Besides becoming…a real boy."

Humor sparkled in Jared's gaze, turning his eyes into a winter landscape on a sunny day. "It's a good thing I already nicknamed you. Pinnochio isn't half as good as tiger, but it would've stuck." He held up two chips, taking one for himself and offering the other to Noah. "Thank you for your respect. You have more goals than you think, but you probably ignore them because they never felt possible. We can daydream together."

"I'd like that." Noah ate the chip, then glanced at the bean bag chair. "I think my uncle brought that for you, but he should sit on it and you should lie down on the bed with me to read. You'll be able to stretch out. I'll be a perfect gentleman, I promise."

Rhodey lifted his brow, catching Jared's eye. "Hmm. If not for the last part, I'd probably have to object, but whatever you're most comfortable with, my man."

"It couldn't hurt for a bit. I've been cramped up on that plane. Next time, I demand a jet. That thing was a two-seater. My knees were in my face." Clearly joking, Jared hopped to his feet, scooping up the book from the pile of items Rhodey had left on the floor, which included a blanket he took with him to the bed. He eyed Noah. "Can you scooch over without hurting yourself, tiger?"

Hands under his shoulders, Noah nodded as he pushed up, carefully moving himself to the other side of the bed to give Jared space. He lowered back down, panting a little as sweat beaded at his temples. "There. I didn't ruin your work, did I? Is it still pretty?"

Weird thing to say about stitches, but not one of the more concerning things the kid had ever said, so Rhodey let it go, rising himself to position the bean bag chair near the head of the bed and plunk down on it. The thing had originally been for Noah, but he'd gotten it big enough that he could sink in and get pretty good support. He'd never had anything like this before, but...he kinda liked it.

"Hmm..." Jared ran light fingertips over a patch of unsutured skin, the rainbow colors of the thread winking playfully as Noah's back twitched. "They'll hold up as long as you don't get too active. Thank you for taking care with my work, and with yourself." He sat on the edge of the bed to kick off his loafers, then positioned the white quilt over Noah's lower half before joining him. "Have you read Tolkien before?"

Noah shook his head. "No, but my mom read a bit of him to me when I was young. When my father was away more often. She had all kinds of books and I was able to read any one I wanted. We spent a lot of time just sitting quietly together with our own books. It was nice. But..." He frowned and shook his head. "That's something a child does. I guess it's okay now because I'm injured. And you offered."

Lifting his head from the pillow, Jared frowned at Noah with mock affrontery. "I can't believe you just called my favorite pastime childish." He winked to soften his words. "I have half a mind to do nothing but read to you from now on."

If Rhodey didn't know better, he'd have sworn the sound Noah made was a giggle.

But he was probably imagining things.

The bright smile on Noah's lips was definitely real, though. "If you do it, it's got to be adult and manly and all that. I stand corrected." He lowered his voice, for some weird reason, like he was afraid someone outside of this room might hear him. "I would never tell my father he's wrong about something, but...I'm glad he was. About this. My mother was sad when he got rid of all her books. I hated that. I..." His expression closed off abruptly. "Nevermind."

"Too many feelings to want to share at once?" Head turned on the pillow, Jared held the book against his bent knees, opened to the first page.

Noah nodded and pressed his face against Jared's shoulder. "Yes. And bad ones start making things dark. I don't want to go there. I don't want you to see me like that. I want to stay here with you."

"I have a trick for when you don't have an emery board." Fanning the pages, Jared made the book rustle. "Tell me one thing you hear, one you smell, taste, touch, and see."

Not moving his head from what looked like his new favorite spot, Noah spoke into Jared's arm. "I hear Rhodey hardly breathing because he doesn't want you to see it either. Tell him that's not at all helpful."

"Especially because if he passes out from lack of oxygen, he's gotten too big for me to scrape off the floor." Jared slid him a sideways look, not turning his head. "Breathe, man. We're all fine over here."

Thankfully, Rhodey could tell that they were. For now, anyway. He let out a noisy breath, grumbling a little because he couldn't stop himself. "Since you like honesty so much, here's one for you, kid. It's creepy when you do that. It's fine if you keep some observations to yourself."

Lifting his head a little, Noah glanced up at Jared. "Do I have to? I'm not doing it to be creepy. I'm doing it because I thought paying attention was good. And being aware keeps things balanced."

"Paying attention is excellent, and asking for help is heroic. Perhaps a color system." Jared met Rhodey's gaze, likely thinking of something completely age inappropriate, but making sure that its adaptation wouldn't freak him out further. "Or numbers. You get to a five and we know you need serious intervention. At three, we try some of my tactics. If we check in with you and you're at one, then you're okay."

Noah looked so relieved it was a little hard to watch him and accept such a simple solution would've done a lot of good from the start. He rubbed his cheek against Jared's shoulder and let out a soft sigh, actually sounding a little bit like a tiger cub when he adjusted with a huff. "Yes, please. I can't always see it coming, but if you can help me stop from going there... I'd really appreciate it. Some topics are an automatic ten and it's too late, but five...I could come back from a five."

"Is there a way for you to safely give us a list of the automatic tens? Or is even thinking about them too much?" Book folded over his index finger, Jared gave his full attention to Noah.

Head tucked almost completely under Jared's arm, Noah spoke in a whisper. "Seven. I can't..."

"Good boy. I'm going to kiss the top of your head." Jared's tone was so gentle it was hard to believe he didn't speak to a very young child. He pressed a kiss on top of Noah's crown, briefly burying his nose in his curls. "Such a brave thing to say. Thank you."

Staying where he was, knowing what those numbers meant, took all of Rhodey's strength. He made sure not to stop breathing again, resisting the urge to order Jared away from the small, sweet looking piece of dynamite he was holding. But he was prepared to move if the fuse ended up lit.

Whether Jared likes it or not.

Progress was one thing. But Jared's safety wasn't something he was gonna mess with.

"Talk." Noah made an irritated sound, more petulant than dangerous. "You're both making this weird. I just need…just talk."

Opening the book, Jared began to read. His deep voice took on an almost lyrical quality, caressing each word like poetry. Words in a rhythmic pulse, then paragraphs becoming pictures, their colors and sounds a soothing music. Adjusting his arm, he gave Noah a larger section of himself, exposing his flank and running his free palm up and down Noah's arm as he read.

Without being asked, Noah glanced up at Jared a chapter in, his tone holding a note of awe. "Two. And it…really works. I didn't fall in."

Which earned him a kiss to his forehead and a warm look from Jared. "It's very nice to have you here."

"It's nice to have you, too." Noah closed his eyes. "I think Rhodey likes it almost as much as I do. He's still on edge, but not as much. Maybe when you're here for a bit, he'll get down to a two. And actually sleep."

Rhodey huffed, shaking his head. "I sleep. And I'm not on edge."

Wrong thing to say. Noah glared at him. "Five. Don't lie."

"Rhodey, your definition of sleep and relaxation has always been sideways to normal, and Noah might not realize this." Turning the page, Jared gave Noah a small mischievous smile. "He can't help being strange. He grew up with me."

Noah wiggled into Jared a bit more, letting out another huff. "Then he was really lucky. But I guess I can be patient with him. You are and you've put up with him for a lot longer."

"Would it help to know he's saved my life more than once?" Placing the book, open, on top of his bent knee, Jared settled back into the pillow.

Eyes locked on Jared's face, Noah stared at him, unblinking. His brow furrowed as he finally nodded. "Yes. You're worth saving. Not many people are. He risks his life a lot for stupid people. I don't have much tolerance for things like that. It's a waste."

Was the kid saying he wanted Rhodey to be more careful? That he worried about him?

Don't be an idiot. He's mocking you.

Only...the kid wasn't using that tone he did when he mocked Rhodey.

He's not exactly shy about it.

Nodding once, which could've been agreement or acquiescence to Noah's point, Jared lifted the book again. He raised his brows in question. "Shall I continue?"

"Yes, please." If Noah moved any closer to Jared, he'd be lying right on top of him. But apart from his awkward flirting earlier, he didn't seem to be doing anything to get an inappropriate kind of attention from the man. He was just a lot more cuddly than expected. "Do you need a drink first?"

"No, thank you, but are you thirsty? Those meds can give you one hell of a cottonmouth." Jared already reached for the root beer. "Here." He held the straw to Noah's lips. "Sip."

How quickly Noah responded, obeying almost automatically, had Rhodey wishing his nephew was a bit older. But it was fucked up to think about how surrendering different kinds of control might help. This, just being cared for in a way he welcomed, from someone he'd formed an immediate connection with, was already making a huge difference. They'd deal with an older, stronger Noah when the time came.

Fuck, I hope he doesn't end up as big as me. We might need an actual zoo.

His lips twitched as he pictured it. Which didn't go much

further than Jared in a safari outfit that wouldn't suit him at all.

Setting the soda back on the floor next to the bed, Jared caught Rhodey's eye with a frown. Then shook his head. "Whatever you're thinking, stop. The last time you had that look, I ended up stealing Bobby Flak's pet snake and putting it in Lysle Hurley's locker."

Which hadn't ended well for Jared. A month of detention had definitely been excessive.

"A snake? Those are beautiful. What kind was it?" Noah rose up, a little too fast, like he'd gotten excited and forgotten about his back. Stopping short, he sucked in a breath. His eyes teared as he shook his head. "I didn't mean to. Please don't stop reading. I'll be still. It's fine. I didn't ruin your work."

"Shhh, love." Sitting up, Jared didn't set the book aside. "You're who I'm worried about, not my work. Let me see." He settled Noah against the mattress, running gentle fingers down his shoulder. "Rhodey, hand me the white tube from the med kit. I'll give him a topical and take out the IV since he's had the full bag of fluids." Adjusting his position so he sat on the edge of the bed, he straightened Noah's arm across his lap. "A piece of gauze and some tape, too, please."

Rhodey nodded, pushing off the bean bag and stepping out of the cell to fetch the med kit. He closed the door behind him, then opened it and closed it again when he returned. In any other circumstances, this shit might be overkill, but since he had a better idea of *why* Noah needed that from him, he didn't mind the extra steps.

He went to the side of the bed, opening the med kit and handing Jared the supplies he'd asked for. His tone was a bit gruff as he glanced down at Noah, all tense again. It was hard to see how quickly he ended up back here. "Stitches can be tricky. Next time, we'll make sure you don't need so many."

That got him a cold look. "Six. If you're serious about helping me? You'll do it. Just like this. When I need it."

"You know what they have absolutely the worst version of in military med school?" Holding gauze over the IV port, Jared pressed down on Noah's elbow and pulled out the plastic needle. "Ice cream. It's full of air and too much sugar. I don't think there's real milk in it. I haven't had a decent sundae in a year." He applied tape over the gauze, then bent Noah's elbow by his side. "I think it can be a retroactive payment for me stealing that python. You'd better get some peanut butter sauce and M&Ms too. Whipped cream."

Attention shifting from where he might actually have been picturing Rhodey as the one under a whip, Noah watched Jared, his expression softening and his lips curving slightly. "That sounds delicious. You should…go visit my mom one day. She used to make her own ice cream in one of those old-fashioned machines. I bet she's doing it again…" He trailed off, then met Jared's eyes. "Don't talk about me going to visit her. That's almost a ten."

"I've never met your mother, but I helped Rhodey figure out how to find her." Dabbing lidocaine on Noah's back, Jared bent over his work. "Do you think she'd like me? I don't know if I'll get to meet her, but if she makes ice cream, then I'll have to make it a priority to try someday."

Closing his eyes, Noah went almost motionless. Which was concerning until the small, soft smile appeared again. "She'll love you. She's somewhere safe. Rhodey told me. A place like she always wanted. I didn't want to hear about it before. But I like imagining you with her. She'd hug you a lot. And talk to you about all kinds of stuff. And feed you every delicious thing she can think of. She's nice. You will meet her. You deserve to."

"I'd like that very much." Jared capped the tube, placing it on the floor near the bed and picked up the book again before he settled next to Noah. "Comfy?"

"Mhm." Noah opened his eyes, nodding even though he

wiggled over again, plastering himself to Jared. "Are you? This is…it's okay?"

"Better than okay." Lips twisting, he shot Rhodey a wry look. "Though I can't promise not to fall asleep mid-page." He glanced back at Noah, using the hand that held the book to push his glasses up on his nose. "You'll need to wake me if I nod off. I don't wish to be rude."

Noah gave him a serious nod, as though he'd been given an important mission. "I'm on it."

Two pages later, he was the one fast asleep, letting out more soft, contented sounds Rhodey'd never heard before.

Maybe it's the drugs.

"Come on." Rhodey pushed to his feet and stretched. "I'll let you crash in my bed while you're here." His lips quirked. "And I'll be a gentleman, too."

Gently extricating himself from Noah's side, Jared left the book on the bed, a clear promise of his return. He tiptoed out with Rhodey, waiting until the door was closed before he answered. "If you don't have both of us naked and fucking each other's mouths in ten minutes, I'll be pissed."

All right, Rhodey could definitely go with plan B. He pulled out the key to lock the cell, casting Jared a hooded look. "I figured you were getting your fill of high quality medical ass at that school. Your pick of Army studs. How can I compete?"

"By shutting up." Backing Rhodey up to the wall, Jared slanted their mouths together in a crashing mess of a kiss that was all need and zero finesse.

Like he'd gotten nothing but writer's cramp and self-inflicted hand jobs for all the time they'd been apart. Which might've been smarter than Rhodey with his homicidal exes, but with Maddox controlling so much of his life for so long, like fuck wouldn't he gorge a little when he could.

Besides, this gave him the perfect opportunity to show his gratitude to Jared.

With something more than a sandwich.

Chapter Eighteen

PAST

Rhodey dug his fingers into muscles thickened since the last time he'd held this man, sliding his hands down Jared's back to take in the newness. And the familiar. He continued down to his ass, squeezing as he pressed the length of his erection against Jared's through their clothes. "Fuck, this body. I didn't think it could get any more perfect, but… Upstairs. Now. Or I'm going to fuck you in front of my nephew's cell. Which will be an eleven and neither of us will get any sleep."

"Your sense of humor is sick." Biting Rhodey's lower lip hard enough to draw blood, Jared headed up the stairs two at a time, shedding clothes as he went. First his shirt, a few buttons popping off and bouncing down the stairs, then his belt, which hit the kitchen floor with a slither and thud. "I hope you have lube. We're going to need lots."

Moving in complete silence, Rhodey crept up behind Jared without warning and whispered in his ear. "I have some, but if it's not enough, we've always been good at improvising. I happen to keep a lot of coconut oil I bet would taste amazing on your ass."

"As long as it's not melted marshmallow again. That's a

hard limit." Jared kicked off his jeans, stumbling backward and catching himself on the bedroom door frame. "No matter how good you tasted, I thought I was going to turn into a Campfire Girl."

Rhodey spat out a laugh, shoving Jared the rest of the way into the room and onto his bed. Fuck, the man looked good there. "Shut up about the fucking marshmallow. And Campfire Girls. And anything other than how fucking turned on you are just thinking about what I'm going to do to you."

Grabbing his wrist, Jared slapped Rhodey's palm over his dick, thrusting upward into his grip. The hard length of him was all flesh and no underwear. He'd gone commando. "Whatever you're going to do, do it so I can have my turn. I'm not gonna go easy on you. Fair warning, you'll have to struggle to walk tomorrow."

"Promises, promises." Rhodey pulled off his shirt, tossing it somewhere in the general direction of the hamper. He undid his jeans, hoping he could keep the man's focus on his dick instead of the tattoo he'd never seen. Leaning over Jared, Rhodey grazed his teeth along his jaw. Raked his fingers into hair too short to get a good grip on. He nipped Jared's bottom lip and let out a soft growl. "I'm gonna need to stash you away someday to grow this back. I miss how good it feels, holding it while I'm fucking you."

Using both hands at Rhodey's hips, Jared shoved his jeans past the swell of his ass. Fabric brushed roughly over sensitive areas, Jared not slowing down to make sure he didn't damage the fun bits before Rhodey got a chance to use them. "Were your jeans always this tight? Or are you just happy to see me?"

"I'm obviously happy to see you." Rhodey pushed forward, aligning his dick with Jared's and wrapping both in his hand, stroking them together. He spit to make the strokes a bit more slick. "I need to stop buying clothes off the rack. Never fits this big body of mine quite right."

Jared made an incoherent sound, either a grunt of

agreement or appreciation. He slid his hand between Rhodey's ass cheeks, hitting his mark with practiced ease and sinking two fingers without lube or mercy. "God. Fuck, yes." His concession to swearing prolifically during sex reared—something Maddox had never even attempted to train out of either of them. "You're going to feel so fucking good."

A slight nod was all Rhodey could manage as he thrust his length against Jared's, trying to breathe and take deep, bruising tastes of his mouth at the same time. He groaned at the burning stretch, a sensation he hadn't felt in a very long time. "You're fucking lucky. I don't let just anyone do that. I get to be in control." He smirked against Jared's lips. "But I don't mind letting you pretend now and then. Only you."

Teeth clacking against Rhodey's, Jared grinned. His laugh gusted warmly, giving back the air he'd taken with another deep kiss. "Only you." He pulled back, meeting Rhodey's eyes, his own growing a shade more serious. "For anything. I don't need a condom."

"Jared..." Rhodey held Jared's gaze, ready to tell him all the reasons they couldn't let things get complicated. But not now. Fuck, he needed this. He needed one damn person near him who didn't want to see him bleed—in a not-so-fun way. Bleeding for Jared was a whole different story. A lazy smile slid across Rhodey's lips. "I have to get tested a lot for...reasons. So we're good. Take what you want."

A starved expression ghosted Jared's eyes, the same specter of need Rhodey identified within himself. "Lube?" Withdrawing his fingers, he sat up, glancing around the room like he saw it for the first time—probably not very well with how his glasses didn't quite sit on his nose. "Where?"

Gesturing vaguely toward the boxes he used as a nightstand, Rhodey shifted up the bed a bit so he could stretch out more comfortably. "In the top one. Other than the bed, I don't have much set up for me. I was...focused on the kid. I thought things would be—yeah. Later. I can't wrap my brain around taking care of anyone right now besides you."

Half-flopped over Rhodey, Jared reached for the box, dragging the tube into his fingers and flipping the cap. He turned his head, the shaft of sunlight toying with the edge of the curtains catching his eyes. The tender look his best friend threw his way had no place in what they were about to do. In the next instant, Jared seemed ready to prove exactly that. A feral smile stretched to expose his canines. He pulled off his glasses, carelessly tossing them aside.

"Me first." Rolling and dipping at the same time, he nipped hard at the inside of Rhodey's thigh, not stopping until he had his face buried at the apex. Heat and slick moisture speared Rhodey's hole, Jared using his tongue to do the job of the apparently forgotten lube. His approval came in the form of a warm hum, then a growl. "Yes. Mine."

Tipping his head back into the pillows, Rhodey let out a soft, breathless laugh, his blood doing a damn quick job of leaving his brain to slam down into his throbbing dick. The urge to grip it, to get himself off, was strong, but that would be too fast. He ignored the ache spreading out from his balls, parting his thighs a bit more to give Jared better access. When he did reach down, it was to put his hand on the back of Jared's head to urge him on. "Fuck, that tongue of yours. I always knew it was good for more than verbally slicing people to pieces. God…you're good at that."

Saliva ran down the fleshy curve of Rhodey's ass, from his hole to the sheet, Jared sparing no inch of the sensitive surrounding skin from the pleasure offered by his teeth, lips, and tongue. Hands gripped, fingers dug in, Jared hanging on tight as he nudged Rhodey's sac with his nose. Nuzzling his seam with his lips to suck his balls much more gently into his mouth, he toyed lower with his fingertips in whisper-light caresses.

"Don't tease me, you bastard." Rhodey huffed out another

laugh, bringing his hand down a bit more, stretching so he could latch on to the back of Jared's neck. "My dick's feeling neglected. I think I remember you saying something about wanting it in your mouth. Or that might've been the voice in my head. Either way, do it. I want to see those sexy lips around my cock."

Jared rolled his eyes up to meet Rhodey's gaze, pulling off his sac with a satisfying slurp as he sank three fingers into Rhodey's ass. "Well, we can't have that. You feeling neglected, husky, is the last thing I want."

Curving his fingers, he nailed Rhodey's prostate, dipping to take him in one smooth glide to the back of his throat all at once. The hum of approval he let out went from Rhodey's dick all the way down to his toes.

A rush of sensations swerved through Rhodey like a getaway car on a rain-soaked street. Bowing his back, he clenched every muscle to get a secure hold on his body's reactions. He moved his hands to his sides, gripping the sheets and gritting his teeth against a shout. Speaking, breathing, probably sounded like he was getting a slow kind of torture. "Yeah...like that. Jared... Just like that."

Taking the cue, Jared swallowed, then swallowed again, working Rhodey's dick past the back of his throat in waves of increasing pressure. His fingertips pressed and caressed deep inside, stimulating just enough to keep him right on the edge. Neither shoving him toward release or pulling him away from it.

Long past when any lesser mortal would've passed out from lack of oxygen, Jared rose up, taking several ragged, gasping breaths. Then went right back for seconds.

Those kiss reddened lips wrapped around the thickness of his dick was a sight Rhodey would never get tired of. Usually, if he got with anyone like this, naked and the least bit vulnerable, they'd be tied up and he'd just fuck their mouth until he was ready to fuck their ass. It should've given him a clue things weren't all that great with his last partner. They'd never shared this kind of trust.

But with Jared, Rhodey didn't have to have the part of his brain—so fucking keyed to any threats—on high alert. He sank a bit deeper into the mattress, zoning out on the pleasure, whispering words he hoped were tender. Or sexy. Or at least coherent.

"Need to—" Kissing up Rhodey's shaft, Jared gripped himself, the pressure he applied to his balls obvious as he staved off his own orgasm. "You're too damned sexy. The taste of you. That look on your face—" He breathed deep, gaze locked on Rhodey, and jacked himself a couple times. "Yeah." He groaned. "That one... Tell me. Tell me you want me to fuck you, husky. Tell me you missed this so fucking much. As much as I did."

Reaching down, Rhodey wrapped his hand around Jared's wrist, yanking his hand off his dick and tugging Jared over him. He trapped him between his thighs, locking one calf over the back of Jared's to keep him in place as he slammed their lips together. Rhodey didn't give a damn where Jared's had just been. He would take every inch of him, however he could have him. "Fuck me, Jared. That dick gets nothing unless it's inside me. Don't make me remind you who's better at snatching up all the control. Enjoy what I give you."

"You're an imperious bastard." The hooded look Jared gave him as he nudged against Rhodey's hole belied the bite of his words. He gripped the still-open lube that had miraculously not jizzed itself all over the bedspread, and reached between them to squeeze it over the length of his shaft. "I'm going to enjoy watching this. Watching you take every inch of my dick."

Rhodey let out a rough sound of agreement. "Good. I like it when you enjoy yourself. I'm very entertaining." His lips curved as his gaze trailed over Jared, his skin much paler than his own, only the muscles stacking his body, almost as big as

Rhodey's, keeping him from looking delicate. "I need to fuck you outside while we're here. You need some sun."

Lip between his teeth, Jared kept his focus on the press of his dick against Rhodey's hole. "You'll ruin my chance to play a vampire in some teen drama." The stretch and burn were part of a slow invasion, Jared taking him inch by agonizing inch. "Fuck, you're tight." Gripping Rhodey's dick with his free hand, sweat beading on his forehead, Jared stroked him with the same maddening slowness. "Want this. Just like this. Forever."

"Jared…" Rhodey couldn't do much more than say his best friend's name, but seemed like a good enough answer. He panted, riding out the pain that was a lot more intense than he remembered. Gasping out a laugh, he pressed his eyes shut. "I swear your dick got bigger in med school. Fuck… Don't stop, but…*fuck*."

"You hurt so pretty for me, husky." Jared's voice held more than a little awe, and Rhodey could feel his searching gaze. "Thank you. I've got you." Thighs met, pelvises snugged together as Jared seated himself the last few inches with the same slow glide. "For you. All of this." Panting now, sweat dripped onto Rhodey's stomach as Jared braced himself and rolled his hips before slamming home. "So fucking good."

Rhodey grunted, sucking in air through his teeth, gliding into the space where pain and pleasure melded together. The side of him that craved all the power wanted to twist around, bring Jared under him. But another side, the one he let take over now, reveled in the vision of Jared in a more dominant position. He'd always had it in him, they both had, but honing it on one another had made it something more.

"Look at you." Rhodey brought a hand up to brush his fingers over Jared's sweat slicked cheek. "So fucking fierce. It's hot. I need to see this, one day, with someone…someone who can surrender more than I can. Will you let me?"

Pupils already blown ate up the last of the blue in Jared's gaze, the hunger and need turning carnivorous with Rhodey's suggestion. A throaty growl accompanying his, "Yes," Jared moved into a rhythm that slapped their bodies together, his forearms caging Rhodey's thighs and shoving them high to expose the thickness of biceps that had seen more than basic training. "Fuck. Yes."

Pleasure stole anything else Rhodey might've said, his hips rising automatically to meet Jared's thrusts, taking him in deeper. Harder. He let out another growl, lust and arousal tangling around him like so many vines, leaving him nowhere to find any relief. As much as he wanted this to last, the fiery sensations building up were hauling him over the edge.

He grabbed Jared's neck, jerking him close, refusing to go without him. "Come when I do. I want to feel it. I want to see how much you've been waiting for this moment."

Tenderness warring with lust and battling pain culminated in a feral kind of bliss to claim Jared's expression. Gaze locked with Rhodey's, he rolled his hips to perfect the angle of their bodies so he caught the sweet spot deep inside. Words weren't required, as the movements tightened to short, sharp shocks of sensation. Winding the world on its axis, tilting everything toward one inevitable point.

There had been maybe a handful of times in Rhodey's life he'd come without his dick being touched. Not all had been pleasant, but this…this tossed him into a space where everything was heat and haziness and pure fucking bliss. He wrapped his arms around Jared, holding him close enough so he could feel him everywhere, soak in every jerk, every muffled cry, and add it to everything else he was feeling.

Forgetting to breathe while he was giving Jared long, drugging kisses had him more than a little dizzy. He didn't mind it, though. Wasn't like he'd be shooting at anything tonight.

Lips and teeth nuzzled Rhodey's neck, Jared's love bites leaving stinging heat in their wake. His rhythm faltered, growing frantic, the fingers he dug into Rhodey's hip a signal as he dragged over his prostate in strokes that seemed never to quite leave that spot. A gasp, head thrown back, the corded muscles in Jared's neck exposed, were about as much of a warning as the man seemed able to give.

Overstimulated already, Rhodey only added to his own discomfort as he tightened around Jared. But it was worth it. He smirked against Jared's lips, flicking his tongue over the bottom one. "I should keep you here. Inside me. Until you get hard again. Wouldn't that be nice?"

The incoherent word Jared growled sounded like *asshole* but it was hard to tell, because it morphed into a shout as his features screwed up into an expression of pure bliss. Mouth forming a perfect *O*, he stiffened in Rhodey's arms, shuddering again and again.

"Mmm, I love seeing you like this." Rhodey relaxed into the mattress, trailing his fingers up and down Jared's back, over muscles still hard from riding out the waves of his release. They were both sticky and slick and it was a strangely wonderful way to be, with limbs wrapped together, the feel of Jared's pulse all over. He huffed a laugh. "Didn't I tell you this was a great bed? We can keep testing it out all night. It won't break."

Jared's "Unpf..." sounded promising.

Collapsing his weight along Rhodey's torso, the evidence of Jared's orgasm lubed the place where their bodies joined to the point his dick slipped free. Flopping over onto his back, he breathed deep, even breaths, his eyes still closed.

"I'm going to need a minute, or you'll be fucking a ragdoll." A weak chuckle followed Jared's admission. "But you might like that."

Rolling his eyes, Rhodey pushed up on his good arm to lean over Jared and kiss his stupid mouth. "I can't feel a rag doll struggling not to fall apart when I'm fucking them..." All right, that sounded strange. "Or, I'm guessing anyway? I won't be finding out, thanks. You said a minute, right? Standard time?"

The back of Jared's forearm thumped against Rhodey's ribs. "Which planet? Jupiter has very long minutes."

"You know I don't know shit about that kinda stuff." Rhodey bit Jared's bottom lip hard, just to make him pay a bit for being an idiot and way too smart all at once. "Does the sun have short minutes?"

"Good question." Jared opened one eye, flicking his tongue over the spot Rhodey had bitten. "It's pretty huge. But it spins fast." He didn't sound quite as intelligent in his lust-drunk haze. "But it doesn't have days. It is the day." Waving his hand in a vague motion, he let it flop back to the mattress. "I think it rotates all the way around in twenty-seven days." He squinted, nodding. "Yeah. A minute would be longer on the sun."

Rhodey shrugged and pushed off the bed, walking across the room naked to the adjoining bathroom as he spoke. He grabbed a small towel and wet it with some warm water. "Then let's not let the planets decide. I'll fuck you when I'm hard again. You'll be ready." He made a face at the mess on his stomach, grabbing another cloth to wipe himself off before returning to the room with the other one to clean Jared. "I should probably thank you again for coming. I don't mean while you were fucking me, I mean...in general. Being here. I was...getting pretty desperate."

Pushing himself to a sitting position against the headboard, Jared squinted at him, likely seeing a large, blurry mass of bronzed skin moving toward him. He was a spectacularly sweaty wreck, but looked relaxed enough it was surprising he hadn't started to drool. "You could've called me...anytime. Or, answered my emails. Why didn't you?"

The emails again. Rhodey shook his head as he wiped Jared's stomach and chest with the cloth before moving down to his dick. Which was still big, even completely drained of all signs of life. "I didn't get any emails. Not that I use that form of communication much, but I wouldn't have ignored you. And I...couldn't call before. I probably shouldn't have this time. I was...Hell, I don't know. Having second thoughts about just killing the kid. Or letting him die. Especially when...he cried."

Concern lined Jared's brow as he studied Rhodey's face. "Cried?"

"Yeah, you know? Tears and stuff? Not like that usually gets to me." Rhodey lifted his shoulders. "I didn't think he was capable of real tears. Killing him back then woulda been simple. He was...empty."

Adjusting one of the pillows, Jared made himself more comfortable and patted the space next to his hip. "I won't pretend I understand why you chose to beat him that way, but I saw what you were up against, only in part. I trust you to do what's best." He lifted the covers to bring both himself and Rhodey beneath. "What I'll ask of you, though? Is not to kill him. I'll do what it takes, go AWOL if I have to. But that boy is worth saving."

Rhodey nodded slowly, hating to keep what'd really happened from his best friend, but the truth didn't really matter. He leaned back against the headboard, staring up at the ceiling. He'd have to continue the work Maddox had done to keep the part of Noah that was 'worth saving.' Which would probably be easier if he didn't try to see what Jared did in him.

He blew out a breath. "I don't think I'll have to kill him anymore. There are ways I can control him now. I won't use them unless I don't have a choice." No point in making himself look like even *more* of a monster. "But once he's more...stable, I might be able to start taking him out of the cell. I ain't letting you go AWOL, but...whatever help you can give me while you're here would be great. I didn't expect him to respond to you as well as he did."

Jared's huff was self-conscious as he plucked at a stray thread at the edge of the comforter. "I figure anyone as feral as Noah needs a safe spot to land so he can sort himself out. That's a lot of anxiety in that kid."

"You really…" Rhodey shot Jared a sideways look, trying to read him. This was one of those times it was kinda tricky. "You don't get it. And I love you for that. Even with all the shit you've been through, you wanna see there's still good in people. He might actually deserve it now. I hope he continues to." Sitting up a bit, Rhodey showed Jared his arm. The wound Vani had stitched up was healed, but still ugly. She was decent as a 'nurse' but much better as a butcher. "He got me to let my guard down. We used to hang out. Watch movies. I told him stuff." He nudged his chin toward his arm. "He did that with a piece of the bedframe he used to have. If I wasn't as well trained as I am? He would've killed me."

"You weren't safe." From Jared's expression, the way his lips thinned, it was clear he recollected some of the lessons Maddox had taught them. "How could the boy trust you to take care of him if you weren't taking care of yourself?" Jared ran his fingers over the scar, his gaze transfixed like he could see the scene as it had played out by the angle of the wound alone. "You should've commended him for his strike, told him you would teach him more. About strategy. About things that engage his mind. He would respect that and would have known you weren't attempting to put one over on him. Trust is what Noah needs, and he can't trust you because you don't respect what he's capable of. You've modeled yourself into his jailer rather than his teacher."

Rhodey resisted the urge to jerk away. To snap at Jared. If nothing else, his time with Crispin—more than Maddox—had taught him not to let his pride do the talking for him. But he wouldn't mince words. "I *am* his jailer. And I'm dealing with a child, my sister's child, not one of Maddox's recruits. I was trying…" He sighed and shook his head. "When he did this, I was trying to treat him like a kid. One *Tracey* would be safe to welcome back into her life. I still want to get there, but...yeah. It's going to take a lot more time and effort than I thought it would. Not sure I want to teach the little fucker how to become a more *effective* killer, but...we'll see."

Rather than appear offended, Jared simply gave him that look. The one with infinite patience that Noah seemed to respond to so well. "Give yourself some time, Rhodey. He's not the only one traumatized by this situation. If you need to lock him away—to control him—then your job will never end. You need to teach him how to control *himself*." Jared leaned in to kiss his lips with lingering softness, speaking against them. "I'll help you. We can do this together."

"Yeah, but I've been trained to deal with all sorts of shit." Rhodey shrugged, sliding down to lie on his side, bracing his elbow on the mattress and his head on his hand. "It's selfish as fuck, dragging you into all this now that you've got a normal life. But I appreciate you being here. Like this." His lips curved into a small smile. "I missed you. *This* you. You're like you were before...everything. Only a bit older and less obsessed with bugs."

Jared's smile turned into a bark of laughter, his head tipping back to expose the column of his throat. "Oh, husky. Those were the days..." He settled in a little closer, making a warm, contented sound that oddly suited him. "Yeah... Yes. I am less obsessed. With a lot of things." Claiming a kiss, he breathed his next words against Rhodey's skin. "But I'll always be very obsessed with you. It's not selfish. You're where I've always wanted to be."

Grunting, Rhodey let himself indulge in another kiss before sighing and shaking his head. "No, you don't want to be stuck somewhere like this—I mean, with the kid is one thing, but the rest..." He met Jared's eyes. "Tell me about school. About your life now. I always got a kick out of picturing you facing those snooty fuckers in a nice city, with...

all those degrees, and trust funds, and the works. I bet you're real good with the patients, too. Even the stubborn bastards like me."

Rolling to his back, Jared slid one hand under his head and stared up at the ceiling. His lips curved. "It was fun blowing them all away in both basic *and* exams. The drill sergeant kept trying to break me, and I would one-up him by doing the push-ups one-handed. When a bunch of the recruits tried to jump me, they got a nasty surprise. People pretty much leave me alone now." Turning his head, he searched Rhodey's gaze. "I like it that way. Fewer complications. And the stuff I'm learning is where I want to focus my attention. My time. I don't need people."

"I'm people." Rhodey poked Jared in the shoulder, grinning as he rose up over him. "You gonna tell me you don't need me? That's fine, I'll just put this dick back in cold storage."

Rather than laugh, Jared cupped Rhodey's cheek with his free hand. "You're not people, husky. You're my person." His thumb traced Rhodey's lower lip. "Who I very much want to fuck me. Hard. Until I can't see straight. Or walk. Or think about anything else other than you."

This was better. There was probably all sorts of stuff they could rehash, or catch up on, but if Jared was going to help with Noah, there'd be plenty of time for that. Except… Rhodey couldn't have Jared sticking around for *too* long. His presence might draw attention from Maddox neither of them wanted.

And Rhodey wouldn't chance the man's influence on either Jared or Noah. For now, Rhodey had control over the situation and he could make sure Jared's methods for getting Noah to a better place gave the kid every opportunity for some kind of a future. Without risking the one Jared had built for himself.

But like fuck would Rhodey take anything for granted.

Maddox was too good at snatching up every ounce of power the second Rhodey got comfortable. There was no avoiding him retaining a certain amount when it came to the job—he had decades of establishing himself on Rhodey and, when it came down to it, those resources could do a lot of good.

Rhodey would do whatever it took to prevent the 'Master' from having power over Jared again.

Which meant never letting him too close.

Except like this. This, just the two of them in this bed?

No matter what Maddox has taken from me...

He couldn't take away tonight.

Chapter Nineteen

PRESENT

One move, one choice, broke all the rules of an existence constructed over months. Discipline thrown out the window, a temporary escape Ezran Leonov would end up regretting later. Who fucking cared anyway? If shit was getting to him, he still had a long fucking way to go before he'd be as sharp and deadly and untouchable as he needed to be.

Inside The Asylum, the mask of indifference fit so comfortably. The Master had trained him to a level where he could face fucking anything and feel nothing.

I should have felt nothing.

But the act made his skin crawl. The way Curtis, of all people, had looked at him, desperate to see something of the boy he'd known, was worse than getting stabbed in the guts. He was a stranger to everyone who'd once made up his whole world. He'd told Maddox he could handle it.

I fucking lied.

His Master saw right fucking through him. The man *knew* he wasn't ready. But when Ez asked to be sent on a mission, to be given the name of some faceless monster he could eliminate so he'd go back to the perfect numbness he craved...

Maddox said, 'No.'

Fine, Ez got it. This was part of his training. A way to get rid of his weaknesses, his attachments, and turn him into a soldier who could take on anything without hesitation or regret. It would be better for everyone if they saw he wasn't that kid they'd had so much hope for anymore. Kinder to force them to let him go.

But...I'm not ready.

It was Maddox's job to fucking get him there, so why wouldn't he? Why did they have to do this shit now?

Running away probably wasn't the most mature way to handle the situation, but...Ezran couldn't stop himself from doing what felt natural. And Maddox hadn't chased him. No, that would be 'undignified'. He'd probably figured he could find Ez wherever he went.

A smirk curved Ez's lips as he crunched the tiny tracker he'd cut out of his forearm between his teeth, then spat it into the first gutter he passed. The sting from the small wound gave him something to focus on beside the sick, shaky sensation built up in his stomach from the second he'd walked through the doors of The Asylum. Home. It was still home.

Except...it couldn't be. Not anymore.

Past the last of the closed down shops on the rougher side of Anniston Falls, Ez made his way to the train tracks. Balanced on one track to make sure he didn't leave a trail in the snow, he breathed in the crisp air, letting out a white cloud with his exhale. Winter around here always gave the illusion of something...*pure*. A blanket of white hiding the neglected yards, masking the stench of trash tossed into abandoned lots.

This far from the city was even better. There was nothing to disturb the smooth, pristine glow of snow covering the landscape. Nothing to crush it, or make it dirty, something for people to bitch about when it got on their fancy boots that were more for show than practical and warm.

Ez's boots were military grade and could take a lot worse

temperatures than this. So could his jacket, but he'd left it unzipped because he wanted to feel the chill.

Yeah, he was a bit of a mess. Wanting to feel nothing and everything all at once.

Maddox could fix it, so easy.

But he wouldn't do that either.

Fine then, Ez would handle shit his own way. Walking far enough along the tracks so even the tallest buildings in Anniston Falls were out of sight, he finally reached his destination. The place he'd found one of the many times he'd run off when he was living with Tracey…with *Mom*. The ache in his chest got even worse when he thought about her, but that was okay here. Here, he could sort out all the tangled shit in his head. He didn't have to worry about being too messed up for anyone to want to deal with. Or get all twisted about them feeling like they *had* to.

The building was half burnt down, black marring the red brick walls, wood beams sticking out like broken bones from where the structure had collapsed. But the other half was solid, strong enough to hold the rest up. All three stories of the place were filled with some really cool old shit—he'd even found some newspaper clippings from the 1800s, and luggage filled with dusty clothes partially eaten by moths. None of the walls were tagged, so the gang had never found it—too fucking lazy to walk all the way out here to do some damage.

Someone must've been here at some point, no way was Ez the first to find it after it'd been abandoned, but they'd left it undisturbed. And none of the stuff Ez had left here over the years had ever been touched, so he figured he was one of only two people who knew about it now.

Snatching up a stick from the gravel by the train tracks, Ez stepped off them, walking backwards and sweeping away his footprints in the snow. Might be a waste of time, not like anyone would know to come looking for him here…except maybe Garet. Only, Garet was off in Seattle at school.

Which was good. The guy was doing something he loved. Working on cars. And he'd meet the right kind of people. *Normal* people. Maybe a guy who could be fun and all cuddly, the way Garet liked 'em.

Nothing like me, but...yeah. I tried.

His best friend deserved better than the half-assed effort Ez had been able to give him. As much as Ez worried Garet would end up stuck with some asshole, them being fuck buddies had been a stupid idea. The only time Ez didn't mind sex was when it could be a bit detached. He'd fuck someone, then leave, hoping he'd at least made it good for them. So long as they didn't touch him too much, it didn't bring back any shit he didn't want to deal with. Shit he'd mostly managed to stick in a vault in the back of his head. With Garet, there was no ducking out after and pretending they'd never met. Not like he wanted that, but it was a careful balance, leaving emotions out of it.

Garet ended up being a lot better at that than Ez, which he hadn't seen coming. Sure, the whole deal was no commitment, and they both did their own thing, but...seeing him with Sin had been rough. Why? Hell, Ez had no fucking clue. It *shouldn't* have pissed him off so much. Sin might be the exact kinda guy Garet could fall for.

Being home for the first time, having messed around with Pike and keeping things all on the level, got Ez setting up how things were supposed to be in his head. Like he could stuff the people he cared about in different boxes, which was dumb. Wasn't as if he told them what box they were in, he just... kinda assumed they knew. And understood the rules.

Don't get attached. I won't let you know who I'm doing, so it won't hurt. And home is...sacred.

Those were the rules of a young man who didn't get to live the way Ez did. It'd taken a lot of training, but he'd finally been able to look back on who he'd thought he was, who he'd wanted to be, and...let go.

Kinda.

Ez shook his head as he got to the side of the building, where he had to force the door a bit to get in, but it was the best access point for not leaving a trace he'd ever been here. During the summer, he liked going through the big front doors, or hanging out on the wrap-around porch. Reminded him a bit of Tracey's, only hers wasn't charred and falling apart.

He passed through the kitchen, about twice the size of the one at The Asylum, completely wrecked. There were some pots and pans and rusted cans under the collapsed ceiling, and he was pretty sure he could get the old stove working with the right tools, but he never stuck around here long enough to bother.

Up the winding staircase to the third floor, his boots sounded loud in the silence, leaving prints in the dust on the worn wood floors—no need to hide his passage anymore, since no one came in here. He got to the room he'd always hung out in, the one missing wall giving him the perfect fucking view of the woods surrounding the city. This place used to be a railway hotel, so there was a bed with an old lumpy mattress, and some other random furniture, including a dresser he'd kept a bunch of food in he'd stolen from Tracey's place, just in case he ever needed to stay here for a while.

Eventually, he'd gotten over thinking she'd toss him out on his ass with nothing, but the urge to have a stash never really went away. Sliding open a drawer, he grabbed one of the chocolate bars he'd left there years ago, piled up beside cans of corn, peaches, and different kinds of crackers. Probably all stale as hell.

Unwrapping the chocolate bar, he went to the end of the room, sitting on the floor where the wall was completely gone. He dangled his legs over the side and took a careful bite of the KitKat so he didn't break his teeth on it. Was a bit hard, but not terrible. Still had plenty of flavor, only not enough to overwhelm. His bland diet made his taste buds super sensitive. Helped to avoid getting poisoned, but he missed being able to enjoy food.

Tell Crispin and you're gonna end up eating nothing but porridge for a month.

The wind picked up, brushing the angled bangs he'd kept styled the way he liked it, part of the goth look he always went for that had Maddox thinning his lips whenever he didn't slick his hair back. The man wouldn't send him on another mission, so who fucking cared what he looked like? He wore what his Master wanted. Every move he made was exactly what his Master expected. His hair was the only thing he'd defied him on.

Well, that and running off.

"Guess I still got some work to do before I'm a perfect merc." Ez laughed to himself, taking another bite of chocolate and working it between his teeth until he could chew through the cookie center, the subtle sweetness melting in his mouth lightening his mood. "Fuck, this is better than rations. I think I'm gonna go on strike until I get some real food again, even if it gets me the whip. Totally fucking worth it."

Actually, Maddox would whip him if he caught him talking to himself. Then put him through some more intense conditioning to set his head straight.

Maybe it'd work this time.

Movement back by the train tracks snapped Ez's focus to the figure coming into view. His eyes narrowed as he looked over the man, huddled into himself, dressed like it was early fucking fall instead of the middle of winter. Sneakers mostly hidden in the snow, bright blue ratty old Nikes. An oversized brown corduroy shirt, blue jeans, the whole outfit had him sticking out against the landscape like a sore thumb.

Too noisy to be a threat, and from here, Ez could take him out with one shot if he pulled out his glock. Wasn't the best weapon—Maddox said he still hadn't *earned* anything better—

but it did the trick in a pinch. And anyway, getting up close and personal with a blade was a lot more fun.

Only with the right target, though. Master decides those. I trust him to pick the right ones.

Smartest thing would be to slip away before the fucker spotted him, but Ez didn't want to give up his spot. He scowled, leaning forward and speaking loud and damn clear. "Turn around the way you came, popsicle. You get *one* warning."

Head jerking up, lips parting, the guy—*Garet*—stopped dead. Surprise widened his eyes further when he spotted Ez. His customary grin never appeared. Unbelievably, he turned, nodding once, and began to walk away.

"So that's how it's gonna be?" Ez cursed under his breath, tossing the rest of his chocolate bar to join the snow covered, crumbled wall below. "Fine! Fuck you, too! I didn't know it was you, but whatever. Go run home and tell Curtis I ain't his problem anymore."

Garet slowed, turning again to stare up at Ezran. The frown partly hidden beneath his bangs was apparent even from here. "You told me to leave! And you know I don't tell Curtis shit."

"Did you miss the 'I didn't know it was you'?" Ez let out an irritated growl, jerking off his jacket and flinging it as far as it would go in Garet's direction. "Stop being a fucking punk. Put this on and get up here."

Snow crunched, Garet wading into a deeper drift after the jacket. On his way around the building, he shoved his arms in, the zipper being jerked up ripping through the snow-dampened silence. Floorboards creaked, the sound of footsteps coming closer. If the guy made any more noise, he'd register as a fucking earthquake in Peoria.

"What're you doing here?" Blowing on his hands, Garet ducked under the half-fallen beam outside the doorway and stepped just inside.

Bracing his hands behind him on the floor, Ez glanced at his once best—and *only*—friend over his shoulder. "Sunbathing. You?"

Gaze on the open wall, Garet shrugged. "Thinking about shit."

"Sounds like fun." Tone dry, Ez patted the floor beside him. "Grab us some snacks and come do your thinking here. Just be careful when you bite. They're kinda like tasty rocks."

That, at least, pulled a snort from Garet, who moved to the dresser. "I left my Halloween candy here that last year we went trick-or-treating." He bent down, opening a door to a cubby that looked like maybe it had been for hats. "Oh, score! I forgot about the Sweet Tarts." Plastic crinkled. "Too bad we didn't think to put Twinkies in here. They'd survive the apocalypse."

The edge of Ez's lips quirked as he turned a little to the side so he could watch Garet without straining his neck. "I need to get a list of shit to stash away so this place is better stocked. But if you come here without me, don't eat it all."

Orange plastic pumpkin dangling by its strap from his fingers, Garet picked his way across the floor. "As if. I bet you're the one who trained Pike to hoover up everything in sight." He handed over the bucket. "Leave me a few scraps, please, sir. I'm a poor starving waif."

"Ew, don't 'sir' me, dude. What the fuck?" Ez snatched the bucket, digging his hand in and plucking out a few hard candies. He almost put the red ones back, because those were Reed's favorites, but…Reed wouldn't come here. He didn't know about this place and there was no reason for him to now. Sighing, Ez unwrapped one of the red candies and popped it in his mouth. Immediately spat it out. Yeah, *way* too fucking sweet. "Pike started eating like that a few days after he moved in. He's…yeah, hard to say. Had a fucking chaffeur, but ate like every meal was his last. Didn't bother me so long as I had my own stash."

Selecting a Tootsie Roll, Garet shook his head. "Nah. You're not a 'sir'. That was supposed to be Oliver Twisted. Or whatever his name was." Candy unwrapped, he popped it in his mouth and tried to chew. "Ow. Motherfucker." Hand slapped to his jaw, he spit the brown candy out into the snow. "Those things really *are* rocks."

"Told ya." Ez snickered, offering Garet a Jolly Rancher. "Here, these stay pretty good. But don't bite it. Pretty sure you've lost all your baby teeth and the big boy ones are expensive to replace."

"Tell me about it." Tearing into the wrapper, Garet studied the candy like it was his last shitty meal. "Whatcha been up to? How's...things...you know...there?"

This was gonna be tricky to answer. Ez had gotten a briefing about the club, strictly what Maddox thought he needed to know. Which wasn't much. From the looks of things, security had gone way up, and there'd been some renovations, but Garet must've heard about all that from Matt. So what he really wanted to know was what Ez had seen, first hand. No holds barred. "Better than I expected, to be honest. I thought people would be all...the way things get when shit happens and it's like, tense. But seemed like the only thing that made it weird was me walking through the front doors. Wasn't a social call, so..." He lifted his shoulders. "How about you?"

Blinking a few times, Garet seemed to parse out what Ez was saying. "Oh. That makes more sense." He spoke around the candy that poked his cheek outward. "You just get back, too? It always feels that way when you've been away awhile. Don't read too much into it, you know?"

Ez snorted, shaking his head. "No, man. It wasn't like that. I was inviting everyone to the opening of a rival club. Not sure it was the 'hey, I'm back' shit they were expecting. And my Master doesn't have many fans there, so..." He lifted his shoulders. "They'll accept it's not gonna be a problem once things get running. Not that I'll expect a 'thank you' card or anything for clearing out the trash, but...yeah. A lot's changed."

"That was like, a whole baggage car to unpack, dude." Garet took the candy from his mouth, sucking on it between his fingers with lips dry enough they had to hurt. "What'd you open up a club for? Can't be a rival because the Core wouldn't see you as a threat. You guys could even do cross-promo and shit. There's enough room for everyone." He sucked on the candy again, then waved it around. "And what trash?"

Lips pressed together, Ez brought his gaze back to the horizon, the sun beaming off the snow making his eyes ache, but it was nice to be out in the sun. "I probably shouldn't have said all that. Forget I did. I'd rather hear about what you've been doing. Have you gotten to work on any exotics? I bet your first one made you hard."

"Um..." Garet shook his head, palms curving around the lip of the floor. He didn't speak for a really long time. "I gotta get back before dark. Want to meet here again sometime? Maybe on Sunday or something?"

Rubbing his own hands against his thighs, Ez nodded slowly. "Yeah, I'll...try. I'm gonna hang around here for a bit longer, but...keep the jacket. Just...be careful out there. There's a switchblade in the inner pocket and some cash. Some of it's American. Buy yourself something pretty."

Garet's lips curved, his eyes lighting up a bit when he felt around the inside. "Thanks. You sure? I can't keep the knife, I'll get into shit. But, the rest would be awesome. I can bring the jacket when I get back here, and if you're not around I'll leave it in the snack cupboard?"

"Naw, I'll get another one. It's no big deal." Ez wouldn't tell his buddy how many had been sacrificed to bullet holes, it would freak him the fuck out. He held up his hand. "Give me the knife, then. Wouldn't want Matt giving you shit."

"Yeah. Matt." Making an entire sentence of looking away and clearing his throat, Garet slipped the knife out of the pocket. He stood and handed it over. "Thanks, man. Take care, and—" He gestured to himself, indicating the jacket. "— this. Yeah. Take care."

Inclining his head, Ez reached out to grab the pumpkin bucket, wiggling it a bit so the candy inside rattled. "I'm keeping this, but I'll save you some. And next time you come, there will be Twinkies."

"Twinkies." Huffing a laugh, Garet gave him a fond look that crinkled the corners of his eyes. He looked a bit older, but not. "You got it. Eat all you want. The jelly beans might make good ammo for a pea shooter."

Ez snorted, jabbing his thumb in the direction of the closet, the door so swollen with moisture, it would take some work to open it again, but it had once been the perfect hiding place for all the shit they weren't supposed to have. "One of these days, we'll have to take them out again. And the slingshots. I promise, I won't come anywhere close to taking out your eye this time. But I still say I would've hit the apple on your head if you'd fucking stopped moving."

"*Me?* You had your damned tongue in your teeth and your eye all screwed up like one of those fucking gargoyles on the cathedral." Laughing, Garet shook his head, already on his way to the door. "I couldn't stop busting a gut looking at you."

Making a face, Ez popped open the switchblade in his hand, twirling it a few times. He wasn't even sure why, he'd learned not to fucking fidget months ago, but being around Garet... Yeah, it was like part of him was returning to who he'd once been. Which couldn't last, but here? He'd let himself have it. "I was a kid. But that was...it was a good time. I'm glad you showed up, man. This was...pretty cool."

"Yeah. It was. The best." Hand on the doorframe, Garet watched him for a minute, seeming like he wanted to say something. Finally, he shook his head. "Where's your club? I'll drop by for the grand opening, and we'll see if you own knowing me, fancy pants."

Ez shoved to his feet, turning to face Garet, his eyes narrowed to slits. "Don't you fucking dare. You don't set foot in that place, do you hear me? It's not for you. Promise me, Garet. You swear to me, right fucking now, no matter what you hear, you won't *ever* go there."

Taking a step back, Garet dropped his hand from the doorway. "Yeah. No problem. Sorry I mentioned it. But good luck, right? I hope it goes really well." The shadows ate up what Ezran could see of him, making it almost like he simply disappeared. Or had never been there at all.

Back at the broken wall, Ez kept his gaze on the tracks until Garet came into view again. He wished he'd been able to say the right thing, to make things...easier, but he couldn't. Their lives were too different now. Garet needed to go back to his brother, to the family they'd once shared. He needed to stay where it was safe.

If Ez was a better man, he'd cut the last of the ties they had to one another, but he couldn't do that either. Not yet. Maybe after more training. Maybe once Master got all those lessons he had to learn through his thick skull. Until then, Ez would keep the last connection he had. Even if the bond he shared with his childhood friend had changed, for a moment, they'd been right back where it'd all began. Easy laughter and smiles, comfortable silence, a finding softness in one another when the world around became harsh and unforgiving.

Only here. In the place he and Garet had claimed for their own.

Chapter Twenty

PAST

Not here. Not again. Noah couldn't fucking do this. Sure, when he'd been out of control and ready to kill his uncle—or anyone who looked at him the wrong way—there wasn't any other options, but he'd grown past that. Working with Jared had gotten him to a place where he wasn't some rabid fucking animal.

Except Jared had left. Had been gone for months this time. Maybe he wasn't ever coming back. Which meant Noah was stuck here because he'd snapped at the wrong time and lost his uncle's trust.

Happened way too easy and Noah was always waiting for it to happen. Until he'd gotten too comfortable.

Pacing along the length of the cell, damp cement all around him, the air like breathing in stale moisture, Noah ground his teeth. From the other side of the cell door, Rhodey said something, but it wasn't reaching him. Not past the buzzing in his head or the darkness creeping along the edge of his vision. If he let himself go, let himself drop into that void, maybe he wouldn't have to come out this time.

Wouldn't that be nice? It's quiet in there. You don't have to care... about anything.

There was a loud bang, like Rhodey had slammed his fist into the door. This time, his words came through. "Sit down, Noah."

"Fuck you." Noah hadn't even noticed the folding chair before, but spotting it now, he grabbed the thing and wrapped his hands around the metal. Cracked it into the door so hard, the metal bent. But of course, the door didn't budge. "I'll fucking slit your throat the second you let me out of here. You're a dead man, Uncle."

"Let me try, Rhodey." Coming from further away, like Rhodey blocked him from getting too near the door, Jared's voice drifted into the cell. "He's not going to hurt me, dammit. Just... Did you bring me back from the dead to watch him suffer? Because if so, I want a goddamn refund and my pennies to cross the River Styx."

Noah smirked, holding his breath at the silence that followed. Was this the plan all along? Why hadn't he figured that out? Rhodey had pretended Jared was gone to test him.

Yeah, and you failed, asshole. Good job.

"Shut up." Noah dropped the chair, backing away from the door, knowing it wouldn't open until he did. The rules had changed, but not those ones. The wild dog had to heel before anyone would come close.

Until then, he got to be alone in here. Alone until he surrendered to his uncle or the void.

Jared gave you another option. Maybe...maybe he will again?

"No... It's a new game." Noah laced his fingers behind his neck and leaned against the far wall. "I'm ready to play."

Voice closer now, like he pressed his mouth to the door, Jared spoke in his familiar, steady tone. Only his voice held a rasp now. Ragged, and a little out of breath. "Noah. Tell your uncle you want to have lunch with me."

"If he expects me to beg on my knees, he can go fuck himself. How about that?" Noah bared his teeth, sure both men could see him. "I'd rather eat that disgusting slop every day for the rest of my life. But I'll share some with you if you come in here. If you're a good boy, he might let us have salt and pepper with it."

Any other man would have at least sighed with annoyance. Not Jared. "If you insist. Though I would have preferred these raspberry turnovers and roast beef."

This had to be a trick, but...Jared didn't do that. Or, he hadn't, back when...when he'd come before. Memories could be spotty between the cell and the void. When Noah drifted too far, chunks of time went missing. Which he fucking hated, but...but he couldn't complain. His uncle did what he had to. What he'd *sworn* to.

Except what remained fucked with Noah sometimes. Because it meant he'd lost some of his time with Jared. And he never had any clue how much. Or whether the result was intended. On Jared's part, from the pain in his eyes which he quickly hid? It wasn't.

Inhaling roughly, Noah swallowed, his mouth watering. "What do I have to do to have that? I'm not begging."

"Sit in the chair and invite me in as your guest." Jared's voice said it was simple, really. Just something normal, polite people did when having someone over to their home.

Glancing at the chair, Noah hesitated. Blew out a breath. "I broke it. I don't have anywhere comfortable for either of us to sit, but..." He closed his eyes, attempting the calm, level tone that used to earn him a warm smile of approval from the man. Fuck, he'd missed him. "The floor is clean. No matter what my uncle tells you, I do a good job washing it. I'm not a slob."

"A picnic it is, then." The smile was there, just beyond the door.

Another deep breath, slow exhale, and Noah nodded. If this was a trick, he was pretty fast. He'd figure out a way around it. He wouldn't let anyone fool him. But if it wasn't... He kicked away from the wall, going to pick up the chair and place it by the door. Then he returned to the center of the room and sat with his legs crossed.

As unthreatening as he could be without becoming someone else entirely. "Yes, please. A picnic would be very nice. I'd…really like it if you'd join me."

"Thank you, tiger. It would be my pleasure." There was a pause and a grumble from Jared. "I'm taking the damned basket in there with me, Rhodey. I'm not carrying everything on top of my head like an armless washerwoman."

This time, Rhodey's voice was loud enough to be heard, all cold and sharp. "He gets spoons. Nothing else. And if he comes after you, I'll fucking shoot him. I'm not risking you. Not when I just fucking got you back."

This sounded familiar, but not. Poking to understand why only made shadows lengthen in his mind's eye, so Noah stopped. Rubbed his fingers against the rough texture of the cement floor until they retreated.

"Let's let him get over the shock of what I look like before you start tossing around threats." Tone warmer, like he might enjoy being fussed over just a little by Rhodey, Jared grunted. "I think I overpacked this thing. Open the door, please, Rhodey."

That bit of information was almost too fucking tempting. Noah eyed the door. If Jared was telling the truth, he wouldn't be able to grab him. Neither would Rhodey. He could make a run for it.

Except…I don't want to. Not really.

He wanted Jared in here. He wanted what they'd had back, that comfortable, strong presence. That hope that maybe…maybe one day, Noah could be something more than what he was now.

Sliding his hands under his thighs, he sat on them so he didn't…react too soon. He could wait and see what the next move would be. Then he'd decide.

But as the door opened, he couldn't stand the silence any

longer. "It's not a threat. I almost killed a cop. He's already written me off. I bet he's just waiting for you to do the same."

Backing into the cell, like he wasn't joining a dangerous animal, Jared entered with his arms around the largest wicker picnic basket Noah had ever seen. "Yes, well, I like edging, and I rarely let my boys come. So he'll just have to be disappointed and sport a homicidal hard-on for the rest of his days."

A smile tugged at Noah's lips as he glanced at his uncle, who held the door for Jared, his big shoulders blocking the entire hall from view. His smile faded when those dark, emotionless gray eyes met his. For the briefest instance, months that had passed in a blur, his uncle had started looking at him a little differently. There had been some pride in those eyes. Trust even. It had taken fucking forever to get there, and a split second to lose it all.

This time, Noah didn't think he'd ever get a chance to earn it back.

How long would it be before the same happened with Jared? Was that why Rhodey'd let him live? So he could get the one last door slammed in his face before he died?

Setting down the basket, Jared straightened, still facing Rhodey. "Thank you. If you don't mind, I'd like some privacy for this." He pronounced the word 'privacy' with a short 'i' like he always did, but sounded strange with the gravel in his voice. "We'll be fine."

"You're a fool, Jared." Rhodey pressed his eyes shut, then nodded slowly. "Fine. But I see so much as another mark on you, this is over. The boy is right. I'm not making fucking threats. I'm not sure what you think is left in there worth saving, but…" He opened his eyes, glancing at Noah in that dismissive way he did, like whatever worth he'd had was long gone. "Both he and I know better."

"Get out, Rhodey. And if you have aspersions to cast, I

suggest you never hurl them at him again in my presence." Tone colder than Noah had ever heard him, Jared remained still and calm.

Without another word, Rhodey gave a stiff nod and shut the door behind him. His footsteps echoed down the hall and another door opened and closed.

Brow furrowing, Noah stared at the door. "Did you piss him off? Is he leaving you here to teach you…something? I don't understand this game."

"It's called trust." Jared still hadn't turned. He faced the door, head tipped so it was obvious he looked at the basket and not the door. "I asked him for privacy, time alone with you, because…this is difficult for me. For you to see."

Noah frowned, his gaze shifting to the man in front of him. Almost as big as his uncle, with massive shoulders and tons of muscles, but somehow not as much as he'd had the last time he'd been here. Six months, two weeks, and five days. For some dumb reason, Noah had kept track—if the markings on the tiger calendar his uncle had given him were accurate. Maybe he would've stopped after a few years.

Maybe not.

"Show me." Noah kept his hands under him, but it was hard to stay where he was. He wanted to force Jared to face him. Half wanted the man to knock him on his ass when he tried. "Is this why you were gone so long? You promised you would come back. Sooner. It was supposed to be sooner than this."

"Yes. It was. I apologize." Though he didn't so much as change his breathing, tension in the air thickened, something about Jared's energy telling Noah this was a struggle for him. He turned with painful slowness, lifting his head at the same time so Noah could see his face and throat clearly. "It's much better now…"

Shoving to his feet, Noah started toward Jared, then

stopped short. The man wouldn't let a dangerous creature close to him, especially not when he was this hurt already. Scars, some of them still dark red, marked once smooth and perfect skin. Jagged along his throat, smaller ones on his face. Whatever had done the damage hadn't left much of him untouched.

No wonder Rhodey was ready to kill Noah rather than chance having him anywhere near Jared. If his uncle loved anyone besides Noah's mother, it was this man right here. He'd have Noah in a shallow grave in the blink of an eye before he'd risk losing him.

Which made Noah's jaw clench. His uncle didn't deserve Jared. He was a coldhearted motherfucker and his kind of love…it wasn't good enough. Jared should have someone wonderful. Someone sweet and caring who'd take care of him.

Now, more than ever.

"Please…" Noah bit hard into his bottom lip. "Can I… can I take the basket? You should sit down and…relax. Why did that asshole let you carry it at all?"

Relief washed over Jared's face. "Of course. I would be grateful." He stepped to one side, getting out of the way, but also bringing himself to within six inches of Noah. So close, the sharp woodsy scent of his soap teased Noah's senses, along with the natural heat coming off his skin. "There's a blanket inside."

Noah inclined his head, moving slowly, even though there was nothing he could do to make himself less of a threat. Maybe Jared would feel it, though. That Noah didn't want to hurt him. He eased the basket out of the man's arms and lowered it to the floor. Knelt beside it to take out the blanket.

His voice came out a bit rough and his eyes burned. He kept his gaze lowered so Jared couldn't see. "I didn't give up. I was…trying. The cop…I didn't expect him and he was close. I grabbed his gun without thinking."

With stiff movements, Jared nodded and lowered himself

to the floor. The paleness stealing all color from his skin showed his pain, but his expression didn't reveal a thing. "That fight or flight response is a tricky one. You're all fight, tiger. Don't worry. We'll work on it. This is just a piece of information we can use now to build up your tools."

"I guess." Noah rubbed his cheek with the back of his hand, glaring when his skin came away damp. He kept his gaze locked on the containers he spread out over the blanket. "My dad would've been impressed. He hated fucking cops..." He snorted. "And he was one. But you knew that."

"Mhm..." Weight on his palms, Jared leaned back, studying him. His lips curved at the edges, humor warming the cold blue of his eyes. "There's something very Freudian there. And it's not a cigar." He nodded at the hamper. "Though there are some in there."

Surprise lifted Noah's head. He blinked at Jared, rubbing his fist against his eyes when one look at him had more stupid tears spilling. As if he was the type of person to cry over someone else being injured. He latched onto the more comfortable topic. "I can have one? You said you'd let me, on my eighteenth birthday..." He scowled. "You missed it."

"I know. I'm sorry. It's why I brought them. And a present." Jared tipped his chin toward the basket. "Food first though. Then I have a question to ask you."

Lifting his brows, Noah grabbed a plate—paper, because his uncle was an asshole, not an idiot—and plunked a few different things on it. He held out the plate to Jared. "Ask me now."

"All right." Taking the plate, Jared nodded his thanks, and placed it on his lap to wait for Noah to dish out his own. Always polite. "I'd like to train you as a Dom. But to do that, I'd like you to be my sub first. In all ways. So you know what your boy or boys will experience under your control."

Noah tilted his head to one side, weighing each word to see if there was some hidden meaning behind it. But as much as he struggled to trust much of anything, Jared had never been part of that. Not after the first few days. And even if it might be a mistake? Not now. "You would never touch me. You always said I was too young. I wanted you to."

"Yes. I know." Jared used his plastic knife to cut into the tender roast beef, juices welling into his potatoes and gravy. "You were too young. But you're of age, and I think learning control would be good for you. It would give you something to push against as well, in a safe way. Something to fight, because you're not a natural submissive. Overcoming that will make you stronger. Steadier." He chewed and swallowed the bite of beef. "It is, of course, not the only option. And we wouldn't engage in those activities as long as you are confined in a cell. Nor will it be a condition of your release."

Huffing, Noah dropped his plate at his side and picked up the meat with his fingers. Something he knew Jared didn't like, but he wanted to piss him off. Because without even getting a chance to put his pieces on the board, he was already losing. He spoke around the mouthful. "So you'll take over whipping me for Rhodey? Sure. Sounds like fun. Maybe you can make it interesting. I'm bored of the same old shit."

"Is that what you think wearing my collar means?" Tone mild, Jared took another bite of food, then leaned over to take a metal flask from the hamper. He held it up. "Wine?"

Noah sucked his fingers clean, grabbing for the flask with his other hand. "Sure. And yeah, what else would it mean? You won't do anything else with me as long as I'm here. I'll be here for a long fucking time. My bank is in the fucking minuses."

"With Rhodey? I suppose it is." Jared produced a plastic wine glass from the basket, holding it out. "Don't tell your uncle. I'm not allowed this on the pain medication, but I'm a damned doctor. I can mix drugs and alcohol if I want. At least I'm not shooting heroin in my eyeball."

Despite wanting to keep a hold on his emotions, Noah

looked at Jared's neck again, blinking fast as he laughed. He dropped his focus to the glass, filling it. "Some people actually do that shit. It's gross. I'm glad my dad went with guns instead of drugs. Or..." He shook his head, hissing in air through his teeth. "No, I'm not. I'm…frustrated, but I still know…I know that was wrong. The things I did, the people I hurt…I still know it was wrong."

"I know you do, love." Sipping the wine, Jared regarded him over the rim, then lowered the glass to his side. "I would like to show you pleasure and control. How to take it and give it. Both. It isn't all sex and pain, the way you imagine." He flipped up his hand, resting it on his knee like he might be inviting Noah to take it. "We can leave that out, if you like. And I will still be able to teach you. But it is entirely up to you and you will always be the one holding the reins."

Wetting his bottom lip with his tongue, Noah looked from Jared's hand to his eyes. "You'd… You want that from me? But…" He shook his head. "My uncle won't allow it. I'm sure whatever the two of you have going on, he doesn't want to share you. Least of all with me."

"What we have…" Jared trailed off, shaking his head as he took a sip of wine. "Would end if you were my boy. We have an understanding, and while we once might have been something more, that hasn't been a possibility for a very long time." He reached out, placing the silver cup down near Noah. "As I said, however, sex is not something that is necessary for me to teach you what you need to know. That will be entirely up to you, and will not affect the outcome."

Out of all the decisions Noah'd ever had to make, this was the easy one. His feelings about his uncle were all kinds of complicated, but he was a little sad for him. Losing 'something more' with Jared must've been hard. But that was the difference between him and his uncle.

Whatever had come between them had been stronger than what they'd shared. Maybe Rhodey couldn't see a way to manage close connections with anyone, because of his job and…well, who he was.

On his own, Noah had trouble thinking he could either, but Jared told him otherwise.

And no matter how challenging it might be?

I might not be able to believe in myself. But I'll always believe him.

Chapter Twenty-One

PAST

Noah always relaxed way too easy around Jared. Why? Because he didn't lie. Maybe there were times Noah missed when people did lie, but rarely. He'd been working on finding those little clues his whole fucking life. Because lies...lies were dangerous. Lies meant the whole reality around him would collapse, leaving him vulnerable.

Which was unacceptable.

Being vulnerable with Jared would be by choice. Not like he had the first fucking clue *how* to be, but...something inside him wanted it. He reached out and put his hand in Jared's. "I don't understand why it's...like this with you. When you're not here it's like, inside me is all coiled up. Then you're here and I...can let that go. I know it sounds stupid."

"Does it? We all need a safe space. I'm flattered I'm yours." Warm hand squeezing Noah's fingers, Jared leaned in. He slowly lifted one hand, gaze questioning before he brought it to Noah's cheek, brushing a crumb from his lips with the pad of his thumb. "I won't always be your Dom, but I promise you this. I will never be far again. When you need me, I will be there. For one year, if you agree, I will teach you everything I know, and then I will watch as you do the same with someone else. I love you, and because I do, I will let you go. When you are ready to fly."

For a second, the touch had Noah stiffening. Not because Jared had never touched him, but because it was rare anyone did. When it happened, it usually hurt. Which didn't bother Noah. Pain made sense. This was different, though. Soft and warm, not a pat on the shoulder or a hand brushed over his hair in the affectionate way he'd craved so much in Jared's absence.

Relaxing a bit, Noah held still, prepared for Jared to move away from him, but wanting to hold the contact for as long as he could. "I...I love you, too. As much as someone like me can love anyone. I won't ever be ready, though. When you let me go, I'll be waiting for you to come back. Like I always do."

Jared's thumb moved up to Noah's cheek, tracing the plane of his face until he was surrounded by the warmth of Jared's palm. "Then that is an unfathomable amount of love, because you love more completely and more deeply than any person I've ever known. I will treasure that gift until my last breath. There is no coming back, for me, because I will always be right here. By your side."

"Good." Noah met Jared's eyes, giving him a slanted smile. He was pushing his luck, but why shouldn't he? There was no better time than when they were being honest with each other. "If you're not out of the military, I want you to quit. I want you somewhere safe. I want..." His voice caught and he pressed his eyes shut. "I want to never see you hurt like this again. You almost left me for good. You can't promise to be by my side if you die. It'll be the first lie you've ever told me and I trust you, so don't...don't lie to me."

"I had... I've been discharged." The words grated across Jared's vocal cords, like they cost him something to say, but perhaps not because he missed the military. His gaze grew briefly haunted before he banked down the emotion and stroked his fingers through Noah's hair. "This is how I know you're not a natural sub. Toppy thing. I will never lie to you, but I won't live forever. None of us will. However long I have, I am in your service. If only so I can watch you soar."

Grinning, Noah moved a little closer and let out a quiet sound in the back of his throat, enjoying the way Jared touched his hair. Maybe he really did remind Jared of a tiger, one not quite tame, but he could still pet. He didn't mind that at all. "Shut up about dying. You're a doctor, you'll figure out a way around it. And cats don't soar. I'm agreeing to be your sub, but you can't order me to grow wings."

That earned his hair a tiny, painless tug. "Cheeky. It's a good thing you're not wearing my collar yet." Jared glanced toward the door. "Rhodey is going to be pissed that he actually has to put up those bunk beds in here. I meant it when I said I'm not leaving your side."

"Bunk beds?" Noah lifted up a bit to stare into those icy blue eyes. Was the man joking? "No. One bed. You'll sleep with me." He looked over at the plain, solid metal bed frame with its flimsy mattress. Too small for two people. Which could be easily fixed. "I bet he'll give us something nice, because you'll be using it, too. But it might take him a few days to weld all the pieces together so I don't try to make my own weapons out of it. Again."

Releasing Noah's hair, Jared leaned back to wag his finger at him with a playful cluck of his tongue. "No, no, tiger. If I share a bed with you, neither of us will get any sleep. You'll earn that right, and many more. Starting with the one that gains us freedom from this cell by showing your uncle and me that you can behave."

Well, that didn't sound like much fun. Noah had a feeling he had a lot to learn about what being a sub actually meant. He rolled his eyes, closing the last of the distance between them, rubbing his cheek against Jared's. "Do you really think putting me in another bed will save you? You'll be lying there, thinking of me, just out of reach. Why not spare yourself being all hard and alone when you don't have to wait at all?"

Turning his head that critical fraction of an inch, Jared brought his lips to Noah's ear. "You forget. I have much more experience with denial. In fact...I get off on it. You never know." His teeth skimmed the shell of Noah's ear. "I might never fuck you."

Noah eased back, sitting on his heels. He studied Jared's face, not sure if he should go for strategy or seduction. The man was right. He had a lot of experience and Noah had... none. But he had a pretty good imagination. "You want to fuck me. Admit it. You've thought about all the things I've been telling you for months I want to do to you. Maybe not then, because it was *so* very wrong, but it isn't anymore. You don't want to deny yourself, you want to put me in my place." He cocked his head. "Is on my knees good enough?"

"Let's start with something you already *do* know." Jared lifted his plate, digging back into his lunch. "I never lie, yes?" He waved his fork a little, the most egregious breach of table manners he'd ever made. "Ergo, when I tell you that absolutely *nothing* will happen between us until we are free of this cell, you can take that to our bank."

Scowling, Noah stayed where he was, in Jared's personal space. He hadn't expected this to be simple, but he couldn't accept being offered everything he'd ever wanted and letting it stay just out of reach. "You're basically letting Rhodey decide when I can suck your dick. Which means it will never happen. I thought Doms called the shots. Is he yours?"

Chuckling, Jared shook his head. He took a sip of wine, swallowed, and tipped his head as if considering. "I only had one Dom, and I never will again." Another sip of wine followed the first. "You need to own your power and responsibility in this situation. You, in fact, hold the keys. When you choose to acknowledge that, you'll be well on your way to freedom. And so will I. With you."

"Being your sub is very frustrating." Noah finally moved back to his own place on the blanket, slouching back and grabbing his roast beef again. He used his teeth for another big bite, then gestured at Jared with it. "Freedom is conditional. I need better motivation. A vague offer of sex isn't enough. I mean..." He effected what he considered a pretty good imitation of Jared's mildest tone. "For all I know, you're terrible at it."

Jared's mouth turned down at the corners. "Possibly. I hadn't considered that fact." He shrugged, taking the pastry container out of the hamper, revealing a black velvet box at the bottom. "Is it a gamble you're willing to take? Learning how to be a submissive who deserves my attention and time, to show up and try to please me, with the off chance that I might, how do you say it? Suck in bed?"

Again, the wrong move. Noah dropped the meat on his plate and wiped his lips with the sleeve of the plain gray sweater—part of the boring uniform his uncle kept him in, whenever he stayed in the cell. Maybe that was the problem. In gray jogging pants and this sweater, he wasn't exactly appealing. Could this be why the man wasn't taking up his challenge?

"Can I start over?" Noah didn't like making mistakes. He hated when he caught himself playing the wrong game, ending up with a checkmate when he'd been going for a full house. He rose back up on his knees. Took off his shirt for good measure. "I...do want to please you. And I don't think you suck in bed. It's *you*. You're fucking good at everything, you wouldn't allow for anything less. But what you see is all I can give you. I am offering it, however and whenever you choose to take it."

Container set aside, Jared pushed to his feet, stumbling a little as he stiffened in pain, but didn't make a sound. He motioned for Noah to rise. "Come here, tiger."

"Why did you do that?" Noah stood and reached for

Jared's arm, pulling back at the last second. "I'm not...I won't hurt you. And I won't ask for anything I just...you should sit. On my bed, you'll be more comfortable. I'll stay on the floor. I can't...I can't watch you in pain. I won't."

"You may touch me. I enjoy your touch." Jared caught Noah's fingers in a loose grip and tugged him closer. "As much as I might want to, two things are preventing me from taking the gift you're offering. One is honor. The other is my somewhat broken body." Cool lips touched Noah's forehead. "I won't take what I want until you're truly free to choose it. In this cell you are not. I know it's confusing, and it feels horrible. I don't like it either." Leaning back, he held Noah's gaze. "But it is a fact we must face so we are able to move past it. Can you trust me in this, love?"

Lifting Jared's hand to his shoulder, Noah nodded slowly. "I trust you. Only you, Jared. But you're going to do what I say now. I'm telling you, respectfully, to come sit on my bed." He gave Jared a sideways look as he wrapped an arm carefully around his waist. "Aren't I an awesome sub? If you sit nicely, I'll grab the wine and a cigar and get you all set up."

The gust of laughter from Jared was both joyful and strange. He pressed a hand to his side, wincing this time. "No smoking in bed. Being lit on fire once a year is my limit." However, he did allow Noah to lead him to the bed where he sat on the edge. "You will be a wonderful Dom, Noah. I dare say, you'll even be able to mimic being a stellar submissive, but no. You will never be a sub. I know this with every fiber of my being."

"I'm not sure if you're daring me to prove you wrong or giving me a compliment." Noah made a thoughtful sound as he fetched the wine and cigar, then the rest of the food and the blanket so he'd have somewhere comfortable to sit. At Jared's feet, where any good sub would, of course. He set the cigar between his teeth and dug into the basket for the clippers and lighter he knew he'd find there. Jared was a practical man.

"If you don't want to share, that's your right, but I'm pretty sure you could manage not to set yourself on fire with it."

"Even I am susceptible to the effects of narcotics mixed with wine." Propped against the wall, Jared studied Noah as he trimmed the cigar. "I see you've been paying close attention. I'm impressed, my boy."

Glowing from the inside out at the praise, Noah sucked hard on the cigar as he held the lighter in front of it. At first, the taste was nice and heady. Like the scent that lingered around both Jared and his uncle sometimes. But when he breathed it in, air blazed his lungs in his chest. He coughed, gasping and holding the cigar away from himself before it could catch on his clothes or the blanket.

"Hell. I'm sorry. I forgot to mention." Lips twitching, Jared reached out to pluck the cigar from Noah's fingers. "You don't inhale cigars. Roll the smoke around in your mouth, then blow it out."

Eyes tearing, Noah coughed a few more times and nodded. "Yes, that would have been good to know. You're lucky you haven't put the collar on me yet, I'd have to say you're a terrible Dom. You're supposed to take care of me, aren't you?"

"I also get to teach you lessons." Jared handed him the cigar. "Try again. You'll never forget."

Noah narrowed his eyes at the cigar before taking it, refusing to let the thing mock him again. He set it between his lips, pulling at it carefully this time, so only a little smoke filled his mouth. Let it out after a brief taste. "Yes, that's better." He licked his lips. "If that was a lesson, have I earned a reward? I think that's definitely how this works."

"Yes. You may tell me your safeword." Arms folded, Jared regarded him with lazy interest. "And get the box from the hamper. The velvet one. Bring it here, please."

Handing Jared the cigar, Noah gave him a slanted smile before crawling over to the basket. He returned a bit slower, curious if Jared liked the look of him with his shirt off. His muscles weren't huge, but they were well-formed and he'd been working hard on getting even more definition. While he was in the cell, there wasn't much else to do, so...he could thank his uncle for that at least. The workouts were paying off.

He smirked at Jared as he put the box in his mouth for the remainder of his crawling, offering it to him that way. Another very sub-like thing to do.

Sliding the box from between Noah's lips, Jared gave him a heavy lidded stare. The smoke from the cigar twirled through the air, curling past his face. "Very handsome. Next time, when we are out of this place, I will show you how pretty I think such displays are." Setting the box aside, he patted the bed. "Come up here. I want to see you open it."

Since Jared liked that display, Noah decided to give him another. Back to the bed, he brought his arms up behind him, lifting himself up so all his muscles swelled. He lowered himself to the bed beside Jared, stretching his arms over his head. "It's good to know you like what you see."

"Mhm... I do. Please take care not to stir my interest over much. The scar tissue still needs work at my groin, and I know you don't wish to cause me pain." He held out the cigar to Noah. "You're a picture."

Sitting up, Noah ducked his head, chewing on his bottom lip. Fuck, how could he have been so careless? The man had always seemed so powerful to him, like nothing could ever bring him down. Even after seeing him suffering, part of his mind kept latching on to that. Kept wanting to keep that image from changing. "I'm sorry, I wasn't thinking. I'll be more careful...sir."

At the last word Noah spoke, Jared closed his eyes, a tiny smile on his lips. Looking totally blissed out, he inhaled deep. "That. Right there." He opened his eyes, pinning Noah with his stare. "Is the best music. Your voice. That one syllable. I love hearing it. Thank you."

Cheeks heating, Noah bit harder into his lip until he tasted blood, using the pain to ground himself. He inhaled roughly, willing his blood to cool, and ignoring his dick, which was hard. Like the stupid thing hadn't been paying any attention to the conversation. "It feels strange to say, but I'll get used to it. It makes me happy, knowing it pleases you."

"Good boy." Voice deep, throaty, and thick, Jared shifted his legs like he might be experiencing a bit of his own discomfort, but maybe not the fun kind, even though he still looked happy. "Here. Open it. If you don't like it, I can get a different one made."

Licking the coppery blood off his bottom lip, Noah opened the velvet box. He blinked when he saw the tag within. The gleam of the metal told him it was platinum, a beautiful piece, with an engraving in elegant letters that read 'Jared's boy'. Lifting it out, Noah turned it, grinning as he took in the tiger head on the other side.

He met Jared's eyes. "I love it. But…where's the collar?"

"It's on my dresser at my apartment. Waiting for you." Making sure Noah saw his hand before touching him, Jared ran his fingers lightly over the ridge of Noah's collar bone. Like he pictured the leather against his skin. "We'll spend time here getting to know your limits and my expectations, discussing what we'll be doing together. When you're familiar and I'm prepared for the responsibility of being your Dom, then I'll offer you my collar there."

Noah lifted his hand with the tag in his palm, his brow furrowing as he considered how his freedom being uncertain put another obstacle between them. "This…will go on the collar? And I will accept any safeword you want, but I don't need it. I won't put any limits on what you can do to me. I said I trust you and I meant that."

Those fingertips ran up and down Noah's arm, now, light scrapes of Jared's nails deliberately raising goosebumps in their wake. "While I am flattered and not so secretly preening at the idea, I need your help. I am not omniscient. I cannot read your mind. As much as it pains you to see me hurt, you will understand when I say that hurting you would be the worst pain of all. Therefore, I need you to respect *my* limits and to choose and to use a safeword so that I may know I am using my property with all the care I would wish."

"Fine, but I think you'll like hurting me." Such a careful line he had to walk, but Noah couldn't help himself. The way Jared touched him scrambled his brain. He slowly tugged his bottom lip between his teeth again, this time, letting the blood trickle down. "I'll respect any limits *you* have, sir."

"Any?" Jared raised one brow at Noah, warning him to be very careful where he went with his next words.

Noah lifted his shoulders. "Why not? I'm giving you the control. That's my choice, isn't it? The power I hold? How much and how little I'm willing to surrender?" His lips curved. "I choose to give it all."

"All right." Jared nodded to the cigar. "Put that away. It has gone out. While you clean up our dinner, I'll tell you what I expect, starting now. A few rules to see if you're up for giving me that kind of control. We'll save the enforcement of them and others until we're out of here. However, these three, if you cannot obey them? I will know you're not ready to give up that level of control."

Inclining his head, Noah used his thumb to swipe away the blood from his chin. "Yes, sir. I am yours to command." He leaned in to whisper against Jared's lips. "I'll show you *exactly* how ready I am."

The sharp nip to Noah's self-inflicted lip wound was as quick as it was unexpected. "Rule one." Jared drew back. "No marking my property or damaging it in any way. That is my privilege. You will not bite your lip, abuse your body with lack of sleep or drugs or too much alcohol, or by eating too much or too little. This—" He motioned to Noah's body. "—is the altar upon which you worship your Dom. Respect it. Respect me."

"Okay, I can do that." Noah tried to make his expression serious, but a smile kept tugging at his lips. "If you'll admit you found it hot and you're looking forward to making me bleed yourself."

"Oh? Are we negotiating that absolute power exchange you just offered me so soon?" Jared did *not* sound impressed. In fact, he looked like he might be contemplating throwing Noah over his knee.

So fucking tempting, but Noah didn't want to fail at submission on his first try. He shook his head and rubbed the rest of the blood away with his fist. "No, sir. I will obey you without…the rest. I was just… I'll go pick up everything and stop…you know."

"Good." Jared's smile made a reappearance. Briefly. "Then I will tell you that, yes, I like the sight of your blood. But I will like it better when *I* am the one safely controlling how it's spilled."

A wide grin spread across Noah's lips as he rose from the bed, bending down to grab the blanket. A few containers rolled onto the floor, but their tops were on, so they were fine. He straightened to fold the blanket to the standard his uncle expected, pretty sure Jared's would be the same. "I knew it!"

"Rule two." Jared launched into his next item, pushing himself up a little higher and resting one arm around his middle. "No swearing. Of any kind. Not in the traditional or non-traditional sense. That includes *damn* and *ass* and any other exclamations you can dream up. If I believe a swear word could be substituted, I will penalize it as such."

Taking a knee by the basket to start putting the containers in it, Noah took a deep breath. "I can do that. Has it…always bothered you? I would've stopped before if I knew. Rhodey swears all the time so…it just became natural."

Following Noah's movements, Jared shook his head. "Not

as such. Being able to control one's language is a sign of self-control. My controlling it, is a sign of *my* control. It pleases me to see you restrain yourself in that way, and it also pleases me to have the mouth that I own as clean as possible. If you can't keep it clean, I will clean it for you."

"I can, sir. You won't need to worry about that. Words are...easy." Noah was tempted to learn about some of the punishments Jared might come up with, but at the same time...not. Because they would mean he wasn't holding up his end of this exchange. "I enjoy the...more playful times we've had, but I don't ever want you to feel this isn't important to me. Because it is. I usually consider very carefully before I say anything, so this is...just another level of the same."

"I know, love. And I wouldn't ask you to do something I thought you would fail at, unless it was part of a *fun* game that you were fully aware of." Jared's warm smile told him he appreciated the level of submission Noah was willing to give on this. "I expect you to keep your language clean even when I am not within hearing distance, and that includes with Rhodey."

Throat working, Noah placed the blanket on top of the hamper. This was a different kind of challenge. His mind raced as he grasped for a way around it, but that would only be taking the control back he'd said he wanted Jared to have. He pressed his eyes shut. "I'll look weak to him. He'll think he's broken me and...I don't know if that's better or worse than the alternative. I need to be strong enough not to...slip up. When I do it's...bad."

"Help me understand." Patting the mattress, Jared invited Noah onto the bed, lifting up his arm to indicate he'd welcome Noah there. "You think Rhodey regards swearing as strength. Yet, I don't swear *much* and you believe he respects and loves me."

Noah lowered to the bed at Jared's side, close enough so there was no space between them. "I think he...is hard on me because I need to be…solid. Inside. And I get that. I push back and he wants me to, on some level. To show him that I'm still *me*. If I stop telling him to go f—you know what I say, you've heard it plenty—he might wonder if I'm still strong enough. He doesn't have to with you, you're not…" He gestured to himself. "*This*."

Resting his arm around Noah's shoulder, Jared pulled him in a little tighter with a thoughtful sound. "You remember I told you I knew him as a boy?"

"Yes." Noah lifted his head, looking into Jared's eyes and trying to picture him any other way than as he was now. A soft smile curved his lips. "You were a tough kid. Intelligent. And very patient to have put up with him."

"Ha!" Jared's laugh tightened his arm around Noah's shoulder. "I tried to get him to rob a bank with me. I also made him hold down the live frogs I dissected for medical experiments. I was *not* the patient one. He was. In his own way…" Gaze going distant, Jared smiled like he saw something soft and tender in Rhodey, a side of his uncle Noah had never known. "The thing he wants most in life is the thing he has never allowed himself to have. Love. The kind of respect that comes from it. Not the respect that is beaten into someone. If you gave him *true* respect—and I understand why that isn't possible given your relationship at this point—he would find it wonderful, not weak."

Looking down at his lap, Noah rubbed his thighs, clearing his throat as it tightened. "When we were training in Russia, before I met you, things were…were better. I thought we might be able to be like family. He showed me so many different things. How to fight, how to survive…hell…" He lifted his head, blinking at Jared. "Sorry, is that a curse?"

"It is." Jared tapped him on the nose. "One free pass."

Noah snickered, wrinkling his nose. "Thank you. But… yeah, so he even taught me how to use a gun. He trusted me. But the second he brought me around other people, things changed. I kept…losing control. I didn't mean to. Anyone too close, the wrong move—I never know what will set me off. And that…I lost his trust. I don't think I'll ever get it back again."

Nodding a little as Noah spoke, Jared made a thoughtful sound. "Trust is a funny thing. It is elastic, but it gets stretched out of shape. It's easy, when you're younger, to bend it into a certain shape that people have trouble seeing another way." He shuddered a little. "That was possibly the worst analogy I have ever laid out. I apologize. My point is, alcohol and narcotics notwithstanding, that you're very young and you're going to make mistakes. When you get older, your relationship with Rhodey will shift. He will treat you as the adult you legally are now, and if you show him that you respect him and yourself, he will respect you too."

"Maybe… Maybe that's possible, now that you're back." Noah rested his head on Jared's shoulder. "It feels different when you're here. Usually, I'm just…waiting. I want to live. I want to get out of here and do…so much. But not if I'm dangerous. I trust Rhodey to decide that. When you're here it's like…maybe he'll think about it a little longer. Because you have different tools to fix me that he doesn't."

"Such as?" Shifting, Jared pressed a kiss to the top of Noah's head.

Noah gave him a slanted smile. "This? He doesn't cuddle. Not that I expect him to, but sometimes… It feels like I need to be close to someone safe. Like maybe I wouldn't freak out as much around strangers if I was more used to…contact. Is that strange?"

"It makes perfect sense, actually." Other arm coming around Noah, Jared gave him a tight hug. "I'd like to bring you to a dojo that just opened up in the town your mother lives in. Would you like to study martial arts more? I know you are versed, but I believe leveling up, teaching some younger students, you might find that you gain confidence and inner balance that helps you see yourself as I see you."

Eyes widening, Noah shook his head before he even realized he was doing it. Then he stopped and groaned. "I do, but I can't. You're safe, Jared. Not only because you feel that way. It would be much harder for me to hurt you. I mean, maybe not *now*, but I'm not...I'm okay in my head again. Not like before. With kids or even...my mother? The last time I saw her, she hugged me and I was scared. There's so much she doesn't know. She *can't* know. It would hurt her so much."

"We're going to get there. I promise." Those strong, warm arms still hadn't loosened their grip. Jared tightened them further in a quick, extra hug. "I can see how close you are, even if you can't. It's always difficult to see the twists and turns of the path we're on, so we often need others who've been there before to help guide us. Which brings me to my third rule. Ready?"

If not for how Jared was holding him, Noah might have said no. As much as he wanted this, opening up had revealed all his flaws and he wasn't sure why Jared even *wanted* him as a sub. But for some reason, he did. And Noah wouldn't let him regret it. "Yes. I'm ready, sir."

"You always tell me the truth, and if you're not ready to tell me the truth? You don't ever lie. You simply tell me you're not ready to tell me." Tipping his chin down, Jared pulled back a little to meet Noah's gaze. From this angle it was possible to see the shiny burn scars and how they must've gone very deep. "I need to trust you as much as you trust me. It makes *me* feel safe and good, too."

Without hesitation this time, Noah nodded. "I can do that. I hate lies. I can tell when people are lying and it ruins any chance of me wanting to let them close. So I won't have any problem with that, sir. I promise."

"Good boy. You have no idea how proud of you I am, but I wish you did. Someday, you will. Someday, my dream for you will come true." Pressing a kiss to Noah's cheek, then forehead, Jared hugged him again. "To be proud of yourself."

Noah shook his head, giving Jared a level look. "That won't ever matter as much as what you think of me. If you're proud of me, it's more than enough. Have bigger dreams. Like…one day, when I'm not your sub, I'll get you a house like my mom's. And a rocking chair. And you won't have to be a doctor anymore, because I'll be taking care of you. Doesn't that sound good?"

"Can I have a cute little pain slut twink instead of the rocker? I think I'd get more use out of him." Quiet laughter rumbled from Jared's chest into Noah's ear. "Or my own private dungeon? That would be lovely."

A slow smile curved Noah's lips. "Consider it yours. And I suppose I could share you with a little pain slut or two. So long as they understand that you're mine. If they forget, I'll remind them with all the tricks you'll teach me."

"It's a deal. You're mine, even if no one else knows it. Always." Jared's smile pressed against Noah's cheek. "It's going to be all right, Noah. We're both going to have a beautiful life. Wait and see. That's a promise I intend to keep."

Chapter Twenty-Two

PAST

*D*reams and promises. Noah didn't realize how much he'd enjoy sharing those with anyone. Or even believed he'd ever get a chance to have them. But with Jared, nothing seemed impossible.

He let out a ridiculously happy sigh. "I never really...think about the future. I don't expect to get there. But I want to. With you. I'm already picturing your apartment. It's probably too small. And it doesn't have all the...stuff you love. I imagine..." His brow furrowed as he glanced toward the cigar. Jared's shoes. The basket. "You like fancy things, but not just for showing off. Quality. You'll have to give me more details to fill in the blanks so I can make this dream bigger. Maybe even...if Rhodey will let me have some art supplies, I can show you the palace I want to build you and you can tell me what it's missing."

"You're very perceptive." Jared's breath puffed against Noah's skin, warm and soft. "I love Gothic antiques and dark wood, the scent of brandy and the taste of bourbon." His tone was hypnotic, painting a picture of everything he said. "I have a few things in storage, but you're correct. My place is a motel room off the highway exit. Well, a suite, really."

Jaw working, Noah shifted back to stare at Jared. "And Rhodey allowed you to stay there? I'm going to kick his...him. We're not waiting until I can manage a palace. He'll find you somewhere better to live. Immediately. If he's listening, he better know that I won't tell him twice."

"Well done." Jared skimmed his fingers along Noah's waist. "I knew I'd be coming here, and that I wanted to stay with you. I hadn't given it up because I wasn't sure you'd want me to after..." He paused, hand stilling. "Well, after."

An evasion and Noah couldn't allow that either. Apparently, subs had a lot of stuff they had to keep on top of, but he was up to the task. "You'll need to elaborate. You're not the only one who can't read minds—though, I'm not sure I'm totally convinced that you can't. After what?"

Shifting away a bit, Jared lengthened his neck, motioning to his skin. "I wasn't sure you wouldn't be too upset for me to be around you."

"You're silly." Noah leaned in, carefully brushing his lips along Jared's throat. "You've seen me roughed up. You've given me stitches. I hate that you suffered, but nothing would make me want you to stay away. You're still...as beautiful as you ever were."

Sighing with pleasure, Jared leaned back again, sliding down on the mattress and drawing Noah to lie on top of him. "Beautiful. That's a new one." He searched Noah's gaze, where at this distance it was possible to tell his eyelids had scarred as well. "I'll take it."

"Of course you will. You know it's true." Noah braced his hands and knees on either side of Jared, which was difficult, because the man was a lot bigger than him, but if he grew just a few more inches, they'd be closer to the same height. Still, even if he wasn't huge, he was heavy enough to aggravate his still healing wounds. "I demand you take better care of yourself. This is not a very good position for you."

Chuckling, Jared shook his head, his thick dark hair rustling against the pillow. "Careful, tiger, or you'll have me calling *you* 'sir' before long. That could be problematic, since you haven't trained up as a Dom yet."

Lips slanting, Noah lowered so he could speak just above Jared's mouth, tasting the heady sweetness from the cigar they'd shared. "You won't. Before long, we'll be equals. But I'll still take care of you. Because you need someone to, very much."

"Then I hope you're good with reciprocation, love." Cupping Noah's cheeks, Jared placed a chaste kiss on his lips. "Because I intend to do the same for you."

The kiss hadn't been enough, but Noah wouldn't get greedy. He was enjoying the closeness too much. Every inch of him could feel Jared's warmth, like the end of each nerve was soaking it in, changing it into something almost electric. He let out a contented sound, rubbing his cheek against Jared's again. "I can let you have that, but you'll probably be worn out, making sure I'm tame."

"Never tame, that would be tragic." Arm around Noah's waist, Jared rolled them both to their sides so they faced one another. "Almost as tragic as this bed. Where are the pillows, Rhodey? I'd like to take a nap, but this is too rough and ready even for someone who slept on a cot for years."

Shifting his gaze, Noah searched his mind for the right way to explain the situation. He didn't exactly like defending his uncle, but...yeah, this part he got. "I did mention he doesn't trust me. And I wouldn't do anything to... But he wasn't taking any chances. There's nothing in here I could use to hurt anyone. Or myself."

Cheek braced on one hand, Jared used his other to smooth Noah's hair back from his forehead. "If the pillows and blankets..." He glanced toward the mattress. "And sheets come back, will you hurt me or yourself? Or Rhodey?"

"No, of course not. I'm just saying... Ugh, this is not the type of conversation I enjoy. The truth is, if I die? Rhodey will make sure it's quick. Painless. If there's pain it's because he sees I'm still salvageable." Noah tipped his head back. "When I go into the void, he's not sure what I'll do. I don't blame him for that, but I usually don't damage myself. Unless I forget walls are solid and I didn't suddenly gain super powers."

"And you're feeling steady? Not on the precipice of your void?" Jared waited for his response, seeming to want to say more.

Closing his eyes, Noah buried his face between Jared's neck and the mattress. "Not now, no. Before...yeah. I can't always see it coming. My uncle's been working on that. I both love and hate him for it, but...I guess that's stupid. It's not his fault it doesn't work for long."

"What would make you want to stay here, with me?" The caresses moved to Noah's back, between his bare shoulder blades, Jared's palm smooth against his skin.

Voice muffled by the mattress, Noah shrugged. "It's not about what I want. I'll *always* want to stay with you. I don't like feeling...like I've lost myself and do bad things. But..." He took a deep breath, turning his head a little as he eased back enough to meet Jared's eyes. "The whip helps. After, it's like...I can center myself with the pain. But he won't do it unless things are really off. When it heals I always end up slipping away again. He shouldn't wait so long."

"Your back feels healed now." Tracing lines that would never go away entirely, Jared seemed to test the firmness of Noah's skin. "But you're with me."

"For now. Or...do you mean you'll do it instead?" A very good option. Maybe then, Noah would never slip into the darkness again. "I'd like that. You can go further than he does and I'll be me for longer. I accept."

"We'll talk about what you need, and I expect I've got several tricks up my sleeve that will keep you in check. If needed." Jared's thumb skimmed along Noah's bottom lip, pulling it away from his teeth ever so slightly. Gaze on that spot, he licked his own. "Pain. Pleasure. Mixed. I don't think I'm someone you need to fight against, but if you care to, it will be in the ring. I will teach you how to fight the right way."

Pressing his tongue into his bottom lip, since his teeth weren't allowed, Noah held Jared's gaze. "Do you…really understand what you're signing up for? You've seen me lose it, but…not all the way. Not to the point where… I don't remember anything that happens. Rhodey tells me after and I can tell he's ready to give up. You're not, but if you see *that?* You might be."

"There are other ways to keep you grounded. Present. And yes. I have seen you lose it." Jared glanced toward the cell door. "Rhodey wanted me to be one-hundred-percent sure, just like you want me to be." His attention returned to Noah's gaze. "I will *never* give up on you. You will always come back, and when you do it will be to me."

That sounded almost too perfect, but right now, Noah wanted to believe. He'd drive himself crazy, searching for all the things that could go wrong. Focusing on what could go right gave him a reason to keep fighting. And now he could do it *with* Jared again. He smiled, dropping his gaze to Jared's lips. "If my uncle is listening, he's probably already looking for a place for you. And he'll go over the top because it's you and he'll feel like he needs to prove *he* can take care of you." His lips twitched upward. "We might end up with bunk beds there."

Jared snickering was a little bit strange, but his head shake cleared the moment from his expression. "Don't give him ideas, tiger. He has enough all on his own." He raised his voice. "And one of them had better be to land us in Anniston Falls."

A huff near the door was the only warning before an armful of bedding was tossed in the general direction of the bed. "I'll think about it." Rhodey's brow lifted slightly when Noah tensed and glared at him. "A 'thank you' would be nice, but don't bother. You haven't earned this, but I won't make Jared suffer for your bullshit."

Breath a hot wash, Jared growled a little, whispering in Noah's ear. "Wouldn't it twist his mind if you were kind and sweet right now? Show me how you know the game works, tiger."

Kind and sweet? Me?

Usually, Noah would laugh at the very idea, but Jared was his Dom. And if he wanted kind and sweet, he'd damn well get it. Fuck what Rhodey expected. He drew in a slow, measured inhale, drawing away from Jared and rising from the bed to collect the thick pillows, sheets, blankets and...hell, even one of those nice mattress pads that got all thick and comfy when you opened them up.

He looked up at his uncle. "Since you've asked me not to, I won't thank you. But I appreciate this. You're right, Jared is taking a chance on me and he should be comfortable."

Rhodey's eyes narrowed as he studied Noah, like he was looking for any sign that this was some new way to fool him into letting his guard down. Finally, he inclined his head. "Good. I'm glad you know that. I don't give a fuck what you two get up to in here, but you better damn well remember he's hurt. Don't be a pushy little shit."

"I'm not." Noah's cheeks heated when Rhodey folded his arms over his chest. "I'll be more careful."

"He's taking very good care of me, husky." Jared rose from the bed, using a nickname Noah had never heard him apply to anyone before. "I'll move so you may make the bed, tiger." He took Rhodey in. "A little politeness goes a long way. Would you please get my pain medication? I believe, judging by the fire crawling up my legs, that it's time."

Cursing under his breath, Rhodey turned abruptly, striding out of the cell. Without bothering to close the door.

Stomach twisting, Noah ground his teeth and unzipped the thick plastic bag holding the mattress pad. He laid it over the mattress, smoothing it right to the edges as it expanded. The only time Rhodey left the door open was to test him. To see if Noah would accept that he still needed to be in here.

If he walked out before he was ready... Sometimes, he'd get the whip. It was his way of telling Rhodey he needed it. Other times, he'd just get dragged back in. There was no right move except...not making one at all.

But if Rhodey was telling him he'd whip him if he needed it...? Would that be better? Maybe he was offering so Noah could do better with Jared.

He let out a soft groan. "Has my uncle...? Do you know all the ways things work around here?"

Shoulder propped against the wall, Jared studied him with a little frown. "I know many ways they work, but I'm not all-knowing. Tell me. What do you need from me?"

"It's not... You wouldn't have to do anything." Noah did his best to keep his tone light. "I can finish making up the bed. Rhodey will bring your meds and...he left the door open. I might be able to get something to make everything...stable. Easier for you."

"I see." A ghost of disappointment and sadness edged Jared's expression. "I haven't found you difficult or unstable, but I don't wish to prevent you from having the care you need. The one request I would make as someone you've agreed to submit to is that you ask Rhodey for what you need rather than taking it or demanding it, then accept his answer graciously no matter what it is. If he says no? I will find a way to take care of you."

Noah paused with the fitted sheet in his hands. "I don't understand. Leaving the cell *is* asking." He made a face. "I don't like talking to him. This keeps things simple."

"We all must do things as adults that we find distasteful. Talking is asking. Leaving is disobeying. One is mature. The other is—" Jared lifted one shoulder, flipping his hand side to side. "Being childish. A brat. Brats often don't get what they want. At least not when they are under my care. I am not attracted to children. Those who are? Well, they are the ones who need a bullet that I'd gladly allow you a gun to administer."

Sucking his teeth, Noah snapped the sheet over the mattress. "I'm not a child. Or a brat. If I'm denied what is necessary, I find a way to get it. Being smart isn't bratty, it's simple…smart. I won't play dumb to entertain anyone."

"Do you trust me?" Jared's tone was mild.

Noah straightened, lifting his chin and folding his arms over his chest. "I've told you I do. And I will obey you. But I want you to speak plainly. Rhodey will either whip me or he won't. Asking nicely doesn't make any sense to me. It's better when he's angry in any case."

"Your uncle is a human being. You've proven you have a kind heart by taking care of me." Pushing away from the wall, Jared approached him. "If you think your words don't have an effect then you're mistaken. Your words hurt. They wound. Perhaps not as visibly with someone like Rhodey, but if you are aiming to cut into him then you succeed. If you ask for what you want, you prove you respect his humanity, and that you are willing to accept what someone else's boundaries are. That you are adult enough to see that he has a right to make decisions that are good for him and in this case, though they affect you, they might not meet your needs. If they do not, then I have given you my word that I will make certain you're taken care of."

There were times when no matter how many different ways Noah approached a situation with logic, the things he didn't know, or hadn't considered, blew every argument out of the water. Rhodey didn't usually bother debating with him, but Jared…yeah, Jared always seemed to manage to pinpoint all the things Noah missed.

Seeing his uncle as human? That was a big one.

"I don't..." Noah pulled on the last corner, then plunked down on the edge of the bed. "It's easy to forget he has feelings. I think we both prefer it that way. I'm aware that you do, right deep down in here." He pressed a hand to the center of his chest. "Not only because it's been explained to me. I *know* it. Other people are harder. He's impossible."

Lips slanting, Jared nodded. "Yes. He is. And it's one of the things I love about him. He is himself, unapologetically. He's earned that right with me. But—" Glancing over his shoulder, then back to Noah, Jared mouthed his next words. "I have seen him cry." He pressed a fist to his heart. "If he didn't love you? In some way, no matter how undetectable to you? You wouldn't still be here. And I definitely wouldn't have been asked to be here with you."

Pushing off the bed, Noah rubbed his hands against his jogging pants and grabbed the flat sheet. The bed was starting to look nicer already, even though Rhodey choosing white was strange. He stared at the sheets, then lifted his gaze to Jared. "You really think he loves me? That it's...hard for him to..." His throat worked. "He gave us white sheets."

"He is rough with you because he can't stand to get close to you, because he might lose you. If he doesn't harden himself, he'll never be able to survive your relationship as it stands now." Jared glanced at the sheets. "You can meet him halfway, Noah. You might need to take the first few steps, but if you do? Rhodey will be there for you forever. Just like me."

Noah took a deep breath, sensing his uncle's approach even before he saw him. He glanced toward the door as Rhodey walked in, holding out a black leather overnight bag. "I threw out the one you brought with you. It was a piece of shit. I swear, the military likes showing you how expendable you are from day one. Fucking canvas."

"Thank you." Jared didn't just say the words. He lifted his gaze from the bag, appreciation written on his face in the lift of his lips and the sheen in his eyes. "To them, we are. But it makes it very nice to be where I'm not."

Rhodey grunted, his gaze shifting toward the bed. "Finish with that, nephew. I'll give you two days. Impress me and I'll have you and Jared set up somewhere better. Fuck up and we'll start going by weeks. Which will piss me off because *he* needs better rest than he'll get in here. But he's too fucking stubborn to listen to a damn thing I say."

Back to Rhodey, Jared winked at Noah, mouthing, "True."

Pressing his lips together, Noah bit back his laugh, speaking as he continued making up the bed. "If you need me to prove myself to get him out of here, I'll do it, uncle. I don't want him staying here any longer than necessary."

"Say that again." Rhodey's stare was almost like a hand on his shoulder, forcing Noah to turn around and look him in the eye. "Why do you want this?"

"For him." Noah didn't blink. He wouldn't lie to Rhodey and he didn't give a fuck if it was the wrong answer. "I don't want him stuck here."

There was a long moment of silence, Rhodey holding still, just watching him. Then he gave a sharp nod. "Good. Two days. I'll see you in the morning."

Until the door shut, Noah couldn't breathe. Even then, he was a little afraid to move.

What the fuck just happened?

"May I touch you, my boy?" Jared had moved next to him.

Nodding, Noah tore his gaze from the door, trying to stop himself from trembling. He was confused and that was… worse than almost anything. "I don't know this game."

"It's the most complicated one there is." Jared folded him into his arms, pressing Noah's face into his shoulder. "Master it, and you will have conquered something very few do."

Noah blew out a breath, wrapping his arms around Jared's

waist. "I know you wanted me to ask, but…he'd already said no. With the sheets. Was that the right move?"

"It was the kind and respectful one." Jared's rough fingers tangled in Noah's hair giving a little tug before he began a softer, rhythmic stroking. "As I said. I'll give you what you need. A way to ground yourself that will leave you floating after. It's called subspace."

"Hmm…I'm not sure if you're making that up, but I'm willing to try." Noah let out a heavy sigh. "Two days. That seems very long and also…not long enough. How do I prove anything in two days?"

"By doing tomorrow exactly what you did tonight, and again the day after that. One moment, one decision, at a time." Using the hair at Noah's nape as a lever, Jared forced his head back to meet his gaze. "What I am about to do isn't punishment. It is a reward. That doesn't mean it won't hurt. Your safeword is 'asylum'. I am breaking my word to you, playing this way, but there is no sexual activity. I mean that. Not until we're out of here. Tell me you can respect that."

The edge of Noah's lips twitched. "Wait two days for you to f— Ugh, I didn't realize there are some times it *will* be hard not to swear. But since I am such a good boy, I will say, yes, sir. I can manage to wait two days for you to make sweet sweet love to me. It will be pure torture, but I'll manage. Somehow."

"Cheeky sub. I'm going to enjoy making it difficult for you to sit down for the next two days." Latching onto Noah's wrist, Jared drew him gently toward the bed where he sat. Then patted his thighs. "Over."

Eyes going wide, Noah stared at Jared. Then looked around the room. Then at Jared again. "Over? Your lap? We did agree that I'm not a little kid? What in the world would you want me there for?"

Lips twitching, Jared raised his brow. His hand remained on his muscular thigh. "If you were a child, I wouldn't lay a finger on you. This isn't a punishment, it's pleasure."

"I think we need to help you find new ways to get off. Me laying on your lap isn't gonna do anything for either of us." Noah's brow furrowed as he went to Jared's bag, opening it and fishing around until he found a pill bottle. "But if you insist, I'll do it. Meds first."

"Thank you, love. Meds after. I can't do this when my judgment or perception is impaired." Holding out his hand, Jared folded his palm in half in a 'come here' motion.

Arching a brow, Noah stepped forward and opened the bottle. "Rhodey's right, you are stubborn. It'll take like twenty minutes for it to hit you. This is not a negotiation, you're already in pain. You can have my ass however you want it after."

"I promise you I'll take it twenty minutes before I end this. So we'll both be blissed out at the same time and I'll be the worst Dom ever for not seeing to your aftercare." This time one brow went up. "Look at me, not stubborn at all. Negotiating."

Head tipped to one side, Noah kept holding out the bottle. "Now you've made it even more clear I need to stand my ground. You intend to continue this for *more* than twenty minutes? In your condition? I might have to call Rhodey in here to spank *you*. I would try, but you're still a little big for me. Another year or so and that won't be a problem."

Laughter shook Jared's shoulders. "I'd like to see him try to spank me. In fact, I'd want footage." He curved his arm, motioning Noah closer. "Come on. Sooner we do this, sooner it's over with. I want to touch you. The endorphins will be good for me too. Just promise me you won't deny me any delicious sounds you'd like to make. If I get your tears, I'll be in complete bliss."

That did sound nice, but Noah wasn't ready to give up just yet. Changing tactics, he moved toward Jared, straddling his lap. He plucked out two pills, hoping it was the right amount, and pressed them to Jared's lips. "Open wide. Next time, it'll be my turn. With something much *much* bigger."

Sighing, Jared leaned back on his elbows, bringing his mouth out of range to speak. "Noah, I won't compromise on your safety. I could injure myself as well, believe it or not. If I didn't notice you'd cut off my circulation, for instance. Be a good boy and I'll take one half-way through and the other when we're finished."

"But..." Noah lowered his gaze to the pills. Would it be selfish to agree? To ignore the pain Jared was in. But the man was a doctor. He let out a soft groan, dropping the pills back in the bottle. "Fine. You win. But if I sense any pain or tension I'm using my brand spanking new safeword. For *you*."

"I would expect nothing less." Jerking his head toward the pillow, Jared sat up again. "You'll want that under your head. Get comfy. You're going to be here a while. I plan to thoroughly enjoy myself."

Slipping off Jared's lap, Noah repositioned himself over it, grabbing the pillow and trying not to let how awkward the position felt show. His cheeks were blazing, so he buried his face in the pillow. A bit better. And that Jared would enjoy himself made him happy. He didn't quite understand *how* he would, but maybe this was another lesson.

"Good boy. Tell me your safeword." Jared's hand smoothed up and down Noah's back, exploring his skin in rhythmic circles.

Noah huffed into the pillow, smiling a little. "*Your* safeword. And it's 'asylum'. I won't forget to use it as needed."

"I'm sure you won't." Fingertips digging into a few pressure points, Jared began a deep massage of Noah's muscles, starting at his nape. "If I go too hard, tell me."

Snorting, Noah turned his head as much as he could, lifting his face from the pillow. "Sir, you *can* see those scars, right? I can take whatever you want to give me. Don't worry."

"And if I wish to give you pleasure?" Jared's thumb dug

harder at a knot at the side of Noah's neck where it met his shoulder.

That was an interesting question. Noah's brow furrowed. "You're touching me. That feels good. But there won't be sex, so I'm not sure what you mean. I don't need much, the opportunities for...well, *anything* have been kinda limited."

"You masturbate, do you not?" Those strong hands both worked his shoulders now, kneading and squeezing his flesh.

"Of course, when it's necessary." Noah struggled to keep his tone level. And not sound embarrassed. But this wasn't exactly something he talked about with...anyone. Not that he'd ever had anyone to discuss it with. "I don't find it necessary often, but...you know. It's whatever."

"I have thought about you pleasuring yourself many times. The idea of watching you. Of telling you when you may come. If you may come." There was no heat to Jared's words, his hands working magic to melt each knot in Noah's muscles. "I want you to remember that while I'm giving you this feeling. The same feeling you have as you float down and up on arousal and its aftermath."

Shifting a bit as blood began pulsing low, Noah inhaled roughly and nodded. "I think...it would be a lot hotter, if you're watching. If you tell me you want that from me. It won't be something I just want to...get it over with."

"Shh... I will tell you exactly what I want, which is for you to submit to what I'm giving you." Hands moving lower, Jared brushed his fingertips under the waistband of Noah's sweats, loosening the elastic to nudge them down past the crest of his ass. Fingernails scraped lightly along each cheek. Then harder.

The sensation was very different than anything Noah'd felt before. He closed his eyes, drawing all his focus to the spots where his skin heated. He let out a thoughtful sound. "There will be some nice marks. Do you think they'll last until we get somewhere where I'll be able to look at them?"

"Yes. When I'm finished you will have a lovely mass of bruises here—" A light fingertip trailed from Noah's left ass cheek all the way down under the sweats to the backs of his thighs. "—and here. And I promise to make certain you ruin Rhodey's white sheets."

Noah snickered, resting his head on the pillow. "I don't think he'll mind it so much if you're the one doing it. And I don't need too many stitches."

"No stitches." Flicking his forefinger against Noah's seam, where his ass met his legs, Jared set up a deep sting before he raked his fingernail over the spot. Wetness welled, hot. Sticky. "Very nice."

Hissing in a breath, Noah adjusted himself so his dick wasn't at a weird angle, but the way it pressed against Jared's thigh wasn't much better. The stimulation, along with the stinging heat, drew out a soft groan. He adjusted again, moving his dick so he was almost fucking Jared's leg. "Yes, I like that."

Nails raked Noah's back. A full set from each of Jared's hands, down his shoulders clear to his lower back. Fire followed in their wake. Then again. And again.

Body jerking with the motion, Noah sucked in a sharp breath, hands gripping either end of the pillow. This. *This* was what he needed. His head wouldn't go anywhere when it was so connected to everything happening to his body. Except it usually didn't feel good in any way. Pain centered him and kept his mind from drifting into the dark. Like each bit of hurt was a red flare, guiding him back to where he belonged. With Jared's touch it was so much more.

A shift of Jared's leg lifted Noah's hips a little higher. Then Jared's arms were under him, temporarily holding him aloft. The soft, heated point of Jared's tongue licked at the scratches on Noah's ass, lulling, soothing. Before the sharp points of teeth bit hard into his flesh.

"*Fuck.*" Noah gasped, shaking his head and groaning into

the pillow, so close to coming it was like his body had decided to leave his brain behind altogether. Only not in a bad way. He struggled to rein it in, latching on to the word he wasn't supposed to say. "I'm sorry...I'm so sorry, sir. I couldn't...I didn't mean to."

"I know, my love. We'll take care of that. I'll teach you control. While you fly." The lowering of Noah's hips was accompanied by the tap of Jared's open palm against the lower part of his ass. First one side, then the other. Just minor impacts. Rhythmic. Again and again. Back and forth in the same spot every time. "I'll have to punish you, of course, but then all will be forgiven. Won't it?"

Noah growled, pressing his forehead into the pillow. "Not unless I can prove I can do this. I can. Please don't stop."

"I wouldn't dream of it. We will be talking about forgiveness, later, but not now. Right now? I am enjoying my boy's ass." The rare and subtle profanity dropped from Jared's lips, sounding all the more shocking because it came from him. "Which is, I must say, the nicest canvas I've ever had to work with. You redden so easily. I wonder if you will in a few months' time once I've used more than my hand on you with regularity?"

"Mmm, I hope so." Noah wanted to see every bit of what Jared had done to him, but part of him also wanted to view it from a different angle. To be standing beside him while he worked his magic. Only...he wouldn't feel that, which would suck. He laughed at himself, feeling a bit high. "I'm going to paint one of your little pain sluts one day. And then you're going to hurt me to show me how much you love it."

A shift of Jared's weight, the lift of his hips, brought his Dom's erection in contact with his hip. "I imagine I would, if you did something so lovely." The spanks grew harder, faster, still impacting Noah's sit spots in precisely the same place each time. "I would enjoy putting a permanent scar where your shoulder meets your neck. With my teeth. Where I can see it when I look at you."

That sounded like a really good idea. Noah nodded, grinding his hip so he could enjoy the pressure of Jared's thigh and let his Dom feel the movement as well. Fuck, knowing he made Jared hard was the best thing in the world. He wanted to see him. To touch him, everywhere. Except now wouldn't be good. Because… "Am I hurting you?"

The way Jared's weight shifted said he shook his head. Voice a little breathy, he answered. "No. I feel what you feel. Tell me. Are you ready to fly, tiger?"

"Yes, sir. I'm ready for it all." Noah slowed the movements of his hips, the edge so close, he would set himself off if he kept it up. But he wanted this to last. "I want to come so bad, but what you're giving me is…better. It's everywhere."

"You may come anytime you like, love." Full impact now, Jared drew back his arm, striking Noah so hard his body jerked forward with each blow. The crack of Jared's palm was like a thunderclap, searing into his skin, and rocking his hips against the meaty portion of Jared's thigh. "And then I will mark you. Again."

Instead of the impact grounding him, it threw Noah right off the cliff into a space that wasn't dark at all. It was brilliant, like staring into the sun, the intense burn lasting long after he closed his eyes. His whole body shook as he reached climax, the intensity more than anything he'd ever managed alone. The pillow muffled most of his sharp cry, but the sound seemed to echo around him as his whole body glowed with pleasure.

Before he even began to spiral downward, Jared's teeth sunk into his shoulder, deep and hard, cementing the sparklers of heat and pain and awareness of his Dom. "Beautiful." Jared whispered against Noah's skin, kissing and laving the mark. "So beautiful."

"I feel…floaty." Noah shook his head, because that wasn't

the right word, but there wasn't a better one. His laugh sounded a bit like he'd downed a bottle of his uncle's vodka. The whole world had gone light and shiny, like even the gray walls of the cell couldn't keep it out. "I don't think I'd ever hurt anyone again if I stayed right here. Isn't that a good idea? I come up with great ones sometimes."

Chuckling, Jared breathed in heated puffs against Noah's skin. "I will make you feel this way as often as you like." He patted Noah's ass, reactivating the nerve endings there. "Scoot up. I need to get you some water."

"Yes, we can both float in the water." Noah dragged himself in the direction he hoped the bed was, except his legs ended up somewhere else. His hand brushed over something and he held it up. "This is yours. You need your…" He squinted at it, his brain deciding it didn't want to give him the right words for anything. "Tic Tacs?"

More laughter from Jared, a little more distant, as he rummaged inside the hamper. A bottle cap cracked, and he approached the bed, joining Noah with what looked like a chocolate bar and some water. "Let me help you. Sit up just a little. I can't lift you right now." He tipped the bottle to Noah's lips. "There we go. That's right."

A few droplets spilled to Noah's chest, which was nice. Cool. The cell wasn't usually this hot. And he wasn't usually this sticky. He wiped one hand over his brow, then blinked at his fingers. "I'm sweaty. I'm sorry, that must've been gross."

"On the contrary." A package crinkled, then chocolate pressed against Noah's lips. "It was gratifying and, as you say, *hot*."

Noah smiled, sucking the chocolate, and Jared's fingers, into his mouth. Sweetness burst over his tongue, along with the saltiness of Jared's flesh. "Mmm, you're tasty. You have to try…you."

"I've already gorged myself on *you*." Smiling down at him, Jared set the chocolate aside and traded it for a square package that he drew a few wipes from. "Let's get you cleaned up."

Frowning, Noah looked around. There was something he was supposed to be doing. Water? No, he'd had that. Jared wanted him to drink it, not float in it. Chocolate hadn't been on the list, but was a great surprise. He shifted over as Jared wiped him down with the cool cloth. Also not on the list, but nice.

The Tic Tacs. No... He gave Jared a hard look as his brain snapped into place. "Your pills. You were supposed to stop and take some. You have to take the full dose now."

"Hush. I took them, as I said I would." Grin widening, Jared continued to clean him, rolling him with a gentle push. "You were too far gone to notice. As I will be too, soon. Let's get you settled so we can share this bed since your uncle was too lazy to set up the bunk beds and apparently enjoys a bit of sadism himself."

Noah snorted, shaking his head. "It would've been silly to set them up for two days. Because it's gonna be just that. I'm getting you out of here." He brought his hand up to his shoulder, rubbing at the teeth marks and grinning as heat flared there. "This will help a lot. Thank you, sir."

"I can sincerely say it was my pleasure." Standing, Jared placed the wipes into a plastic bag, then tossed it on top of his duffel before drawing his shirt over his head. As he did, a few of his scars pulled dangerously, like they might split, but he didn't seem to be feeling much other than blissed out. At least judging by his dreamy expression and curved lips. "I hope you don't mind if I wear pajamas. I usually do." Holding up a pair of black silk trousers and a matching top, he indicated the clothes. "I get itchy against sheets."

Shaking his head again, Noah threw his feet over the side of the bed, bending down to grab the small roll he kept there, which had one change of the same outfit he was wearing. Rhodey usually grabbed his old clothes every day when he brought him food, or led him down the hall to the bathroom. The same old routine. Tonight, the big difference was, Jared was part of it.

He laid the clothes on the corner of his bed. "I've already had my shower today. When I was still...calm. But if you need one, I'm sure he'll bring you. Or...for the bathroom or whatever."

Dressed in his pajamas, Jared turned, looking around the room as if seeing it for the first time. His brows pulled together. "Isn't it customary to have at least a toilet in these places?"

Noah shrugged, lowering his gaze to the floor. "One of the other cells had one. It probably made things easier. But Rhodey always comes right away when I knock. He gets pissed if I do it just to bitch about being in here, but...he always shows up."

"Hmph." Jared's mouth twisted to one side. "Ah. Time to lie down." He swayed a little, holding out an arm to Noah. "Would you...?"

Moving fast, Noah caught Jared around the waist and gently eased him onto the bed. He slid the covers over his Dom, smiling as he stroked his black hair. "You can rest now, sir. Thank you for taking care of me. Now it's my turn. Whatever you need, all you have to do is say the word and I've got you."

"That's lovely." Jared blinked at him, smiling back. "I had antiseptic wipes. Your scrapes should be disinfected. Oh, that's right. I did it already." His smile broadened. "Would you lie down next to me? I'm a little cold. These pills mess with my metabolism. And to reward you..." There was a long pause. "I shall recite poetry."

Grinning, Noah pushed to his feet, quickly changing into his clean clothes, and bringing the ones he'd worn all day to put on top of the folding chair Rhodey would probably grab later. "I can do that. And I'd love to hear your poems..." He stilled as the door opened, tripping back so he wasn't so close to it. "I didn't hurt him."

Rhodey glanced toward Jared, then back at Noah. "I know. He's not a fool, he would have let me know if you'd tried. Get some sleep. The door won't be locked. You can show him where the bathroom and showers are. I won't be far if you think he needs me."

"Okay, but..." Noah rubbed his hands on his thighs, drying his sweaty palms on his sweatpants. "Okay."

"I'm not saying you can't manage, Noah." Rhodey gave him a level look. "I'm asking you to understand that if you can't, I'm here. Got it?"

He gave his uncle a sharp nod. "I've got it. I wouldn't let him be hurt or whatever for my pride."

The edge of Rhodey's lips curved. "Yeah. That's why I'm unlocking the door. Have a good night. And if he doesn't need to call me in here, maybe I'll let you have breakfast at a table."

From the bed, Jared mumbled, rolling to his side. "Tyger tyger burning bright..."

Shooting him a worried look, Noah jumped when Rhodey put a hand on his shoulder. When his uncle immediately pulled it back, he almost told him it was fine, but the man was already headed out the door.

His tone made it seem like nothing was wrong. "Go on. You'll want to hear this one. It's one of his favorites."

When the door closed, Noah climbed into bed with Jared, laying down facing him. He pulled off his Dom's glasses, folding the arms gently and reaching down to lay them on top of Jared's overnight bag. Seeing Jared like this was strange. The scars, the pain, was something Noah wished he could take away, but the rest... He was relaxed. Still so powerful, a force in his own right, but more...human. Less like someone untouchable and all knowing.

And it made Noah feel a bit more human himself, just having him close.

Two days. Yes, Noah could definitely pull off two days for more of this, away from the cell.

He might never have to come back because Jared was here.

Best of all?

He's here to stay.

Chapter Twenty-Three

PAST

Sitting at the kitchen table on the first floor of the house he'd never gotten to see much of, for the second morning in a row, Noah picked up his glass of orange juice and took a sip. Yesterday, he'd gulped it down, liking having something to drink with flavor and the way the glass was cool against his palm.

He even had cutlery. *Metal* cutlery. He grabbed his fork, spearing his eggs with it, the tines scraping noisily against the plate.

Rhodey shot him a sideways look, then brought his focus back to Jared. "I swear, he's housetrained."

"Careful, husky. You don't want me revealing how long it took you to learn how to hold your utensils in something other than your fists." Demonstrating, Jared balanced a bite of pancake on the back of his fork, which was in his left hand.

He didn't switch up the knife and fork the way Noah had always seen people do, instead making the act of eating look like an elegant dance or high-wire act. Each movement was quiet. Serenely so. Without saying anything at all, Jared showed him how to behave. How his Dom would like him to behave.

Repositioning the fork, Noah slid it into the eggs, sitting up a bit as he mirrored Jared's posture too. When he caught Rhodey watching him, he took a very proper bite and gave him a smug look. "I'm a very fast learner, uncle."

"Yeah, but your attitude still needs some fucking work." Rhodey used his fingers to bring a breakfast sausage to his mouth and bit it in half. "Just because you're leaving today doesn't mean you don't have a lot to work on. Don't get cocky. Don't start thinking you're in the clear. Because you're not, and not because I'm an asshole. There's no fix, Noah. Just the right tools, used the right way."

"We all have our own scars." Jared kept eating, his movements fluid and not threatening in any way. "They become part of us. But they don't define us." He pushed his juice glass over a little, trading it for Noah's and giving Noah his own full one. "As long as we don't let them."

Rhodey inclined his head, polishing off the sausage and using a napkin to wipe off his fingers. "True. And maybe he'll get there. Right now, he needs to be very aware of himself, keep working on shit. Since he's doing a good job of it with you, he can continue somewhere nicer. I got you a decent-sized condo in Anniston Falls. Stay there as long as you want. Tracey told me to remind you you're welcome to her guest house whenever you—"

"No. The condo is fine." Noah's fork clattered on his plate as he pushed away from the table. "If this is a test, stop. I'm not ready. I'll stay in the cell. You can't..."

"We can stay in there as long as you like, tiger. But it's not a test, and you *are* ready to come home with me." Jared's warm voice was still very much *him*, but the raspiness in it hadn't gone away since that first night. "I asked to be there because I want to live there. Not to test you. We can go somewhere else if you like."

Pressing his eyes shut, Noah forced his mind to calm and

his breaths to fall back into a steady rhythm. He caught Jared breathing the same, slowly, more obviously now, guiding him into it. He opened his eyes and gave Jared a small smile of gratitude, lowering back into his seat. "I don't mind being close to her. Just…not that close. Not yet. When the time is right, I want to…be a good son to her. I'll get there."

Palm up on the table, Jared offered his hand to Noah. Not like he *had* to take it, but more like he was welcome to that bit of comfort if he wanted to claim it. "I know you will, love."

Noah took Jared's hand, holding it as they finished breakfast. Then whenever he got a chance while they packed up the things Rhodey'd collected for their new place at some point—obviously not watching Noah as closely as he used to. Not since his declaration about the steps Noah needed to take to get out of here. The SUV ended up pretty full, and Noah had to squeeze into the middle seat, but Jared reached back to give him his hand again as they drove.

The ride wasn't that long, which caught Noah off guard. He'd expected Rhodey to bring him to one of his remote safehouses, on the other side of the country. But before long, they were pulling into an underground parking garage. Unloading and taking an elevator up to the top floor, where the condo seemed to take up most of the space.

Already fully furnished in a clean, modern style, the things they brought in only added some necessities and comfort. Noah kept his focus on moving packages and boxes, not saying a word until Rhodey handed Jared the keys with a few quiet words, then left them alone.

In their new home.

"This is…" Noah took a deep breath, walking over to the floor-to-ceiling windows, looking over the edge of the city and the woods beyond. "It's really nice. I don't even know what to say." He turned his head to grin at Jared. "Thank you, sir. There's no way I'd be here if it wasn't for you."

"Thank you for wanting to be with me enough to work for this." One hip leaned against the white waterfall island, Jared seemed to be taking Noah in more than the surroundings. Like he got more pleasure from Noah's joy than from the space itself. "Come here, please."

Wetting his lips with his tongue, Noah approached Jared slowly. His Dom had been moving a bit easier, but still…not without pain when his meds started to wear off. He stopped in front of Jared and met his eyes. "Sir, just because we're here now, it doesn't mean… We don't have to…" His cheeks heated. "Make sweet sweet love. We can just watch a movie or listen to music. Or…I think I saw some paints?"

"You did. But there's something I'd like to do more than any of those things, first." Reaching around, Jared pulled open a drawer that was fitted seamlessly into the marble and drew out a flat, long box wrapped in dark red, shiny paper with black ribbons around it. "This is for you."

Noah took the box and rested his hip against the island, close to Jared. He gently tugged the ribbon, then laid it on the counter beside him and went to work on the tape. Once that was set aside as well, he opened the box. Inside was a cuff, made of heavy platinum links.

He cocked his head, lifting his gaze, his lips twitching. "Sir, I don't think this will fit around my neck without some serious effort. But we can try."

Huffing, humor in his eyes, Jared shook his head. "I decided on a cuff rather than a collar for a very good reason." He pointed at the floor. "You may still kneel, however, while I put it on you."

"Hmm." Noah moved in a bit closer. "I need something first. Before I can be a very good *official* sub for you, sir."

Jared raised one brow. "Oh? Are we negotiating again?"

"Yes, sir. Respectfully. And at your pleasure." There. Saying the right things should help. Noah could play with

Jared, so long as he behaved himself. Mostly. He was skirting the edges of what his Dom would tolerate, but it would be worth it. "You've marked me and I love it. Everything you've done. But something's missing and you've asked for my honesty. So I'm giving it to you."

Inclining his head, Jared folded his arms. "I did. Go on."

"A kiss." Noah held Jared's gaze, not willing to be a coward now that he'd come this far. But his throat worked, because part of him was afraid he'd taken more than he should have. And not being sure was damn frustrating. "I need…to feel more than those small kisses you've given me. I know I'm being pushy and it's up to you how much I get, but it's driving me crazy. I want that more than anything and I'm sorry if that's…wrong."

Placing a finger against Noah's lips, Jared shook his head. "You had me at 'a kiss', my boy." His hand moved to Noah's nape, gathering in the curls there, tugging with just the right amount of pressure to activate the rush of tingling down his spine. Jared angled his head just so. "Like this?" Soft, teasing, a mere butterfly brush of contact across Noah's lips. "Or…did you mean, like this?" Tongue darting, Jared licked the seam of Noah's mouth. "Tell me, love. What do you really need?"

"More." Noah pressed up against Jared, whispering against his lips. His whole body had focused on the taste of the man. On the heat of his mouth, as though everything Noah could want in the world was right there for him to savor. "I need it all."

"Then you shall have it."

Jared's breath mingled with his own before his mouth came crashing down with a needy groan. His tongue parted Noah's lips in a show of ownership, leaving no doubt in that moment as to the control he could and would wield. One hand on Noah's hip, the other in his hair, Jared snugged their bodies together.

Tongue dueling with his Dom's, Noah smiled, letting out his own quiet sound of pleasure. Something about kissing this man was purely fucking intoxicating. Even more than he'd thought it would be. He gripped his hands into Jared's shirt, sliding his mouth to an angle, drinking in the air passing between them like the richest hard liquor, except the burn flowed right through his blood.

Adjusting, Jared slid his hand down to Noah's ass, cupping one cheek and digging in his fingers. Bruises and scrapes all still fresh activated, Jared seeming to know exactly where to press. He lifted his head on a gasp, pulling away from Noah's mouth with a smacking sound. "Sweet sweet love on the kitchen counter isn't what I had in mind, but that's where this is headed."

"Mmm." Noah gave Jared a hooded look, dipping in to nip his bottom lip. In the back of his mind, something nagged at him, but right then he was too drunk on Jared's kisses to shift his attention anywhere else. "There's a nice couch somewhere. It exists. And probably a bed."

"*This* is the reason I got you the cuff." Jared's laugh puffed across Noah's cheek. "So you can start wearing it on your left wrist when you're in the mood." Sharp teeth nipped his earlobe. "For now, on the right though, you have a lot to learn."

His Dom had a point, but Noah couldn't help sighing a bit before he lowered to his knees. Except, from here, he had something else to distract him as he held up his wrist. "I submit to your judgment, sir. And I love the gift." He rubbed his cheek against the outline of Jared's dick in slacks that fit him *just* right. "Should I show you how much?"

"Hold up your right wrist, tiger." Jared's voice held a certain amount of strain. "Let's get this and the tag on you."

Ah, yes. Right wrist. Noah switched the hands he offered up and used the other to pull the tag out of the pocket of his jeans. Normal clothes were nice. But multitasking was even better. He ran the tip of his nose along the length of Jared's dick while handing him the tag. "Here you go, sir."

"Good boy." The metal was cold and heavy as Jared worked the cuff around his wrist and closed the solid clasp with a *snap*. Taking the tag, his Dom threaded its loop through one of the links, then let it go so it clinked brightly. "I'd say that deserves a reward." He stepped back. "For you. Not me."

Frowning, Noah lifted his gaze and sat back on his heels. "Why not both? It would be a shame to have me down here for nothing, wouldn't it? I mean…not *nothing*." He lowered his arm, smiling as he brushed his fingers over the cuff. "This is precious and I'm grateful to be yours." His one track mind had him looking at that firm, hard length pressing against smooth, dark fabric. "But your dick is. Right. There."

Jared inhaled sharply, then slowly, almost hesitantly, stepped within reach again. One hand gripping the counter edge, he inclined his head. "Since you ask so prettily. You may."

Glancing up, Noah studied Jared's face. His brow furrowed. "Sir, you will always be honest with me, right?"

"I will." Sweat dotted the top of Jared's upper lip, but he didn't appear to be in pain. There was no tightness around his eyes or paleness to his skin.

Still, Noah had to make sure. "Will this hurt you? If it will, I don't want to do it. I'd be fine with more kissing. On the sofa. Or the bed. Where you can be comfortable and I can enjoy your mouth for as long as I'm awake. You can nap if you want, I won't mind."

Jared's fingers slid into the hair at Noah's temple. "You are such a sweet boy to be concerned. The answer to your question is that I don't know if it will hurt me. I know I can't make a thrusting motion without pain. I've not…" He cleared his throat. "I've not yet successfully ejaculated since the explosion."

Nodding slowly, Noah brought his hand to the back of

Jared's, holding it there as he pushed to his feet. "Then when we try this, you'll be lying down. No thrusting. Your very good sub will do all the work and you'll keep very *very* still."

Breaths even, Jared searched Noah's face. "You won't blame yourself if I experience pain or can't continue? If I lose my erection?"

"No, but you haven't lost it yet." Noah lifted his shoulders, grinning as he laced his fingers with Jared's and lowered it so he could tug him in the direction of where he hoped the bedroom was. First door was a small bathroom. Second was the laundry room. The third was an office. "I swear, if my uncle somehow manages to cockblock me without even being here, I'm going to...do something drastic."

Jared snorted. "He's always been big on grand gestures. Tell me something? Is the space something you like? Would you choose it for yourself?" Peering into a coat closet, Jared clucked his tongue. "I don't know who has this many coats. What will we put in there?"

At the end of the hall was one final door. Opening it, Noah understood why the place was so big. His lips parted as he took in the massive bed, and furnishings right out of a magazine. He shook his head slowly. "It's not...what I would have chosen. I don't know what I would choose, but this is... it's really nice. Almost as good as what I would picture giving you. Only...for you it would be something darker. More wood. I don't mean that as anything else, I just... Still, he chose well."

Behind him, Jared tucked his arms around Noah's waist, placing his chin on Noah's shoulder. "Well, then." It was all he said for several minutes, clearly needing time to take in Rhodey's gift. When he spoke, the gravel in his voice had thickened. "I love that stupid bastard. For this. And for letting me have you."

Noah grinned, turning in Jared's arms and curving his

hands under his elbows to draw him over to the bed. The comforter was pretty plain, white with thick, dark blue stripes, but it was plush and looked like heaven to lie under. He folded it over so Jared could climb in. "You get to enjoy it first. I bet it'll be awesome after my 'room' and…the motel and everything before that."

Inclining his head, Jared lifted his arms a bit from his sides. "I would appreciate it very much if you would undress me." His gaze softened as he ran it over Noah, taking his time with his perusal. "Occasionally, it will please me to do the same for you, and to dress you."

"Really?" Noah moved closer to Jared and got to work on the buttons of his silk shirt, dark, like most of his clothes, but this was black with a dark red sheen when it caught the light. He brushed his fingers over the fabric between each button he released. "I guess I wouldn't mind that, but not until you're fully healed. Until then, the pleasure is all mine."

"I believe I can tolerate that." Humor edged Jared's words, tipping up his lips. "We'll be going to a club to observe some of the submissives there. I expect you to speak only to me, no matter what. When you're ready, of course. But when we do, I would like to hear your views on the submissives there, and what you believe would make a good submissive."

The edges of Noah's lips tightened as he gently slid the shirt down Jared's arms, then laid it on the end of the bed. He took a knee to undo Jared's shoes. "Much later, maybe I'll be ready. I don't think I'll mind you having your pick of subs, but…not yet. I need to know what you and I have…that no one can come between us. Not them, not Rhodey. No one."

Curving his hand under Noah's jaw, Jared gently lifted his face. "*No one.* I have no desire to be with anyone else for as long as we're together. You are mine. I am yours."

Noah lifted his brow at his Dom. "Sir, you get a bunch of little pain sluts, remember? I'll be a Dom some day. Your equal. I'll enjoy watching you toy with them. Then remind you why you kept me."

A small huff of amusement escaped Jared's nose. "I meant after you are no longer *mine.*" He glanced meaningfully at Noah's cuff. "And you *are* my equal, Noah. Never doubt that. Dom and sub do not mean unequal. They are simply different roles in a dynamic."

"All right, fine. I guess that makes sense, but I don't want to think of anything changing right now. I'll learn all the stuff I need to, but what I do know?" Noah gave Jared a little push onto the edge of the bed so he could finish taking off his shoes. "Is what I need to do for you at this moment. Get you nice and comfy."

"As you wish, love." Leaning back on his hands, Jared tipped his head back to stare at the high ceiling. "I've never seen so much bright white. Everything in the desert was brown and tan."

Setting Jared's shoes aside, under the edge of the bed, Noah turned his attention to his socks. "Maybe that's why Rhodey chose it? He probably knows what you like, better than I do." The idea of that irritated Noah, but he did his best to keep his tone light. "I'll learn, though. No matter how long we're here, I'll make sure it's up to your standards and becomes a place you can call home."

"That *we* can call home." Jared lowered his gaze, glancing around the giant room with its empty corners. "Over there. That looks like a good spot for an easel. The light in here is good. Do you think you might let me pose for you? Or do you not enjoy figure drawing?"

Noah cocked his head, rising up a bit so he could undo Jared's slacks. "I don't know, I've never spent much time doing it. I can do pretty good sketches of people, but most of my paintings have been landscapes and animals. I really like painting animals. It reminds me of..." He took a deep breath and shook his head. "But, yeah, I'd love to paint you." He tugged lightly at Jared's slacks, lowering them when his Dom lifted his hips. Not staring at the scars all over his thighs was hard, but he managed to focus on his task. "You're like…the purest image of strength I could ever imagine. I don't know if I'd ever let anyone else look at the painting, but it would be… an honor to be allowed to do it."

Listening to him, hanging on to every word Noah said, like he always did, Jared nodded slowly. "Thank you, my boy. I'm glad I can be that to you." He ran his fingertips through the front sections of Noah's hair, playing with the curls and widened his thighs. "You may remove my underclothes."

Even though Noah had been practically naked in front of Jared, there was something a lot more intimate about the positions being reversed for some reason. Hooking his fingers to the waistband of Jared's boxer briefs, Noah tried to keep the conversation going like this was no big deal. He was tending to his Dom. Good subs did this all the time.

"You know, it's kinda weird, because sometimes it's like you're super old, but other times it hits me that you're not even ten years older than me." He glanced up at Jared. "But you've been all over the world. You know practically everything. I have a lot of catching up to do."

"I'm flattered, but I do not know nearly everything." Jared lifted his hips a little to assist Noah with the boxer briefs. "I'd like to get you a library card and as many books as you like. There's a wonderful used bookstore in town. One of those ramshackle places where the books are in piles everywhere and you never know what treasures you'll find. You can travel anywhere in a book."

A spark of excitement flared in Noah, but he tamped it down with some much needed caution as he drew Jared's boxers off and set them with the rest of his clothes. "Rhodey brought me books a lot. I wouldn't mind going to the bookstore…at some point. But not the library. There could be a lot of people there. Innocent people. I need to stay away from them."

"We'll work on that. And any books that are in the library are also in their online catalog. You can choose any ones you like for now and I shall get them for you." Scooting back on the bed, Jared reclined against the many thick, fluffy pillows, sinking into the pile and held out a hand to Noah. "Come. I want you up here with me. Where you can look at me. All you like."

"Yes, sir. I just have to take off my boots." Crouched down, Noah made quick work of removing the sturdy leather boots his uncle had provided with the rest of his new clothes. After setting them beside Jared's shoes, he climbed onto the bed, leaning over Jared to brush a soft kiss to his lips. "You're really comfortable with being naked. I like that. I probably wouldn't like knowing *why*, though."

Pushing Noah's hair back from his forehead, Jared chuckled. "I'm a physician. A surgeon. I view the body as a machine. It is who we are on the inside that we seem to be best at hiding, while we pretend the outside is a big mystery."

Noah considered Jared's words carefully, inclining his head. "True, but you wear gloves during surgery. Touching skin, showing it like this is...special, isn't it? You wouldn't put your hand on someone..." He rested his palm on Jared's chest, right over his heart. "Unless you were examining them, right?" He caught himself wanting to growl at the idea of *anyone* touching Jared at all and rolled his eyes at himself. "I'm sorry, I'm being possessive and I have no place doing that."

"I've given you that right, love, and I would struggle with anyone but me touching you as well." Jared ran his hand down Noah's flank, gripping his hip to pull him closer. "As for examinations, no, I don't do them naked. If someone forced me to, I wouldn't be uncomfortable. Amused. Perhaps a little worried about scalpels getting too close to my tender parts.

Being naked with you like this? You being here? That's what makes it special."

Kissing Jared again, Noah hummed his agreement. "I won't ever stop you from doing your job. But your little sluts won't be allowed to touch you. They'll have to wait for how you want to use them. Maybe you'll wear gloves and they only get you from a distance. It'll drive them crazy."

Something flickered in Jared's gaze, but it was an emotion or thought that was difficult to pinpoint. His voice was quieter, thoughtful, when he answered, again, "As you wish." He patted Noah's hip lightly. "I believe you were going to have a look at me and then I was going to teach you how to pleasure me with that beautiful mouth."

"Mhm." Noah shifted so he was half over Jared, lowering to graze his teeth along Jared's jaw. "I look with my mouth too. It's a special talent of mine I've just discovered. I can memorize every inch of you with it."

"Noah?" There was a strained note in Jared's tone.

Lifting his head, Noah met those icy blue eyes, like the smoothest frozen lake reflecting a cloudless sky. His blood was already pulsing down low, but not so much he couldn't bring his focus back to his Dom. "Yes, sir?"

Jared skimmed the back of his hand over Noah's right pec, his gaze searching. "I need you to look at me and know you see all of me. No one has. Not since... I'm sorry. I need that. May I ask it of you as both my boy and a friend?"

"Friend?" Noah felt silly repeating the word, but it threw him off. Of everything Jared had ever said to him, that was the part he'd never expected. "I... Of course. I've seen a lot of you and I don't know if the scars are bugging you. They only bother me because I know they must've hurt a lot. But they're...part of the strength I see in you, all the time." He looked down at Jared's throat, skimming his fingers over one of the longer scars. "I hate that I came so close to losing you.

But each of these..." He moved his fingertips to another scar, this one on Jared's chest. "Is proof that you survived."

"For you." Capturing Noah's wrist, Jared brought it to his lips to trace the veins one at a time with his tongue. "I tried to leave, but—" He smiled, gaze going distant, and kissed Noah's pulse point. "I think I knew you needed me. Somehow. I remember thinking of you. Of getting back here."

The lump in Noah's throat made it hard to swallow, but he brought his attention back to Jared's chest, touching another scar a bit lower. "I'll always need you. If you can't find any other reason to hold on, then know that. Without you, I won't...I won't have any reason not to slip into the void. I'll let myself stay there. I won't believe there's any light to come back to, because there won't be. I'll just keep being a monster."

"Then it looks like we'll both need to stick around for a very long time." Jared cleared his throat roughly. "Now, where were we?"

"Kissing?" Noah glanced up at Jared before bringing his lips down to his chest, close to one nipple. "I'm serving at my Dom's pleasure with my mouth. It's gonna take a while."

Deep, rumbling laughter vibrated from Jared's chest, buzzing against Noah's lips. "We have all the time you need. Though I will insist on both of us being fed at some point."

Flicking his tongue over Jared's nipple, Noah nodded, then moved lower, trailing light kisses over Jared's ribs. "That's a good idea. I'll need my energy so I can keep this up. You're not a small man."

More laughter, warm and rich, shook Jared's frame. His abs rippled, skin flush with pleasure. "True. I, like every good youth, have measured up against my peers. I have no illusions about my above-average size and am unashamed to admit it."

Noah shot Jared a sideways look before turning all his focus to his Dom's dick. Nice and long and thick. Dark hair surrounded the base, some still growing back where it must've been shaved before various surgeries. The head of his cock was a deep red, and almost seemed to strain toward him. He moved down so he could brush his fingers over it. Aside from his own dick, and the ones in the magazines Rhodey gave him without comment, this was the first one Noah had ever seen.

He followed the path of his fingers with his tongue, loving how smooth and hot the length was, a little salty near the tip. He licked at it again, curving his fingers around the base to give himself better access.

Absolutely quiet, barely breathing, Jared threaded his fingers in Noah's hair, applying a little pressure at the back of his skull. The gentle direction, a subtle increase or decrease of tension told him when and where to focus, and for how long. Not like Jared didn't trust him, but like he enjoyed showing Noah what he found pleasurable. A part of the dance.

"Don't forget." Noah circled his tongue over the head of Jared's dick, taking a few inches into his mouth before drawing back to give his Dom a pointed look. "You have to stay still and let me do all the work. No thrusting."

Jared nodded, passing his tongue over his lips. "That will be impossible if you bring me to climax, but I will do my best not to gag you. We'll take this slow. If I tug on your hair, you need to stop so I can take care of things in a way that won't be overwhelming to you for your first time."

Brow lifted, Noah gave Jared a few long strokes. "What would be overwhelming? And if you move, I'll hold you down, so you don't have to worry about that. This is your chance to just let go."

A long groan followed. "Noah. Do you feel how full my balls are? I've been thinking about this for days. Without relief. You will drown. It's not the typical situation for a first time. I am your Dom. I certainly get to take care of you as well."

"You're challenging me. I accept." Noah grinned and kissed the tip of Jared's dick. "I'll just have to swallow really fast. Or make a mess. Or both. I don't have a problem with that. Besides, you can take care of me some other time. You took care of me in other ways in those cells…" His voice got a bit rough as he gave his Dom a pleading look. "Please? Let me do this for you."

Gazing down at him from his reclined position, Jared fisted both hands against the mattress. "All right, tiger. Because you ask so nicely, and because that lower lip is going to look so sweet covered in my come."

This time, Noah couldn't hold back his smile, every part of him heating up, warm from the praise, and almost blazing with lust. He shifted his position, kneeling between Jared's spread thighs. One hand on Jared's hip as a reminder to not move, he wrapped the other around his Dom's dick. Held his gaze as he lowered his mouth to take him in. The first time, he drew back with a wet slurp, the thickness filling his mouth taking some adjustment. Dipping down again, he slid until his lips reached his hand. There was nothing like the sensation of having Jared in his mouth like this, of the trust, the pleasure, they were finally sharing. He dragged back up slowly, repeating the motion a few times.

Moving his hand, he took him a bit deeper, growling with frustration as he rose, struggling against the urge to gag and gasp, like his body couldn't figure out if he was being smothered or had swallowed something the wrong way. Stupid thing.

"You feel so fucking good, tiger." Jared spoke through clenched teeth, his hand coming to Noah's shoulder, thumb pressing into the new bite he'd left there only last night. "When my cock hits the back of your throat, swallow. Get a good breath, and swallow again. I've never felt…" He panted, grip tightening. "Anything so good as your mouth."

His Dom's words renewed his determination as he sucked in a deep breath and slid all the way down. His eyes teared as he fought his body's reaction, swallowing, following Jared's instructions, keeping him at the back of his throat for as long as possible. He fisted his hand against Jared's hip, not letting his instinct to pull away quickly take over. Rising up slowly, he gave himself a second to take another breath, then slipped his lips over Jared's length again. And again, until he found a rhythm, rewarded with the taste of slick saltiness every time his tongue glided over the head of Jared's cock.

Sweat soaked Jared's skin beneath Noah's fist, his Dom's thighs vibrating with the need to thrust. Deep groans drawing out, Jared shook his head against the pillow. "Right there. Yes. Like that." His praise sounded like a prayer and a plea. "God, Noah. Fuck. What you do to me." Hips coming up, he hissed, lowering them quickly, but a spurt of precome flooded from his shaft onto Noah's tongue. "I don't think it's possible to come without moving."

Narrowing his eyes, Noah smacked Jared's hip. "It is. Don't do that again." He fixed his Dom with a hard look. "I could probably make you come if I tied you up, but I don't think you'd be quite so comfortable. Maybe we can try it some other time."

Jared's bark of laughter echoed in the large space. "You do not tie up your Dom unless you want the un-fun kind of spanking."

"I'm starting to think you're making up all these rules. And the 'un-fun' spanking." Noah huffed, laying his hand flat and firm on Jared's pelvis. "Now behave yourself and let me drive you out of your mind. You totally ruined my flow."

"I believe all that matters is that my dick is still hard enough to pound nails." Jared tapped his cheek, but not too hard. "Get back to work, lovely boy."

Preening a little, because that had definitely been a win, Noah lowered his mouth over Jared again, this time picking up the pace. Maybe if he got Jared close to the edge quickly, his Dom wouldn't be tempted to take over. The motion, the sensation of a quickening pulse under his tongue spurred him on. After a while, he didn't seem to need to take as many breaths, letting him keep Jared down his throat for longer and longer. He hummed with pleasure as the powerful thrum of control and arousal spilled over him, his own dick throbbing from just the subtle rocking of his hips and the fabric of his jeans rubbing it through his boxers.

He closed his eyes, willing it to wait. This time was all for Jared.

"So good. Noah—" Jared's fingers dug into Noah's shoulder with bruising pressure, his short nails cutting into skin. "Noah!" The shout rang, every muscle in Jared's body tensing. "So good— Yes!" The last word was drawn out, Jared's head thrashing against the pillows, as he came.

At first, the same swallows were enough, but then Noah jerked back as the slickness covered his tongue and spilled over his lips. He swallowed again, using his hand to stroke Jared, laving him with his tongue until he managed to get the rest. A mess, but not one he couldn't manage. He smirked up at Jared as he swept his thumb over his chin and sucked on it. Then flicked his tongue over the head of his dick again.

He was nothing if not thorough. "See, sir? I told you I could do it. And so could you. I'm very proud of you."

"Put the damned cuff on your other wrist." Snickering with a certain amount of breathy humor, Jared latched onto Noah's arm and pulled him up for a deep kiss, his tongue delving to catch the lingering slickness. "Stay with me while I catch my breath."

Letting out a happy sigh, Noah nodded, but ignored the command about the cuff. He rested his head on Jared's shoulder. "Tell me what a good sub I am. I've earned it."

"You are the best sub in the history of subs. In your own way." Tipping his chin down to look at Noah, Jared winked. "And you will make an even better—one of the most amazing —Dom. I'm proud of you for your attention to detail, your care, and how you attuned yourself to my needs. It was one of the most blissful moments of pleasure and forgetting I've had in a long, long time."

Noah rubbed his cheek against Jared's shoulder, stretching out against his side and laying one arm across his chest. "I like hearing that, sir. I'll have to do it to you a lot. It was a decent performance, but with practice I bet I could be even better. You could prescribe yourself a blowjob or two a day as part of your recovery. Maybe more."

"May the gods have mercy. If you get any better, the top of my head will come off." Jared placed a smacking kiss on Noah's cheek. Color and eyes bright, he appeared completely happy for the first time since Noah had seen him walk through the cell door. "Thank you, my boy. Truly."

"Don't thank me, sir. It's...I enjoyed it. I love sharing this with you." Noah curled his fingers into the hair at the center of Jared's chest, toying with it a bit as he smiled up at his Dom. "I still can't believe we're here. Together. That I get to have this. I'm going to need some time for it to feel real and giving you a lot of blowjobs to keep myself occupied would be a very good idea. That and kissing. Maybe a shower at some point, when I get too sticky."

"All of this and more." As the haze of arousal, as well as the endorphins that came with it, receded, the tightness around Jared's eyes that had seemed normal before, but not now, returned. "Let's get you undressed so I may return the gesture and enjoy my boy the way he deserves."

Watching Jared closely, Noah caught the signs of his pain, and slipped from the bed. He'd probably earn a spanking at some point for being so bossy, but that was a worry for later. "You're still under my 'don't move' rule, sir. I also believe you said something about refueling? I'll see what Rhodey got us for food. Bring you something to take your pills with." He tugged the blanket over Jared, smiling as he pressed a kiss to his cheek. "No wine this time."

Narrowing his gaze, Jared pressed his lips together. "I'm

keeping count, you know. Of all the times you get your way. There will be a comeuppance."

"I'm counting on it, sir." Noah breathed out a laugh as he kissed Jared's cheek again, closer to his lips. "If there wasn't, I'd be completely out of control and you're too good of a Dom to put up with that. But anyway, the important question now is do you just want water, or water, then some tea?"

"Water and tea, please." Grumbling under his breath, Jared straightened the covers. "I will not mention unflattering comparisons between you and Rhodey. You are far more controlling and the pushiest sub. I'm going to take great pleasure in making you suffer." The smirk he couldn't quite hide gave him away, before he waved his hand to shoo Noah out of the room. "Go. The sooner you do, the sooner I'll have you close to me."

For the first time ever, the mention of Rhodey didn't make Noah grind his teeth and scowl. He left the room, going to Jared's bag first to get his pills, then to the fridge for a bottle of water, taking note of how well-stocked the thing was with everything they could need for at least a few weeks. His uncle was a lot of things, but the one Noah admired—even though he wouldn't say so out loud—was he didn't fuck around when it came to the people he loved.

Noah wasn't one of them. Which might change, one day, but the important thing was Jared being on that very short list. Between him and his uncle, the man who was so important to each of them in different ways would heal. He'd become just as strong as he'd been before, a strength no longer wasted on a battlefield. Jared's time in the trenches was over.

All that power, that control, would be used for whatever future would bring him back the joy he'd lost at some point, out in the damn desert. He could have anything he wanted now. Keep being a doctor or spend his days training Noah if he enjoyed that. Eventually have subs who were much more... sub-like, just to entertain him.

There had never been any kind of future Noah dared to hope for, but Jared had given him one. One he was starting to see clearer with every moment they spent together.

And in return?

I'm going to give him the world. On a silver platter.

But for now? Hopefully a decent cup of tea.

Chapter Twenty-Four

PRESENT

Garet finished tying up his sneakers by the halfway house's front door, Ezran's jacket a warm weight on his shoulders. Sensing someone watching him, he peered over his shoulder to find the guy who'd been his welcome shadow for the past day lingering in the kitchen.

Between the two of them, they'd made the place fucking shine. To the point even Mal had left Finn alone this morning.

They'd made 'pancakes a la Curtis', and drawn stupid faces on them with whipped cream and chocolate chips. While bacon was a luxury they didn't have, the smoked fake bacon bits added a little something when dunked in maple syrup. Not the real stuff, but still better than nothing.

Outside, flurries fell, but nothing like the storms of the past several weeks. The windchill clocking in at truly bone-chilling temps made it too cold out for much more. The kitchen felt extra warm and cozy with the stove running, even if the rest of the place was cold enough to freeze balls.

"Hey." Standing, Garet motioned Finn closer. "You remember what you're doing while I'm gone, right? And our plan?"

Staying up until two a.m. with a stolen flashlight and a pad of paper, they'd drawn and redrawn Finn's dream car. All the while, Garet told his new friend stories about The Asylum, his friends, and how much Sin was going to like him once Finn served out his house arrest and could come for a visit with Garet. No matter what, Finn would always know where to find him and how.

Nobody was going to abandon his friend again.

A bit of mischief in his smile, Finn straightened and cleared his throat. "No stealing anything, even a lawnmower, no matter how fun it seems like it would be in my head. I can't draw good like you, but I'm gonna make a whole scrapbook with all the parts for my car. And read that manual you gave me so I'll be able to legally drive it when it's made." He cocked his head. "You ever think about how dumb most laws are? How am I not supposed to break the ones I don't agree with? People should get better at sharing."

Snorting, Garet shook his head. "Not that I don't agree, but how about we focus on learning all the cool ways to legally get free stuff?" Leaning closer, he made sure Mal wouldn't hear his next words. "There are dumpsters behind the shops, and you can get all sorts of cool shit to refurb and sell. It's like stealing but legal and a total rush. Because you realize how stupid the people who just tossed it are. Lazy bastards."

How excited Finn got at the idea of dumpster diving was pretty close to the expression on his face when he got into details about finding cars rich people left unlocked. He glanced toward the street like he was tempted to go start digging into the nearest bin. "I love you, man. You've got me excited about the future and...never thought that'd happen. Don't get so wrapped up in this guy that you'll forget to come back and dig in garbage with me? *Expensive* garbage. I can't fucking wait."

Garet zipped up Ezran's coat, still loving how it released his best friend's scent, close to his skin. So fresh it was like Ez stood there with him and Finn. "You keep your cell charged and I'll send you a selfie of me and Sin, and tell you what we're up to, yeah?"

"I will. I stole Vinnie's charger, so I'm good to go." Finn flashed him a brilliant smile. "I've never been on a date—you gotta give me all the deets. I won't even bitch if you gotta keep it age appropriate. Just, like, say 'fade to black' like they do in sappy romances. I'll fill in the rest."

"If it comes to that I will, but we're just having coffee today." Though he and Sin had done a lot more in the past, Garet totally knew his... *No, not Dom...not boyfriend...* His *date* was good for his word. He paused, hand on the door knob. "And, Finn?"

Gaze snapping up from where he'd been digging into the pocket of a jacket by the door that was definitely not his, Finn blinked at him. "Yeah?"

"I believe in you. You can do this." Garet's lips tipped up. "And I love you, too."

Drawing his hand back, Finn stared at him, then jumped forward and wrapped his arms around Garet's waist. "Fuck the demerit points. Gotta hug you. Go have fun. And make coffee sexy."

"You got it, my dude." Turning, Garet opened the door, letting in a blast of arctic air. "And remember. You have five minutes less than you did five minutes ago. It's now four weeks, six days, twelve hours, and fifty-five minutes."

Finn eased back and took a deep breath. "Okay. I can do this. Follow the house rules, don't get caught stealing anything, and think about my car a bunch. Easy peasy."

"Or, you know, don't steal. Plan, instead." Waving, because he was already late for Sin, which was not a good look for a first date, Garet threw Finn his biggest smile and leaped off the porch into a giant snowdrift just to make his friend laugh.

The bright laughter was followed by Finn talking in a rush. "No stealing, starting now. The money I put in your wallet is just borrowing. For emergencies. Mal won't mind if he never finds out. See you!"

Groaning internally, Garet shook his head and kept trudging through the snow, his hands held over his head Rocky style as he picked up his pace. If he came back with the money, he'd get Finn in trouble. Better to give it back to the man when he wasn't looking with an, 'Oopsie. What's this on the floor over here? Did someone lose some cash?'

Running practically all the way to Sin's shop, Garet was out of breath but toasty warm in Ez's jacket. He unzipped it a bit, taking the wooden stairs up to the porch two at a time and leaned into the doorbell to the upstairs apartment.

"Down here, my boy." Sin waved at him from below, wearing nothing besides a sleeveless white T-shirt and a pair of jeans, all his tattoos on display. He shot Garet an apologetic look. "I was about to text you to let you know I was running late. A client spotted me on the street before I could make it past the door and begged for a consult. I'm gonna have my schedule full within the next few days if I don't put my foot down. Nice to feel missed, even if it's just because people need ink therapy."

It didn't matter that dates weren't supposed to hug and kiss and stuff the first time. Garet saw Sin and it was like seeing home. All the rawness of the past several months, the aching need to be with family and those he loved came rushing in to fill the void. He went airborne off the porch, trusting Sin to catch him. Snow and wind ruffled his hair, making the rush about more than the beat of joy-driven adrenaline in his veins.

Strong arms wrapped around him, drawing him against a muscular chest, Sin's lips covering his like he sensed what was needed in the moment. Like he needed it too. Lowering Garet to his feet without breaking the kiss, he delved his fingers into Garet's hair, letting out a hum of pleasure as he tasted his lips with gentle dips of his tongue. Slanting his mouth to deepen the kiss, he held Garet still, every bit of pressure, every breath he allowed, a reclaiming of everything they'd shared and more.

Gloveless hands slipped into Sin's back pockets, Garet allowed himself to be a greedy boy for just a moment. He used his tongue in a tentative greeting that flavored the kiss with submission and the barest hint of need. It might be against the first date rules, but Sin would tell him when they needed to back up. There was nothing Garet didn't trust about this man, especially that he'd guide them both exactly where they needed to go.

A breathless laugh was the first clue of Sin's intentions to keep both of them from taking any more steps, even when he backed Garet into the closest brick wall and braced a hand above his head. "Exactly as irresistible as I remember. Damn, I missed you. Playing the field is a lot less fun when you've already won and the team clears out. Or something like that. Give your Dom a minute, his brain needs some oxygen."

Head tipped back, Garet ran his tongue over his lips to gather up the taste of Sin his Dom had left behind. *Pun very much intended. Curtis would be proud.* Grinning, he reached up to brush the hair from Sin's forehead. "Hi, sir. It's good to have you home."

"It's very good to *be* home." Sin pulled him in close again, squeezing him gently and pressing his face into his hair. "And you were a very good boy, fixing up my place all nice. First reward? Coffee. And only because I want to show you I have *some* self-restraint." He winked at Garet as he eased back and took his hand. "Not much, but some. I'll save tying you up and flogging your ass for date number two."

Garet's hand spasmed, a full body shiver walking up his spine. Not like he hadn't had any sex since the incident that had brought his life crashing down, but those flings hadn't meant anything. What if he choked? Had a flashback? Panic heated his skin just below the surface and he automatically dropped into the space in his head where his mantra lived, repeating it to himself until the rhythm of his heart normalized. When it did, he realized he'd been standing still in the middle of the pavement for who knew how long. Long enough for Sin to reach in his shop to grab a well-worn leather jacket and shrug it on.

"Sorry." Throwing Sin a sheepish smile, Garet shook his head. "Coffee?"

Sin nodded, studying his face for a moment, continuing to walk with a light tug on Garet's hand. His tone remained casual, but there was an understanding warmth beneath it. "We'll save the tying up and flogging talk for later. For now, let me know if this is all right." He nodded toward their hands. "You don't need to safeword. Just give me a head's up."

Squeezing Sin's large hand with fingers that barely wrapped his palm, Garet returned Sin's nod. "It's good. I just haven't...been with anyone who mattered. I don't want to screw it up."

"You won't." Sin leaned in and kissed his temple as they continued down the street at a relaxed pace. "You can't screw up me wanting to spend time with you. Unless you hadn't shown up. That might've made it a bit trickier. I might be a modern guy, but I'm not into having a coffee date with an empty chair. Or a phone screen."

"That would be less satisfying than that blowup sheep in the back of the dungeon closet. The birthday one that Ez and I used to steal all the time as a joke and put in Curtis' bed." Gared grinned so hard his face hurt. Between the memory and walking down the street with Sin, this day couldn't get any better. "We named it Bob."

Giving an exaggerated shudder, Sin stopped Garet steps away from the door to the small, nondescript coffee shop about a third of the size of Matt's. He met Garet's eyes and lifted his brow. "If you even put something like that in my bed? I won't be giving you lines. Have you seen what those guys did to that poor sheep?" His lips curved slightly. "If not, I'd give you a play-by-play. And have you reenact the whole thing. On top of the bar."

Hearing those details would've been better *after* he'd had the chance to slip into the booth in the coffee shop, but if walking into the place with a hardon was the price he had to pay for being given that image, Garet would take it. "Bah?"

"Hmm." Sin tilted his head slightly, then nodded. "I was right. No threatening my little porn star with exhibitionism. I'll have to get creative. Part of me was enjoying the idea of fucking with Curtis a little bit. Look at the little boy you used to babysit, all grown up and fucking blowup sheep. Just handing him a switch—the one with the handle, not another *him*—would be boring. But I like a challenge."

Grabbing the door handle, Garet opened the door for his Dom, following him into the shop. Didn't smell nearly as delicious as Matt's, but had his favorite powdered donuts under a cake dome on the counter. "I dunno if you can scare Curtis that way. He's engaged to Reed."

"I never said scare. Just mess with him a bit." Sin shrugged, nudging his chin toward a corner table near the back. "I should probably save it, I haven't been in Reed's good books in a while and opinions in The Asylum tend to spread a bit like his glitter. Only a lot less fun." He pulled out the first chair for Garet, then took the one facing it, with his back to the wall. "We'll figure out how to navigate the place again. Poor guys have probably been bored out of their minds without us. I mean, aside from getting blown up. But we'll remind them entertainment can hurt in better ways."

Toying with a brunch menu in a little plastic stand, Garet nodded in agreement even though he had no clue how Sin might get him back into The Asylum. "You know my membership got torn up, right? I've never known them to let someone back in. After." He licked his lips, wondering if he should offer to go get the coffee. "It's not like I'm mad at anyone. Not even me. I wish I hadn't done all that stuff, but I get why I did it. Past me was full of bad decisions, but they were the only way I knew how to cope then. I have better ways now. It's not like I can expect anyone to welcome me back, though. I saw Matt yesterday. It didn't go well." Words tumbled from his mouth like they couldn't get out fast enough. "Then I went out this morning and I saw Ezran by accident. He doesn't know. He'll probably kill me *for* Rhodey when he finds out."

Sin shook his head, glancing past Garet's shoulder and nodding to someone. "You let me worry about your membership. Sure, there's a lot to sort through, but you haven't done anything you can't come back from, far as I'm concerned. You're right, we can't have any expectations for how anyone will react. Some people, like your brother, might need time to deal with their own feelings. Matt's a good man and he loves you, so in the end? I have a feeling that's all that will matter." He smiled at the perky young waitress who skidded up to the side of the table on little ballet flats, the perfect match for the black tutu and silver vest of her unique uniform. "A couple of your favorite coffees that have whipped cream on them. And a dozen donuts. I'll bring whatever we don't finish home so I don't have to order out again."

At the promise of donuts, Garet's stomach gave a whine despite all the pancakes he'd eaten with Finn earlier. "Oh, hell to the yeah." He patted his belly. "Can I have some chocolate sprinkles on my whipped cream, please?"

The ballerina waitress looked at Sin, then blushed and ducked her head without answering.

Sin's lips curved as he nodded. "Chocolate sprinkles on both, Cindy. Good girl. I'll let your Domme know we were very happy with your service."

Eyes going wide, Garet looked the sub over again. He hadn't really run into a lot of girl subs, so he wasn't sure how to tell. It seemed easier to tell on guys, maybe because he paid more attention to them. There was a vibe. Leastwise, around The Asylum, where most everyone played. There were members who only came for the food and the fighting, but those were fewer.

"Thank you, sir. I'll be right back with everything." Cindy twirled and practically danced on her way around the counter. She greeted another couple as they came in, without the deference she'd shown to Sin.

Watching Garet, Sin gave him a slanted smile. "My poor sheltered little sub. I'll have to teach you how to spot kindred spirits. More importantly, their Doms. Cindy's Domme is scary, though. I don't think you'd have any trouble."

Garet let out a low whistle under his breath. "Anniston Falls. Kinkiest town in the Northeast. But it's a good thing. It gets cold here. We gotta stay warm somehow." He threw Sin a saucy grin, lifting a few sugar packets to make a tiny fort. "How's your mom doing?"

"A lot better now. My sister indulged me by answering all my questions the second I landed, so I actually believe it now. Not that I don't trust her, but...it's hard. Since my mother can't tell me herself." Sin inhaled slowly, letting out a noisy exhale. "It'll take a while to relax about the whole situation. With Bethany there, at least I don't have to rely on the staff to keep my mother safe. And the place really is beautiful. Better than anything I could afford on my own."

Reaching out, Garet covered Sin's hand. "Does your mom know when you're talking with her? Do the docs expect any improvement?" Before all the therapy and rehab, he would've avoided the questions, but one of the things he'd learned was how important it was to talk about things. Or at least to be given the opportunity. It always helped to have someone who you knew would listen. "I don't know a lot about these kinds of things. My mom went so fast."

Smile a little sad, Sin turned his hand to lace his fingers with Garet's. He stroked his thumb back and forth over the inside of Garet's wrist. "No, she'll have good days and bad, but she'll remember less and less over time. We're all...just making sure she's as comfortable as possible with the time she has left and always has one of us around. It's hard sometimes, not seeing any recognition in her eyes, or when she calls me one of my brothers' names. But...she got me, and them, where we are today and I'm...grateful for the time I had. The time I still have, even if the mother I love isn't always with me in that room."

"Is it okay that I believe in souls? I think about my mom and how she's always there for me to talk to. I don't know if you believe in that stuff, but I think your mom is there hearing you in a way, even if she can't express it with her body." Garet leaned back as their drinks came, the waitress—Cindy—placing them gracefully on the table with her gaze respectfully lowered. "I'm glad you're all there for her."

Sin's smile warmed as he inclined his head. "Thank you, my boy. It's nice to discuss this with someone other than my siblings. I love them, but sometimes I want to shake them when they act like I have the most right to be upset, since I'm her biological child. And Tay...fuck, that whole situation makes me so angry. Not with her or him, but... That aside, yes. I believe in souls. Not sure if she'd be hanging around the hospital if she had a choice, but I think she knows we're around." He laughed and shook his head. "If she were hearing me getting all down while on a date with a handsome young man, I'd get one of her disapproving finger wags. Almost as brutal as a bullwhip."

Tipping his head toward the plate of donuts, Garet brought Sin's attention to the food. "Well, I think this is a cure for the blues. Even though I think the best way to get to know someone is to peek inside their sad as well as their happy." He released Sin's hand with a squeeze, plucking up one of the honey glazed creations to take a big bite. He melted back into his chair with a sigh of pleasure. "Ohmigod."

Selecting his own donut, Sin took a smaller bite, licking his lips as he chewed, looking like he enjoyed Garet's reaction more than anything. "I'm good with the happy and the sad, but you learn a lot about a man by the way he eats. You're in for it now, my boy. I know all your secrets."

"Yeah?" Unable to hide his grin, Garet stuck his thumb in his mouth, sucking the glaze off his skin with a wet, slurping sound. "Like how I have filthy table manners?"

Sin chuckled, swiping the rest of Garet's donut, holding it close to his mouth. "You know very well I don't mind my boys a bit messy. If I wanted good table manners from you, I'd say so. And you'd do it."

Voice low, throaty, Garet barely pressed his lips to the donut, speaking against it in a way that would vibrate into Sin's fingertips. "And how about now? What do you want...sir?"

"I want you to take another bite and make that sound again." Sin moved the donut out of reach, leaning across the table to claim a deep kiss, easing back slowly with a little smirk. "Then tell me how much you want me to restrain you in the dungeon and make you hurt as good as that tastes. First date talk and all."

Swollen length growing even harder with the words gave a good hard kick against the seam of Garet's jeans. He moaned even before his teeth tore into the doughy treat. Images of Sin doing the same to his inner thigh, while Garet hung restrained from the iron rings sunk into the dungeon's rough brick, blossomed in a heady rush. "Oh God, yes, please..." The words came out in a breathless spill, memories of the taste of Sin's dick rolling through next on his emotional landscape. "No fair. I told Finn we weren't even going to kiss. He's going to know and pump me for all the deets. Dude's a minor."

"Finn?" Sin's gaze went from interested to surprised when he cut in before Garet finished and seemed to absorb the last. "Ah...yeah. I will not be offering to give you more explicit 'deets' to share with him. I don't mind my subs getting into a little trouble, but…not that kind."

Taking a sip of his coffee, Garet nodded his agreement. "Yeah. He's eighteen in a couple months, but he's young up here." He tapped his finger to his temple. "You can tell he never had anything steady, you know? I promised to build him a car if he can keep out of trouble long enough to get off house arrest so you guys can meet. He's totally sweet in his own way. He needs us."

Expression very serious now, Sin lifted his own drink to his lips. He took a long swallow before lowering it. "He's lucky to have you. And I have plenty of experience with all sorts from the kids my parents fostered, so I wouldn't mind helping in any way I can. Giving him goals and someone he can build trust with will go a long way."

"Curtis did that for me." Staring at the metal table's scuffed surface, Garet remembered all the firm lines the man had drawn for him so he had a map to direct him rather than just a bunch of speed bumps he would be more likely to trip over, and his heart squeezed. "I miss him. I know they miss me, but they've all given up."

Shaking his head, Sin set his cup aside and took both Garet's hands between his own. "They haven't, my boy. Not if they're the men I believe they are. Like I told you, I have my own reservations with how involved Tay has gotten, but that's mostly because he needs more security and stability than I believe River can give him. The rest? They keep that place going. For men like you and me. I truly believe once they can see past how much you scared them? They'll remember that. Because you wouldn't have if they didn't love you. That kind of love doesn't just disappear."

Garet really hoped Sin was right, and of course he was. He was a smart man. Knowing how much to tell anyone was tough. The counselor had said to say as little or as much as he needed to, and his actions were most important, along with acknowledging the harm he'd done.

"Can I...ask your advice as someone who knows them?" Garet looked up from under the fall of his bangs, using them like a shield to cushion his world.

Nodding, Sin lifted one hand, holding up a finger and picking up the last bit of the donut to feed it to him. "Yes, but finish that and absorb my words while you chew. I meant it when I said I want to start something serious with you, Garet. That means I want us to get to a place where you won't ever have to ask me a question like that again. You can always ask me, or tell me, anything you need to."

Donut crumbs landed on Garet's tongue as he swept them from his lips, doing exactly as Sin had commanded. He hung onto every word, letting them fill him up. "Thank you, sir. I feel the same." A small smile played about his lips. "And really, really lucky. To have you. To get to know you better. I saw you for a long time before we even played together and I know how rare that is for you. Letting people all the way in."

"It is. I enjoyed keeping things light, and I had no intention of settling down, but it started feeling a little too shallow. Especially when I had to face I almost lost someone very special to me." Sin traced his thumb under Garet's lips. "You deserve someone who will give you more. I intend to be that someone."

Happy tears forced Garet's sniff and he laughed. "Ugh. Mean Dom."

"Sometimes." Sin chuckled, sitting back and taking himself another donut. "Would you feel better if I confess to liking it a whole lot more to hurt a sub I get to cuddle after? You can thank Reed for showing me a sub that's 'fine' without aftercare isn't easier. And...well, pretty bruises should be right there for me to admire whenever I please."

"I don't know if it makes certain parts of me feel better, but they sure are interested." Garet poked his finger suggestively, slowly, and very deliberately, into the nearly closed hole of a fat old-fashioned donut. lifting it up to take a nibble without breaking Sin's gaze. "I don't even remember what I was going to say."

Sin's lips twitched with amusement. "Well that just won't do. I'll hold off telling you what else I intend to do to you until it comes back to you. For now, you'll just have to continue seducing your donut."

Bursting out with laughter, Garet rolled his eyes. "Fine. You win." He set the donut on a napkin and slid his gaze to the window, where darker clouds had rolled in. The wind rattled the panes, but inside was warm, so he shrugged off Ez's jacket and twisted around to lay it over the back of the chair, like Sin had done with his. When he faced Sin again, he'd sobered. "I don't know whether it'd hurt Matt and Lawson, everyone, more to know I started using after someone dosed me and date raped me at a party."

Inhaling roughly, Sin clasped his hand to Garet's again. "They're your family, my boy. They deserve whatever truth you can give them, whenever you're able. And you deserve their support. I can't tell you what to do, but I don't believe any of them would want a lie to spare them any kind of pain."

Garet swallowed, throat tight, his gaze affixed to Sin's fingers twined with his own. "I don't want to make excuses. The guy said he thought I'd like it, want it, because of the porn. I felt like maybe he was right. So instead of getting help, I hurt myself more by going deeper with the drugs." He lifted his gaze, searching Sin's eyes. "I couldn't afford them, so to pay off a debt, the cartel started using me as a mule—once they learned about my record with the gang here. I was totally fucked."

"They are very good at using whatever vulnerabilities they can find. You didn't deserve any of the things that happened to you, but I think you know that." Sin's gaze rested on his face, his tone gently encouraging. "From what I've heard, you did finally get the help you needed. I'm proud of you for that. I know they will be, too."

"I put in the work, but it definitely was Rhodey's ultimatum that got me to the place where I could. I didn't tell him or anyone about this, unless you count my therapist." Garet lifted the donut, taking a few small nibbles to ground himself in the taste of vanilla and nutmeg. "I think I just need them to stop being so angry...for Matt to stop...before I can tell them about this part. It's not the 'poor me' that I want to lead with, you know?"

Sin inclined his head. "I get that. You've come a long way, put in a lot of work, and you need them to see that. You can't control how they react, how they feel, but you can show them the effort is there. Let them get to know who you are now. Regaining that mutual trust will be worth it in the long run. Getting there is the hard part."

"Tell me about it." They'd deliberately planned in their texts for their date to be shorter, ending before group, but Garet found himself not looking at his phone, wanting to draw it out until the last sweet moment. Guilt that he hadn't sent Finn a snap of him and Sin yet bubbled up, and he sighed knowing instinctively it was almost time to go. "I promised my new little buddy I'd send a selfie of us together. You mind?"

Scooting his chair over with a few, very noisy jerks and a slanted smile on his lips, Sin shook his head. "Not at all." He put his arm around Garet's shoulders. "Another first. I've never gone out with someone and taken a selfie. I have had a few guys ask for dick pics, but you're not getting one of those in the café. Your Dom has *some* limits."

Phone at the ready, Garet burst into laughter, snapping the pic at the same moment. The result was nothing short of spectacular. Sin's eyes sparkled with humor, his lush lips parted as

Garet—eyes crinkled at the edges—leaned into him with a warmth that couldn't be faked.

"I'm keeping this forever." He turned his head, tipping his face up to meet his Dom's dark hazel eyes. "Thank you, sir. This was really nice."

"I agree. Self-restraint has its place…for the first date. I make no promises for what I'll plan for future ones." Arm still around Garet's shoulder, Sin curved his hand under his jaw and claimed a long, slow, kiss. "Mmm, definitely something involving whipped cream. And restraints. Maybe an ice cream shop?"

Garet blinked at the last part. Images reared of being laid out on the marble countertop of the hand-mixed ice cream and soda fountain place deeper in the heart of the city. "You know somebody there, or we gotta break in to fulfill that one?"

"I don't, but that would definitely make for a memorable date." Sin's tone said he was only half serious. Maybe. Either way, he definitely enjoyed playing with the idea. And Garet. "I'll come up with something, but since it's time I walk you home, I'll just leave you with a reminder that I am a sadist. Not as hardcore as others…maybe. Depends on what you consider hardcore. But if you like needleplay, or are interested in it?" He grazed his teeth along Garet's jaw, then nipped his earlobe. "You can come see one of my demos at the club. Once that whole situation is handled."

A breathless, "Yes, please, sir," ended with an embarrassing lift of Garet's hips. Needy and raw, he couldn't have hidden his desire from this man if his life depended on it. "I'd really like that. And I like most things, especially when they please someone else. It feels extra good to know you're getting off on what you do to me."

Sin eased back with a reluctant sigh, taking out a few bills to cover their coffee and donuts, along with a generous tip. He held Garet's hand, helping him to his feet, then grabbed his jacket to dress him as though it was the most natural thing in the world. "You're exactly my kind of sub, but I already suspected as much. You know there will be more conversations before I have my way with you, but I'm looking forward..." He did up the zipper, letting it skim dangerously close to Garet's throat. "To seeing your reactions when I push you right to the edge."

Moistening his lips with the point of his tongue, Garet hung onto every word, every gesture, unable to break Sin's gaze. His nod was a slow, mesmerized, agreement he had every intention of honoring. "We've...played before. But this feels different. Does that sound weird?"

"Not at all. We fucked, my boy. I kept things light because you were new, and young, and had a stable of overprotective big brother types. Along with your *actual* big brother. But since you're mine?" Sin lifted his shoulders, his lips curving. "I intend to play with you *my* way. And not be quite so concerned how anyone else feels about it. They can feel free to look away."

"If what we did was light, I can't wait to see your next level." Scooping his phone from the table, Garet remembered to shoot the photo to both Sin and Finn, along with, "Headed home. See you for group." He chuckled. "Your names rhyme."

His own jacket on, Sin put his arm back around Garet as they started out of the café. Let out a soft laugh while he pushed the door open, holding it above Garet's head. "My parents used to stick with 'Sinaan'—Jared's called me that on occasion—but when I was a teen? There was no way I'd've miss out on just being 'Sin'. It suits me." He smirked. "But you know that."

Sneakers crunching through the crusty layer of older snow, Garet nodded. His stomach sank, growing heavier the closer they got to the halfway house. The only reason he had to stay there was because he didn't have anywhere else to live. For the first time, he found himself resenting Matt not bringing him back to The Asylum. If he had, then the date with Sin might've lasted longer.

Except then he wouldn't have met Finn. Or known he could find a way to make it on his own.

"My mom used to call this feeling 'a case of the Sundays'." Heaving a sigh, he stopped at the end of the walk to the ramshackle house. Lights glowed a warm yellow from behind thin gingham curtains, which someone had put up in an attempt to make it feel more homey. "Can I text you later?"

Facing him, Sin brought his hands to Garet's arms, rubbing them and giving him a bracing smile. "If you don't, I'll start questioning if I'm any good at this first date thing. Text me whenever you want, the only time I won't answer is if I'm with a client. Possibly when I'm sleeping, but I wouldn't mind being woken up by you. I'll enjoy it even more when it's because you're right next to me." He leaned in to brush a soft kiss over Garet's lips. "Just so you have something to look forward to. It'll come, my boy. All this, what you're dealing with now? Is a step towards so much better."

Cupping Sin's face with one cold hand, and one warmed from being encased in his Dom's larger one, Garet returned the smile. "I'm going to work so hard and come back to you an even better version of me. Someone you can be proud to call your boy."

"I already am, Garet." Sin frowned as the front door of the halfway house swung open. He pulled Garet to his side when Mal stormed out, looking absolutely furious. Plucking his phone out of his pocket, Sin glanced at it. "He still has another ten minutes."

Thin gray hair mussed, like he'd been raking his fingers through it, Mal stepped up to the edge of the porch. "He has *no* time left. And no second chances. Not for this. Garet, get inside. I've already made the call. You will be returned to county as soon as the officers come to take you in. Of all the… *Stealing?* We provide everything you could possibly need and you decide to steal from me?"

The donuts and hot chocolate threatened to revolt, a sick feeling spreading until Garet's limbs were numb. He realized too late his hand had automatically gone to his wallet, which contained the money Finn had given him on his way out the door. There was no way to explain it being there without giving Finn up. Finn, who needed all the second and third chances he could get, but who'd been even lower down on Mal's chance-o-meter than Garet.

There was no time to think of a better alternative. Fessing up his only option.

Even if it meant an awful end to the most perfect day he'd had in a long, long time. Maybe ever.

No way would he leave Finn out to dry. He'd promised to take care of the kid, and he'd do just that.

Like Matt did for me, time and again.

Garet never really appreciated exactly how much guts it took to step in the way of trouble for another person. Until he lifted his chin and confessed. Hoping beyond hope he could begin to make amends for all those times he'd let someone he loved shoulder the worry.

And carry the burden of his fall.

Chapter Twenty-Five

PRESENT

"I'm sorry. I didn't know it was yours. I was going to ask when I got home, but I found the money when I was on my way out the door." Garet's hands shook as he took out his wallet and withdrew the money to hand to Mal. "It's all there. I swear. I wasn't going to spend it."

Mal snatched the money and took his time counting the bills, even though there were only three twenties. His eyes narrowed. "Unfortunately for you, I don't believe that explanation. Maybe you'll have better luck with the police."

"No, I don't think he'll have to worry about that." Sin wrapped his hand around Garet's wrist and tugged him back to his side. He met Garet's eyes, dismissing Mal as though the man had abruptly fallen off the face of the planet. "Do you have anything here you need? We're leaving."

Finn...

Garet shook his head, knowing he couldn't take his friend with him. "No, sir."

"All right. Then let's go." Sin turned, then paused, as though suddenly recalling Mal's existence. He gave him a cold look over his shoulder. "If anyone needs to discuss this matter further, leave a message for *me* at The Asylum. If you need the number, look it up. They have a website and everything."

"I really didn't take it..." Garet began, feeling like he was ten years younger, trying to explain to Matt that he hadn't stolen his big brother's gi and gotten grape juice all over it, right before a tournament. "Please, believe me, Sin?"

Not slowing until they'd rounded the corner, Sin stared straight ahead, his jaw ticking. He finally took a deep breath and glanced over at Garet. "I do, but I know the story was bullshit. I'm not mad at you either way, he should have fucking given you the benefit of the doubt after how hard you've been working..." He closed his eyes and ran his hand over his close-shaved dark hair. "Sorry, I've seen this so many times with the kids my parents fostered. Someone tossing them aside over the smallest thing and leaving them feeling...worthless. Over and over. I won't let that happen to you."

Sirens wailed in the distance, a reminder of Mal's phone call. Garet shook his head, tempted to run. "You can't save me, Sin. I'm not gonna tell them a different story, and you're right that it's bullshit. I didn't take the money, but I'm not gonna give Finn up. He's messed up, but his heart's in the right place. They'll put him away for *years* over sixty bucks."

"I *can* save you, but one step at a time." Sin tightened his grip on Garet's wrist as though worried he might be tempted to go back. He continued down a side street, then across to another in the general direction of The Asylum. "If this kid has a good heart, and he's the one who took the money? He'll confess. Text him and tell him to keep his mouth shut."

Nodding, Garet took out his phone, nearly fumbling it from his post adrenaline shakes. He shot off a cryptic message to Finn, not wanting Mal to see it and figure out everything.

Stay put. I've got it handled. Sin's taking care of me. 4 weeks, 6 days, 6 hours, 14 minutes. BE GOOD.

The text came so quickly, it was obvious group with the

other house monitor, Jordan, must've let out the second the cops showed up.

You're coming back though, right? I'll still be able to see you? I'm sorry, I fuck things up. But I didn't want to fuck things up for you.

"Ugh. This kid needs a damned hug." Swiping at the tears running in cold trails down his cheeks, Garet sniffed hard and shot back another text, nearly stumbling as he walked as fast as he could to keep up with Sin.

You didn't fuck anything up. You made it so I could go home. I'll see you, and you'll have a place with me always. Just stay out of trouble so I can get you when your time is done. I miss you.

Coming to a stop half a block from The Asylum, Sin pulled Garet to his chest and wrapped his arms around him. "He'll get tons of hugs, he has you. And when I get to know him well enough, I'll have a few for him, too. I'm not too bad at them." He stroked his hand up and down Garet's back. "Next step is making sure *you* never have to go back there. I'm going to talk to Rhodey. Are you ready for this?" He leaned back and gave Garet a sheepish grin. "As badass as your Dom is, I don't have any magic pull with the cops. Otherwise, I would've told them where to fucking go right then and there."

Garet swallowed hard, remembering his last conversation with Rhodey. "Yeah. If this doesn't work, do you know anyone in Canada?"

"Nope. But it'll work." Sin shook him lightly, holding his gaze. "Trust me?"

"Always." That one was easy. "With everything."

With a satisfied nod, Sin slid his arm around Garet as they crossed the rest of the way to The Asylum's front gates. He buzzed in and the gates opened to let them pass. Which had Sin's lips quirking. "I'm going to be honest. I wasn't sure we'd get this far without some smooth talking. Should we take this as a good sign?"

"Either that or they saw Ez's jacket and wondered what the fuck—er..." Remembering the rule against subs swearing on the premisis, Garet twisted his mouth nearly inside out trying to take the curse word back, but it hung out there like a stink bomb in summer air. "Sorry. I don't have a clue."

Staring up at the building's brick façade with its gray granite window sills, all that clean glass and the perfectly tarred and plowed parking lot, he felt a pang. Remembered all the times he and Ez had snowball fights with Reed and Matt, how the bar always smelled like sugar, and the way the warm air would puff against his face when he walked in the door on a frigid day like today. The lump in his throat dissolved with painful slowness and he lost his ability to speak at all.

The front door opened, Keiran's face unreadable as he motioned them in. "Come on, don't stand there in the cold. I'm heating up some stew for you. Rhodey will be down in a bit."

Keeping mute, Garet tried to blend in with Sin, wishing he could suddenly become a tattoo. The idea would've been kinky if he weren't so freaked out. Inside, everything was the same but not. Where sugar had once hung on the air, everything smelled like new wood and new paint. A hint of wet plaster and the faintest tinge of cigars and alcohol mingled with the spicy, meaty-sweet scent of stew. Breathing deep, he tried to memorize everything in case he wasn't allowed back again.

Sin led him to the bar, lifting him up to sit on a stool. When he went around the bar and grabbed a couple glasses, he got a raised brow from Keiran, which brought a slanted smile to Sin's lips. "I am still staff, my boy. An extended vacation doesn't change that. Do you want me to pour you something, too?"

"No... Actually, yes, please, sir." Keiran sighed and rolled his neck, moving to Garet's side and turning his stool to look him over. Finally, his expression softened. "You look really good. I wish we'd had a chance to talk after...everything. And that I'd known... If what we did together caused any of this, I'm sorry. So damn sorry, Garet."

Getting the denial past his lips was difficult, because he had a feeling Keiran wouldn't see it that way if he knew the entire story. Instead, Garet shook his head, his arms automatically flinging themselves around his friend's neck. "I missed you. So much. God."

Holding him close, Keiran spoke quietly, his lips brushing Garet's cheek with soft kisses every few words. "I missed you, too. And I don't give a damn that you're not supposed to come back here. If Sin's building a team to fight for your place in The Asylum? Consider me on it."

So many tears Garet had shed over the past months had been gut wrenching sobs filled with misery and shame, longing and loneliness. The ones he cried now were in gratitude, mixed with happiness, and sheer exhaustion. As if his entire being had been walking a wire until this very moment, where on one side was his messy and terrible past, and on the other a future that was completely unknown. For the first time in forever, he was just in the moment, feeling all his feels and not fearing a single one.

"Thank you. I promise I won't let you down like that ever again. I'm so sorry, Keir. I love you and I didn't mean to hurt you." Garet spoke into the vee of flesh where Keiran's neck met his shoulder, smelling cinnamon and the spicy soap all of Rhodey's crew used when they were home. "I don't expect you to forgive me automatically, but I'll do what I have to so I can earn your trust."

Keiran made a dismissive sound and eased back to cup Garet's cheek. "I can't speak for anyone else, but as far as I'm concerned? You're forgiven for scaring the hell out of me. Because I can see, just looking at you, just listening to you, that you're in a much better place. That's all I want. Along with the chance to help you stay there." His own eyes glistening with tears, he kissed the tip of Garet's nose. "Swear to me you'll let me and we're good, dulzura."

A lopsided and very wet grin tugging at his lips, Garet nodded. "It might involve a lot of marshmallow squares and chocolate chip cookies?"

"Now *that* I can definitely do." Keiran looked over when Sin slid two drinks to them, sputtering a protest. "You can't give him—"

"It's a Shirley Temple." Sin arched a brow at Keiran. "You think I don't know how to take care of my own sub? Give me some credit. And drink your vodka like a good boy."

"Jamie's gonna be mad at me, eating his safewords. You gave me extra cherries." Popping one in his mouth, Garet separated it from its stem to chew the plump sweetness. He looked around the bar, then at the bar clock. "Everyone eating upstairs tonight? Or did they leave before I came in?" Picturing Lawson ushering his quad out of the bar, Garet felt a wash of shame. "I'm sorry."

An irritated grunt came from right behind him before Rhodey leaned over and snatched Keiran's untouched vodka. "Everyone was already in their own lofts, you didn't cause a mass exodus, my boy." He glanced over at Sin. "This is *my* shit's gone sideways drink, not Keiran's. Keep up or I'll have to bury you under the bar instead of letting you work behind it."

Sin raised his hands, his lips twitching with amusement. "My bad. I'll keep that in mind. Your subs don't drink much."

"I get them sick of it during training." Rhodey shrugged and tossed back the vodka. "I should be pissed about you leading the cops to our door—I wasn't planning on playing with them today. Dallas, tell Towne to make them disappear. However he wants. There's new recruits coming up any time now, aren't there?"

In the time Garet had been away, Dallas must've done some serious leveling up, because it was impossible to see him until he stepped out of the shadows near Lawson's office door. He opened his phone to fire off some texts. "Two. One from Cleveland, a cousin of Vani's, and another who owes Tracey a favor for getting her mom a place at that exclusive assisted living situation in Boca Raton for half price so they could afford it. You really want the others gone?" It sounded like Dallas thought so. "I can have Avery sneak out to plant something illegal in their pockets."

"No, he didn't mean that." Keiran groaned when Rhodey tapped his chin like he was seriously considering a more permanent solution. "Two recruits are not enough to cover all of Anniston Falls. As terrible as some of them are...damn it, do *not* make me argue on their behalf, sir. I won't make snickerdoodles for a month."

Sighing, Dallas put his phone away after shooting off the text to Towne. "It's true. He won't." He gave Sin a put upon look. "I tried to force him once and he put salt in with the cinnamon."

Sin made a face, taking a long swig of beer. "When they say subs have all the power, they're not joking." He pointed at Garet, a gleam of humor in his eyes making it clear he was joking. "You ever try something like that and you will not like what happens when I take back control." He tilted his head. "Or maybe you will. Some subs enjoy weights attached to their balls. That's going to be the fun part of getting to know one another."

Under the circumstances, it shouldn't have been possible to get a fat dick, but there Garet was, feeling his own pupils blow and all his blood racing south. "I don't know how to bake. But I could learn?"

"No. You are not saying yes before I decide what the fuck I'm doing with the boy." Rhodey shot Keiran a sharp look when his lips parted, an edge to his tone saying the fun and games were over. He set down his glass and studied Garet for a long moment. "You are aware the second you left that place and the cops were called, I was alerted? Give me one good reason I should change my mind about our agreement."

Begging with Rhodey wouldn't help, and Garet wasn't sure he could stomach being that emotionally underhanded anyway. With Keiran there, it wasn't possible to tell the full story, but maybe if Rhodey sent him away? No, that wasn't the way he wanted to be let back in.

"I did the work, sir. Please give me another chance. I don't know what I'd have to do to prove to you I won't backslide, but if it's speech restrictions or leashes or scrubbing urinals with toothbrushes, I'll do it." Definitely not looking at Sin, Garet took a juddering breath. "If I set even a toe out of line I'll pack my own bags and I promise I'll never ask again. For anything."

Rhodey nodded slowly, making a cutting motion with his hand when Sin tried to jump in. "He's not wearing your collar yet, my man. And even if he was? This is his life he's trying to rebuild. You can't do it for him. And if you argue with me, I'm going to shoot you, so don't." He rubbed his jaw with his finger and thumb, his focus on Garet. "You don't touch even a fucking bottle of beer. You will do your work and continue your therapy—I'll arrange it. You will live here and you'll be on the same curfew, but if I see you so much as wave hello at the few remaining ex-gang members, you're done. I also don't want to hear any whining if the Core is *mean* to you. Within reason, but don't fucking expect the welcome mat laid out from everyone. You deal with that shit like you were taught to. Understood?"

It wasn't as if Garet didn't know what he was in for coming here, staying here. Their welcomes wouldn't be all like Keiran's. Hell, he'd be lucky if Noah didn't *try* to make him fuck up just to have the satisfaction of throwing his ass out on the street.

"I can do that, sir." Garet sat a little straighter. "I should tell you Matt threw me out of the café a coupla days ago. I think he's going to be pretty upset. I won't get in his way, but in case you want to give Lawson the final say or something, I get it."

That got him a dry look. "No. I've already decided. You and your brother will figure shit out. He'll be grumpy for a while. That's not my problem. So long as neither of you changes that, I've said all I have to on the matter."

"I'll be staying with him." Sin held Rhodey's gaze, gesturing with his beer bottle to the other Dom's empty glass. "He'll be wearing my collar because we've already discussed it. And as his Dom, I *will* have a say if someone disrespects my sub."

Rhodey lips slanted as he slid his glass across the bar for a refill. "Fine. But don't forget that when it comes to *your* little brother. You aren't his Dom, so you won't meddle when it comes to his relationship with Seth and River."

Lips parting, Sin ended up pouring half the vodka on the bar. "Excuse me, what? What the hell does Seth have to do with any of this?"

"Sir, Seth tagged him, but he's a very good Dom and takes excellent care of him. You don't need to worry." Coming out of the galley with two bowls of stew on a tray, a thick load of steaming bread beside it, along with a selection of cheese, Keiran set it down on the bar. He spoke in a rush, his tone reassuring. "You'll see, he's doing well. And other than some of the other Core subs sorting through their feelings about what happened, I'm sure they'll just be happy to see Garet and…you being here will be good, but he doesn't need you to protect him from us. He's family."

In a hesitant gesture, Garet laid his hand on Sin's bare forearm over one of his Celtic shield tattoos. "It's real sweet, all of them. You'll see. I promise, sir. He rocks a onesie."

Sin rubbed his free hand over his face. "I… Yeah. I'm going to need some time to wrap my mind around that. But you've got yourself a deal, Rhodey." He lowered his hand and met Rhodey's eyes again. "I'll stay with Garet, and I won't cause any waves. I'm here to make sure he doesn't feel alone while everyone sorts through their feelings. Present company excluded."

Garet knew better than to question a Dom. He'd been around The Asylum long enough to know the drill, even if he'd never had a Dom of his own. But— All rational thought cut off as the realization hit him between the eyes like lead shot, and his jaw dropped as giddy exaltation sent his stomach into freefall, then bouncing up again.

"Holy shit! I have a Dom!" He whooped, arms going in the air and tapped his feet in a dance rhythm against the bar rail. Laughter tripped from his lips, and he threw his arms around Sin's neck to hug him in a flurry of kisses. "Mine. Mine. Mine-mine-mine."

Sin laughed and patted his back a bit awkwardly, shaking his head when Rhodey lifted a brow at him. "Hey, he's had a rough day. He gets to be excited."

"Not to be an asshole, but…Wait, no, I don't mind being an asshole." Rhodey smirked, tipping his glass to his lips. "You'll be getting regular blood tests, my boy. So I suggest the first men you make nice with around here are the doctors."

"I can do them." Wren poked his head out from the stairwell, creeping quietly into the bar. "I am quite proficient. I can also examine his rectum as needed."

Garet's greeting stuttered to a grinding halt. He wasn't sure what kind of tests might require a rectal exam but…

Oh. Yeah. The drug smuggling.

Face flaming, he ducked his head, hoping no one saw him put two and two together.

"Glove up, buttercup." Dallas squeezed Wren's shoulder, catching him before he could duck away from the touch and managing to snatch his hand back before Wren's snapping teeth could sink into skin. "We probably should give him a full once over before he comes in. That way there's no doubt and you have a baseline."

Letting out a string of Spanish curses, Keiran gestured with the butcher knife he'd been using to cut the bread. "*Look at him.* He's healthy. He's been working hard to stay away from anything dangerous. He's here to avoid being treated like a criminal."

Wren blinked at Keiran, leaning back a bit against Dallas as though needing to feel his presence in the confusion. "I wouldn't treat him like a criminal, I am concerned for his health. He had a terrible addiction… Please don't be angry. I hoped he would be comfortable with me."

In the past, Garet found the almost ten years difference between himself and Wren really obvious, but at times like these, when the other sub was unsure of himself, that age gap lessened. Reaching over, he hooked a pinkie with Wren's.

"It's okay." Ducking down, he met Wren's doe brown eyes. "I don't mind. It'll make Matt feel better, I think. It's not about me being comfortable. You're all letting me into your home. It's about making sure everyone else has what they need."

Lips drawn into a firm line, Wren shook his head. "Not with this. I will…likely be taking a very different stance than my Doms, but hopefully I can help them understand what you were…what you *are* dealing with. Nothing will erase the hurt and fear and uncertainty caused, and there are things to process. But you will have the accommodations you need to manage your addiction, the same way I did…and do. Different methods might work for you, but those with more experience will make those decisions. I would not be very good at navigating the emotional impact, but…I can…relate to some of the struggles you'll face."

Sometimes, Wren having his own addiction was easy to forget. Garet didn't seek the rush of gambling, rather the oblivion drugs provided. An escape from the fear, loneliness, and uncertainty that had dogged him his entire life, which the assault had just made worse. If the fuckers hadn't dosed him, he probably would've found his way out, but the drugs… Yeah. They had their own way of hiding the truth even better than he'd ever been able to hide it from himself.

Focused on Wren, he forgot the rest of the room existed. "Do you…did you want to get out of your own head? Or was it something else?" He wanted to understand, to connect with this man who he'd had so little contact with, but who seemed like he might get him better than anyone else here. "Do you still want it or do the craving go away?"

"I wanted…for the longest time, it was all I had to offer. My only value. Then it made me feel…invincible." Wren wrapped his arms around himself, his gaze going a little distant. "When the outside world was overwhelming, confusing, I could go online and lose myself to it. Most would have faced financial ruin, but even that wasn't a deterrent for me. Only…only drawing the wrong kind of attention. If I hadn't gotten arrested, one of them…would have likely killed me. But I never worried about it. It felt…too good to stop."

Garet found himself nodding, unable to break Wren's gaze. Even hearing about Wren's struggles made that yawning pit open in his own middle—that insatiable hunger that made him desperate to do, be, *take* anything in an attempt to fulfill his cravings. "Sometimes…when I scened here, when people would play with me, it went away. That need. You?"

A soft smile curved Wren's lips as he nodded. He appeared more present, his expression taking on a kind of wistfulness. "When I was first with Noah, then with Jared, it became more…solid. But even with the Doms online, the ones who were not terribly *in*ept, the scenes would…settle something in my mind. I realized when the exchange came with a connection, that feeling was more constant. I was able to find it in other things. Caring for others in small ways. Service and medical treatments. And anything…a little dark and twisted, but with play it must be under someone else's control. I find I am not very good at drawing my own limits. Any more than I was with my addiction."

"God, I get that—"

Inching closer to Wren as he spoke, Garet jerked his head up when the door to the gym opened, and Jared's sharp, "Wren," echoed from the large space beyond. He snapped his fingers, gaze swinging from Garet to his boy. "To heel."

Wren blinked, moving in a quick, smooth pace to his Dom. He took his place a step behind him, seeming to sense something was off. From the way his brow furrowed, he wasn't sure what. "Sir?"

Ignoring Wren, Jared lasered in on Rhodey. "I thought we had an agreement?"

"I dealt with the situation. I'm still dealing with it." Rhodey straightened from where he'd been leaning against the side of the bar while Garet and Wren were talking, silently observing along with his men and Sin. He folded his arms over his chest. "If the boy hadn't put in the work, I wouldn't even consider letting him come back. But he has. And he's family. I won't leave him to the fucking wolves."

Jaw working, Jared turned glacial before Garet's eyes. "And have you considered the ramifications to Noah? Matt? The stability of this place after—" He cut himself off, breathing through flared nostrils. "He stays in his loft."

"I always consider *every* angle, my man." Rhodey's tone took on a warning edge as he closed the distance between himself and Jared, his gaze locked on the other Dom's. "Will it fuck with them? Probably. We can handle that. What we can't handle is serving up another member of our family to be used against us. So consider *that* before you start making goddamn ultimatums."

"Ultimatums. Get a dictionary, Rhodey." Hand on Wren's shoulder, Jared drew him back, turning to leave the way he'd come. His next words, he addressed to his boy on his way into the gym. "Not a word to him. Until I say, he doesn't exist to you."

Rhodey strode forward, slamming his hand into the gym door to keep it from closing. "That snide shit is beneath you, Jared. 'He stays in his loft' and 'he doesn't exist'. If he stays, that's how you're gonna be. Pissy and fucking petty. If he goes, you'll play nice. Pick another word, it's the same damn thing. He stays. And don't forget who your boy fucking works for."

Eyes snapping with shard-like sparks, Jared rounded on Rhodey. "An ultimatum, if you must, comes with a stated cost or option. Such as, if he stays, you'll need to choose between him and me. Which I did not utter. I gave a *directive*. An *order*. I know you're familiar with those words." He leaned in. "Stay in your lane."

Letting out a bitter laugh, Rhodey inclined his head. "I know I've really pissed you off when you try to make me feel stupid. Got it, my man. But Garet needs a physical. And Wren offered to give it to him."

"Sirs, if I may." Leaving both Pike and Tay standing just inside the stairwell, Quint stepped forward. "As skilled as Wren is, he's not qualified to give that kind of exam in any official capacity. I'd like to volunteer my services. I'll make sure he has whatever care, tests, and treatment might be required."

Chewing his pinky nail down to the quick, Garet watched the argument between two men who were rumored to have been friends since childhood. Coming between them seriously sucked. Quint was dope for stepping in, but it wasn't going to solve everything. "I mean, I could stay in my room. My loft. I don't wanna upset anyone."

"You won't be a prisoner here." Keiran nudged Garet's stew closer to him, motioning for him to eat, speaking quietly enough so only those around the bar should be able to hear him, but the shift in Rhodey's stance made it obvious he hadn't missed a thing. "The Doms like growling at each other sometimes, niño. You'll get used to it."

Obediently picking up the fork, Garet toyed with a piece of meat, then put it in his mouth to make Keiran feel better. He wanted to lean into Sin, to find a place to hide, but being a needy baby would only be a turnoff.

From the doorway, Jared watched him, expression hawkish. Like maybe addiction was catching. After a moment he tore his gaze away to consider Quint. "All right. Thank you, my boy. That would be acceptable. Standard institutional regimen and cadence."

"Yes, sir." Quint stood almost at attention, like he was addressing a commanding officer, rather than a Dom. But his calming smile wasn't at all military-like. "I believe it will console everyone to know this situation is being addressed with all the necessary precautions. I'll have a file ready within the hour and make all my findings available for both yourself and Seth."

Chewing slowly, Garet had the momentary feeling of panic he always did before a drug test. Like maybe someone had slipped him something and he was going to test positive. His therapist said it was natural, given how he'd gotten to this in the first place, but it still felt like the floor under his feet wasn't quite substantial.

"Upstairs, Wren. I meant what I said, but you may get the spare loft ready." Jared gently prodded his boy toward the stairway.

"Spare loft?" Garet frowned. "I stay in Curtis' old place."

"It's a schoolroom now." The Dom seemed to take a bit of evil delight in letting him know the home he'd lived in since he was sixteen was no longer available. "Quint, let him know when you're ready for him. Come to me if he gives you any trouble."

A bottle clinked hard on the bar surface, Sin blowing out a breath like he was trying very hard to remain calm, but he'd reached his limit of standing on the sidelines. "He won't give anyone trouble. And *I* will be there if anything comes up. For *my* sub." He tilted his head slightly and let out a soft laugh. "Nice to see you, Jared. I'd say it's good to be back, but I'm thinking my timing could've been better. If things had gone the way I hoped, you'd all've had time to plan a party. Maybe next time."

"You're always welcome, Sinaan." Jared using Sin's formal name felt...weird. The Dom nodded to Keiran. "The stew smells lovely. I'll return for some in a bit."

Gaze shifting from Rhodey to Jared, Keiran appeared torn, but a silent communication, conveyed in a glance from Rhodey, visibly relaxed the other sub—though his smile was still a little shaky when he nodded. "I'll have some ready for you, sir, along with some freshly baked bread. I'll go...do that now."

Dallas stood, leaving the table where he'd been cleaning his gun, all the pieces back together almost faster than Garet could follow. "I'm on watch now. I'll see you all in the morning." He snagged Keiran's belt loop, bringing him around for a kiss on the forehead. "Good boy."

"Thank you, sir." Keiran closed his eyes, leaning into Dallas and speaking in a mock whisper. "I'll be making an extra batch of snickerdoodles just for you. I'll have Avery bring them up."

"Mmm..." Dallas breathed deep, like he smelled the cinnamon on Keiran's skin even now. His gaze slid sideways to Garet. "Or you could have my boy Garet bring them up. We haven't been able to catch up in a while."

Warmth spilled into Garet's vacant middle, pushing his lips into a lopsided grin. "Yes, sir. I have Ez's coat to keep me warm, so I won't even freeze my balls off up there. He won't let me go to his club opening, but if you go will you say hi for me?"

A burst of cold spilled into the bar as the front door opened, Reed's laughter cutting off at Garet's words. Or maybe at the sight of him. He gave his head a hard shake, snow coming off his sparkly purple knit hat as he skidded on wet boots toward the bar. "You saw Ez? How is he? And what're you doing here? Ish is gonna hit the fan." He glanced around the bar and sighed. "Or did it already start flying?"

Making a vee of his arms over his head, Garet mimed a poop emoji. "I'm the King of Kaka." He hopped off the stool, tipping his head back to look up at the guy who was his second big brother. A man he was even closer to than his own. "He's good. He's opening a club. I got kicked out of my living sitch for getting caught not-stealing. I missed you."

"I missed you, too, kiddo." Reed pulled him into a rough hug, the snow on his puffy pink jacket soaking into Garet's T-shirt and dampening his cheek. He brought his lips close to Garet's ear. "No matter what anyone fucking says, you promise me you're gonna tough it out and stick around. They go too far and I'll mess them up, got it?"

Nodding against Reed's chest, Garet hugged him so hard it was like they melted together. He closed his eyes, soaking in the scent of candy and snow. "Come have popcorn and cocoa with me later like old times...if it won't get you in ish with my bro? He's not cool with this...or he won't be when he finds out."

"Tough fucking titties." Reed put his hands on Garet's shoulders, his bright blue eyes flashing with anger. "I'll be there. He can deal with it or not, but me and you? We're Gucci."

"We'll work it out. He gets to have his feels." On tiptoes, Garet brushed a kiss over Reed's cold cheek as the door opened again. "You might be Gucci, but I rock the Prada."

Curtis stepped inside, blowing on his fingers, then slipped in a puddle and sat right on his ass with a floor rocking thud. "Ow. That hurt. I might've hit my head. I'm seeing Garets."

As though his cousin's fall broke the tension, giving him permission to stop hovering in the stairwell behind Quint like a toy soldier, Pike tripped into the bar with a laugh and scrambled to Curtis' side. "I'm contagious. But yeah, you're seeing him. He busted into this place like 'Yo, what's up mofos?' and it was kinda epic. I like him better like this and not...well, like the first time we met. Also, Keiran's making more bread. Drama haven around here is awesome for my poor, empty stomach."

Hopping to his feet, Curtis lifted Pike to throw him over his shoulder. "Can't have that. Reed, you want pancakes and Pop-Tarts for dinner? I'm buying." He closed in on Garet and Reed, lifting Garet to throw him over his other shoulder so the world flipped upside-down. "Sorry, Sin. I'm claiming parental rights and feeding this waif."

"You won't get any argument from me, my man." Sin grinned at them, then looked over at Tay, who hadn't moved. "Do I get a hello or do your new Doms have you on some kind of High Protocol shit?"

Tay shook his head, bolting forward and throwing himself against Sin's chest. His voice was muffled when he spoke. "No, my Doms are awesome. I just...things can get... I missed you. So damn much. And I've got a lot to tell you."

"Yes, you do." Sin crouched down a bit to meet Tay's eyes, glancing at his collar, his lips curving slightly. "So long as they make you happy, I guess I won't give them too much grief. The second that changes, I'll have to kick some ass, though. Just giving you a head's up."

Wrinkling his nose, Tay punched Sin in the shoulder. "No beating on my Doms. You'll have to get through me. And I've seen some pretty intense fights around here. Might've picked up a thing or two."

Sitting Garet on the bar next to Pike, Curtis got out the toaster and the hot plate along with his premade pancake batter he liked to keep in the bar fridge. "Who wants chocolate chip smiley face pancakes? With whipped cream."

"I do, obviously. And Tay, too." Pike spoke around a piece of bread he'd torn from what was left of the load from Garet and Sin's dinner. "Garet's gotta do some kind of medical thing with Quint. That's gonna make him hungry. It always makes me hungry."

Garet raised his hand. "Me. I'd like some, please, sir." He leaned his shoulder against Pike's to whisper, "I'm really sorry about everything. I didn't mean to hurt you."

Chewing slower, Pike shook his head. "You didn't, really. I mean, that whole thing really sucked, but you more…I was scared. And…I figured I always get in trouble, so it'd be more of the same. But that's not your fault." He stared down at the piece of bread in his hand. "You…my family hurt a lot of people like you. Everything I had was…from that. So I got no room to judge."

"You still get to be hurt and pissed off. That's not judging. But all the same?" Digging into the jar of chocolate chips, Garet handed a few to Pike to nibble. "I'm really thankful you helped save me. And I can't wait to get to know my…Curtis' cuz."

In private, sometimes, when he was a kid, he teased Curtis calling him 'Dad' and 'Old Man', secretly wishing he'd had a father as cool as him. He wasn't old at all, but he had the kind of wisdom in his eyes that made him seem way older than he was. A life well lived, or at least experienced and seen.

"You'll like him, he's pretty great." Reed reached over the bar, snagging a multicolored unicorn lollipop. Hopping up to sit on Garet's other side, he spoke low. "You're lucky Sin's your Dom, I won't have to warn you against all the trouble this little rascal can get you in. Sin won't mind."

Sin snorted, lifting Tay onto a nearby stool. He leaned over to claim a kiss from Garet, speaking against his lips. "No, Sin won't. Within reason. It'll be fun to watch you guess what those limits are."

Poking his tongue out, Garet tasted the beer on Sin's lips, then nipped the lower one with a breathy laugh. "It'll be fun finding them, sir." The scent of pancakes rose, along with the warm hum of the conversation in the bar. "Because they mean I get to be near you."

"Mhm." Sin kissed him again. "All things considered, I think this went better than expected." He rapped his knuckles on the bar. "And I hate to break up the family reunion, but I wouldn't be a very good Dom if I didn't handle the priorities. Let's go get that exam done so it's one less thing to worry about."

Hopping to the floor, Garet obediently headed toward the clinic, trying not to show any nerves. If he wobbled, everyone would think he had something to hide. He didn't, except for the cloud of memories that haunted him every time he went through this ordeal.

The gym was like he remembered it, except not. Everything was gleaming and new, with none of the stale beer and old sweat smell once underlying all the floor wax and bleach. The cage lights gleamed, and the windows on the high perimeter of the far wall had new steel shutters that looked like they'd slide closed to bomb-proof the place. And the clinic was super different, with more rooms, wider spaces, and brand new equipment. Thankfully, the man who'd taught him the science knowledge he'd needed to pass his college entrance exams was nowhere to be found. He'd never been particularly close to Jared—the Dom seeming to prefer keeping him at arm's length—but earning his respect all those years back had been something Garet had strived for, and it hurt not to have it now.

"Hello?" Garet called out, not sure which room to go into off the main one.

Inside, quiet voices came from one of the offices. "I know it's not as pretty as your boy would've gotten it, but I don't mind a few scars to show off." The voice was unfamiliar, with a warm, teasing undertone. "Don't look at me like that, it was one bullet. And it's almost all healed."

Sin huffed and wrapped his arms over Garet's chest.

"Sounds like we're not the only ones back from our great adventures. That's River. And he better not have gotten any holes in the ink I did for him or I'll be pissed."

"Is River a sub?" Uncertainty in his tone, Garet tipped his head back to look at Sin upside down. "Do you have a thing?" He tried to remember where he'd heard the name before, then laughed at himself because his nerves had made him blank. "Oh. Nevermind. He's Tay's Dom. That's right. We never met."

"No, you weren't around when he joined the club." Sin brushed his lips along the side of Garet's throat. "I met him in the Air Force and I did a piece on his back. Also got him in the club. He's a good man, but I'm still deciding if he's good enough for my brother."

"I never had that problem. I always knew Lawson was good for Matt." Giving Sin greater access to his throat, Garet sighed happily. "Do you think they're really gonna do a rectal?" He wiggled his ass against Sin's front. "Maybe you could let Quint show you how."

Huffing out a laugh, Sin nipped his neck hard enough to sting. "Cheeky sub. You think your Dom needs a sub to teach him how to handle his boy's body? If I didn't know better, I'd be hurt that our time together was that easy to forget."

This was good. Lighthearted and easy. Everything with Sin seemed as effortless as breathing. When so much in life had been a struggle it was fucking beautiful to have something that very much wasn't. "Well, you know. We never played doctor."

"That is not why you're in here." Quint came into the clinic, carrying a box and clucking his tongue. "There's a medical sceneing area in the dungeon if you'd like to try it out, but in the clinic we keep things professional." He looked over as the office door opened, and let out a heavy sigh. "Sir, please don't tell me you have as much difficulty keeping your clothes on as our little angel. There are hospital gowns for a reason."

Wearing only a pair of snug, black boxer briefs, a tall, muscular man with light brown skin strolled barefoot into the main part of the clinic with a teasing smile on his lips. "No, but now that I know you like it so much, I'll make a point of doing it more often."

Sterile gloves on, Quint gave the Dom a long look before approaching him, turning him with a gentle hand on his arm to examine his shoulder. The wound was a bit red around the healing flesh, but whatever stitches had closed it were long gone, and River didn't appear to be in any pain. Actually, he seemed more surprised at Quint touching him than anything.

"You're right, I could do a better job. If you'd like, I'll set some time aside tomorrow to make sure you won't have a nasty scar." Quint traced his finger around the edge of the bullet wound, smiling as his gaze shifted to the tattoo of a jungle, with a single jaguar...no, a jaguar with her cub hidden away...and crisp Roman numerals beneath the elaborate piece created by Sin on the man's flesh. Glancing over his shoulder, Quint gave Sin a reassuring look. "It won't impact your beautiful work, sir."

Before Sin could say a word, the door to the clinic swung open, tense voices pouring in as Lawson held it open with his shoulder. Rhodey's tone held an edge that usually made everyone around him sit up a bit straighter and make sure they hadn't done anything to draw his ire. But Lawson didn't seem the least bit deterred.

Rhodey made an irritated sound. "The decision's already been made."

"It wasn't your decision to make." Lawson's jaw worked as he looked at Garet, then returned his attention to Rhodey. "We will handle this our way."

Tone detached and much lighter than the other two men, Noah spoke as though they were all discussing something vaguely amusing. "It's fine, my man. I'm sure my uncle's taken everything into account. We should have a 'Welcome Home' party. Invite everyone. My mother, Rhodey's son—"

"Noah, ostanovis' seychas zhe—"

The words Rhodey snapped out were cut off as Lawson's casted arm cracked into his mouth.

Yeah...Garet was definitely home.

And the welcome wagon is full of hornets.

He had a bad feeling he'd kicked it over...and was about to get stung.

Chapter Twenty-Six

PRESENT

*T*he *CRACK* of Lawson's cast into Rhodey's jaw made Garet jump. While Matt's husband usually only wielded a paddle—and occasionally a whip—when dealing with the subs, Garet had a feeling the man definitely saw him as less of a sub in need of discipline, and more of a threat to the safety of his family. Which meant he might be next in line for a faceful of plaster.

Every Dom in the room tensed, as though prepared to jump in when Rhodey grabbed the front of Lawson's shirt.

Hand up to keep them back, Lawson stared at Rhodey, unblinking. "You knew what this would do to him. What this would do to *all* of us. You don't get to take the easy way out because you made a decision without consulting anyone. You won't ruin all his progress because you've decided to play God."

Shoving away from Lawson, Rhodey took a step back and closed his eyes. He swiped at the blood spilling from his bottom lip, leaving a fresh trail to drip to the floor as he inhaled a measured breath. "I'm not fucking trying to ruin anything. I won't do to the boy what I did to *him*. Play God? Like when I decided Noah wasn't worth the effort and I either end him or let—?" He cut himself off and opened his eyes, the gray within dark with regret for a split second, before he regained his composure. "The damage I did can't be fixed, as much as you want to believe it can. Fucking think about that before you turn your back on the damn kid."

"No, Uncle, that's one thing you don't need to worry about." Noah's lips curved into a slow smile. "We won't turn our back on him, that would be foolish."

Expression pained, Lawson turned to Noah, putting a hand on his shoulder. "Security will need to be tightened, in case there's more to this than the boy wanting to come home. Why don't you take watch on the roof?"

Noah nodded, humming to himself, a song not hard to recognize as *Every Breath You Take* by The Police, even though it sounded eerie and wrong. The Dom didn't even look Garet's way now, though the spine tingling sensation of being watched never faded. Shifting his focus, Noah stroked Matt's cheek with his fingertips. "I won't let anything hurt you, pup. I promise. No more graveside tears. We'll paint much prettier ones."

Keeping silent in the face of the opposition mounted against him in the room was impossible. Rhodey was a formidable ally, but allies weren't what Garet needed. He needed his family. His friends. Winning them back wouldn't happen overnight, or at all, if he threatened their happiness and well-being. Standing from his seat on a plastic waiting-room chair, he squeezed Sin's fingers.

"It's okay. I get it. I don't want to rock anyone's world. I love you, bro and I never meant to hurt you. I'm sorry." Garet took a deep breath, trying to subdue the shaking in his voice as he looked Matt in the eye. "I hope you can forgive me someday, but I totally get it if that's not possible."

Matt's chin notched, the set of his jaw so much like their father's Garet had to force himself not to take a step back. "You didn't want to *hurt* me? That's a new one." His laugh was bitter. "I'm done bailing you out and waiting for the other shoe to drop with you, *bro*. It's easier to pretend you don't exist than to wait to get kicked in the head again when I least expect it. I hope you have a nice fucking life, as long as it's nowhere near me or the people I care about. Who I *trust*."

Out of all the apologies Garet had made, this one sucked the most. Mostly because he didn't blame Matt one bit for his reaction, but being loved by his big brother was the holy grail of his recovery. They'd warned him about this. About how there'd probably be a desperation at some moment to fill himself up with someone else's forgiveness. An interaction that would rock his self-worth to its core. He couldn't let it, even though the craving for the drugs and alcohol reared so hard, and so fast, for the first time in months, it made him nearly gasp aloud.

Taking a step away, he didn't lower his gaze. "I mean it. I'm sorry. I love you, and I'll go."

"If you were sorry, you never would've shown your face here in the first place." Matt didn't give an inch, his blue eyes steely as he stood with Lawson and Noah at his back.

Garet would have to make it past all three of them to return to the bar.

One day at a time became one moment at a time. One step at a time.

"I just need to get my coat." Garet made his apology with his expression, motioning to Sin as he attempted to move past the three men—past his brother—to the door.

Matt blocked his way. "I saw it. It's Ezran's coat. Not yours. We all thought he was here."

His brother's tone told Garet he'd have preferred if their visitor had been Ez instead. "Yeah. No. I saw him the other day at the old abandoned hotel we used to hang out in." *God, that seems like a lifetime ago.* "I didn't have one, so he gave it to me."

"Am I supposed to feel sorry for you?" Matt folded his arms over his chest. "You obviously didn't tell him why you were walking around without one, or he wouldn't have given you the time of day. Did you even consider, Garet, when you were out using and selling, fucking with the gang who almost *killed* you both—who *did* kill people here, and got Noah thrown in prison and taken away from the people who cared about him and needed him—that you were shoving a red hot poker up the asses of the people who'd loved and comforted you, provided you with shelter and food and a goddamn education? Did you even ever for one fucking moment give a thought to how your actions affected them all?"

Tears, hot and pregnant with all the emotion he tried to stuff back, sprang to Garet's eyes. "No." Giving a bark of laughter, Matt threw his head back, but Garet continued, cutting off his reply. "I was too busy trying to forget getting dosed with my first hit while I was out at a college bar, and waking up bleeding from a rape I couldn't remember. The drugs became a way to cope. Then dealing became a way to get my next hit so I *could* cope." He lowered his voice, realizing he'd been close to shouting. "I'm sorry. I know it's not an excuse for what I did to you all, but I can't change it. I can't change *anything*, and I've got to live with that. I get it—" Swiping at his eyes, he choked back more tears, not wanting to open up a vein, only to be accused of making a selfish attempt for sympathy. "Please. I'll go. Can you just let me by? I promise I won't come back."

Rhodey grunted, putting a hand on his shoulder, nodding to Sin when Garet's Dom drew him back to hold him to his chest. Tone rough, Rhodey glanced at Matt, then Lawson, as though deciding he might be the level-headed one, even though the guy had just busted his lip open. "He stays. You need space? He'll give it to you. He won't say a goddamn word to a single one of you if you're in the same room. But whatever you're feeling about this situation? Is yours. Don't make it my fucking problem." He gave Garet a little shake and glanced down at him. "Finish your medical shit and head up to the loft. You need a break from all this." He gestured vaguely at the other men. "Get the fuck out of the clinic. None of you is bleeding."

Garet held his breath, wondering whether more blows would be exchanged. The revelations had momentarily floored Matt, widening his eyes with brotherly terror, then anger on Garet's behalf before he seemed to remember that he wasn't to be trusted and shut down again. But not before his next thoughts flashed across his face. He thought Garet was lying. That he'd say or do anything to gain the empathy and forgiveness that Matt was no longer willing to give.

"Garet, Sin. In here." Seth stood in the doorway to one of the clinic rooms. "I'll take care of you."

Inhaling slowly, Lawson brought his hand to the back of Matt's neck, his thumb stroking along his throat as he guided him out of the clinic. Voice low, Lawson's words were clearly for Matt alone. "Let's head over to the café for a bit. I could use a good cup of coffee and we can see how your new hire is working out. We all need some time to...process."

As the three men left the clinic, Quint gave Garet a sympathetic smile. "Seth will take good care of you. Go with your Dom and get this over with. I'll clean up this mess..." He lifted a brow at Rhodey. "Since I doubt you'll let me take care of that lip."

Scoffing, Rhodey went to the counter and grabbed a few tissues from a box there. He pressed them to his bottom lip, his slanted smile a little bloody. "You're a smart sub. This is my reward for forgetting the bastard's got some grit under those snazzy suits. I'll have to repay him. That'll be fun." He eyed River. "Go take watch with Noah. You're decent at not setting him off. Except that one time, but you're still breathing so I'll consider that a win."

"Hey, it's worked for me so far." River grinned at Rhodey, then reached out to ruffle Garet's hair, sobering as he lowered his hand. "I don't know you well enough to say anything useful about the situation, but I'm sorry. For everything you've been through. What you just did took a lot of strength, no matter how...fucked up some people's reactions were. You might not feel it right now, but I know a lot of people are happy to have you back. The rest...will come around."

Gratitude to the man for reaching out—for sticking his neck out—to comfort someone he didn't know, had a steadying effect. Garet inhaled deeply, nodding as he exhaled. "Thanks. That's more useful than you know. I'm a little..." He gave a shaky smile. "Frayed around the edges right now, but I'll do the work and get back to center."

Maybe if he kept telling himself that, it'd all be true. Having Sin, Keiran, Reed, Rhodey, and Dallas—and now maybe River—to help support him made The Asylum feel less like the relationship equivalent of Humpty Dumpty and more like a Rubix Cube. He might not have all the right moves to get the colors on the correct side, but he'd keep working at it. With a little luck and a lot of persistence, he might get it all aligned again.

Matt, though... That one hurts.

And it should. He'd been a complete asshole in the way he'd treated his brother for a really long time as a kid. That was the thing though. He *had* been a kid, and there was a certain amount of forgiveness he could give himself, and he'd hoped Matt had given him for those things. A clean slate. Which he realized as he walked into the sterile clinic environment was something no one owed him. Their feelings were theirs.

His phone buzzed in his pocket, and he took it out expecting to see a text from Finn.

Instead, it was from Matt.

Heart lifting a little, he opened the conversation. Maybe it was an offer to talk later, or something that would offer an eventual place to meet on common ground. It was none of those, though. Seeing that it was a group text, he scrolled, his heart jamming up into his throat as his knees nearly buckled under him.

Garet was banned from The Asylum for using and dealing for the gang. Thought you should know before you give him the rest of the clothes off your back.

A sense of loss beyond just missing his brother set up a heaviness in Garet's middle. His friendship with Ezran would never survive this. No matter the reason. Matt had done more than reject him, he'd fired the first shot in an attempt to make Garet a complete outcast from his friends and family.

Afraid he'd puke if he saw Ez's reply, he shut off his phone entirely and stowed it away to numbly begin undressing. "Can I have some water, please?"

Prepping some blood tubes and a syringe, Seth nodded toward a drinks fridge near the door. "There's juice too." He glanced over his shoulder Garet, frowning. "You're pale. Do you have a problem with needles?"

Garet forced a smile. "No. Today was just a lot, you know?" On top of the counter there was a plushie puppy sleeping on a haphazard mountain of connected Lego. "Um..." He laughed despite the heaviness in his chest. "There's a three-headed dog guarding some kind of...stegosaurus?"

On hands and knees, gloves on, Quint cleaned and disinfected the floor, a soft look in his eyes as he followed Garet's gaze. "Tay's on a dinosaur kick and Pike's been getting Wren to tell him about different mythologies. Naturally, Wren is most interested in those concerning the underworld."

Sin's brow furrowed as he opened the small fridge and took out both a bottle of water and a variety of juice boxes. He came to Garet's side, holding them up for him to select one. "My parents turned one of the rooms in the basement into a den full of all kinds of toys. The rest of the kids had a riot messing around down there, but Tay always stayed away —he liked sketching and doing those word finder things. I used to save the ones I found in the newspaper whenever I was home. My mom got him a few of the books full of them from second-hand stores, but…well, most of them were already done."

Remembering his own childhood, Garet looked over the plushie. "I was into cars." He didn't mention how those kinds of toys had stopped being a thing once his mom had died. "It's cool. I bet satanic dinos are a total thing. Why else would they have horns?"

Stepping up to him, Seth swabbed his arm. The alcohol's astringent scent stung Garet's nostrils, but he was used to the prick of the needle and how his arms constantly had black and blue marks. He barely felt Seth's work though. "I'll get your chart from the state." The Dom doc gave him an encouraging glance, switching out the tubes. "And if you ever want to play with some of the cars in Pike and Tay's collection, you're welcome."

Heat crept up the back of Garet's neck at the thought of lying on his belly making the cars zoom around. He shook his head quickly in denial. "Thanks. That's cool of you to offer."

Opening the bottle of water and leaving the rest of the drinks in Garet's reach, Sin kept his gaze locked on the needle. "He'll be joining your boys. Because I'd like to get a better idea of what little play is like. And if it gets him squirming and blushing, all the better." He tipped the bottle to his lips, swallowing down half in a few long gulps. "Besides, it gives me an excuse to keep an eye on you and River."

Seth capped the last tube, nodding at Quint to do the honors with the gauze. He met Sin's gaze with his steady dark blue stare. "Why do you need an excuse? You're family." He labeled the tube, leaving it near some kind of machine where presumably it'd be processed. "Have dinner with us. Every night if you want. Tay would be happy to see you, and what makes him and my boys happy, makes me happy."

"We just might take you up on that." Sin polished off the

water, wiping his lips with his sleeve as he watched Quint gently tape the gauze to Garet's arm. "I don't want to impose when we just walked in the door, but if I can't be with Garet, for *any* reason, I'd appreciate it if you or one of your men could stay with him. I've seen how things get around here when someone is persona non grata, and I won't have that happening to him."

The amount of trouble people here would need to go to if Quint and River, and Seth, agreed boggled Garet's mind. At first, he'd thought Sin asked so someone would make sure he wouldn't be tempted to use. When the rest of the explanation came out, Garet ducked his head, flexing his arm just to have something to do that would look normal.

Seth tore his gaze away from Quint's. "My boy has my permission *if* he's willing. I won't speak for him." He leaned out of the door. "Or you, my man. It's up to you, of course. I'm good with it for my part. I enjoy poking Jared in the eye."

The soft chuckle from River made it obvious he'd decided to stick around for a bit, rather than head straight up for security duties. He strolled into the office, leaning in to brush a kiss to the edge of Seth's lips. "Get myself right in the middle of an Asylum mess? I can't think of a better way to make sure no one forgets I'm home."

Groaning inwardly, Garet tried to decide whether or not this situation would work for or against him. Other than someone spiking his blood test results, he probably couldn't get in deeper shit.

"Thank you, sirs." He glanced between the three Doms, then to Quint, who hadn't answered. "I promise I won't be any trouble."

Quint gave him a sad smile and cupped his cheek. "Since you have a lot of people who likely won't believe that at first, I need you to know I do. And I will do my best to shield you from some of the...*harsher* reactions from the other Core members. I won't get in between my Doms, though. Jared has his reasons for how he's taking all of this and I love him too much to stand against him. He's a reasonable man, I'm sure he'll come around. The best I can offer for now is to keep the peace."

Squeezing Quint's shoulder on his way toward a computer screen on a desk at the room's far end, Seth gave his boy an approving look. "Well said. One of us needs to keep him from losing his cool. And you're much better at it than I am." He winked at River. "We all need to do what we're good at."

"Absolutely. And if we come up with some good distractions, the little mechanic won't face too much heat." River folded his arms over his chest, his expression thoughtful. "Having him around our boys will help. They can't seem to avoid getting into a bit of trouble. And when they decide to behave, I'll just have to get creative myself."

Garet leaned into Sin's side, soaking up his Dom's heat, shivering a little at the reminder there was someone in this world that he was *allowed* to seek that comfort from. "If I'm really quiet, no one will notice I'm there. They didn't even when I was loud, so this should be a piece of cake."

"None of that, you don't need to make yourself invisible. For *anyone*." Sin gave him a one-armed hug. "We'll ease into things here and if Seth and River's crew can give you some space to adjust, all the better. You have other allies, too. Let's focus on spending time with them, showing the rest they can't scare you away, and hopefully get them to pull their heads out of their asses."

Grabbing a juice box, Garet peeled the wrapper free of the straw while he considered Sin's advice. The little tinfoil circle at the top proved a pain in the ass, resisting his first few attempts to stab it. "I can do that, sir." He handed the box to his Dom. "I could use some help, sir. I think the juice boxes here are Pike-proofed."

Seth snorted. "No. My little pixie would've squeezed the box hard as he slid the straw in, and gotten a faceful of grape juice. We do it for him now. Or rather, Quint does." He glanced up from the computer screen as the machine where Garet's blood was being processed stopped whirring, then the app beeped and a line of green bars came up. "Very good. You're in the clear. We'll do this at random intervals. Your arms need a rest and I'd rather not start using your feet. Keep up the good work."

"If you need to use his feet, it could be fun." Sin poked Garet in the side. "They can be very sensitive. Having him keep perfectly still while you're doing it would entertain me very much."

Rolling his eyes, Quint put his hand over Garet's. "Don't worry, we don't let Doms indulge in their kinks while we're handling patients. If he can't behave himself, he'll have to wait outside while I finish your exam."

Blinking at the last part, Garet pulled his bottom lip between his teeth. *We're not done?* "Please don't make him leave. I'm good."

"I remember that scene Jared did in the dungeon a while back. Needle play when a sub has a full bladder is very entertaining." Seth seemed not to notice anything at all unusual, or that Quint had just said there was no indulging of kinks in the clinic. "I've been thinking how cute it would've been if the boy had worn a pair of briefs with that truck print Pike has on his pajamas."

Garet's face went so hot he got a head rush. "Can we finish? Sorry. I'm hungry."

"Yes, let's get this over with." Sin pressed a kiss to Garet's cheek. "But I love that blush. It's adorable. I'll be finding a lot of reasons to get you all nice and red for me."

The idea of which only made Garet smile as he tipped his head back to beg a kiss on his mouth. "Promise, sir?"

"Promise." Sin dipped in to claim a deep kiss, leaving Garet's lips tender when he finally drew away. He moved back as Quint motioned for Garet to stand. "I won't make any more kinky suggestions, but I'm not leaving. Whatever you need to do, you can do in front of me."

Quint's lips thinned slightly. "If Garet is comfortable with that, sir, I don't object, but I would remind you that in this room? You do not make the orders."

Grinning, River headed for the door. "Now you're in for it. Don't mess with the docs, Sin. They're better with sharp things than you are."

"You need me to stay, smiley, or can I go make sure our littles haven't set the loft on fire?" Seth stood from his rolling seat, the sound of the metal and rubber rollers squeaking in a way that would have Curtis reaching for his lifetime supply of WD-40. "Which reminds me..." He lifted the plushie and the Lego-saurus. "I should deliver these as well."

Donning a fresh pair of gloves, Quint gave his Dom a warm smile. "I'll be fine, sir. After Garet's cleared, I'll update his file and close up here…unless someone manages to hurt themselves in the next ten minutes. Otherwise, I'll head over to the general clinic—I have a patient who works odd hours and couldn't make the time to see me during our regular hours. I shouldn't be long."

"Take someone with you. Curtis maybe." Concern skated past the shadows in Seth's eyes as he looked Quint over. "I don't like you being there alone when the building is empty." He lingered in the doorway. "Come see me when you're back. I'm making fresh pizza dough and might need help unsticking it from Pike's hair."

Quint breathed out a laugh and nodded. "I can almost guarantee it. I will, sir." He crossed the room, careful not to touch anything, and brought his lips close to Seth's, speaking softly. "I might not be a merc anymore, sir, but I can handle myself. Please don't worry."

"Humor me." Seth spoke the words against Quint's lips before he nipped the bottom one then smacked his boy's ass hard enough to make him stumble forward into his chest.

"Mhm. I'm *definitely* going to want to see you when you come home."

Making a quiet sound of pleasure, Quint nodded and touched his forehead to his Dom's. "I am looking forward to being seen, sir." His tone took on a teasing note. "Almost as much as I'm looking forward to that pizza."

Seth snorted. "It'll need to be seen, to be believed. We'll find out if I can pull it off. YouTube videos have assured me I can." Claiming a last lingering kiss, he broke off the contact with clear reluctance to jerk his head toward Garet. "Go on. I think I smell smoke."

Huffing, Quint returned to the exam table, his eyes dancing with laughter. "You're not going to frighten me out of leaving, sir. I'm sure, between you and River, Pike will be in one piece when I get back…" His brow furrowed slightly as he sniffed, like he wasn't sure whether or not Seth was joking. "But you should probably get up there."

Cerberus and 'steggy' in hand, Seth saluted with the plushie and pivoted on his heel to exit the clinic. "Everything is under control. I'm sure of it. Don't you worry…" The door closed on his, "Much!"

Garet snickered. "Not a lot has changed, except now you have two 'kids' to take care of." He eyed Quint's dark blond hair. "How are you not gray?"

"I use the bit of spare time I have to meditate." Quint winked at him, then laughed and shook his head. "Honestly? I love it. Even though I can't stand seeing Pike hurt, or anything upsetting him or Tay, they…give me something I've always needed. Someone who I can take care of. Who takes care of me in so many ways. I was craving something soft and tender, and I found it."

Nodding, Sin slid his arm around Garet's shoulders, pressing a kiss to his hair. Something in Quint's words had him more relaxed, as though concern for his brother remained, but every exchange with the men Tay loved lessened it a little more. "When you find someone who fulfills those kinds of needs, who you can give that to as well? It's worth...*everything*. It can be fucking rare, but this place?" His smile was in his voice as he looked around. "Being here, it's like you beat the odds. Because it draws in a lot of good. A bit twisted, a little rough around the edges, but...good."

They got through the rest of the exam, Garet having endured it enough times before that Quint's clinical touches, even in front of Sin, didn't embarrass him or make him in the least bit aroused. The first time in jail had been kind of a shock, but he'd long since learned to go somewhere outside of his body. Especially since the assault.

Pulling up his pants, he kept his eyes on his shoes while listening to the sounds of Quint moving about the clinic. When he looked up, he found Sin watching him and smiled. "Ready, sir?"

Sin nodded and held out his hand. "Ready." He glanced over at Quint, raising his voice a bit. "I'll let Curtis know you need an escort." He lifted his brow when Quint frowned at him. "We both heard your Dom. This isn't a medical thing, so no pulling doc rank on me. I might've been gone a while, but I haven't forgotten how things work around here. When subs try to outmaneuver the Doms, they always find themselves...very *very* sorry."

"Yes, sir." Quint grabbed his jacket, pulling it on. "I wouldn't presume to contradict you, I'm aware you are a well respected member of The Asylum." His lips curved as he pushed the back door open. "I appreciate you letting Curtis know he can meet me there. Have a good night, sir. And I'll see you later, Garet."

When the door closed, Sin shook his head and sighed. "I don't think the Core's been beating their subs often enough. I'll have to mention that. Maybe it'll keep them busy enough to stop analyzing everything *you're* doing."

Smirking, Garet circled Sin to hop up on his back and

wrapped his legs around his Dom's middle to wordlessly claim a piggyback ride. Chin on Sin's shoulder, he turned his head enough to whisper hotly in his ear. "Or, you know, beat me enough in front of them that they *think* you're keeping me in line...sir."

"You get Toppy. I'll definitely have to beat that out of you." Sin slapped Garet's thigh as he shouldered into the gym. He walked at an easy pace, heading for the bar. "I'll be keeping you in line my way. And enjoying every minute." Stopping by the stairwell, he gestured to Curtis. "Seth wanted you with Quint while his boy's at the clinic. I assume he was supposed to wait for you. Why don't you do our man a solid and let his sub know how *impressed* you are that he didn't."

Lips thinning, Curtis nodded, already hopping over the bar to land with a solid *thump* on the other side. He grabbed his parka, checking the pockets for his keys, and shouldered it on. "On it. I swear. You'd think Avery and Keiran landing in a lye pit and Rhodey getting shot would've had the man showing more sense." Walking fast, he nearly broke into a jog. "Tell Reed for me. He's in the loft."

"Will do." Sin continued into the stairwell, glancing over his shoulder at Garet. "I'm glad you're not a merc. I think I could handle pretty much anything else. They seem like a handful."

Garet's eyes went wide. "I didn't know you knew. About the stuff that goes on here." He glanced up at the dungeon door as Sin ascended the stairs. "Can I ask you something?"

"Always, but just so you're aware? There's a lot I *don't* know. I've heard things here and there. Enough to figure out the basics. But I don't expect you to break any confidences you have with your family. So long as it doesn't drag you into anything you're better off avoiding? I'm good." Sin stopped at the next level, his gaze going to the one loft door that had been propped open. "Do you want to ask before we go in? It sounds like Wren and Reed are both still in there."

Licking his lips, Garet nodded, his chin rocking against Sin's shoulders. "Yeah. For starters. It's a longer convo. But about the other thing, you should know that if you're gonna live here that Rhodey'll let you know everything you're gonna need to know in order to stay safe. It's not straightforward. We go everywhere in pairs. And you're gonna need some training."

Sin reached back, pulling Garet down to set him on his feet, facing him. He tilted his head slightly, as though thinking over his words. "I was in the Air Force, my boy. I've had plenty of training, but if Rhodey thinks I need more to do my part in protecting you and this place? I'll do it. That wasn't a question, though."

"No, sir." Garet shook his head, leaning back against the wall with his palms flat against it behind his ass. "I wanted to let you know that, but it's not my question." He breathed deep. "I was wondering something that I probably should ask later, but I'm afraid I'll chicken out."

One hand braced on the wall above Garet's head, Sin moved in close, his lips curving. "If it's whether or not I'll fuck you tonight, the answer is no. We're still on our first date." He brushed a kiss over Garet's lips. "But it would please me very much if you have trouble sleeping because you can't stop thinking about when I will. We've never actually slept very much when we've shared a bed, anyway."

Rapid breaths had Garet sipping air like a fine wine. He let the taste of Sin roll over his tongue like he tested his Dom's bouquet. Whimpering softly, he slid down a bit as his knees softened. "No, sir. I forgot we were on our first date, but that wasn't it. Do...I'm going to ask later though, okay?"

Kissing him again, Sin nodded, his smile in his voice. "Whenever you're ready to ask whatever's on your mind, I'll be here. Until then, I'm having fun finding different ways to make it difficult for you to stand. And breathe. I never knew having a sub would give me so many opportunities to play in all my favorite ways. You're a damn treat."

"Oh, god..." Hearing the praise and all of the twisted ways he pleasured his Dom had Garet voicing a prayer aloud that he'd be able to find the strength to remain on his feet instead of his knees. "I really really hope you say yes." Diving in, taking a chance, Garet lifted his gaze. "Okay. Here goes. Do you enjoy...all kinds of sadism? Like...dark stuff? And the chance to make me squirm for real? Because I never knew I might, and downstairs...I got curious." He covered his face with his hands, turning fuschia if his skin temperature was anything to go by. "It's okay if you don't. Forget I asked. It's too soon."

Sin blinked at him, leaning back a bit to meet his eyes. "I'm not going to forget you asked, so get that thought out of your head right now. Yes, I like a variety. And I'll fucking love making you squirm. These are the things we'll need to discuss before we go there, so it's definitely not 'too soon'. I might've set some first date rules, but I'm still a Dom. You're my sub. I need to know your limits before I accidentally trample all over them. And if I hit one—which is bound to happen at some point—I need to know you won't be afraid to stop everything and tell me so."

"I can definitely promise to use my safeword, sir." Garet peeked through his fingers. "So, it's okay to talk about what we both like or want to explore? I want to know what makes you happy, if that's all good with you. When you're ready to talk about it all. And it's a nice escape from other stuff. Thinking about pleasure."

Lips curving, Sin tugged Garet's hands down. "It really is. And we'll be doing more talking than anything else for a little while, so it's good to know you're comfortable with that. It makes me happy to get you hard, and blushing, and more than desperate to find some relief, but knowing you won't find any until I allow it." He patted Garet's thigh. "In case you get any ideas about jerking off in the shower. I'm old school like that. Your pleasure belongs to me."

Old school, in school, out of school, Garet never found himself so glad to be a fan of lifelong learning. And he had a feeling, with this man?

There'd be no shortage of lessons.

Class was very much in session, and he had every intention of getting all A's.

Chapter Twenty-Seven

PRESENT

A fucked up mixture of longing and contentment rolled down Garet's spine to pool in his tailbone. He shivered, unable to break his Dom's carmel-kissed gaze with those deep green shadows seeming to dance in the overhead lights. Finally, he got enough oxygen to his brain to remember Sin telling him his body and its pleasure were all his Dom's.

"Yes, sir. It belongs to you." Having Sin's warm bulk surrounding him with so much ink-covered muscle was like something straight out of Garet's best dreams. "I'll do my best to please you."

"It won't take much. I like you, Garet. Very much. I like having you close and being able to explore every fantasy we both have." Sin lifted his shoulders and cupped Garet's cheek. "Do what comes naturally. We'll have fun getting to know each other better. I'm pretty easygoing, until I'm not. And I think you'll secretly love it when I keep you guessing."

A slower nod dipped Garet's chin this time. "Yes, sir. I don't think it'll be a secret though."

Voices rose from the loft, Jamie's coming in a muffled whisper. "You're not supposed to be in here, Wren. I like him, but Noah's gonna freak and Jared's gonna freak harder. Then it'll be a freak fucking fest. Come *on*. It's clean enough."

"Jared said I could prepare the room, so I don't believe he'll 'freak'. He was uncomfortable with me handling the exam, which I understand. I don't have the experience Quint does...I'm not sure how I'll get it if I'm not allowed to observe, but I'm certain our Dom has a plan." Wren sounded distracted. "It will be perfect with a few less throws. Can you help Reed take out at least half of them?"

"It's chilly in here at night." Reed let out a heavy sigh. "Look, if you guys gotta go, it's cool. This time. But don't start running off every time he's existing in your space. We're not fucking doing that shit again. Not to him. That ish wasn't cool any of the other times and this time? He's not a fucking stranger. He's...he's a kid who got in a fucked up situation."

Head turned toward the loft door, Garet listened in, wondering if Matt had told Reed what he'd said. About what had happened. It was hard to believe his brother would've mentioned him at all after what had gone down in the clinic.

"Rhodey said we're not supposed to talk...and that seems really mean, but we're not supposed to upset anyone." By *anyone*, Garet figured Jamie meant Noah. "Why does this happen when anyone new...even if he's not new...comes in here?"

The sound of a vacuum cleaner echoed into the hall, along with Wren's raised voice. "I believe Rhodey expressed that we shouldn't speak to him until we have our Doms' permission. It may be a temporary arrangement for security purposes...actually, I believe I might be on speech restrictions. Please excuse me, I won't be able to continue this conversation... Reed, where did those come from? I have no idea where you store all those plushies...I'm going to be quiet now."

Reed laughed and the vacuum cut off. "You did that already, Poe. And he needs at least a few teddy bears to cuddle with when people are being dicks." He went quiet, then sighed. "You're...partially right. Security is why a lot of new people get the third degree and the whole...like walking through a minefield thing. This is different, though. It's... Everything about Garet right now could hit several triggers. For Noah, Curtis... I think they'll be okay when they get that it's *him*. The same little boy they knew, not a representation of...all the pain from their past."

Ducking under Sin's arm, Garet rounded the doorway to push it open and walked up to Reed to put his arms around his 'other brother's' waist. Face buried in Reed's chest, he breathed in the cotton candy sweetness of his clothes. "I love you. I'm sorry."

"I love you, too, kiddo." Reed hugged him tight, kissing the top of his head. "And stop apologizing...to me, anyway. Do what you've got to do when it comes to Matt and the rest. Including kicking them in the nuts if they overdo the whole, 'you fucked up and now you gotta pay.' Fuck that noise. I get people being a little pissy, but it's, like, over-the-top. And you ain't gotta deal with all that. I won't let you."

Nodding with his cheek against the glitter-rough fabric of Reed's colorful shirt, Garet tightened his hold and closed his eyes. He had to know. "Did Matt tell you?"

"Tell me what?" Reed leaned back, his arms still around Garet, and met his eyes. "I think he's at the café with Lawson. We haven't...talked a lot. Nothing he says will make me change my mind about you, if that's what you're worried about."

"Oh..." Wrinkling his nose, Garet shook his head. "Forget I said anything. I just...something you said made me think... Ugh." He blew out a breath. "I told him why all that ish went down with me and I just thought..."

Sin stepped to his side, motioning to Jamie and Wren. "You two should get going. I agree with Reed, I don't want you turning the other way when you see Garet, but let's not rock the boat just yet. It's been a long day. Thanks for getting the room set up." He bent down, speaking softly in Garet's ear. "If you want to tell Reed, I think now's a good time. Better he hear it from you than have it all twisted by someone else."

Looking around the well-lit, plushie and rainbow-hued, throw-strewn place the subs had somehow managed to decorate and make feel cozy in a very short amount of time, Garet gave Wren a soft smile. "Thanks for putting this together. I know you're on speech restrictions, but it's good to see you and I really appreciate everything you did tonight for me and Sin." He glanced at Reed. "And you, too, big bro."

In the middle of folding a small blanket into a neat square —as though making it into a kind of throw pillow would be a good compromise for the excessive number of them—Wren smiled back at him. He glanced toward the fireplace, his brow furrowing slightly, then looked at Reed and made a few distinct motions with his hand.

Reed nodded and patted his pockets. "I'll light the candles…soon as I find my lighter. And my phone." He blew out a breath and gave Garet a sheepish grin. "I'm glad you like it. Me and Jamie put some stuff in the closet for you—I snagged a few of Curtis' things for you, Sin. I don't think he'll mind. Just until you guys get a chance to bring all your own stuff."

Rubbing Garet's arms, Sin nodded. "I appreciate that, my boy. And I also appreciate that you haven't let how things were before impact you welcoming Garet back. I know you were angry with me—"

"Yeah…that's ancient history." Reed shrugged, lowering his gaze. "I can't blame either of you for Ez not being around. He's got his own ish to work through and…I need to accept that."

Garet cringed inwardly, remembering Matt's group text. His hand went automatically to his phone in his back pocket.

Before he could figure out what to say, Jamie tugged on Wren's sleeve, gesturing at the same time toward the kitchen situated —unlike the other lofts—more toward the back, while the bedroom was to the right side.

"We had a ton of extra chocolate and a lot of pistachios that Noah and Curtis got on sale for some reason... And whiskey from the bar. There's a lot of pasta, too. I've been practicing cooking with it, but everyone's kinda tired of it. Even Connor threatened to beat me with wet rotini if I tried to feed it to him again." The sub wrinkled his pert nose, raking his fingers through tufts of snowy white hair Wren probably loved for its color alone. "Keiran sent up leftovers in containers, too. Come on, Wren. Let's go up to the roof and see if it's snowing yet."

Excitement filled Wren's eyes and he nodded, lacing his fingers with Jamie's and giving Garet and Sin a little wave on his way out the door. He stopped by the doorway, bending down to straighten one of the multiple pairs of slippers lined up there, then let out a sound of protest when a small bundle of fur darted past him, disappearing under the sofa.

Reed chuckled and waved them on. "I'll get him, don't worry. You go enjoy the snow. I'll make sure our new housemates don't get a winged visitor in the middle of the night."

The only 'winged' sub Garet could think of was Avery, and he wasn't sure why the dude would come chasing after what hopefully had been a cat and not a ferret or a pet rat. Or maybe a guinea pig. Those were fluffy, weren't they?

"As long as L.D. doesn't come chasing after him, you should be good." Jamie settled a knit cap on Wren's head, pulling it and another out of his pockets. "Come on. We'll get our coats on the way up. That'll make our Doms happy."

Going to the door to close it after the subs, Sin looked at Reed, who was crawling beside the sofa, making kissy noises. Garet's Dom was clearly thinking along the same lines he was. "'Winged visitor'? I think I'm missing something."

"Stephan's raven. I don't know if you met him…Stephan, not the raven, but him, too. He claims visitation rights with Pike's kitten every once in a while." Reaching under the sofa, Reed drew out a calico kitten, about half the size of Jamie's cat, L.D. and apparently a lot more cuddly. When Reed cradled the kitten to his chest, a contented purr filled the room like he was holding a miniature motor boat. "Sin, Garet, meet Fresco. He takes after his owner, so don't be surprised if he gets into all kinds of trouble. Usually, it's harmless." He flipped a lighter between his fingers. "Other times…well, at least he doesn't have thumbs, because he found my lighter."

Making a delighted cooing sound that surprised even himself, Garet held out his arms. "Oh, hello, precious baby…" He smiled uncertainly at Reed. "Can I hold him?" Never having had a pet of his own—and definitely never having held L.D., the Demon from Cat Hell—Garet wasn't sure of the etiquette around bundles of floof. "Will he bite?"

Reed shook his head and gently slid the kitten, who on closer inspection was a little pudgy and gangly in an adorable way, into Garet's arms. "He doesn't really bite or scratch, unless it's by accident. I think Pike got him hooked on buttons, though, 'cause he'll chew on those. Or your hair."

There wasn't much about Garet's outfit Fresco could ruin, what with the long-sleeved T-shirt being a bit rumpled already and definitely buttonless. "Hair?" He took the kitten in his hands, surprised at the warm weight of him, and how he rumbled. "Oh!" Laughing, he tucked the animal to his chest in the way Reed had. "Oh, wow. He's so…alive and like a plushie, but better. I want one."

"I can give Tracey a call if you want? She's always trying to find homes for the kittens she rescues. And other animals, but Lawson put his foot down when someone jokingly asked about adopting a baby goat. My Dom can be mean." Reed lowered his head to let Fresco bat at his curls, the kitten catching one and bringing it to his mouth. "I bet she'd love to hear from you, though."

Paling at the thought of what Noah would do to him if he reached out to the Dom's mother, Garet shook his head, stroking under Fresco's soft chin with two fingers. "Maybe if things ever get...normal? And I don't want to piss people off, bringing other animals into the club. I'm gonna lie low, ya know?" He gave Reed an apologetic smile. "But I could use a favor if you don't mind? I could...is there still a free box with all the clothes and stuff people've left around here? I only got what I'm wearing, and I could use some socks." He held up one sneaker covered foot. "My shoes stink from wearing them without them."

"Dude, I told you..." Reed hooked his fingers to Garet's elbow, tugging him to the bedroom, which was just as colorful as the rest of the loft. He drew him to the large dresser, opening a few drawers, then let him go to cross over to the closet, swinging the door open with a broad grin. "Me and Jamie got you covered. There's even some cool clubbing stuff, mostly mine because Jamie's stuff would be too small." He rushed back to the drawers and snatched out a pair of bright green socks. "There's plenty of these. And boxers. You'll need pajamas for after you shower..." He yanked open another drawer, tossing a few items of clothing. "Not sure where Wren put them, but they're somewhere. If you're missing anything, let me know, but you shouldn't be. He made a whole list."

Lowering slowly to the edge of the bed, Garet stared at the abundance. "Reed. This is...too much. Thank you." Struggling to find words, he focused on the bundle in his arms as Fresco settled in and his purr became a shallower rumble, like he might be falling asleep. "I love all of it. It'll be fun to dress up again." He caught Sin's shadow blocking the light from the doorway and lifted his head. "It's a comfy bedroom. We're going to be cozy when you're not at your place, sir."

"Did you miss me telling everyone I'll be staying with

you?" Sin lifted a brow at him. "If you think you can get rid of me and claim the spot closest to the window for yourself, you're sadly mistaken, my boy. As for the kitten, I'll get you one. If you're good. Once things have settled here, I think your little fluff ball will be a welcome addition to the kitty brigade."

Garet's bounce woke Fresco, who yawned with a curl of pink tongue and stuck out one paw in a languid stretch. "Really, D— Sin?" Catching how his ears turned pink in the dresser mirror, he cleared his throat. "I heard you, but I figured you'd stay at your shop in bad weather or whenever you want to be home. You know...like if you have other guests or chores or..." *Oh my god, dude, shut up!* "I don't want to get rid of you."

Chuckling, Sin came over to sit on the bed beside him, mussing Fresco's fur in a way that had the kitten twisting to swing his paw, with his claws sheathed, at the Dom's hand. The move had him almost rolling out of Garet's arms, but Sin held the furry bundle in place with his other hand. "I stayed above the shop with Tay so we didn't have to travel to my mom's old house every day. It's a long drive, and when we had clients, or wanted to come here, it got to be a bit much. I haven't told Tay yet, so please don't mention it, but I'm going to sell the house. It'll help cover some of my mom's treatment, and since I didn't work for a while..." He blew out a breath. "Anyway, I'll be going to the shop when I have clients and to make sure it's not buried in snow. Other than that? I'm fine right here."

Never having had constant companionship, it was difficult to imagine. Someone to wake up to, to fuss over, and cook breakfast for. A person who could grump at him in the morning or be cajoled into wakefulness with a cup of coffee and a wake-up blowjob under the covers on a cold and snowy day.

Grinning like an idiot, Garet nodded. "Yes, sir. I won't tell him." He sobered. "I'm sorry I can't help much, but I'll make sure you have everything a boy like me can offer."

"That's more than enough, my boy." Sin curved his hand around the back of Garet's neck, drawing him in for a kiss. "Have your chat with Reed, then go jump in the shower. This will be the last one you'll be taking alone."

Garet drew in a sharp breath, a sex-soaked hum roaring to life in his veins. He didn't care if Sin wasn't going to let him shower alone because he didn't trust him not to jerk off. In fact, he almost hoped that was part of the reason why—it was damned hot.

His, "Yes, sir," came out as an unintended throaty promise.

"He doesn't have to chat with me right now. I'll be around." Reed held out his hands for Fresco, wincing when the kitten darted up one and perched on his shoulder. "See? Not on purpose. But...yeah. You're happy right now, so... hang on to that. You're allowed to be happy. The sad, stressful stuff isn't going anywhere, it just...doesn't own all your time."

Reaching out, Garet hooked his fingers to Reed's belt loops to keep him from leaving. "No. Please? I need to tell you."

Reed took a deep breath and nodded. "Okay. I'm listening and...whatever it is, don't forget that I love you. If you killed someone, I'll get the shovel. Prada and Gucci, remember?"

Laughing was tempting, but the moment called for a kind of brotherly solidarity. Nodding with a sageness feeling about twenty years ahead of his time, Garet repeated the words. "Prada and Gucci." He scooted back against the pillows, patting the bed for Reed to join him, and grabbed a porcupine plushie with soft felt quills to cuddle. "I love you, too, and there's no hole I wouldn't dig for you to bury your enemies."

"Glad we got that cleared up. Except...well, Avery and Keiran would probably tell us both we're doing it the wrong way—something about lye, but they're no longer *quite* so big fans of it." Reed shook his head and plunked down on the bed on his stomach, while Sin claimed Fresco and settled in his chosen spot, closer to the window. "Tell me. Whatever it is."

Garet let out a long breath and hugged the plushupine closer. He passed his tongue over his lips to wet them before he met Reed's gaze. "You remember that Saturday night when I called you all excited to go to the frat party with William?"

Reed's nod was a bit hesitant. "Yeah, I was happy for you, but Matt reminded you not to overdo it and focus on your studies. Lawson said to focus on making good connections. Curtis started telling us all a story about beer pong regrets."

"I'd forgotten that part." Snickering, Garet pulled up his knees with the plushie pressed to his stomach. "I didn't overdo it, and I was telling Will I needed to leave. He said he wanted one more round, and since we were walking I didn't think it was a big deal you know?" Those days and that night seemed like so long ago. So innocent, the world was full of possibilities he'd never feel like were within his grasp again. "So, I went to the bathroom while he got the beers, and when I came out some guy I didn't know handed me a drink he said was from Will. I didn't think about it at the time, but it was so obvious in hindsight." Throat tight, he put his cheek to his knees, curling around the plushie. "I shouldn't have drunk it."

Shifting into a seated position, Reed shook his head and reached out to grasp Garet's hands against his knees. "No, but…you couldn't have known…" He pulled in a slow breath between parted lips. "It was spiked, wasn't it? God, Garet, I'm…so fucking sorry. Is that how this all started? We shouldn't have let you and Ez leave. I thought you guys would have a whole experience, but… Do you know who it was? Did you tell Rhodey? If some asshole's out there spiking drinks to get people hooked that's…that's gotta end."

Misery wet Garet's lashes with his tears. He sniffed, sitting up a little. "No. I think Will set it up, but I could never prove it and by the time I saw him again I didn't care." Unable to meet Reed's gaze, he stared at the far wall with its rough, unglazed brick. "I woke up in I guess what you'd call a flophouse? I was..." He shrugged. "You know? They did things while I was out of it, that I only kinda remember. Bits and pieces. And I was desperate for a hit. Like they knew I would be, and they gave it to me. That was the beginning of the end." Everything went a little out of focus as he tried to remember details that had never been entirely clear. "I told Matt tonight. Rhodey was there. I don't think there's anything he can do, and Matt...he's still too hurt to think I'm not lying."

"Fucking hell." Reed yanked Garet into his arms. "You okay with this? I need to...just hold you. I'm sorry, so fucking sorry I wasn't there when you needed me. I wish I'd known. I wish..." He let out an angry sound. "*You* were hurt. You faced all this shit by yourself. I don't give two shits how anyone feels when you were...you were trying to survive something horrific. But you won't be doing it by yourself anymore. I swear it, kiddo. I've got you."

Arms around Reed, Garet soaked in the contact. All the hugs he'd missed and needed so much it was like a bottomless well that he'd fallen into and just kept falling and flailing—his arms reaching for anything and anyone in a silent desperate bid for stable ground—he soaked in during that moment.

"I think I came here that night knowing someone would figure it out." Voice muffled, he spoke into Reed's chest. "I wish I'd told Lawson, anyone, but it never occurred to me until I was clean. I could've asked for help and I didn't. I did all the wrong things. And I hurt everyone."

The way Reed's chin brushed back and forth against his hair made it clear he was shaking his head. "How were you supposed to think of all that when you were trying to escape everything that was done to you? Sure, I get it, looking back, maybe you're seeing all kinds of bad choices, but...they were because of what happened. No one can have the right answers after that. You could have...you could have done so much worse, Garet. So much worse and I wouldn't blame you. Not one bit."

Hearing Reed's words, wishing they had been Matt's and Lawson's, wrecked him. All the pain came spilling out. The fear and loneliness, wondering what would happen next after Rhodey dropped him off. How awful the abandonment had been, and how much he'd blamed himself for causing it. He *had* caused it, and owning that was a huge part of his recovery.

Still, he'd needed this so damned much. To be loved and not to feel like the world had dropped out from under his feet. Like it had the day his mom had died, and the day Matt had disappeared from their house and the gang had become the family he'd missed so much it was like having a hole blown open in the middle of his chest.

When he finally could breathe, he didn't know how long he'd been sobbing, trying to get out all his thoughts, while in Reed's arms. It might've been an hour—probably was. Hiccups fought him for air in his lungs, and he gasped with each one. Somewhere along the way, he'd begged Reed not to leave him, not to stop holding him. To forgive him. Worries about how maybe his mom had died because she'd known he was going to be a disappointment and wouldn't want to see how he'd turned out. All his deepest fears—things he hadn't said to anyone else, even his counselor—were just *out there*, making a mess of his brain, just like his snot had made a mess of Reed's sparkly shirt.

"Hey." Curtis' voice was a warm blanket, his hand joining Reed's on Garet's back. "We've got you, sweetheart. We're not going anywhere. Neither are you." Shifting the covers, he pulled them back, and lifted Garet to lie down with him. "Come snuggle, Reed. We'll make a Garet sandwich."

"Sin." Garet managed to mumble his Dom's name, already pulled toward sleep. He half rolled, attempting to sit up to go look for the man.

Not that he didn't want Reed and Curtis there, but the

face that swam in his half-awake mind was handsome and caring in all the edgiest and gruffest ways. He wanted to be surrounded by a sea of skin covered in tattoos, and beefy arms that were big enough for him to get lost in.

"I'm right here, my boy." Sin slid close, wrapping his arms around Garet and speaking softly to Curtis. "You can stay as long as you want, both of you. But what he needs…is going to be support outside of this loft. I'll stand against every one of them if I have to. It'd be better if I don't."

Positioning himself near Garet's thighs, Reed stroked his hand up and down his leg. "Either way, you won't be the only one."

Through eyes half shut, Garet saw Curtis lift his head to meet Sin's eyes. "It's going to get complicated, but Garet is like a son to me. You have my word he won't suffer."

"Good. That's what I hoped you'd say." Sin's voice took on a quiet, teasing note. "And I have a feeling it's not in the same way Tay calls his Doms 'Daddy', so I won't have to worry about the competition."

"No, and I think several people here would pass out if he started calling me that." Curtis kissed the top of Garet's head, turning him so he was nestled even more snugly against Sin, with his back up against Curtis. "Ezran… He had something similar happen to him at the hands of the gang. So let's keep this as quiet as we can. We don't want him to stumble into the information unprepared."

Garet groaned into Sin's chest. "Reed…can you turn on my phone? Check my texts?"

Giving him a confused look, Reed patted Garet's pockets, plucking his phone from the back one. "Still gotta find mine. And get you some PJs. Forget the shower, you can have one in the morning…" He tapped the screen and scowled. "Motherfucker. I'm going to kick his ass."

"Who?" Scrubbing his face, Curtis sat up, not even commenting on the swearing.

"Did Ez reply?" Garet's voice was as swollen as his head and eyes.

Reed shook his head, handing the phone to Curtis before he pushed off the bed. "It doesn't look like he saw it yet. I'll try to give him a call and head this off, but...he hasn't been in touch in a while. Either way, Matt had no fucking right."

One arm looped loosely around Reed's waist to hold him close by the side of the bed, Curtis scrolled through the text. "Fuck." He glanced up, holding the phone out to Sin. "If Lawson doesn't beat his ass black and blue, I will."

Shaking his head, Sin briefly scanned the screen, then pulled Garet even closer. "I don't think he will, from how things went down in the clinic. And I don't think he'll let you, either. He cracked Rhodey in the face when he said something in Russian to Noah...not sure what that was all about, but it's clear which side he's chosen."

Garet's, "But I don't want there to be sides," blurred with Curtis', "Oh, this is a monumental shitstorm." Curtis' bulk left the bed, making the mattress briefly dip and then rise with a creak. He leaned over to smooth a hand down Garet's back. "I'm going to be as calm as I can about this. It'd be better if people didn't know which side I was on, so I'm going to work behind the scenes to unruffle people's dicks."

"Feathers." Garet corrected.

"Nope. Dicks. They're jousting with them and all the pubes are tangled." Speaking from the doorway, Curtis motioned Reed with him. "Come on, sparkles. Let's go see if we can throw some vision obscuring fairy dust on the sitch and fix a few things."

Inhaling roughly, Reed knelt on the bed, bending over to hug Garet and kiss his cheek. "I guess we're handling this the non-violent way. For now. Either way, it'll be handled. And Ez..." His throat worked. "He's a hot mess, but he loves you. I don't think anyone, or anything, will ever change that." He looked over at Sin, his lips quirking as he hopped off the bed. "Enjoy untangling *that*, sir."

Sin rubbed his cheek against Garet's, letting him feel the scruff there. "I just might. I'm not an idiot, Reed. I know what I'm getting into. And whatever comes next? Garet and I will face it. Together."

And the comforting thing about that? It wasn't complicated in the least.

He and Sin just made sense. So no matter how snarled all the lines got around him, Garet wouldn't get caught in them or tripped up too often. But when he did, he could count on one thing.

He had someone there—several someones—to catch him when he fell.

Chapter Twenty-Eight

PRESENT

*L*oneliness. A feeling Ezran couldn't indulge in, but lingered at the back of his mind. Something he should've been cured of by now, but going home brought the weak emotion back.

No. Not home. Not anymore.

Snow melted in his hair and on his cheeks as he stepped into Otium, a place that was everything The Asylum wasn't. The living areas were all high end and classy—making it more like a hotel than a home—but the main part of the club contained a very specific design feature. Everything was easy to clean. Nothing ever stained. With smooth black and metal surfaces everywhere, anyone's presence could be erased with little effort.

Curtis would be proud of how good he'd gotten at cleaning. Or disturbed. Maybe a little of both. At least he could hold on to some of what the man had taught him.

The strobe lights in all different colors flashing over the hazy dance floor would be Reed's favorite part of this place. He'd get a kick out of all the different light effects, how they could make every movement seem faster or slower, blinding flashes of blue or hypnotic pulses of red. Usually, he avoided the area, because Otium had an unwritten policy whenever anyone walked into the dancing crowd.

Everyone was fair game.

Considering most of the patrons were either skilled mercs or hardened criminals, the freedom to touch didn't necessarily come without consequences. Bodies could be writhing in a languorous fuck a few paces to the left, while a bold motherfucker who'd grinded up against the wrong chick could be bleeding out to the right. Kinda like graduating to the next level at Maddox's mansion, only on crack.

A shudder walked down Ezran' spine as he gave a couple of gangbangers doing lines on a high top table wide berth. Those two would likely be in the furnace by morning, once someone got done torturing them for intel. Sloppy fuckers had probably come in with a shitload to sell, thinking they'd score big at a place with such 'lax policies'. Those policies were meant to draw in people like them so they could squeal then die. Not the job Ezran had been recruited for, so he did his best to ignore them.

Ezran couldn't avoid seeing Noah in his mind's eye, though. His expression whenever he'd talked about his student, Andrew, who'd died because of bastards just like them. Sucking in a sharp breath, Ezran tried to banish the sight of one of three men who'd become like fathers to him, standing in front of a grave, speaking softly, struggling to hold back tears. Telling him and Reed all about a young man with so much potential, a life taken too soon by poison used to make heartless fuckers rich and broken people desperate. Curtis had been groomed from a young age, so his involvement was different. He'd atoned for his sins a thousand times over.

The whole situation might've been messy as fuck, but far as Ezran was concerned? Curtis' family had killed Andrew. And left him to suffer the consequences.

These two weren't kids raised by the mob, or helpless

addicts, so Ezran couldn't spare an ounce of sympathy for them. They wouldn't be here if they weren't high level dealers with connections leading to valuable targets.

One of the reasons the mayor turned a blind eye to what Maddox let happen within these walls? The Master was cleaning up the streets, literally and figuratively, and the crime rate taking a nosedive would keep him in power for a very long time.

Moving closer to the edge of the dance floor, Ezran curled his lips at the stench of expensive perfume and cologne, avoiding the inquisitive gaze of a voluptuous woman in a mesh dress and the beckoning curve of her red claw-like nailed fingers. Some of the mercs liked to play with one another, and the results weeded out the weak, but Ezran wasn't in the mood for that now. He was hunting a very specific kind of prey.

A hand on his hip and a breath stirring his hair made every muscle tense. Even with all his training, he couldn't stand to be touched unless he was familiar with someone, and there were only two people in this place he could tolerate. This was good, though. Let the fucker get close. Watching the light fade from his eyes was the perfect cure for all the emotions Ezran couldn't seem to shut down.

Knife palmed, Ezran spun, aiming for the tall man's throat. Too slow. The return strike stopped him short and the room whipped sideways. Pain burst through his wrist, the blade hitting the floor as his back slammed into the closest wall. Baring his teeth, Ezran glared as the man gave him a lazy smile, his big hand fisted in Ezran's shirt.

Not a target, another fucking merc. One Ezran didn't know and way out of his fucking league, damn it. Twisting to break the man's grip, he let out a growl of frustration when the asshole jerked him forward and shoved him against the wall again even harder.

The pain didn't bother him, he'd been taught to use that.

To find the pleasure and peace in it he couldn't find anywhere else. But being trapped still messed with him. The Master would not be pleased if he found out, so Ezran couldn't react. Couldn't let the panic slithering over his skin like a hundred slimy leeches show.

"Let him go, Mitchel." Amusement hinted at Maddox's tone as he stepped up to the man's side, patting his arm. "This one is not for you to toy with."

"Yes, Master." Stepping back, Mitchel lost his combative attitude.

Wearing a skintight pair of black leathers and a silver mesh shirt that showed off spiked nipple piercings, Mitchel fit right in with the Otium's atmosphere. He looked like he'd clean off easy if hosed down, even his skull hugging close-shaved haircut leaving nothing to chance. There was something about his eyes though—a watchfulness that said his actions had been part of some kind of internal script that he'd very much written himself. He was no follower. He was a planner. A guy who did things by the book just so he could throw it out the window later when you least expected it.

Ezran ground his teeth, resisting the urge to cuss the guy out, or go on the attack. If the Master wanted either of them dead, he would've said so. Besides, if he ever ended up on a mission with the guy, trying to slit his throat first would probably leave some hard feelings.

He shoved his hands in his pockets, falling into step behind Maddox when his Master continued through the Club to the less frequented rooms in the back. This one had a nice, big comfy leather sofa, a few sleek armchairs, and what Ezran always thought of as tall, narrow fish tanks, a few feet apart in the center, stretching from floor to ceiling for optimal viewing pleasure. Inside, thick smoke caressed the bodies of the dancers, what Maddox liked to call 'Mes Homme Fatale', who would show off their moves for hours in here before going out and seducing any mark they set their sights on.

Their missions could last for months, sometimes even years, before they eliminated the target. They weren't as brutal as many of the other mercs, but just as deadly. Ezran had done some training with them, losing some of the bulky muscles he'd spent way too much time building and toning to a more natural, wiry form. He was tall enough to be intimidating when needed, but still well under six feet, which Maddox said gave him an advantage with stealth if he learned how to use it.

But he didn't have the patience to do what those guys did, and the only time he used sex as a weapon, he ended things before they got…too far. Besides, Maddox had other plans for him.

Plans he hadn't shared yet.

Hopefully, he would now.

"I need to get out of here." Ezran pressed his lips together when Maddox glanced over from where he was pouring himself a drink at the minibar in the back corner of the room. Making demands of the Master never led to anything good, so he had to choose his words carefully. Something he wasn't all that good at, but, fuck, he tried. After months of learning to adapt to this new life, to people who were unpredictable, even cruel for nothing but their own amusement, Ezran stopped expecting much of anything. He was just happy when he was given a goal to accomplish. Or the gift of oblivion when he pleased the men who he'd surrendered all control. "Please, Master. I'm useless here. If I could just go on a mission I'd—"

Maddox lifted a hand, cutting him off as he came around one of the armchairs, settling in with his drink. "You may entertain yourself in the club or you will go to your room. Those are your options."

A prickle of irritation crept up the back of Ezran's neck. He drew in a measured breath, fighting to keep his tone neutral. Respectful. But he'd always been shit at acting. And if he got a beating for slipping up?

Even better.

"Is there someone in the club you need me to—?"

"No."

"But—"

"Crispin." Maddox sighed, his gaze on the sensual display in the fish tanks, not bothering to check if his top lieutenant was around. One rarely went anywhere without the other. "Deal with this."

Fuck.

Nothing good ever came from drawing Crispin's attention. When Ezran had begun training, he'd actually managed to avoid it. He kept to himself and did what he was told. The rewards were an endless supply of targets, without the risk of jail time. His family wouldn't have to worry about him ruining his life.

Except...in some ways, he already had.

For once, however, the guy didn't heave a sigh or pull out some pins to stick under Ezran's nails. Instead, he approached with a calm expression, lifting his hand to run a fingertip lightly along a loose tendril of hair that had fallen over Ezran's forehead. "Come with me, my boy." His voice was almost tender. "Let me take care of you."

"Okay..." Ezran backed up a step, not sure what to make of this side of the man. Maybe it was a mindfuck before he took out the whip? That'd be fine. Or whatever other tool he wanted to use. So long as the sensations were all physical and he didn't have to think about...anything. "Thank you, sir."

"We'll head to the quiet room." Speaking to the Master as much as to Ezran, Crispin adjusted the fall of his suit jacket— an expensive Italian job with sleek lines and fabric an apprentice tailor would piss himself to take the shears to.

That curt, dismissive nod from the Master always set Ezran's teeth on edge, but he knew better than to let that show, too. Squaring his shoulders, he followed Crispin out, keeping close to the wall so none of the mercs or their special 'guests' got the idea he wanted to play. Unless he got the green light to do it with his machete, but so far?

Doesn't look like that'll happen tonight.

Everyone who was in the know didn't exactly look Crispin's way, but somehow there was never a press of bodies when the man walked past. His heeled boots snapped against the polished floor despite the music, then were muffled by thickly padded flooring in the quiet room. The man snapped his fingers at a couple who lounged in the middle of the eerily hushed space, and they scattered, bringing their toys with them.

Tired of the silence, even though he could deal with it for days on a mission, Ezran huffed and plunked down on the floor. "Do you need me to take off my shirt, sir? Do you have any orders or is the torture you being all quiet? Because, with all due respect, that ain't gonna cut it."

"Sit there." Crispin pointed to a chair that was two feet from the far wall and the only piece of furniture in the place. Wooden, high-backed, and scarred from rough play over the years, the thing wasn't purchased specially for the club, but rather part of the Master's private collection. "And no."

Scowling, Ezran shoved to his feet, crossing over to the chair, tempted to kick the damn thing over. Instead, he sat on it, but the frustration, the pure rage the Master spent so long teaching him how to cage, were slamming against the damn bars. "I've done *everything* he's asked of me. Why am I being punished? Why don't you let me do what I'm good at? Me being here is a waste of time."

"I couldn't agree more." Crispin sounded bored, as if he'd seen nothing new in Ezran's behavior and knew exactly how to deal with cranky recruits. Who reminded him more of children than mercs. He knelt before Ezran to buckle leather straps around his ankles that had been concealed in compartments in the chair legs. "Now." He stood, beginning the action of binding Ezran's wrists in a similar way. "Let us chat. Shall we?"

Ezran rolled his neck, inhaling as deep as he could without making it obvious. He searched for the calm he always found after a kill, or after a good beating, but having neither left it out of reach. If he didn't find some other kind of distraction, he'd imagine stepping through the doors of The Asylum again. Imagine his family, so close. How he was a stranger to them now.

And the emotions that would bring could not be allowed.

Jaw clenched, he met Crispin's eyes. "I have nothing to say."

"For once?" Amusement lit Crispin's gaze, a rare show of emotion. He took out a knife with an odd curve to it, as if it would fit nicely against a skull. Examining the blade, he stepped around the chair and stopped at Ezran's back. "Conversations don't always need to involve words. Why don't you let me do the 'talking'." Cool fingertips touched Ezran's cheek, then walked up his temple, before the flat of Crispin's hand soothed his hair back in an almost motherly gesture. Soft. Gentle. Rhythmic. So kind it took a moment to notice the dark hair beginning to fall around his shoulders like rain. "There we go. Such a good boy. Look how good you can be."

Ezran swallowed hard, shaking his head. He didn't know why *this*, of all things, got to him. Of everything he'd had to leave behind, had to surrender to become...worth *anything*, being able to look in the mirror and see even a ghost of the boy his family had loved was all he'd dared to hold on to. "Please...don't."

"Don't what, lovely boy? Don't make you into the man you crave to be?" More locks fell, thicker, making rustling noises. In the dead silence of the room, his own heartbeat and the pulse in his neck seemed loud, along with the rasp of the blade and the shushing sound his hair made as it fell. "We'll keep you this way from now on. When I've finished here, we'll get you comfortable and take care of the rest of the hair on your body. I like my boys bare..." Crispin leaned down, flicking his tongue over Ezran's ear. "Just like the little ones they behave like. So precious."

Growling, Ezran jerked to one side, twisting his wrist, his body, so he could look the man in the eye. "No. Back the fuck off, Crispin. The only men I let even *consider* getting that close to me are the ones I bleed out. You want to fuck with me by messing up my hair? Go for it. But if you touch me any other way, this night ends with one of us in the ground."

"I know." Heat trilled down Ezran's neck, a river of brandy scented breath both reminiscent of Jared...and not. "But I promise I'll give you the screams you crave before I slit your throat."

Another twist and Ezran freed his wrist, tipping himself and the chair as he ripped open the other restraint. Moving with the speed this very man had taught him, he tore open the ankle restraints. Went for the knife, but Crispin was faster than him. That he'd let him get this far was probably part of his fucked up games. "I won't let you touch me again. Not like that. Not while I'm still alive, so you might as well use the knife now. I'll make a hot fucking corpse."

Crispin rolled his eyes, nodding toward the door. "Go upstairs. We'll decide what to do with you. I've had enough. Loose cannon. You're worse than Leonov was. Either of them." He motioned with his thumb. "I wash my hands of you."

Backing up a step, Ezran stared at the man. "I'm not a loose cannon. I do my work. I'm damn good at it and you know it. Just give me another fucking job and you won't have to deal with me anymore."

"Whine whine, bitch, complain." Slipping away the knife, Crispin mimed a yapping dog with his fingers. "It's all about you in that family, isn't it? What *you* need. The jobs *you* deserve. How *you* should be given something." Making a disgusted sound at the back of his throat, he dropped his hand to his side. "Grow the *fuck up!*" A man who never yelled, sent spit flying with the enraged bellow, then grew very quiet. "It's not about you. Is it?"

Blinking at him, Ezran wiped away the wetness on his cheek with the side of his hand. "No. It never was. I was told I could do what I was doing and...stop those men. Others like them, before they could hurt anyone. That's why I'm here." He let out a bitter laugh. "*That* family? Is why I cared to even try to make something of *this*." He slammed his fist to the center of his chest. "What's left of me. But not in a way they'd understand. And I guess not in a way you do either."

"Again. About you. Why are you doing this? Why do you wish to bring those men to justice? Because you've been wronged? Hurt? Had a bad experience with the bad, bad men?" Crispin mimed crying, then barked a laugh. "You either set that aside and realize you're here to do a job that has nothing to do with rescuing what is unrescuable—namely, your past—or you and I are going to take a nice long walk to the basement and I'll make sure you never have to think about those dark things that bother you so much ever again."

Somehow, the callousness brought back some of the calm Ezran couldn't reach before. His lips quirked as he nodded slowly. "You want it to be that simple, don't you? Then you can brush me off as another failure. And I'm a lot of things, but not that. I don't give a fuck what those men do to me. If they're coming for me, they can't go after anyone else, ever again. I'm a weapon. That's all." He shrugged. "But since you don't care about using me or keeping me sharp, I guess we're both wasting our time. Let me know when *you* remember why we do this. Because it's supposed to be about saving people. Not being superior assholes who get high on the power they've gained from controlling more powerful men."

"You're no weapon. You're a mess." Righting the chair, Crispin sat in it, legs outstretched, hands steepled. "Your emotions are all over the place. It takes nothing at all to ricochet you from emotional to calm and back again in a moment. I've just proven that. You care more about your pubic hair than you do about saving someone else from the hell you experienced. I have zero trust that you won't shatter if someone manages to get you in the wrong hold. It would take you five minutes to undo five years of *our* work with the wrong decision. I'm not releasing you to another job until we do this scene again and I don't so much as smell a hint of sweat on your naked skin. Right now? Frankly?" He sniffed the air. "You reek."

Ezran really wanted to find something hard and heavy to throw at the man. There were days when he'd been able to emulate his complete detached bearing—which always drove the other recruits fucking nuts. He'd been grateful, back then, for someone to give him an example of how to behave. He hadn't trusted himself not to either freak the fuck out or turn on the wrong person.

No better way to end up in the furnace than to kill one of Maddox's favorite pets when he intended on them serving a higher purpose. Some recruits were disposable, but figuring out which ones was not a guessing game anyone wanted to play.

Pacing with his fingers laced behind his neck, he searched for any way to prove Crispin wrong. To show him he didn't need another round of training to do what he was already good at. "I'll never be like those guys in the fish tank. That's not what I'm here for. But if you want me to shave my fucking pubes, I'll do it."

"The first mistake you made, and continue to make, is to make it about yourself and not the work." Crispin's bald head shone in the dim overhead lights, the brightest object in the room. "You'll never be this, you aren't here for that. You'll do what we want you to if we give you a prize. No, my boy. Not until you learn to remove yourself from the equation." Sitting forward,

Crispin rested his elbows on his knees, wrists loose. "You sound like a mewling lion cub. But you're no king of the jungle yet."

Ezran stopped and let his hands drop to his sides, shaking his head. "I am trying to keep my tone respectful. If you'd like something else from me, please, tell me what that is, sir. I want to understand where I went wrong and all you're doing is complaining about the way I'm talking. Should I not say 'I'? Pick a damn word for me to use. We'll do a goddamn grammar lesson instead of, you know, focusing on the job I'm apparently good at, but not good enough."

"You're a beautiful killer, Ezran." Crispin unfolded from the chair, standing to tower over him. "But you do it to avenge yourself. To forget yourself. Not to be the instrument those we protect need you to be. When you become a knife, we'll wield you. Steel, with a lethal edge. Until then, you have as much of a chance of being a prop with a blunt retractable blade as you do completing enough missions successfully to be worth the risk and the investment. We will control you. And you need to control yourself. So we can."

Lifting his chin, Ezran met Crispin's eyes. "You didn't have an issue with my work until we came here. Is that the problem? Because I could have stayed at The Asylum. I could have tried to be the person they remember. It would've probably even felt good for a bit, until they saw the truth." He lifted his shoulders. "But I didn't. I stayed with the Master. I know where I belong and who I serve. I don't know how the hell else I'm supposed to prove that."

"Why didn't you? Since you are so fond of running off to half-destroyed buildings to eat nearly inedible candy with old friends?" Crispin opened a portion of a leather padded wall, revealing a wet bar and an assortment of bottles and garnishes. He plucked out an olive, considering it. "And if your next job is to eliminate your friend?" He met Ezran's gaze. "What then?"

Ezran spat out a laugh, folding his arms over his chest. "We don't kill the innocent. Another pop quiz? I left my old life behind. What exactly would it accomplish to even entertain the thought of killing someone under Rhodey's protection?"

Chewing the olive, Crispin swallowed as he poured gin into a cocktail shaker to begin making martinis. "Under Rhodey's protection? Living in a halfway house as a recovering addict and an on-probation drug dealer? That is amusing." He glanced over his shoulder. "No, my boy. He was banished from your family's nest for bringing that poison there. It was quite a thing. You should have seen Noah's reaction. Curtis? Now, he may have been gutted. We shall work on him once we have you sorted."

"You're lying." Ezran strode forward, knocking the drink out of Crispin's hand, the glass exploding against the wall. "Garet wouldn't do that. Leave my fucking family out of this. You have me, because I want to be here. I...this is the purpose you trained me for." His throat tightened as rage and confusion boiled to create the exact emotional mess Crispin had accused him of being. This was what happened when he went too long without anything to bring him back to center. He couldn't tamp it all down. When he was on his own, he could've gone out and hunted. Or at least found some underground fights to release some of the chaos in his mind. Instead, he was trying to negotiate, another thing he was shit at. And against Crispin? Yeah, he might as well be a toddler, throwing a fit, even if he did it in a whisper. "Please, sir...? I'm sorry. I'll work on...whatever you need me to. You're right. I'm not good enough. I can't...focus on what I should be."

Carrying on making another martini as if he weren't wearing half of the last one on his expensive gray suit, Crispin nodded slowly to himself. "I would never lie to you, my boy.

Test you, yes. But not with something like this." He glanced up at Ezran. "Would you care for a lager?"

"Yes, please, sir." Ezran braced his shoulders against the wall, dropping his head back to stare at the ceiling. "You would have beaten the fuck out of any recruit who acted the way I just did. Why won't you do it? I deserve it."

"In this life, we often get neither what we want nor what we deserve." Handing him the cold glass of lager with a perfect head of foam, Crispin turned with his glass in hand. "I never act out of anger or emotion. I do what the situation requires. Because I am entrusted with the care of my Master's finest weapons." He clinked his glass against Ezran's, then spoke over the rim. "You will be sent back to The Asylum when the time is right. You will also get close to your former friend. Encourage him to go back to his gang, back to the men he was working for before his incarceration. You will get every ounce of information he can obtain." He sipped. "Then eliminate him. *That* is when the Master will give you everything you could possibly want, need, or desire."

Sipping the lager, which was nice and cool, but had a rich flavor he couldn't stand, Ezran eyed Crispin over the glass. He managed an unsteady grip on calm again, the unbalanced undercurrent always rocking his foundation when he went too long between kills making his hold even weaker. But not so weak he'd turn on Garet to get a fix.

From how the conversation had been going so far, explaining all that wouldn't get him anywhere. And he didn't want to open up to Crispin, of all people, about his...*feelings*. Refusing the mission—not the kind he'd ever fucking signed up for—would only have someone else sent in his place.

Like Avery had been, only his family wouldn't be so lucky next time. Men with his skill didn't usually come out with any of their humanity left intact.

How long will it be before I lose the rest of mine?

A strange coolness spilled over him. Not exactly the control he needed to find, but close enough. "When?"

"Soon." That was the only answer he was likely to get, tonight, at least, given the chill that had re-entered Crispin's eyes. He raised his glass. "I shall look forward to your graduation."

Ezran lifted his own glass, then took a sip. "No you won't. If the Master let you, you'd be enjoying some time by the furnace, roasting marshmallows over my body. You've already decided I'm too pathetic, too unstable, to bother with."

"Have I? I appreciate you letting me know." Eating another olive, Crispin sucked the juice off the pad of his thumb. "Your uncle was like you. I got through to him eventually. No. I am fairly certain if I end up roasting marshmallows over your body it will be when we dispose of you after you are shot by one of the others for being a damned sentimental fool."

Licking a bit of the foam from the top of the glass, Ezran let the bubbles tickle his nose like he used to when he was little, the face he made getting Reed laughing every time. But he didn't make the face in front of Crispin. Just shrugged. "So far, all your good boys have missed every time they tried. I guess you trained me well, in all the wrong ways. You want to shut down my emotions, you know how to do it. Since you won't, you get to deal with this. Or kill me yourself. Whatever's easiest."

"We will see." Not taking the bait, Crispin nodded to someone behind Ezran. "Escort him to his rooms. He will stay there until the morning meeting with the Master." He gave Ezran a rueful look full of apology. "If you will excuse me, I must suffer for your transgressions now."

Ezran's brow furrowed. "No one else suffers for me. If I have to be punished, then do it. It's your job."

"Oh, sweet boy." Crispin's laugh was light. "Someone always suffers for us when we are unable to perform. Your failures are mine. Rhodey's were Jared's and, well...I believe in a way Noah's were Rhodey's. You have no one..." Both arms held out from his sides, the man shrugged lightly. "But me."

As much as Ezran hated the man on days like today, he loved him in a way that made no fucking sense. Like his brain wasn't sure where he belonged, but since he was a constant in Ezran's life, providing the only bit of certainty and security he had left, it put him in a weird spot. Not friend, or lover, or family, but warped shards of each. He shook his head and put his mug on top of the mini bar.

Closed the distance between them and wrapped his arms around Crispin. Not a hug, but...kinda. Also kinda trying to hold him right there because he needed him to stay. "I'll do whatever I have to so you don't have to pay for me being a fuck up. Please...I'm sorry. I'm so fucking sorry. We can start over. You can cut my hair or...or whatever you want to. I'll keep my mouth shut."

Setting his glass down on the wet bar's obsidian ledge, Crispin lightly ran his fingers through Ezran's hair. No coolness touched his scalp, meaning the man must've left him with a bit of a ragged cut. Knowing him? Something more punk than Ezran had before, just to fuck with him. "Do you know how many acid scars I have on my skin from all of the curses you've uttered? I feel the scars pulling even now. Think of that. Think of me, suffering for you, and that will make me happy. It will make the Master happy. And then, perhaps, I won't be required to suffer any more."

"But I...I didn't mean to. There has to be a way. *Please*, sir." Ezran released his desperate grasp, afraid he might be hurting the man. "I'll learn not to...say the wrong thing. Do the wrong thing. It always...it always happens when it's been this long. The Master said he understood. He made sure I wouldn't get like this. And now...now I don't know how to..." He made a frustrated sound, his pulse thrumming in his ears at the reminder of how much simpler things could've been. "I'll learn, though. I swear."

"Yes, my darling boy. I know you will." Leaving the room with one of the guards, Crispin laced his hands behind his head, walking with elbows out like a prisoner.

Snarling as something in his mind snapped, Ezran grabbed one of the bottles from the wet bar, smashing it in two. He had other weapons on him, but this? This would be more satisfying. He locked his focus on the guard, the world becoming a blur. Then sharpening when he managed to draw that first drop of blood.

More. A little more and his mind would be his own again. He could shut out anything that didn't belong in this place. Anything the Master wanted to remove from him. Every bit of weakness.

The woman he fought danced out of the way, her short blond hair flecked with blood. "It's only your bedroom. Christ, Leonov."

"I'm not going to my bedroom." Ezran wet his bottom lip with his tongue, tasting copper, still a bit warm. "We're going downstairs. Master wasn't happy with the collateral damage from your last mission. This will please him."

"What?" The question gusted from the merc trainee's lips. She glanced over her shoulder, but her companion had left with Crispin, taking him to wherever the Master had decided. "I haven't left the club in three weeks."

No, that can't be right. Ezran shook his head, his grip tightening on the bottle. Someone had pissed the Master off. He was saving them for Ezran. It had to be her. He wouldn't put someone who wasn't guilty in his reach.

But what if this was another test? There were so many of them. Different ways the Master and Crispin expected him to prove himself. To show he could be lethal, but not to just anyone. He let the bottle slip from his hand.

"I'm sorry." Back to the wall, Ezran slid down, pressing his hands to the side of his head. "I just...need a minute. I don't...know what I'm doing. I had a purpose and now I have...nothing."

Snow and mud covered boots appeared inside the frame of his folded arms, their owner crouching in front of him. The scent of cigars and brandy brushed his senses as he was lifted into strong arms. Black leather gloves caressed his face before chilled lips kissed his forehead.

A familiar voice, reminding him of a more innocent time, cut through the haze. "It's time to come home, my boy. First, we will make it better."

This had to be some kind of fucked up dream, which Ezran usually didn't have. He always craved the clarity found right before he took down his prey. There was no past. No present. Only the moment. He didn't have any excuses for what he did, Master said he didn't need them. Because the prey deserved to die.

But part of him knew damn well no one else would understand. Not his family.

Which is why...

"I can't go home. Ever. Because I can't stop. They'll want me to stop and I can't."

"Let them worry about that, my boy." The voice was a cool rasp. "You are nothing we haven't seen before. We take care of our own."

Despite himself, Ezran relaxed a bit in the hold. If only this dream remained of all he'd lost, all he'd never have again, he'd cling to it for as long as he could. Reality would return, bringing him right back where he'd started.

Alone. With only two men who held control over the depraved thing he'd become. They were tired of him. He had no more value.

But the cold called to him. In the voice of one who'd never have left him feeling so useless...

And it has other plans.

Chapter Twenty-Nine

PRESENT

Outside of Sin and Garet's loft, Curtis waited for Reed, motioning him toward the one place he could think of that wasn't bugged. The broom cupboard. No cameras necessary to keep an eye on Mr. Clean. Inside was warm, dark, and smelled like old shoes. Which it really shouldn't, considering.

"Close the door." Keeping his voice low, Curtis crowded back against the shelves, trying not to knock over the only thing in the space that qualified as a broom—the upright vacuum cleaner Wren treated as a kind of second pet. "We need to talk."

Reed sidled past the door, easing it shut behind him, his curls falling over one eye as he spun around and laced his fingers behind his neck. "This is... I'm sorry, Daddy-o, but I'm going to claim my free passes for the next fucking year. I can't believe Matt did that. I could've been cool with a lot of things. Him being a grumpy asshole. I was *just* gonna do the grownup thing and have a chat with him about what went down with him and Pike and now *this*? I'm not sure I can even talk to him without giving him a couple black eyes."

"Wait. Something happened with Matt and Pike?"

Palming the back of his own neck, Curtis massaged tight muscles as a headache began to throb behind his eyes. Could this day possibly get any more fucked?

Eyes widening, Reed stopped the rapid pacing he'd been doing in the small space in front of the door. "Pike lost a tooth…I don't think anyone besides that little brat could pull it off as a fashion statement, but… Anyway, getting off track. Matt said something to Tay, kinda dickish, you know? And Pike responded by dumping popcorn over his head. Then fell on his face trying to get away. And Matt started wailing on his ass. I knocked him off and we got into it and Matt ended up punching Jamie."

By the time Reed finished, Curtis pretty much figured his eyebrows were hiding in his hairline. Permanently. "Does Lawson know? Why didn't someone tell me? Or him?" He let his hand fall to his side, looking past Reed and wondering why they weren't already halfway to Stephan and Drew's place. "What the actual?"

"Noah talked Matt down, from what I heard. He handled everything, but between the blackout and the generator catching fire and everything since…I don't know. I figured Pike would've told you, but…yeah. To your family, that whole thing probably doesn't seem that serious." Reed lowered his hands to his sides and shrugged. "I thought Matt was cool with everything with us, but…he wasn't. So it's my fault all that ish went down."

Head merry-go-rounding faster than one of Reed's fidget spinners, Curtis gave Reed his best, most patient, 'Please explain' look. "Cool with every *what* thing with us? The popcorn incident had something to do with…me and you? Or someone else? There are a lot of us-es in this place."

Stuffing his hands in his pockets, Reed shrugged again, staring down at his sneakers. "He snapped at Tay because he's mad at me. Probably because he feels like I'm trying to steal Lawson and… I didn't know it would bother him. Lawson being my primary. I should've figured it out, but I thought... he seemed..." He let out a frustrated sound. "I don't even know. I hate when shit gets messy. And it's like I stepped in shit and left it everywhere without realizing it."

"Hm..." Deciding there was probably enough room to sit as long as his ass didn't hit the robot vacuum and turn it on, Curtis gingerly slid down with his back against the wall and motioned for Reed to join him. "You didn't. Matt's feelings are his, and Law's been your primary in everything but name pretty much ever since I got back from my trip across Canada and the middle states. As much as it kills me to admit it, I've been a crap Dom for you. I'm sorry, my boy. I love you, and I failed you about as hard as anyone could fail another person. I feel like shit about it, but it's not your shit. Otherwise I'd look like unicorn poo and not the brown turd emoji."

Reed plunked down on the floor facing him, twisting his legs into one of his favorite pretzel positions, so one knee was bent in front of him, with the other angled underneath. He crossed his forearms over his knee and rested his chin on them.

"I didn't mind us all figuring out the dynamics, letting them shift a bit for what...works for all of us. I love you and I want you to be happy, too. I was less scared when I saw how you and Noah figured things out. How Lawson was dealing with that. I felt like...I was the only piece out of place and it was an easy fix." Reed shook his head and sighed. "Only it wasn't. I want...I want you to be able to switch whenever you need to, without worrying about me. Or anyone else. It's not fair when you can't. Unless someone's dying, it shouldn't be a thing. You gotta go all merc Dom when there's lives at stake? Totally cool, too."

Surrounding Reed with his feet, Curtis squeezed to give his boy a leg hug. "I don't know that I ever explained this, but I'm going to give it a go. Bear with me if I need a few tries, and ask all the questions you want, 'kay?" He waited for

Reed's nod, then continued. "I don't have a 'sub' side. I have a need to submit to two people. Because I feel safe when we have that dynamic. It's what works in my relationship with Lawson and Noah. Sometimes, I need that safety more than others. I never exactly lose my Dom side. It's there, along with the need to take care of my boys, and pretty much everyone else here who taps into that side of me, like even my cousin—except he doesn't turn me on and it's not sexual. Thank fuck." He snorted. "We had an uncle like that. My family dealt with him in the usual O'Rourke style. Not a big loss and the only thing they ever did right in my mind. But does any of that make sense?"

"Yeah, but, like...you go in pretty deep with Lawson, with Noah. And...I love seeing it. I know how it feels and I want you to have that. I also...when something yanks you out of that space, I can see how uncomfortable it is. I don't ever want to be the one to do that to you." Reed trailed his fingers under the hem of Curti's jeans, toying with the elastic band of his sock. "I was all like, 'Lawson's collar is the perfect solution,' and just went for it. I should've...it was a mistake. I didn't consider how much it would hurt you. Or piss Matt off. I'm sorry."

"I'm not sorry. I'm proud of you." Curtis let out a long breath. "Look. Do I wish I could have made you feel safe and cared for, and like you didn't need to care for me instead in that way? Sure. Do I wish I could be your number one? Yeah. But I'm not, and it's going to be okay. I'm getting there, and eventually I'll stop kicking myself. That's not your fault though. You get that, right? You need to take care of my boy, and I'm glad you learned that lesson. The rest is just adjusting. For all of us. Lawson has enough love to go around, and if Matt would pull his head out of his ass for one minute, he'd see that he's the only one who can fuck up what we've all got, for himself."

Reed snapped Curtis' sock against his ankle and gave him

a sideways look. "Sir, I'm gonna tell you again how much I love you. So I can tell you that you drive me crazy, but I kinda love that, too. We take care of each other. Hell, maybe it sounds cocky as fuck, but I think we do it better than a lot of people. We try, anyway. And sometimes we get it wrong, but… then we can sit here, like this, and sort out the rough spots. You *are* my number one, in…well, every way people like us have any numbers stamped on anyone, because we've got these oversized hearts and room for more than just one. You've been my best friend since as long as I can remember. You were my hero when I was a kid and you still are. Only…a more *real* hero. One who fucks up and reminds me I can and it's not the end of the world. All the ish I can face that I couldn't before? Is because of you."

A lump formed and dissolved in Curtis' throat. "That's pretty special." He held out his arms to beckon Reed into them. "I really worried I fucked us over."

"Naw. I thought I made that clear when I didn't pull a *Runaway Bride*. Was kinda tempting, because I thought I had to walk down the aisle, like, ASAP or you'd think I didn't love you anymore and it got me all panicky. That would've been awkward as fuck." Reed unfolded his knees and leaned in, wrapping his arms around Curtis' shoulders and meeting his eyes. "I want to spend the rest of my life with you, in every way we can come up with. But I don't want a collar, or a ring, to be the…deciding factor. I want us. In all the twisted, screwy ways we just work. I don't want to try to fit in anyone else's box. I want…I need us to be like those Christmas presents under the tree, that you can't figure out what it is and it's wrapped all funky, but you know it's gonna be special."

Lifting his chin, Curtis nuzzled Reed's lips with his own, bumping their noses just to feel the warm puffs of their mingling breaths. He spoke against Reed's mouth, with the barest hint of laughter. "If Pike wraps up pizza for us all again this year, it'll definitely be funky." Tongue darting, he licked the seam of Reed's lips, then leaned back. "I'm not sure whether or not you just broke off our engagement or one-upped Lawson and Matt by marrying me in an uber private ceremony, but I'm on board either way. You're mine and I'm yours." He kicked the vacuum hose away with his toe. "No broom jumping required."

Reed wrinkled his nose and rested his forearms on Curtis' knees. "I don't know. Is that weird? Being engaged feels like we're making it clear we're not just boyfriends, but we don't gotta go through all the paperwork that makes it feel... It's like, the contract between a Dom and sub I get. It's to keep things safe and consensual and all that. But marriage? I guess..." He looked down into the small space between them. "My dad only bothered with me after my mom died because he felt obligated. Until he found someone else and moved on. I guess it feels like that kind of contract is some kind of obligation and it only means so much. It can't stop the bad stuff. It can't make anyone stay, but there's this idea it can. And...I hate that. I want to know we're good without adding a step that's...not always all it's cracked up to be."

Listening to Reed as close as he could, Curtis tried to put himself in his boy's shoes. The leather was a little tight, a couple sizes too small, and definitely not his color, but it didn't make the shoes any less wonderful.

"I hear you, and I don't feel the same way, but I understand why you do. So, I'm not hurt and I'm on board. Whatever you need and what works is what matters." Curtis gathered Reed's hands between his own, brushing his thumb over Reed's knuckles. "For me, in my family, marriage was nothing special. A contract of another kind. A way to show loyalty and ownership. But...I always wanted something more. Those words and vows to mean something. Like a magic spell that would make the air sparkle as much as you do when you smile." Lips quirking, he shrugged. "I'm not saying it right, but I guess there's a mega romantic in me and I wanted to have that with you. It's not what's important though, and I can get on board with your vision because making you happy is all I really want."

"One day, I think...I could get with the magic spell. I just...are we on the same page with a long engagement? And when we're both in the right place, and it feels good and easy, we can do the whole ceremony?" Reed ducked his head. "I did get pretty excited talking to Jacks about the different outfits. And wondering what we could do for the honeymoon. Something a bit wild and fun and just...*us*. But I need to know it's not a fix, you know? We don't need to be fixed, or have all this as some kind of...I'm not sure how to explain it except, I keep picturing the colorful bandages Pike's turned into a painful fashion statement. I want to know when I walk down the aisle, it's because we're doing this thing. And the people we love are happy. We're happy. And it's...another step for us together."

Nodding, Curtis held Reed's gaze. "We'd better stop adding people to this place, because every time we do, my chances of making everyone happy at the same time and carrying you over the threshold to our pirate themed honeymoon suite gets lower and lower. Can we maybe pick five or six people who need to be, maybe, I don't know, ecstatically happy first?"

"Okay, I could go for that." Reed's lips slanted as he leaned in and rubbed his slightly cold nose against Curtis'. "I'll even let one of them be your cousin. He's ecstatically happy whenever there's cake, so it's an easy homerun."

"Why are you so cold?" Leaning in, Curtis licked the tip of Reed's nose to warm it up. "Do you and I count? Or are we extra? Besides in the obvious meaning of the word?"

Snickering, Reed nodded. "We're extra. Because we both do that thing where we get all up in our heads, trying to make things cool for the people we love. We couldn't enjoy anything if we couldn't get most of 'em to a good place." He brought a hand up to rub his nose. "Wren said having surgery could've messed with my immune system. Or something. I don't feel sick, but maybe I'm not as good at staying warm anymore. I don't know, my body is just gonna keep kicking my ass for letting anyone near it with a scalpel."

"It's just an excuse to keep you warm." Curtis suggestively waggled his eyebrows, then leaned back so Reed would know it wasn't an actual come-on. "So, if we're gonna get everyone around here in a happy place sometime before we start collecting Social Security, maybe we should come up with a plan to help Matt feel more secure? And Noah less...I don't know...Noah?"

Lips twisting with irritation, Reed scooted in and rested his head against Curtis' chest. "I don't know what to do with the situation with Matt, yet. If I wasn't pissed at how Jared and Noah are handling things, I might've stayed at their place, but...asked you to come with. I can't even wrap my head around what to do about them. Maybe we should go talk to Keiran and start serving a whole bunch of tea. It'll buy us some time, anyway."

Cheek pressed against Reed's soft curls, one arm wrapped around his boy's shoulders, Curtis took a moment to drink in his closeness. Eyes closed, he allowed himself a moment of sheer contentment and happiness that he hadn't felt so completely in a very long time. In the dimly lit closet it was easy to believe only they existed.

"Mhm..." Not moving, Curtis spoke with his eyes closed. "No tea. We might get caught and then we'd have all that to deal with. But...I think we start with getting Lawson to see he might be being unreasonable about Garet and about how Matt needs to see what he has before he crushes it. With us, I mean. And Law." Cracking a yawn, he forced himself to lift his head. "That made no sense. I think we should make sure Lawson knows what Matt did to Pike."

Reed peered up at him, head tipped back against his arm.

"Do we...get to be mad about this? Because I am. If I wasn't worried someone would find an excuse to throw Garet out on his ass, I would've gone a few rounds with a punching bag. And only because if I busted up my knuckles again, Seth might bring Jared in and...I can't pretend I'm not pissed at him. Or at Lawson. Or Noah. And the longer the list gets, the more I start questioning if I fucked up somehow, but then I look at Garet and it's like, fuck that. He doesn't deserve this. Not after everything he's been through. He deserves another chance. He's earned it."

Curtis didn't disagree with his boy, but he needed to hear Reed's reasons for having room for that grace for Garet. "How come? How'd he earn it? Not by being a victim. Just to be clear, I agree with you but I want to make sure you're not confusing work with wounds."

"I'm not. I felt that way before I knew...everything." Reed sat up and hugged his knees to his chest. "Walking through those doors, wanting to be here, even when it would be easier to stay gone? He could've written us off. Done the work he needed to do for himself and started a new life. He didn't. He's sorry for the hurt he caused, even though it happened because of something he didn't ask for. That has to count for something."

"It does count for something. It counts for a lot." Licking dry lips, Curtis broke Reed's blue eyed stare to gaze at the far wall. "Try to think of it from Matt's perspective for a minute. Just to help balance things out. When he got here, Garet was a part of the gang, he'd had a lot of chances and messed up every single one. He gets in a stable place with Matt working his ass off to send him to school, then, from Matt's perspective, throws all that hard work down the toilet to go back to them. That's a lot of past shit to kick up. To process. From a time when Matt had no one, not any of us or a family."

Tipping his head back, Reed stared at the ceiling. "So I don't get to be pissed at Matt? Because, like, I get it. And if he'd just…I don't know, stormed off and thrown some shit, or punched something and refused to look at Garet for a bit, I would totally understand. I'd talk to him and let him rant and rage and get it out. But the cruelty…that's what I can't deal with. I'm not saying I love him any less. But I don't like him very much right now."

Curtis began shaking his head before Reed finished speaking, but heard him out. "No. You get to be pissed. Just like Matt gets to be pissed at Garet. Feelings are feelings, and you never shove those in a box." Taking down a roll of paper towels, he tore off a strip and began shaping it into an origami heart. "Everything you said to me just now you should absolutely say to Matt. Without yelling and with all the love you can muster, because maybe he'll hear it. But punching things and destroying your own fists is like Matt hurting Garet and Ez. That's not okay. You're lashing out and that doesn't fix stuff. Believe me. I have broken enough bar stock to understand. The fractures only get bigger, and sometimes you end up being the one walking barefoot over broken glass."

"I don't feel like it's the same." Reed rubbed his hands up and down his thighs, his gaze a little distant as he stared at the side wall. "Yes, I know hurting myself is bad. In any way. I try not to, but in the end? I'm not making everyone else feel my pain. This is like…like punching someone who didn't know they were in the ring. And catching them off guard. Neither Garet or Ez agreed to be punching bags. So…Matt's got some work to do. And he needs love and support, totally. I can't give it to him. Not right now. If I've gotta not put how I feel in a box? I can't pretend any of this was okay. Not with Pike. Not with Jamie. And not with Garet."

Holding the heart between his thumb and forefinger, Curtis handed it to Reed. "You shouldn't pretend it was okay. Say everything you said to me, but say it like you said it to me so it becomes about his actions, not about your actions. And you know very well that when you hurt yourself you hurt all the people who love you. It's like a splash effect. You might not mean it, but it's catching all of us off guard, and making us have to deal with your emotions and our hurt in a way that makes everyone feel scared and awful. Talking like this? Or asking for a round in the dungeon to safely work out some feels? Sure. The ring too. I'm down. Destroying the man I love or hurting him in any way is not okay."

"Can we?" Reed lifted his head to meet Curtis' eyes, his own sheened with tears. "Because I want to. I need to…do something to get this feeling out of my chest, because it's tearing me up. And I'm sorry it hurts you when I hurt me, but sometimes it's all that keeps me from shattering into little pieces. I'm not ready to find the right way to talk to him. I don't even want to yell at him. I need to stay away from him until I can say something that won't finish the tears in our family that started with…all of this. I need to get in the ring. Then I need to…can we crash somewhere? Maybe we can both squeeze onto Danny's dog bed in the galley?"

Just the vision of Keiran coming down in the morning to find them there had Curtis snorting. "No, but I know of a loft in a snazzy cathedral we could hang out in for a bit. We can tell everyone we're practicing for our honeymoon and don't want to make them jealous."

Already shaking his head, Reed grabbed Curtis' hand, scrambling to his feet and letting out a choked laugh. "I'm not leaving The Asylum. And I'm gonna be here when Garet wakes up so he's not tiptoeing around, wondering what shit's gonna be thrown at him next. We can always have a few cups of coffee and not sleep at all."

"Because that always goes so well." Curtis kept his tone light, phone out. "Law's going to notice something's wrong if we don't go back to the loft. Then there will be questions you're not ready for. Want me to talk with him, then meet you in the ring? We can ask Sin if we can crash on the fold-out couch in his loft."

Reed shook his head again. "He's gonna think we don't trust him with Garet and they're in the lovey dovey stage. Let them enjoy their time together. Yes to you talking to Lawson, though. We can...Seth has a spare room. Can we ask him about staying there?"

"Shacks has a spare room, too. So I guess it's a matter of whether you want to wake up to the sound of barking or bawling." Curtis pushed open the closet door with one hand, hoping there wouldn't be someone in the hall to see. "I'm good with either. As long as Pike doesn't set his hair on fire again, it shouldn't smell as bad as it did the last time I was there."

Amusement lit Reed's eyes as he walked backwards in front of Curtis, bouncing down the steps in a way that would've given half the Core heart attacks if they didn't know how agile he was when he was in good form. "Wren felt horrible for telling him what a good weapon hairspray and a lighter can be. He didn't think to mention it wasn't a good idea to try when you've just *used* the hairspray. Or for Pike to try it at all. He was focused on all the other things that make good weapons. Thankfully, Pike was distracted by then. By the way, Keiran wanted me to ask you to put locks on all the cabinets in the galley so no one tries to see what else is flammable."

Paused on the landing near their own loft, Curtis tried to process all the ways that scenario could've gone worse and decided, after stumbling over several, he really didn't need to give himself any more PTSD than his family and The Asylum had already instilled. "I learn the most fascinating things talking to you. Remind me to put you on speech restrictions more often." He winked, motioning toward the bar. "I'll see what Shacks are up to. Waking up to a dog licking my face is suddenly very appealing. Go change and I'll be down." One finger held up, he shook it. "Don't hurt my boy. Or I'll be spanking that cute butt."

"I won't, sir. I'll be getting ready for you to do it for me." Reed grinned and held out his arms. "You are gonna bring it, right? Not sure, but you were pretty rusty the last time we got in there. I'll give you plenty of time to warm up. I know you need it."

Curtis mock narrowed his gaze with his growl. "Now that I know you can take it, you'll be getting the full treatment. Don't think I won't take you down."

Blowing him a kiss and wiggling his fingers, Reed practically skipped down the rest of the steps. "We'll see. But either way? Looking forward to it, Daddy-o."

Curtis pretended to catch the kiss and eat it. "See you there, sparkles."

At the loft door, he took a deep breath, unsure what he'd encounter inside or—despite what he'd said to Reed—how he'd handle the situation. Pausing, he looked to his right, toward the stairway, and made a snap decision to change course. There was more than one set of nerves to settle around here, and taking the temperature of the man at the top, so to speak, wouldn't be a bad idea. Taking the steps two at a time, he rounded the banisters with a wide arc, tromping up to the roof and bursting outside in a way that would mean Noah had to hear him coming from several flights down.

"How's the weather, sir?" The cold-enough-to-freeze-balls temperature already seeped into Curtis' skin through the sleeves of his Henley, but he pretended otherwise, face lifted like it was a sunny day. "I swear. It gets any warmer there'll be palmtrees up here to go with the monkeys in Seth's loft."

Noah lifted a brow at him, then returned his gaze to the street below. "Enough snow and ice to be a good obstacle. Not many have the training to maneuver in it well. I've always been fine in most weather, but I didn't understand what cold really was until my uncle took me to Russia."

Plunking his jean-clad ass down on the low wall surrounding the rooftop nearest Noah, Curtis nodded. "I heard you need special parkas." He looked the man over, wishing like hell there was something he could do to settle his mind. "How long were you there?"

"Eight months." Noah's brow furrowed slightly before he shook his head. "Maybe. Apparently this fucked-up head of mine decided it didn't need to retain basic things like memories. Until it was convenient. Or *in*convenient, depending on where you stand. I can't remember the first time I made love to Jared. But I remember standing by that grave…" His jaw ticked. "Which is cruel to bring up, but I can't stop seeing it. Whenever I look at that boy. More bodies in the ground, despite everything you, Lawson, and Matt did to keep him off that path. Advantages you never had."

Risking showing his hand, Curtis took a deep breath and used it to speak. "I never was date raped and dosed with heroin. Who knows what I would've done. Rhodey pulled him out, though. The kid wanted to be saved. Your uncle has guided us all, along with you, so far. Maybe we see if he's right about Garet, too?"

Eyes narrowing, Noah braced his foot on the ledge by Curtis' hip and held his gaze. "You were conditioned your entire life for one purpose. Don't fucking dismiss that like it will soften me toward the boy. It won't. You were abused, you were twisted up, and did everything you could to survive. And you are a damn good man. Whatever stories you've been told, don't repeat them to me. You believe what you need to, I know you love him. But he brought that poison *here*. Into our home." He let out a bitter laugh. "I wonder if you'd be so forgiving if Pike had decided to 'party' with him, instead of blocking the toilet with the drugs. At least you got to know him first, and he won't be yet another faceless O'Rourke who needed to be eliminated."

Blinking against the wind and Noah's stark reality, Curtis managed not to look away. "What does he need to do to prove himself, sir?"

"Don't 'sir' me right now, Curtis. I know you. You couldn't be further from a submissive headspace if you tried." Noah ran his tongue over his teeth. "And you don't want me to answer that. Not at this moment. Not while I see nothing but headstones."

Curtis bit back the crazy desire to clue Noah in on the ways he and Wren were like two peas in the same coffin. Standing, he nodded slowly. "All right. But...to be clear? My thinking of you as my Dom isn't something I take off and put on like a suit of clothes. I'll cut the honorific, but only because it's making you uncomfortable." He started toward the door. "I'll have someone bring up some hot coffee."

"I can't be your Dom while we're discussing this. So it is clear. Maybe I'm incapable of seeing you as a sub in this moment, because if I did? I'd do the same thing I intend to do with my other subs." Noah looked over his shoulder at him. "I'd order you not to speak to him. Not to be alone with him. But you'd hate me for that. And as fucked up as I am? I don't want that. I won't ever want that."

Arms folded over his chest to keep his remaining core body heat stable, Curtis shook his head slowly. "I wouldn't agree with you, but I wouldn't hate you. You'd end up with me safewording and a lot of drama, but I'd never hate you. Never have. Never will. So you can check that worry off your list."

Noah inclined his head, then motioned to the door. "Get inside. You're not built like me, thank fuck. Go be human, and sympathetic, and good. And stop trying to find something in me that isn't there."

"I found it a long time ago." Hand on the door, Curtis used his other to gesture to his heart. "I'll keep it here until you're ready to feel everything again. Until then, it'll be safe right here and so will you. We've got this, Noah. All of us. Right beside you."

Expression softening, only enough for someone who really knew him to catch, Noah nodded. "Thank you. That's exactly where you belong." His gaze shifted, and his light gray eyes went distant. "If you see Jacks, tell him I want some knitting needles. And...you should go now. Don't let anyone else come up here."

Inclining his head, Curtis turned to leave, closing the door softly behind him. As he walked down the stairs, he found one of the cameras and spoke to it. "What's the significance of knitting needles? Should I ask Jacks for them for him or not?"

"Not." Rhodey stepped out of the shadows of the stairwell, his gaze going over Curtis as though checking for injuries. He gave a satisfied nod. "I was gambling I'd get there in time if he accidentally pushed you off the roof. Or slit your throat. I only let him keep a small knife. Would've hurt like fuck, but your head would still be attached."

"Um...thanks?" Life as a Jack-o-lantern had never really appealed, and there were really just so many things you could do with a human head wall mount without getting arrested. "Wren will be disappointed, but I'm glad to say I'm not on Noah's shit list. Apparently." Gesturing to the stairs, he started to move past Rhodey, then paused. "Did you jam Matt's message to Ezran? Is that why he hasn't responded?"

Sighing and shaking his head, Rhodey put a hand on Curtis' shoulder, prompting him to continue down the steps beside him. "No, but considering Garet has Ezran's jacket, I'm willing to bet Maddox wasn't happy about them hanging out. He'll keep Ezran away until he eliminates the weakness. Not by killing Garet. By removing it from Ezran. He might try to have Ezran kill Garet himself. Let's not let that happen."

Pain at the thought nearly took Curtis' breath away and he stumbled, his foot slipping off the step so he started to pitch head first down the stairs. The feeling wasn't unlike the loss of control he felt at not being able to protect two kids who were like sons to him, or brothers at the very least. Arms pinwheeling, he found himself as unable to rescue himself as he was them.

A firm grip on the back of his shirt jerked him backward, Rhodey lifting him off his feet with the fabric, his voice gruff as he carried Curtis down the remaining steps like an errant puppy. "Sloppy. I'll have to have Wren erase that. Vani will take it personally if she sees you getting thrown off like that. Literally. And we don't need you away on another training exercise."

Heart still hammering wildly, Curtis placed one hand on the nearest wall and nodded. "Thanks. That was…" He shook his head to clear it. "I love those boys. There has to be a way, Rhodey. Tell me what it is and I'll fucking do it. Just… Not Ez. Please."

"When I figure it out, I'll let you know. For now, we need to keep Garet out of reach. For both his and Ezran's sakes. You have no clue what Maddox is capable of. The things he can make those he controls do." Rhodey's jaw tightened, and he brushed his fingers through Curtis' hair, as though using him as a touchstone. "I wasn't sure we would get Garet back from this, but we have. Focus on that. The other one won't be completely lost unless he takes that step, so…there's hope. Or whatever you idiots want to call it."

Needing the touch as much as Rhodey seemed to, Curtis leaned closer, breathing in the man and the musky sweetness surrounding him—only detectable if he let you get this near. "You're the asshole that keeps giving it to us. I'm a grateful idiot."

Lips curving, Rhodey gave his hair a light tug. "Good. I wasn't expecting you to be one of the level-headed ones about this whole shitshow, but it's fucking nice to see. I've got too much to deal with to go down and clean those damn cells so I can lock half the Core up. It's tempting, but we'll see how the talking and feelings thing works first. Even though it takes a lot longer. And it's not nearly as fun to watch."

"I'm not sure what the other options are, but count me in for a show if it's half as kinky as that sounds." Returning the grin, Curtis straightened, doing a pop-snap with his fists and palm. "As for being level headed? I'm trying to hold my boys together, and make sure Lawson doesn't lose his shit. I'm in a position I don't often find myself in. Being the relatively sane one. It's a lot of fucking work. I hope I don't have to do it too much in the future."

Rhodey grunted and poked at a swollen, split spot on his lip, rolling his eyes when his fingertip came away with blood. "Fucking thing. You better handle your man. If this shit doesn't work out, I'll regret not shooting him. And reconsider how pretty he'd look with a few extra holes. Then you'll be doing that work a whole bunch. For a very long time."

"This is not a situation requiring ventilation." Worried Rhodey might be half serious, Curtis gave him the best mock stern stare he'd learned from Tracey. "Let's not and if anyone asks we can say we did and he dodged."

Chuckling, Rhodey nodded. "I wouldn't mind seeing if he could, the man is faster than he looks in those fucking suits. But fine. We'll save the bullets for last resort, since you want to be a killjoy."

One hand on the door to his loft, Curtis gave Rhodey a thumbs up. "Killjoy was here. It has a ring to it." He saluted the man. "I'm goin' in. Wish me luck. Reed and I are going a few rounds in the ring in a bit. Stop by and watch. He's mad as hornets and might actually kick my ass this time."

"Good. Maybe an asskicking will keep you on your toes and not falling down the stairs." Rhodey smacked the wall on his way down. "These things should be padded."

"Save that for the cells." Door opening, Curtis called out, raising his voice. "Oh! Noah needs some hot coffee. You'd better bring it. He likes you best."

Rhodey snorted. "And I thought you loved us both. If I go up there, only one of us will come back down. Since you've become Switzerland, give Jared a shout. Or send Wren. Either of them will survive."

"Not Jamie, huh? Afraid he'll serenade him into a semi-automatic showdown with the street?" Knowing the answer, Curtis winked. "Wren or Jared. Got it!"

Giving him a dry look, Rhodey glanced back at him. "I'm trying to be nice and not traumatize the little kitty. That'll teach me. If you've still got a beef with Connor, go ahead and try that on for size. He can bring the boy home in a straightjacket."

"Cruel." Snickering, Curtis left Rhodey in the stairwell and went into the loft to kick off his shoes by the door where Reed's pile of slippers, boots, and glittery sneakers were in a relatively neat jumble. "Honey! I'm home!"

While he might be going a few rounds with Reed in the ring, the fight started here.

And this was one challenge he knew he'd need every ounce of finesse he possessed to get through. Lawson was a formidable opponent, but when he protected his own? Getting him to back down and tap out?

Not fucking likely.

So Curtis needed to use the one thing against him that his man didn't have in his possession.

The truth.

Chapter Thirty

PRESENT

*C**oming home shouldn't feel like stepping into the ring.*
   Sighing inwardly, Curtis squared his shoulders and threw a few prayers to the fuckers upstairs. For better days and a dash of innocent happiness he wasn't entirely sure he'd recognize if it bit him in the ass.
It better come with a fanfare and a skywriter.
Stepping out of the kitchen, holding a steaming black mug and wearing only a pair of dark green flannel sleep pants, Lawson gave him a weary smile. "Welcome home. Do you want some coffee? Matt just put some on."
"Wouldn't mind a cup." Rubbing his hands together, Curtis determined the feeling had come back to them. The loft was warm, the lights in the living space casting golden pools over the sturdy but elegantly appointed furniture Lawson and Matt seemed to prefer. "What are you two up to?"
Lawson motioned him into the kitchen, where there were a couple of decks of cards set up in the middle of the table, and a few scattered around the surface. "We're playing every card game we know. I felt like it would be a good distraction."
Glancing over the table, Curtis noted the bowls of snacks

and the neat piles of red and black cards laid out in what appeared to be a game of gin rummy. "My gran used to love cards. Pike and I knew how to play crazy eights before we could talk. Might explain a lot, come to think of it."

Farther into the loft a toilet flushed, then water ran. It seemed a shame to ruin Lawson and Matt's comfortable evening, all things considered. But he'd promised Reed he'd try to remove at least one thorn. Taking out a beer, he popped the cap and propped his hip against the counter to take a sip.

"So... Has Matt mentioned anything to you about knocking Pike's tooth out and decking Jamie?" Trying to go for casual, Curtis wiped a thumb over the corner of his lip to gather up some drops of beer. "Something about being pissed about the whole reconfiguration of our power dynamics?"

Frowning, Lawson glanced in the direction of the main bedroom. "No, but I heard there was some kind of scuffle. Obviously I noticed Pike's tooth, but your cousin is very accident prone. As for Jamie, he's asked Matt to work with him in the ring several times. I don't see our boy hurting him— hurting *either* of them—intentionally."

"You're probably right. Reed mentioned having been there, but maybe he didn't have the whole story. Something about Noah wanting Matt to talk to you about it but the power going out and the generator going *The Avengers take Manhattan* on The Asylum." Shrugging, Curtis took another sip of beer as Matt walked into the kitchen in his own checked green and white pajama bottoms, barefoot and shirtless. "Maybe he can clear it up himself."

Lawson inclined his head, then lifted his brow at Matt. "Yes, that's a very good idea. Matt, were you fighting with Jamie and Pike? Is there an issue there I should know about?"

Turning red to the roots of his sandy blond hair, Matt took an automatic half-step back, his hands going to fists by his sides as his chin came up. It was such a tell that the evil demon on Curtis' shoulder wanted to snicker, but the part of him—

the bigger part—that loved Matt felt a wave of disappointment.

"Pike was being Pike, and I didn't mean to hit Jamie. The tooth...wasn't intentional." Matt licked his lips. "He threw a bucket of popcorn over my head and I just sort of snapped. I apologized."

"By beating his ass like you were his Dom?" Curtis popped up one brow. "Or did the apology come after?"

"A-after. I apologized to Jamie and to Noah. Noah said I had to tell you, but I forgot." Matt folded his arms around his middle. "It was a weird day."

Rubbing his hand over his face, Lawson sighed. "You... spanked Pike? Because he threw popcorn on you? Matt..." He reached out and pulled a chair away from the table, closer to him. "Come sit down. Needless to say, you will be apologizing to Pike *and* his Doms as well, but first we're going to discuss what started all this. You didn't lose your temper over popcorn."

Dragging his feet a la Pike would have been kind of cute if Curtis wasn't so pissed at Matt. The situation with Ezran foremost in his mind, he'd forgotten some of the details Reed had related until he'd started to open up this whole can of worms for Lawson to examine.

Matt plunked down on the chair, arms still folded. "I mean, to be fair, he surprised me with an entire bucket over my head. Like the thing was *on* my head and covering my eyes."

"Please explain to me how you consider that 'fair'." Lawson curved his hand under Matt's jaw. "You're quite a bit bigger and stronger than him. And, as Curtis mentioned, you are not a Dom to be taking something like that on yourself. Did Jamie try to stop you? Is that how he ended up getting hit?"

"No." The whites of Matt's eyes grew wider as it apparently dawned on him exactly how deep the shit pile he'd landed himself in was. "Reed."

"You tried to hit Reed?" Curtis' blood began to simmer. "Because he defended Pike."

"It happened so fast." Matt tried to pull his jaw from Lawson's hold. "And Pike tripped. I didn't knock his tooth out. I think somewhere in my head it seemed better to whack his ass than to do what I really wanted."

Firming his grip, Lawson gave Matt a hard look. "Be still. I want you to look at me while you tell me what you really wanted to do. And why you didn't get a hold on yourself *before* taking a swing at your best friend. Your partner. I'm glad you apologized to Jamie, he didn't deserve to get hurt for what I assume was an attempt to de-escalate the situation. But I'm not hearing you finding any fault in your actions. You are better than this, my boy."

White splotches appeared against the red of Matt's skin where Lawson's fingers held him still when he tried to shake his head. "I got blindsided. By Reed. The whole thing with you and him. How he didn't want Curtis anymore. I never s-saw it coming, okay? That he'd want you, and that people could just divorce each other here and decide t-t-to do things on a whim. I thought it would be you and me next and I'd never see it. That it'd be just like with my mom and one day I'd have you and the next..." Swallowing convulsively, Matt closed his eyes. "Please let go of me."

Lowering his hand, Lawson sat back. "It won't be you and me next, Matt. Not unless it's something you decide you want. Because it's not what I want, even though I am very disappointed in you. And I'm hurt that you chose…you chose to lash out at others, to take out your pain and frustration on them, rather than discussing any of this with me."

"I'm sorry." Matt's voice was a pained whisper as he met Lawson's eyes, his expression bereft.

Curtis leaned over, taking Matt's mobile from the table

and flipped it over. "Put in the passcode and show him your text messages."

"What?" Going from contrite to freaked in a split second, Matt shook his head. "Why?"

"Damn it, Matt, what else are you hiding? Or not telling me?" Lawson shoved his chair back, pacing across the kitchen. He stopped at the far end and turned. "I feel like you are attempting to make your worst fears into a self-fulfilled prophecy. What am I supposed to do if you close off communication with me? If you turn to…to *violence* rather than open up to me? If I didn't see this is because you're struggling, with several things, if I let myself go there for one fucking second, I'd be reliving my own nightmare. But I won't allow it. And I need to know you won't continue down this path because it will only get much more difficult."

With shaking fingers, Matt poked at the series of numbers that would open his phone.

Curtis leaned down, one palm on the table to open the text app to the group message with Ezran. "For the record? You don't get to lock your phone any longer until I say. I'll be getting you a phone without a text app and you can earn this one back." He handed the phone to Lawson. "You and me, we're going to work on that attitude, the anger, and you can sit back and trust that I've got you."

Reading over the text, Lawson shook his head with disbelief. "This… Yes, I think that would be a very good idea, Curtis. I'll also be speaking with Stephan and making you an appointment, Matt. Your family will be here for you. *I* will be here for you. But this kind of behavior…this needs a support system that includes more than we can give. This isn't you, my love. This is…I don't know what to say."

"It *is* him, Lawson." One hand on Matt's shoulder, Curtis squeezed gently. "Just like all the good things he does are him. And most of them *are* good. But pretending it's not all him will only land him in the same cycle. I know you don't want to hear it, but I think Garet had it right owning up to what he's done. There's awareness and strength in being able to say we're not entirely in the right all the time and that we can fuck up. Especially when the people who love us make it safe for us to do it. When we feel all that and let ourselves feel their hurt and disappointment, it makes us understand we don't want to feel that way—we don't want *them* to feel that way—again."

Closing his eyes, Lawson returned to the table and sat heavily. "You're right, my man. I know you're right. Part of me..." He opened his eyes and looked into Matt's. "I wasn't aware you were capable of going this far. Now that I am, I would like to see you work on it. But first...I need to hear you understand. How very wrong your actions were. The message, the violence, the behavior. When you are fighting a threat, or a perceived threat, as you and the other Core subs do with the... 'Misfit Mafia'? I do not approve, for the most part, but I have no tolerance for bullies and they've crossed those lines several times. But now...you are the bully, Matt. And you can do better."

A myriad of emotions from shame to betrayal and fear skated through Matt's blue eyes, the fall of his bangs obscuring one. Lips parted, his breaths were shallow sips. When he spoke his voice shook. "If Garet stays..." He tossed his bangs off his forehead, closing his eyes. "No one asked me what I wanted. About anything. What I did was wrong. I'm sorry. For all of it. Maybe I am the bully. I don't know. I trust you. So I must be."

"I see." Lawson gave Matt a long look. "I don't feel like you truly understand why it was wrong, but we'll get there. I'm not sure what you'd have liked me to ask you about. Concerning Reed? He did ask you. But I understand there being some complicated feelings and we can discuss it again as a family. As for Garet, you know I don't want him here. I didn't want you to have to go through everything you have with him, all over again, when you'd just begun to heal. But I don't have the final say concerning that and I'm sorry. I will do everything in my power to make sure he can't hurt you again." He glanced at Curtis. "Can you have Reed come here? Maybe...we can at very least resolve the situation that concerns all of us."

Giving a slight shake of his head, Curtis let Lawson know with his gaze that his suggestion was a *very* bad idea. "He's working out some feelings of his own at the moment. I promised him I'd get in the ring with him after I came in to chat with you. We spent the last little while talking about what he needs, and I'm very proud of him for using his words. I'd like to respect them and the time and trust he put in by giving him the space he needs."

"Space... You mean more than the time in the ring." Lawson rubbed his hand over his mouth. "How much space?"

"From Matt? It's difficult to say. At least until Matt seems able to apologize and hear Reed out without his own feelings getting in the way." Curtis dropped his hand from Matt's shoulder, taking a step back to retrieve his beer. "You hurt his brother, Matt. Did you think about what it might do to Ezran to have all that history brought up when he's already struggling to feel like he can come home and trust us? Were you looking out for The Asylum or for yourself? Because you tore through a lot of good will tonight from people who love you very much. Including me."

Staring at his hands, Matt shook his head. "No, sir. I wasn't thinking about that. I just wanted Garet away from everyone."

"Including someone who isn't here, my boy. I have a feeling your intentions were much darker than you're willing to face. But as your other Dom mentioned, you need to face it, or you'll only repeat it. Garet hurt you." Lawson put his hand over Matt's. "And you needed to hurt him back."

A fat tear dropped onto the back of Lawson's hand. Then another. Matt swallowed audibly, but didn't reply at first. Curtis remained silent, letting him feel the weight of the emotions in the room until Lawson's boy took a juddering breath. "I tried so hard. I'm tired of trying. I can't rescue him. I can't even rescue myself."

"You don't need to, love. If he is going to stay, we will reserve judgment. Many are saying he's put in the work. We'll let him continue to do so. It will be up to you to decide if it's enough. I won't allow anyone to pressure you, even if you decide it never will be. That is your right. As we discussed, forgiveness is not something to be demanded. It's something to be given, if it's right for you." Lawson used his fingertips to wipe away Matt's tears. "But I need you to consider, very carefully, that the same goes for anyone you've hurt. And the effort you put in to mend those relationships needs to be because you know it's the right thing to do."

"I know." Matt lifted his watery gaze, finally meeting Lawson's eyes. "I was just thinking that, sir. I can't forgive me, and you shouldn't either. I don't think I can change, just like I don't believe my brother really can. We're the same."

Lawson stood, clasping Matt's hand in his and pulling him to his feet. "I have a lot more faith in you than that, my boy. Until you can find it for yourself, I'll have to have enough for the both of us."

That was just like Lawson, and Noah, both. Always carrying everyone else's burdens. Exactly what Curtis loved about them most, and what worried him. Both were likely to let other people's stuff bury them six-feet under before their time.

"Hey, person here who offered to take some of that load. Hello." Waving the beer bottle, Curtis gave Lawson a lopsided grin. "I'll even give him his daily beating if you want. Reed's been far too good. I need practice."

Lawson breathed out a laugh and nodded. "I would appreciate that. At some point, I may have to ease off on the painkillers and ask one of our good doctors to take a look at my arm. Rhodey has an incredibly hard face."

"I know. He's let me sit on it." Not really, but what Lawson didn't know wouldn't hurt him. Smirking, Curtis took out his phone. "Want me to call Seth down here to take a look?"

Hesitating, Lawson glanced over at Matt. "I'm sure it can wait until morning. Matt needs some rest." He pressed a soft kiss to Matt's temple. "He'll need his energy for all those beatings."

It was impossible to tell whether Matt knew they were teasing, his expression remained so even, like he'd decided if he couldn't conquer his anger he'd just never feel a damned thing again.

Curtis ruffled his hair on the way by, then mussed Lawson's for good measure. "I'm sending Seth. I need you back in the ring. My rep is on the line if I don't get someone in my weight class to fight soon who's actually worth a damn."

"Until I'm cleared, get some time in with Dallas." Lawson gave Curtis a warm smile as he guided Matt to their bedroom. "Let me know when, I would very much like to watch."

Inclining his head, Curtis gave Lawson a reassuring look. It was going to be okay. They'd all been through worse. Matt might feel like shit at the moment, but that was only natural. Because he damned well should. That he did meant he wasn't unfixable or even broken. He was just a human going through a hell of a time and spilling all his feels on the rest of the people around him. Helping him to build a dam to contain them so they could be dealt with appropriately was something both Noah and Lawson, as well as Stephan, had helped Curtis with. It was time to return the favor.

Could have been worse, and the fuckers upstairs could've assigned him someone like Paris to fix. Then he would've had to beg Rhodey for his bowie knife and a length of rope. "Get some sleep. I'll bring you your paddle with your coffee in the morning."

"I'll see you then." For a second, sadness filled Lawson's

eyes, but then he shook his head and cleared his throat, keeping his tone light. "Where will you and Reed be staying?"

Perceptive.

Curtis paused, glancing up as he'd bent over to put on his shoe. "With Shacks. If they say yes. Otherwise Seth."

Matt's inhale was sharp and pained. He turned, the emotion in his eyes returning in a flood. "I'm so sorry."

"I know you are, mo ghrá." Other shoe on, Curtis gave him a bracing look, taking out his phone to text Seth. "Now we just need to help Reed to believe it. Piece of advice? Giving your brother the time of day, if not your forgiveness, would go a long way."

"I'll try." Matt's response was unexpected, but proved one thing. He might not trust his brother, but he loved Reed a metric fuck-ton.

Some of the barely visible tension eased from Lawson's shoulders. He put his arm around Matt and gave him a light squeeze. "That's all anyone can ask, my love. Now, go get me another cup of coffee and my pills. I'll put the heated blanket on the bed. It will be missing some heat without our men in it, but we'll make do until they return."

Lawson was the only man Curtis knew who could drink coffee and fall asleep after. Finished texting, he slid his phone into his back pocket, shaking his head. "You're bizarre and I love you, my man."

Saluting on his way out, Curtis didn't wait for Lawson's response. He had a boy waiting for him downstairs, and another upstairs who was counting on him to figure out how to put his world back together again. Time was awastin', as his gran would've said, and he wasn't the kind to let moss grow under his testicles.

"Okay. That was too far even for me." He shuddered, pushing his way into the gym. "Reed, do you know if it's possible to have mossy balls? If so, I want a preventative."

"Ew, I hope not. But with the way the locker rooms smell

before Wren gets done murdering all the nastiness?" Reed shuddered, stretching his arms on the ropes, his bright orange tank and shorts making him glow in the spotlight like a wiry fireball. "It's possible. I betcha he could give you all the deets."

There was a faint scratching sound, Wren coming around from the other side of the ring to hand Curtis a pad of paper with the words, *'Not moss, but several different kinds of fungus,'* written on it.

"Did you put yourself on speech restrictions again, Freaky Friday?" Curtis glanced up from the paper to meet Wren's owlish gaze. "I thought there were rules against that for nurses. What if I couldn't read? How would you cure me?"

Wren made a pained sound and looked over at Reed.

Vaulting over the ropes, Reed landed beside him. "Jared put him on speech restrictions. He forgot for a bit, so I think he's doubling up on it now. Think I can use my Head Boy status to get him off of it? That'd be handy."

"Why'd he put you on speech restrictions? Wait. Was that in the *bar* all those hours ago?" Curtis made a frustrated sound. Reaching over, he jangled Wren's tags. "I'm taking you off them. He would've, too, if you'd seen him since then. Come on, you can ref the fight and we need your voice for that."

Worrying his bottom lip with his teeth, Wren nodded slowly. "I don't know if he would, sir. Things are very complicated right now. But I would very much enjoy reffing for you. A fight in the ring would be much simpler than…everything else."

Stripping down to his boxers after kicking off his shoes, Curtis made sure to leave plenty of mess for Wren to straighten. He took his phone out of his pocket and placed it to one side on the stairs to the ring. "I think they'll get a little simpler. With Matt at least." Dropping his shirt to the floor, he glanced at Reed. "Matt said he'd try with Garet. And he's sorry for being a…what do you call it? Wafflebutt?"

"Dick waffle. Or whatever variety pops into my head at the time." Reed pulled a neon green elastic from his wrist, smoothing his hair away from his face and tying it into a small bundle at the base of his neck. "If he tries I guess I can...we'll see. It's hard to be mad at him, I miss him. But the whole thing messed with my head. I hate when I can't tell...where anyone stands, you know? One sec things are cool, the next there's a huge blow-up and it's like...*whoa*."

"I think we're all a little tired of that." In the ring, Curtis sat on the mat, doing his stretches and warm-up. "Look, if you'd been in my family, the times people were shouting at you were when they were *least* likely to walk up behind you and shoot you in the back of the head." He mimed the gesture with his thumb and forefinger to his skull. "So for a real long time I was loud when I was mad around here, and I think maybe Matt has some kind of similar damage. He likes to see things coming, and he likes to assert his boundaries hard so he sees *them* coming. But it's time for him to get a different coping mechanism." Bounding to his feet, Curtis did a quick jog in place to warm his blood. "We're gonna do better around here, sparkles. Not just saying."

Reed nodded, tugging at the hem of his tank top, then hopped up to sit on the ropes. "I wonder sometimes, when things go sideways, if our damage kinda...you know, crosses some wires? When I was a kid, being too loud got the wrong kind of attention from my dad. Or he'd just walk out until... he did it for good. Living with Tracey helped with a lot of that, she taught me it was okay to...well, *exist*. Be a bit loud sometimes. Or bright and happy and..." His lips curved. "Sparkly."

Grinning in return, Curtis made jazz hands with wiggly fingers. "I like the sparkly. I definitely see you coming, and going, and you make me see there are good ways to be loud." Meeting Reed at the ropes, he looped his arms loosely around his boy's waist. "Want to glitter me, my little glitterbug? I'm looking forward to wearing you on my skin."

"Yes, sir." Reed held up one hand, wiggling his own fingers to make the sparkles from his lotion catch the light. "I'm glad you don't mind me getting this on you. Wren isn't so cuddly right after I put it on."

On the steps leading up to the ring, Wren sighed and shook his head. "I am very rarely cuddly. And I prefer waiting until your skin absorbs most of it. Otherwise, you are very…slimy."

Curtis bit his lips to keep from laughing as he met Reed's eyes. "Glitter and slime. I'm looking forward to you wrecking me." He stepped back, beckoning Reed with him. "Now let's see what you got, my little one-man sparkle party."

"It's on." Reed bounced off the ropes, his bare feet landing lightly on the canvas. Continuously moving, he shifted into position, holding up his guard in the way they'd been working on for years. His gaze followed Curtis' movements, likely searching for any tell of tensing muscles before a hit or a kick. He snapped his first punch toward Curtis' middle, testing his response time. "We haven't done this as much as we used to. I missed it."

"Same." Coming out of his dance away from the hit, Curtis realized he hadn't put in his mouthguard. Hopefully, Noah wouldn't decide now was a good time for a break. Tracking Reed's footwork, he waited for the expected kick, skirting sideways as it grazed his side. Following through with a grapple, he went for a maneuver meant to take Reed down to the mat, but came away with air. "Nice!"

Disguising his intent with his grin, he came in fast with a head-butt to Reed's middle. Before he could get a good grip, Reed twisted, the lotion making him more than a little slippery.

And left him holding nothing but the flashy orange tank top.

Eyes shining with laughter, Reed went for a leg sweep, bounding behind Curtis when he evaded. "You taught me never to let a bigger fighter trap me. Or land a good hit. I don't have all the muscle I used to, but I got fast again. Comes in handy."

Humor was a balm to the last several hours, and something Curtis had very much missed with his boy. "Good boy."

Testing Reed's reflexes with a few quick jabs and an uppercut, he missed when Reed ducked and weaved to evade them all, and jumped out of the way of the leg sweep Curtis returned. He picked up the pace, using a deliberately missed side-kick to maneuver Reed closer to one corner of the ring so he could trap him where he wouldn't be able to get away from the hits.

As a distraction, Curtis kept the conversation going—a trick Lawson disdained, but any port in a storm. "I'm using that lotion trick. What is that, strawberry?"

"You've got a good nose, sir. Strawberry candy cream. It's all natural—the lady Keiran gets his cheese from…well, they're a couple, but she makes this as a little side business. It's actually a 'body butter' and it feels really good—she added the glitter just for me. I bring her some butterscotch candy from Phil's whenever I swing by with Keir-bear—" The distraction absolutely worked, Reed too caught up in the topic to realize the direction he was headed until his back hit the corner. He cut himself off, catching his breath and using his hands on the ropes to lift himself onto the corner, thrusting forward to throw himself onto Curtis, attempting to use the momentum to knock him off his feet. "Tricky Dom."

Catching him around the middle, Curtis landed a stinging smack to Reed's ass. The drop filled the gym with a resounding *SLAM* as Reed's back hit the canvas. Following him down, Curtis laughed, wrapping his legs around his boy. Barred his throat with a forearm to hyperextend his neck and cut off his airflow.

There were several options open, but if Reed weren't up for the fight he could tap out without losing face. "Give and we'll start again. I might let you get in a hit this time."

Reed shook his head, bracing his elbow against the canvas and twisting his body, ramming his shoulder against Custis' face and forcing him to adjust his hold. Reversing the move, Reed gasped in air, locking Curtis' arm behind him rather than using the opportunity to escape and regroup. The better choice for a fighter against an opponent out of his weight class. And with much more experience.

By Reed's tone, he was well aware he was going *against* all he'd been taught by grappling with Curtis this way. But he was having fun. "Give because I can't breathe? Come on, sir. You know me better than that. If I can still move, I don't stop."

Being this close to Reed when there had been so many months without physical intimacy between them, affected Curtis' body like a live wire in water, sending trills of electric sensation down his spine and outward to his thighs, fingertips, toes, and especially his groin.

"If it's any consolation, I am very good at CPR. I cut open one of the dummies out of curiosity, which Jared said is not at all how the procedure works…" Wren crouched down next to them, as though convinced he would need to call the match any second. "I don't believe I'll need a scalpel to treat either of you if there's an injury, but I am prepared for any outcome."

The energy changed as Curtis looked in Reed's eyes, but Wren's words—thank fuck—helped him to head the moment off at the pass. Releasing his opponent, Curtis bounded to his feet, yanking Reed with him.

Surprise gave him the advantage, and he managed two hits, stumbling Reed back again. Hard enough to register as not pulling his punches, but not so hard Lawson would kick his ass for being brutal. Keeping the fight upright from here on would be important. No need to risk crossing the line Reed had drawn around himself.

Smile bright with the pure rush of adrenaline from their sparring, Reed swung around with a high kick easily blocked. Snapped forward with a rapid sidekick. His expression changed and he cut it short before it connected with Curtis' ribs, tripping backward out of reach.

Holding up a hand, as though to let Curtis know he was okay, he bounced in place, giving his head a hard shake. "Come on, you've got this. Don't psych yourself out, damn it. You won't break him."

"You *will* insult my ego, however, if you don't land at least one bone bruising hit." Considering for a moment, Curtis held his arms wide. "Let's break the seal. Come on, my boy. I'm your bag. You get three before I block. Keep 'em comin' fast and hard. I'll block as many as I'm able after."

Wrinkling his nose, Reed bounded forward and poked Curtis in the stomach. "You can't *let* me hit you, I just…" Curls had come loose from his ponytail and Reed shook them away from his face. Several strands stuck to the sweat and lotion slicking his skin. "I keep hearing that crack, from when I kicked Jared. I don't want to hurt you like that, too."

"Then you don't belong in this ring, and you're not giving your Dom enough credit. Either of us." Keeping his arms up, Curtis didn't back down. "Come on. Show me you deserve the title of Head Boy and the First Sub Royal. I want to see who I tagged all those years ago, not the shadow of him."

Eyes flashing, Reed landed a punch right in Curtis' stomach. "I do belong here. I've worked fucking hard to get here." The next two jabs struck Curtis' sternum and his side. "It's not my fault you keep getting hurt. That everyone's always hurt. And angry. And miserable."

Taking a chance, Curtis kept his arms up, and raised his voice. "How do I know that? Maybe it is. Maybe it's because you won't fight. What if it's you who's making us all pissy because you're hiding your head in the sand? That didn't even tickle."

"I'm fucking trying!" Reed slammed his shoulder into Curtis' middle and drove him back into the ropes. Slapping his hands against Curtis' shoulders, he stared at him for a second, then turned and walked to the other side of the ring. He gripped the ropes there, hanging his head between his arms. "I know how bad shit can get. And maybe I should just…stop looking for the good stuff. Be miserable, too. But I can't. I need to know there's still…something worth fighting for. Otherwise, what's the point?"

Curtis slowly lowered his arms. "I should've known that wouldn't work on you the way it used to on Law." He crossed the ring to put his hands on Reed's shoulders and shook him gently. "If you were miserable, *I* wouldn't have anything left to fight for. I fight to be the man you want and need every day, just to see that smile or hear your giddy laugh. I miss it, Reed. I miss *us*. Please…I know you're tired, but I need you to fight. Because I can't keep fighting without you."

Turning to face him, Reed met his eyes. Shaking his head, he threw himself forward, this time without any hits, just wrapping his arms around Curtis' waist. "I am fighting with you. But it's like…I get it, you're on the front lines. You don't see me there. But I am. I always am."

"I know, love." Sighing into Reed's hair, Curtis held him close. "Did you know…" His tone thoughtful, he kept his gaze on the far wall. "When Noah picked up you and Ez…that's when I made my real decision. To become a better man. The way you looked at me, how you seemed to see no one but me and not my past was everything. I wanted to be that person you saw, and to show you there was someone you could count on in this shitty world. I'm still trying, because you're still here."

Reed lifted his head, laughing as he swiped at the tears gathering on his lashes. "Well, yeah. I'm not going anywhere. You're here. This is our place. And I'd be a crappy future-partial-owner if I took off." He placed his hand on the center of Curtis' chest. "I still see that man. The awesome one who's strong and sometimes a bit goofy, and protective, and dangerous in all the right ways. You'd do anything for the people you love and I'm damn grateful to be one of them. I'd do the same for you, any day of the week, even when things get a bit rough. Or...well, don't get rough because I just developed a really fucked up aversion to kicking people in the ring. And it's one of my best moves."

"It was a one-in-a-thousand hit, Reed." Leaning back with his arms looped around Reed's waist, Curtis dipped his chin. "And Jared's, like, *ancient*." He mimicked Jamie's voice, doing a fairly good job. "He has to have osteoporosis by now. So you can't blame yourself. Come on." He dropped his arms. "I'm ordering you to fight. We're not going to bed until you try to kick me at least three times and land one. Let's go."

Light throat clearing came from behind him, along with the flipping of pages, from what looked like a fighting manual Wren must've slipped away to fetch from Lawson's office. "Jared does *not* have any such ailments. He is in very good shape, and he is not at all ancient. I believe you may be misusing that word, sir. It's all right, Jamie does that all the time. Sometimes, I do get the gist of what he's trying to say. Almost like with your puns." He frowned at the book. "There is absolutely nothing in here about how a ref is supposed to handle fighters stopping to hug. That's very short-sighted."

Bursting out laughing, Curtis shook his head. "That's in the special Asylum rule book." He tapped his temple. "Up here. It only happens in late January on a full moon."

At Wren's solemn nod, Curtis went to the center of the ring and waited for Reed to take up his stance. Bumped fists and came out swinging, forcing himself into the mindset where he had a full crowded gym and ten-grand on the line.

His moves became tight and quick, leaving Reed no time to think. Only to react.

Breaths coming fast, Reed held up his guard, smoothly blocking and dodging, moving faster as though escaping into the flow of the fight. He managed to skid around Curtis and snap a solid kick into his ass. The playful light usually in his eyes while between the ropes returned. "That's one. You really shouldn't let your opponent get behind you, sir. I thought we were being serious now?"

Curtis growled, whirling with an attempted leg sweep, used to distract Reed long enough to land a solid hit to his boy's jaw. Almost guaranteed to leave a bruise he'd be able to show off. "You want to smack it? You gotta earn it, sparkles."

"Only in here. So you'll have to enjoy getting a beating from me while you can." Reed did a jump and a roll to evade the next strike, kicking Curtis' calf before rolling again to keep out of reach. He sprang to his feet, sweat sheening his bare chest. "Two. And in case you forgot? Outside of the ring? I like being on the other side of the pain."

"Do you? I hadn't noticed." Curtis winked, then barreled in with an elbow strike to Reed's middle. Followed-through with a grapple to flip him, letting his boy's back slap the mat.

Immediately scooting over to give himself space to catch his breath, Reed grinned as he shook the rest of his hair loose, the elastic having pretty much lost all purpose at this point. "This is what I needed. Fuck, you're awesome like this. If I wasn't planning to kick your ass...*again*...I'd totally stay here and stare at you. Good strategy. Just stand there and look hot."

It was rare Curtis felt ten-feet tall, but when Reed looked at him like that? Yeah. He was a dog-damn giant. "What? No tricks of your own?" Pacing to his corner, he picked up the water bottle Wren had left for him and cracked the cap to pour half of it over his head. The rest he guzzled, before he turned. "Round two?"

"Yes, please, sir." Reed went to his own corner, snickering when he attempted to hug Wren and the other sub ducked and side-stepped, shaking his head. Grabbing a towel to wipe his face, Reed gave him a thoughtful look. "You know, you're pretty quick. If you wanted to spar sometimes—"

Wren blinked at him. "I would hope you would bring me to the clinic to have my head examined. That is not at all for me. I'd much prefer to observe. From far enough to avoid getting sweat on me."

"Biting is allowed." Giving Wren a wide grin and a brow pop, Curtis returned to the center of the ring.

Polishing off his own water, Reed nodded, then joined Curtis. "You have to get sweaty during training, anyway. Could be fun, but if you don't want to, having you watch is nice. It sucks that you can't be here for the big fights."

"I'm satisfied seeing fights like this. It's much less enjoyable with all the members around. They are very noisy and many seem to have terrible hygiene." Wren tucked the fight book under his arm and waved between Curtis and Reed. "Please continue hitting one another."

A shadow moved overhead before a long length of deep purple silk dropped from the rafters. Avery slithered down halfway, bundling the remaining material into a sort of hammock swing and settled in to watch.

Biting back a grin, Curtis couldn't resist considering several suitably 'Addams Family' names for the sub. 'Thing' or 'Cousin It' would have Rhodey feeding him bullets. Lurch didn't quite fit.

Wednesday has a ring to it...

Fist held out for Reed to bump, Curtis latched onto his wrist. Spun him around for a standing nelson. Knowing Reed would use the position to leverage a backflip, he braced one knee into the back of Reed's to get him off balance.

Cursing under his breath, Reed dropped his weight, the lotion on his skin still giving him enough wiggle room to free one arm. He jabbed his elbow back into Curtis' ribs. Then froze.

Not giving Reed time to panic, Curtis brought him to the mat, rolling him to pin him on his stomach. Switching to a half-nelson, he immobilized his boy to growl in his ear. "You better fucking break this hold. I know you know how to do it."

Reed growled back, baring his teeth as he wrenched himself to one side, hooking his leg to Curtis' thigh and rolling them both over. He lifted his upper body, pressing his forearm against Curtis' jaw and tightening the leg lock. "I'm also not supposed to let anyone get me down here, but I guess I can improvise."

Neck extended, Curtis shouted as he yielded and let Reed go. He laughed, bounding to his feet at the same time Reed did. He punched hard, connecting with Reed's shoulder and forcing him back. Keeping close, he guarded his face rather than his middle. The very place his boy needed to connect with to get past his fear.

Spinning swiftly, Reed took the opening without hesitation, landing a roundhouse kick right into Curtis' ribs. He followed through with a punch to his jaw, completely engaged in the fight, with no room to second-guess himself. The exact mentality he needed whenever he faced a bigger challenger in the ring.

Curtis shook out the hit and blocked the next, circling away and bouncing on the balls of his feet to give himself a moment to absorb the disorientation. He forced Reed to come to him, ducking a kick and landing one of his own to Reed's left side.

Stumbling, Reed went on defense, dancing out of reach with a bit less grace, but no less speed. He came in with several jabs, then skidded back again, swiping his hair out of his face and panting, the spark of excitement never fading from his eyes. "I'm not letting you get me down again. If you plan to win, you're gonna have to catch up."

There's my boy.

Sweat slicked his chest, running in rivulets down his face to sting his eyes, but Curtis telegraphed one-hundred-percent lazy coolness with his grin. "Don't issue a challenge unless you plan to defend it and win." He rushed Reed, arms wide like he intended to grapple, but instead pivoted with a leg sweep.

Jumping up, Reed almost managed to avoid the sweep, but it clipped him enough to send him landing hard on his side. He groaned, pushing back before laughing. Too stunned to get away any faster. Not ready to give up just yet. "Sneaky Dom."

Chuckling, Curtis stalked closer, placing a solid foot on Reed's sternum, just heavy enough to show him how quickly he could lose if he stayed down like that, but light enough to be playful. "Someone has to keep the Head Boy on his toes. If I don't do it, who will?"

Reed lifted a brow at him, grabbing his ankle and rolling to tug him off his feet. Without waiting for Curtis to land, he vaulted to his feet and bolted to the other end of the ring. "Why yes, please, sir. You lie there and I'll just be over here, getting ready to knock you down again."

Tongue poking at the inside of his cheek, Curtis nodded slowly. "What I want to know is why you're not down here with me, beating the piss out of me?" He bounded up, making a come-hither motion with both hands. "I don't want you over there. I want you here."

"I know, but maybe if I make you chase me, it'll tire you out." Reed blew out a breath, closing his eyes and shaking himself out. When he opened them again, he began to circle along the length of the ropes. "Would you believe me if I told you the lighting's better over here?"

Wren had the book open again, his brow furrowed as he scanned the pages. "Stalling must be against some kind of rule. Fights would take a very long time if that was permitted."

"I'm starting to think he's flirting. Which is definitely

allowed." Curtis purred the last bit to rile Reed. Give him a last burst of energy to finish with a kick to some tender part of his anatomy. Any longer and it'd be too much. They'd already gone much longer than their match with Jared and Noah. "Too bad I forgot to mention 'the usual'."

Jaw hardening, Reed squared his shoulders, bouncing against the ropes and rushing forward. He met Curtis with a few rapid jabs, gasping between each one. "You didn't forget. If you want me to bring it? I'll bring it. I can...I'm still strong. I can do this."

Letting his guard down just a fraction, slowing his reflexive duck a hair, Curtis made sure his boy could land two solid hits. One to his shoulder. And the other to his nose. Blood sprayed, and he laughed, shaking his head to decorate the canvas as he whooped and lifted Reed up in his arms in a fireman's carry.

"Ow." Blood dripped down his chin onto Reed's cheek. "You win."

Slapping his shoulder, Reed shook his head. "You can't *let* me win. I saw that. Sugar. Finish it. We're not following any of the rules and you know it."

"I am finishing it, my Toppy McTopperson. You're going to let me Dom you into winning and let *me* win by showing you that you didn't break me." Lifting one brow, Curtis stared Reed down. "I'm learning to compromise. Humor me."

Reed's lips curved into a hesitant smile as he slowly nodded. "Okay, fair. And...you're really okay? Aside from the nose?" He tugged his bottom lip between his teeth. "I wouldn't beat you for real, I know that. But I didn't do too bad and it felt...really good."

Kissing the tip of Reed's nose, Curtis breathed a laugh with his, "Mhm. It did." He carried Reed to the ropes, stepping over them onto the stairs. "And there will be a time again soon when you can hold your own against me. I recall several times when the outcome wasn't certain. You did good, my boy. I'm fucking proud and feel higher than Avery in his silks."

"That was fun. Can I kick your butt tomorrow, sir?" Avery munched on some real popcorn, flicking a few kernels onto Reed's chest from above. "My Dom would beat me if I lost. But I promise not to mess you up too bad."

Shaking his head, Wren came to Curtis' side and pressed a fresh towel to his nose. "I will not clear him for a fight until this heals. And you are not cleared until your back is no longer tender. You will need to wait to schedule another fight." He tilted his head to one side. "That is one I'd like to watch as well. You have some advantage with your moves, but the outcome, I believe, would not be at all what you would expect. Thankfully, you don't mind it too much when Rhodey beats you."

"Yeah, I do. Even though it doesn't really hurt. I don't like disappointing him." Avery slid the rest of the way down his unraveled silks to land lightly at Wren's feet. He held out the paper tub. "Popcorn?"

Wren shook his head. "No, thank you. I do not like eating crunchy air."

Over by the other side of the ring, Shea chuckled and nudged Danny, who had his face covered with his hood. "You can look now. And I owe you a hundred bucks. Under protest. Curtis had that."

"Yes, sir, but there were no conditions to *how* either of them won." Danny lifted his hoodie and grinned up at his Dom. "Besides, Reed's been training a lot. You and Jacks used to bet on him all the time, you told me so."

"I always knew you were a smart man." Setting Reed on his feet, Curtis took the blood-soaked towel from Wren. "Wow. That was a good hit." He tipped his head back, trying to stem the flow. "Nice. I haven't had a gusher like this in a while. Get me the styptic pencil, Freaky Friday."

Reed scuffed his bare foot against the wood floor. "I was expecting you to block, so I didn't hold back."

Walking at a quick pace, Wren headed for the clinic,

glancing back at them over his shoulder. "I don't believe you are supposed to hold back. There is absolutely nothing about that in the manual. And the blood isn't nearly as terrible as the popcorn. It certainly smells better."

Snickering, Curtis held the towel to his nose. "If he'd held back I would've beaten *his* ass. Seriously, Reed. I am fine. I've had a thousand nosebleeds, and there's no reason to worry. If I need to order you back into the ring with Shea to give him one, I'll be seriously put out."

"Hmm…" Reed breathed out a laugh and leaned against Curtis' side when Shea arched a brow at him. "No, I'm good, sir. I've got a rush and I don't mind a bit of blood. It…really helps. Seeing you like this. I mean…still laughing and in one piece. Just a bit messy, but I'm good with that, too."

Curtis swiped the blood droplets from Reed's cheek, noting the red blotch from his hit. "You're going to have a pretty trophy of your own, sparkles. I'd say I was sorry, but I'll enjoy the reminder of tonight. This was everything."

"It really was. And I love those kinds of trophies." Reed gazed up at him, a brilliant smile on his lips. "I love you. Thank you for not treating me like I'm fragile either. I needed that."

"I love you, too. And any time. I mean it." Catching Reed's fingers, Curtis lifted his hand to kiss the tip of each one. "Shea, can we use your spare room tonight?"

Nodding, Shea lifted Danny into his arms and came over to stand with them as Wren returned with the styptic pencil, several packages of gauze, and a few ice packs. Shea smiled at Curtis. "Sure, we wouldn't mind the company. As long as you don't mind the sound of the sewing machine. Jacks has a new design he's working on, so he'll probably be at it for a while."

"It's not that loud, though, sir." Danny spoke quickly, as though afraid Curtis might change his mind about staying over. "And it's a cheat day, so Keiran made all kinds of treats. If you're there, I won't have to feel bad about not finishing them all. And we can watch a movie and chase my ball and snuggle."

"What do you think, my boy? Perfect end to a perfect fight night?" Curtis tipped his head back, letting Wren poke at him with the pencil and fuss with the gauze.

Reed slipped his hand into Curtis', smiling up at him. "I'd like that. Very much. I'll go get those light up balls Noah got. Pretty sure Jacks'll have something for me to change into for the night. All I'll be missing is a few plushies, but I can steal a few of his throw pillows and you're a pretty good teddy bear to snuggle with. If that's not enough, we can always steal Danny."

"And leave me in that big bed by myself? I don't think so." Shea brushed his nose against Danny's cheek. "You want to cuddle during the movie, that's fine. But I'm keeping this one to myself for a bit."

Feeling a bit selfish himself, Curtis smiled into Reed's hair. "I'm not quite big enough to be considered a bear, but if you ask nicely I bet Jacks'll make a satin teddy for me to wear. We can pretend." He snickered. "As for Jacks? Have you ever considered that the next time he needs to take out a bunch of stitches, you can call him Jacks the Seam Ripper?"

"First of all, no satin teddies tonight, please, sir." Reed hugged Curtis' hand to his chest. "I want to fall asleep to the image of my badass Dom, just like this. If it pleases you." He tipped his head back. "And you gotta tell Jacks that one. I think he'd get a kick out of it."

Close to Curtis' other side, Wren laughed quietly. "'The Seam Ripper'. That was a very good one, sir. You can be very clever."

Gobsmacked, Curtis stared wide-eyed at Wren. "Yeah? You liked that? I need to buy a lottery ticket. I'm on fire today."

"Jack the Ripper was a notorious serial killer. I find everything about him terrible, but fascinating. I never considered he could be used for a good joke. Taking apart teddy bears with a sharp implement is very much like murder." Wren appeared to be picturing it, a small smile curving his lips until he glanced at Danny's shocked expression. "I am certain your Dom would not do it in front of you, don't worry."

Danny took a deep breath and tucked his face against Shea's neck. "We're watching a happy movie. I don't want nightmares about dead teddy bears. Those poor things."

A bark of laughter escaped Curtis' lips. "My cousin is a cereal killer. He kills at least a box a day."

"I know. He keeps sneaking into my stash, the little brat." Reed's tone said he didn't really mind. He reached out to take Wren's hand. "If you don't mind watching a movie where nobody dies, you should come with. Seems like Noah and Jared are busy with stuff, and Jamie's with Connor. You can hang out until someone comes looking for you."

Head tilted to one side, Wren let out a thoughtful sound. "I don't know that I'll be interested in the movie, but I would like to play with my puppy. Thank you, I accept your invitation."

"To my place." Shea huffed, then motioned for them to follow. "And with *my* puppy. My sub. Ugh, you know what I mean. But yeah, you can join us. Danny made sure to keep some of the stuff you like around for when you visit, so you won't have to suffer evil popcorn."

Curtis glanced around for Avery, intending on stealing some of the stuff from the sub's seemingly bottomless tub, but Rhodey's boy had already silently disappeared back to whatever dark place he'd chosen to hole up in for the evening. "Make sure to text Noah to let him know. We can stop by your loft and grab what you need, Wren, and let Jared know where you'll be."

When Wren opened his mouth, Reed held up his hand. "No phone. I don't got mine either, it escaped again. Shea, can we borrow yours?"

"I've got you." Shea palmed his phone, tapping at the screen, his lips twitching. "'Hey, Noah. Keeping your sub for a bit. Have fun guessing which one. Catch you later.'"

Curtis cringed, mentally counting the seconds and waiting to hear the roof door. No, scratch that. In Noah's present mood, Shea would never hear or see him coming. "Uh. You might want to put on your, 'Just kidding, I'm harmless,' face. Our man is walking the edge tonight."

"Sir, that was *not* funny." Danny glanced at the screen and poked Shea in the chest. "Tell them you didn't send it. Please. And…maybe I should write the message. I really don't want Noah to snap you into little pieces tonight."

"Just tonight?" Shea chuckled, then kissed the tip of Danny's nose. "All right, all right, I'll send a nice, civilized message. How about 'If you ever want to see your boy again, transfer—'"

Danny snatched at the phone, but didn't get it before Curtis did.

Unfortunately, in the grapple, his thumb hit the SEND button. It was like watching a slow-mo of his own death. Heart pounding, he quickly fired off another message, reading out loud. "It's Curtis. Bad joke. Abort."

Several, very long, seconds passed before the text came back.

Tell Shea he doesn't get another pass. Is Wren with you?

Keeping Shea's phone, Curtis tucked it away with a dirty look at the man. He took out his own to answer.

Yes. About to watch movies and have a sleepover with me and Reed at Shacks'. I'll let Jared know when we go grab Wren's things from your loft.

This reply came faster.

Thank you. It will be good for him. Tell him I love him and I'll see him in the morning.

Knowing a response wasn't strictly necessary, Curtis sent one anyway.

You got it.

Sighing in relief, Curtis put away his phone. It looked like the feathered fuckers were in the mood to grant a few miracles tonight, and they were going to have a good rest of the evening.

Movies, popcorn, and a warm bed to sleep in.

What could possibly go wrong?

Chapter Thirty-One

PRESENT

A night with his boy, within a cozy loft where real drama rarely lived, sounded like the best one Curtis had hoped for in a long, long time. Perhaps nothing terribly dramatic seemed to come Danny and Shacks' way very often because the sub cast a smoke screen with his catastrophizing that blocked upstairs from seeing exactly how vulnerable and ripe for the picking those three really were.

Letting out a long breath, he headed toward the back of the gym. "Yeah. Let's all just...not poke the bear, okay?" Handing Shea back his phone, he shook his head, realizing again how close they'd come to true disaster with Shea's unintended text message. "Seriously. Do me a solid on this one. Just leave your need for speed at the door where Noah's concerned in the future, okay?"

Regret filled Shea's eyes as he nodded. "Sorry about that. Things have been tense and seeing you and Reed in the ring, having things feel a bit more...like *our* normal? It got me wanting to mess around. I wouldn't have sent it, I'm not a complete idiot. Just a partial one sometimes." He gave Curtis a grateful look. "Thanks for having my back, there."

"Sorry for accidentally sending it." One arm around Reed

and the other around Wren, Curtis ushered them toward the elevator. "Let's take the easy way up. My bruises are starting to complain. Besides, I want to make sure the repairs to this baby are all good."

Pulling up his hood, Danny sucked in a sharp breath. "Shouldn't we test it *before* we ride it? What if it goes down and crushes us all and catches on fire? It always makes weird noises."

Tucking himself a bit closer to Curtis, Reed nodded. "Yeah, because it's haunted. But we can get some salt. Hold the door, I'll go grab some."

Wren stepped up to the elevator door, peering at the ceiling. "If such a thing were possible, the ghost would be extremely bored in there. And there is nothing to ignite. Unless one of us spontaneously combusts, but the chances of that are very low. It seems very safe. Being killed by appliances in your own home is much more likely."

"Also, the elevator isn't an original part of the building, and neither is the gym. So, the ghosts don't know it's here." Curtis tipped his head to one side, listening to the cables squeak as the elevator came down from the top floor. "Probably needs more oil in the colder months. Or a different weight oil. I'll have to call the manufacturer tomorrow."

Brow furrowing, Reed followed his gaze, then glanced back toward the gym. "I never thought of that. That actually...makes me feel a lot better, sir. Thanks. So we only have to worry about the ghost in the stairwell. And Bram, pretending to be a ghost."

"Seems like." The elevator door slid open, chilly air rushing out from its lack of use. "Come on. We'll drop you off on your floor and go up to Noah's and Jared's. Meet you back at your place, Shea."

"Sounds good." Shea stepped onto the elevator, rubbing Danny's back. "You know neither me or Curtis would take you on this thing if it was dangerous. How about you think about which movie we're gonna watch? No deaths and no explosions. And when it's done, you get to play a bit. Like Curtis said, perfect end to the night."

Danny nodded, relaxing in his Dom's arms. "I'd like that. And I'll try not to be scared of the elevator anymore. It's really good that you put it in, sir." He smiled at Curtis. "Jacks likes using it when he's got big loads of fabric."

The door slid shut, Curtis reaching out to chuck Danny under his chin with one finger. "Your Dom's right. I wouldn't harm a hair on your head. Speaking of human teddy bears. You're like The Asylum mascot. We might have to start worrying about other clubs stealing you."

Huffing, Reed shook his head. "They'd have to go through all of us. Good luck with that. Since we're keeping things PG, I won't go into details. But no one messes with what's ours. Or…who's…you know."

"Word." Gravity tugged, doing its work to make Curtis' feet feel heavy against the floor as the elevator rose, then lurched to a halt at Chez Shacks. "Your stop, my boy."

"See you soon, sir." Leaning forward in Shea's arms, Danny kissed Curtis' cheek. "We have some of the beer you like. Can we toast Reed's win? I wouldn't have bet against you, usually, but I had a feeling and I had to go with it. That's how my Doms always place their bets."

"I think there's something in the rule book about it being mandatory to toast when one fighter takes the locker number of another top tier fighter." Curtis booped Danny's nose. "You were wise to place your money on the winner. No hard feelings."

Not speaking until the door closed behind Shea and Danny, Reed gave Curtis a long look. He ran his tongue over his teeth, then shook his head. "Sir, I'm not taking your locker. None of that was official and… Damn it, please don't call me Toppy again. We both know how things are here. You need to hold on to your status."

"It's okay. I'll win it back from you before we open tomorrow." Curtis winked at Reed. "Let the boy have his fun, mo ghrá. We know what we're doing."

Reed blew out a breath and nodded. "All right, I just don't want this causing any more issues. And as much as I like winning…" He ducked his head. "Even though it used to be close sometimes, I kinda liked knowing you could take me down. It makes me feel like…I can be strong, but it's okay to not always be the strongest one in the room."

Tipping his boy's chin up with two fingers, Curtis met his gaze. "I've got you. Always. Trust me?"

"I do, sir." Hand braced against the wall when the elevator jolted to a stop, Reed glanced over, as though to check on Wren, and snickered. The other sub was reading over the fight manual, not seeming to have noticed a thing. "You're gonna have that whole thing memorized before you ref again, aren't you."

Humming his agreement, Wren stepped onto the landing as the door opened, nose still in the book. "It would be good if I can serve my position to the highest standards. It is not a very long book, so it shouldn't be that difficult. Then I will request some time with you, sir. If I may." He lifted his gaze to Curtis'. "To learn all the secret Asylum rules."

"The secret…" Curtis caught the laughter in his eyes from his reflection in the loft's entryway mirror. Entering Noah and Jared's space always felt like a second homecoming of sorts. Now that many of Jamie's fluffier things had made their way to his and Connor's place, the masculine vibe made it even more so. "I see. Yes." He cleared his throat, not wanting to offend Wren. "Well, you do know that we'll need a 'quiet room' for that."

Wren inclined his head as though that made perfect sense. He gave the sofa a wide berth, likely because L.D. was sprawled out on it, eyeing them all, and slipped into the main bedroom. Then his office. "We could arrange some time in here, it is very quiet." Coming out, he frowned, heading to Noah's art room next. "I believe Jared must have decided to go to the clinic with Quint. Some of the special patients need more care than others. Maybe I should stay here and wait for him."

Shaking his head, Curtis frowned at the cat as it stood with a languid stretch. "No... I went and came back with Quint. Jared wasn't there." He snapped his fingers. "He's probably on the roof or in the bar keeping Rhodey or Noah company." Taking out his phone, he texted Rhodey and Noah. "I'll just ask them which. Your Dom doesn't like text messages much."

Reed went around behind the sofa, reaching over to pet L.D. Jumped back before the cat could swipe at him. "I don't think he's with Rhodey, they're...I don't think I've ever seen them like this. The rest of us butting heads sometimes is one thing, but with them it's like watching someone rig explosives. And not having anywhere to run."

Deleting the text, Curtis nodded, opening the tracker app on his phone instead. He brought up the list to isolate Jared's dot from the rest, then went back to the map. Frowning at it, he searched for the red blinking indicator to show him where in Carmen Sandiego Jared might be.

"Fun game, but...is it broken?" He held up the phone to Wren. "I can't find Waldo."

Expression troubled, Wren shook his head. "No, it's a simple program. The only way it wouldn't show where he is, is if he went somewhere that blocked the transmission. Or his tracker is damaged beyond repair." He gave a firm nod and strode to the door, grabbing his jacket. "We should go find him. I will go speak to Noah. Can you please see if any of the vehicles are missing?"

"Whoa there, Freaky Friday." Curtis snagged the back of Wren's jacket before he could walk out the door. "Noah's not in any mental condition to be freaked out over Jared going AWOL. Let's take door number two and ask Rhodey."

Chewing on his bottom lip, Wren turned and gazed up at Curtis. "But if they're angry with one another...? What if that's why Jared left? What if Rhodey won't help? What if...? No, I can not start thinking of worst case scenarios. My Dom is strong and smart. We will find him."

"Yes, we will." Rhodey spoke even as he opened the door, scanning the living room as though looking for anything out of place. He brushed his hand over Wren's hair as he passed. "You're not leaving the building, Misha. Head to the security room and go over the footage. Avery's already there. Reed, go with him." He turned to Curtis. "Come with me, we'll see if he decided to get clever about slipping out without Noah or River catching him. He knows their rounds. River's good, but he's not as familiar with this place as Noah is. I have a feeling Jared might've taken advantage of that."

"And gone where, in this weather? To catch the ballet?" Grabbing one of Noah's spare jackets, even though it was a bit large, Curtis realized he'd taken his phone with him but hadn't put his clothes back on when he'd left the gym. He swore softly. "I'm underdressed for the show. Gimme a sec."

Rhodey inclined his head, holding the door open for Wren and Reed to pass. He glanced over at Wren when he spun around, giving him a soft smile of understanding. "Go ahead, my boy. But don't let this mess with you too much. I love that bastard, even when he's being a pig-headed fool. I won't let anything happen to him."

Throat working, Wren nodded, then hurried to the bedroom. He knelt in front of the nightstand, pulling open the drawer with quiet reverence and taking out Jared's old glasses.

With a soft sigh of resignation, Curtis went to Noah's dresser and took out some clothes and socks for himself, dressing without comment other than to gather Wren to his chest for a hug. More for himself than for the boy, since the sub hated the things, but dammit there should be more cuddles around the place. "I love you, my boy. We've got this. I bet Rhodey knows where he went, and I'm starting to think I do, too."

"I love you, too, sir." Wren held the glasses carefully against his chest, not pulling away, speaking barely above a whisper. "He's not here. If he didn't want us to see him leave…there's no way to know when he'll be back. Or…if."

Imagining any circumstance under which Jared wouldn't return to his men was difficult, so Curtis had every faith he'd do what was in his power to come home. Either way, one thing was certain. There were people here who would do what *they* had to in order to make sure he did.

"He'll be back. He's our very own Asylum T2-1000. Right?" He probably had the Terminator model number completely wrong, but that didn't matter. Much. Even though Tay would remind him it very much did. "We won't let him get melted down."

Despite his nod, Wren didn't look convinced. Something about the situation was troubling him. "I don't think he intended for us to have that option, sir. But I will…I have my orders. Please be careful out there. The cold is powerful, and beautiful, but can do irreparable damage if you're unprepared."

Reaching past Wren, Curtis opened Noah's top nightstand drawer to take his gun and tucked it in the back of his jeans. Wearing the man's clothes and his firearm were an odd sensation, like those first days at Tracey's, when there hadn't been any other options. Of course, they'd both been less bulky then, but all the same, having the scent of the man wrapped around him was a reminder of why he fought so fucking hard for this place, and could make the promise to bring back the man both Noah and Wren loved.

"I'm prepared. Remember. Step carefully around Noah right now. Don't go up to the roof to see him." Smoothing Wren's hair from his forehead, Curtis winked. "No bear baiting until I get back. I don't want to miss the fun."

Wren smiled a bit at that, rising up on his tiptoes to kiss Curtis' cheek. "I know how to walk in the darkness with him, sir. But for now...I want to spare him the pain. For as long as possible. He doesn't need any more. The snow will numb what he's already feeling and...and he will be with us again. He will focus on holding our home together."

Nodding his agreement, Curtis knelt to adjust his heel when his foot didn't entirely sit right in Noah's spare boots. "Huh. If my feet are bigger than his, I wonder if my other parts are too?" Keeping it light, because if he started to blubber they weren't going to get anywhere fast, he stood and grimaced at the pinch. "This is going to be a fun training exercise." He made the comment as he re-entered the living area with Wren and shouldered on Noah's coat. "Ready as I'll ever be."

At the door with Rhodey, Reed reached out to take Wren's hand, his expression completely closed off, the way it often was when things got serious. His tone was rough when he glanced at Curtis. "Check in when you can, sir? I'll keep an eye on things here. I won't say anything to Lawson yet so he can focus on Matt. We should probably let Seth know, though. So we can tighten security...just in case."

"Let Rhodey worry about that. And...I know you and Matt will find your way, right?" Cupping Reed's cheeks, Curtis searched his boy's gaze before dipping in for a sweetly lingering kiss. He drew back with his, "You are my heart. Keep it safe. I love you."

"I love you, too, sir." Reed slid him a reassuring smile before continuing out with Wren. "And don't worry about me. I'll be fine."

Rhodey grunted, closing the door behind himself and Curtis, nodding to chatter only he could hear. He plucked something out of his pocket and handed it to Curtis. "My men have already taken their positions. Put this in so we'll be able to communicate with them without wasting any more fucking time. Seth's already been alerted."

Taking the ear piece from Rhodey's palm, he inserted it. The Asylum came to life in another dimension as conversation between Keiran and Avery buzzed in his ear. "What are you thinking?" His boots became silent on the stairs down to the bar as Vani's training kicked in and his mind went into merc tactical mode. "What's the plan?"

"I'm thinking our man doesn't like problems he can't solve. So he went for the one goddamn solution I told him not to." Rhodey's jaw ticked as he strode down the steps, his boots striking each one like a violent drum beat. "This is the one time I really hope I'm wrong, because I can't do a fucking thing about it without destroying every bit of protection I've managed for this place. For...for you. Jared's boy. Your cousin. Not without some careful planning."

Curtis pushed into the bar, half afraid to utter his next question. "Do we need to clear everyone out to a safehouse before we go do this thing?"

Shaking his head, Rhodey cut across the bar and shoved the front door open. "No, this is the safest place. Besides, an attack won't come here. We're not dealing with anything that messy. It'll be strategic. And if we're not careful, we'll never see the impact until it's too fucking late."

"I—" Cutting himself off as Dallas' voice rumbled in his ear, Curtis paused in the swirl of snow in the parking lot, the rest of the world beyond the gates cloaked in the city's version of darkness.

"We have foot traffic outside the gate." Though Dallas could be heard, Curtis couldn't pinpoint his location. "Avery—"

"I'm on him."

For a moment, Curtis' heart leapt. It was Jared. Come to his senses and come home. Maybe he'd been visiting Jamie and his tracker had failed? It wasn't like the things were foolproof, especially with the amount of wear and tear the Core put their bodies through. He gave Rhodey a hopeful look, but the man wasn't focused on him.

Drawing out his gun, Rhodey aimed it at a spot in the shadows of the gate, where the security lights didn't quite reach. He spoke as someone landed soundless, not big enough to be Jared—not that the man had a habit of jumping over fences. "Put it away, boy. I don't have to kill you to make you regret showing up like this."

"No, but why make more work for the doctors you have left?" Ezran let out a cold, bitter laugh. "Take it. I don't give a fuck. I'm sure it'll make you all more comfortable if you can see me as weak and pathetic."

Ezran's tone was so familiar, it was impossible not to hear Noah in it. Something about his aspect, his stance, had all of those sharp edges but without the honed quality that usually loaned the man confidence and power. This was pure hurt and bravado lurking under layers and layers of pain Curtis recognized as having been within himself not so long ago.

"Ez." Putting his own gun away, Curtis approached the boy with his arms open. "Where's Jared?"

Eyeing him suspiciously, Ezran held out the glock, barrel wrapped in his hand and handle within Curtis' reach. He audibly ground his teeth. "He's visiting Maddox. They had some catching up to do. Under the condition that I come back here."

Dammit, Jared.

He asked the next question—one he really didn't and did want the answer to. "For how long?"

"I don't know." Ezran shoved the gun at him. "Fucking take it. And I have other weapons on me, so you should take them all before you let me into your castle. Don't insult me by pretending I'm not a threat."

Taking the gun, Curtis handed it back to Rhodey before he patted Ezran down. Sarcasm wouldn't work here, and neither would a hug. As much as he ached to give the boy one, there was too much space and time between the last one and now for him to take those kinds of liberties. Too much he didn't know or understand. He handed each knife, throwing star, and another smaller firearm to Rhodey with an impressed sound.

"What'd I miss?"

That, at least, got a barely contained smile tugging at Ezran's lips. "There's a switchblade in my boot. But not bad."

"Thanks." Standing, Curtis took a chance. "Have a beer with me?"

Ezran glanced at Rhodey, then nodded slowly. "Yeah, I can do that. But you can take the place off high alert. No one's coming to get you."

"No, I didn't think they were." Rhodey jutted his chin toward the front door. "Get him inside. But don't let him out of your fucking sight."

Not highly likely. Curtis couldn't get his fill of looking at the kid he thought of like a son. Ezran was home, and if there was anything he could do to manage it, Ezran was there to stay. Glancing back at the gates on his way inside, he tried not to think too hard just yet on what they'd lost to achieve it, but the prayer he sent to the fuckers upstairs was more of a warning.

Don't get too comfortable...
We're coming for our man.

Chapter Thirty-Two

PRESENT

The luxury in The Asylum appealed to Sin on so many levels. Not something he'd ever have considered indulging in during his time in the military, or for a long time after. His needs were simple, but the ones he had as a Dom were what got him looking into the place, then jumping on the chance to work here to cover a membership he couldn't have afforded otherwise.

Elegant bar fixtures and a well stocked dungeon weren't why he'd stayed a member for so long, though. Hell, not even just the kink. Sure, he enjoyed every bit of it, but the community created here, fucked up as it could be, was something he'd always wanted to be part of, if only on the fringes.

Something he'd wanted for his little brother, no matter how awkward accepting he was a grown man with similar—albeit opposite—needs. Bringing Tay to the Club meant he could have them met somewhere safe. Where Sin would never be too far.

Looking down at Garet, Sin suspected his family had started with the same intentions, then tried to go in a different direction when things started to get messy with the gang and…well, a fuckton Sin still didn't have a clue about. But like him with Tay, life could throw all kinds of curveballs. Sin couldn't be there for his brother every waking moment, and Garet's family couldn't shield him from the harsh realities of the world by sending him away from the hardcore one they lived in.

Every single person, at some point, had to figure out where home was.

He had a feeling, for Garet, this was it.

Head rested on the plush pillow, on a bed even nicer than the one he'd slept in at the hotel in Santa Fe—and fucking ten times more comfortable than his own—Sin did something he never thought he'd do with anyone. Sure, the times he and Garet had been together in the past, he'd woken up sometimes and looked at him for a bit, smiling at how sexy and rumpled he was before slipping out to head back to his own place. The one time he *hadn't* left, he'd been exhausted after a long shift in the club and only got a clue that shit had gone sideways after he found out Ezran had walked in to see them together.

Even then, he hadn't fully grasped the impact, but he'd dealt with his share of guilt since. There was still a lot of work to do to fix things with the other young man, because Sin couldn't imagine Garet not wanting him in his life.

But if nothing else, The Asylum was the perfect place to figure that out. And he'd meant it when he'd told Reed he would.

Sin lightly brushed his fingers over Garet's hair, admiring the hints of gold in the soft strands. Maybe he was a fool, but having his boy—and no, he wouldn't slow down in that regard, he'd spent long enough holding Garet at arm's length —here with him, like this? All he could think of was how he'd give him everything he could ever want. Ever need.

And if it wasn't in his power?

I'll get fucking creative.

Rolling to his side away from Sin, still asleep, Garet huddled in on himself. The covers fell away, revealing the sliver of pale skin playing peek-a-boo between his shirt hem and pajama pants. It was apparent the boy wasn't used to seeking comfort, but the way he drew up his knees said he very much craved it.

Arm sliding around a slender waist, Sin drew his boy in, nuzzling his neck and breathing him in. He huffed out a laugh, catching the scent of unwashed hair, sweat, and the familiar, unique scent of clothes from second-hand stores and church sales before they'd been thoroughly washed. Not to be mean, but…

"Nope." Sin sat up, giving Garet's ass a light slap. He took care of his subs, even the temporary ones, and *especially* the one he'd now claimed. That 'care' might sometimes look like something closer to what a drill sergeant would enjoy, but he didn't want Garet getting *too* used to a soft Dom when he was with a sadist. Poor thing wouldn't know what hit him.

Which could be fun, too, but we'll wait until he's not fucking half traumatized before we get to the good stuff.

Throwing his legs over the side of the bed, Sin stood, then leaned down to lift Garet into his arms. "Come, my boy. You'll sleep a lot better if you're clean. I've been a bad *bad* Dom, letting you in bed like this. Let's fix that."

Garet shook his head, making an aggrieved sound Sin's shoulder muffled. "Good here. Sleep now." Apparently, his sub had a mind of his own when semi-unconscious. "Love you. Night."

Making a sympathetic sound, Sin kissed his boy's temple as he carried him into the bathroom. "You're precious. I love you, too. But you can't stay here, you're about to get very slippery." He sat Garet on the counter by the sink, steadying him with one arm as he peeled off his shirt. Tossing it over his shoulder, he kept his tone cheerful. "Now, the question is, can you wake up enough to make one last decision before I make it for you?"

Cracking open blue eyes, Garet squinted at him. "Why am I a toothbrush?"

"Focus, my boy." Sin grinned as he touched his forehead to Garet's. Sleepy subs were fun to fuck with. He'd have to do this more often. "Hot or cold?"

Humming a little of that Katy Perry song, Garet nodded. "Hot please. Are we going to have beach umbrellas? Sand gets in weird places." He cracked a giant yawn, sagging back against the mirror. "You're cute. I like cute."

Sin lifted his brow. He hadn't expected Garet to respond this way, but the boy still wasn't used to his style. And there was only one way to fix that. "Hmm, that might've been a mistake. A good Dom doesn't leave such important decisions to their sub. But don't worry, I'll take good care of you." He lifted Garet up again, stepped into the shower, and turned the faucet.

On cold.

Garet grew heavy in his arms right before the water hit him, saying he'd fallen completely back to sleep. The spray hit his clothes, soaking them, and plastering his hair to his face. His mouth opened with his gasp, his entire body growing rigid. "Fuck! What the fuck!" He twisted nearly out of Sin's arms. "Cold!"

Standing his boy in front of him under the spray, Sin nodded, very seriously. "It is. Very cold water. One of my favorite things about winter, it's got such a nice bite to it." He leaned down to kiss Garet's trembling lips. "There, does that help?"

Arms around himself, Garet made a valiant attempt to tip his head to one side and gave Sin his best version of a considering 'Elsa'. "M-m-m-maybe? Try a-g-gain."

Sin clucked his tongue, spinning Garet away from him and gripping the back of his neck to hold him steady. The wet smack on his ass made an incredible sound, the sting on impact spreading over his palm. He followed it with two more.

Body heat and all that. "My subs don't tell me what to do. Just in case you've forgotten. Now, where were we?" He shoved Garet's sopping wet pajama pants down, admiring the bright red of his handprints. "Warming you up, right? That looks nice and hot."

Dancing from foot to foot, Garet rubbed briefly at his ass. "Sorry...yes, s-sir." He looked over his shoulder at Sin, hair darkened by dampness, a different kind of warmth in his gaze. It was probably close to impossible for him to get hard in this chill, but his dick had stopped trying to climb up inside his pelvis like a living Greek statue with those tiny little pricks. "And, ow."

"Mhm. I love spankings in the shower. The marks are so pretty and always have a perfect sting to them." Sin slapped Garet's ass again, rubbing his hand over the mark so the heat would linger. "It's also better than coffee for getting you wide awake. I'm pretty sure there's been studies on it. Stand up straight now so I can wash you. My boy should smell as sweet as he is."

Hissing air between his teeth, Garet wrapped his arms around his torso and ratcheted himself up so he stood under the deluge. The shower made a waterfall of his eyes and lips, both of which were screwed shut. He briefly unwound the latter to speak. "Gotta be clean by now."

"You're wet, not clean. Didn't any of your pseudo daddies teach you how to scrub up properly?" Sin selected a bottle of shampoo with a very happy looking strawberry on it. He popped the top and sniffed. "Not what I would have grabbed for myself, but..." His lips curved as he kissed the hollow behind Garet's ear. "Do you know how much it will fuck with everyone to have you smelling like Reed? Is it evil that I'll enjoy that very much?"

Garet's huff of laughter shook his shoulders. "I had a crush on Curtis at one point when I was like six months into being here." As he spoke, he relaxed, legs widening and arms unfolding to his sides. "I spent about a month stealing Reed's clothes and toiletries, imitating him, until the guy told me people would like me better for myself. It was sweet."

"I'm glad he did, because I like you very much for you. So it was good advice." After pouring some of the shimmy pink shampoo into his palm, Sin worked up some suds between his hands, then brought them to Garet's hair, massaging it in and rubbing his fingers in circular motions against his scalp. "We'll discuss you playing with other Doms at some point, I wouldn't want to be *too* greedy. But we'll get them all worked up first. Let them see what a sexy little thing you grew up to be. I imagine there will be some interesting mixed feelings for a while."

For a moment, it looked like Garet's self-doubt would tip him over into saying something that would impugn Sin's taste, but something shifted and he stood a little taller, preening at Sin's praise. "That will be fun, sir. I like them seeing your property and knowing they can't touch unless you say."

"Good boy." Sin rewarded him by deepening the massage, rinsing his hair, then doing it all over again. He even turned the hot water on, just enough to make the temperature a bit more pleasant. "Things will be challenging for a bit, but we'll find the fun in every day anyway. Because I say so."

"Because you say so." Garet repeated Sin's words, making them sound more like a mantra, then mouthed them again to himself. He was such a natural submissive, his need to please and to understand what was wanted of him showing a promise that would have many Doms wishing they'd snapped him up first. "Feels so nice. Thank you, sir."

Sin smiled softly, kissing the side of Garet's neck. "It's my absolute pleasure, my boy. Though I might end up developing a sweet tooth if this keeps up." He breathed in, the aroma of the strawberry shampoo in the building steam strangely alluring. Even more so now that it was all over Garet. "I plan to add feeding you to my routine. My boys might suffer for my pleasure, but they...*you*, will always be taken care of." He shook his head as he rinsed Garet's hair again, then grabbed the bodywash. The bottle was sparkling. This could get interesting. "Like I mentioned, we do have some things to discuss. Namely me *not* having a revolving stable of subs, because I'm not interested in anything that shallow anymore. But when I slip up, know it's out of habit, not desire."

Reaching out, Garet lightly raked his fingernails down Sin's pecs, bringing to life the soap that had gotten caught there. Damp lashes lifted, his boy's attention riveted to his face. "Is it okay that I only want to make you happy? As long as you're enjoying watching someone use me, or hurting me, I want to give it all to you. Pleasure, my pain, obedience. I will take care of other boys for you if you want them, whether it's deep or shallow with them. I never felt like this before. Just like you're the sun and you're eating up all the darkness."

"It's okay, to a point." Sin smoothed the body wash over Garet's chest, the sensation of getting to know his body all over again making him linger on smooth flesh. Along the dip of his throat, then the curve of his collarbone, down the center of his chest where light, springy hairs were a faint trail down to his stomach. And lower. "If I think another Dom is worth sharing you with, I'd hope you'd want to please him, too. I really need you to hear me. I do not want anything shallow. I don't want it for you. And the other subs...you have your own bonds already. Cherish them. Not for me. Because they're worth holding on to."

Garet's ready nod began before Sin finished speaking. "Yes, sir. I do. I will. I meant anyone you owned or played with, but yes. I love Reed and Jamie, though they're like brothers, but Keiran and Dallas are...have been...more." Picking up a bar of rainbow striped soap that appeared to have a plastic smiling frog trapped inside, Garet ran it over Sin's chest, releasing the scent of grape bubble gum. "I want you to not worry that what we had before, and how we had it, is going to mess with me, because it doesn't. I trust you enough that I think about doing all the things I secretly wanted but that scared the crap out of me. Even making bacon. And...sexy things."

"Sexy bacon. Not sure how that'd work, but I'm down to try." Sin chuckled as he plucked the bar soap out of Garet's hand, replacing it with a good, old fashioned bar of Irish Spring. Probably Curtis, being all thoughtful. "Subs get to smell like candy and flowers. Big tough Doms smell like... whatever this smell is. Manly stuff."

"Manly stuff." Garet seemed to like repeating shit Sin said, like he was trying out his Dom's clothes for size. Clutching the soap, he began painting Sin's skin with the pungent smelling lather. "What's three things you've never done with a sub that you always wanted to try? You tell me yours and I'll tell you mine."

Sin arched a brow and lowered to his knees. In this position, he was aware of what his boy might be expecting, and stayed just like that long enough to reinforce the idea, even letting his breath skim over Garet so his growing length twitched. Then he lifted Garet's foot and bent his own knee to set it in the perfect place for a good scrub. "We do Q and A over coffee, my boy. New rule. In the shower, we get you nice and clean while I come up with random dirty things to talk about. New and old. Or more serious stuff if I feel like it." He leaned in to nip the tip of Garet's freshly washed big toe. "I don't want to discourage conversation, but I can tell you've developed some habits from group therapy and all that. I want you to have something more natural with me, okay?"

One hand on Sin's shoulder to steady himself, Garet nodded. His cheeks were pink all the way to his ears. "Yes, sir. No quizzing my Dom." He twitched his foot, nearly jerking his ankle out of Sin's slippery hold. "Eek. Tickles." Grip tightening on Sin's shoulder, he hopped up and down on the foot Sin didn't hold. "Mean Dom."

"Very. But you love it." Sin slapped Garet's thigh to warn him to keep still, then resumed washing the rest of his leg. Even with the touches being very practical, they were definitely drawing the interest of both his dick and Garet's. Not one to be ruled by anything other than whatever the fuck he felt like doing in the moment, he intentionally stretched out the very thorough cleaning. "It's a good thing we don't have trouble communicating. The list of things I can torture you with is going to get very long. Restraints and merciless tickling. We're definitely doing that one."

"Matt used to tickle me until I wet my pants. It was gross." Garet snickered. "But I always got the last laugh." Switching to his other foot, he wiggled his toes. "I mean, if you're into watersports, sir, I could go there. But that's on you. Literally."

Sin huffed out a laugh, meeting Garet's eyes as he pinched the tip of his dick. "No, it won't be on me, cheeky brat. If you want to pee on yourself, I'll just hose you down after." He pinched again, a bit harder. "What I like, I'll take from you. Unless it's a hard limit, but we'll discuss those before doing anything intense."

Top lip between his teeth, Garet nodded, his gaze on his dick and Sin's fingers. "Hurts good." His voice was breathy and even in the shower it was possible to see his dick drooled precome. "If I beg, will you let me give you my mouth to use, sir?"

"No." Sin tugged Garet a bit closer, using his dick as a handle. He gave it the same attention he had the rest of him, the soap nice and slippery as he stroked his boy's length, then his full balls. He continued to his taint, taking his time there. "Begging is fun when you can't help it, because I've got you bound and desperate. You're not that desperate yet. You're just trying to control where this goes. And I don't play that way." He pressed two soapy fingers against Garet's hole, swirling them to tease the sensitive nerves. "Your Dom is making you all clean. Say, 'Thank you, sir'."

Garet's response was thready with need. "Thank you, sir." His knees wobbled, his eyes fluttering closed as he sank toward Sin's fingers with a keening hum that seemed to say, *Yes. Right there. Just like that.*

"Stand up straight, my boy. We wouldn't want you to fall in the shower. I prefer the bruises on your body to be ones I had the pleasure of putting there." Sin let his fingers glide up between Garet's ass cheeks, then rubbed over each one. "I suppose, to make things easier for you, we should include lessons in shower time. Lesson one? Don't tell a sadist, with your mouth or with your body, what you really, *really* want, right now. You just make it so much more appealing to deny you for as long as possible."

Both hands on Sin's shoulders now, Garet held himself upright, but if he'd been any younger or less experienced he might've stomped his foot. That much was clear. The pout he was obviously unaware of gave him away. "How long is it possible for you to deny me, sir?"

"Probably an infinite amount of time, but we can test it if you'd like? I'm all about giving subs *some* choices." Sin withdrew his hands and rose to his feet. He tipped Garet's chin up with his knuckles. "I won't use spankings to punish you, I enjoy them too much. I will warn you with a smack if you're toeing the line. You will learn to tell the difference." He brushed his lips over his sub's. "If you force me to make denial a punishment, instead of something I do for my pleasure? I will not be pleased."

Blinking up at him, Garet hung onto his every word, not looking away for a second. It was as if Sin were his textbook and he memorized him line by line. "Yes, sir. I don't know how to make sure that's the way it goes, but I'll do my best. I don't want to deny you pleasure."

"You make sure of it by never trying to force my hand. And if you know you've done something to piss me off, intentional or not, don't be cute about it." Sin shrugged, flicking off the shower and picking Garet up. He wrapped his boy's legs around his waist, grabbing a couple of towels on the way out of the bathroom to spread over the bed before dropping his sexy little bundle on top of them. "You know I'm pretty easy-going, so I don't see it being a huge issue. But some subs like to test their Doms. Don't be one of them."

The line of Garet's throat convulsed with his hard swallow. Lips parted, he didn't look away. "No, sir. I don't mean to.. You're too important. I—" He passed his tongue over his lips. "Did I do those things?"

Sin lowered to the bed over Garet, hands braced by his shoulders to keep his full weight off of his smaller form. He smiled as he kissed Garet's damp lips and shook his head. "Not quite, but I can tell the impulse is there in the tiny nudges and some of the things you say. I'd rather make sure you're aware of them now, before they become an issue. We'll both get to have a lot more fun." He kissed Garet again, whispering against his lips. "Wouldn't you rather let go and have me be fully in control? No guessing, no pushing for what you think you want. Just trusting me to get you where you need to be."

Garet's answering, slow nod, brushed his lips up and down over Sin's. It wasn't a taking, more like a leaning into what he'd been given in a way that showed he was conscious of where the line had been drawn. His breath was warm and sweet when he spoke. "Yes, sir. I want that, if it pleases you. It's hard to let go sometimes. But I want to. Especially with you."

"I'll help you with that, in every way possible. Make it hurt in good ways. And…bad." Sin sucked Garet's bottom lip into his mouth, biting down hard enough to draw a nice, sharp bit of pain, but no blood. He aligned their bodies, fisting both their dicks in one hand. "But only bad when you need it. To get out of your head. Or to be my good boy."

"Good boy…" Garet's repetition of Sin's words was

completely breathless, his hips jutting in an automatic movement so his dick notched against the head of Sin's in a way that made the heat undeniable. "I'll be that." Desire flared in his sub's gaze, a tiny nod saying he'd probably turn into a prince or a toad, he didn't care which. As long as Sin kept touching him like that. "Your hand is so fucking huge. When I look at it holding us both I want to look at it forever."

Rising up so his boy could enjoy the view even more, Sin thrust into the circle of his hand, the damp glide not slick enough to get a smooth motion going, but the friction made up for it. That and the reactions from Garet. Sin didn't want to rush, didn't want to spoil what they were building, by taking too much, too soon, but it was a heady feeling, knowing he could. Knowing he'd had this body under him before, enjoyed it in every way, but now…now he was sharing a whole different level of intimacy with his sub.

Mine. All fucking mine.

For the moment, anyway. Sin wouldn't focus on that until the situation changed, though. He was too wrapped up in how much more intense every touch, every kiss was, with all the meaning behind it. "Fuck, you're gorgeous. Not just your body. I never could get enough of it, but you… Move with me, my boy. I want to feel you give it all up. Everything you've ever held back. Give it to me now."

Undulating, slowly, then rhythmically, Garet's lithe form danced for him. The rapture in his gaze was as mesmerizing as it was open and giving. Lips parted, skin flushed from the exertion, he breathed Sin's name over and over. A mantra and a promise. Arms raised, he crossed his wrists and tipped back his head to expose his throat. The lines of his ribs expanded and contracted, each gasp morphed into moans, his body creating music from that one note, a symphony all for his Dom. All for Sin.

"Beautiful. One of these days, I'm going to mark you. Leave some stunning artwork on your skin, something that reflects everything you are." Sin's breathing came out in harsh rasps, and he leaned down to kiss Garet between each thrust. "But first, something a little less permanent. Come for me, my boy. Come with me. No more holding back."

Short, sharp cries tore from Garet's chest, his hips jerking almost as soon as Sin said the word, 'Come.' His boy's torso lengthened, ropes of muscles trembling with tension as his young, perfect body focused its energy on that one point, that one moment of bliss, and he gave over to Sin's command. Pulses of his release jerked his shaft in Sin's fist, the spill of milky come painting his chest, and slicking Sin's hand.

Gathering up a bit more, Sin used it to lube them both up, his fist moving faster as he joined his boy in climax, his vision spotting as the pressure burst from the base of his spine. The rapid motion overstimulated him as he continued past the deep throb of pleasure, likely almost painful to Garet at this point, but dragging out the sensations always gave Sin an intense rush. One he could cling to when his body demanded rest.

And also something that tended to make sweet little subs very tender and obedient if he decided to toy with them while they were still recovering. He couldn't fucking wait to see how Garet responded, since he'd never played with him quite this way.

All right, so my 'slow' is a bit fucked up.

He laughed as he released their dicks when he managed to draw a whimper, rolling to lie on his side next to Garet, trailing his fingers through the mess on his chest. "You really are a treat, you know that? I haven't had that much fun in… way too long."

Still panting, eyes glazed with lust and the drowsy afterglow of release, Garet rolled his head to gaze up at him adoringly. "Missed you. So much, Sin." Voice throaty, he licked his lips, looking every bit as sexy as his film with Dallas and Keiran, except with something more. The light in his eyes, the connection in them, was a tangible force. "I feel alive with you. Whole. Is that too much?"

Sin shook his head, laying his hand flat on Garet's chest. "Not at all. It means I'm doing my job as your Dom. Job isn't the right word, but it's a big part of what I need to do for you. Make sure you feel everything I give you, everything you give me, in a way that feels complete. So it's a true exchange. I won't settle for anything less. Ever again."

A new kind of awareness entered Garet's gaze, his lids fluttering with the moment of realization. "Me either. This is what it's about. I think. I want this. For both of us." Pushing up so he sat against the headboard, he hooked a finger to Sin's pinky. "I thought you were in the pool that night. I went in to find you. Then, at the bottom, it was so quiet. I knew I'd find you, but I was looking in all the wrong places."

"Yes, you were. But you won't have to look anymore." Sin lifted their connected pinkies to his lips, kissing the link between them. Such a small gesture, but to him, to Garet, the meaning behind it was clear. "You won't ever have to look for me again, Garet. No matter what else happens beyond our control? You'll always know where to find me. I promise."

And he meant every word, on a level he'd have to examine at some point, because this was something new. A soul deep need to protect what they were building. Even when it got hard, which it no doubt would. There were still too many challenges ahead of them to count. He wished he could smooth the way for his boy, but that was beyond his control.

Keeping his promises?

That was in his power. Regardless of who or what he had to fight, Garet would never have to wonder where he stood. If he'd ever be alone. Because Sin would be there, one way or another.

Even if only in these precious moments, painting memories like intricate designs drawn in ink. Permanent. Lasting.

A promise of forever. Starting right now.

*P*AST JUSTICE: PART 2, COMING VERY SOON!

This story is simply too big for one book. Rest assured, we'll give you plenty of spoilers and sneak peeks in our lively **Facebook** groups and **Discord** server!

*W*ant more time with the fellas of The Asylum Fight Club?

Turn the page to view the Asylum Fight Club Reading Order List, where you'll find links to over 20 books and counting!

Come hang out with readers just like you in The Asylum Fight Club Facebook Group at https://www.facebook.com/groups/asylumfightclub where you can also ask to join our Discord server!

We also post updates on our Web site at https://www.asylumfightclub.com, where you can sign up for our newsletter at https://www.subscribepage.com/j4m0q5 for free reads, contests, and more!

Keep turning the pages in *this* book to find links to Bianca and Tibby's backlists.

We've got you covered!

Asylum Fight Club Series Reading Order

Flawed Justice

Beyond Justice

Hard Justice

Cold Justice

Raw Justice

Dark Justice

Uneven Justice

Deserted Justice

Stolen Justice

Out of the Ring

Double the Heat Brewed

Love & Stitches at The Asylum (Book 1)

Love & Stitches at The Asylum (Book 2)

Love & Stitches at The Asylum (Book 3)

Love & Stitches at The Asylum (Book 4)

Broken Justice

Sub 101, Book One, Part One

Sub 101, Book One, Part Two

It Had to Be You

Past Justice: Part One

Past Justice: Part Two

About Bianca Sommerland

Tell you about me? Hmm, well, there's not much to say. I love hockey and cars and my kids...not in that order, of course! Lol! When I'm not writing—which isn't often—I'm usually watching a game or a car show while networking. Going out with my kids is my only downtime. I get to clear my head and forget everything.

As for when and why I first started writing, I guess I thought I'd get extra cookies if I was quiet for a while—that's how young I was. I used to bring my grandmother barely legible pages filled with tales of evil unicorns. She told me then that I would be a famous author.

I hope one day to prove her right.

For more of my work, please visit: www.Im-No-Angel.com

- facebook.com/BSommerland
- instagram.com/biancasommerland
- amazon.com/Bianca-Sommerland
- bookbub.com/authors/bianca-sommerland
- goodreads.com/Bianca_Sommerland
- youtube.com/biancasommerland

Also by Bianca Sommerland

Sign up for my Newsletter for monthly prizes and teasers

The Dartmouth Cobras

Blind Pass

Game Misconduct

Defensive Zone

Breakaway

Offside

Delayed Penalty

Iron Cross

Goal Line

Line Brawl

Overtime

Tag Up

Off Ice Collection

Butterfly Style

Cocky Shot

Neutral Zone Trap

Winter's Wrath Series

Backlash

Diminished

Inversion

Off Beat

New Rules Trilogy

Polished

Gilded

Damasked

Also

Deadly Captive

Collateral Damage

The End

Celestial Pets: Evil's Embrace

Forbidden Steps

Rosemary Entwined

The Trip

Untamed (Feral Bonds)

Solid Education

Street Smarts

Upper Class

About Tibby Armstrong

Librarian, tech geek, and professional cat herder by day, Tibby Armstrong becomes her author-cape wearing alter-ego by night.

A native of Connecticut with a love of armchairs and chocolate, she has always been an unashamed and avid Romance reader.

Tibby is a frequent traveler to London and has made it her life's mission to search out every pub with a fireplace, where she sips hot cocoa and plots to take over imaginary worlds.

For free reads and giveaways, news about new releases and events, connect with Tibby in her Facebook Group, Tibby Armstrong's Seekrit Clubhouse, and via her blog and newsletter at TibbyArmstrong.com.

- twitter.com/TibbyArmstrong
- instagram.com/tibbyarmstrong
- goodreads.com/Tibby_Armstrong
- amazon.com/author/tibbyarmstrong

Also by Tibby Armstrong

Be the first to hear about new releases and free reads. Sign up for Tibby's newsletter where she also serializes her latest story in the SIN & world, titled SIN & COFFEE.

Hollywood

No Apologies

Acting Out

Full Disclosure

Outtakes

Numbers Game

Boston After Dark

Surrender the Dark

Taste the Dark

Ingram Content Group UK Ltd.
Milton Keynes UK
UKHW042021090323
418309UK00001B/163